The Emperor of Lies

Steve Sem-Sandberg was born in Oslo in 1958 and now divides his time between Vienna and Stockholm. He is a literary critic and translator as well as a prize-winning novelist. *The Emperor of Lies* is a bestseller in Scandinavia and won the August Prize, the Swedish equivalent of the Man Booker Prize, in 2009.

Further praise for *The Emperor of Lies*:

'Sem-Sandberg's achievement is that this history becomes but a background to a multitude of vivid characters, the ordinary Jewish people of the ghetto, whose experiences he weaves expertly into a mesmerising whole . . . (They) become as familiar to us as every character in *Great Expectations* or *David Copperfield* . . . When the deportations begin in September 1942, we cannot bear to see each one go . . . *The Emperor of Lies* is a novel about heart-wrenching suffering and extraordinary evil.' *Guardian*

'In this vast and impressive book, the Swedish novelist Steve Sem-Sandberg revisits these five years of barbaric history. The chronology from April 1940 to January 1945 is handled with great skill . . . [and] the book is immeasurably strengthened by its multiple points of view . . . Yet the book is not a mere recitation of crime and evil. There are compound ironies in the fact that Rumkowski insists to employ the authorities acknowl   erhaps the book   e these complex

'The author uses *The Ghetto Chronicle*, a 3,000 page archive set up by Rumkowski in 1940, to give this novel an extraordinary immediacy and power.' Kate Saunders, *The Times*

'Steve Sem-Sandberg's extraordinary novel is set in the Łódź ghetto during the German occupation. The story has been told many times before . . . yet rarely with such imaginative empathy . . . *The Emperor of Lies* is a brilliantly sustained work of fiction.' *Sunday Telegraph*

'This brutally vivid narrative, superbly translated by Sarah Death . . . a compelling homage to a community wiped off the map.' *Scotland on Sunday*

'Sem-Sandberg's recreation of the Łódź ghetto, utterly convincing, rich in sympathy and understanding, is more a lightly fictionalised documentary than a work of the imagination. Nevertheless, it needed that form of imagination which goes by the name of empathy to enter this world of horrors and show how individuals sought to survive or succumbed . . . [*The Ghetto Chronicle*] is a harrowing document into which Sem-Sandberg breathes life, presenting us with an extraordinary range of characters . . . Sem-Sandberg sentimentalises nothing. There is courage in adversity, heroism and examples of selfishness, but there is also meanness, cowardice, dishonesty . . . the translation is clear.' *Scotsman*

'Steve Sem-Sandberg has achieved something monumental, but with a strange and necessary lightness of touch. It is sobering, scarifying, and, in its hunger for the truth enthralling.' Sebastian Barry

The Emperor of Lies

STEVE SEM-SANDBERG

Translated by Sarah Death

faber and faber

First published in Sweden in 2009
by Albert Bonniers Förlag as *De fattiga i Łódź*
First published in the UK in 2011
by Faber and Faber Ltd
Bloomsbury House
74–77 Great Russell Street
London WC1B 3DA
This paperback edition published in 2012

Typeset by Palindrome
Printed by CPI Goup (UK) Ltd, Croydon, CRO 4YY

A CIP record for this book is available from the British Library

ISBN 978–0–571–25921–2

This translation has been published with the financial assistance of the
Swedish Arts Council

Contents

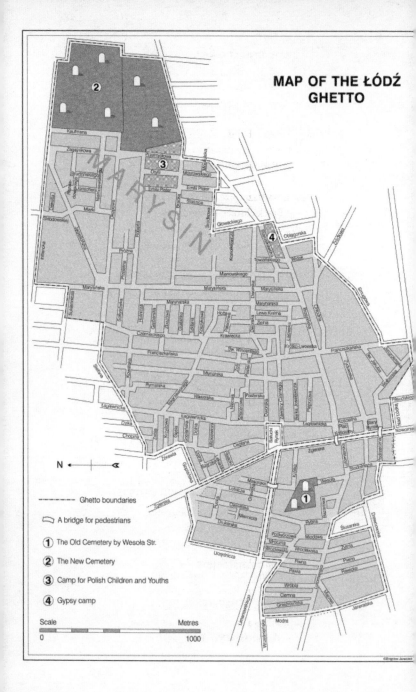

MAP OF THE ŁÓDŹ GHETTO

MARYSIN

N

Ghetto boundaries

A bridge for pedestrians

1 The Old Cemetery by Wesoła Str.

2 The New Cemetery

3 Camp for Polish Children and Youths

4 Gypsy camp

Scale
0

Metres
1000

Litzmannstadt Ghetto 1940–1944

Some streets in the ghetto,
with their Polish and German names

Bałucki Rynek – Baluter Ring (Bałuty Square)
Plac Kościelny – Kirchplatz (Church Square)
Radogoszcz – Radegast

Bazarna/Bazarowa Street – Basargasse
Bracka Street – Ewaldstrasse
Brzezińska Street – Sulzfelderstrasse
Ceglana Street – Steinmetzgasse
Ciesielska Street – Bleicherweg
Czarnieckiego Street – Schneidergasse
Drewnowska Street – Holzstrasse
Drukarska Street – Zimmerstrasse
Dworska Street – Matrosengasse
Franciszkańska Street – Franzstrasse
Gnieźnieńska Street – Gnesenerstrasse
Jagiellońska Street – Bertholdstrasse
Jakuba Street – Rembrandtstrasse
Karola Miarki Street – Arminstrasse
Łagiewnicka Street – Hanseatenstrasse
Limanowskiego Street -Alexanderhofstrasse
Lutomierska Street – Hamburgerstrasse
Marysińska Street -Siegfriedstrasse
Mickiewicza Street – Richterstrasse
Młynarska Street – Mühlgasse
Pieprzowa Street – Pfeffergasse
Podrzeczna – Am Bach
Próżna Street – Leeregasse
Rybna Street – Fischgasse
Szklana Street – Trödlergasse
Urzędnicza Street – Reiterstrasse
Wesoła Street – Lustigergasse
Zagajnikowa Street – Bernhardstrasse
Zgierska Street – Hohensteinerstrasse

The Emperor of Lies

Memorandum

Łódź, 10 December 1939
Confidential
Classified

Establishment of a Ghetto in the City of Łódź

There are, at a reasonable estimate, some 320,000 Jews living in the city of Łódź today. This number cannot all be evacuated simultaneously. A thorough study undertaken by the relevant authorities has shown it would be impossible for them all to be concentrated in a single, closed ghetto. In due course, the Jewish question will be solved as follows:

1) All Jews living north of the line marked by 11 Listopada Street, Plac Wolności and Pomorska Street must be placed in a sealed ghetto, ensuring firstly that a strong German centre around Independence Square (Plac Wolności) is free of Jews, and secondly that this ghetto can also be extended to the northern parts of the town already inhabited exclusively by Jews.
2) Able-bodied Jews who live in other parts of Łódź will be organised into special labour units and housed in barracks under close supervision.

Preparations for and implementation of this plan are to be the responsibility of a staff consisting of representatives of the following:

1. NSDAP (the German National Socialist Workers' Party)
2. The Łódź representative in the Government Presiding Committee in Kalisz
3. The Łódź City housing, employment and public health departments
4. The Schutzpolizei, responsible for local law and order
5. The security police
6. The Death's-Head Units (SS forces)
7. The Offices of Trade and Industry
8. The Offices of Finance

The authorities will also take the following preliminary measures:

1) Assess the action required to close off streets and barricade entrances and exits from buildings, et cetera.
2) Assess the resources required to position guards around the perimeter of the ghetto.
3) Hold ready material from the Administrative Development Agency for the closure of the ghetto.
4) Make preparations to ensure health-care provision in the ghetto – particularly the prevention of epidemics – by transfer of drugs and medical equipment.
5) Draw up regulations for future removal of refuse and waste from the ghetto and transportation of dead bodies to the Jewish cemetery, or for setting up a similar burial site within the ghetto.
6) Be equipped to supply the amount of fuel required by the ghetto.

As soon as these initial measures have been taken and a sufficiently large security force is available, I will fix a date for the implementation of the ghetto scheme, i.e. at a given point in time the boundaries as specified in advance will be manned by guards and the streets will be sealed with barbed wire and other obstructions. At the same time, house fronts will be walled up or otherwise blocked off by workers within the ghetto. Inside the ghetto, Jewish self-government will be established. This will consist of an Eldest of the Jews and an expanded community council (*kehila*).

The Department of Food Distribution in the City of Łódź will supply the ghetto with food and fuel, which will be transported to designated places within it where they will be given into the charge of the Jewish administration. The scheme will operate on the principle that the ghetto can only pay for provisions and fuel with goods, fabrics, textiles and other such items. Thus we will extract from the Jews all the valuables they have misappropriated and amassed.

Other parts of the city will be searched so that all Jews unfit for work can be transferred to the ghetto immediately it is in operation, or very soon afterwards. Those Jews fit for work will be placed in special labour units in supervised barracks constructed by the City authorities and security police.

With reference to the above, the following conclusion is to be drawn. All Jews placed in special labour units who prove unfit for work or fall ill must be transferred to the ghetto. Those Jews inside the ghetto who are still able-bodied must carry out whatever work is required within the ghetto itself. I shall reach a decision later about the extent to which able-bodied Jews are to be moved from the ghetto to the labour barracks.

Naturally, the establishment of the ghetto is only a temporary measure. I reserve the right to decide when and how the City of Łódź is to be purged of Jews. The ultimate aim must be to burn away this infectious abscess entirely, once and for all.

[signed]

Übelhör

The Chairman Alone
(1–4 September 1942)

Whatsoever thy hand findeth to do, do it with thy might;
for there is no work, nor device, nor knowledge, nor wisdom,
in the grave, whither thou goest.
Ecclesiastes 9:10

That was the day, engraved for ever in the memory of the ghetto, when the Chairman announced in front of everyone that he had no choice but to let the children and old people of the ghetto go. Once he had made his proclamation that afternoon, he went to his office on Bałuty Square and sat waiting for higher powers to intervene to save him. He had already been forced to part with the sick people of the ghetto. That only left the old and the young. Mr Neftalin, who a few hours earlier had called the Commission together again, had impressed on him that all the lists must be completed and handed over to the Gestapo by midnight at the latest. How then could he make it clear to them what an appalling loss this represented for him? *For sixty-six years I have lived and not yet been granted the happiness of being called Father, and now the authorities demand of me that I sacrifice all my children.*

Had any one of them an inkling of how he felt at this moment?

('What shall I say to them?' he had asked Dr Miller when the Commission met that afternoon, and Dr Miller had extended his ravaged face across the table, and on his other side Judge Jakobson, too, had looked him deep in the eyes, and they had both said:

Tell them the truth. If nothing else will do, you'll have to tell them that.

But how can there be Truth if there is no Law, and how can there be any Law if there is no longer any World?)

With the voices of the dying children roaring in his head, the Chairman reached for the jacket Miss Fuchs had hung up

11

for him on the hook on the wall of the barrack hut, fumbled with the key in the lock and had scarcely opened the door when the voices overpowered him again. But there was no Law standing outside his office door, and no World either, merely what remained of his personal staff in the form of half a dozen clerks exhausted by lack of sleep, with the tireless Miss Fuchs at their head, neatly dressed on this day as on all others in a freshly ironed, blue-and-white-striped blouse, with her hair in a chignon.

He said:

If the Lord had intended to let this, His last city, go under, He would have told me. At the very least He would have given me a sign.

But his staff just stared back uncomprehendingly:

Mr Chairman, they said, *we are already an hour late.*

*

The sun was as it usually is in the month of Elul, a sun like the approaching Judgement Day, a sun that was a thousand needles piercing your skin. The sky was as heavy as lead, without a breath of wind. A crowd of some fifteen hundred people had gathered at the fire station. The Chairman often made his speeches there. On other occasions it was curiosity that brought people to listen. They came to hear the Chairman speak of his plans for the future, of imminent deliveries of food, of the work awaiting them. Those present today had not gathered because they were curious. Curiosity would hardly have induced people to leave the queues for the potato depots and distribution points and walk all the way to the square in front of the fire station. Nobody had come to hear news; people had come to listen to the sentence that was to be passed on them – a life sentence or, God forbid, a death sentence. Fathers and mothers came to hear the sentence that was to be handed down to their children. The elderly summoned the last of their strength to listen to what fate had in store for them. Most of those gathered there were old people – leaning on thin sticks or on their children's arms. Or young people, holding their children tightly by the hand. Or children themselves.

With heads bowed, faces distorted with grief, with swollen eyes and throats constricted by tears, all these human beings – all fifteen hundred assembled in the square – were like a town, a community in its final moment; waiting under the sun for the Chairman and his downfall.

Józef Zelkowicz: *In jejne koshmarne teg*
(*In These Nightmarish Days*, 1944)

*

The whole ghetto was out on the streets that afternoon.

Although the bodyguards succeeded in keeping the majority of the mob at a distance, a few grinning whipping boys found their way up into his carriage all the same. He leant back against the hood, too feeble to brandish his stick at them as he usually did. It was as malevolent tongues were always saying behind his back: he was done for, his time as Praeses of the ghetto was over. Afterwards they would say of him that he was a false *shoyfet* who had taken the wrong decision, an *eved hagermanim* who had acted not for the good of his people but just for the power and profit he could engineer for himself.

But he had never acted for anything but the good of the ghetto.

Lord God, how can You do this to me? he thought.

People were already filling the fire-station yard in the scalding sunlight. They must have been standing there for hours. As soon as they caught sight of the bodyguards, they hurled themselves towards him like a pack of ferocious animals. A line of policemen formed a human chain at the front and wielded their batons to drive back the crowd. But it was not enough. Sneering faces still hung over the policemen's shoulders.

It had been decided that Warszawski and Jakobson would speak first, while he waited in the shade of the platform, to temper as far as possible the pain in the hard words he would be forced to speak to them. The only trouble was that, by the time he came to climb up onto the speaker's rostrum they had improvised for him, there was no longer any shade, and no platform either: just an ordinary chair on a rickety table. He would be forced to stand on this tottering pedestal while the loathsome black mass jeered and gaped at him from down in the shade on the other side of the yard. Faced with this body of darkness, he felt a terror unlike any he had ever felt before. This, he now realised, must have been how the prophets felt the moment they stepped before their people; Ezekiel, who from besieged Jerusalem, the *city of blood*, spoke of the need to cleanse the city of evil and all filth and set a mark on the forehead of all those who rallied behind the true faith.

Warszawski spoke, and he said:

Yesterday, the Chairman received an order to send away more than twenty thousand of us . . . among them our children and our very oldest people.

Do not the winds of fate shift strangely? We all know our Chairman!

We all know how many years of his life, how much of his strength, his work and his health he has devoted to the upbringing of the Jewish children.

And now they demand that he, HE, of all people . . .

*

He had often imagined it possible to converse with the dead. Only those who had already escaped the incarceration could have said whether he acted rightly or wrongly in letting people

14

go who would not have had any other life anyway.

In the first, difficult period – when the authorities had just begun the deportations – he had ordered his carriage so he could visit the cemetery in Marysin.

Endless days at the start of January, or in February when the flat country round Łódź, the vast potato and beet fields, lay shrouded in a raw and pallid haze. At long last, the snow melted and spring came, and the sun was so low on the horizon that it seemed to cast the whole landscape in bronze. Every detail stood out against the light: the stark mesh of the trees against the ochre shade of the fields, and here and there a splash of bright violet from a pond or the line of a brook hidden in the undulations of the plain.

On days like these he sat huddled and unmoving in the rearmost seat of the carriage; behind Kuper, whose back assumed the same curve as the horsewhip balanced in his lap.

On the other side of the fence, one of the German guards would stand stiffly, or pace restlessly up and down around his sentry box. Some days a fierce wind would blow across the open fields and pasture land. The wind swept sand and loose soil along with it, and also blew a litter of paper over the fence and walls; and with the smoking soil came the the cackle and mooing of poultry and cattle from the Polish farms just the other side of the fence. At times like these it was so evident how arbitrary the drawing of the boundary line had been. The guard stood impotent, head down into the persistent wind, with his uniform coat flapping pointlessly around his arms and legs.

But the Chairman sat there as still as ever while the sand and soil whirled around him. If all that he saw and heard had any effect on him, he did not show it.

There was a man called Józef Feldman who dug graves as a member of Baruk Praszkier's gang of diggers. Seven days a week, even on the Sabbath since the authorities had ordered it, he was there digging graves for the dead. The graves he

15

dug were not large: seventy centimetres deep and half a metre wide. Just deep enough for a body. But considering there was a requirement for two, perhaps even three, thousand graves a year, it was obviously heavy work. Usually with the wind and loose soil whipping him in the face.

In winter, digging was out of the question. The graves for the winter had to be dug in the warmer half of the year, which was therefore the time when Feldman and the other diggers had to work hardest. In the colder months, he retreated to his 'office' for a rest.

Before the war, Józef Feldman had been the owner of a small plant nursery in Marysin. In two greenhouses he had grown tomatoes, cucumbers and green vegetables, salad leaves and spinach; he had also sold bulbs and packets of seeds for spring planting. Now the greenhouses were empty and deserted, their glass broken. Józef Feldman himself slept in a simple wooden cabin off one of the greenhouses, which he had formerly used as an office. There was a low wooden bunk along its back wall. He also had a wood-burning stove, with a flue sticking straight out through the window, and a little hotplate that ran on propane gas.

All the plots of land and former allotments in Marysin were formally owned by the Eldest of the Jews, to be let out as he chose. The same applied to all land previously in collective ownership: the Zionists' *hachsharot*, for example, twenty-one fenced-off allotments with long rows of meticulously pruned fruit trees where the ghetto's Pioneers had toiled day and night; Borachov's kibbutz, the Hashomer collective's decaying farm on Próżna Street where they grew vegetables; and the youth cooperative Chazit Dor Bnej Midbar. Also the large, open areas behind the tumbledown old toolshed that went by the name of Prazkier's workshop, where the few dairy cows left in the ghetto grazed. All this belonged to the Chairman.

But for some reason, the Chairman had let Feldman keep

16

his. The two of them were often to be seen in Feldman's office together. The big man and the little man. (Józef Feldman was diminutive. People used to say he scarcely reached to the top of the graves he dug.) The Chairman would be talking about his plans to transform the area round Feldman's nursery business into one huge beet field and plant fruit trees on the slope down to the road.

It was something often said of the Chairman. He basically preferred the company of ordinary, simple people to that of rabbis and Council members in the ghetto. He felt more at home among the Hasidic Jews in their school in Lutomierska Street or among the uneducated but deeply devout Orthodox Jews who continued making their way out to the big cemetery on Bracka Street for as long as they were allowed to. They would sit there for hours then, crouching between the graves with their prayer shawls over their heads and their well-thumbed prayer books held to their faces. Like him, they had all lost something – a wife, a child, a rich and prosperous relation who could have been providing food and lodging now they were old. It was the same eternal *shoklen*, the same lament down the years:

Why is the gift of life given to one tormented so bitterly;
to one who waits for death but waits in vain;
to one who would delight if he could find his grave;
to one whose path is wreathed in darkness:
pervaded, immured by God?

From the younger visitors, less lofty sentiments were heard:

— *If Moshe had left us in Mitsraim we could all have been sitting in a café in Cairo instead of being trapped in here.*
— *Moshe knew what he was doing. If we hadn't left Mitsraim we would never have been blessed with the Torah.*

— And what has our Torah given us?

— Im eyn Torah, eyn kemakh, it is written; without the Torah, no bread.

— I'm quite sure that even if we'd had the Torah, we still wouldn't have had any bread.

The Chairman paid Feldman for the winter upkeep of his summer residence in Karola Miarka Street. Virtually all the members of the Council of Elders had 'summer residences' in Marysin at their disposal, in addition to their town apartments in the ghetto, and some were rumoured never to leave the area, like the Chairman's sister-in-law, Princess Helena, who was said only to leave her summer residence if there was a concert at the House of Culture or some rich business owner was giving a dinner for the *shpitsn* of the ghetto; then she would always put in an appearance, wearing one of her many elegant, flat, wide-brimmed hats, with some of her favourite finches in a hemp-rope basket. Princess Helena collected birds. In the garden round the house in Marysin she had her personal secretary, the versatile Mr Tausendgeld, construct a large aviary to accommodate no fewer than five hundred different species, many so rare that they were never sighted at these latitudes and certainly not in the ghetto, where the only birds generally to be seen were crows.

As for the Chairman, he shunned all excess. Even his enemies could testify to his modest lifestyle. Cigarettes, however, he consumed in great quantities, and when he was sitting up late, working in his office in a barrack hut at Bałuty Square, he not infrequently fortified himself with a glass or two of vodka.

And sometimes, even in midwinter, Miss Dora Fuchs would ring from the Secretariat to say the Chairman was on his way, so Feldman had to take his coal scuttles and march all the way up to Marki Street to light the stove, and when the Chairman got there he would be unsteady on his feet and cursing because it was still cold and damp in the house, and it would fall to Feldman's lot to get the old man to bed. Feldman was more intimate than most with all the swings of the Chairman's mood, and well aware of the oceans of hatred and envy that lay behind that silent gaze and sarcastic, tobacco-stained smile.

Feldman was also responsible for maintenance of the Green House, on the corner of Zagajnikowa and Okopowa Street. The Green House was the smallest and most outlying of the six orphanages that the Chairman had set up in Marysin, and here it was that Feldman would often find him, sitting hunched in Kuper's carriage opposite the fenced-off children's playground in the garden.

The old man clearly found it soothing to watch the children at play.

The children and the dead. Their horizons were limited. They took sides only on the basis of what was right before their eyes. They did not let themselves be duped by the machinations of the living.

They talked of the war, he and Feldman. Of that immense German army which seemed to continue expanding on all fronts, and of Europe's persecuted Jews who had to submit to life at the feet of the mighty Amalek. And the Chairman confessed that he had a dream. Or rather, he had two. He spoke of one of them to many people; that was the dream of the Protectorate. He spoke of the other to only a few.

He dreamt, he said, that he would demonstrate to the authorities what capable workers the Jews are, so they would let themselves be persuaded once and for all to extend the ghetto. Then even other parts of Łódź would be incorporated into the ghetto, and when the war was over, the authorities would finally be forced to admit that the ghetto was a *special* place. Here the lamp of industry was kept burning, here there was production such as had never been seen before. And everyone had something to gain by letting the incarcerated population of Litzmannstadt work. Once the Germans had realised this, they would declare the ghetto a Protectorate within the borders of those parts of Poland that had been incorporated into the German Reich: a Jewish free state under German supremacy, where freedom had been honestly won at the price of hard work.

That was the dream of the Protectorate.

In the other, the secret dream, he was standing on the prow of a big passenger ship on the way to Palestine. The ship had left the port of Hamburg after he had personally led the exodus from the ghetto. Exactly who, apart from himself, had been allowed to emigrate was never clarified in the dream. But Feldman understood that most of them were children. Children from the vocational schools and from the ghetto orphanages, children whose lives the Praeses had personally saved. In the background, on the far horizon, was a coast: faint in the strong sun, with a strip of white buildings along the shoreline, and above them rolling hills that merged imperceptibly with the white sky. He knew it was Eretz Israel he could see, Haifa to be more precise, but he could not make anything out very clearly because it all melted into one: the white deck of the ship, the white sky, the refracting white sea.

Feldman admitted he found it hard to see how the two dreams could be compatible. The dream of the ghetto as an extended Protectorate, or the dream of the exodus to Palestine? The Chairman answered, as he always did, that the ends depended on the means, that you had to be a realist, and see what opportunities presented themselves. After all these years, he was familiar with the Germans' way of thinking and behaving. And even he had acquired many confidants among their number. But one thing he knew for sure. Every time he woke up and realised he had dreamt the dream again, his breast filled with pride. Whatever happened, to him and to the ghetto: he would never abandon his people.

Yet later, that was precisely what he would do.

The Chairman rarely spoke of himself or where he came from. That's all over and done with, he would say when certain events from his past were brought up. But still sometimes, when he gathered all the children around him, he found himself coming back to certain events that had presumably taken place when he was a child himself, and that he had obviously never got out of his mind. One of these stories was about one-eyed Stromka, who had been a teacher of Talmud classes back home in Ilino. Just like blind Dr Miller, Stromka had a stick, and that stick had been long enough for him to reach any pupil in the cramped school-room at any moment. The Chairman showed the children how Stromka used to deploy his stick, and then rocked his own heavy body just the way Stromka would rock up and down between the desks where the pupils sat hunched over their books, and every so often the stick would shoot out furiously and rap some inattentive child on the hand or the back of the neck. *Like that!* said the Chairman. The children had nicknamed the stick the extending eye. It was as if Stromka could *see* with the end of his stick. With his actual, blind eye he could see into another world, a world beyond our own where everything was perfect and without distortion or imperfection, a world where the pupils formed the Hebrew characters with complete accuracy and rattled off their Talmud verses without stumbling or hesitating in the slightest. Stromka appeared thoroughly to enjoy looking into that perfected world, but he hated what he could see on the outside.

There was another story, too – but the Chairman was not as fond of telling it:

21

The little town of Ilino where he had grown up was situated on the River Lovať near the town of Velikiye Luki, for which many fierce battles were to be fought during the war. The town consisted at that time almost exclusively of narrow, rickety wooden houses, built close together. On the short slopes between the buildings, which swelled into shapeless areas of mud when the rains came in spring and the river burst its banks, there was room for little garden plots. The mainly Jewish families who lived there traded in cloth and imported comestibles and other goods from the colonies, conveyed all the way from Vilna and Vitebsk. The district was poor, but the synagogue looked like an oriental palace with two substantial pillars in front; all made of wood.

The bathhouse stood on the riverbank. On the far side of the bathhouse was a stony beach, to which the children often went after Talmud classes. The river was shallow just there. In the summertime it looked like the stagnant water from the well that his mother used when she was washing clothes on the front porch; he loved dipping his hand into the water, warm as his own urine.

At low tide, a little island would appear, a flat streak of land in midstream, on which birds would stand spying for fish. But the bank's shallow appearance was deceptive. On the other side of the 'island', the muddy riverbed fell away sharply again and the water grew suddenly deep. A child had drowned there. It had happened long before he came into the world, but they still spoke of it in the village. Perhaps that was why his schoolmates were drawn to the place. Every afternoon, crowds of children competed in daring to go out to the island lying bare and exposed in the middle of the fast-flowing river. He remembers one of the boys waded in almost to the waist and stood with elbows raised far out in the choppy, glittering water, shouting to the others to hurry up and join him.

As he remembers it, he was not among the boys who then,

laughing, ploughed their way through the water.

Perhaps he had volunteered to join the game but been rejected. Perhaps they had said (as they often did) that he was too fat; too clumsy, too ugly.

That was when he had a sudden inspiration.

He decided to go to Stromka and tell him what the others were up to. Afterwards he could only dimly recollect the effect he had hoped to achieve. By turning informer, he would somehow win Stromka's respect, and if he only had respect, the other children would not dare to exclude him from their games any more.

A brief moment of triumph followed, as blind Stromka came stalking down to the river, his long stick swinging in front of him. But the moment of triumph was short-lived. He did not find himself in favour with Stromka after all. On the contrary, the evil eye stared at him from then on with even greater contempt and ill will, if that was possible. The other children avoided him. They would stand aside and whisper each day when he came to school. Then one afternoon, when he was on his way home, they came too, crowding round him. He was surrounded by a whole crowd of shouting, laughing children. That was what he remembered afterwards. The sudden surge of happiness that ran through him when he thought himself accepted and included in their circle. Though he realised at once that there was something forced and unnatural about those smiles and comradely thumps on the back. They joke and play around, they tell him to wade out into the water, they say they bet he doesn't dare.

Then it all happens very quickly. He's standing up to his waist in water, and behind him the children closest to him are bending down to pick up stones from the beach. And before he realises what is happening, the first stone strikes his shoulder. He feels dizzy, tastes blood in his mouth. He does not even have time to turn round ready to run out of the water before

23

the next stone comes flying. He flails his arms, tries to get to his feet, but falls again; and the stones are landing in the water all around him. He sees they are aimed in such a way as to drive him out towards the deeper channel. The moment it dawns on him – that they want him dead – the wave of panic breaks over him. To this day, he has little idea how he did it, but by frantically pushing aside the water with one arm and holding the other over his head for protection, he somehow manages to get back onto the beach, find his feet and shuffle or limp away, as the stones rain down on him.

Afterwards he was made to stand with his back to the class while Stromka beat him with his stick. Fifteen brisk strokes on his bottom and thighs, already swollen and blue where the stones had hit him. It was not for missing lessons but for telling tales on his classmates.

Yet what he would remember later were not the informing and the punishment but the instant at which the smiling children's faces down by the river were suddenly transformed into a vengeful wall, and he realised he was, in effect, in a cage. Yes, over and over again (even in front of 'his own' children) he would come back to that barred cage with spaces through which stones and sticks were perpetually thrown or poked at him and he was a prisoner with nowhere to retreat to and no means of protecting himself.

When does a lie begin?

A lie, Rabbi Fajner would say, has no beginning. A lie runs downwards like a rootlet, branching an infinite number of times. But if you trace the rootlets down, you never find a moment of inspiration and vision, only overwhelming desperation and despair.

A lie always begins with denial.

Something has happened – yet you do not want to admit that it has.

That is how a lie begins.

*

The evening the authorities decided without his knowledge to deport all the old and sick people from the ghetto, he had been attending the House of Culture with his brother Józef and his sister-in-law, Helena, for a celebration of the foundation of the ghetto fire brigade, precisely one year before. The following day it was exactly three years since Germany invaded Poland and the war and the occupation began. But naturally they did not celebrate that.

The soirée opened with some musical impromptus; these were followed by some turns from Moshe Puławer's 'Ghetto Review', which had on that same day received its hundredth performance.

The Chairman generally found musical performances extremely trying. The deathly pale Miss Bronisława Rotsztat wound herself around her violin is if an electric shock were passing through her over and over again. Miss Rotsztat's musical expression was, however, much appreciated by the women. Then it was time for the Schum sisters, who were twins. Their act was always the same. First they rolled their eyes and curtseyed. Then they rushed out into the wings and came back as each other. Since they were exactly alike, this naturally presented no problem. They simply swapped clothes. Then one of them vanished – and the other sister began to look for her. She looked in bags, she looked in boxes. Then the missing sister popped up and started looking for the one who had been looking before (and who had now vanished), or maybe it was actually the same sister looking all the time.

It was all extremely disconcerting.

Then Mr Puławer himself came on stage and told *plotki*.

One of his stories was about two Jews meeting each other. One of them was from Insterberg. The second man asked: What's new in Insterberg? The first one replied: Nothing. The second: Nothing? The first: *A hintel hot gebilt*. A dog barked.

The audience laughed.

Second Man: A dog barked in Insterberg? Is that all that's happened?

First Man: Don't ask me. A big crowd of people seems to have assembled.

Second Man: A big crowd of people assembled? A dog barked? Is that all that's happened in Insterberg?

First Man: They've arrested your brother.

Second Man: They've arrested my brother. What for?

First Man: They've arrested your brother for forging bills of exchange.

Second Man: My brother's been forging bills of exchange? That's not news, is it?

First Man: Like I said, nothing new in Insterberg.

Everyone in the hall convulsed with laughter, except Józef Rumkowski. The Chairman's brother was the only person in the hall who failed to realise the joke was about him.

There were also stories about Rumkowski's young wife Regina and her incorrigible brother Benji, whom the Chairman was said to have locked up in the mental hospital in Wesoła Street for 'causing too much trouble'; that is, for saying things to the Chairman's face that the Chairman did not want to hear.

The most popular stories of all, however, were about the Chairman's sister-in-law, Helena. Moshe Puławer told those himself, coming forward to the edge of the stage with his hands stuck impishly into his trouser pockets. For example, the fact that he referred to her as the Princess of Kent, making play on the Yiddish verb for knowing a person: *Ver hot zi gekent un ver vil zi kenen?* He asked, and suddenly the stage was full of actors shading their eyes and spying out for the missing princess: *Princess of Kent? Princess of Kent?* The audience went wild, pointing to the front row where Princess Helena sat blushing bright red beneath the curved brim of her hat.

The other actors went on scanning the audience:

Where is she? Where is she?

Another actor came on stage, shamelessly imitating Princess Helena's duck-like gait. Addressing the audience, he reported that there had been a distress call from the district fire station in Marysin. An unusual case: a woman had locked herself into her home and refused to go out. She had her husband bring food home for her. She ate and ate, and when it was finally time for her to go to the privy, she had ballooned up so much that she couldn't get out of the door. The fire brigade would have to come and lift her through the window.

SO THAT WAS THE UNKNOWN PRINCESS OF KENT!

Upon which the whole ensemble dashed on stage, linked hands and burst into song:

S'iz keyn danken keytn
S'iz gite tsaytn

Kayner tit zikh haynt nisht shemen
Yeder vil du haynt nor nemen;
Abi tsi zayn tsu zat*

It was the most malicious and shameless song-and-dance act Mr Puławer had ever put words to. Within a hair's breadth of lese-majesty, and typical of the mood of despondency and chaos that had prevailed in the ghetto over the last months. Though the Chairman tried to put a brave face on it and clap in the right places, even he felt a distinct sense of relief when the acting was over and the musicians returned to the stage.

Miss Bronisława Rotsztat concluded with a turgid Liszt scherzo and drew a line under the whole deplorable business with her well-rosined bow.

*

The following morning, Tuesday 1 September 1942, Kuper was waiting with the carriage as usual outside the summer residence on Miarki Street and the Chairman got in as usual, a scarcely audible grunt his only greeting. **WAGEN DES ÄLTESTEN DER JUDEN**, says a silvery-white plaque on each side of the carriage. Not that anyone could be in doubt. There is only one carriage of its kind in the ghetto.

The Chairman often toured the ghetto in his carriage. Since everything in the ghetto belonged to him, he was naturally obliged to look in from time to time, to assure himself that it was all in good order. That *his* workers were queuing properly at the foot of one of the ghetto's wooden bridges, waiting to cross; that *his* factories stood ready with their vehicle access doors open to admit the vast flood of workers; that *his* police officers were on hand to prevent unnecessary altercations; that *his* workers went straight in and stood at their tools and

---

* There is no one to be thanked, / These are good times, / No one need feel ashamed, / Taking is all we want to do; / Just to satisfy our hunger.

machines waiting for *his* factory whistles to sound, ideally all together, at the same moment.

And so the factory whistles did, that morning. It was a perfectly ordinary dawn in the ghetto, clear but a little chilly. Soon, the heat of the day would burn away the last remaining moisture from the air and it would be hot again, as it had been all that summer and as it would remain for the rest of that dreadful September.

He did not notice anything amiss until Kuper turned off Dworska Street and into Łagiewnicka. The road in front of the barrier guarded by the Schupo, the German police, at the entrance to Bałuty Square was thronged with people, and none of them were on their way to work. He saw heads turn in his direction and hands reach out for the hood of the carriage. One or two people shouted at him, their faces strangely projected forward from their bodies. Then Rozenblat's Jewish constables came running, the forces of law and order surrounded the carriage, and once the Schupo lifted the barrier, they could calmly continue into the square.

Mr Abramowicz had an arm out ready to support him as he stepped out of the carriage. Miss Fuchs came rushing out of the barrack hut, and after her came all the clerks, telephonists and secretaries. He looked from one frightened face to another and asked: *What are you staring at?* Young Mr Abramowicz was the first to pluck up courage, stepping forward from the knot of people and clearing his throat:

Haven't you heard, Sir? The order came last night.
They're emptying the hospitals of all the sick and the old!

There are several eyewitness accounts of the Chairman's reaction on first receiving this news. Some said he did not hesitate for a moment. They had seen him head instantly, like 'a whirlwind', down Wesoła Street, rushing to try to save his

29

nearest and dearest. Others thought he had received the news with a look that could best be described as derisive. He was said to have denied to the very end that any deportations had occurred. How could anything have happened in the ghetto without his knowledge?

But there were also those who thought they could see the uncertainty and fear suddenly breaking through the Chairman's authoritarian mask. After all, was it not he who had said in a speech: *My motto is always to be at least ten minutes ahead of every German command.* An order had been issued sometime during the night; Commandant Rozenblat must have been informed, since the ghetto police force had been called out to the last man. All of those most closely concerned had been informed, except for the Chairman, who had been at the cabaret!

When the Chairman got to the hospital, just before eight on Tuesday morning, the whole area round Wesoła Street was closed off. At the hospital entrance, Jewish policemen were forming a human chain, impossible to breach. On the other side of this wall of Jewish *politsayen*, the Gestapo had brought up big, open-topped lorries, with two or three large trailers attached behind each vehicle. Under the supervision of the German police, Rozenblat's men were in the process of dragging the old and the sick out of the hospital building. Some of the sick were still in their hospital clothes; others were dressed only in their underpants, or nothing at all, with their emaciated arms crossed over their chests and ribcages. A few individuals managed to break through the police cordon. One white-clad figure with a shaven head rushed towards the barrier, its blue-and-white-striped prayer shawl flowing out behind like a banner. The German soldiers immediately raised their weapons. The man's incomprehensible cry of triumph was cut off abruptly and he fell headlong in a shower of fabric shreds and blood. Another fleeing patient tried to take cover in the back seat of one of the two black limousines that had pulled up alongside the lorries and trailers, beside which a handful of German officers had been standing for some time, impassively observing the tumultuous scene. The escapee was just attempting to crawl in through the back door of the car when its chauffeur alerted SS-Hauptscharführer Günther Fuchs to the presence of the intruder. With a gloved hand, Fuchs dragged the wildly resisting man out of the car and then shot him, first through the chest and then again – when the man was already prone – through the head and neck. Two uniformed guards immediately rushed over, grabbed the man's arms and threw the body, still bleeding from the head, up onto the trailer, where a hundred or patients already stood crushed together.

While all this was happening, the Chairman, calm and composed, had gone up to the officer in charge of the operation, a certain SS-Hauptscharführer Konrad Mühlhaus, and asked to be given access to the hospital building. Mühlhaus had refused, saying this was a *Sonderaktion* led by the Gestapo, and no Jews were allowed to cross the police line. The Chairman had then asked for access to the office to make an urgent telephone call. When this request, too, was turned down, the Chairman is supposed to have said:

> You can shoot or deport me. But as Eldest of the Jews, I still have some influence over the Jews in the ghetto. If you want this operation to run in a smooth and dignified way, you would be wise to grant my request.

The Chairman was gone for scarcely thirty minutes. In that space of time, the Gestapo brought up more tractors and trailers, and an extra handful of Rozenblat's men were ordered to the hospital gardens, to find any patients who had tried to escape out of the back entrance. Those patients who had been hiding in the hospital grounds all this time were felled with blows from batons or rifle butts; those who had strayed out into the road were cold-bloodedly shot by the German guards. At regular intervals, screams and stifled cries could be heard from the cluster of relatives outside the hospital grounds, who were powerless to help the infirm as they were led one by one from the hospital building. Meanwhile, more and more eyes turned to the upstairs windows of the hospital, where people expected to see the Chairman's white-haired head appear, to announce that the operation had been suspended, that it had all been the result of some misunderstanding, that he had spoken to the authorities and all the sick and the old were now free to return home.

But when the Chairman reappeared at the main entrance after those thirty minutes, he did not even glance at the column of loaded trailers. He just walked briskly back to his horse and carriage and got in, and they set off back towards Bałuty Square.

That day – the first of the September operation – a total of 674 in-patients from the ghetto's six hospitals were taken to assembly points around the ghetto, and then onward out of the ghetto by train. Among those expelled were Regina Rumkowska's two aunts, Lovisa and Bettina, and possibly also Regina's beloved brother, Mr Benjamin Wajnberger.

There were many who wondered afterwards why the Chairman had done nothing to help his own relations, in spite of the fact that everyone had seen him standing outside the hospital talking first to SS-Hauptscharführer Mühlhaus, then to SS-Hauptsturmführer Fuchs.

Some thought they knew the reason for his compliance. In the course of the brief telephone conversation Rumkowski later had from inside the hospital with ghetto administrator Hans Biebow, he was allegedly given a promise. In exchange for agreeing to let all the old and sick people of the ghetto go, the Chairman would be allowed to compile a personal list from among those on the expulsion list, a list of *two hundred fit and able-bodied men*, men indispensable to the future operation and administration of the ghetto, who would be allowed to stay in the ghetto despite being formally above the age limit. The Chairman was said to have agreed to this pact with the Devil because he believed it was the only way to secure the continued existence of the ghetto in the longer term.

Others said Rumkowski realised that the time of promises was over, as far as he was concerned, the minute the deportations began without his knowledge. That everything the authorities had promised until then had turned out to be lies and hollow words. So what did the lives of a few family members signify, when all that was left for him was to look on, bewildered and powerless, as the whole mighty empire he had built slowly crumbled?

I

Within the Walls
(April 1940–September 1942)

Geto, getunya, getokhna, kokhana,
Tish taka malutka e taka shubrana
Der vos hot a hant a shtarke
Der vos hot oyf zikh a marke
Krigt fin shenstn in fin bestn
Afile a ostn oykh dem grestn

[Ghetto, beloved little ghetto
You are so tiny, and so corrupt!
Whoever has a hand so strong
Whoever bears a certain mark
will choose from the loveliest and the best
and at least the greatest, too]

Jankiel Herszkowicz: 'Geto, getunya'
(composed and performed in the ghetto, around 1940)

The ghetto: as flat as a saucepan lid between the thundercloud blue of the sky and the cement grey of the earth.

If geographical barriers were no concern, it could go on for ever: a jumble of buildings on the verge of rising up out of their ruins or tumbling back in again. But the real extent of the ghetto only becomes fully obvious once you are *inside* the rough barrier of planks and barbed wire that the Germans have put up all around it.

If it were, in spite of everything – from the air, for example – possible to create an image of the ghetto for yourself, you would clearly see that it consists of two halves or lobes.

The eastern lobe is the larger of the two. It extends from Bałuty Square and the old church square with the Church of the Most Blessed Virgin Mary in the middle – its tall, twin spires could be seen from everywhere – through the remains of what was once the 'old town' of Łódź and out to the garden suburb of Marysin.

Before the war, Marysin was little more than a run-down area of allotments and small dwellings, filled in with a random collection of huts and workshops, pigsties and outbuildings. After the ghetto was cut off from the surrounding area, Marysin's little plots of land and cottages have been turned into an area of summerhouses and convalescent homes for the ruling elite of the ghetto.

Also situated in Marysin is the big Jewish cemetery and, on the other side of the fence, the railway yard at Radogoszcz where the heaviest goods and materials arrive. Units of the *Schutzpolizei*, the same force that guards the ghetto round the clock, lead brigades of Jewish workers from the ghetto every morning to help load and unload at the platform, and the same police company ensures all workers are led back into the ghetto at the end of the working day.

The eastern lobe of the ghetto comprises all the districts east and north of the main thoroughfare of Zgierska Street. All through traffic, including Łódź's north–south tram link, is routed through this street, which is guarded by German police at virtually every street corner. Of the ghetto's three, wooden-vaulted bridges, the two busiest cross Zgierska Street. The first bridge is down by the Old Square. The second bridge, called Hohe Brücke by the Germans, goes from the stone base of the church of St Mary over Lutomierska Street to the other side of Kirchplatz. The western lobe comprises the districts round the old Jewish cemetery and Bazarowa Square where the old synagogue (now converted into stables) once stood. The four blocks of flats in the ghetto that have running water are located in this area.

Another main road, Limanowskiego Street, leads into the ghetto from the west, thus cutting the western lobe into two smaller sections, a northern and a southern. Here there is a lesser-used wooden bridge: the bridge at Masarska Street.

In the middle of the ghetto, at the point where the two main streets, Zgierska and Limanowskiego, meet, lies Bałuty Square. You could call this square the stomach of the ghetto. All the materials the ghetto needs are digested here, and then taken on to its *resorty*, the factories and larger workshops. And it is *from* here that most of the products of the ghetto's factories and workshops go out. Bałuty Square is the only neutral zone in the ghetto where Germans and Jews meet, totally isolated, surrounded by barbed wire, with only two permanently guarded 'gates': one to Łagniewnicka Street and one out into 'Aryan' Litzmannstadt at Zgierska Street.

The German ghetto administration also has a local office

at Bałuty Square, a handful of barrack buildings back to back with Rumkowski's Secretariat: Headquarters, as it is popularly known. Here, too, is the Central Labour Office (*Centralne Biuro Resortów Pracy*), headed by Aron Jakubowicz, who coordinates labour in the *resorty* of the ghetto and is ultimately responsible for all production and trade with the German authorities.

A transitional zone.

A no man's or, perhaps one should say, an *everyman's land* in the midst of this strictly monitored *Jewish land*, to which both Germans and Jews have access, the latter however only on condition that they can produce a valid pass.

Or perhaps simply the specific *pain node* at the heart of the ghetto that is the explanation of the ghetto's whole existence. This gigantic collection of dilapidated, unhygienic buildings around what is basically nothing but a huge export depot.

He had discovered early on that there was a sort of vacuum of muteness around him. He talked and talked but no one heard, or the words did not get through. It was like being trapped in a dome of transparent glass.

Those days when his first wife Ida lay dying.

It was February 1937, two and a half years before the outbreak of war, and after a long marriage which, to his great sorrow, had borne no fruit. The illness, which perhaps explained why Ida had remained childless, made her body and soul slowly waste away. Towards the end, when he took the tray up to the room where she was in the care of two young maids, she no longer recognised him. There were times when she was polite and correct, as if to a stranger; and others when she was curtly dismissive. On one occasion she knocked the tray out of his hand and shouted at him, calling him a *dybek* who must be driven out.

He watched over her while she slept; that was the only way he could convince himself he still completely owned her. She lay tangled in her sweat-soaked sheets, lashing out in all directions. *Don't touch me*, she screamed, *keep your dirty hands off me*. He went out onto the landing and called to the maids to run for a doctor. But they just stood down there, staring at him, as if they did not understand who he was or what he was saying. In the end, he had to go himself. He staggered from door to door like a drunken man. Finally he got hold of a doctor who demanded twenty złoty before he would even put his coat on.

But by then it was too late. He bent over and whispered her name, but she did not hear. Two days later, she was dead.

He had once tried his luck as a manufacturer of plush in Russia, but the Bolshevik Revolution had got in the way. His hatred of all manner of socialists and Bundists stemmed from that period. I know a thing or two about Communists that isn't fit for polite company, he would say.

He saw himself as a simple, practical person, without any sophisticated *airs and graces*. When he spoke, he said what he thought, loud and clear, in an insistent, slightly shrill voice that caused many people to look away uncomfortably.

He was a long-standing member of Theodor Herzl's party, but more for practical convenience than out of any burning belief in the Zionist cause. When the Polish government postponed the elections for the local Jewish councils in 1936 for fear that the socialists would take over those, too, all the Zionists in the Łódź *kehila* resigned and let Agudat Israel run the council on his own. All except Mordechai Chaim Rumkowski, who refused to put his place on the community council at anyone else's disposal. His critics, who responded by expelling him from the party, said he would collaborate with the Devil himself if it came to it. They did not know how right they were.

There was a time when he had also dreamt of becoming a rich and successful cloth manufacturer, like all the other legendary names in Łódź: Kohn, Rozenblat or the incomparable Izrael Poznański. For a while, he and a partner ran a textile factory. But he lacked the sort of patience needed for business. He lost his temper over every late delivery, suspected deception and swindling behind every invoice. It ended in altercations between him and his partner. This was followed by the Russian venture, and bankruptcy.

When he returned to Łódź after the war, he took a job as an agent and salesman for various insurance companies including Silesia and Prudential. Curious and terrified faces crowded the windows at his knock, but no one dared open the door. They called him *Pan Śmierć*, Mr Death, and he also wore the face of Death as he dragged himself through the streets, for his stay in Russia had made him sick at heart. He often sat alone in one of the fashionable cafés on Pietrkowska Street which were frequented by the doctors and lawyers in whose distinguished circles he would have liked to be seen.

But no one would share a table with him. They knew he was an uneducated man who resorted to the coarsest of threats and insults to sell his insurance. He told a paint dealer on Kościelna Street he would drop dead if he did not sign up his family at once, and the next morning he was found dead under the flap of his own shop counter, leaving his wife and seven children suddenly with no means of supporting themselves. At Mr Death's café table, people with confidential information came and went; they sat with their backs to everyone and dared not show their faces. It was said he was consorting even then with certain people who would later be part of the ghetto's *Beirat* – '*third-rate "personages" with little appreciation of the public good, still less of ordinary honour and decency*'. It was as if wherever he went, he found himself trailed not by the 'great men' he envied, but by a pack of wasters.

But then something happened: a conversion.

He was later to tell the children and the nurses at the Green House it had felt as if the words of the Lord had suddenly and unexpectedly revealed themselves to him with the force of an *exhortation*. From that day forward, he said, the sickness had left him, like some mere, fleeting illusion.

It happened in winter. He had been dragging himself dejectedly through one of the dark, narrow streets of Zgierz, when he came across a girl sitting huddled under a sheet-metal shelter at a tram stop. The girl had stopped him, and asked him in a voice shaking with cold if he could give her anything to eat. He took off his long overcoat and wrapped it round the girl, then asked her what she was doing out so late, and why she had no food. She replied that both her parents were dead and she had nowhere to live. None of her relations had been willing to take her in or give her anything to eat.

Then the future Chairman took the girl with him up the hill, to where the client he was on his way to visit lived on the top floor of a grand house. This man was a business associate of the well-known cloth merchant and philanthropist Heiman-Jarecki. Rumkowski told the man that if he knew the meaning of Jewish *tsdóke*, he would at once take care of this orphan girl, give her a nutritious meal and a warm bed to sleep in; the businessman, who by that stage realised death might be his fate if he refused, dared do nothing but follow Rumkowski's instructions.

From that day, Rumkowsi's life changed dramatically.

Reinvigorated, he acquired a dilapidated estate building in Helenówek just outside Łódź, and set up a home for orphaned children. His intention was that no Jewish child would have to grow up without food, a place to live, and at least some rudimentary schooling. He read a lot, and his reading now included for the first time works by the founding fathers of the Zionist movement, Ahad Haam and Theodor Herzl. He dreamt of creating free centres, where children could not only work the soil like proper kibbutznikim but also learn simple crafts in preparation for the vocational colleges that awaited them when they eventually left the homes.

He acquired the funding to run his *Kinderkolonie* from various sources, including the American–Jewish aid organisation JDC, the Joint Distribution Committee, which donated freely and abundantly to all manner of charitable institutions in Poland. He raised the rest of the money the same way he sold life insurance. He had his methods.

So here's Mr Death again. But this time it's not life insurance he's selling, it's sponsorship, for the upkeep and improvement of orphan children. He has names for all his children. They are called Marta, Chaja, Elvira and Sofia Granowska. He has photographs of them in his wallet. Small, bandy-legged three- and four-year-olds, with one hand thrust in their mouths, while the other gropes the air for some invisible adult.

And there's no escaping behind kitchen curtains for the prospective policyholders this time. Mr Death has found himself a profession that means he can set himself above life and death. He says it is every Jew's moral duty to give to the weak and needy. And if the donor does not give what he demands, he threatens to do all he can to blacken that person's name.

His *Kinderkolonie* grew and flourished.

Six hundred orphan children were living in Helenówek the year before the war, and they all saw Rumkowski as a father; they all greeted him joyfully whenever he took a trip out to see them and came driving up the long avenue. He would have his jacket pockets full of sweets, which he sprinkled over them like confetti, to make sure it was they who ran after him and not him after them.

But Mr Death is Mr Death, whatever coat he chooses to wear.

There is a particular kind of wild beast, he once told the Green House children. It is woven from little bits of all the animals the Lord ever created. This beast's tail is forked, and it is to be seen walking on four legs. It has scales like a snake or a lizard and teeth as sharp as a wild boar. It is unclean; its belly drags on the ground. Its breath is as hot as fire and burns everything around it to ashes.

It was a wild beast like that which came to us in the autumn of 1939.

It changed everything. Even people who had previously lived peacefully side by side became part of the body of that wild beast.

The day after German tanks and military vehicles rolled into Plac Wolności in Łódź, a group of SS men, drunk on cheap Polish vodka, went along the main road, Pietrowska Street, dragging Jewish tradesmen from their shops and cabs. Cheap Jewish labour was needed somewhere, it was said. The Jews were not even given time to pack their belongings. They were rounded up into big groups, ordered to form columns and marched off in various directions.

Those who ran businesses quickly closed their shops. All those families who were able to barricaded themselves in their homes. The occupying German authorities then issued a decree allowing the Gestapo access to all homes in which Jews were hidden, or were suspected of concealing their wealth. Anything of value was confiscated. Anyone who protested or offered resistance was forced to perform some humiliating task in full public view. A senior Gestapo officer walked along the street, spitting. He was followed by three women, who were forced to fight each other to be the first to lick up his saliva. Other women were put to cleaning the city's public toilets with their own toothbrushes and underwear. Jewish men, young and old, were harnessed to wagons and carts fully loaded with stones or refuse and forced to haul them from one place to another. Then to unload them, and then to load the whole lot back on again. Ordinary Poles stood silently alongside – or gave stupid cheers.

Jewish Community Council members tried to negotiate with those now holding power; collectively and individually, they made vigorous representations to the German city commissioner, Albert Leister. Leister finally agreed to receive a certain Dr Klajnzettel at the Grand Hotel, where he was having a meeting with Friedrich Übelhör, the chief of police. Dr Klajnzettel was a lawyer, and brought with him a long list of expropriations of Jewish land and property that had occurred since the German invasion.

49

There was a large walnut tree in front of the hotel. After twenty minutes, Klajnzettel was escorted from the hotel by two SS men, who took a long rope, tied the doctor by the ankles and knees and hoisted him up, leaving him hanging upside down from the tree. Around the tree, a crowd of Polish men and women had gathered, and they were at first horrified, but then began to laugh at Klajnzettel, writhing upside down in the tree. There were also a few Jews among the crowd, but no one dared to intervene. Some unoccupied soldiers on guard outside the hotel began throwing stones at Klajnzettel to make him stop screaming and yelling. After a while, some of the Poles in the crowd joined in. In the end, a hail of stones was flying into the tree and the man dangling there like a bat, his own coattails over his face, was no longer moving.

One of those who witnessed the stoning of Dr Klajnzettel was Mordechai Chaim Rumkowski. He had his own memory of where stoning could lead, and what was more, he thought he knew something about the nature of the monster that seemed to have absorbed the city's Polish inhabitants into its rough, lizard skin. He thought he knew that when the Germans spoke of Jews, they were speaking not of human beings, but of a potentially useful though basically repulsive raw material. A Jew was a deviation in himself; the very fact of a Jew asserting some kind of individuality was a monstrosity. Jews could only be referred to in *collective* form. In fixed numbers. Quotas, quantities. This was how Rumkowski thought: *To make the monster understand what you meant, you yourself had to start thinking like the monster. See not one, but a larger number.*

At that point, he applied by letter to Leister. He was careful to underline that the letter expressed his *personal* understanding, which was therefore not necessarily shared by the other members of the Łódź *kehila*. But the letter nonetheless contained a proposal:

*If you need seven hundred workers, turn to us: we will give
you seven hundred workers.*

If you need a thousand, then we will give you a thousand.

*But do not spread terror among us. Do not tear men from
their jobs, women from their homes, children from their
families.*

*Let us live quietly and in peace – and we promise to assist
you as far as possible.*

Then somebody did listen to Rumkowski at last, after all.

On 13 October 1939, Albert Leister issued a proclamation
that he had dissolved the old *kehila* of Łódź and in its place
appointed him, Mordechai Chaim Rumkowski, to the position
of Chairman of a new, governing Council of Elders, answerable
only to him.

The march into the ghetto –

It is February 1940. Snow on the ground. The sky bright white, poised motionless above.

Across the snow trundle creaking wagon wheels, barouches with sagging suspension, carts loaded high with suitcases and precariously lashed items of furniture.

Some are in front, pulling the carts, others push from behind, or walk alongside to make sure the huge mountain of bags and cases does not tip over.

Tens of thousands of people in motion, grand folk and workers. The grey winter's day does not differentiate between them. Despite the cold, some are wearing skirts or in shirtsleeves, perhaps with a blanket or coat round their shoulders, driven out of their hiding places by the Gestapo, which is continuing its search of every Jewish home. Sporadic shots are heard from inside the buildings. There is broken glass lying in the snow.

He sings as he escorts the children from Helenówek.

They have brought everything with them: even housekeepers, cooks and nurses.

They are like a travelling company. Dangling pots and pans clatter.

They have five horse-drawn vehicles at their disposal, among them the carriage that will later become his own *dróshke*, with the fold-down step and the silver plaque on each side.

He sits in the front carriage beside the coachman Lev Kuper, along with some of the children; they are wearing thick winter hats and coats trimmed with fur. They drive past the ruins of the Temple Synagogue in Kościusz Street.

He tells the children about the town he came from.

It is like the town they are heading for.

A *teeny tiny* town, he explains. So tiny it fits into a matchbox. He holds up his tobacco-stained hands to show them.

He has a high, almost squeaky voice. It is the combination of his thin monotone and his bodily bulk (he is not tall or burly in any way, but *heavy*) that makes such an overwhelming impression on the children who have had the misfortune to encounter him; this and the anger that could suddenly suffuse him, overpowering in its intensity. With eyes open wide and spittle spraying from his lips, he sends a hail of sarcastic comments over whichever apprentice or clerk or day labourer has not completed his task, and, a second later, his stick follows. Even when his voice is mild and temperate, it is clear he will brook no contradiction.

He is also very conscious of the effect he has on others; in the same intuitive way that an actor is conscious of the range of expression available to him on stage. Playing the childish idiot. Or the tough, dogged, loyal worker. A wise old man with semi-blind eyes and a cracked voice, who has seen his whole life pass by. He is almost uncannily clever at assuming these different guises and at falling into others' way of speaking, so he sounds just like them –

There was a cobbler in this little town, and a blacksmith.

(He mimics:)

There was a baker and a lacemaker.

There was a cooper and an apothecary.

There was a cabinet-maker and a rope-maker.

And of course there was also a rabbi.

(who lived right at the back of the synagogue in an unheated room full of books and papers)

And there was a teacher there, too, a teacher who wasn't like your teachers but had one good eye and one bad.

(with the good eye he looked to all those who were of any use –

and with the bad eye at those who drifted round idly with nothing to do)

When he talks to, or in front of, the children, his thin voice is as smooth and flat as a stone, but with a slightly pedantic ring. His tongue and palate linger a moment on every syllable, to make sure the children are listening.

And the children truly are.

The older ones with a look of blind fascination on their faces, as if they can't get enough of the perfectly judged, rhythmic, metronome beat of that thin voice.

For the younger ones, the voice is if anything more hypnotic. As soon as the Chairman starts to speak, it is as if the person behind the voice disappears, leaving just the voice, hanging disembodied in the air like the glow of the cigarette he would at some stage in his story produce from his silver case and light.

And then there was someone who could do a bit of all the things I'm going to tell you about: he was called Kamiński.

He skinned and flayed oxen and sheep.

He even had the skill of tanning the hides the old way, by rubbing fat into them and burning them over an open fire.

He also had the art of repairing clocks and watches.

He used mixtures of herbs to make decoctions that cleaned wounds and eased swellings.

He knew exactly what kind of clay to insert between the oven stones of stoves that had burnt through.

It was said that he could even tame wild wolves.

The Chairman went quiet for a little while.

The end of his cigarette glowed red and enlarged before fading again when he took a puff, and then another. *He was called Kamiński*, he added quietly to himself.

In the light of the glowing cigarette, the furrowed old face softened, and assumed a sort of introspective look. As if he could see quite clearly in front of him the man he was attempting to conjure up for them:

He was called Kamiński . . .

And everybody got angry with this Kamiński.

(the rabbi got cross, because he saw him as an envoy of Satan, but so did the baker, the tanner, the paver, the locksmith and the apothecary, because they all thought he was stealing their customers from before their very eyes . . .)

So the members of our kehila *unanimously decided to have him deported from the village.*

But it was decided that he would first be shut in a cage and put on show in the market place.

He sat in the cage for forty days, a trapped animal baring his teeth like a wolf, while he showed the children who flocked around the cage how to make matze –

Pat pat, with both hands

(*like this!*)

The Chairman clamped his cigarette between his lips. Held up his own hands and demonstrated by clapping and patting his hands together.

Bread, he said, and smiled.

The Lord took seven days to create and order the world.

It took Rumkowski three months.

On the first of April 1940, a whole month before the ghetto was sealed, he opened a tailor's workshop at 45 Łagiewnicka Street and put the energetic manufacturer Dawid Warszawski in charge of operations there. This was the *resort* later to be known as the Central Tailors. Shortly afterwards, in May, another tailoring workshop opened at 8 Jakuba Street, close to the ghetto boundary. On the eighth of July, a shoemaker's opened in the same premises as the Central Tailors.

And so it went on:

14 July: a cabinet-maker's and a factory for wood products at 12–14 Drukarska, with a timber store for the latter in the yard.

18 July: another tailor's workshop, at 18 Jakuba.

4 August: a workshop for upholstering furniture at 9 Urzędnicza. Mattresses were also made here, as well as sofas and armchairs (stuffed with dried seaweed).

5 August: a linen factory at 5 Młynarska Street.

10 August: a tannery at 9 Urzędnicza. (This dressed soles and uppers to be used for shoes and boots for the Wehrmacht.)

15–20 August: a dye works; a shoemaker's (actually a slipper factory) in Marysin; and another tailoring workshop, this time at 53 Łagiewnicka Street.

23 August: a metalwork factory on Zgierska, manufacturing among other things metal tubs and various kinds of bucket and pail; as well as containers for wood-gas fuel, primarily for military use.

17 September: a (new) tailor's, at 2 Młynarska Street.

18 September: another tailor's, 13 Żabia Street.

8 October: a furrier's, 9 Ceglana.

28 October: yet another tailor's, 10 Dworska Street.

Apart from uniforms for the German army, the tailors produced (for the same army): protective and camouflage suits; footwear of all kinds: shoes, heavy-duty boots, marching boots; leather belts with metal buckles; blankets, mattresses. But also various kinds of women's underwear: corsets and brassieres. And for men: earmuffs and woollen jackets, the model known at the time as golfing jackets.

Under the authorities' direction, Rumkowski set up his administrative office in a number of interconnecting wooden barrack huts on Bałuty Square. The German ghetto administration had its local office in a couple of similar blocks. The section of the ghetto administration under the city's jurisdiction was in Moltkestrasse, in central Litzmannstadt.

The head of the ghetto administration was Hans Biebow.

Biebow supported Rumkowski's plans from the very start. If Rumkowski told Biebow they were a hundred cutting-out machines short, then Biebow arranged delivery of a hundred cutting-out machines.

Or sewing machines.

Sewing machines were hard to get hold of in wartime, in an economic crisis. Many of those fleeing Poland before the German invasion had taken their more basic machines with them.

But Biebow managed to organise even sewing machines. They might not arrive in full working order, for Biebow always tried to pay the lowest possible price. But Rumkowski would reply that it didn't matter if the Singer machines were in a usable state or not. He had foreseen the problem and set up two sewing-machine repair workshops in the ghetto: one at 6 Rembrandtstrasse (Jakuba), the other at 18 Putzigerstrasse (Pucka).

This was how their collaboration initially worked:

Whatever the one saw a need for, the other procured.

And that was how the ghetto grew: suddenly, out of nothing, materialised the German army's most important stock supplier.

*

Here's Biebow. He's holding a garden party for his staff in a leafy inner courtyard near the offices of the German occupying authorities in Moltkestrasse.

In the background: a long table, decorated with wreaths and freshly cut flowers. Rows of tall, fluted glasses. Piles of plates. Platters of cakes, pastries and fruit. People are standing in a crowd round the table, most of them in uniform.

Biebow himself in the foreground, wearing a light-coloured suit with narrow lapels to the jacket, and a dark tie. His hair is in the military style, shaved right up the back of his neck, and parted to one side, accentuating the angular shape of his face, with its pronounced chin and cheekbones. Beside him, one can glimpse Joseph Hämmerle, the head of finance, and Wilhelm Ribbe, who was in charge of goods deliveries and stock purchase in the ghetto. The latter's narrow, foxy-looking face looks out from between two rather plump women, while his arms are round their waists. The two women have permed hair and very obvious dimples. The reason for their laughter is the Torah scroll in Biebow's hand, which he has been given as a birthday present.

In actual fact, it is one of the scrolls the community rabbis were able to save at the last moment from the burning synagogue in Wolborska Street in November 1939, scrolls which the German authorities have now, as it were, confiscated all over again, this time with the express purpose of giving them to Biebow as a gift. It is widely known among senior German officers and officials in Łódź that Biebow has a comical weakness for Judaica of all kinds. He even considers himself something of an expert on Jewish questions. He has already, in a letter to the Reichssicherheitshauptamt in Berlin, offered to take over the running of the concentration camp in Theresienstadt personally. There are cultivated Jews there, as opposed to the poor and uneducated workers who jostle for space here.

By this stage, Rumkowski thinks he has got to know Biebow quite well. *Er ist uns kein Fremder*, is how he often describes him. Nothing could be further from the truth.

Biebow is an erratic administrator. Sometimes he is absent from the ghetto for weeks on end, only to turn up with a huge delegation and demand immediate stocktaking in every factory. With his bodyguards in tow, he then goes from workshop to workshop, searching their stores of materials for anything hidden away on the sly. If, on his way back to Bałuty Square, he happens to pass a wagon or handcart of potatoes or vegetables en route to the soup kitchens of the ghetto, and a single potato falls off the back, he gestures majestically to halt the vehicle, and goes down on hands and knees to retrieve the dropped potato. Then wipes it on the sleeve of his jacket before replacing it carefully, almost reverently, on the pile.

You must look after what little you have.

This concern for every overlooked detail in the ghetto is not easy to reconcile with Biebow's personality as a whole, which is expansive, to say the least. He is seldom sober when he comes into the office, and when he is in what he calls 'a delicate condition', he often summons his Eldest of the Jews. One day when Rumkowski comes in, he is sitting at his desk howling like a dog. On another occasion he is crawling around on all fours in front of the desk, doing imitations of a chuffing steam engine. It is the day after the first removal order has been issued: the order for the first train convoys to the death camps in Chełmno.

Biebow generally adopts a considerably more friendly tone. He wants to *talk things over*. He wants to talk production quotas and food deliveries. That kind of discussion could sometimes lead to a strange, false intimacy between them. *Well I must say, Rumkowski, you've developed quite a belly*, he might say, for example, throwing his arms round the other man's girth.

That certainly was a sight: the coffee merchant from Bremen clinging to the ghetto's Eldest of the Jews as if to a reluctant pillar. Rumkowski stood there, hat in hand, his head bent subserviently as always. Openings like that gave Biebow the excuse to expand on his thesis that the hungry are the best workers.

Workers with full stomachs get bloated, he said.

They can't keep a firm grip on their tools, he said.

They fall on their arses.

And if they don't fall on their arses, they can't tear their eyes away from the clock on the wall telling them when they can leave their seats and let their overfed bodies get some rest.

No, he went on theorising, the thing is to keep the swine at a level where they've got a little but never quite enough. When they're working, they think about food all the time, and the thought of soon being able to eat makes them work a bit more, give up a bit more, always on the verge of getting by and yet never quite there; *on the verge*, Rumkowski, on the verge.

(*You see?* he said, looking at the Chairman as if appealing to him, as if still not entirely sure Rumkowski had understood the full implication of what he had said.)

*

There was a Debt. Biebow constantly reminded him about it. The outward manifestation of this Debt was a loan of two million Reichsmarks made to Rumkowski by Leister, the City Commissioner, allowing the former to expand the industries of the ghetto. This loan was now to be paid off in instalments, with interest; the payments were to be in the form of Jewish possessions that had been confiscated and goods that had been produced, and these were now streaming through the export depot at Bałuty Square at an ever-increasing rate.

But the Debt also had an internal dimension. It was used to establish the value of work within the ghetto. The amount for subsistence for each inhabitant of the ghetto was reckoned at *thirty pfennigs*; no one living there was to cost more than that. It was Biebow's head of finance, Joseph Hämmerle, who had worked out this *Jew allowance* on the basis of what it cost to supply food and fuel to the ghetto.

Families with children or old people at home faced the added burden of the cost of milk, if available, plus electricity and fuel. The Chairman set one of his colleagues to working it all out. To guarantee the survival of a single adult in the ghetto it took a food ration costing at least one mark and fifty pfennigs per day, that is to say, five times as much as the daily quota fixed by the authorities.

Most of the food supplies reaching the ghetto were also of poor quality or downright inedible. Out of a ten-thousand-kilo consignment of potatoes that reached the ghetto in August 1940, only 1,500 kilos could be salvaged. The rest of the shipment was entirely rotten and had to be buried in the cesspits at Marysin.

So how did one set about feeding a ghetto of 160,000 people on 1,500 kilos of potatoes?

It could only be a matter of time before hunger riots broke out.

In August 1940, the unrest began.

The demonstrators were not initially violent, but they were vociferous. Wave after wave of impoverished Jews in rags came welling out of the buildings in Lutomierska and Zgierska Streets, and it soon became impossible to move in the ghetto except by going with the flow of the marchers.

Rumkowski knew at once that he was facing a serious dilemma.

Leister had made it plain from the outset that if he,

Rumkowski, was not able to maintain peace and order in the ghetto, then the Gestapo would dissolve the whole Council of Jewish Elders with immediate effect, and the autonomy he had dreamt of for the Jews of the ghetto would be nothing more than a memory.

He had, however, no proper police force of his own to deploy. Armed only with their own fists and a rubber truncheon each, the fifty ghetto policemen Commendant Rozenblat had managed to assemble did not even venture among the ranks of demonstrators. They opted instead to erect barricades along the streets and then make themselves scarce. But the demonstrators paid little attention to barricades. They were soon massed outside Hospital No. 1 in Łagiewnicka Street, where the Chairman had his 'private quarters', shouting, swearing and chanting slogans. They also despatched a messenger to demand that the Chairman come out and 'speak' to them.

Down in the hospital, Wiktor Miller, the blind doctor, was on the telephone urging more doctors to come on duty. Dr Miller had served in the Germans' last war as a field surgeon, and just as he was helping to carry away a soldier who had fallen in a French artillery onslaught, an ammunition store close by had blown up. The explosion took off his right leg and bits of his right arm, and shrapnel penetrated his skull through both eyes, permanently blinding him. For this contribution, the Germans had awarded him the Iron Cross for 'courage in the field'. But it was for his contribution during the hunger riots in the ghetto that he definitively earned himself the epithet Justice. With the scar tissue in his mangled face shiny and sweating behind his dark glasses, and with only his stick and a couple of bewildered nurses to aid him, he ran to and fro calming the most hot-blooded demonstrators while helping the wounded onto stretchers so they could be carried into improvised surgeries in the waiting rooms. For now, most of the wounded had only themselves to blame: they had been trampled by the crowd, or collapsed with exhaustion or dehydration. They had nothing to eat, after all, so how could they find the strength to demonstrate? Outside the waiting room, a man lay bleeding copiously from a gash to his head caused by a piece of paving stone intended for the Chairman's windows on the first floor.

It was now clear that the revolt had spread throughout the ghetto.

In the meantime, Rumkowski's brother Józef and the latter's wife had arrived at the rooms where the Chairman lived. From the first-floor windows they could see Rozenblat's men wielding their harmless batons, hitting out in a pathetic attempt to make inroads into the crowd. Fights broke out here and there, where isolated knots of men refused to flinch from the baton blows and continued their offensive with stones and sticks.

On this occasion, Princess Helena was highly agitated and declared to everyone around her that it was just like the revolution in Paris, when the people 'lost their senses' and turned against their own kind. She tottered back and forth between the window and the desk, giving little screams and flailing her arms. The sight of the scenes of tumult outside was eventually too much for her: *They're going to kill us all*, she shrieked hoarsely, and then staged one of her more extravagant fainting fits.

As always when Princess Helena was afflicted by some *malaise*, Józef Rumkowski stalked over to his brother. And just stood there: right up close to him, with his gaze fixed accusingly on him. He had done it ever since they were little.

Well, what are you going to do about this? he said.

And Rumkowski? As always on such occasions, he sensed his feelings of inadequacy and shame being diluted by an unreasoning hatred: of his brother's rigid reproaches; of his subjection to a wife who was trying with all the means at her disposal to divert attention from the situation that had arisen onto her own interminable self-pity. In normal circumstances, his anger would have erupted at that moment. But no angry outburst ever made any impact on Jósef. His brother just went on staring. There was no way of retreating from or evading that unyielding stare.

Luckily, neither of them needed to do anything.

The Germans were already on the way.

From further down Zgierska, the sound of emergency vehicles could already be heard – and a discernible sense of alarm spread not only through the ranks of the demonstrators but also among the policemen Rozenblat had called in, most of whom had already been knocked to the ground or taken shelter against the walls of the buildings along Spacerowa Street. Should they exploit the situation and try to look as though they were 'responding forcefully' when the Germans came, or copy the demonstrators and try to run away as fast as possible?

Most of them opted for the latter but, like the demonstrators, did not get very far before a whole commando of German security forces blocked all the surrounding roads with riot-squad vans and strategically parked jeeps. Rounds of submachine-gun fire issued from the vehicles to confuse the fleeing demonstrators, who didn't know which way to run, and seconds later soldiers came surging from every corner and alleyway. In the space of a few minutes, Łagiewnicka Street had been completely cleared, leaving only a handful of bodies lying there among a pathetic collection of broken paving stones, abandoned caps, and trampled leaflets and banners.

That night, Rumkowski called a meeting, attended by Commandant Rozenblat, Wiktor Miller and Henryk Neftalin the head of the Population Registration Bureau. Plus some of the district police commanders in whom Rozenblat claimed to have particular confidence.

The Chairman urged them all to take a sensible view of the situation.

Ordinary people, particularly men with a family to support, did not take to the streets en masse unless exhorted to do so. There were troublemakers in every district. And it was these agitators they needed to get at: Communists and Bundists and activists from the left wing of the Poale Zion; countless secret party cells had been formed inside the ghetto. *Treacherous* people. People who did everything in their power to prove there was no difference between those in positions of trust in *his* administration and the odious Nazis. Rumour had it that there were even men in his own Council of Elders trying to exploit the situation for their own gain, individuals who had ways of discreetly stirring up the troublemakers with the aim of making the Germans dismiss the whole *Beirat*.

What the Chairman wanted from Rozenblat and Neftalin was *names*. The lists of names would be divided among all police units, which would be detailed to swoop on the suspects' homes the following night. It made no difference whether they were socialists, Bundists, or just run-of-the-mill criminals and troublemakers. He had already ordered prison chief Shlomo Hercberg to prepare special examination cells for interrogations.

The strategy proved surprisingly effective. Between September and December there were no further incidents; the ghetto remained calm. But then winter came, and winter was his enemy's best friend.

Hunger.

The discontented were driven out onto the street once more, now so desperate that they stopped at nothing, least of all a simple baton blow.

*

That was the first ghetto winter.

They said in the ghetto that it was so cold the saliva froze in people's mouths. Sometimes people did not turn up for work because they had frozen to death in their beds during the night.

The Fuel Department sent out teams of workers to pull down ramshackle buildings and salvage the wood. On the Chairman's express orders, all fuel was to go to the workshops and factories, and also to soup kitchens and bakeries which would not otherwise have had anything to heat their ovens with. Allocating fuel for private consumption was out of the question. Which naturally had the effect of increasing the black-market price of fuel tenfold within just a couple of days. It was here, on the black market, that the majority of sawn wood ended up. As the fuel crisis deepened, deliveries of flour to the bakeries of the ghetto failed to materialise. When the Chairman took it up with the authorities, they said they were not even getting their own emergency supplies through, because of the snow and ice. He tried to play for time by temporarily reducing rations, but he was aware of trouble starting to brew out in the factories again.

Every day brought the same sights. Snowbound streets, carts and sledges that could not be shifted because their wheels or runners had frozen fast in the snow. It took the shoulders of at least four men to get the handcarts back into the tracks worn by other wheels. And at the soup kitchens in Zgierska Street, in Brzezińska, in Młynarska, Drewnowska, sat rows of backs, male and female, huddled tightly together under coats and shawls and bedcovers, drinking down the increasingly watery soup as dense clouds of fine snow blew through the streets and alleys.

The disturbances that now broke out were of a different kind.

The mob was fully mobile this time. It had no set destination when it gathered in the streets, but moved swiftly from district to district.

Rumour was what drove it.

A ratsye iz du, a ratsye iz du!

Wherever these words were heard, people turned and followed the crowd to where the incoming food convoys were thought to be heading.

A food delivery would scarcely be through the Radogoszcz

Gate before it was attacked. The driver of the horse-drawn vehicle would be pulled to the ground, and as five or six men put their shoulders to it, the whole cart went over, to great cheers. By the time the Schupo lumbered up, the overturned load had been plundered of every last potato or swede.

There was a rumour going round that timber was available for collection from an address in Brzezińska Street. The timber consisted of a dilapidated hovel somehow overlooked by the Fuel Department when it drew up its inventory of the ghetto's wood reserves.

And the mob was immediately on the spot.

Somebody took the lead by getting lifted up onto the roof of the ramshackle building, while others used axes and ripping saws to attack everything that could be hacked or pulled loose, and the building promptly collapsed. Of the men and women inside, half a dozen were trampled to death. When the police arrived, they were faced with men determined to fight them off while their comrades grabbed as much of the highly prized wood as possible before running off.

At that point, the staff of the six ghetto hospitals decided to go on strike. They worked in three shifts – round the clock, and what was more, in premises so cold that the surgeons could scarcely feel the knives in their hands – trying to save frightened, starving adults and children who were brought in with frostbite damage or with crushed or broken arms and legs from being struck or trampled down outside the ghetto's distribution centres. Only a fraction of the food convoys coming from Radogoszcz got through. Those that were not intercepted on their way from the goods station were attacked once they were in the ghetto. A handful of men jumped over the low wall running round the central vegetable depot, and even though Rozenblat had by then ordered his officers to work double shifts to protect every food delivery (there were now two policemen to every convoy of provisions and at least three at every depot), they could not prevent the mob from getting in, and out again through the gates, so that in the course of just a few hours it had been stripped entirely bare.

Hunger was the problem.

Whatever measures the Chairman took to tackle the lawlessness in the ghetto, he would never bring it under control until he got to grips with the hunger.

To give an impression of strength and decisiveness, the Chairman abolished all extra rations and increased the collective bread ration. Everyone employed in the ghetto, regardless of profession or position in the ghetto hierarchy, would be entitled to a ration of four hundred grams of bread a week.

Abolishing special rations initially seemed a wise move. It would later turn out to have been the Chairman's biggest mistake, one that very nearly led to open revolt against his rule.

Ever since the ghetto was sealed off from the outside world, distribution of what food there was had been in accordance with a clear hierarchy of privilege.

First, the so-called *B rations*.

B stood for *Beirat*, the central ghetto administration. B rations were allocated to people in positions of particular trust – divided into categories from I to III, depending on their position in the ghetto hierarchy: from members of the Chairman's own Secretariat down to business leaders and technical instructors, lawyers, doctors and others.

There were also so-called C rations.

C stood for *Ciężko Pracujący* and was given to manual labourers with particularly heavy jobs. They did not amount to a great deal more than the normal worker's ration: the heavy workers were given fifty grams more bread a day than the ordinary factory workers, and possibly an extra ladleful of soup. But it was a symbolically important extra allowance because it was proof that hard work paid.

When word got out that the C ration was to be stopped to finance an increase in everyone's bread allowance, the joiners in Drukarska and Urzędnicza Streets decided to go on strike. They demanded not only no cut in the C rations but also an insignificant wage rise.

It was naturally impossible for the Chairman to agree to this. If the joiners of Drukarska were allowed to keep their extra rations, then a host of other workers would soon be insisting that their jobs, too, required a supplementary food ration. He ordered Rozenblat to have his forces ready. Rozenblat sent seventy men, led by a police inspector named Frenkel, to the Drukarska Street joinery shop. A few of the workers left the building when they saw it was surrounded by the police, but most barricaded themselves in on the first floor and refused to evacuate the premises despite repeated appeals, first from Frenkel and then from Freund, the factory manager. When the seventy-strong band of police finally stormed the upper storey, it was met with a hail of wooden furniture at various stages of manufacture. Stick-back chairs struck the policemen on the head; these were followed by shelves, sofa legs, table tops. Shielding their faces with their arms, the police made their way up the stairs and attempted to overpower the workers one by one and drag them out. Not a single worker gave in without a fight. In fact, reported the agitated factory manager Freund on the telephone to Rumkowski afterwards, several of the arrested workers subsequently needed hospital treatment. They were in such a starved state that they collapsed with exhaustion even before Inspector Frenkel's men got the handcuffs on them.

Freund had no sooner hung up than Wiśniewski, manager of the tailoring workshop that made uniforms at 12 Jakuba, rang to report that they had also stopped work there, in sympathy with the joiners in Drukarska and Urzędnicza. Wiśniewski was desperate. His workshop was just about to complete delivery of an order of some ten thousand Wehrmacht uniforms, each with shoulder boards and collar insignia. How would the authorities react if they did not get their uniforms on time? And Wiśniewski was scarcely off the line before Estera Daum at the Secretariat put through a call from Marysin. This time it was the chairman of the Funeral Association speaking on behalf of a company of gravediggers who had announced that they did not intend to dig any more graves unless they could keep their extra rations of bread and soup. Why, they argued, should the gravediggers be singled out and punished with sub-standard soup? Did their work somehow count as less strenuous and important than that of other workers who had previously been receiving C rations?

'What do you expect me to do about it?' was all Rumkowski said.

Unlike Wiśniewski, who had been almost in tears as he poured out his anguish over the phone, the representative of the Funeral Association, one Mr Morski, took a more humorous view.

'Well, even the dead will have to wait their turn now,' he said.

That same morning, the temperature in Marysin had been recorded as minus twenty-one degrees, Mr Morski told him; he had been informed of this by Mr Józef Feldman, who of course was also a respected and trusted member of his digging team. Twelve bodies had arrived from the centre of town that morning. His *grobers* had attacked the ground in their usual way with picks and iron bars, but had not even penetrated the surface of the soil.

'And what do you expect me to do about it?' repeated the Chairman impatiently.

But Mr Morski was far too preoccupied by his own difficulties even to listen. 'I suppose we'll have to stand them on end,' he said. 'If we stand the bodies on end instead of stacking them on top of each other, they'll take up less space.'

But now the Praeses of the ghetto had had enough. He pushed

his way through the Secretariat's sea of industrious telephonists and typists, threw open the door and yelled to Kuper to
get the carriage ready at once. Then he was taken the short
distance to Jakuba Street. Mr Wiśniewski met him at the door,
rubbing his hands together, though it was not clear whether
this was from cold or from a desire to show the Chairman into
his factory as soon as possible.

The striking seamstresses sat obediently in their places at
their workbenches, looking up at Mr Chairman expectantly.

Wiśniewski: I gave them a beating.

The Chairman: I beg your pardon?

Wiśniewski: I gave them a beating with my stick. Those who
  wouldn't work, that is.

The Chairman: But my dear Mr Wiśniewski, I don't understand
  how you imagine you can take such liberties; if anyone is to do
  any beating, it is I!

And whether it was David Wiśniewski's burning red ears
at that moment, or the strange atmosphere in the freezing
factory building, where Wehrmacht uniforms marched
in rows along the far wall (a whole army of brown tailor's
dummies, admittedly nothing but chests and trunks, but all
on the march!), suddenly it was as if inspiration struck the old
man, and before anybody knew it, before anybody could rush
forward to offer a supporting arm or elbow, the Chairman was
up on one of the rickety benches, speaking with clenched fist
held high, for all the world like one of those socialist agitators
he had just been condemning; and the speech he made was
subsequently acknowledged by all those present to have been
one of his most stirring ever:

*You are the first to condemn me, you women – you may take
the part of all those agitating against me. But tell me honestly:*

what would you have thought of me if you had known that I only favoured the few in the ghetto and forced the rest to work for slave wages . . . !

Every hour, I am focused exclusively on what is best for the ghetto. Order and calm in our workplaces is the only salvation for us all . . . !

(Shame on those who think otherwise!)

Don't you know that it is the GERMAN MILITARY POWERS you and I and all of us are working for; have you considered that for a moment? And what do you think would happen if at this very second – right now, as I am speaking – German soldiers rushed in and took you at gunpoint to an assembly point for deportation?

What would you say to your poor parents, your husbands, your children . . .?

[The women crouched behind their workbenches.]

From today, I am imposing a WORK BAN at this and all other workplaces in the ghetto where agitation and rebellion have occurred.

MR WIŚNIEWSKI! SEE THAT ALL WORKERS ARE IMMEDIATELY REMOVED FROM THESE PREMISES. SEAL THE FACTORY GATES!

No rations will be distributed from this point on. All strikers will surrender their identity cards and work logs. Only when you accept the fact that whatever serves the ghetto's best interests is also in your best interests are you welcome back to your former places of work!

The strikers held out for six days.

On 30 January, Rumkowski let it be officially known that the factory gates stood open again for those who pledged to accept existing conditions. All the strikers went back to work, and the whole story could have ended there.

But it did not end there.

Two days after the strike was called off, on 1 February 1941, Rumkowski took his revenge. In another speech, this time to the ghetto's *resort-laiter*, he announced his intention to have deported from the ghetto all 'vermin and disturbers of the peace'* who could be proved to have taken part in the strikes. Among the 107 people whose names went on the list that day were some thirty workers from the joinery workshop in Drukarska, and the same number from Urzędnicza Street.

One of those who was 'sacked' and left the joinery on Drukarska Street that day was thirty-year-old cabinetmaker Lajb Rzepin.

Lajb Rzepin had taken part in the strike action, even been one of the workers who barricaded themselves in the upstairs rooms and thrown things at the police.

But Lajb Rzepin's name never featured on any of the deportation lists.

On 8 March 1941 – the same day the first transport of forcibly ejected workers left the ghetto – Lajb Rzepin started a new job at Winograd's *Kleinmöbelfabrik* in Bazarowa. Around him at the long workbench, where he stood with his gluing tools, you could have heard a pin drop. No one raised their eyes from the work of their hands, no one dared look the traitor in the eye.

From that day, it was as if treachery began to cast its long shadows into the ghetto, Jew against Jew; no worker could be sure that he would not have his work permit withdrawn the next day and be expelled from the ghetto, without having done anything more than claim his right to his own daily bread. But Chaim Rumkowski knew how words and rumour could run through the ghetto. In his speech to his *resort-laiter* he had said that he never had more to give than there was to give. But the very fact that he *gave* meant he was also entitled to *take*. Namely

* The Polish transcript of the Chairman's speech uses the word *szkodnicy*; the German uses *Schädlinge*.

from those wicked, irresponsible people who misappropriated the bread that everyone had a right to demand.

In that respect, he said, quoting the Talmud, *he stood on solid ground.*

And so it was decreed from the highest quarters: everyone in the ghetto was to work.

By earning your keep, you also served the public good.

Yet there were many in the ghetto who couldn't care less about the public good and preferred to provide for themselves. Some of them dug for coal behind the brickworks on the corner of Dworska and Łagiewnicka Streets. The yard behind the works had been used as a dump for years. It often took several hours just to get down to the coal level. First you had to dig down through a slimy mess of vegetable tops and other food waste that lay rotting under a covering of angrily buzzing flies. Then down through layer after layer of waterlogged sand and mud full of smashed crockery with shards that cut into your hands.

Among the dozen or so children who dug here were two brothers, Jakub and Chaim Wajsberg from Gnieźnieńska Street. Jakub was ten years old, and Chaim six. They had picks and shovels with them, but sooner or later they always had to resort to their hands. The wide jute sacks they wore tied over their shoulders then fell forward so they were hanging at stomach level, and all they had to do was stuff the prized black gold straight into the sacks.

Nowadays it was rare for anyone to come across coal from the brickworks' own firing kilns. But if they were lucky, the mud might yield an old chunk of wood or rag, or something else, all covered in coal dust. If you put a rag like that in the stove, you could make the fire burn for at least a couple of hours longer, a good, evenly burning, settled fire; a rag like that fetched twenty or thirty pfennigs if you sold it down at Jojne Pilcer Square.

Jakub and Chaim usually worked as a team with two brothers from the tenement next door, Feliks and Dawid Frydman, but that was no guarantee they would be left to work in peace. All it took was for some of the adults who were also on the lookout for coal to come by their patch, and their coal sacks were gone in a flash. That was why the children had collectively employed Adam Rzepin to keep guard.

Adam Rzepin lived on the floor above the Wajsbergs and was known in the streets around Gnieźnieńska Street as *Ugly Adam* or *Adam Three-Quarters*, because his nose looked as if it had got squashed when he was born. He always used to say that his nose was crooked because his mother had got into the habit of twisting it every time he lied. But everyone knew that was a fib. Adam Rzepin lived alone with his father and his mentally retarded sister; nobody had ever seen a Mrs Rzepin.

All Adam could remember of the first years in the ghetto was the hunger, like a permanently aching wound in his belly. Just being watchman for young gold-diggers was not enough to assuage the pain of the wound in the long run. So on the fairly rare occasions when Moshe Stern came round to the brickworks and asked Adam to run an errand for him, Adam leapt at the chance and left his guard duties to take care of themselves.

Moshe Stern was one of the many thousand Jews who made a fortune after the ghetto was sealed off from the outside world by dealing in combustible material of all kinds. Most responsible fathers of families tried to build up a stock of coal or briquettes, which they kept locked up in various convenient places. Some of the locks could be picked – and then the desirable black gold was out on the market again. There was also money to be made from trading in minor timber items, such as old wooden furniture, kitchen cupboards and drawers, skirting boards and window frames, banisters and anything else that could be sawn up and bundled as firewood. In the summer months, the price of such bundles sank to about twenty pfennigs a kilo, but it went back up to two or three rumkies as winter approached. In other words, it was a matter of waiting for the demand. In the very worst winters, when even the coalmines were inaccessible, people quite literally made fires of whatever they sat and slept on.

Time after time, the police pounced on Moshe Stern. His mother tried to hide him in the drying attic above the old people's home, where he was rumoured to have his secret stores. But the local police came and drove him out.

Rumour had it that Stern was aiming to become the new Zawadzki.

Zawadzki was the smuggler king of the ghetto. He was also known as 'the tightrope walker' because he was in the habit of escaping over the rooftops. It was the only way of gaining access to the ghetto from the Aryan parts of the town, because the buildings closest to the ghetto boundary had no underground water or waste pipes.

Perfumes, ladies' soap; flour, sugar, rye flakes; canned goods, everything from German sauerkraut to pickled ox tongues: these were some of the items that found their way into the ghetto with Zawadzki as their intermediary. Late one evening in 1940, he was apprehended by the Jewish police on the Lutomierska side of the ghetto with a rucksack crammed with chocolate powder, cigarettes and ladies' stockings. The police took him for interrogation to the headquarters of the first police district at Bałuty Square. When the Germans heard that the Jews had caught Zawadzki themselves, they rang for a car from the centre of Litzmannstadt. The Jewish officers realised this was the end for Zawadzki and asked him if he had a final request. He replied that he wished to go to the toilet. Two policemen escorted Zawadzki to the latrines out in the yard. They handcuffed Zawadzki to the latrine door and then stood guard outside, keeping a careful watch on the shoes clearly visible beneath the locked door. The policemen stood staring at Zawadzki's shoes for a good hour. Then one of them plucked up the courage to break down the door. The shoes were still there, and the handcuffs, but no Zawadzki. An open roof hatch showed which way he had escaped.

Zawadzki the smuggler was a legend. Everybody talked about Zawadzki. But Zawadzki was a Pole – he came from the *Aryan* part of the town. And when he had been in the ghetto for as long as he wanted, he *got out again!* Whenever Adam Rzepin dreamt he was free, he dreamt he had a rope and a rucksack, like Zawadzki. He dreamt that one day he would hit the big time like Zawadzki, be something more in life than a mere *luftmentsh*.

Adam's dream very nearly came true one morning when Moshe Stern sent one of his many messengers round to the brickworks, where he was at his usual post, keeping guard on the kids. The message was that there was *pekl* to be fetched. *Pekl* could be almost anything – a bundle, a packet, a consignment – from coal briquettes to dried milk. Adam Rzepin had learnt not to ask questions. But when he got to the address where he had been sent, some empty basement premises in Łagiewnicka Street, all he found there was Moshe Stern, no *pekl*.

Moshe Stern was a small man, but walked as if he were several sizes larger. When he handed out orders and instructions, he crossed his arms on his chest like a resolute bureaucrat. But not this time – Moshe Stern took two firm steps towards Adam Rzepin and gripped his shoulders. As always when he was worried or nervous, he licked his lips.

The parcel in question, he said, was to be delivered to 'a very important person'. This person was so important that if the police stopped him or started asking questions, Adam was *in*

78

no circumstances to reveal that he had been given the parcel by Moshe Stern. Could he promise that?

Adam promised.

Moshe said Adam was the only person in the ghetto he could rely on; then he handed him the parcel.

In the middle of the yard of the house in Gnieźnieńska Street there had once stood a chestnut tree with mighty roots and trunk and a huge crown that made the tree look as if it had found its way there from one of the grand avenues in Paris or Warsaw. Beneath the chestnut, puppet-maker Fabian Zajtman had his workshop: an adjoining pair of wooden sheds, so cramped that there was only room for the puppets inside. From long metal hooks along the roof and walls of the sheds hung rabbis with long *kapotes* and peasant women with headscarves, all equally smiling and helpless. In summer, when it was hot under the wooden roof, Zajtman preferred to sit out under the chestnut tree with his tools. There he sat among the children, carving puppet heads and watching the clouds drift across the pale-blue sky of the yard. *Do you know where the thunder goes to rest?* he had once asked Adam, there on a visit to the Wajsbergs, and had nodded meaningfully up into the crown of the tree, behind which the tall mass of dark clouds was gathering. From that day on, Adam had lived in permanent terror of what really lay hidden in the crown of the chestnut tree; particularly on hot days when the leaves hung motionless and the air was as hot as a baker's oven in the narrow streets.

Fabian Zajtman had died just before the war. They found him lying sprawled across his workbench, almost as if the thunder had turned back in anger to smite the chisel and plane from his hand. There were many orthodox Jews around Gnieźnieńska Street who spat on the ground and said it was an abomination for a Jew to devote his time to idols as that Zajtman had done.

Then the Germans came; the wire surrounding the ghetto ran

just outside Zajtman's wooden huts and Mrs Herszkowicz, *die Hauswärtin* as she was now called, had the chestnut felled and split for firewood. She also had both Zajtman's sheds sawn up.

Now I've got enough wood to see me through the war and even longer, she boasted.

In Gnieźnieńska Street, people got used to the hole in the sky where the chestnut had once stood, but Adam couldn't stop thinking about the tree and the thunder. Where would the thunder go now there was no chestnut to rest in? There were no trees in the ghetto. Adam imagined the thunder circling aimlessly, getting wilder and wilder in all its din. There was no relief from the perpetual crashing anywhere, no way out. On this side of the wire there was only one route to freedom, as Zawadzki had proved: it went *upwards*, though hatches and windows that didn't exist or that one was forced to invent in order to get through.

Adam Rzepin stood with his parcel on a treeless plot of land not far from the tailor's at 12 Jakuba and waited for the 'very important person' to show up.

The first person to put in an appearance was a very young man, wearing a hat and a suit, and an elegant, light-coloured gabardine raincoat that made Adam think of the American gangster films they used to show at the Bajka cinema before the war. The man could have been standing on a street corner anywhere in Europe if it had not been for the two others following him like a shadow. Two rugged men: they looked like *politsayen*, though they had no caps or armbands.

Have you got the goods? asked the man in the light-coloured raincoat.

Adam nodded.

Only then did a fourth person step forward.

Adam Rzepin asked himself afterwards how it could be that he had immediately known the fourth man to be a German officer. The new arrival was dressed in civilian clothes, but

80

the uniform he wore when on duty was still evident in the watchful way his whole body followed when he turned his head or looked to the side.

The man in the gabardine addressed him as Mr Stromberg. That meant he must be Kriminaloberassistent Stromberg, one of the most notorious police commanders in the whole ghetto. Stromberg was a Volksdeutscher, one of the Germans who had been living a settled life in Łódź long before the Nazis came.

Stromberg had a permanent smile on his face; but he moved as if wading through sewage. Stromberg did not as much as glance at Adam, just turned to the young man in the gabardine mac and repeated in his vaguely sing-song Polish:

Has he got the money?

And when his question elicited a confirming nod, Herr Kriminaloberassistent Stromberg finally seemed to relax inside his civilian clothes.

Adam interpreted this to mean that the moment had come to hand over his parcel; he gave it to the raincoat who passed it in turn to Stromberg, who immediately started tugging and ripping the paper like an impatient child at Hanukkah. A few moments later, he was holding a shiny gold link between his fingers. The raincoat hurriedly gestured to Adam, beseeching him to turn his back, the way you turn your back on a woman so as not to embarrass her as she gets dressed; then he swiftly thrust a ten-mark note into the palm of Adam's hand.

Then they were both gone – the young Jew in the gabardine raincoat and the German police chief. Only the two guards remained, their hands threateningly at their hips, as if to assure themselves that Adam was not following the other men.

It was several months before Adam discovered the identity of the man in the raincoat who had sold gold objects to Stromberg. By then, the whole ghetto was talking about Dawid Gertler, the young Jewish police commander who seemed to be on such a good footing with all the officers of the occupying force.

Adam was in the queue for the baker's in Piwna Street. Every bakery was by now baking its own bread, and it always went fast; you had to get up early to be sure of getting your ration.

In Piwna Street. Bread queue. Some *dygnitarzy* push their way to the front.

The young man in the gabardine raincoat is suddenly there again. As before, he is accompanied by two bodyguards. There are sounds of protest from the queue. The bodyguards step resolutely forward, ready to wield their batons to silence the noisemakers. But this time the normal course of events fails to unfold. It is the men in suits from Rumkowski's *Beirat* who have to give way.

'Even in the ghetto, those who have had to wait longest will get their bread,' says the man in the raincoat.

Gertler, Gertler, Gertler . . . ! shout the people in the queue with their hands in the air, their heads straining forward as if they were cheering on a sports star.

And Dawid Gertler presses his hat to his chest and bows like a vaudeville artiste in a circus ring. Adam is not giving up his place in the queue at any price; nor does he raise his eyes, for fear of being recognised by the powerful man. Would the people in the bread queue have carried on applauding if they had known that the young Dawid Gertler was ready to sell their very souls as long as he could stay on intimate terms with the odious Germans?

But perhaps it didn't matter.

As long as the bread could be shared out fairly and everyone got the same.

One of the regular daily columns in the *Ghetto Chronicle* was a record of the number of births and deaths. This was sometimes followed by an entry giving the names of those who had died by their own hand.

That was how the *Chronicle* put it: *died by their own hand*. But in the ghetto they just said that he or she had *gone to the wire*. The phrase expanded the ghetto's already rich vocabulary with an expression that meant not only taking your own life but also transgressing all the limitations the authorities imposed on how life should be lived inside.

In the first week of February 1941, according to the *Chronicle*, seven people went to the wire. Some of the suicides were striking, to say the least. A middle-aged clerk in Rumkowski's housing department took it into his head to crawl right under the fence of planks that reinforced the barbed-wire barrier on the north side of Zgierska Street. Of all the places he could have chosen for his escape attempt, he opted for the most closely guarded stretch in the entire ghetto. It still took some time for him to be detected. There was time for several of the trams that carried Germans and Poles straight through the ghetto to pass by the man's head and shoulders, wedged under the fence, before the police in the lookout two hundred metres away realised something was up. The clerk just lay flat on the ground, waiting for the terrified guard to start shooting.

Other cases were less clear.

They generally involved workers returning home from their evening shift.

Everyone moving through the ghetto had orders to stay as

far away from the boundary as possible. Two hundred and fifty metres was the recommended safety margin. But if you couldn't avoid approaching the wire, you were recommended to do so in broad daylight, right under the eyes of the German guards and for some explicit purpose (if, contrary to all expectation, anyone should ask you).

But for worn-out shift workers there was always the temptation of saving a block or a few hundred metres by taking a short cut along the ghetto boundary to the nearest wooden bridge.

And maybe it was dark. The person taking the short cut couldn't see.

The sentry on the other side couldn't see very clearly, either.

And maybe the man or woman on their way home didn't speak German.

Or he or she couldn't hear what the sentry was shouting because a tram came past at the same time.

Or perhaps there was no tram. The sentry just shouted, and the man or woman who should have been home long ago panicked and started running.

Which the sentry interpreted as an escape attempt. And the shot rang out.

At least four of the seven individuals who went to the wire in February 1941 were killed that way. Did they deliberately seek death, or were their senses dulled by fatigue? Or was there perhaps no distinction between conscious intent and unconscious choice? Perhaps they made for the boundary because they knew there was quite simply nowhere else to go.

A few weeks later, in March 1941, the *Chronicle* reported that forty-one-year-old Cwajga Blum had succeeded in taking her life that way after no less than thirteen attempts to go to the wire.

Cwajga Blum lived in Limanowskiego Street. The only

window in the flat she shared with two other women looked out directly over the cordon. Limanowskiego Street was the main thoroughfare for the German transports of foodstuffs and materials for the factories, for unloading at Bałuty Square, and was for that reason very closely guarded. A little way up stood the third wooden bridge, the one that linked the northern and southern lobes of the ghetto with each other, with red-and-white-striped sentry boxes clearly visible at each end of the bridge. It was to the box at the southern end of the bridge that Cwajga Blum went with her request.

Shoot me, she said to the sentry in the box.

The sentry pretended not to hear. He lit a cigarette, let the strap of his rifle slip from his shoulder, laid the rifle across his lap and pretended to take an interest in the detail of its stock and muzzle.

Please, she pleaded. *Shoot me.*

It was the same guard on duty night after night. And the same Cwaiga.

After this nuisance had gone on for several weeks, the guard's commanding officer asked the local Jewish police to take the matter in hand.

The harassment simply had to stop.

From then on, the front entrance of Cwajga Blum's block of flats in Limanowskiego Street was guarded round the clock by two of Rozenblat's men. As soon as Cwajga ventured over the threshold, the Jewish policemen were there, dragging her back to safety.

Cwajga Blum tried to get out the back way instead. But the policemen had already seen through her. The minute she emerged from the courtyard they were there, hauling her back into the building. This game of cat and mouse was repeated twelve times. At the thirteenth attempt, Cwajga Blum succeeded in outwitting her supervisors, and it also so happened that the Schupo had just changed its rota of sentry duties. The embarrassed police guard from Limanowskiego Street had been moved to Marysin and a rather more outspoken colleague had taken his place in the Limanowskiego Street box.

Please shoot me, said Cwajga Blum.

Do a little dance for me and then we'll see, said the new guard.

Before Rozenblat's men realised what was going on, Cwajga Blum performed a desperate, crazy dance on the other side of the barbed wire. When she had finished, the guard took aim with his rifle and shot her twice in the chest. When her body insisted on continuing to twitch even though it was lying on the ground, he fired another shot to be on the safe side.

The story of Cwajga Blum was told in different versions around the ghetto. One version had it that she had previously been an in-patient in the psychiatric ward of the Wesoła Street hospital, but had been forced to give up her bed to some high-ranking person in the *Beirat*.

In another variant, Cwajga Blum was said to have been so confused that she was not even aware she was in a ghetto, and what she said to the guard in Limanowskiego Street was actually not *shoot me, shoot me*, but *shut me in, shut me in* – because she thought she recognised the soldier as one of the ward attendants from the hospital.

(In that case, the guard must have thought the lady was making fun of him. Why would she ask him to shut her in? She was already well and truly shut in.)

At any event, these tales of men and women who went to the wire became so legion that the Chairman felt obliged to issue a special decree (Public Notice no. 241), in which he expressly forbade any unwarranted approaches to the ghetto boundary. And particularly outside normal shift-working time.

But people went to the wire even so. One way or another.

In April 1941, the *Chronicle* reported a reduction in the number of fatal shootings along the boundary. The statistics showed that would-be suicides now preferred to throw themselves out of high windows, from flats or stairwells. Most of them chose, moreover, to do this from buildings other than those in which they lived. Possibly because they wanted to be sure the drop would be long enough, or perhaps to avoid causing their neighbours any unnecessary bother.

In May 1941, according to the *Ghetto Chronicle*, no fewer than forty-three such suicides were recorded. But even those who died by throwing themselves out of windows were said to have gone to the wire. They had simply been too depressed, or too weakened by hunger and illness, to drag themselves there under their own steam.

One morning, the German police reported that the body of a female had been discovered on 'Aryan territory' alongside the barbed-wire fence, right by the now infamous sentry post in Limanowskiego Street. The woman was lying on her back, with her head resting on the ground and her arms sticking out at an unnatural angle.

The two German guards who found her had initially thought she was dead, yet another of those Jewish suicides. But when they bent down to deal with the body, they discovered she was still breathing. They searched through the woman's clothing for identity papers, but found nothing. The German guards were now faced with a real dilemma. Having found no identity papers, they could not say for sure whether the woman was from the Jewish or the Aryan side of the wire; whether she had been escaping from the ghetto or, on the contrary (and these things still happened – just look at Zawadzki!), had been trying to force entry through the wire.

In consultation with their superiors, they decided to take the woman to the office of the Eldest of the Jews, so its employees could take over the matter. The Kripo also demanded to see the daily reports of all the guard commanders, so they could see whether any Jew had been reported missing in the ghetto. The admittance books of all the hospitals were checked, as were the patient records of the psychiatric clinic in Wesoła Street, to which many of the more well-to-do ghetto inhabitants had their mentally or physically enfeebled relatives admitted. But nowhere had any report been filed of patients going missing.

They therefore felt it safe to conclude that the woman had *not* come from inside the ghetto.

One of the first to examine her was Leon Szykier, the 'workers' doctor'. He was known as the workers' doctor because he was the only physician in the ghetto who did not demand shamelessly high fees of his patients, so even ordinary people could afford to consult him. During the examination, Dr Szykier palpated the woman's body, and found it 'a little wasted and emaciated' but without any other signs of dehydration. There were also scratches and abrasions to the lower legs and arms, indicating that the woman had tried to climb over an obstacle of some kind. The body showed no other injuries. No swellings in the throat. No fever. Pulse and breathing normal.

It was later hinted that the good half-hour Szykier had spent alone with the woman had been enough to 'damage her'. Others naturally disputed this. But it was quite clear that the woman had been lying calmly and peacefully on the stretcher when the German police guards carried her into the Secretariat, whereas half an hour later – when Dr Szykier left her – she was writhing on the barrack-bed in feverish convulsions and mumbling incoherent words of prayer in Hebrew and Yiddish.

Some even thought they could hear traces of the prophet's words on her lips:

ashrei kol-chochei lo –

For the LORD is a God of justice;
blessed are all those who wait for Him.

News of the paralysed woman and her strange utterances spread rapidly. The Chairman had her taken to the Hasidic School in Lutomierska Street, where she was put into the care of a *rebbe* named Gutesfeld and his assistant Fide Sajn. The Hasidic Jews would later claim that Reb Gutesfeld had already seen the incapacitated woman in his dreams. In these dreams she was apparently not paralysed but went stumbling from house to house in a burning city. She did not enter the houses, merely touched the mezuzah on the doorpost of each one – as if to give a sign to those living there that they should leave and follow her.

In the eyes of the Hasidic Jews, there could be no doubt about the matter. She was a *tzadika*, perhaps a messenger, come to offer the incarcerated Jews of the ghetto a little comfort after two years' war and a dreadful winter of hunger. The ordinary people of the ghetto would later refer to her as Mara, *the sorrowful one*. For a period of time, she was the only one of the ghetto's inhabitants – almost a quarter of a million at that time – who had no fixed address or bread-ration card. She did not even feature in the register of the Kripo, which otherwise included every soul in the ghetto and was updated monthly by the *Meldebüro* of the Statistics Department.

On the face of it she was clearly a matter for the rabbinate, though they were only too happy to entrust her to Reb Gutesfeld's care. But even the Hasidic community dared not let her stay, so the *rebbe* and his helper were often seen making their way through the narrow streets of the ghetto with the woman on a litter between them. Fide Sjazn would be at the front while Gutesfeld, who had problems with his legs and could not see very well either, stumbled along behind in his black cassock. They could cover quite a few kilometres that way, in rain, in icy winds or blinding snowstorms. Every so often the *rebbe* stopped to try to work out their location by running his fingers along a wall or the side of a house, or to let Fide Szajn (whose lungs were diseased) finish coughing.

Why were they on the move? Why did they keep on moving?

Some said it was because the woman would never keep still. As soon as they put down the litter, a piercing cry would force its way from her throat and she would thrash her arms about, as if to fend off invisible demons. Others said that every house, every block, concealed an informer who would not hesitate to go to the Kripo if they knew the woman was there; and what would happen to the sorrowful one then?

There were days, however, when the *rebbe* brought the litter back to the prayer room, and on those days a wan but hopeful band always gathered outside the front door in the hope that a touch or a look from the paralysed woman would cure the pain in their arms or heal wounds that refused to heal, or even lift from them the curse of hunger that made formerly strong and healthy men move like ghosts through the streets of the ghetto. Dr Szykier, who was a convinced socialist and loathed all superstition, tried to make the local police drive away the crowd, but the *rebbe* insisted, saying that his dream had also predicted the arrival of these people, and that it would be blasphemous to turn away Jews who had come in the belief that the God of the Scriptures could perform a miracle through even one of his most distant representatives.

One of the people queuing was Hala Wajsberg, Adam Rzepin's neighbour in the building in Gnieźnieńska Street, and mother to Jakub and Chaim who spent their days hunting for wood and coal dust at the old brickworks in Łagiewnicka Street. Hala Wajsberg had heard of Mara's gifts from her friend Borka at the Central Laundry and persuaded her husband Samuel to try a visit to the woman for his painfully aching lung.

In the first months after the ghetto was sealed off, there had been no wooden bridges, and the German police guards opened the fence every morning to let through workers like Samuel who had to move from one half of the ghetto to the other to get to work. The fence was opened at specific times and workers had to make sure they were there punctually. It seemed to Samuel that he was always the last man hurrying across the street before the two guards who presided over the opening lifted the barbed-wire barricade back into place, and one morning he really was the last man out – before he realised what was happening, he was alone in the middle of the 'Aryan' corridor, and the ghetto was closed to him in both directions.

There was a finely developed sadism among those bored German guards with nothing to do all day but shift barbed wire, and every time they managed to catch a Jew between them in 'the corridor' it was a moment of pure and unalloyed pleasure.

Samuel stumbled and fell, and one of the policemen hit him several times with the butt of his rifle across the back and in the belly, and kicked him straight in the chest with the steel-capped toe of his boot to make him get up again. As the traffic was allowed to start flowing again, they grabbed hold of the now semi-conscious body and heaved it between them over the barbed-wire barrier. Even long after his broken ribs had healed, the imprint of the policeman's boot remained as a physical mark of oppression in Samuel's left lung. And things scarcely got any better when the wooden footbridges were built.

Every step he took up the bridge was suffocating, every step back down a torture. Forty-seven steps up, forty-seven steps down. With every step, less air was left in the wheezing, aching lung. By the time he got down to the foot of the bridge he was wet with sweat and quivering like an eel, and everything went black; but through the haze of hunger the heavy, metal-shod voice of the guard rang out again:

Schnell, schnell . . . !
Beeilung, nicht stehenbleiben . . . !

If Mr Serwański at the joinery in Drukarska Street had not been aware of Samuel's problems with his lung, he would un-doubtedly have let Samuel go, and what would become of the family then? Hala was thinking primarily of herself. The ghetto was already full of men hollowed out by hunger until they were beyond recognition, who spent their time lying at home, pale and staring, while their wives had to provide for the family alone.

The morning Hala Wajsberg took her husband Samuel to the Hasidic prayer house it was a raw, pallid winter day with mist hanging so low over the ghetto that the three wooden bridges appeared to vanish straight up into the sky. There was chaos in the back room that morning. Guards, the same guards that normally oversaw the ghetto factories, were doing their best to push back the swarm of people pressing its way in from outside and growing larger by the minute. Half a dozen women had managed to elbow their way to the litter and were now hanging over the face of the paralysed woman with their sick children in their arms.

There was such dreadful shouting and clamouring that nobody noticed that the woman on the litter had herself stopped shouting some time before. Dr Szykier had opened his big, black doctor's bag and given Mara an injection in one of her thin arms, their many red, infected grazes illuminated by the glow of the candles Fide Sjajn had placed round the litter.

At that moment, Helena Rumkowska and her retinue entered the room.

Princess Helena, too, had latterly begun to feel the effects of one particular ghetto illness, that *malaise au foie* which according to her private physician, Dr Garfinkel, afflicted many of the 'chosen few' in the ghetto. As its French name indicated, it was an illness primarily affecting the liver. Since an attack of jaundice many years before, Mrs Rumkowska's liver was officially sensitive. The obscure symptoms generated by this liver provided an inexhaustible topic of conversation at the dinners she regularly gave at the Soup Kitchen for intellectuals in Łagiewnicka Street. Only ghetto dwellers with coupons for

B rations, *respectable people*, as she put it, had access to this kitchen, and it was certainly a gift from above to be able to see Princess Helena pause in one of her tours of inspection, lean kindly over some diner's shoulder, pull out a chair or perhaps even sit down and engage in a little well-bred conversation.

An even more highly prized favour, out of most people's reach, was to be invited as a *personal* guest to Helena and Józef Rumkowski's 'residence' in Karola Miarki Street in Marysin. The couple's home was not much to boast about in itself: a run-down *dacha* with lots of poky rooms, heated by wood-burning stoves, with carved wooden banisters, Russian carpets and single-glazed veranda windows that steamed up when the winter cold breathed on them, turning them as shiny white with frost as the outside of Dr Miller's removable china eye.

But from the ceiling hung the crystal chandelier which Princess Helena had brought with her from her old home in the centre of Łódz – and that was a relic. Those who had been guests of the Rumkowskis spoke not only of the 'generous spreads' Princess Helena was known to provide, but also of the way the flecks of light cast by the chandelier spread shimmering colours across the cramped room, from the simple tulle curtains to the cane furniture and matt sheen of the linen cloth.

For many in the ghetto, Karola Miarki Street came to symbolise the *pogodne czasy*, the 'golden days' from before the war. It was beneath that very chandelier, for example, that Princess Helena one memorable evening had ordered a sack to be slit open, releasing a flock of finches collected on Mr Tausengeld's instructions from the aviary out in the garden: the aim was a symbolic driving out of evil, not only from Princess Helena's own body but also from those of all decent ghetto dwellers. But not even this dramatic medication had any effect. Princess Helena continued to be tormented by her liver. She lay shut in total darkness in her bedroom for ten days, until Dr Garfinkel appealed to her to try as a last resort to see the woman everyone was talking about, to whom for some reason they attributed powers of healing.

So in great pain, and with a good deal of fuss, she had herself taken in one of the ghetto *dróshkes* to the Hasidic prayer house. She was dismayed to find other people already there, and she ordered the *opiekuni* to drive them all, the crippled and the lame, out into the yard. Only when the room was empty did she bend over the poor, pitiful creature lying there on the litter.

That was when *it* happened, the thing Princess Helena's people found so hard to explain afterwards. Someone was to write later that it was as if 'sudden tribulation' had descended on the paralysed woman. Others described it as being like when you cover a light with your hand. The woman's pure and limpid gaze was suddenly clouded with a dark, shifting anxiety. 'A *dybek*!' screamed Mr Tausendgeld. Perhaps it was simply that Mara had briefly managed to fight her way up from the heavy, morphine-drenched sleep into which Dr Szykier had sunk her, and Helena Rumkowska, ever prone to sentimentality, had felt her heart wrung by something she felt she had glimpsed a moment earlier in the sick woman's clear, liquid eyes. Had been so moved, in fact, that she took a little handkerchief from her handbag, carefully dampened its edge with spit and leant forward to wipe away – *what?* – yes, *what* had she thought to wipe away (afterwards, not even Helena Rumkowska could remember with any clarity)? – perhaps the saliva at the corners of the woman's mouth, the tears on her eyelids, the sweat on her brow.

But Princess Helena's trembling hand and handkerchief never reached their goal.

At that moment, spasms shook the woman's body again. Dr Szykier, who had been working from the outset on the assumption that his patient was suffering from epilepsy, rushed forward to prize her jaw open. But instead of resisting his action, she opened her mouth even wider and at the very moment the *dybek* (so Tausengeld claimed) left the body, the whole frightened crowd crushed into the backyard of the prayer house could stare right into the swollen orifice and see the thick, white coating on the woman's palate and throat. Then Mara was said to have uttered two short sentences, or in some versions just two words, forced out with great difficulty – though this time in fully 'comprehensible' Yiddish:

Du host mikh geshendt . . . !
A bayze riekh zol dikh und dayn hoyz khapn . . .*

That was all. In her initial, terrified confusion, Princess Helena had put the handkerchief to her face, realised what she was doing and then hysterically tried to shake it out of her hand:

She's sick! She's sick!
They have sent sickness to us!

In the course of a few seconds, the room emptied of people, leaving only the police behind. Leon Szykier pleaded with them to send for an ambulance, but they returned instead with the news that the Praeses' brother – Józef Rumkowski – did not in any circumstances intend to let any of the ghetto's hospitals admit the woman. The official line was that the woman could not be treated because nobody knew who she was. There was no written record card for her at the *Meldebüro*. And if there was no name under which she could be entered in the books, how could anyone be sure she was a Jewess and not some person in disguise sent by Amalek to spread sickness and disintegration to them all?

For four days and nights, the first lady of the ghetto hovered between life and death as a result of her meeting with the sick woman. Józef Rumkowski took Helena's favourite birds to her

* You have violated me . . . ! May the demons of evil take you and your house!

96

room: the linnets that liked to sit in the fruit trees; the comical starling that sounded just like Marshal Piłudski.

But the birds, too, sat silent and dejected in their cages.

In the prayer room in Lutomierska Street, Dr Szykier had established a quarantine station. It was the first in the ghetto, and was presumably viewed as extremely provisional, for a big crowd had again begun to gather outside the room. This time, however, it was considerably more aggressive and consisted mainly of men demanding that the woman be sent away.

Shame, shame on any who bring sickness to the ghetto!

The Hasidic *rebbe* finally had no alternative but to lift up the woman on her litter and carry her round again. She spent the first two days and nights in the kitchen of Dr Szykier's home. But the furious mob soon found its way there, as well. And so they set off on an unsteady journey between various houses and addresses, that would not end until 5 September 1942, the first night of the *szpera*, when the Chairman took his protective hand from the ghetto and the German police under the command of SS-Hauptsturmführer Günther Fuchs went from house to house, taking with them all the weak and sick, all the children and old people.

And for Samuel Wajsberg there had been no remedy.

Nor for his wife Hala, who three days after the curfew was announced was to lose her most beloved son, Chaim.

It was indeed like losing life itself.

*

Two days after the uproar in the Hasidic prayer house, the Chairman called all members of the medical profession to a meeting to decide once and for all how to deal with the epidemics threatening to destroy the ghetto from within.

The meeting generated some heated discussion.

Doctor Szykier dismissed all the rumours that the woman had brought the infection with her, and he was supported in this by Wiktor Miller, the ghetto's Minister of Health, who maintained that in the case of diphtheria, there were in fact phases or preliminary stages that sometimes resembled neural paralysis. What was more, Dr Miller claimed, diphtheria constituted a threat above all to the children of the ghetto, but the illness could only be transmitted from mouth to mouth, which did limit the threat. It is a different matter, he said, when the infections are carried by the water we drink and the food we eat and the bugs crawling in our walls, and we can do nothing to root them out short of sanitising the whole ghetto.

To combat dysentery and typhus we need doctors; nothing but that – doctors, doctors, doctors!

Dr Miller was to make the battle with the epidemics of the ghetto into his own, private crusade. 'People complain they can't keep kosher any more, but it never occurs to them to boil their water or keep the floor under their own stoves clean!' With his iron-tipped white stick, the blind man tirelessly measured the depth of the ghetto's open drains, used the few remaining fingers on his hand to trawl through piles of rubbish and latrine trenches; he stuck his thumbs behind swollen or bulging wallpaper in search of typhus lice. At the least suspicion of typhus or dysentery, the whole building would be quarantined.

His efforts were eventually crowned with success. Over the course of a year, there was a tenfold reduction in dysentery cases, from 3,414 in the second year of the ghetto's existence to scarcely 300 the year after. Typhus traces a similar downward curve, with a peak of 981 cases in the period January–December 1942, and a gradual falling away in the two years that followed.

As for the outbreak of diphtheria in the ghetto, however, something remarkable happens. In the first twenty-four hours after the rumpus in the Hasidic prayer house, the out-patient clinics of the ghetto register seventy-four new cases of diphtheria, but only two the day after, and then no more at all. Just like the hazy image Mr Tausendgeld thought he saw sliding across the sick woman's face, sickness comes and goes in the ghetto like the briefest of whispers. Not even Princess Helena feels its effects, despite lying upstairs in Miarki Street day after day, shaking with fever, waiting for the ghastly voice that called out to her from Mara's swollen throat to take her in its grip, too.

But nothing happens. At least, not yet.

Early on the morning of 9 May 1941, Rumkowski's newly appointed Minister of Propaganda, Szmul Rosensztajn, climbed onto an upturned beer crate outside the barrack-hut office at Bałuty Square and informed all those who cared to listen that the Chairman had gone to Warsaw to find doctors for the ghetto. Wherever people gathered, from Wiewiórka's barber's shop in Limanowskiego Street to the tailors' workshops in Łagiewnicka, the word spread: *The Chairman has gone to Warsaw to find a way to cure and save the sick of the ghetto.*

The Chairman had scarcely left before they began the preparations for his return. It was all to be on a grand scale – *po królewsku* – with a carriage and a guard of honour, and crowds of cheering onlookers kept at a safe distance by ghetto police. Though in fact it was only one of the routine transports organised by the Gestapo, who travelled the 130 kilometres to Warsaw in convoy every day, and who had no objection at all to letting a Jew come along, if he was stupid enough to pay twenty thousand marks for his ticket.

Rumkowski's trip to Warsaw lasted eight days.

He was courted day and night by members of Czerniaków's Jewish Council, and also by resistance workers and couriers, who tried to pump him for all he could possibly tell them about German troop transports and conditions for the Jews left in Wartheland. The Chairman, however, had no interest in hearing how the Jews of Warsaw were faring, how they organised their *aleynhilf*, how they dealt with the distribution of food, educated their children or engaged in political agitation. Wherever he went, he lugged a large trunk with him. In the trunk he had brochures and information leaflets prepared at his request by the lawyer Neftalin, head of the Department of Statistics, and printed by Rosensztajn. They detailed how many corsets and brassieres his ladies' tailoring workshops produced each month, and how many military greatcoats, gloves, uniform caps or fur-lined camouflage caps the German *Heeresbekleidungsamt* had ordered from him. The old man with the trunk made an indelible impression on the Warsaw Jews who encountered him:

A person calling himself King Chaim has been holding court here for some days, an old man of seventy with great ambitions, a little crazy [*a bisl a tsedreyter*]. He tells miraculous tales of the ghetto. In Łódź [he says] there is a Jewish state with four hundred police officers and three jails. He has his own 'ministry of foreign affairs' and various other departments. When asked why, if it is that good, it is still so bad, why so many people are dying, he does not answer.

He sees himself as the Lord's chosen one.

For those who can be bothered to listen, he talks of how he combats corruption in the police service. He says he goes into the local police headquarters and rips off the caps and armbands of everybody there.

That is how the Lord's chosen one administers justice in the Litzmannstadt ghetto.

The ruling Council of Elders in Litzmannstadt has seventeen members. They obey his every order and slightest wish. He seems to view everything in the ghetto as his personal possession. They are *his* banks and *his* markets, *his* shops, *his* factories. And also, one presumes, *his* epidemics, *his* poverty, *his* fault that his ghetto dwellers are subjected to such degradation.

Adam Czerniaków and the other members of the Warsaw ghetto Jewish council also met him. Czerniaków writes in his diary:

We had a meeting with Rumkowski today.

The man is unimaginably stupid, self-important; officious. He goes on and on about his own splendid qualities. Never listens to what anybody else says.

He's dangerous, too, because he insists on telling the authorities that all is well in his little reserve.

But Rumkowski had his own eyes to see with, and from what he saw he could draw only one conclusion. Unlike the ghetto in Litzmannstadt, the Warsaw ghetto was in the grip of chaos and decline. People did not seem to do a day's work, merely wandered around aimlessly. Along the pavements, long rows of emaciated children sat beside their starving mothers, begging. From a restaurant – they still had such things! – came raucous, drunken bawling. The contrasts were enormous. Rumkowski was escorted to a grocer's shop that had been converted into a tuberculosis clinic. In the shop window, boards had been laid across wooden trestles; on these primitive beds, old men lay dying in front of the eyes of passers-by. He visited soup kitchens run by Poale Zion, in which people were sitting or lying anywhere they could find room, wolfing down free soup.

Wherever he went, people would moan.

About the dirt, the cramped living conditions; the disgusting state of the sanitation.

In the parish hall, a meeting was called of all the Jews who had fled from Łódź in the opening phase of the war and had ended up here, in Abraham Gancwajch's patronage network, or as Czerniaków's lackeys. There turned out to be thousands of Łódź Jews, old and young, who filled the hall to the last standing space.

He had his travelling trunk with him, its lid open wide.

'There is no argument,' he said, 'absolutely no argument today, against the ghetto as the future form of livelihood for the Jews of Europe . . . !'

There is war in Europe today. But war is nothing new for Europe's Jews. All these years, as dark clouds have loomed over our towns and cities, we have resigned ourselves to the fact that we live cut off from one another, and can no longer move freely.

In years gone by, if there was want or destitution in our cities and towns, if we were short of doctors or medicines, the town councils would agree to send an envoy to find out whether any other town nearby had a doctor willing to return with them to help heal and cure.

SEE ME AS SUCH AN ENVOY – I am an ordinary, simple Jew, coming to you with a plea for help [. . .]

Most of you have no doubt heard about my ghetto.

Malicious tongues claim that my Jews have voluntarily submitted to slavery. That we toil in grime and filth. That we voluntarily break the commandment to keep the Sabbath; that we deliberately eat unclean food. That we demean ourselves by carrying out the occupiers' slightest decree.

Those who claim all this have not learnt to appreciate the value of work properly. For so it is written in the Pirkei Avot: YOU ARE NOT REQUIRED TO CARRY OUT WORK; BUT NOR SHALL YOU REFRAIN FROM IT.

And what does that mean? It means that work is not exclusively about the earnings of you or me. Work is what holds a society together.

Work not only purifies. Work also protects.

Among us, in my ghetto, nobody dies of hunger. All those who work have the right to share what there is to be shared. But with rights come responsibilities. Anyone who misappropriates, who takes from the common store for his own gain, shall be excluded from his khevre, and nowhere shall he find food to eat. Nowhere shall he sleep. And nowhere shall he be able to go to pray.

But conversely, anyone who is prepared to work for the

community will also be rewarded for that. I do not come to you as one who preaches and lectures. I am a simple person. God has given me, as he has everyone else, two hands. I raise them now to entreat you – come back to us in Litzmannstadt and help us to build a home for all Jews.

All your contributions are welcome.

Gifts of money are also most acceptable.

People came to him in the night.

They did not want to hear about his high production quotas or all his successes in the battle against corruption and black-market trading in the ghetto. They wanted to hear what he could tell them of their nearest and dearest, whom they had left behind in Litzmannstadt, of the streets where they had lived; they wanted to know if the houses were still standing, and if those who once lived there were still alive. And he opened the lid of his trunk and distributed letters and postcards, and, to 'refresh' their memories further, he told them of the chestnut trees the Germans were letting them plant in Lutomierska Street this spring. They would make a proper avenue. He told them about the children who went to school each day, about the summer camps he was planning to set up for them in Marysin: seventeen thousand children would be fed three hot meals a day; they would be taught Yiddish, Hebrew and Jewish history by teachers he had trained specially for the purpose; a hospital with all the most modern equipment had been put at his disposal exclusively for the children. In return, the children would work at planting and sowing green vegetables and root vegetables in the spring. He told them there were agricultural collectives where hundreds of kibbutznikim were at work, planting potatoes. They dug three crops of potatoes a year.

From his trunk he produced a copy of *Informator far klayngertner*, a handbook for vegetable-growers that Szmul Rozenzstajn had printed. What mattered was not *who* or *what* you were, he said, waving the booklet about, what mattered was that everyone who came knew their craft and was willing to work.

*

A week later, the Chairman was back in Litzmannstadt. His return could hardly be described as 'royal'. A Gestapo vehicle let him off at the ghetto boundary. That was at about half past five in the afternoon. The ghetto was deserted. At the far end of Zgierska Street, near the wooden bridge, a tram had stopped dead, as if it had been struck by lightning.

Where was everybody? His first thought was absurd: that the population of the ghetto had not been able to bear his absence and had quite simply exploded from hunger and sorrow.

His next thought was more plausible: that some kind of coup had been mounted while he was away. Could it be the Bundists, the Zionist Workers or the lunatic Marxists who had ganged up against him? Or could it possibly be that the favoured Dawid Gertler had persuaded the authorities that he be allowed to take over the functions of the police, as well?

But if that had happened – why was it so quiet and empty everywhere?

Die Feldgrauen were standing there as usual, stiff and idiotic in their red-and-white-striped sentry boxes. They weren't even looking in his direction. He decided to think no more about it, took up his trunk and set off towards the barrier marking the border at the entry point to Bałuty Square.

Outside the long row of ghetto administration huts stood a parked lorry, and behind it – as if taking cover behind bomb defences – his entire staff was waiting, with Miss Dora Fuchs, Mr Mieczysław Abramowicz and the ubiquitous Szmul Rosenzstajn at their head. They looked nervous, as if he had caught them doing something they were ashamed of.

Where is everybody?

There's been shooting in the ghetto, Mr Chairman.

Who? Who's been shooting?

Nobody knows. The shots came from inside the ghetto, that's all we know. One of them, unfortunately, happened to cause some injury to a German official. Herr Amtsleiter is in quite a state.

Where's Rozenblat?

Chief Police Commander Rozenblat has been summoned for interview by the authorities.

So ask Gertler to come.

Herr Amtsleiter Biebow has imposed a curfew on the ghetto until the perpetrator is caught. If that person hasn't come forward by seven o'clock tomorrow morning, he is threatening to have eighteen Jews executed by firing squad.

And where are those Jews now?

In the Red House, Mr Chairman.

Very well, then we shall go to the Red House. Mr Abramowicz, you will accompany me.

The Red House was a building in the district just behind the Church of the Most Blessed Virgin Mary on the big square; it was three storeys high and made of solid, red brick, hence its name.

Before the occupation, the red-brick building had been used by the ministry of the Catholic Church, but as soon as the ghetto was set up, the German criminal police had seen the potential of the place, thrown out all the church occupants and moved their own people in instead. On the top floor, Polish women typists sat writing reports to the Central Staff back in Litzmannstadt. The basement housed the torture cells.

In the ghetto, the Jews were free, mentally at least, to roam any district. And every Bałuty resident could have found their way blindfold to absolutely any passageway, courtyard or side street. But at the Red House, tongues and thoughts came to a full stop. Even uttering the name Roytes Heizl was like touching an abscessed tooth: your whole body flinched from the pain. Every night, those who lived round about, in Brzezińska and Jakuba Streets, were awoken by the screams of the torture victims; and every morning – whether there were corpses to collect or not – Mr Muzyk the undertaker would be waiting outside with his cart.

Szmul Rosensztajn records in his diary that Rumkowski had two meetings with the German authorities the day he returned from Warsaw.

First in the Red House (where he finally got the reception he had hoped for when he came home: eighteen of Biebow's hostages pressing their terror-stricken faces to the bars of the prison windows and shouting out how glad they were that their deliverer had finally returned); and then with Biebow himself in the latter's Bałuty office.

By then, the account of events was rather different.

It turned out that there had not been any shots fired in the ghetto. What had happened was that some blunt and heavy object had been thrown from inside the ghetto fence and hit a tram that was passing through the 'Aryan' corridor beyond. It was the tram he had seen standing on the slope up from Bałuty Square when he arrived. The stone from inside the ghetto had broken one of the tram windows and the splinters of glass had fallen on one of the passengers in the aisle. This might have been overlooked, had not the person involved happened to be Karl-Heinz Krapp, a civil servant from Mayor Werner Ventzki's office, a dyed-in-the-wool Aryan.

The Kripo for their part had worked on the assumption that it was an attempt on his life, and had arrested fifty people who had witnessed the incident, taking eighteen of them to the interrogation suite in the Red House. Starting at seven o'clock the next morning, one of them would be executed every hour until the stone-thrower gave himself up.

'If you intend to do anything about this, I suggest you start at once,' Biebow told Rumkowski.

Rumkowski gave Dawid Gertler orders to search all the districts on the right-hand side of Zgierska Street. Gertler's men decided to approach it scientifically. In order to hit the tram window at that angle, the stone must have been thrown from quite a height, and thus from the second or third floor of one of the blocks of flats along Zgierska Street. That ruled out all the blocks except three.

Gertler's men swarmed up winding, ramshackle flights of stairs, broke down closed or barricaded apartment doors and forced their way in.

By about seven thirty, Gertler could personally report that they had the culprit surrounded. He was in a flat on the top floor of number 87. There were clearly also children in the flat. When the police broke down the door, children's cries had been clearly heard from inside.

'Shall we go in anyway?' asked Gertler.

'Don't do anything,' replied the Chairman. 'I'm coming over there myself.'

87 Zgierska Street was one of the most dilapidated of the blocks of flats looking out on one of the side streets, Flisacka. The three rows of windows along its facade resembled as many cave mouths. Not a single window pane remained unbroken. Most of the apertures also lacked frames, and the only protection they had against the rain and cold was a basic sheet of cardboard or a bit of grubby sheeting.

The police had already ringed the building and as soon as he arrived the Chairman was escorted to a flat right up on the third floor. Two men were squatting by the stove on what appeared to be an upturned enamel washtub; a woman stood beside them, rubbing her hands on a dirty apron. Gertler led the way to what looked like the door to a cloakroom or store cupboard at the back of the room, and thumped his fist a number of times on the frame.

Go away, leave us alone, came a muffled voice from inside.

(A rough, man's voice.)

The Chairman approached the door and said in a commanding voice:

'It is I. Rumkowski.'

There was silence on the other side. Someone thought he heard whispering, and the sound of bodies shuffling. There were apparently several people in the cloakroom.

Rumkowski:

We demand that the person guilty of this deed come out. Otherwise, eighteen innocent Jewish lives will be lost.

Again: silence. Then there was a voice. A very small voice –

Is it really Mr Praeses?

A child. Meaningful looks were exchanged among the men in Gertler's unit. The Chairman cleared his throat and said in a voice that he tried to make sound as stern and authoritative as possible:

What is your name?

Moshe Kamersztajn.

Was it you who threw the stone, Moshe?

I didn't mean it to hit anything the way it did.

Why did you throw the stone, Moshe?

I often throw stones at rats. But this one got away.

The rat or the stone?

Is it really you, Mr Praeses?

It is, Moshe, and I have a present for you.

What sort of present?

You'll see when you come out. I've got the present in my trunk.

I daren't come out, Mr Praeses. They'll beat me.

No one here is going to beat you, you have my word on that.

What sort of present is it? When will I get it?

The rough, man's voice from inside:

Stop that, he's just trying to trick you –

Moshe, who's in there with you?

(Silence.)

Don't say anything!

Is it your dad?

Yes . . .

SHUT UP, YOU LITTLE DEVIL!

It went quiet. Then the Chairman spoke up again:

Moshe, tell your dad that if you show yourself, you'll be able to come to me. There's plenty of room for able boys in my police force.

(Silence.)

Are you a big boy now, Moshe? Tell me, are you a man?

Don't answer!

(Silence.)

Tell me what you're good at, Moshe.

I'm good at killing rats.

Then you can be my rat killer.

Will I be a policeman?

More than that. I'll make you the head of a special rat commando. If you'll just open the door and come out. It's never too late to do something about your life, Moshe.

The door opened and a skinny boy of about thirteen stood blinking in the light. Behind him was a middle-aged man, pale and unshaven. The man looked uncomfortably around him. It was apparent that he did not like the scrutiny of all these people in the cramped room. The boy was as pale as his father, and had a lopsided look. The right side of his face hung out over the left, which looked slack, as if it had no feeling in it. The same was true of the rest of his body: as if someone had put a meat hook through one shoulder and the rest of him dangled from it, limp and lifeless. But the part of his face that did have life in it was beaming with anticipation.

Later, there would be much talk in the ghetto of how good the Chairman was with children. By provoking the authorities, this child had put the lives of hundreds of innocent Jews at risk. No one would have been surprised if the Chairman had proceeded to mete out one of his severest punishments, in the name of discipline. But he did not. Instead he crouched down and took both the boy's hands in his.

'If you had been my son, Moshe Kamersztajn, what do you think I would have done with you?'

The boy was so overwhelmed to find the Chairman there in the flesh that he could only stare down at the dirty floorboards; he shook his head.

'I shall ask you to consider fully what you have done, and then take your punishment with dignity. If you can do that, then you will have earned my respect again.'

He took the boy's hand and led him past the chain of policemen, down the stairs and out into the street. Then they walked together through the ghetto. The Chairman first, gesticulating eagerly (he was clearly busy telling one of his innumerable stories); the boy after him, rolling on his stiff hip.

When they were halfway to Kirchplatz, they came across Meir Klamm with his 'hearse'. Mr Muzyk's undertaking business would later have at its disposal a large conveyance with thirty-six recesses and drawer compartments, but at that time there was just the one cart, with space for one corpse, and it was pulled by an old mare who was always pressed into service if there was a shortage of draught animals in the ghetto: so gaunt that the ribs stood out along her flanks like the strips in a badly woven raffia basket. She was recognisable above all by her walk. She would walk on for one or two steps, then stop; after that she took a couple more exhausted steps forward, and there was nothing old Meir up in the driver's seat could do to speed her up.

The Chairman now seized the reins and asked Meir if he was aware that the authorities had imposed a curfew and that he could be shot as a punishment for breaching it. Meir replied that he had been out with the cart since long before the curfew came into force, and what was he supposed to do about that?

Curfew or no curfew: people kept on dying.

While this exchange was going on, Moshe Kamersztajn would have had all the time in the world to slip away. The Chairman had even let go of his hand. But Moshe just stood there staring. And when the Chairman was done, Moshe's hand found its way up into the Chairman's again, and the two of them carried on chatting about whatever it was the Chairman had been in the middle of saying.

And so they went, all the way to the Red House, where the Kripo's leading interrogators were awaiting their 'perpetrator'.

*

Four days later, the Chairman called his Council of Elders, all the *resort-laiter* of the ghetto, and the rest of his administration to a meeting in the House of Culture. He opened it with a speech about his experiences in Warsaw:

> I have been in Warsaw. Some hold that against me, in view of the high price that the authorities demand for these trips.
>
> But I would still like to tell you what I saw.
>
> In Warsaw there is no one considering what is in the best public interest. People think only of themselves. And those in power in Czerniaków's Jewish Council have no choice but to watch money changing hands behind the backs of the doctors caring for the sick.
>
> Treatment is only available to those who can pay for it.
>
> Food and medicines are smuggled in. But only the rich can

afford the prices being asked.

Let me tell you that criminality and smuggling in Warsaw have grown to such proportions that they are now the ghetto's main industry. Unlike here in our ghetto, smuggling is the only industry that really works.

Not the labour of all for the common good. But everyone fighting it out with everyone else.

Is that the way we Jews should behave to each other?

Is that how you would like us to behave towards one another in my ghetto, too?

I do not believe you do, though I know there are some here who think that would be the solution to all our problems.

Not sharing our burdens equally, but letting everyone take responsibility for their own.

I shall tell you where that leads.

Not to short-term prosperity for anyone, but to public anarchy.

Right at the front of the stage stood a small table covered with a white cloth. On this cloth, the Chairman had placed his big trunk. Two police officers were guarding it, one on either side, to prevent any robbery. This despite the fact that the trunk – as the Chairman was careful to emphasise – did not contain any items of value, but only letters, greetings (scribbled on scraps of paper); photographs in faded frames; a lock of hair in a little box; a necklace; an amulet.

Even so, they stormed the table as soon as the lid was opened.

The duty police superintendent had to call for reinforcements. The door to the hall opened, and into the midst of all the tumult came the chief of police himself, Mr Leon Rozenblat, holding young Mr Kamersztajn firmly by the scruff of the neck.

Moshe Kamersztajn's split face was red and puffy on both sides; his cheek was swollen to double its normal size and appeared to hang right down to his collarbone. But the torturers of the Red House did not seem to have made any impact on his fundamental defect. The boy still limped as though he had a painful hook stuck in him, somewhere between his cheek and the back of his neck –

He says Mr Praeses promised him a present from Warsaw.
The Chairman generously swivelled the open trunk.

Step forward then, young Mr Kamersztajn;
Step forward and choose what you would like –

Three weeks later, as yet another *geshenk* from Rumkowski to the ghetto, a transport with a total of twelve doctors from Warsaw arrived. The Chairman had signed their contracts already, while he was there, and the bribes and transport costs had been prepaid to the Gestapo. The *Chronicle* lists all twelve doctors by name and specialism:

Michał Eliasberg and *Arno Kleszczelski* – (surgeons);
Abram Mazur – (throat specialist);
Salomon Rubinstein – (radiographer);
Janina Hartglas and *Benedykta Moszkowicz* – (obstetricians);
Józef Goldwasser, Alfred Lewi, Izak Ser, Mojzesz Nekrycz;
(Miss) *Alicja Czarnożyłówna* and *Izrael Geist* – (general practitioners)

Then, in June 1941, the Germans launched their invasion of the Soviet Union: Operation Barbarossa.

All that summer, people queued for hours at Wiewiórka's barber's shop to hear the news read aloud from a copy of the *Litzmannstädter Zeitung* that one of the Schupo had been persuaded to leave behind. Herr Wiewiórka read the German himself, while one of his apprentices interpreted into Yiddish. 'The conquest of White Russia', translated the young barbershop apprentice in an increasingly shaky voice, 'has proceeded by *leaps and bounds*; German troops are *already marching on Moscow*.'

What was going to happen next?

Earlier that summer, on 7 June 1941, SS-Reichsführer Heinrich Himmler had paid a visit to the ghetto. Among the factories and textile workshops inspected by Himmler were the Central Tailors at 45 Łagiewnicka Street and the uniform-maker's in Jakuba Street. After his visit to Warsaw, the Chairman had concluded that he could never again interrupt his supervision of the ghetto, and had on his own initiative imposed a curfew from eight o'clock on the evening before Himmler's visit. The motorcade of SS guards and Himmler's limousine passed through open, empty ghetto streets in which not a soul was to be seen.

In his diary, Szmul Rosenzstajn noted the following exchange between Rumkowski and Himmler:

Himmler: So you are the renowned rich Jew of Litzmannstadt, Herr Rumkowski.

Rumkowski: I am rich, Herr Reichsführer, because I have a whole people at my disposal.

Himmler: And what are you doing with your people, Herr Rumkowski?

Rumkowski: With my people I am building a city of workers, Herr Reichsführer.

Himmler: But this is not a city of workers – it is a ghetto!

Rumkowski: It is a city of workers, Herr Reichsführer; and we will carry on working for as long as you have demands to make of us.

The Chairman told the members of his Council of Elders afterwards that the German successes on the eastern front had taken some of the *pressure* off the ghetto. There was a sense of calm among the occupying powers that he intended to take advantage of. The time had come to request the expansion of the ghetto.

Overcrowding leads to social misery, and the wretched, in-sanitary conditions allow disease to take hold – diphtheria, above all, has proved an intractable problem. I have personally arranged for more doctors to join my ghetto, but that will not help unless I can put whole buildings, even whole districts, in quarantine.

In front of the authorities, Rumkowski always adopted a more moderate attitude. In front of them, he always stood the same way, with his hands at his sides and his white-haired head meekly bowed –

Ich bin Rumkowski. Melde mich gehorsamst zur Stelle.

It was two days since he had submitted his request for the ghetto to be extended for 'sanitary reasons'. Now Mayor

116

Werner Ventzki leant down from the high platform on which he sat with Amtsleiter Biebow and administrator Ribbe, and gave his solemn promise:

You shall have your wish, Rumkowski. The ghetto is to be expanded. It is to be expanded by twenty thousand Jews. Berlin has decided to send them from the annexed areas of the Reich, both the old and the new.

Twenty thousand more like you, Rumkowski.

You can scarcely let your ghetto get any bigger than that.

From his vantage point on the roof of the brickworks Adam Rzepin could see the 'foreign' Jews arriving at the ghetto. Thousands of people in a single line, like a rope stretched across the low horizon. Above this long rope of humanity, the October sky arched wide and desolate over the treeless plain. One minute the sky was almost stingingly open and blue, the next it was all but covered in a rapid swell of black cloud. And a few moments after that, the file of people disappeared into the dark mass of cloud as if it were swallowing them up. When the new arrivals emerged once more, their baggage, the clothes they were wearing, everything was covered in a fine layer of snow.

Adam cupped his hands into a funnel and shouted down to Jakub Weisberg – *The foreigners are coming! The foreigners are coming!* – He saw Jakub's face turn upward in dismay; then he swung himself, like Zawadzki the smuggler, in one fluid movement from the roof down to the ground, with its still pristine covering of snow.

But hundreds of ghetto dwellers seemed to have had the same idea. The streets and alleyways leading to Marysin were packed with people. Out at Marynarska Street, Gertler's Sonderkommando had erected a roadblock. Nobody was allowed to pass unless they could pay first: twenty marks just to be let through, another twenty if you had a handcart. Adam had only his two lacerated hands, but the fierce guard insisted on payment even for those.

No access for porters unless they can pay their way!

From behind the barriers through which he would never

get, Adam saw one of the newcomers – a short man in a hat and an elegant gabardine raincoat – fishing in the inner pocket of his jacket for money. Beside the peculiar foreigner stood the foreigner's wife, wearing a tight skirt, real stockings and high-heeled shoes, and next to her their three almost grown-up children, two boys and a young woman. The children were looking around them, wide-eyed. They obviously hadn't the faintest idea where they had ended up. With a gesture that was meant to look extravagant, but merely emphasised his bewilderment still further, the newcomer took out his wallet and gave the porter a couple of notes.

Beside them, all the suitcases they had brought with them had already been stacked and lashed onto the porter's barrow: a mountain of luggage.

*

Schnell, schnell . . . !
Mach, dass du hier wegkommst, dumme Judensau . . .

This was the first thing Věra Schulz heard: the German police guard's voice, sharp yet tinny, cutting through many closed wagon doors. Then the doors were pulled open from outside and a sort of dark, metallic *clang* ran through the whole train, and suddenly all was chaos and noise as people who had been sitting stiff and immobile for many hours set their heavy limbs reluctantly in motion.

She wrote the date in her exercise book:
4 October 1941; Transport No. 'Prague II'

It must have snowed during the night; the bright light reflecting off the snow was piercing to eyes that began to water in the unexpected cold. No platform: just bare, frozen ground. Boards like those used for unloading cattle were propped against the open wagon doors. The sick and the old held out groping, disorientated hands and were helped down by passengers who had already made it to the ground. And once they were down, the desperate crush that arises when thousands of people don't know which way to go.

German soldiers driving them from all directions; those hysterically shouting voices can be heard everywhere above the din: *Schnell, schnell! Nicht stehenbleiben! Los!*

Not a moment to rest or get your breath back.

There are some men standing beside the train, all wearing the same uniform caps, and armbands with stars of David, whom she at first took for railway employees but now sees to be policemen of some kind. A number of them are blocking people's way and demanding to see identity papers or insisting that all accompanying *Gepäck* be opened, and that (as she only later realises) is how such huge amounts of clothing and valuables go missing before the newcomers have even properly arrived.

Among the Polish Jews there are also some adolescents, mostly boys, who have bribed their way through the police barriers and are coming up with barrows to offer to carry luggage. Someone in the transport (not her wagon) must have become separated from her husband or son, because she is desperately crying out his name into the crowd. Another woman – directly behind Věra – falls to her bare knees and starts to sob.

Heart-rending, uninhibited sobbing.

Where have they taken us? Where are we?

Standing a little further off is a handful of German soldiers in knee-length, greyish-green military greatcoats, with rifles slung across their backs. They stamp their booted feet to keep warm in the cold, and they are all smiling though they are feigning indifference, pretending not to see. Perhaps they are thinking about the profits to be made now that all the Jews –

all of them from the Reich, with everything they own, stashed or sewn into suitcases and rucksacks and coat linings – will finally be forced to pay back all they owe the German people.

*

Diary entry:

We walk as if in a trance. The march seems to go on for ever. Run-down tenements with smashed or empty, gaping windows. No motorised traffic; but everywhere the same crush. Men and women hauling loaded carts and stinking latrine tanks – two in front, two pushing at the back. Like working animals!

But most of all, children. They come swarming round our legs as soon as we are inside the barricades – and they will not leave us alone until the police marching alongside step in.

We have now got to our 'final destination' – an old school building. The wide archway into the courtyard is flooded with sewage. Some of the younger people put down planks so the older ones can keep their feet dry as they go in, and form a human chain to pass the cases through.

People jostle, push forward; all the classrooms and the corridors from one end of the building to the other have been converted into dormitories. Wooden bunks are lined up under the windows, each bunk 75 cm long, so people's feet have to hang over the end. In that small space, we are also to store our luggage: rucksacks at the head end, suitcases at the foot end. Our room has about sixty people 'living' in it. There are just as many in the corridor outside! When everyone has a place, they give out bread that is meant to last us a whole week.

In the morning: weak black coffee, like brown water.

Young women from the ghetto bring big vats of soup from the soup kitchens.

It's not much of a soup – hot water with something greenish in it. But everyone falls on the food, even those who said earlier that they wouldn't touch it! It turns out to be the only meal of the day.

Washing is difficult. We have to go out into the yard because there's no water in the taps. And then: stand in the snow, queuing for the latrines. Toilet paper – forget it. What little toilet paper we have is reserved for the sick! They say tuberculosis and typhus fever are rife in the ghetto. Every other inhabitant is ill with it. My hands ache right up to the elbows with a constant, dull pain that is made worse by having to wash clothes in ice-cold water. It's the rheumatism again!

Some people have strung lines around their bunks so they can hang up their wet washing. Everyone huddles up as tightly they can; children scream, howl and cry; and many of those who are sick make the sounds sick people make.

So the nights pass, and are followed by the days.

And then it is night again. And in the morning the same thin, beige soup that looks and smells just as rank as before – like ammonia. The smell of the soup stays in the walls far into the night, and it's like the ache in your stomach and the band of hunger round your forehead. Will I ever get used to it?

But the worst thing of all is the regret. The thought that we should have got away to safety while there was still time – that Papa thought it was more important to do his bit at the hospital than to look after his family. That he refused to think of us and of Maman!

But I can't say any of that, because of course now Papa is making himself indispensable upstairs, where they've set up a first-aid post for the sickest people in the transport! They're crying out for doctors here! But I can't sleep, it feels too horrible not knowing what the future holds for us . . .

Somewhere, somehow, there must be some way to get help, otherwise we shall all fade away and die . . . Somewhere, there must be . . .

Adam Rzepin lived with his father Szaja and sister Lida in a flat, just one room and a kitchen, at the top of Gnieźnieńska Street, near the south-western boundary of the ghetto. In the kitchen, they also kept a bed for Szaja's brother Lajb. But ever since the fatal strike at Drukarska Street, it was as if Lajb had some kind of curse on him. He moved from *resort* to *resort*, changing jobs like other people change their clothes, and nobody really knew where he slept from one night to the next. It was said in the ghetto that he was a *Spitzel* for the Kripo and it was best for people to keep out of his way.

Adam's sister now lay in the bed that used to be Lajb's. When Adam got up to fetch water and light the stove in the mornings, Lida would lie there, listening to the angels. The angels often came down from Heaven and spoke to Lida. In summer they sang in the stove-pipe, and in winter they traced their own, delicate wing-quill patterns in the frost flowers on the window panes. Adam and Lida's father Szaja had insulated the frame with old rags but the damp got in anyway, and in winter the glass was sometimes entirely frozen over on the inside, the catch covered in fine hairs of frost. Every so often, one particular angel they called *the big beast* would talk to Lida. Lida's world was populated by the little beasts and the big beast. The little beasts were the bedbugs, who gathered in drifts behind the wallpaper and crawled over your hand as soon as you pulled away a skirting board. The big beast was a bleeding angel of hunger.

When the hunger angel got its teeth into someone, it was as if they were being turned inside out. Every bit of their body was crying out for food; anything would do, as long as it could be chewed and swallowed and taken down into their stomach. When the big beast spoke, its voice seemed to come from a great, ravenously dark pit of hunger. The only thing Lida could do was to open and close her mouth in terror, to let out its tormenting screams.

Whenever the big beast took his sister in its clutches, Adam got a blanket and lay down beside her; he lay so close to her that it was as if he was trying to absorb her body into his own.

Though she weighed no more than about thirty kilos, Lida's face was remarkably unscathed, the skin pale, bluish, and as thin as porcelain. And beneath the rags in which Lida lay swaddled there was, in spite of everything, a body with a distended belly and two small, thin breasts. Where it had not already grown swollen and waterlogged from lack of nutrition, her flesh was covered in sores and bruises. Every morning, Adam carried water up from the yard and washed his sister in a large wooden tub, then wrapped the rags around her again. But even while he was washing Lida, her china face remained smooth and immobile, as if frozen in an expression of perpetual wonder – at the existence of the world, and of her brother, and of the hunger angel beating and beating its hard wings out there in the icy brown darkness.

The Rzepin family had lived in Gnieźnieńska Street since long before the ghetto existed. Back then, they had all helped to provide for the family, even Uncle Lajb. But since Lajb fell into disgrace, Szaja could rely on little more than the daily workplace soup, and you did not get fat by running errands with parcels or keeping watch for children, as Adam did.

Everyone was talking about the new arrivals in the ghetto now. Moshe Stern said the richest Jews were the ones from Prague. According to Moshe, some of them had even had so much food with them when they arrived that they gave away what they couldn't carry to children, and other people who begged for it.

Lying there beside his sick sister in the evenings, Adam Rzepin kept turning this over in his mind. How was it possible that someone could reach the ghetto with such a surplus?

The Prague Jews had been divided into two collectives inside the ghetto. One was quartered in the former children's hospital at 37 Łagiewnicka Street, the other in the elementary school in Franciszkańska Street. Adam opted for the latter, because he thought there were more, and safer, escape routes from there; and a few weeks later he cautiously began to prowl about the area.

The snow that had begun to fall the day the foreign Jews arrived was still coming down, though not as thickly. It had got colder. Down in the Prague Jews' courtyard a few women were busy hauling up buckets of water from the well and carrying them into the school. The women carried their water awkwardly, clumsy in their movements; they were *city Jews* – and it showed. The children, too, were different. Instead of playing with whatever came to hand, they just wandered aimlessly round the yard, barging into each other.

Adam realised at once how much of a stranger he was here. He spoke Yiddish in his daily life, Polish when he had to. But the peculiar, spiky, sing-song Czech spoken by the women in the yard was completely alien to him. He couldn't understand a single word.

Moshe Stern, who had been to the collective several times, said there was only one way to treat the newcomers. You had to smile and be polite. So Adam put on his sunniest smile as soon as he got into the yard. With that smile he pushed past a small group of Czech men on their way out of the building with snow shovels in their hands and thick, hunting-style caps, the earflaps fastened on top. Adam did not need to turn round to be aware of their looks boring into his back. It started to hurt inside his head. The higher he climbed inside the building, the tighter the band of pain around his forehead grew, and when he was at the very top, Lida started to sing.

Lida had only once before started singing for him while he was out. He and some of the kids from his street had gone to look for reject building timber on the empty plot next to the plank store in Drukarska Street. The plot had been fenced off, and the whole storage area was patrolled by local police, on duty in shifts from dawn to late evening. With Feliks Frydman from the tenement next door he had managed to dig a way under the fence along the back of the plank compound, and Feliks was already inside when he heard Lida's voice, as indelibly pure and clear as the sound of a spoon tapping a glass that is half-full. As the tone faded away, a pain ran through his head, as if someone had suddenly pushed a sharp metal wire through it, from one temple to the other. He only just had time to get away before the guards came rushing up, batons raised. They had already caught Feliks inside the compound.

Now he could hear Lida's voice again; like the thin whine of a drill:

eeeeee-eeeeee

He wonders if it is the men with the snow shovels she wants to warn him about. But what has he actually got to hide? He's only here out of curiosity, to look round a bit. And anyway, he has gone too far to turn back now.

There are sleeping places in the classrooms, and the corridors outside them, but to his surprise, Adam sees few people between the screens that separate the various families' spaces. Most members of the collective must have moved out; or the Praeses has already found jobs for them all. He runs his eyes frantically over bunks and improvised tables, sees clothes, blankets and mattresses, spread out or rolled up; sees lots of kitchen equipment, saucepans, frying pans, washing bowls and tubs piled in and on one another, or stowed with suitcases under the narrow bunks. But nowhere can he see anything worth stealing. Then he suddenly remembers something Moshe told them: *at least* one doctor came with each transport, and those doctors were expected to set up a surgery in every collective. Adam has seen no sign of any surgery on the ground floor of the building. So there must be one upstairs somewhere. He is on the second floor now. The rooms are smaller here, the corridor running between them narrower. He notices people tense and turn round to stare after him as he pushes past them increasingly curtly.

He is suddenly aware of how few people there are up here.

Two youngish men approach from one side.

Where's the doctor's surgery? he asks.

In Polish: *Gdzie jest przychodnia lekarska?*

And then, mainly to gain time, in Yiddish as well: *I'm looking for the DOCTOR. Can anybody tell me where he is?*

One of the two men thinks he understands what Adam means, and points uncertainly along a further stretch of corridor. As he walks in the direction indicated by the man, he thinks he is probably not going to get out of here alive.

But the far end of the corridor opens out into something that looks like a waiting room, with people sitting or lying on the floor outside a closed door. He goes up to the door and pulls it open, expecting to see a doctor look up in alarm from examining a patient. To his astonishment, the room inside is empty. A perfectly ordinary office with a desk, and an armchair behind it, and next to the desk a cabinet with some dishes, dressings and anonymous glass bottles on its shelves. He opens the cabinet doors and pulls out its drawers; he pays scant attention to what he is taking, just fills his pockets with as many bottles and jars and packs of dressings as he can cram in; then backs out into the corridor and makes his way out by the same route he came in by.

But now his sunny smile no longer meets with other smiles.

An elderly man he tries to squeeze past opens his mouth and screams.

He starts to run, heedless of anyone or anything in his way. Until he reaches the end of the corridor and his eyes fall on a woman dozing on a wooden stool with her head – all he can really see is a huge mass of hair tied in some kind of headscarf – hanging low between her knees. On the floor beside the woman is her handbag: a *real* handbag. It is large, quite plain, in faded leather with a clasp at the top like the one Józefina Rzepin had on hers when the two of them strolled up and down Piotrkowska on Sundays. It is this sudden image of a mother he otherwise scarcely remembers that decides the matter for Adam. Before he knows what he is doing, he has snatched the bag and run headlong down the stairs. Out of the corner of his eye he sees the men with the hunting caps swarming *up* the same stairs, in an avalanche of indignant voices, but they have come *too late* – taken the *wrong* doors – he knows he will have time to get down and out ahead of them: two more strides and he'll be safe.

Franciszkańska. The sharp, blinding light of the snow in his eyes.

Muddy slush in the streets. Empty facades.

Ten metres down the road, a gap between two buildings leads into a narrow courtyard. At one time, all the inner courtyards of the ghetto were surrounded by tall wooden fences, but those have all been taken down now, chopped up and carried off for fuel. Instead, a whole network of firebreaks, some as wide as avenues, opens up behind the house fronts, affording the fugitive free passage from one part of the ghetto to another. But these internal routes are known only to those who lived here long before the barricades came. Long before there was even a ghetto here.

The name of the woman with the headscarf and the handbag in the collective in Franciszkańska Street was Irena, though no one had ever called her anything but Maman, pronounced not in the French way but with equal stress on both syllables.

Ma-mann! Ma-mann!

It was a cry that had echoed right through Věra Schulz's childhood, through stairwells where the high, stone vaulting intensified the noise of the passing trams, and through the empty rooms in the spacious apartment in Vinohrady in Prague, which at this time of day, in the afternoon, was suffused with warm sunlight and the stately sound of ticking clocks. After she had sat all morning practising at the grand piano, Maman would languish and pine the afternoons away. She complained the heat gave her migraine, and rubbed expensive creams into her skin to stop it drying out. Lying on her back, on top of the bedclothes on the wide bed, she would amuse the children by tying coloured ribbons in her hair. Maman had a shock of curly, almost frizzy hair, which with a little effort she could transform into any look she chose. Maman would step into her wardrobe and came out again in a tennis skirt and Mary Pickford hat, or dress up as Mrs Benešová the President's wife in a tailored suit of 'English cut', with a hat that looked like a military cap.

The fact that her mother was always vanishing and coming back as someone else, even if it was only in her piano soirée costume, had implanted in Věra from an early age a dread of Maman one day vanishing for good. As long as you look after me properly, I won't be vanishing anywhere, Maman would joke, but none of the children – as well as Věra there were two brothers, Martin and Josel – believed her. For as long as they had known their mother, she had always been leaving them in some way or another.

Arnošt Schulz loved his wife in a more pragmatic way: as you love and care for a desirable ornament. According to him, Maman did not have good or bad days, she had different *personalities* (you did that, as an artist), and the family was instructed to stay on good terms with them all: *Now children, please leave Maman in peace for a little while*, he would say as soon as Věra or her brothers raised their voices at the dining table or played too boisterously in their rooms.

After two weeks in the ghetto, Maman had only one of her *personalities* left: a gaunt, hollow-eyed woman sitting crouched under a cloud of frizzy hair, who flinched in terror if anyone spoke to her. She would only eat the *disgusting* soup if someone fed it to her with a spoon, or the way Věra did it: soaked a few bits of dry bread in it and popped them in her mouth as soon as her attention was elsewhere.

But how different it was for her energetic husband.

From the very first moment, Dr Arnošt Schulz had made himself the spokesman of the Prague collective. He had set up a system of guards to tackle the local inhabitants' brazen theft from the new arrivals, and had also composed letters and coordinated petitions to the Chairman's office to complain about unheated rooms, lack of running water and a latrine-emptying procedure that *resembled nothing so much as a farce*. This last comment was made in his capacity as newly appointed general practitioner at Hospital No. 1 in Łagiewnicka Street where he is, as he puts it, *occupied day and night with saving the lives of people who as a result of the inadequate supply of nutrition in the ghetto lack all the prerequisites for survival*.

For a number of weeks after he sent off this missive, nothing happened.

One day, a slim envelope arrived, stamped with the Chairman's postmark. Inside was an invitation to attend a 'musical soirée' to be held in honour of the new arrivals at the House of Culture in Krawiecka Street, and Arnošt Schulz decided to go with his daughter. He went with mixed feelings and no great expectations, and returned 'distressed', as he put it. Věra, too, describes the event, in the diary she was keeping fairly regularly at the time:

Evening Revue in the House of Culture

The first people we meet are a group of *politsayen* with armbands and batons [!] who tell us to step aside and let the *honoratiores* through.

I had not expected to find hierarchies like this in the ghetto. It's as if they have invited us just to show us how little we are worth!

We stood like prisoners behind bars, watching the *honoratiores* arrive. I saw Rumkowski himself, a dour, white-haired man, like a pompous emperor at the head of his praetorian guard. It would have been laughable, but for the fact that everyone in the place leapt to their feet and started clapping.

Then the *show* got under way. A painted backdrop of a synagogue. Some actors dash up on stage and blurt out some lines in loud voices. Since the audience laughs, it must be some kind of joke, but I can't understand a word. The whole thing is in Yiddish.

Between the comedy sketches there are musical numbers. A Miss B. Rotsztat performs some 'light romances' by Brahms on the violin, accompanied by Mr T. Ryder on the piano. Miss B. Rotsztat plays surprisingly well, though her movements are very exaggerated. The embarrassing part is the way the audience reacts – as if it has got to show rapturous delight to prove itself a proper audience.

Then it's the Chairman's big moment, Mr Mordechai Ch.

Rumkowski. You could hear a pin drop in the hall; hearing him speak was clearly the real reason everyone was there.

He turns to those of us standing at the back, and he addresses us not in German but in Yiddish, absurdly enough, since very few of us understand the language. Perhaps it was just as well we did not understand, because I have since found out that *the old man*, as they call him here, spent most of his speech telling us off, calling us 'robbers' because we haven't handed over our valuables to 'his' bank, because we haven't turned up at the jobs he has found for us (that clearly doesn't apply to Papa!), and saying that if we didn't abide by his rules he would *have us deported* at once – where to? – Doesn't he understand that we have just *been* deported?

*

Two days after the 'spectacle' at the House of Culture, the Chairman pays his own visit to the collective in Franciszkańska Street. The women and children down at the latrines see him coming first, or rather, the children in the yard see the white horse that pulls the Chairman's carriage come snorting through the wide gateway at a brisk trot. The Chairman himself appears briefly engulfed in the sea of bobbing caps and berets that suddenly surrounds him. But his bodyguards are there straight away, their fists and batons pushing the crowd back far enough for him to move freely again.

First the Chairman inspects the latrines and the long row of washtubs lined up by the cellar door; then he and his retinue of guards set off up the school's worn marble staircase. He goes along corridor after corridor. In all the places where outdoor clothes have been hung and suitcases and portmanteaux stacked in piles, he orders all the loose bits of clothing to be removed. Suitcases, portmanteaux, handbags: they are all opened and searched. In one of the classrooms, an older woman gives a heart-rending shriek as one of the bodyguards takes out a knife and starts cutting into the mattress on which she has just been lying.

The men of the Prague collective's newly formed security force come rushing from all directions, chief among them the former clinical consultant at Prague's Vinohrady Hospital –Dr Arnošt Schulz.

Schulz: Mr Rumkowski, will you be so kind as to stop these unfortunate proceedings.

Chairman: Who are you?

Schulz: Schulz.

Chairman: Schulz?

Schulz: We have met. You are merely suffering a temporary lapse of memory.

Chairman: Ah, Professor Schulz . . . ! As a doctor, you should know that leaving clothes and other loose items lying around attracts bedbugs.

Schulz: I apologise for this misunderstanding, Chairman. It will be rectified at once.

Chairman (pointing): We are now going to take these things down into the yard and burn them.

Schulz: Mr Rumkowski, you cannot treat people's possessions like that.

Chairman: Who makes the laws here, you or me?

Schulz: But this is madness.

Chairman: I see it as my personal responsibility to deal once and for all with the insanitary conditions that have developed here in the ghetto. All I see on this inspection, apart from the fact that you are flagrantly flouting the rules and regulations I have issued, are the sources of infection you are consciously breeding here in the collective.

Schulz: If you are concerned about the risk of infection, Mr Rumkowski, you should ensure that there is enough gas for everyone or make sure the latrines are emptied.

Chairman: It may be that the toilets are cleaner where you come from, Professor Schulz.

Schulz: Not even animals should be expected to eat the watery soup you give us. The bread is mouldy. What's more, the lives of women and children are threatened by intruders who come in off the street in broad daylight. The other day, some opportunist thief broke into our medical supplies. Money, blankets, pots and pans – they steal them all, in front of our very eyes.

Chairman: If you need protection, my *Ordnungsdienst* is at your disposal.

Schulz: With all due respect, Mr Chairman: your *Ordnungsdienst* is not worth a candle. I have seen some of your men here from time to time. They come at mealtimes; but it feels more as though they are supervising us to make sure we don't steal soup from you, than anything else. That is why we have set up our own guard!

Chairman: Your so-called guard is to be disbanded forthwith.

Schulz: You cannot prevent us defending ourselves.

Chairman: There is a police force in the ghetto, and it answers to me, and I view any attempt to set up another one as treason. Do you know how we punish treason here in the ghetto, Mr Schulz?

Schulz: Is that a threat? Are you threatening us?

Chairman: There is no need for any threats. I may be king of no more than a few latrine tanks in your eyes, Dr Schulz. But I know one thing for sure. One telephone call from me, and you and your family will be deported from the ghetto within twenty-four hours. But I will not make the call. I will let you get away with your insolence, doctor. This time.

Meanwhile, Gertler's men had carried suitcases and loose items of clothing down to the yard, doused them in petrol and set light to them. Within seconds, the flames were at the height of the first and second floors, where people were hanging out of the windows, watching in disbelief as the fire sent black smoke billowing to the opposite wall of the courtyard. A number of families reported afterwards that they had lost not only clothes and suitcases but also valuable personal items such as gold chains, charms and rings. One member of the collective said the Chairman's men had also confiscated his winter coat, cut his watch and watch chain from his waistcoat pocket, and stolen his wife's lace-up boots with winter linings.

At about the same time as Rumkowski was carrying out his inspection of the Franciszkańska Street collective, the Kripo raided the Adria restaurant at Bałuty Square, which had become something of a meeting place for the ghetto's German Jews. Nine people from the Berlin and Cologne collectives, and five from the Prague collective, were caught red-handed transacting various bits of business. One of the German Jews was trying to sell a complete dinner service, another a set of table silverware. It transpired that all the potential buyers were either informants reporting directly to the Kripo, or members of Gertler's intelligence team.

This is the way the Jews of the ghetto look after their own.

Věra Schulz writes of Rumkowski in her diary, the day after the courtyard bonfire (11 December 1941):

. . . that man is a <u>monster</u> –

His only achievement to date: selling out his own people in record time and stealing or embezzling all they own. Yet still a quarter of a million people look up to him as a god! What kind of human being is it who deliberately sets out to demean and dishonour as many people as possible, simply for his own advancement?

I don't understand it!

Adam Rzepin naturally had no idea what kind of drugs he had got hold of, or what use could be made of them. On Moshe Stern's advice, he therefore sought out a certain Nussbrecher – seasoned middleman in all sorts of illicit ghetto deals – and asked for a free estimate.

What Adam did not know was that the market for goods of all kinds had been saturated since the arrival of the foreign Jews, and that the black-market sharks in Pieprzowa Street were fighting like ferrets in a sack these days to hang on to their market share. Every new player in the market was seen as a potential rival. So instead of giving Adam a fair price, Aron Nussbrecher went straight to the newly appointed prison commandant, Shlomo Hercberg, and told him there was a young man by the name of Rzepin who had started selling drugs in the ghetto. Hercberg had just come out of a meeting with the Chairman, in which the latter had reminded him of the need to clamp down on the growing crime and corruption at any price, and it occurred to Hercberg that he could usefully make an example of young Rzepin as a warning to others. It helped that he was under nobody's patronage. In other words, he would not inform on anybody else as a result of himself being betrayed.

The following day, therefore, what turned up at Adam and Lida's flat was not a handful of lucrative offers but a pair of hefty policemen, and Adam was taken for interrogation to the prison in Czarnieckiego Street.

In common with many others in the forces of law and order in the ghetto, Shlomo Hercberg had his roots in Bałuty. He was what the German-speaking citizens of Łódź called a real *Reichsbaluter*.

He had once had a job as a projectionist at the Bajka cinema on the corner of Brzezińska and Franciszkańska Streets. There were still folk in the ghetto who could remember the way Mr Hercberg had anxiously prowled the pavement outside the cinema before performances in a tight, navy-blue uniform with steel-grey braiding, hoping to catch a glimpse of *society on parade*. Hercberg had loved première evenings. Years later at the dinners at Princess Helena's, when he himself was part of the small group that constituted ghetto society, he would keep harking back to how in years gone by you could see the leading families from Poznański or Silberstein or Sachs arriving in their luxurious carriages at the big Temple Synagogue or at the concert hall in Narutowicza Street, ready to take their seats in the boxes.

Hercberg was at pains to convince people of his rank. He would boast that he had served as a captain in one of Field Marshal Piłsudski's cavalry regiments and could, if asked, produce reams of certified copies of call-up and transfer papers, along with doctor's certificates detailing where and how he had been wounded in the field, which field hospital he had been taken to, and where he went for rehabilitation. All these documents were naturally entirely fake; but Shlomo Hercberg knew, just as the Chairman did, that it was not academic titles that counted if you were to build something from scratch, but the ability to invest your office with gravitas and dignity. And if there was one thing Shlomo Hercberg was good at, it was this.

In the Czarnieckiego Street prison, Adam was held in what they called the Pit. The Pit was actually nothing more than a wide, underground space, an oubliette with an opening in the ceiling through which the warders could only insert or remove the prisoners by use of a long metal pole with a forked end, rather like fishing for frogs in a pond. At the end nearest the opening there were some basic, iron-framed bunks around the walls, where the favoured prisoners slept. The rest had to squeeze in as best they could at the far end by the latrine trench.

But that was just the anteroom. Beyond the barred door, the Pit opened out and branched down through the weathered stone. When the mass deportations from the ghetto began later that year, thousands of men would be held prisoner down in its winding galleries. It was as if deep *inside*, or deep *down* (depending how you looked at it), the ghetto had no end. From the meandering shafts, an incessant moan penetrated to the surface, as if the lamentations of all who had ever been incarcerated down there were entwined into a single monotone that continued regardless of the numbers waiting to be deported or let out.

Every so often, Adam was fetched up for interrogation by Hercberg.

He was taken to the so-called Cinema, which on the surface looked more like a private office than an interrogation room, furnished with everything a *Reichsbaluter* could possibly own in the way of luxury and affluence. There was an upholstered leather suite flanked by 'oriental' lamps with silken fringes, a desk with many drawers and compartments, all with keys in them, and a desk blotter with decorative wooden inlays and its own inkwell of real silver. But above all, there was food; the tempter Hercberg had laid out everything a starving prisoner could dream of, in the form of ham and *kiełbasa*, a whole tub of sauerkraut; perspiring cheeses in linen cloths; delicious-smelling fresh bread that the employees of the bakery in Marysińska Street brought in each morning on Hercberg's express orders.

There now, come in, don't be afraid . . . ! said Hercberg to Adam Rzepin, smiling a smile as gleaming as the fat on the ham. And when Adam could no longer resist stretching out a trembling hand towards the piece of bread nearest the edge of the plate, Hercberg grabbed the incorrigible sinner by the scruff of the neck –

So . . . even now you can't keep your hands to yourself, you miserable devil!

– and drove his head hard against the wall.

They abused him constantly. Sometimes with their bare fists, sometimes with long, flat wooden clubs, which they used systematically, working from his backside all the way down the inside of his legs to his ankle bones and Achilles tendons. They wanted to know what he knew about Moshe Stern. They wanted to know who Stern was 'doing business with' these days. They had also heard he was mixed up with the dealer Nussbrecher. Who had Nussbrecher offered to take the goods to? Lastly, they wanted to know everything about the people he had stolen from. They wanted the *names* of all the rich Jews from Prague. Adam had stolen their documents, hadn't he? So of course he knew what they were called.

Adam screamed until he lost consciousness, but Lida added her high note to the song rising up from all the galleries of the Pit; it sounded like the vibrating overtone of a string stretched to breaking point:

Give them nothing, give them nothing, her voice cut through him.

And so he gave them nothing. No names.

Back in the Pit, Adam dreams of the day many years ago when his father took the whole family to see the sea. They went there from Łódź in a little Citroën lent to them by one of the foremen at the sawmill. Szaja had driven it himself.

Sopot. That had been the name of the place they went to. It came back to Adam now.

Alone in the flat in Gnieźnieńska Street, Lida is dreaming of the same sea. And her brother is with her in the dream, just as he is with her in everything she says or does; even when she is sleeping or falling.

In Sopot there was a long wooden jetty known as the Pier stretching out into the sea. On either side of the Pier there were beaches with fine, loose sand strewn with mussel shells, and further up the beach, backing onto the promenade, there were tall, bast-fibre huts with awnings in barber's-pole stripes where the really Rich and Important visitors got changed. Adam remembers several of these Rich and Important people raising their hats to them as they walked along the Pier later that evening, just as if they were not poor people from Łódź, and definitely not Jews.

Lida remembers that when she waded out into the shallow water she suddenly realised the sea was not a flat, even, level surface, the way it looked on postcards. No, the sea was a living creature. The sea moved. It rocked and surged and incessantly heaved itself up onto and over her back and down between her legs and knees. It was constantly changing.

Right now it is like an enormous ball.

She stands there with both arms round the big, shiny sea-ball, but she can't encircle it completely. The surface of the ball is smooth and wet. But the thing with the sea is that it keeps slipping away. Two palms are not enough to hold on to the sea, and her eyes are slipping, too, and when she manages to raise them at last, she sees the sea floating off, all the way to the horizon.

In her memory, she drinks it all up. In great, deep draughts she swallows down the sea, gulp by gulp, and the sea doesn't taste like the soup Adam feeds her with, but harsh and salty, and the more she drinks, the more clearly she can feel that there is something to catch in there, something smooth and slippery; and when she gets it in her teeth it's a fish with a hard, scaly tail that scratches her soft palate and the inside of her cheeks. The fish tastes harsh and sharp and salty, but soft and living, too, and she keeps biting until the bones crunch, and then sucks, running her tongue over rough fish scales and soft, slippery guts.

And in his cell, Adam can also feel his mouth filling with the taste of fish, harsh and salty like nothing he's tasted before; and he must have screamed because all of a sudden he hears the guards outside.

They come rushing in a jangle of keys, arms already raised to strike.

Shut up you devil,
Or do you want to be sent away as well!

And they stick down the pole with the long snare at the end, and when he shrinks back to avoid getting the hook in his face, it has turned into a calloused warder's hand that grabs the scruff of his neck and rams his face into the cell floor. An intoxicating numbness rises from the back of his neck. His mouth is full of blood and he can barely swallow. But when he does, everything tastes of fish, and he is one big blood-dream of fish and living water.

*

When they came for him, Adam Rzepin had been in the Pit for over four weeks. One of the warders who came to unlock the grille had a form with him. Adam had to give his name, address and father's name. Then they got the pole with the snare and hauled him up.

It was cold outside! A month before, there had only been grey slush in the streets; now the whole ghetto was encased in smooth, gleaming white snow. He saw the sun sparkling on the banks of snow, the light so sharp and blinding that he could scarcely tell earth from sky.

There was as much commotion in the fenced prison compound as in any market place; people were dragging heavy suitcases around with them, or carrying mattresses and bedclothes strapped to their backs. But there was none of the incessant, busy hubbub of the market. People moved almost reluctantly, like rows of convicts; strangely quiet, disciplined. The only sound plainly audible in the clear, frosty morning was the hollow, bell-like clatter of the pots and pans hanging from belts and luggage straps.

'What's happening?' he asked one of the guards.

'You've had it, you're being sent away,' said the guard, and without further ado handed Adam's workbook to an official sitting at a desk to one side. The official briskly stamped the document, and a minute later Adam was given a bit of bread and a bowl of soup, and ordered to go and wait at the far end of the compound, where around a hundred men were already standing guard over their possessions.

That's how it is, said one of the other prisoners, who already had his food and was gnawing at his bread with almost toothless jaws. *They're letting the foreigners into the ghetto and sending us residents away.*

Adam opened out his papers and looked at the stamp:

> **AUSGESIEDELT**

it said in big, black letters all over the top half of his work log, where his name, address and age had been filled in by hand. *Resettled.*

Then suddenly, and somehow reluctantly, everything fell into place.

They hadn't brought him up from the Pit to let him go, but to deport him from the ghetto.

Adam looked round. Several of the men inside the compound knew each other, or at any rate seemed superficially acquainted, but as the ritual of calling the names, stamping the papers and dishing out the soup and bread continued, none of them said so much as a word. It was as if they felt ashamed to see each other there.

Adam realised they must be waiting for the contingent of deportees to be big enough to march off. Where to? To assembly points somewhere else in the ghetto, or all the way to Radogoszcz? If he were deported, what would happen to Lida? Would he ever see her again? In his nervousness, Adam wolfed his piece of bread whole. It was dark and surprisingly juicy: the first proper meal he had had for a month. He felt his stomach being warmed by the soup.

That was when he caught sight of his uncle Lajb on the other side of the fence.

*

When Uncle Lajb still lived with them, he had a bicycle. He had been the only one in the whole of Gnieźnieńska Street to own a bicycle, and, just to prove what a remarkable possession it was, he would get it out, take it to pieces and lay out all the parts on a piece of oilcloth. Each component separately: the chain, the tools in their case with special pleats and slots for every spanner and clamp. Then he would put the bike back together again, with the local children all standing round him in the yard, watching.

Several evenings a week were devoted to this ritual. But never the Sabbath.

On the Sabbath, Lajb stood with his face to the wall, prayer book in hand, praying. Lajb spoke the Eighteen Blessings with the same ceremonious precision as that with which he took his bicycle apart and reassembled it. When he put on his prayer shawl he spoke the blessing over the prayer shawl; when he put on the *tefillin* he thanked God for the gift of the phylacteries. Each element separately. And Adam thought when he saw Lajb's face at prayer that it looked just like the cycle saddle with its little eyelet holes, and the tendons in his neck just like the two-pronged front fork sticking down to the hub round which the prayer wheel spun with its smooth-running spokes, imperceptibly and silently. Without wanting to be or indeed being aware of it, Lajb always stayed at the centre of the circle. Wherever he went, people gathered round and regarded him with reverence and admiration. Back then in Gnieźnieńska Street, it had been little boys. This time it was prison guards. They were approaching Lajb as if he were some holy rabbi. Just a few minutes later, a happy guard came over to Adam with some freshly stamped documents, his whole face beaming with joy:

> *Rz-zepin! It's your lucky day today, Rz-zepin.*
> *Your name's been c-c-crossed off the list.*

*

They walked in silence, he and Lajb.

Coming in the opposite direction they met several more knots of men and women who had just been notified of their deportation and were on their way to the assembly camp at the Central Jail, and once again a sort of circle or vacuum formed around them. Adam dared not look the deportees in the face. He dared not lift his eyes any higher than their knees. Most of them had no shoes, just bits of cloth wound round and tied at the ankles, or feet stuck into primitive, loose-fitting clogs that they were dragging through the snow as if they were fetters.

Adam thought about the new shoes he had seen Uncle Lajb putting on, the day after the Praeses announced that all the workers behind the strike in Drukarska Street were to be deported from the ghetto.

144

That was the way it went: some had been deported; others had got new shoes.

Just as with Uncel Lajb's bicycle, no one in the ghetto had ever seen such shoes: proper lace-ups of smooth, glossy leather, with a substantial heel and sole, and punched, stitched decoration to the uppers. When Lajb walked up and down the flat in Gnieźnieńska Street wearing them, they creaked against the floor just as their steps were creaking on the dry snow now.

In normal circumstances, the flat would have been empty at this time of day, with his father at work. But Szaja got up self-consciously from the kitchen table when they came in. Adam's eyes went involuntarily to the bed where Lida usually lay. Where the bed had stood, there were now a table and two spindly wooden chairs, and on the chairs sat a man and a woman, with a girl of about ten or twelve on the floor between them.

This is the Mendel family, says Szaja in a formal, Littvishe Yiddish of a kind he would never normally use; and, as if to clarify (in Polish):

They are from the Prague collective. They have been billeted with us.

Mr Mendel is a short man with a bent, almost hunchbacked posture; bald-headed, with round spectacles. Adam gazes into his eyes, but the look behind the spectacles is entirely blank. He sees, and yet does not see. His wife sits beside him, fiddling with something in a handbag.

Where's Lida? Adam asks.

Szaja says nothing.

Adam turns round, ready to ask Lajb the same question.

Where's Lida?

But Lajb is no longer there. A mere minute before he was standing close beside Adam, his face as mute and expressionless as ever. Now it's as if he had never been there.

When Józefina Rzepin died, father and son learnt to carry out their respective duties silently and with the minimum of fuss. In the mornings, Szaja would generally light the stove while Adam went down to the yard to fetch water. Since Szaja was the only one of the two with a proper workbook, he was usually the one to queue at the food distribution points when new rations were announced; while Adam was the one to make the soup for dinner, wash the clothes, feed Lida, and talk and sing to her.

This is the first time for many years they both realise the silence that has arisen can only be broken with words. Adam has a huge hole in his chest. The hole is called Lida. But it's too big to fill with words like missing or anxious or afraid. Or rather the words, if he were to dare to utter them, would simply disappear down into it.

I've never asked for help, Szaja finally says, nodding in the direction of the door through which Lajb has just gone.

Adam says nothing. At the other end of the room sits the Mendel family, following their interaction with worried looks. Though they understand none of what is being said, it is as if they, too, have been caught up in the tension between father and son.

They said they'd deport the lot of us. (At the word *deport*, Adam's father lowers his voice still further.) *Even Lida was on their list.*

So I asked Lajb to help me

I've never asked anyone for help in my whole life

Adam looks his father in the eyes.

Where's Lida, is all he says.

They were going to deport Lida, too

Adam glances over at the Mendel family. He wonders if Mr Mendel recognises him as the *criminal* who broke into their collective. Presumably he does. It's just taking a while for the realisation to sink in. That he is now to be the lodger of the very same man who tried to rob him of all his worldly possessions.

146

Lajb's found a job for you

Adam stares at his father.

At Radogoszcz Station. They need people for the unloading. Well paid.

Insight has deepened into horror in Mr Mendel's face. He is looking straight at Adam now, and Adam looks back. (Defiantly, scornfully: what can he do?) Then to his father:

Where's Lida?

You don't know what it's been like while you were away

Where's Lida?

Adam hurls himself forward, leaning across the table to grab his father by the shoulders, shaking him as if he were some rag doll. At the other end of the room, Mrs Mendel gets to her feet and presses her daughter's face to her bosom as if to protect her from attack. Plates and cutlery crash from the table to the floor.

In a rest home, is all Szaja says.

Lajb found her a place in a rest home

*

For Adam, as for many other Bałuty residents, Marysin was more or less unknown territory. A place for the others: the wealthy, men with power and influence.

Ordinary folk only went to Marysin if they had business there: at the shoe factory, for example, which was one of the few *resorty* in Marysin; or at the warehouse behind Praszkier's workshop, where people with special coupons queued for allocations of heavy-duty timber, or coal briquettes. Or if you were dead, and were going to be buried. Day in, day out, Meir Klamm and the other members of the Funeral Association could be seen driving funeral director Muzyk's horse-drawn hearses back and forth along Dworska and Marysińska Streets. On the other side of the wall in Zagajnikowa Street, the kingdom of the dead stretched away, such a vast expanse that it was said you could not see all the way from one side to the other. The air in Marysin was also full of death, the putrid smell of raw, open earth, crumbling concrete and refuse; and when the snow melted to grit and mud, and the wind was in the wrong direction, it was filled with the bittersweet stench of saltpetre from the cesspits where the excrement workers were applying quicklime. You could see them in the distance. A long row of men with shovels was outlined against the sky, like tattered crows on a telegraph wire.

Adam had never set foot in the area round Okopowa and Prożna Street, where the Praeses and the other powerful men in the *Beirat* had their homes. But he knew from Moshe Stern's reports that there were ghetto residents who rented out 'casual rooms' here, and they could sometimes be seen prowling up and down Marysińska Street, touting for custom.

It was bitterly cold the evening Adam Rzepin set out to look for his sister. The snow was piled in big drifts between the buildings where vehicles could no longer get through. Adam did not encounter many of the room touts. Those he asked instinctively turned their backs on him. For them he was presumably just a ragged tramp: a man 'with no shoulders', as they said in the ghetto. Without some elevated *dignitary* to support you, you were quite literally nobody out here.

If it had not been for Lida's voice, it is hardly likely he would have persevered, alone in the cold. Lida's voice was as faint as the flimsiest shadow through glass; but it was alive, and talking to him constantly.

I shall take you home, Lida, he told it.

Don't be afraid. I shall take you home with me.

Wispy smoke was rising from a few of the houses. Police from the Fifth District were on guard, wearing their armbands and tall, shiny boots. He saw them talking to some of those with rooms for hire. He didn't know whose protection these particular streets were under. Above the empty gables and tops of walls along Marysińska Street, the sky shone a pale red with the reflected light from the parts of Litzmannstadt that were not blacked out.

All at once he saw a cab, coming from the centre of the ghetto. He heard the high snorting of the horse and the jingle of its bridle and halter: a sound so familiar and yet so unusual out here that it was enough to startle anybody. The snow was so deep that the horse's hoofs made scarcely a sound. The driver pulled up the horse. Climbing down from the springy step of the cab was Shlomo Hercberg, wearing a big, thick coat of fur that looked like beaver or some wild animal of the kind. Two bodyguards had followed in another cab, and they both instinctively moved towards him, as if to clear away this troublesome obstacle that had suddenly materialised in the Prison Commandant's path. But Hercberg was in a hurry this evening, and the guards contented themselves with shoving Adam out of the way; Hercberg disappeared into a little house slightly further up the left-hand side of Marysińska Street, scarcely more than a shack behind two tall wrought-iron gates, which were unlocked by someone from the house as Hercberg approached.

The cab waited. The horse snorted and stamped in its harness. After a while, the driver climbed down and started walking up and down, slapping and hugging himself to keep warm. Adam didn't know what to do. He dared not leave, for fear that Hercberg would get away. Nor did he dare to go any closer, for fear of being caught by the cab driver and guards.

After barely half an hour, Hercberg emerged again. He spoke in commanding tones to someone beside him; then climbed into the cab and was borne swiftly away. The man who had come out with him, and who presumably rented out the room, stood there for a few moments; then he shut and locked the big wrought-iron gates. Adam waited until both were out of sight, then threw all his weight against the gate. The lock did not yield. Around the house was a stone wall with metal railings with big, sharp spikes. He managed to get one foot up on the wall, then gripped the railings as high as he could reach, and launched his body forward and up, over the sharp metal points. But he had no time to ready himself for landing. His foot twisted sideways on impact, and an intense shooting pain seared his leg. He limped swiftly to cover at the foot of the house wall. Waited. Nothing.

Now he could see the window through which the stove-pipe protruded. A thin, pale light from inside cast a faint square on the snow.

He went up to the front door and knocked. Nothing.

He had hardly expected anything else. He knocked harder.

Open up, it's the police! he said.

The door opened. Inside stood Lida. It was so cold that the light streaming out was entirely blue. Lida's body was blue, too – from her porcelain neck, all the way down to the blood between her legs. He could not comprehend why she had no clothes on.

Lida, he said.

She smiled at him, briefly and cheerlessly as one might at a total stranger, took a step forward and spat in his face.

The first meeting about the resettlements of the ghetto ordered by the occupying powers was held on 16 December 1941, according to Rosensztajn's records. Just as on previous occasions, the meeting had not been preceded by any correspondence; Rumkowski had merely been summoned to the offices of the Ghetto Administration, to receive his orders directly from the authorities. Others present at the meeting, apart from Biebow himself, were his deputy Wilhelm Ribbe, Günther Fuchs and a handful of representatives of the police and security services, whose task it would be to supply transport and supervise the actual loading.

Rumkowski stood as he always did, and always would, in front of his superiors. With his ageing white head bowed, his eyes on the floor.

Ich bin Rumkowski. Ich melde mich gehorsamst.

They were friendly and correct, but came straight to the point and made it clear to the Eldest of the Jews that they were now facing yet another long, hard, wartime winter, and that in the long term it was impossible for them to ensure supplies of food and fuel for all the Jews who had been given sanctuary in the ghetto. For that reason, the *Gauleitung* in Kalisz had decided to move a proportion of the ghetto population to smaller towns in the Warthegau, where the supply situation was less acute.

He asked how many people this would involve.

They said twenty thousand.

He stood there at a loss, saying the ghetto could not possibly spare as many as twenty thousand.

They replied that unfortunately the supply situation demanded it.

He reminded them that the authorities had very recently allowed twenty thousand foreign Jews to move *to* the ghetto.

They replied that the decision about the foreign Jews had been taken in Berlin.

What was at issue here was how they were to deal with the regional supply problem in the Warthegau.

He then said he could offer them *ten thousand*.

Their response was that they could consider limiting the 'initial evacuation' to ten thousand people, provided that he could guarantee that the transports could begin without delay. It was naturally understood that he himself, together with his council, would be responsible for the selection of those to be deported and for moving them to the assembly points at Radogoszcz, where the German police would take over.

Those who saw the Chairman after this meeting said he certainly seemed upset, yet also, in some strange way, self-controlled and decisive. It was as if the meeting with supreme authorities, along with the fact that he alone had been called upon to put that power's intentions into practice, had breathed new life into his body, soul and mind.

He repeated this over and over again:

Ten thousand Jews will be obliged to leave the ghetto. This is perfectly true. It is what the authorities have decided. But we must not let ourselves be paralysed by the fact. It makes more sense to turn the question round instead, and see the opportunities it has to offer us. If it is entirely unconditional that ten thousand must leave, then which people can the ghetto best afford to lose?

On the Chairman's advice, they decided to set up a Resettlement Commission to deal with all the questions arising from the impending mass move. The Commission's work would be led by the head of the Population Registry, lawyer Henryk Neftalin, and its members, in addition to Rumkowski, would be Leon Rozenblat, head of the ghetto police, Szaja Jakobson, chairman of the presiding committee of judges, and prison commandant Shlomo Hercberg. The Commission would have the task of going through the population registers *from cover to cover*, cross-checking them against criminal records and the lists of patients in the ghetto hospitals, and it would then determine who had to leave the ghetto.

They decided to try wherever possible not to leave individuals to be deported on their own, but to *let whole families go*. A decision was also taken to prioritise the removal of so-called *undesirable elements*. When somebody asked what the criteria were to qualify as 'undesirable', the Chairman referred them to the criminal record department. Notorious black marketeers; known criminal recidivists, prostitutes, thieves – those who saw dealing in other people's vulnerability and despair as their 'meal ticket' – these would be the first to go.

And if the person or persons considered undesirable were, contrary to all expectation, found to have no criminal record? Then their cases were to be referred to him. The decision to initiate the deportations might have been the authorities', but, just like last time, he reserved the right to make the final decision on who should go.

They said this was a time when the Chairman never slept.

Day and night he sat agonising over the Resettlement Commission's lists.

His room: a single, illuminated cube in the barrack-hut offices on Bałuty Square. The rest of the offices were in darkness because of the blackout. But as long as he was still there at his desk, some of his staff stayed at their posts, too. They crept about in the dark, lurking behind doorposts and office furniture, ready to obey his least command. As the hands of the ghetto clock on the corner of Łagniewnicka Street moved towards midnight, he closed the file and asked Miss Fuchs to order his carriage. He was intending to visit the children in the Green House and then spend the night at the Residence in Miarki Street.

(But it's late, Mr Chairman. It's almost twelve.

He brushed aside her objections:

Ring Feldman, too, and ask him to go on ahead and light the stoves.)

Despite the anguish of the job in hand, there was something deeply satisfying in leaving the office so late. The tall facades with their rows of darkened windows gave him a sense of tranquility. Here and there, at a street corner or outside some factory, he saw a policeman on guard. Outside the Kripo's red-brick castle, the black limousines of the Gestapo stood parked in long, shiny rows.

And so on through the empty night-time streets of Marysin.

He had the brim of his hat pulled well down and his collar turned up over his ears. The only sounds at this dark, midnight hour apart from the creak of the carriage wheels and the muffled clatter of hoofs were the repeated cracks of the whip as the driver urged the horse on.

And Marysin was something else, of course. Whenever he was being driven out there, he always had the sensation of the ghetto dissolving around him. The houses shrank in height, and spread themselves out behind walls and railings. Houses, outhouses; little workshops and sheds. Squeezed in here and there were cultivated plots that had belonged to the cottages, but that he had now given away as individual parcels of land to his most loyal colleagues. Then came the kibbutzim that the Zionists used to operate: large, open fields in which young men with spades and hoes moved among precise rows of potatoes, green cabbages and beetroot.

The Green House was the most outlying of the summer villas he had converted into young people's hostels and children's homes. Altogether there were six children's homes like this in the ghetto, plus a newly established children's hospital and large dispensary to go with them. But his heart belonged to the children in the Green House. They were the only ones who reminded him of the free and happy years in Helenówek, before the war and the occupation.

There was nothing particularly remarkable about the building: a dilapidated, two-storey house with damp in the walls and its roof in a state of disrepair. As soon as his *Kinder-kolonie* had moved there from Helenówek, he had had the house repainted. The only colour of paint available in the ghetto had been green. So the walls had been painted green, the roof, the front porch, the window frames; even the handrails of the steps. The house became so green that in the summertime it was scarcely distinguishable from the creeping vegetation behind.

But this was his kingdom: a *shtetl* world of little, tightly clustered houses in which the lamp of diligence burnt late into the evenings. He would really have preferred to visit unannounced. That was how he saw himself. The simple man, the unknown benefactor who, in spite of the lateness of the hour, just happened to be passing.

The transports to the ghetto in recent months had included many children who had lost all their close relatives, or perhaps never had any. One of them was a girl called Mirjam, another a boy with no name.

The girl was eight or nine years old, and turned up at the Green House with a little cardboard suitcase that she refused to be parted from, in which Miss Smoleńska later found two carefully ironed dresses, a warm coat and four pairs of shoes. One pair was patent leather with silver buckles. The girl's identity papers were in a pocket inside the suitcase, neatly folded. According to them, her full name was Mirjam Szygorska. She was born and registered in Zgierz. (But that was not where she had come from.) Her case also contained some toys, a doll, and a couple of books in Polish.

The boy was delivered to the Green House by brothers Jósef and Jakub Kohlman, acting on direct orders from the coordinator of transports in the Cologne collective. The boy had arrived with one of the last transports from Cologne, on 20 November 1941. He appeared on the transport list as number 677. But that figure said no more about him than the fact that he had been the 677th person registered for the transport. On one side of the next column was a forename, WERNER, followed by a question mark, then the designation SCHUELER, and finally, under JAHRGANG, the year 1927. Assuming the columns had been filled in correctly, SCHUELER was just the neutral term for 'student', and the young man had no surname.

They called him SAMSTAG, since it was on the Sabbath the Kohlman brothers brought him to the front door of the Green

157

House; and that was the name under which Dr Rubin, the superintendent of the children's home, entered him on the roll:

SAMSTAG, WERNER, geb: 1927 (KÖLN);
VATER/MUTTER: Unbekannt

From the very start, there was something unruly and pent-up about him. He could not pass a wall or a doorpost without knocking into it. If his eyes had anything in them at all, it was as if they were constantly searching for something behind or to the side of what he was looking at. And then there was his smile. Werner smiled a lot and, thought Rosa Smoleńska, the person who generally had to deal with him, in an almost brazen way; it was a smile full of gleaming little white teeth.

When they brought him, the Kohlman brothers explained that he spoke neither Polish nor Yiddish. But when Rosa Smoleńska tried talking to him in German, she got only cross grimaces in return. It was as if the words were there, and he understood what they meant, but could not comprehend why she was saying what she said or addressing him the way she did. If they tried to force him to do something he didn't want to, he had terrible fits of rage. One day he overturned a full washtub Chaja had brought into the kitchen; on another occasion he started throwing furniture out of the window of the Pink Room. When Superintendent Rubin went over and tried to calm him down, he bit him in the arm. And sat there with his jaws clamped, refusing to let go, although four of them, including Chaja who weighed at least twice as much as he did, threw themselves into the fray and tried to separate the two bodies. His closely spaced little teeth embedded in Superintendent Rubin's arm looked like like those of a shark, all sharp and shiny.

He did not seem to have any problem communicating with the other children. He liked being with the younger ones, and best of all he liked being with Mirjam. When they were out in the grounds, he would just hang around in a corner, almost comical in his oversized shoes, twice as tall as his playmates. But if Mirjam was going anywhere, Werner would always follow, a couple of paces behind. He played cops and robbers with two of the younger boys, Abraham and Leon. He would chase them with a stick and shout *ikh hob dikh gekhapt* – Gotcha! – like all the others, but in a strange accent that revealed he had never spoken the language in his life before.

(Later, Rosa would remember how peculiar she found it from the outset that someone who had never spent any time in the ghetto could mimic pitch and intonation so closely; she had even said this to him on one occasion – in German of course, as that was the language the two of them still used with each other at that stage: *Du bist doch ein kleiner Schauspieler du, Werner . . . !* Only to see his face stiffen the next instant into that horrible smile she had learnt to fear. Nothing but teeth, no mouth, and no expression of any kind behind those pale-blue eyes.)

*

Rosa Smoleńska had worked with homeless or orphaned children all her life. She held her post in Helenówek for eight years, and was always in charge of the very youngest children. Apart from the head of the home, Superintendent Rubin, she and Chaja Meyer the housekeeper were the only ones who had come to the ghetto with the Chairman after the occupation. The other nursery nurses had fled to Warsaw when war broke out. But they had all been married and had *other options*. Rosa had never had either a husband or any other option: just all these children! There were forty-seven of them now, including the latest arrivals, Werner and Mirjam.

Rosa Smoleńska was among the first to get up in the mornings. In winter she was up by four or five, to light the fires. Once she had the big stove in the kitchen alight, she went to the well a little way down the slope where the enclosed part of the Big Field started. As dawn broke, there were usually pale streaks of light above the banks of cloud in the eastern sky. The reflected light of the rising sun made the brick wall round the cemetery cast long shadows across the snow. A couple of hours later, the sun rose above the top of the wall and the light glittered on the frosted wires running between the telegraph poles along Zagajnikowa Street. At six or seven in the morning she often saw knots of workers on their way to or from their shifts at Radogoszcz Station. They walked in a huddle, as if to preserve as much heat as they could in the cold, and without saying a word. The only sound was the hollow clatter of the empty tin mugs tied to their belts. At regular intervals, German tanks and lorries would also rumble their way through the frosty silence, and distrustful-looking soldiers with submachine guns would patrol the pavement on the ghetto side. The Germans seldom came any closer than that. The black, horse-drawn hearses that came from Bałuty every morning were a more familiar sight. Sometimes there were no horses available, and the carts were pulled, just like the excrement tanks, by men hitched or harnessed to the shafts in front, while other unfortunates had to push the carts from behind.

Once she had carried in the water, she would go back out to wait until she saw Józef Feldman trudging up Zagajnikowa with his buckets of coal. Summer and winter he was bundled up in the same yellowing sheepskin coat and leather cap, his face almost completely covered. Rosa knew the Chairman had given Feldman instructions always to see to the fires in the Green House first, and to be ready to drop what he was doing at any time, if help were needed *up there*. Feldman's actual job was in Baruk Praszkier's gravedigging team. Rosa never dared go too close to him – she thought she could smell death on his hands – but she helped him carry the coal buckets down into the cellar so he could pour in the coal and get the fire going.

Meanwhile, Malwina would wake all the children. They stood shivering in the narrow hallway, waiting for their turn to come forward and wash. Rosa would decant some of the cold water she had fetched from the well into a big tub that Chaja always set in the doorway from the kitchen to the dining room. They had to wash before they were allowed to take their seats on the benches, where Chaja cut the bread for them. The slices grew thinner all the time, but there was always a slice for everybody, spread with a thin layer of margarine.

One morning Feldman brought with him a small figure, pale and shy, whose name and origins nobody knew. But unlike Werner and Mirjam, he did not seem to have come with the transports. When Rosa Smoleńska asked him who he was and what he was doing there, the boy just took a few cocky steps into the room and announced, as if singing or declaiming a poem:

I have heard there is a piano here that needs tuning!

He was the son of an instrument-maker by the name of Rozner, so well known among the upper classes of Łódź that no one ever called him anything but 'the piano tuner'. But Mr Rozner also repaired other instruments: flutes, reed instruments, trombones and percussion instruments for military orchestras. He had put some of his many instruments on display in a luxuriously fitted showroom next to his workshop. The workshop itself, however, was cramped and basic, as anyone who spent any time in it could see; but those just passing in the street saw only the showroom with the smooth, shiny instruments laid out on cushions of silk and plush. Since Rozner was a Jew, he was naturally rumoured to have money squirrelled away in his shop. A drunken mob of Volksdeutsche, led by two officers of the SS, forced their way into the instrument-maker's premises one evening and demanded he hand over the money on the spot, and when Rozner denied having any hidden away, they attacked the shop with clubs and batons until all the instruments were in pieces and Rozner himself lay in the middle of his demolished showroom with a smashed skull and every bone in his body broken. Rozner's son escaped at the last minute with the most valuable thing his father owned. This comprised two bags made of coarse sailcloth, joined together, in which Mr Rozner kept his tools when he went round the rich families of Łódź, tuning their pianos. The son was now to be seen with the pair of sailcloth bags over his shoulder in all sorts of unlikely places in the ghetto, going round trying to complete his dead father's work.

The piano in the Pink Room had been badly affected by damp, so now they had to keep a bowl of water inside it to stop the wood cracking and the strings coming loose from their pegs. The piano tuner paid careful attention to these and other defects. He tested the pedals of the piano, ran his palm carefully across the lid and down the sides, tapped all along the body of the instrument. Only when he had satisfied himself that this did not produce any unexpected sounds did he ask Kazimir to hold open the lid while he himself opened the back of the piano and climbed inside. He was so small that he could hang like a monkey within the exposed tangle of strings, loosening and tightening, slackening and pulling taut. When he climbed out of the piano apparently unscathed, he had worked his way through the whole keyboard from the inside, from one hammer to the next. With an expression of barely concealed triumph on his wizened face, he set a tuning fork on top of the piano lid, and gestured smilingly to Debora Żurawska to come forward to the piano stool.

So Debora took her seat, and struck a firm and ringing C-Major chord that was clearly taken up by the tuning fork and amplified.

The children clapped, and as Debora proceeded to play a Chopin étude, the piano tuner sat down beside her and added strange trills and arpeggios of his own, in a higher register. It was plain he had never learnt to play properly, but just by imitating chord sequences and key changes: as if he had scraped together into his cloth bags every phrase and motif Chopin had ever used and then scattered them all back over the keyboard, according to his own taste and in random order. But at that particular moment, it did not matter. Debora played, and the piano tuner followed, and soon the playing of the two was so intertwined that no one could hear where her chord finished and his began.

Within a few days, music and vocal items had been written; the 'orchestra' had rehearsed; a theatre troupe had even been formed, consisting of all the children from the home with a Mr SAMSTAG, Werner (*dyrektor teatru*) at its head, and they went round distributing hand-written invitations:

☛ Actors' Collective **'Grine Hoiz'** presents ☜
<u>Der kleyner Wasserman</u>
Play in One Act
By S. Y. 'Ritter'

Young Adam Gonik read the poem 'Spring is here' in Hebrew, and a small choir of children, led by Superintendent Rubin himself, performed songs and poems by Bialik. During this overture, the spider-like piano tuner ascended a ladder in the hallway and removed the metal cover from the bell mounted on the wall outside the kitchen. With one of the little metal hammers he kept in his cloth bags, he was able to short-circuit the device and set it off, so the Green House echoed from top to bottom with a shrill and piercing note:

riiiiiiiiii-iiiiiiing

That was the signal: the children in the choir ran to pull back the green drapery that the actors' troupe had strung across the room as a curtain. Kazimir stumbled onto the stage, dressed up as a rich Polish nobleman, and told the group of Jews driven from their home town in Galicia by the troops of the Russian Tsar that he would of course hide them in the biggest cellar in his castle. Debora hammered a quick succession of dramatic chords on the piano while the piano tuner stood atop his stepladder, declaiming loudly – THE RUSSIANS ARE COMING! THE RUSSIANS ARE COMING! – and all the children sang:

Umglik, shrek un moyres
Mir veysn nit fun vanen
Oikh haynt vi in ale doyres
*Zaynen mir oysgeshtanen!**

Then Werner Samstag came clumping on stage, dressed in a full-length black coat like a proper *rebbe*, and a big black *shtraiml* he must have made all by himself, since bits of the velvet lining were hanging down over his eyes. His beard was also home-made: a scrap of grey material through which his smile shone as white and gleaming as ever, with a total lack of lips. Debora thumped the keys with both hands, deep down in the lowest octaves, and as the children's voices soared in bold descant above her, Reb Samstag raised an admonitory finger, first to the audience and then to Heaven, and declaimed:

Shrayt yidn, shrayt aroyf
Shrayt hekher ahin dort;
Vekt ir dem altn oyf –
Vos shloft er kloymersht dort?
Vemen vil er gor gevinen?

* Misfortune, terror and dread / We know not from where / Today and down the generations / Suffering has been ours!

164

Vos zaynen mir – a flig?
Loz er undz a zkhus gefinen
Oy, es zol shoin zain genuk*

When Rosa Smoleńska went over the whole scene in her mind afterwards, it seemed to her as though the bell on the wall outside the kitchen had jangled all evening, and she had gone up to the piano tuner several times during the performance and asked him to please turn off the racket, and in future keep his hands off things that did not belong to him.

But perhaps the angry, jangling rings had not, apart from that first and only time, been the piano tuner's work. Perhaps it was just as Miss Estera Daum later said: the Chairman's staff had been trying to get through to the Green House all evening, but received no answer. Their last attempt had been long after midnight. By then, Rosa had finally managed to get the sweaty, overexcited children out of their costumes and into bed, and even had time to go to bed herself.

Riiiiiiiiiii-iiiiiiiing . . . !

went the peremptory signal again.

She heard Superintendent Rubin in the office on the floor below, stamping around in search of the telephone receiver which was somewhere under all the papers and books on his desk; then his voice answering, and immediately assuming a submissive tone, with a *yes* and an *of course* and an *at once, Mr Chairman*. She realised straight away what was happening, pulled on a cardigan over her nightdress and went from room to room, to try to shake some life into the children again:

Hurry up and get dressed, the Praeses is on his way!
Hurry up!

* Raise your voices, you Jews, / Let your call rise higher; / Rouse up the Old One – / He is surely sleeping there? / Who is he hoping to win? / What are we – a mere fly? / Let him give us a just reward, / It must soon be enough.

The staff of the Green House normally had between thirty and forty minutes to wash and dress all the children, and comb their hair. That was about how long it took the Chairman to get all the way out to Marysin from his office once Miss Estera Daum had rung to alert them.

The children were by this point so exhausted that she had the utmost difficulty getting them back on their feet. By the time she and Malwina finally had them lined up in fairly neat and tidy rows, with the youngest at the front and the older children ranged in rising order of size on the stairs behind them, the Chairman was already out of his carriage and on his way into the house. Without so much as a glance to his right or left he swept past Mirjam, who was trying to give him the album of illustrated Talmud verses which the children had prepared in case of a visit. But for now, the ghetto's highest of the high had no eyes for young Mirjam, or any of the other children either; he just handed his hat, coat and walking stick to Chaja and addressed Superintendent Rubin in a loud voice.

Be so kind as to accompany me to your office, Dr Rubin.
Yes, at once . . . ! And bring the lists of all the children!

Ever since the time in Helenówek, Miss Smoleńska had tried to read the old man's many shifting moods as one might the weather. Was he calm and pleased with himself today? Or was he once again in the grip of the strange *fury* that occasionally overcame him?

There were nearly always clues. Like the way he moved his hands: whether they were calm and assured, or restless and fumbling, as they felt for cigarettes in his jacket pocket. Or if he had what Chaja Meyer called his 'joker look': that knowing little one-sided smile, a hint that he had *ideas* or *plans* for one of them, or even one of the children.

But on this late visit she detected no sign. The Chairman

appeared strict, grave, resolute. What was more, he was closeted in the office with Superintendent Rubin for an unusually long time. Several hours passed. Then Chaja, apparently acting on orders from the office, started filling buckets with hot water from the big pan in the kitchen, and Miss Malwina went round the tables, laying out towels. It was by then *half past two* in the morning, and since no contradictory order had been given, the children were still lined up on the stairs. Some were already asleep, their heads propped on each other, or the wall or banisters; or they had subsided into a sitting position on the stairs, like Samstag, who had his hands between his knees and his knees drawn up to his ears like a cricket.

Then the Chairman appeared again. In one hand he had the *Zugangslisten* Superintendent Rubin had asked for.

Rosa Smoleńska would later remember the empty, lifeless expression on the Chairman's face, and the fact that when he finally opened his mouth to speak, he could not initially find the words he was looking for. Was it then – only then, having sat in Rubin's office and gone through the lists of all the children's names with Rubin – that the full extent of the fate awaiting the incarcerated Jews of the ghetto hit him? Not just the children, but them above all, since the children were *his*. After that, it was unclear whom he was addressing, the dozing children on the stairs or the staff of the Green House, worn out and short of sleep. But he *stammered* as he spoke. He had never done that before.

I am only going to say this once, and I shall say it now, to explain once and for all the gravity of the situation in which we find ourselves:

The authorities, whose rules we must all obey, have decided that without exception, everyone in the ghetto must work – including children and young people – and that those who do not work will be sent away from the ghetto immediately.

I do not say this lightly – because I have be no wish to frighten
people needlessly – but beyond the borders of the ghetto there is
no one who can guarantee the safety of you or any other Jews.
Only in the ghetto, under my protection, since I have secured
the lasting trust of the authorities, can you be safe.

I have therefore in consultation with Mr Warszawski
decided to create special apprentice places for all ghetto
children old enough to work. Even those who have not yet had
the compulsory health inspection are from now on expected to
start as trainee cutters and sewers at the tailor's workshops of
the ghetto!

At his words, a degree of alarm spread among the older children on the stairs.

Have we got to leave? Debora Żurawska was heard to cry
from somewhere behind Werner Samstag's legs. And from
behind her, a chorus of muttering. But now the signs were
unmistakably there in the old man, the signs she had long since
learnt to recognise: the smile at the corner of his mouth, the
darting eyes, the hand going in and out of his jacket pocket:

It's your young lives at stake here, and you dare to set yourselves
against me?

A deathly hush descended on the hall and stairway.

Superintendent Rubin took a step forward so he was at the
Chairman's side. Rumkowski's reaction was to grab the lists out
of his hand in exasperation.

The particulars of a number of the children which should be on
these lists are missing. I have also just seen with my own eyes
that many of the children arriving have been entered under
incorrect or even false names . . . The day the authorities call
on me to account for all the children under my protection, we

are all doomed! Children! Please now be so good as to come forward one by one when Superintendent Rubin calls you out, tell us your names and where you come from, and then go into the kitchen where Dr Zysman will examine you.

No one wonders why this procedure had to be gone through at three o'clock on an icy cold winter's morning. They all know that if the occupying authorities had carried it out themselves, considerably worse things could have happened. Even so, some of that same sense of terror and unreality creeps under their skin as Superintendent Rubin clumsily adjusts his glasses on his nose and starts to read the list out loud:

Rubin (reads): Samstag, Werner. *Geburtsort*: Köln. *Vater/Mutter – Unbekannt.*
Chairman: And what does *Unbekannt* mean?
Rubin: Samstag arrived in the second transport. There were no accompanying relatives and he has not been able to tell us of any since.
Samstag: My name's not Samstag.
Chairman: It doesn't say Samstag here. It is you, Superintendent Rubin, who wrote in Samstag. Didn't you? That's what happened, isn't it?
Rubin: We thought we ought to give him a surname.
Chairman: What crap! Go on.
Rubin (reads): Majerowicz, Kazimir. *Geburtsort*: Łódź. *Vater/ Mutter – Unbekannt.*
Chairman: *Unbekannt* again. How is that possible?
Rubin: It was your order that children who had been separated from their parents were to be brought here.
Chairman: How old are you, Mr Majerowicz?
Kazimir: I'm fifteen going on sixteen, thank you for asking Mr Chairman.
Chairman: It says here that you were born on 12 January 1926.

Rubin: There may be a few mistakes, Mr Chairman.

Chairman: Very well. Next.

Rubin (*reads*): Szygorska, Mirjam. Vater/Mutter –

Chairman: Let me guess. *Unbekannt.*

Rubin: How did you know?

Chairman: Do you know what, Mr Rubin. Do you know how
   many lives your appalling lack of accuracy could cost me in the
   next few days?

Rubin: No, Mr Chairman.

Chairman: Would young Miss Szygorska please step forward . . . ?

Mirjam came forward. Since she was still holding the album
of illustrated Talmud verses, she tried once again to present it
to the Chairman. This time the Praeses, clearly taken aback,
accepted the gift. Then he stood staring at her, the smile at one
corner of his mouth becoming more marked:

Chairman: And how old is young Miss Szygorska, then?

Rubin (*anxiously*): Young Miss Szygorska can't speak, Mr
   Rumkowski.

Chairman: Talkative or not, perhaps Miss Szygorska would be so
   good as to answer for herself.

Rubin: Miss Szygorska is eleven, Mr Chairman.

Chairman: She looks big for eleven. Or is this just another attempt
   to get out of my apprentice scheme?

Rubin: Young Miss Szygorska unfortunately doesn't have the gift
   of speech, Mr Rumkowski.

Chairman: Doesn't have the gift of speech? It seems to me that in
   other ways nature has been more than generous in its gifts to
   Miss Szygorska.

Then he takes Mirjam by the arm and drags her roughly into
the office. In the doorway he turns and imperiously beckons
Chaja to bring him one of the washbowls and a towel, waits

impatiently for her to bring them and then shuts and locks the door behind him.

For quite some time they just stand there – frightened, nonplussed – staring at the closed door. After a time they hear faint noises from within. Chair legs scrape; something heavy hits the wall and then rolls slowly across the floor. The thudding and rattling are repeated several times. Then they hear the Chairman's voice, muffled and angry. And superimposed on it, a descant – Mirjam's. So she does have a voice, after all! It sounds as if she has something loud and urgent to say, but something or someone stops the words getting out.

Chair legs scrape the floor again, and once more it sounds as if something heavy is hitting the floor or falling over.

Then it goes quiet. Appallingly quiet.

Debora is the first to break out of the collective paralysis. She runs back to the Pink Room and starts pounding the piano keys. Then the rhythm emerges and the whole keyboard bends to the notes of the old Jewish protest song that the theatrical troupe performed earlier:

Tseshlogn, tseharget ales
Tsevorfn, yedes bazunder
Fun khasanim – kales
Fun muters – kleyne kinder
Shrayt, kinder, shrayt aroyf.
Shrayt hekher ahin dort;
Vekt ir dem tatn oyf
Vos shloft er kloymersht dort?
Far dir herstu veynen, klogn
Kinder fun der vig
Zei betn doch, du zolst zey zogn:
*Oy, es zol shoyn zayn genuk!**

* All beaten, all killed / Discarded, one and all / Taken from bridegrooms – brides / Taken from mothers – little children / Raise your voices, you children

171

Kasimir beats time on the drum, loudly. Out in the other room, the younger children are racing round in an increasingly frenzied dance. Natasza Maliniak has put her hands over her ears and is screaming, while Liba and Sara climb up onto the piano and try to grab hold of Debora's hands from above, as if they were perched on the edge of a well, trying to catch butterflies.

Rosa remembers that Chaja usually keeps the spare keys to the office in one of the kitchen drawers. When she gets back, key in hand, she sees Werner Samstag lying flat on his back on the floor outside the office. He has unbuttoned his flies and is masturbating with long, convulsive movements of his right hand, while the fingers of the left open and close like a throbbing heart. He has caught her eye long before she realises what he is doing, and she sees that he is smiling, in the middle of the long ascent to his orgasm: the shiny, saliva-wet smile, shameless and full of the certainty of the initiated.

Then it happens, the thing she has always known would happen. When she looks up, she sees the piano tuner has climbed to the top of the stepladder again. His face is as black as mud, or as if someone has poured soot over it and then given his eyes and mouth a perfunctory wipe. She can now plainly see that he is considerably older than the fifteen or sixteen she had assumed him to be: a little gnome, a child who has stopped growing and prematurely aged into the body of a grown man. But with skilful hands. It takes him only two seconds to short-circuit the bell with the tuning forks from his sailcloth bags, and the ringing cuts like an acoustic tidal wave right through the house . . .

Riiiiiiiiiiiiiiiii-iiiing –

Let your call rise higher / Rouse up the Father – / He is surely sleeping / You hear yourselves crying, lamenting / Children in their cradles / They ask you to tell them / It must soon be enough!

172

And suddenly it is as if the entire storm has abated.

Then the Chairman is standing among them again. He is bright red in the face, and his otherwise pedantically neat suit is crumpled and unbuttoned.

Somebody seems to have rung . . . ?

It is more a question than a statement. It is obvious he does not know what to say.

Through the half-open door to Superintendent Rubin's office, Rosa can see the enamel bowl Chaja Meyer took in lying upturned in the middle of the floor, surrounded by pools of water. Of Mirjam, who was in there with him, there is no sign.

Superintendent Rubin, says the Chairman.

It sounds as if his most immediate need is a name on to which he can hook his confusion. But once having pronounced that name, he seems suddenly to reach a decision, and repeats his command, with renewed authority:

Superintendent Rubin, you will come with me!

And holds the door and waits for Superintendent Rubin to go in with him, then locks the door behind him again.

Chaja the cook is the first to rally after the shock. In two strides she is at the piano and pulling Debora's hands away from the keyboard. Rosa Smoleńska goes down on one knee beside Werner Samstag, who is still lying there on the floor with his trousers undone, and though he is twice as tall as she is, she is able to get his loose-jointed body over her shoulder and carry it backwards up the stairs to the dormitories above.

In all the ensuing uproar, nobody remembers Mirjam. It is in fact only long after Rosa and Malwina have got the children to bed again that they realise Mirjam is missing.

They search the whole house. Even the coal cellar, where the piano tuner has made himself a sort of nest, in which he sleeps under a couple of mangy blankets. In the spilt washing water under Dr Rubin's desk, Rosa later finds the welcoming gift, the album, with the carefully coloured-in pictures of Hagar and Lot ripped out and torn in two.

But they don't find Mirjam.

At about five in the morning, Józef Feldman comes up to the house as usual, walking his bike with the buckets of coal dangling from the handlebars. Superintendent Rubin hands Feldman a battery-operated torch, and Feldman sets off into the empty dawn to look for her.

As the first light of day reaches over the wall in Bracka Street, he finds the body in an untouched bank of snow between a closed-down grocer's shop and the no man's land leading from the wires and watchtowers at Radogoszcz Gate. Mirjam is still wearing the knee-length black coat she had on when she arrived at the Green House. Lying a couple of metres from the body is the suitcase of dresses and rag dolls and black patent shoes that the other children so admired.

It was a mystery to everyone how she could have got out unseen. Perhaps she went out the back way, up the steps from the cellar, which the previous day had been revealed to be in use not only by Feldman but also by the piano tuner; then cut across the yard at the back of the house that was used as a playground for all the orphanage children of Marysin. But instead of turning right, into town, she must have gone left. Perhaps she had been lured by the light and noise coming from Radogoszcz Station, and then unwittingly walked straight into the restricted zone where the German guard with the machine gun in his high tower aimed straight at her.

The shot must have hit the side of her head, by her temple, for the blood lay cast in a wide arc of almost twenty metres across the snow. From the drift of snow that the wind had piled over her body during the night, one arm stuck up in the air like a pole. There was nothing else to be seen of her.

When they carried the frozen body into the boiler room

of the Green House, Werner Samstag insisted on coming too. As Rosa and Chaja washed and shrouded the dead body, something happened to young Samstag that Rosa Smoleńska would never really be able to explain. He didn't say the Kaddish – presumably he didn't even know the words – but it was as if his face suddenly softened and sank into itself.

Dem tatn oyf, was all he said, and then he curled up beside the stiff corpse.

He adopted the same position as Mirjam, his arm sticking up like an exclamation mark, and was found the next day by Feldman when he came in again with his buckets of coal to get the boiler going. It was below freezing down in the coal cellar, and the insides of the windows had a white covering of frost. Mirjam was dead, but Werner Samstag was alive. He was asleep in the icy cold in the middle of the floor, with his arms clasped around his own body and a bright, utterly peaceful smile on his lips.

Thus Justice and the Law prevailed in the ghetto –

Der gerekhter un dos gezets.

Justice came in the person of blind Dr Miller. Day after day he dragged his body, supported on its false limbs, through the alleyways of the ghetto, putting houses and factories in quarantine, and making sure housewives took themselves off to the gas-fuelled kitchens he had set up especially for them, so they could get their drinking water boiled for the negligible sum of ten pfennigs a litre. The Law was presided over by apple-cheeked Szaja Jakobson, the judge. By now a special police court (*shnelgericht*) had been set up to mete out instant punishments whenever a crime was discovered. Workers caught pilfering shoelaces or misappropriating a few grams of wood chips were brought forward, beret in hand.

(They had two sentences to choose from: *excrement removal duties* or *deportation*. Most chose *excrement removal duties*, so even this proved beneficial to the ghetto.)

By cleanliness and discipline, the ghetto would survive from day to day.

That was what the Chairman, in his infinite wisdom, had decided. As for Love or other extravagances, the ghetto was hardly the place for them in current historical circumstances. Yet Love was to prove capable of getting through the wires anyway, in its own strange and wonderful way, and changing everyone's lives. Not least the Chairman's own.

The Praeses appointed a young lawyer with good prospects, Samuel Bronowski, as the President of his *shnelgericht*, and put at his disposal a secretary named Rywka Tenenbaum. Miss Tenenbaum was one of the many beautiful young women in his Secretariat to whom the Chairman had certain *romantic aspirations*. The two of them had even been seen together occasionally. But then the Chairman went off on his much-discussed Warsaw trip, and it so happened that while he was away, Rywka Tenenbaum went and fell head over heels in love with young law graduate Bronowski.

And as if that were not enough: when the Praeses was back from his trip, she not only owned up to her amorous adventure, but also rebuffed the Chairman's continuing advances, saying she was not the woman he thought she was, and most definitely not *for sale*.

The Chairman was so furious about this deliberate betrayal that he immediately ordered Dawid Gertler to search young Bronowski's home. In the course of his search, Gertler found no fewer than 10,000 US dollars hidden away in various places in Bronowski's many secret cupboards and drawers. The young lawyer whom the Chairman had entrusted with fighting corruption in the ghetto turned out to be the most corrupt of them all. In view of the severity of the crime, the Chairman decided to lead the proceedings himself, and the perpetrator was sentenced to a six-month prison term followed by deportation, for theft, document forgery and accepting bribes.

Two days later, Rywka Tenenbaum hanged herself from the pipework behind the courtroom in Gnieźnieńska Street, one of the few buildings in the ghetto that had running water and a flushable toilet.

*

As far as the Chairman was concerned, it was not so much a matter of being popular with women as of power and ownership. Just as the court and the bank were *his* court and bank, each collective and distribution point *his* collective and distribution point, so every woman in the ghetto was to be primarily *his* and no one else's.

Seasoned female employees in his various offices thought they could tell just by looking at the old man whether he had 'got any' the night before or not. They could tell by his mood. He could be as gentle as a dove if he had had his way. Standoffish, sarcastic, *nasty*, if he had been refused. Some even reckoned they could predict his state of mind from the degree of compliance his chosen ones had demonstrated in the course of the day. Goodwill on the Chairman's part was always dependent on some woman having made up to him earlier. If he was rebuffed, on the other hand, nobody could do anything to mitigate the power and intensity of his fits of rage.

His rage was like the dark edge of a towering thundercloud. His eyes narrowed, the flesh under his chin quivered; the saliva sprayed from his lips.

There was only one person who eventually proved able to curb that anger once it was raging.

She gets to her feet on the defence side of the long table:

We must remember, Regina Wajnberger says to the court that is in session to pass sentence in the Bronowski case, *that this is naturally not about theft or embezzlement; this is a classic* crime de passion; *that is how we must see it, and judge it.*

The Chairman stares in disbelief at the young female counsel who is speaking for Bronowski. She can't be much older than the accused is himself, and moreover so tiny that she looks as though she is having to stand on tiptoe to reach her own face. But his disbelief stems above all from this: that there is a single person in the ghetto who dare assert the rights of Love in a place where treachery and greed reign. It is like a miracle. With just one word, it is as if this wonderful woman has given his life and his life's work new meaning.

Regina Wajnberger was one of those people of whom it is said:

she had a strong soul but a passive heart. She knew that to get anywhere in the ghetto you had to aim for the very top, and from the very outset she had hoped to ensnare the old man. But Regina also had a brother, and that brother did not allow himself to be manipulated so easily. Benjamin, known as Benji, had to be viewed as more or less a Law unto himself. He complied with nobody, least of all his industrious sister; and she answered him with an unconditional love unlike any other love in the world.

Benji was tall and thin with a mane of thick, prematurely grey hair which he was always sweeping out of his face with long, bony fingers. He was generally to be found on some street corner, expounding to audiences of varying sizes on how vital it was that *certain ghetto dignitaries* take responsibility for their own actions and start to practise what they preached for once; and he would add, with a delighted, almost spiteful glint in his eye:

And from now on I count my so-called brother-in-law among those dignitaries . . . !

And those gathered round the lanky loner would burst out laughing. They laughed until they fell over in the street; strong fists wiped away tears and then enthusiastically hoisted Benji aloft.

Why were they in such high spirits? Because someone in the ghetto was finally daring to speak out and say what everyone thought but nobody dared say aloud? And because these home truths came not from some passing stranger, but from the inner circle itself – from someone who might reasonably be expected to know – from the brother of the young woman whom *the old man* had finally chosen to marry – *from the Chairman's own brother-in-law to be?*

Sister and brother. They were each other's opposite and precondition:

Where she was the Rule, he was the errant Exception.

Where she was the Light, shining like a lamp, he was the great Darkness.

Where she was the smiling, perpetual Innocent, he was the Conscience.

Where she (despite her physical frailty) was the Strength it took to overcome all obstacles, he was like a constant Weakness that would punish her until her dying day, and even longer.

If Benji had not existed, Regina would hardly have accepted when the Chairman presented her with an offer of marriage. She might possibly have carried on seeing him 'at the office', as his other lovers did. What was the alternative? Any woman who had once been favoured with the presence of the Praeses scarcely had any option but to bend to his will.

But getting married was another matter. Her father, lawyer Aron Wajnberger, warned her repeatedly of the consequences of allowing herself to be wedded to that 'fanatic' for all time, for all eternity. But for Regina, the ghetto was like slow suffocation. Every day, a little bit more of the life she lived was taken from her. Her aged father was now in a wheelchair; he could no longer get up or walk unaided; and what would happen the day her father – who was, after all, an esteemed and respected lawyer in the Chairman's camp – no longer held his protective hand over them? And what would happen to Benji then?

Her brother meanwhile naturally went round the ghetto in his typical way, doing all he could to undermine the position she had carved out for herself and her family.

Benji was particularly fond of talking to the 'new arrivals', the Jews from Berlin, Prague and Vienna who were seeking out the market places of the ghetto with increasing desperation. To them he could tell it *like it was*: that the deportations which were about to take place were just the beginning of an *exodus on a massive scale*, and that the Germans would not give up until not a single Jew was left alive in the ghetto.

And the new arrivals should not think they were safe just because they had been deported once already, or because they as 'German Jews' constituted some specially spared elite:

On these trains, we all travel in the same class, my friends!

Only the Chairman believes the Germans will treat good, well-behaved Jews any differently. In actual fact, they see the whole lot of us as rubbish to be thrown away – and the only reason they've gathered us all in one place is to make it easier to get rid of us. Believe me, my friends. That's what they want. To get rid of us.

Some of the new arrivals thought what Benji said was dreadful and wanted to hear no more. Others stayed and paid attention.

Benji was one of the few 'real' ghetto dwellers they had met who spoke in a way they could understand – in pure, clear German, in which one could discuss not only Schopenhauer but also practical matters like how to apply for a proper place to live, or where to go in the ghetto for coal briquettes or paraffin. And besides, Benji seemed to have connections in the higher echelons of the ghetto hierarchy. If they could interpret his outpourings correctly, they might get at least some hint of an answer to the question that was plaguing them all. That is: how long would they be kept here? And what did the authorities have in store for them?

And Benji told them willingly – everything he knew.

He told them of the Debt the Chairman had incurred from the authorities when the ghetto factories were built, and of Biebow's constant demands that this Debt be repaid in some form; if not in cash then at least in valuable objects or brigades of hearty, healthy workers who could be sent to labour outside the ghetto. The Debt, he said, was infinite. That was why the new arrivals had to pledge to hand over all their ready money and exchange all their possessions for money at the Chairman's bank for a ludicrous cashing fee, and still it would not be enough:

He speaks to you as if you were a resource, but you are not a resource; in actual fact you have all come here to be slaughtered . . . And do you know how? The same way as animals, put into a pen. First they have to tire themselves out round its zigzag runs and then, when they come out, the club and the butcher's hook are waiting . . . !

Many of those Benji talked to subsequently hung on to their savings and assets. It was said that many also asked whether there was anyone else in the ghetto to hold their possessions in trust for them. Was there a private bank? But Benji was aware of none, and if, contrary to expectation, he had known of anybody, he would never have said so. He simply stared back at whoever asked, looking at them as if they had just crawled out of their own skin, and then strode off.

*

Before the deportations began in the late winter of 1942, the wedding of Mordechai Chaim Rumkowski and Regina Wajnberger was the most widely discussed event in the ghetto.

People talked about the lavish celebration the Chairman was expected to lay on for his bride, and the gifts he intended showering on her family and all the Jews in the ghetto out of gratitude for having been given her. But mainly they talked about his chosen one. They said how *scandalous* it was that she was thirty years younger than him, but most of all that she was 'one of them', and so it followed that it could have been absolutely anybody who was thus overnight elevated to the mighty man's side. Many saw in the image of the young, apparently defenceless Regina a way out of this captivity and degradation that nobody had thought possible until then.

The Chairman's own relatives, however, seemed less responsive. Princess Helena had asked her husband a number of times to talk his brother Chaim out of it. And when that had no effect, she had gone to the rabbis and asked to have the marriage put to a legal test. She thought *that false creature* – as she called Regina – had deliberately set out to seduce a helpless old man, and what was more, one with a weak heart, who could thus scarcely be expected to survive the emotional turmoil that marriage with a woman thirty years his junior would probably entail. But the Chairman said that he had not considered changing his mind at any stage, and had no intention of doing so now. He said of Regina that she was the first woman to come near him who had not made him feel ashamed. In her dazzling smile, he perceived an innocence that redeemed him from all previous taint, and a sublime purity that spurred him on to new duties. Only one thing worried him. Whether her delicate body would be capable of bearing the child he intended to give her. More and more often of late, he had begun to think it his duty not only to discipline and educate, but also to ensure that his inheritance was passed down. In March that year – 1942 – he would be sixty-five. He therefore thought, not unreasonably, that he had no time to lose in bringing into the world the son he had always dreamt of.

The marriage service itself was conducted by Rabbi Fajner in the old synagogue on Łagiewnicka Street and was a simple ceremony, with Rumkowski in a three-piece velvet suit and the bride as fragile and beautiful as spring rain beneath her white veil. In the course of just a few hours, the Chairman and his young wife received no fewer than six hundred telegrams of congratulation, sent from every conceivable corner of the ghetto; and outside the front entrance to the hospital where the Chairman had his 'town residence' at the time, hundreds of *kierownicy*, heads of department, representatives of the local police and fire brigade queued to hand over personally the gifts they naturally dared not come without. Even Princess Helena and her entourage had thought it prudent to abandon their opposition and change sides, and they stood smiling in the doorway to welcome all the guests, including Princess Helena's own administrator, Mr Tausendgeld, who had personally undertaken to set up a present table on which the gifts and greetings telegrams were piled.

Benji was there, too. He went round, pale and composed, asking everyone to give a piece of bread and tip a few drops from their wineglasses into a bowl he was holding pressed to his chest. When the bowl was full, he went out to the forecourt where curious onlookers had gathered, despite the icy wind, to witness the event from a distance. All the wedding guests could see the bride's brother from the window as he, his half-mast suit trousers flapping around his anklebones, handed out bread and poured wine for the poor of the ghetto.

And those with the sense to be ashamed were ashamed.

The rest danced to prohibited gramophone music.

But Regina was not ashamed. She was physically incapable of being ashamed of her brother.

Afterwards, the Chairman told his wife he had earmarked a special place for Benji at the 'sanatorium' in Wesoła Street. Perhaps a stay in a rest home would make him calm down and finally feel more content. Regina asked her husband if she could rely on him keeping this promise. He replied that if that was all it took to make his beloved wife happy, then it was the least he could do.

After six months in the Franciszkańska Street collective, the Schulz family had finally been allocated a place to live. It was a couple of blocks away in Sulzfelderstrasse, or Brzezińska as the street was called in Polish. Two families were already housed in the little flat. In the room overlooking the inner yard lived a young working couple and they had a little girl with long plaits, named Emelie, who never said a word or even looked up when they met in the hall; in the larger room, facing the street, lived a paint dealer named Riemer and his wife, who had both also come from Prague.

On Dr Schulz's advice, Martin and Josel slept in the Riemers' room, while Věra and her mother moved into the kitchen.

Just off the kitchen there was a tiny room, formerly used as a larder or possibly a cloakroom. There were two doors to this cubbyhole: a door from the kitchen that was so small you had to crouch to get through it; and a taller, narrower one from the hall that looked like an ordinary cloakroom door.

Up on the ceiling of this room there was an air vent, which could be opened using a rod fixed to the wall. As long as the vent was open, you could have both doors shut and there was still some light in the cubbyhole.

Maman installed herself in this restricted space. Věra took food in to her on a tray every day, and they also brought her water in a bucket, and an enamel bowl to use as a chamber pot. It was so cramped inside that if Maman wanted to sleep with the door shut, she had to sit with her back against the wall and her knees pulled up. So there she sat. She ate very little; soon she was eating nothing at all, unless Věra or Martin put the food in her mouth and forced her to swallow.

Arnošt tried to use his connections to get Maman admitted, first to the hospital in Łagiewnicka Street, then to the 'special clinic' in Wesoła Street; but he was forced to give up. In a ghetto where everyone is more or less ill, stays in hospital were for *di privilizherte*, and Arnošt Schulz, foreign Jew that he was, still had a long way to go before he could count himself among that select, privileged group.

But he worked doggedly, day after day, to try to get there.

In 1942, he and a Dr Wieneger from Berlin, with whom he had had some correspondence on scientific matters before the war, developed a technique for making a special salt and sugar solution that could be given subcutaneously; it was derived from a decoction of potato peelings left over from the factory soup kitchens.

Potato peelings – *shobechts* – were desirable commodities in the ghetto; they came in 'thick' and 'thin' varieties and were sold in sacks of two or five kilos to anybody with contacts within the administration, and those individuals naturally knew at once what it took to get five times as much for the sacks on the black market. The trade in potato peelings eventually became so widespread that the Chairman had to insist they be put on prescription, just like milk and other dairy products. That was how the two doctors, Schulz and Wieneger, were able to get their hands on them. They simply wrote prescriptions for each other.

Then, finally, something happened to make the Eldest of the ghetto take some notice of the stocky but undeniably quick-witted doctor from Prague. In a speech to the ghetto administration in February 1942, Rumkowski made particular mention of *Prague physician Schulz's brilliant innovation using the waste products of the soup kitchens* as a model of how current problems in the ghetto could be solved if only one were inventive enough and worked out ways of reusing the ghetto's own resources.

*

But it was for Maman's sake, this obsession with potato peelings.

Every morning before he went to the hospital, he fastened the solution he had devised himself onto a stand Martin had made out of old coathangers, and then inserted the tubing that was attached to the drip bag into a vein in Maman's left wrist.

Thus Maman could get her nutrition intravenously.

Věra records in her diary that her mother's body shook with a strange fever and thick, foul-smelling sweat oozed from her pores and made her face red and swollen. Yet despite the side effects, Maman seemed to get back some of her former strength and impulsiveness. In her alert moments, she was still quite convinced she had never left their apartment in Mánesova Street. She told Věra one evening she suspected there were Czech Nazis hidden in the apartment, who at nights, when the family was asleep, sat up writing secret despatches to Berlin on Věra's portable typewriter.

Before they left Prague, that typewriter had been the subject of an argument between mother and daughter. Věra had insisted on bringing it with her, knowing that sooner or later she would have to look for a job; Maman had said no.

Has the girl taken leave of her senses; that blessed machine must weigh at least fifteen kilos!

Was this now Maman's subtle attempt to pay her back after she had been forced to relent?

But as Věra sat with Maman in the tiny room, she too could clearly hear the click of little type bars hitting the narrow cylinder. She looked up at the ceiling and saw a clump of cockroaches – as big as a wasps' nest – clinging to the vent, their hard bodies falling to the floor one by one, *click, click, click*: it sounded just like the typewriter bars hitting the cylinder . . .

By that stage, the authorities had imposed blackout regulations.

Every evening, Martin or Josel would climb up and cover the kitchen windows with a sheet of tin to stop the light spilling out.

But the children dared not cover the vent in Maman's ceiling, despite the fact that the vermin got in through it. When the door was shut, it was her room's only source of light.

So they all sat there together in their dirty, unheated kitchen in a Polish town they did not know, listening to the distant sound of what Josel said were Allied bombers on their way into Germany, and from the darkness of her chamber Maman whispered that she was sure the Allies' disembarkation plan would succeed this time, and when she next went out to buy fresh *rohliky* at the baker's on the corner, she would find that all the hateful Nazis had been driven out of Prague.

<u>Linguistic confusion</u>

I know. It was nothing but trouble, just like Papa and Mama said, for me to bring the typewriter with me. But I could see no point in spending Kč150 on a portable typewriter in working order only to leave it 'in store', which in this case would have been the same as making a gift of it to the Germans.

There was bound to be a demand for secretarial services even where we were going. Łódź is, as Martin explained to us all, a *German* town.

And how right I was! and how wrong!

In the offices here they use *Polish* typewriters, of course, I'd be an imbecile to get a job here – as I understand it, they don't use the German letters on the keyboard here; for a German e they type a Polish ę – or an ą – or an Ł instead of a proper L.

The spoken language is even worse. It's like living in a swarm of bees. Everywhere you hear Polish, Yiddish, Hebrew. The only language <u>not</u> being spoken is German. That's the language of the occupiers, the enemy – the Germans.

As a speaker of German or Czech you are entirely isolated here; you *have no idea* what's being discussed all around you. It makes me feel like a complete illiterate . . .

It was the spring of 1942. The resettlement operation, as the deportations were known, was already fully under way.

For many of the German Jews, the dismay of finding themselves in such a miserable situation had turned into a nagging terror of what might come next. It was reported that even some *Western Jews* were now on the lists of those to be deported, which many felt to be an utter absurdity. Would this misery never end?

It was so cold in these winter months that Martin had to hack chunks of ice out of the well before he could carry water up to the flat. Věra went down on hands and knees and tried to scrub away the worst of the dirt, but the water was so cold that her hands were soon numb and swollen, and all the joints ached dreadfully. They had to hang the washing on a line strung from the stove-pipe to the handle of the door to Maman's little room, but it scarcely dried, and however much they tried to keep a fire going, they were still frozen to the bone.

But it was not so much the cold and damp as the hunger that made life a daily torture. The skin of their bellies and round their wrists and ankles became swollen and heavy, retaining water; weakness was like a weight in every limb. After a few days with nothing to eat but the thin soup that stank of ammonia, lassitude turned to dizziness and dizziness in turn developed into a kind of mania. Hour by hour, minute by minute, Věra had no thought in her head but *food*. She thought about the newly baked bread Maman would bring home in the mornings, with a hard, crusty, aromatic outside, and so fresh that it lay warmly in the palm of your hand when you broke it; or of the deliciously garlicky boiled beef that their housekeeper would set before them on Sundays, with potato dumplings that she mixed and kneaded herself and boiled in a big saucepan and then served with a big, juicy blob of butter on top; or of the proper *palašinky* the children used to have for dessert when they got home from school, with jam and cream; or of the laden plates of *cukrovinky*, little nut and vanilla cakes shaped into balls and twists, that were always put on the table around Hanukkah. None of these visions were of the slightest use for alleviating her torment, in fact they merely drove the hunger animal in her guts even wilder. What was more, Arnošt would brook no compromise: any food that they could spare, however little, must go to Maman.

He talked constantly about Maman to Věra and her two brothers.

And thus, *talking about Maman* became a way of escaping the hunger. It was the only way of dulling your own body's pain: incessantly talking about someone whose suffering and hunger were greater.

Weak, distracted almost to breaking point by pain and hunger, Věra made her way each day with thousands of other workers along the deep, dirty furrows that had been worn in the banked-up snow along the middle of the street.

The carpet-weaving workshop where she had been given a job as a 'Polish' secretary was in a side street off Jakuba. There must have been a dairy or some shop of that kind in the building before the ghetto was sealed, for the imprint of the lettering was still visible in the grey plaster where the sign used to be: *M l e k o* it said, in italic shadow letters above a row of three deep shop windows, their glass broken but the inside still carefully covered with blackout paper.

One small consolation amid all her sorrow was that her skills as a typist had come in useful after all. Instead of sitting at the looms, she had been allocated a little booth, or partially partitioned-off area, next to the office of the manager Mr Moszkowski, and there she spent her days typing out long lists of materials and invoices directed to *Centraler Arbeits-Ressort*, which Mr Moszkowski would sign at the end of the working day.

There was very little elbow-room between her open office and three looms with the warp threads stretching right up to the ceiling; the carpet weavers sat in rows on long benches, men and women in pairs or groups of four. The foreman's name was Gross; he walked round like a slave-driver on a Roman galley, beating time with a wooden stick which he thumped against the wooden frames of the looms, and beside the harrying stick the weavers' hands flew round and round, sending the shuttle and bobbin through the warp, and pressed the wooden treadle right down with the arch of their foot to operate the harnesses, and the weft thread was sent back again; the beater slammed home:

Send, receive; treadle.

The air above them was thick with fluff.

Clouds of damp dust that clogged your throat like a thick, choking sock of cloth, making it hard to swallow and blocking your nose and ears.

Though Věra was behind her protective partition, she scarcely dared breathe for fear of taking more of the foul, dirty carpet dust into her lungs. How must it have felt for the workers at the looms? But the ghetto workers were nothing more than the operations they performed: those urgent hands and treadle-stamping feet working ten hours a day to keep pace with a frenzied tempo that no human being could match under normal circumstances.

At twelve o'clock, *mittags* was served at the tailor's workshop in Jakuba. The serving hatch was not a hatch in the normal sense of the word but simply a window on the ground floor of an ordinary tenement block. Inside the window, a scarcely visible hand dispensed soup from a ladle into the outstretched tin mugs and other vessels.

Those in positions of trust, that is to say the people the woman serving knew or had taken into her confidence, got two ladlefuls. Everyone else, including Vĕra, got one. On producing her dinner coupon she was also handed a slice of dark, dry bread without any margarine. They always had to wait their turn for the food. The workers from the uniform workshop at 12 Jakuba were always allowed to go first. They took priority with the soup, because they were sewing for the German army.

It was as she was standing in the queue waiting for the ladle of the *pani Wydzielaczka* to reach her tin that she realised the deportations were under way. First one of the women weavers said she was 'leaving them' and surprised them by solemnly going round all her fellow workers to shake their hands and say goodbye, and Mr Moszkowski and the foreman Mr Gross and the two policemen from the ghetto Wirtschaftspolizei who had been posted there to make sure *nothing was stolen* all looked away or down at the ground, red in the face with shame. Knowing that you had your work and your living quarters in the ghetto *on charity* was one thing; proving it to anybody and everybody was quite another.

The following day, the Polish working couple living in the other room of the flat were gone. When Vĕra got back from Mr Moszkowski's *resort* one evening in February, another family was standing in the hall, with an almost identical daughter: she, too, had plaits, and kept her eyes on the floor. Vĕra felt like asking her if she knew what had happened to the other girl, Emelie, as if the fact that they were so alike might mean this girl knew something about the other one.

But how could anyone know what was really happening at all? In times like these, all anybody cared about was that their own soup bowl was filled, preferably with *two* ladlefuls; and that the thin slice of bread they ate would last them for at least an hour or two before the terrible hunger cramps came back.

There were evenings when Věra could hardly move, when cups and plates slipped out of her hands as if the latter were nothing more than two useless *objects*.

Martin and Josel helped her scrub the kitchen floor, which to her eyes looked permanently ingrained with grime. Together, they did the washing and hung it up to dry.

The aching persisted, even so. It was as if a deadening chill was biting into her joints, making every bone in her body sag and bend. At nights it felt as if her whole skeleton turned to a block of ice; a body of *pain* within what was left of her own, making her thoughts turn to places and things they would not voluntarily have dwelt on: to Marysin where Emelie and her family and thousands of other ghetto residents were shuffling through the snow with a hastily packed bare minimum in bundles and sacks on their backs, or tied round their waists.

On their way where? Nobody knew.

The resettlement operation continued.

In February, the Chairman was called to another meeting with the authorities and informed that the respite period was over and a further ten thousand Jews would have to leave the ghetto.

His Resettlement Commission was working on its lists round the clock. It just about managed to find the numbers for ten transports during February, but this still was not enough to reach the specified quota. Figures reported to the German administration of the ghetto in February indicated that 'only' 7,025 Jews had left the ghetto, as opposed to the agreed ten thousand.

The authorities expressed their distress at this dilatory behaviour and decided as a result to add what remained of the February quota to that for March, so the Chairman was ordered to arrange by 1 April, in addition to the ten thousand Jews *normally* demanded, three special transports of some three thousand.

The authorities' displeasure also made itself felt in other ways:

There were alarming reports from Radogoszcz of deportees having their luggage taken from them before they boarded the trains. Those who did not immediately comply were beaten bloody by German guards and then thrust into the train by force.

So was all this business of carefully regulated numbers just camouflage, a trick to make people go to the assembly points voluntarily?

What was more, the deportations of February and March 1942 coincided with some of the coldest days the ghetto had ever seen. At the assembly points, stove-pipes and chimney-stacks cracked in the cold and people had to sleep on the floor with nothing to cover them but their clothes. In the second week in March, a violent storm swept in over north-eastern Europe, a cloud of driving snow and bitter cold. That week, nine people froze to death in a former schoolroom in Młynarska Street, waiting for a train that never came. The open trucks that had been shuttling to and fro between Radogoszcz Station and Bałuty Square with the baggage the deportees had been forced to leave behind now came back loaded with corpses, frozen stiff.

It was possible to appeal against deportation decisions.

The applicant had to present his petition to the Commission in person within five days of receiving his notification to leave. To be approved, an appeal had to be accompanied by documents from the employer to certify that the applicant had a job and his work was satisfactory. Such certificates could be bought in the ghetto for a couple of marks. There was also the option of paying a copyist, who would formulate the appeal using approved standard phrases.

This explains the awkwardly formal tone of some of them:

> *To the Resettlement Commission –*
> *Re: Departure Notice NR VII/211-23*

Most esteemed Resettlement Commission,

I hereby apply most sincerely to be granted respite from the instruction to leave on the part of myself, my wife Zora and my four children, and also my mother: Mrs Libkowicz, widow of Mr Paweł Libcowicz, machine operator. I am a professionally trained electrician with a number of years' experience, and my wife Zora works as a hat-maker at Resort No. 14 in Brzezińska Street. Mr

Viekl, her *resort-laiter*, has been very satisfied with her as a dutiful and competent worker, and in our family we have never been in trouble with the law but have each of us always honestly earned our daily bread, for which reason the departure notice has come as a bolt from the blue. I have heard our Praeses say several times that a workbook and a settled home life are the best guarantee of peace and quiet in the ghetto and so I wonder why we have reached a point where ordinary, honest workers are being punished.

I am most respectfully grateful for your attention and ask you, gentlemen of the Resettlement Commission, to please spare me and my wife and also my mother who after a long working life now suffers with her legs and is generally not in a fit state to take part in the resettlement.

Litzmannstadt Ghetto, 7/3 1942
Józef Libkowicz

By March, pressure on the Resettlement Commission had become so great that it was obliged to move to larger, more spacious premises in Rybna Street. The number of secretaries and administrative assistants was increased from four to some twenty, to deal with all the appeals. A telephonist was also engaged to answer enquiries, particularly from the German ghetto administration. Every morning, before the Commission's offices opened at 8 a.m., a queue of over a hundred appellants, or *petenter* as they were called, would form, awaiting their turn at the counter.

In particularly tricky cases, Shlomo Hercberg was even known to make a personal visit to the applicants' homes. There was a special expression for this in the ghetto. It was said that nobody escaped their *tnoyim* until they learnt to *kiss Hercberg*.

Tnoyim – the marriage contract – was what they called the printed forms the Commission sent to those it selected for resettlement, giving the date and time when they were to present themselves at the assembly points. Hercberg could, as a last resort, agree to put off the departure date a little. But the price of such a postponement was high. The price for permission to stay in the ghetto for an unlimited period was, if that is imaginable, even higher, and payment in cash was always required.

Former cinema projectionist Shlomo Hercberg was well on his way to amassing a considerable fortune in a very short space of time. But something must have gone wrong with his calculations.

Or maybe someone with even better *pleytses* set about slandering him.

On the morning of 13 March 1942, Shlomo Hercberg's success story came to an end. The Kripo raided two of Hercberg's addresses: his city apartment in Drukarska Street and his summer house in Marysin. They also entered his offices in Młynarska Street and broke into the prisoner detention areas of the Central Jail, which Hercberg had locked and sealed. The list below details what the German criminal police found in the Cinema, in addition to the equivalent of 2,995 Reichsmarks in US dollars, stuffed in old shoeboxes, and artist Hirsch Szylis's murals of 'famous actors and naked women', deemed by the German treasurer to be 'of no value':

70 kg bacon (salted)
60 kg ham (salted, dried, cured)
12 barrels sauerkraut
120 kg rye and wheat flour (in sacks)
150 kg sugar
24 boxes of sweets and 'jellied fruits'
32 bottles of brandy + vodka
40 preserved ox tongues
1 crate of oranges
242 pkts 'perfumed' soap
262 tins shoe polish (sealed and unopened)

By this time, Adam Rzepin had already started his job in the unloading bay out at Radogoszcz Station that his uncle Lajb had fixed for him; and he had just finished his shift that icy, grey morning when the Gestapo drove up with the man who had been Rumkowski's right hand, the prison commandant and chief of police who had locked up and raped his sister.

It was 17 March 1942; a completely ordinary day in the 'new life' of the ghetto.

That day's transport stood ready for loading. The final columns marched out from the assembly point in Marysińska Street had arrived, and stood stamping their feet in the muddy slush. Disturbances broke out here and there as groups of German guards approached the new arrivals to separate them from their luggage. Rucksacks, bedding and mattresses, rolled and tied, had already been gathered in a huge heap to one side of the low station building.

Just before the train was due to depart, a black car with its hood up swept into the railway sidings, and a deathly pale Shlomo Hercberg emerged from it, handcuffed to a Kripo man in plain clothes. He was not allowed to straighten up or even look around, but bundled directly into the nearest available wagon.

The next morning, the procedure was repeated with Hercberg's wife, mother-in-law and three children. According to those who saw them there, the children looked 'as scared as everyone else'. Which should perhaps have been a comfort to all who had been victims of Hercberg's greed. But for most in the ghetto, it had the opposite effect. It was only when Shlomo Hercberg and his family were deported that ordinary people in the ghetto realised the authorities' sentence on the Jews of Litzmannstadt was in earnest.

If there was no mercy or deliverance even for those at the very top, what hope did they have when it was their turn?

On Sunday 12 April, the Chairman was summoned by the authorities once more. Those present besides Biebow himself were his two deputies, Czarnulla and Ribbe, while the security forces were represented by SS-Sturmscharführer Albert Richter, second-in-command of the so-called Section II B 4, responsible for Jewish affairs in the ghetto.

On this occasion, too, discussions were conducted in a 'disciplined and, in the circumstances, relatively relaxed atmosphere'.

Albert Richter began by explaining that the war effort had made it necessary to concentrate the Jewish population in a few locations of 'strategic' importance in the Warthegau region. It would therefore soon be time for transports of Jews from the rest of the Warthegau *to* the Litzmannstadt ghetto. In spite of these operations – or perhaps rather *because* of them – it was vital that the resettlements from the ghetto continued swiftly and without interruption. Berlin had stated that it was now 'imperative' that only Jews who were part of the labour force could remain in the ghetto. Therefore all non-productive elements among the newly arrived Western Jews would now also have to leave.

Rumkowski was then given the opportunity to speak and asked the assembled authorities how it was to be decided who was capable of working and who not.

Richter replied that a medical commission made up of German doctors would examine all the remaining residents of the ghetto over ten years of age – *Western* Jews as well as *all the rest*. Those who got a stamp to say they were incapable of working would have to go. All the others could stay.

Chairman: May a Jew say a few words?

Richter: Naturally. You are always welcome to give us your views, Rumkowski.

Chairman: At all costs, exceptions must be made to this labour requirement for the sick and weak of the ghetto. I will provide for them from my own resources.

Richter: But of course, Rumkowski. We are not inhuman.

On the orders of the security services, the ghetto administration now allowed a rumour to spread with regard to where the deportees had been taken. They were said to have gone to the town of Chełmno in the Warthbrücken district, *Kulmhof* in German. Once the German population had been evacuated, a camp of huts had been constructed of a similar size to the first labour camps that had been built, outside Lublin. According to the Gestapo, a hundred thousand Jews from Warthegau were accommodated (*verlagert*) here, among them the forty thousand who had already been evacuated from Litzmannstadt. The living conditions were, it was said, *extremely* good. Three full meals were served every day; all those who considered themselves fit could also do a light day's work for a reasonable wage. The men were said to be largely occupied in mending roads, while the women did agricultural work.

The rumour about the 'labour camp in Warthbrücken' spread rapidly by word of mouth and soon everybody knew the official line, but nobody believed it. It was possible the deportees were still alive and in some labour camp elsewhere in Wartheland or the Generalgouvernement. But they were most definitely not in a newly opened labour camp in Warthbrücken.

*

Outside the communal soup kitchen in Młynarska Street, a long queue formed in the early dawn as people waited to be 'stamped'. Most of them were German Jews from the collectives: men, women and children in random order, because the supervisors of the transports said that only those who voluntarily submitted to a medical examination would be allowed to present their coupons afterwards and get their daily ration of soup.

The queue divided at the entrance into a male and a female line.

The men had to carry on shuffling through the ground-floor rooms to a counter at the back, where normally the serving women stood with their vats of soup, but where now a row of grave doctors in white coats was waiting. While the men's workbooks were checked, they had to twist the upper part of their bodies this way and that beneath carefully palpating doctors' fingers, after which the senior doctor stamped them firmly on the chest, back or waist in blue ink.

There was a system of letter codes for the stamps, running from 'A' – which meant fully fit for work – right down to 'E' or 'L', which meant unfit for work of any kind.

After five days, the medical commission had stamped and drawn up lists of a total of 9,956 of the twenty thousand people it was expected to examine, and had begun to transfer in-patients from hospitals and other care homes to the medical stations. The next day, the authorities took the decision to initiate the 'evacuation' of the western European Jews as well.

As soon as this order had been given, Rumkowski said in a speech:

You know as well as I do the old Jewish proverb that the truth is the best lie. Well, I shall tell you the truth: all the Jews from Prague, Berlin and Vienna who leave the ghetto will be given work in other places. I have the word of the authorities that no one's life is in danger and that all Jews leaving the ghetto will be brought to safety.

But those packing the paltry ten kilos they were allowed to take with them asked themselves the perfectly natural question: since they had been examined and stamped fit for work, why now go to the bother of deporting them to put them to work elsewhere?

Then the transports from Brzeziny and Pabianice began arriving, and then came the convoys of lorries loaded with used clothes and shoes, and the root-fibres of the lie were exposed to broad daylight.

A Saturday in May: long, pale curtains of steady rain hang from the sky. In the curiously cold, watery blue light in the courtyard of the Resettlement Commission in Rybna Street, a crowd about a hundred strong stand waiting, compressed into a single mass of stiff shoulders and hands thrust into thread-bare coat pockets.

They had already been standing there for weeks, ever since the announcement that the Western Jews who had still not found jobs were to be evacuated. In his speeches, the Chairman constantly returned to the new arrivals' unwillingness to work. His voice trembling, he referred to them as work-shy parasites who had lost all drive, and said that he had wanted to settle his account with them long since, but the deportations of the permanent residents had got in the way. Now, however, the time had come.

Any time now, he declaimed from up on his platform.

Any time now, it will be your judgement day, too!

The Czech and German Jews in the ghetto were caught napping by the Chairman's aggressive attacks on them. The Central Labour Office at Bałuty Square and the Resettlement Commission's office in Rybna Street were suddenly inundated with people from the collectives looking for work; or claiming they could prove they already *had* work; or brandishing documents to prove they were so ill that they could not possibly undergo another transport like the one they had so recently suffered, which they could verify by producing doctor's certificates and all manner of letters of introduction from their friends and former employers.

Arnošt Schulz had found himself sought out over the past few weeks by numerous former acquaintances from the Jewish congregation in Prague, men who would scarcely have given him the time of day, but who now insisted on his signature on a variety of certificates they said were their only hope of salvation.

There was one woman in particular who came to see them several times: Hana Skořápková, just a few years younger than Věra, who was from one of the Prague families with whom they had shared a room in the collective. Now, Hana's father, mother and elder brother had all been notified that they were on the list and that she alone, as the only one of them to have a job, would be allowed to stay. Věra helped the frantic Hana type out an application for postponement, and Dr Schulz appended a note certifying that Mrs Skořápková, Hana's mother, was suffering from muscle inflammation and was thus unsuitable for selection for transport – *für Transport ungeeignet*. All this was sent to the Resettlement Commission; then there was nothing to do but wait.

That was why they were standing there in the rain in the courtyard of the office in Fischgasse. On the stroke of eight every morning, decisions were announced on the most recently processed applications for postponement.

Věra could later remember the tense intake of breath that ran like a wave through the many-headed crowd as the door at the back of the courtyard opened and the Commission secretary, a short man with his shirtsleeves rolled up and his braces dangling, came out and began shuffling his papers. Standing there beside Hana, Věra could hear the sound of raindrops pattering on a tarpaulin canopy that was sticking out from the wall of the building; and beyond that sporadic dripping the great, deep roar of rain, like an invisible wall in the air around them.

In an unexpectedly loud, almost resounding voice, the

204

secretary began reading out the names, first those of people who had been granted respite, then those whose appeals had been turned down.

At first the crowd stood in complete silence. Although the names were read out in alphabetical order, some people still thought it worth hoping: perhaps the name they were waiting for had been missed by the reader, or was lower down the list; but a vague unease soon began to spread among the crowd. Somebody burst into shrill tears; another started shouting out the name of someone who had just been turned down. And what had until then been just a slight forward movement turned into a huge avalanche, the entire crowd hurling itself at the doorway (through which the lone clerk had already slipped), and the police who had been standing on guard throughout stepped in and formed a human chain across the entrance.

The policemen had seen it all many times before. But not Hana. The girl was inconsolable. All her appeals for postponement, including the one for her mother, had been rejected.

*

The ghetto was getting ready for departure. On pavements and street corners from Jojne Pilcer Square and all the way up Łagiewnicka Street, German and Czech Jews were trying to sell whatever household goods and personal property they had. Only a short time before, the new arrivals from Prague, Luxembourg and Vienna had paid porters with crisp Reichsmarks to carry all the baggage they had brought with them to the ghetto. Now all those indispensable articles were nothing but a weighty encumbrance, worth not much more than the linings of the expensive winter coats they were inviting passers-by to bid for.

And none of the hagglers were interested in money. Those selling wanted to exchange their goods for food; and the 'natives' who had come to barter for the wares all brought their own scales in which they carefully weighed out the amounts of flour, sugar or rye flakes they could spare in exchange for that warm winter coat or a pair of shoes with some wear left in them.

From somewhere in the throng, Věra heard a voice calling her name.

A little way down the road, a man stood waving to her, his arm flapping wildly. That was how she recognised him, by the way he carried himself.

Schmied was his name. Hans Schmied. *Aus Hamburg.*

In the weeks following the arrival of the transports, he and some of the other German Jews from Cologne and Frankfurt had fallen into the habit of coming down to the old elementary school in Franzstrasse for a chat with the Czech Jews who were housed there.

They said they only came to swap news, the ghetto's perpetual *was Neues,* or to make useful contacts in the never-ending hunt for food. But they were particularly complimentary to the women, and Schmied had for some reason immediately latched on to Věra.

Not that Herr Schmied's appearance was entirely against him. The same God who at his birth had twisted his shoulders half a turn out of alignment had also given his long, narrow face an aristocratic look, with a slender nose and an austere downward turn to the mouth. Even on those rare occasions when he did venture a smile, the corners of his mouth were pulled down, which made him appear to be viewing everything with the same vaguely disgusted disapproval. His aristocratic air was contradicted by his voice, however. Schmied talked constantly, and insistently. He had told her that he had almost completed his diploma in electronics when the new race laws came into force. Two years after that, the whole family had been deported to Litzmannstadt. But the family had not lost touch with all its old contacts, he said. His father, who had a shipping firm in Hamburg, had many of the rich textile manufacturers of Litzmannstadt as clients. He was now lodging with one of those clients, a certain Herr Kleszczewski, who had kindly let him have a room of his own in the family's apartment in Sulzfelderstrasse.

Things had, said Schmied (almost boastfully), gone unspeakably well for him in the ghetto.

Yet here he was now, caught up in the crush in the street; with the suit he had worn for courting her now dangling on a coathanger from the wrought-iron railings behind him. He had not even bothered to unpick the hateful yellow Star of David from the back and front.

So you are leaving, Mr Schmied, she said.

It was more of an observation than a question. She didn't know what to say.

But he wasn't listening. With one hand on her arm, he leant forward and whispered that he had something to show her, something important. She would only have to give him a quarter of an hour of her time, twenty minutes at most.

She looked round. She tried to explain that she was needed at home. That her mother was ill, and could not be left alone for any length of time.

But Schmied insisted. His eyes had a moist, strangely evasive look: *I don't know who else I'd dare tell*, he said, with that stiff, disapproving expression on his face, making it look more and more like a rigid mask of bone.

A little while later, Schmied was leading her through an archway that looked wide enough for two vehicles to pass each other. Inside the courtyard, she noticed an abandoned handcart of a rudimentary design, propped against a wall. The cart had a wooden wheel with metal fittings, and long wooden handles, splintered and unpainted. When she tried to find her way back to this address much later, it was the broad gateway she looked for – and the handcart in the yard.

But by *then*, of course, it was all gone, and the archway looked a lot narrower.

That was what the hunger did to you. Anything that was not right before your eyes immediately drained from your memory and all you were left with was the hollow yearning for food. (Was it food he was going to give her? Bread, maybe he had some left over and couldn't take it with him on the journey.) Looking back, she remembered that once inside the building, they ascended several flights of stairs and kept meeting other people on their way down. On the first floor they passed four men who were blocking the whole landing with the big bed they were carrying between them. Everything must be sold now! Tables and chairs from the flats on the floors above were also on their way down.

It was not until they reached the top floor, where the walls closed in and the ceiling was so low that they could scarcely stand upright, that they found themselves alone. Hans Schmied took out a key and unlocked a door with shiny metal fittings.

In the dusky light into which they stepped, tall rafters supported a distant roof from which some kind of rope and tackle hung. Here and there, mattresses and blankets abandoned in corners partially obscured random collections of household items. Schmied went straight over to the far wall, knelt down by a sort of basic fireplace, took out a knife blade and began working loose some of the sooty bricks. Behind the grit and other debris that this generated, a rectangular cavity emerged, and within it – scarcely distinguishable through the cloud of brick dust – a simple, home-made radio receiver.

'I built the whole thing myself,' he said, his voice thick with dust and pride. 'I used old parts Kleszczewski got hold of for me.'

This – he leant forward and pointed –

'This is the valve, and this is the oscillator.'

And this, he said. He brought out a dirty exercise book, brushed the dust off the cover and showed her page after page of closely written notes:

'This is the log of all the news broadcasts I've managed to pick up in the last six months.'

All written in *code*, so even if the radio was found, nobody could link it to him.

And I'll give you the key to the code so you can read it for yourself, everything that's happened since we came here.

Věra instinctively took a couple of steps back. She listened for footsteps following them up the stairs, but all she could hear was the whispering, rustling sound of rain on the roof above; and Schmied's energetic voice as it went on telling her how he would creep up here to the drying attic secretly in the evenings, sometimes alone, sometimes with Kleszczewski. They listened mainly to the German stations transmitting from Litzmannstadt and Posen, but also to the illegal Polish station Świt. In the latter case, Kleszczewski would listen and Schmied would sit beside him, writing things down.

He leafed through the book, letting her see all the pages of notes, made in his own, secret script:

'The German winter offensive is a fiasco, the siege of Stalingrad a war of attrition that only the Russian People's Army can win. The Russian patriots have pushed forward their front line in the Caucasus. Sooner or later, the victorious Russian army will cross the Weichsel and the ghetto will no longer exist. It is only a matter of time.'

He looked gave her a long, intense look, which made her feel distinctly uneasy. 'There are Listeners all over the ghetto,' he said.

Without her noticing, he had taken hold of her right hand, into which he now slipped the key he had used to open the attic door.

'There's nothing to be afraid of,' he said. 'Just look after it for me. It's enough for me to know it's in safe keeping.'

He spoke in a steady voice and with surprising composure. *Now go*, he said, and when she made no move to leave: *I'll stay here until I'm sure you've gone*. She closed her fingers round the key and walked towards the attic door, and when she turned round one last time, he had already slotted the bricks back into the hole behind the fireplace and brushed away all the traces.

Later, she saw him leaving the ghetto.

She stood in the group of curious people that had gathered behind the police barriers, and watched the deportees leave the assembly point in Trödlergasse outside the Central Jail and make their way down the dusty road to Radegast. It was a boiling hot day in May; Hana Skořápková was there, too, walking with her mother and father towards the rear of the column. So in the end she had decided to leave the ghetto rather than be parted from her family.

Schmied walked alone, with that customary aristocratic look on his face and a suitcase in one hand; over his shoulder he had a lumpy bundle of what she assumed to be household items rolled up in towels and sheets. He met her eye as she stood there at the roadside, but gave no sign of recognition and did not turn back, either.

Night after night, convoys of heavy army vehicles drove into the ghetto. Those who lived along the main roads in and out of the ghetto told of headlights so bright that they tore great wounds right through the blackout curtains, and the throb of engines that made the walls shake. There were at least ten lorries in every convoy. Each one was loaded with a hundred twenty-kilo sacks of torn and bloody clothes.

The next morning, the area around the Church of the Most Blessed Virgin Mary was cordoned off. In the open space between the church door and the statue of the Virgin by the steps down to Zgierska Street lay heaps of mattresses and sacks full of sheets and blankets.

Workers were recruited on the spot at Bałuty Square.

Fifty casual labourers loaded the sacks onto wheelbarrows and took them into the empty church. They began by stacking the sacks of clothes in front of the altar; then the space between the pews was packed with blankets and mattresses. Soon they had built a pyramid of sacks so tall that the light falling through the beautiful, lead glass windows above the altar was obscured, the echo vanished and the empty, abandoned church was plunged into darkness.

It was at about this time that the Jews from the neighbouring towns of Brzeziny and Pabianice began arriving in the ghetto. They, too, were brought at night, in small train carriages with sealed doors and windows.

There were a thousand Jews in the first transport – all women. Somewhere along the way, the women had been separated from their menfolk, and their children had been taken from them. Their accounts were incoherent and confused. Some said the Germans had herded them all together, hundreds of them, and made them run to the station, mercilessly shooting down any who tripped over or couldn't keep up.

Those who survived had been shoved violently onto the waiting trains, and some of them beaten in the process. Others did not even seem to be aware that they had been in a railway wagon, still less that the train had brought them somewhere else.

Blind Dr Miller despatched doctors to Kino Marysin where the women had been taken for the time being, to the same (now empty) storehouse area pressed into service just a few weeks earlier during the evacuation of the Cologne and Frankfurt collectives.

There was also some question of the Chairman going out to talk to the women. But he declined to. Instead, he ordered Rozenblat to close off the area and make sure the women stayed in their huts.

But it was too late. A number of them had already got past the barriers, and before long they were in the streets round Bałuty Square. There, they accosted everyone they met, demanding to know if anyone had seen their children and husbands.

The Jews of the Łódź ghetto listened to their stories with growing horror.

Brzeziny, too, had had a ghetto. But it had been an open ghetto, from which people could come and go as they pleased, without being shot. There had been work, as well. Almost all the Jews in Brzeziny had worked for one German company, Günther & Schwartz, which had made them think all the town's Jews were safe. But then, without warning, the evacuation order was issued. The SS commando unit blocked off district after district. They had been promised an allowance of eleven kilos of luggage each. But once they had formed themselves into lines with their scanty baggage, black-coated SS men stepped forward and started sorting people. Young, healthy men and women were put into one group, designated A. Others, children, the old and the sick, were allocated to a group B. Whole families were thus split up. Group B had to stand to one side, and group A was ordered to set off to the station at a run. Before they even got there, they could hear the Germans shooting everyone they had left behind.

Others had even more to tell:

In the village of Dabrowa, three kilometres outside Pabianice, a warehouse had been set up in an old factory, disused since the previous century. Mountains of used mattresses, shoes and clothes had been taken to this warehouse. Some of the young men and women who had been in the group A category had initially been brought here, to carry out the task of sorting, and they had reported that among all the coats and jackets and shoes and underclothes they had also found workbooks with Jewish names, all bearing the round seal of the Central Labour Office and with the official stamp **AUSGESIEDELT** across the photograph and signature. They had also found wallets containing coins and five- and ten-mark notes in the Łódź ghetto's own currency.

For the shocked crowds listening to them, this evidence was incontrovertible. The workbooks could hardly have originated anywhere else but the ghetto, and the currency was only valid here, and not available anywhere else.

*

On Monday 4 May at 7 a.m., the first transport of western European Jews left Radogoszcz Station. The families from Hamburg, Frankfurt, Prague and Berlin who had arrived in the ghetto and endured such hardship just six months earlier were now forced to leave it again.

The resettlement of the collectives took place in much the same order as their arrival:

The first to leave were *Berlin II* and *Vienna II*, *Düsseldorf*, *Berlin IV* and the collective from *Hamburg*. They were followed by: *Vienna IV*, *Prague I*, *Prague III*, *Cologne II*, *Berlin III*, *Prague V*, *Vienna V*, *Prague II*, *Prague IV* and *Vienna I*.

On receiving their deportation order, people were expected to make their way to the assembly point at Trödlergasse. There they had to give up their bread coupons and ration cards, and were registered for a transport whose number matched the one they had been allotted on the Resettlement Commission's list. They then spent the night either in one of the newly erected barrack huts in Trödlergasse or in the Central Jail. At four in the morning, a special unit of ghetto police came and ordered everyone to form up in marching order – in rows of five, with a police guard at the front and back of every group, and others spaced at ten-metre intervals all along the route.

They were forced to march the length of Marysińska Street, all the way to Radogoszcz Station.

At six in the morning, an hour before the train was due to leave, they were ordered to form up again, this time two metres from the train. Half an hour before departure, two Gestapo cars pulled into the station yard, and two officers accompanied by police from the German ghetto guard went along the train, ordering everyone to put their luggage down on the ground. Once they had complied, the doors were unlocked and the passengers helped aboard the train, which this time consisted of nothing but third-class compartments.

The abandoned luggage was then taken in lorries to the premises of the Resettlement Commission in Rybna Street, where two back rooms facing onto the yard were already full of suitcases and mattresses. A few hours later, the same train was back with the same carriages, though the carriages were now empty, ready for the next transport.

All you can see at first is the sharp glare of headlights, hanging out there in the dark. The light rises and falls, as if an invisible arm were raising and lowering a lantern. The lantern swells into a ball of light that suddenly shatters, and at that instant one can make out the heavy chuffs and groans of the labouring locomotive behind. Then the locomotive erupts into the siding in a deafening screech of metal against metal. There are always four or five armed guards on board, and as many again come running along the long platform of the loading bay, or swing themselves aboard, grabbing hold of side ladders or doors. And the commanding officers gather at the front of the train, shouting in gruff, rasping voices until the group of workers who have been waiting behind storehouses and carriage sheds slowly and almost reluctantly approach the wagons that are now to be unloaded from both sides.

On paper, they are *outside* the ghetto boundary now. Adam Rzepin would have felt a degree of elation at this fact if it had not looked exactly the same *out here* as it did *in there*. The same contingent of utterly bored German soldiers from the ghetto guard, in helmets of dull steel and full-length, field-grey military greatcoats, moving to and fro – chain-smoking, passing neutral phrases between them, and looking on with indifference as the workers pulled open the sliding doors of the goods wagons.

On the other side of the illuminated station yard there is nothing but darkness. And flat, open country. And mud. And the certainty of a shot in the back once the marksmen up in the watchtower have caught up with the sweeping beam of

215

the searchlight. Radogoszcz may lie outside the ghetto. But no one has ever escaped from here, or even tried. The ghetto's boundaries are not as simply drawn as that.

Considerably more cheering was the fact that a few Polish railwaymen generally accompanied the goods trains. They would sometimes shout down to the Jewish workers. A mixture of threats, insults and words of encouragement. One of the Poles even addressed him by name:

Psst Adam, A-daam, come here . . . !

A hand reached down from the wagon and brushed against his; a smile vanished into the darkness and chaos as soon as the unloading began. The Poles never did more than slide open the doors or release the locking mechanisms of the loading hatches. The heavy work, the unloading itself, was to be done by the Jews. The only tools they had at their disposal were shovels and simple handcarts. Two men would swing themselves up into the goods wagon; two others would climb onto the handcart and stand ready, and then the sacks of flour would be slung from man to man. Items like white and red cabbage, carrots and potatoes were usually emptied from the wagons loose, directly into the barrows. If they were in a hurry, the Poles simply pulled up the side flaps of the wagons so the load poured out, at worst straight onto the ground. And if you were really unlucky, the commanding officer – Oberwachtmeister Sonnenfarb – would decide at that very moment to squeeze himself out of the little security hut by the loading bay where he sat eating his packed lunch and listening to the radio. Dietrich Sonnenfarb was a German of vast proportions, whose main amusement was imitating the Jews in his charge. If anybody passed him with a wheelbarrow, Sonnenfarb would immediately follow after with both hands outstretched as if he, too, was wheeling a barrow, his great body with its rolls of fat wobbling from side to side as he shouted, and encouraged the other guards to shout:

Ich bin ein Karrenführer, ich bin ein Karrenführer!

The other guards would double up with laughter; and as if that was not enough, Sonnenfarb's underling Henze would follow in his wake and take swipes with his rifle butt at any Jews in the vicinity, to force them to laugh as well. Henze was lower in rank; it was important to him that everybody – Jew or Aryan – did exactly what Sonnenfarb wanted.

But to everybody's relief, there was usually no time for further orgies of laughter. Another wagon would arrive and need 'scooping out'.

Sometimes, other cargoes came welling out of the wagons when the side hatches were opened:

Empty suitcases, rucksacks and briefcases. And shoes, hundreds of thousands of shoes – ladies' shoes, men's shoes, children's sandals – most of them with the soles or uppers torn off. There were rumours that gold objects had been found stuffed inside some of the shoes or sewn into the linings of the suitcases. The German guards were therefore extra-vigilant whenever they saw a load like this arrive. Adam stood alongside, watching a number of his fellow workers root frantically through the bloody items of kit. But this was never allowed to go on for long. *Schluss! Schluss!* Henze would cry. *Aufhören damit!* As soon as a cart was fully loaded, the two men who had been up in the train would jump down and be 'hitched' to the front of it, while the two who had stayed on the ground would go round to push from behind.

The carts were lugged to one of the many wooden store sheds that had been put up round the main building in the railway yard. From here, the produce was taken directly to the big vegetable depot at Bałuty Square. In Radogoszcz there was also a meat store where slaughterhouse waste was kept to await 'processing'. Summer or winter, a nauseous, suffocating stench permeated the space beneath the tall rafters. Into long, shiny tubs at one end they sorted the meat products that were classed as 'seconds': bits of raw horsemeat with bluish veins, beneath which the flesh had already gone grey and sweaty. These 'seconds' were carted off into the ghetto and ground down to make sausages; every time the storehouse door was opened and the carts passed by, they could smell the thick, nauseating stench of the rotting, meaty dross, like a putrid wave hitting them in the face.

There were the severest penalties for attempting to smuggle anything out of the wagons or store sheds. The local police did full body searches of all those working there: first to make sure they were not bringing in any illicit goods; then a second time when they were going home after their shift. But no police force in the world could prevent the unloading gang as they went about their work picking up a potato or turnip that had happened to fall off the cart and swiftly chewing and swallowing it. This was known as 'skimming'. Everybody skimmed. First the workers in the unloading bay. Then those who handled the provisions at the depot. Then the workers who took the food into the ghetto and unloaded it at the central stores. Then the cart drivers who took the food from the stores to the distribution points. Then those in charge of the distribution, who always liked to put a little aside for themselves, or those whose protection they enjoyed. By the time a customer who had queued for three or four hours finally reached the counter and handed over their coupon, they often found that the desirable consignment of *rote Rüben* was all gone –

Aus, they would be told in that characteristically brusque and dismissive tone, *kein Zucker mehr, kein Brot heute* –

Aus –

Adam Rzepin was not stupid, and realised it was a job with privileges his uncle Lajb had wangled for him, despite the night shifts and the arduous physical labour. For as long as the deportations lasted, there were three or four full trains per shift to unload. As well as old clothes and shoes, which were reused in the ghetto factories, materials for the wood-product and metal-goods factories were also delivered this way. And the foreman made no distinction between human beings, old rags, scrap iron and coal briquettes. They were all just freight to be unloaded.

And then there were *the two soups*. Everyone who did a night shift got an extra portion of soup. It was after the second helping of soup one night, when the work gang Adam belonged to had just set about emptying a wagon of scrap metal, that he heard the voice again:

Ugly Adam! – don't you recognise me?

And there, perched on the coupling between two wagons, was Paweł Biełka. They had lived in adjoining blocks of flats in Gnieźnieńska Street, the Rzepin family at number twenty-six, the Biełkas at twenty-four. Paweł Biełka had been one of those louts who went round kicking other kids and calling them *Jewish arseholes*. But now here he was, behaving as if he was absolutely delighted to see him again, a grin plastered all over his face:

Adam, you ugly mug – how are things . . . ?

And Adam, too taken aback by their reunion to reply, just had time to glance quickly over his shoulder to check there were no German guards within earshot.

Only a week earlier, Adam had seen German policemen come charging along the train. The reason: a Pole and a Jew had stopped about ten metres from each other. Adam could not tell if they were talking or not. But one of the police guards had landed a rifle-butt blow on the Jew's head – it was Mirek Tryter – and Mirek had not turned up for the next shift, and nobody had dared to ask about him.

But to Adam's surprise, Biełka responded by grabbing his shoulders and pulling him into the gap between the wagons. They would subsequently often stand like this, pressed as close together as two coins. And Paweł repeated *how are things in there really, we hear the most bloody awful rumours, like you having to lick the shit off the walls because you haven't got enough to eat, is it true Adam, that you eat your own shit, is it true*, as he stood there, feet planted wide apart, rocking to and fro on the coupling that connected the two goods wagons.

Adam didn't know what to answer. It was as if they were still back in the yard by the flats and Paweł Biełka was challenging him. *Come on, you fat Jewish arsehole!*

Biełka swivelled his hips. The whole set of wagons rocked, and Adam instinctively threw himself back down onto the platform. Just in time to shoulder the straps that were passed down to him from the front of the cart of scrap iron, and before *die Feldgrauen*, busy with something further along, had time to notice his absence.

So he took up the straps and pulled.

Two men pulled, and two pushed from behind.

And then a sudden sharp blast on the whistle: the wagons jolted again; then the whole train set off at a slow, almost leisurely pace. Back in the direction from which it had come.

*

Before they had had time to accustom themselves to Lida's crashes, Adam's mother Józefina would put a bucket of water beside Lida's bed and hang a mirror above the head of the bed. This seemed to have a calming effect. She could lie there for hours, running her hands through the water or tracing pictures with her finger in the frost on the inside of the window pane.

Adam got into the habit of doing the same every evening before he went to work: he put out a basin of water by the bed and hung up a mirror and hoped it would do. But Lida had a way of outwitting them all. As long as Adam or Szaja was at home, sleeping, she would lie there peacefully, but as soon as she was left alone in the flat, her crashes would start again.

One morning, as Adam was coming back from Radogoszcz,

he heard her hoarse seabird cry long before he turned the corner into Gnieźnieńska Street, and although he was so exhausted after his night duty that he could scarcely walk, he took the stairs up to the flat at a run. Lida was lying on the first-floor landing with her nightdress pulled up over her malnourished, swollen belly, her arms and legs still thrown out as if she imagined she was flying, and bending over her was the concierge Mrs Herszkowicz. She had a coal shovel in her hand and was wielding it coolly and deliberately, as if trying to tenderise a piece of tough meat; and all around stood the neighbours (including Mrs Wajsberg and her two sons Jakub and Chaim, and Mrs Pinczewska and her daughter Maria), and they all saw what was happening but no one made the slightest move to intervene until he forced himself up the stairs. Then they all moved back, shamefaced, even Mrs Herszkowicz (who dropped the coal shovel as if the handle were on fire); and let him put his arm round his sister to help her crashed, broken body back up to the flat.

The first weeks after Lida came back from the stay in the rest home Lajb had arranged for her, everyone had the impression she was a lot better. The weeping sores on her arms and legs had gone; her porcelain skin had regained a little of its former glow. Above all, she could walk more confidently. Instead of creeping along as if the floorboards were about to give way beneath her, she now ran around with a lively spring in her step. She would nod, and announce in a loud, shrill voice:

Einen schönen guten Tag, meine Herren, or (in Yiddish):

S'iz gut – dos veys ikh schoyn.

Until then, Adam had found lying down on top of her was enough to calm her when she had her fits. He had lain like that for hours, his body against hers as he whispered or sang into her ear. None of that helped now. With a strength he had not known she possessed, she tore herself out of his embrace and began to plummet again. He tried wheeling her round in a wheelbarrow in the yard. It helped for a little while. Long enough, if he was lucky, for him to get her washed and fed and into bed. As an extra precaution, he tied her arms to the headboard. Sometimes she made no protest. On other occasions she resisted so violently that Adam had to ask Szaja to help hold her down while he tied the ropes. But even then, and for a long time afterwards, he could feel the desperate muscle contractions in her body: long drawn-out spasms running from her trunk all the way along her pinioned arms.

Like wingbeats. Convulsive, unfulfilled.

Something inside her was broken.

There were times when she did not recognise him. And that was perhaps what hurt him most.

It was like when she opened the door to him out in Marysin. In her eyes just then, he had been just another of those who came to use her ill.

He tried to bring the subject up with his father, but Szaja refused to talk about it. Above all, Szaja refused to talk about his brother Lajb.

'We must be grateful,' was all Szaja would say.

'We must be grateful that you've got your work, Adam, and we must be grateful that we've got Lida back. Things could have turned out much worse.'

And Adam worked. And he was grateful for the employment Uncle Lajb had found for him. And he decided he would never do anything wrong again or break the Chairman's laws. For Lida's sake. But one morning he heard the familiar whistle from between the goods wagons again, and when he slipped in to avoid attracting the attention of the guards, Paweł Biełka said straight away:

You know Józef Feldman.

It was more of a statement than a question.

I've got something for him.

Biełka delved into his trousers and produced a copy of the *Litzmannstädter Zeitung*: a damp and sticky wad of wood pulp covered in heavy black type. Adam wanted to say they search us every day on our way in and out of the ghetto. But of course Biełka already knew that.

Do like me – stick it in your crotch.

If they catch you, just say you were using the shit as toilet paper then you won't be lying, at any rate!

Adam made as if to jump back down onto the platform, but Paweł grabbed hold of him again and fixed him with a grim look:

What do you want? Cigarettes?

It's too dangerous.

Food?

Paweł, I can't.

Medicines? Azetynil, Vigantol?

That was what made Adam weaken. He thought of Lida. Maybe a few little tubes of vitamin tablets would give her back her faculties and her reason. If he went through the gate with the tubes under his tongue, the guard wouldn't find them. The only time a German shone a light into a Jew's mouth was when he thought he might find gold there, and by then the Jew in question was most certainly already dead.

Give it a go, said Biełka, who could see him hesitating. And he held out the crumpled newsprint at an angle from which it could be seen by every guard on the entire platform, so Adam did what anyone would have done in that situation: snatched it and hid it under his clothes as fast as he possibly could.

*

The sun was up, suspended a bare hand's breadth above the horizon: a red globe of trembling warmth above the grey-scrubbed fields and the thinly scattered rows of shanties and earth cellars overgrown with grass. It was already May, but still cold at nights. Streaks of nocturnal mist lingered in the hollows where the light could not reach. Not much green, either, on the trees and bushes, which seemed to be coated in the same, cement-like dust that was for now lending its colour to the sky.

But there was strength in the sun. He could feel it burning the side of his face. Turning, he saw the daylight running like a knife-edge over the wall round the cemetery. The light cut reflections out of the corrugated tin roofs opposite, of the gravel chips in the road he was walking along, of the bottle glass someone had set in the top of the wall around a *działka*: scrubby fruit bushes behind an iron gate, its lock rusted through. He walked slowly along the outside of the cemetery wall, past the Green House, and went on down the hill some five hundred metres, until he reached Feldman's nursery business. Wisps of smoke rose from the tin chimney fastened to the wall of the main building. A delicious smell of frying was coming from inside. Adam knocked, stepped onto the upturned beer crate that served as a doorstep, and opened the door.

The house consisted of a single large room, lined from floor to high ceiling with desks and bureaux, their compartments and pigeonholes stuffed with invoices and old account books; on top of every cupboard or stack of shelves were books and advertising brochures, their once garish covers now faded and curling in the damp. And above *them*, rows of stuffed wildlife: wood grouse and black grouse with courtship displays of splayed tail feathers; a marten partway along a narrow tree branch, its muzzle lowered as if hunting for prey in the cracks in the floor way below.

Józef Feldman, by contrast, was a small man, a metre and a half tall at most; he seemed to be swallowed up by the thick, moth-eaten woollen overcoat he was wearing. But the eyes peering out of the coat were unexpectedly sharp and steady, and the voice was like a dangling noose as it spat out its *who are you?* before Adam even had the door fully open.

'Mr Feldman?' said Adam tentatively, not yet daring to let go of the door.

Instead of stepping inside, he undid his belt and stood there holding up his trousers with one hand and brandishing the smuggled copy of the *Litzmannstädter Zeitung* in the other.

Feldman, who was busy cooking at his little primus stove, did not take his eyes off Adam's face for a second. *Rzepin?* was all he said when Adam gave his name. *I only know one Rzepin – and he's called Lajb.*

He spoke the name as if it were a swearword. Adam felt ashamed, though he could not for the life of him fathom why.

Lajb is my uncle, he said simply.

The smell of frying sausage suddenly overwhelms him. He wants to sit down, but stays on his feet because there is nowhere to sit among all the clutter. Feldman glances at the newspaper Adam has given him, then folds it up small and stows it like a flat parcel in a slot between the sections of a filing cabinet.

At the far end of the low greenhouse is something Adam at first takes for a big, dirty window; then he sees it is comprised of little boxes or containers made of glass, different shapes and sizes, piled one on top of the other and stacked edge to edge, like a set of glass shelves from the floor right up to the roof. Some of the glass boxes contain gravel or sand, and dried plants; others are empty. As he stands staring at this incomprehensible wall of glass, it suddenly catches fire. Somewhere deep in the labyrinth of glass surfaces dimly reflecting each other, a pinprick of light penetrates, then spreads and bursts out, like a burning sun – the light suddenly so dazzling to the eyes that everything in Adam's peripheral field of vision instantly dissolves.

It is the sun, suddenly rising on the other side of the greenhouse wall.

You must be starving, says Feldman, and indicates a corner of the floor where there are a mattress and a threadbare old horse blanket.

Have a seat . . .

As Adam sits down, the dawn light falls into shadow again, and the glass wall no longer looks so impressive: a collection of silted-up aquariums, their bottoms covered in a layer of greyish mud and their sides caked white with dust.

Feldman later told him that as a young man he had ranged the marshy forests of Masuria with his scoop net, vasculum and a collection of glass jars and other storage vessels, determined to survey every habitat in the whole system of lakes. And how that interest had widened out in the early thirties, when he started experimenting with different ventilation and heating units to recreate other living biotopes in miniature: Brazilian rainforests, desiccated desert landscapes, steppes and prairies.

There was a time when I was obsessed with the idea of reconstructing every landscape and soil type on earth. But then along came the war and the occupation, and you could say I found I had enough to do with my own, and what I've got here.

Feldman transfers the cooked sausage to a plate and starts cutting it into slices. In Adam's brain, an advanced calculation is in progress. Could there be fifty, no it must be closer to sixty, grams of sausage on his plate now? How long could he make the sausage last in his stomach? Ten hours, twelve?

It depends how slowly he eats.

Now he is nearer the fire, he can see that Feldman is much younger than he first thought. Within that dark face there are paler folds; as if the weather-beaten skin were just a mask, pressed onto the face underneath. The expression in that *other* face is boyishly bright, fearless yet somehow strangely scheming. Adam would later describe it as Feldman having a way of looking at people as if measuring them up for their funeral. That was the expression with which he was appraising him now.

There was someone else who used to bring the newspapers. Do you know what happened to him? Adam chews his sausage; says nothing. *Rzepin?* says Feldman after that, as if sampling the taste of the name. Adam carries on chewing. *I'm surprised at Lajb making one of his own into an errand boy. What hold has he got on you?* Adam turns and says: *It was a man called Biełka who asked me, that's all I know.*

Feldman carries on looking at him, as if expecting Adam to say more, now he has finally started talking. When nothing more comes, he turns away again with a sigh that seems to spread through his whole body, and extends a surprisingly long arm from one sleeve of his coat to poke the fire with a block of wood, making the glow in the stove flare up in a shower of sparks.

Adam sits there chewing until there is no sausage left to chew. When no more food is offered, he realises it's time to offer his thanks and go. *Do come and visit me again*, says Feldman, but in a voice and tone which indicate that he has already lost all interest in Adam and the contraband he has brought.

Adam has no sooner re-emerged into the surprisingly bright sunlight than he meets the first column of deportees on their way out from the assembly point in Młynarska Street.

The marchers have been issued with new, machine-made *trepki*, and this practical footwear is stirring up the dust in the road into a gigantic cloud that shrouds them in a pale, chalky veil which then slowly settles again behind their doggedly tramping feet. On their left-hand side, an escort of five policemen is keeping pace with them. Every so often, one of them shouts an abrupt order to keep the marchers on course. *Straight on!* or *Right turn!* Beyond that, there is no sound to be heard. The men plod past in their new clogs, with their cases and rucksacks, and mattresses tied round their waists or slung over their shoulders, and not one of them shows any sign of turning to look at him. Nor does he turn his head to watch them go. It is as if they are moving in two separate worlds, far apart.

But Uncle Lajb's name keeps cropping up, like a nagging toothache. Adam knows his father is right and he should be grateful for the job he has been given. But he still can't help thinking it can hardly be a coincidence that a place in the work brigade at Radogoszcz suddenly fell vacant. Of all the jobs in the ghetto, why should Lajb offer him that particular one? And of all the people he once knew or was acquainted with in the ghetto, why should old Biełka be turning up between the goods wagons? Could it be that he had been entrusted with a task originally earmarked for somebody else? And in that case, who was that other person, and what had become of him?

By the time Adam Rzepin turns round, the marching column has gone; nothing is left but the cloud of chalk-white dust, hanging like a dense, powdery stripe above the sunlit horizon. The sun's disc has risen higher now. The heat has begun to ache in sand and grit and stone. Adam Rzepin has sausage in his belly. He decides not to think about it any more.

It started as a game. He said: Shut your eyes and imagine I'm somebody else. And Regina laughed her clear laugh and said surely he needn't *lower himself.* He was the Chairman, after all. The whole ghetto looked up to him. But he insisted. Shut your eyes, he said, and when she finally did so, he put his hand on her knee and ran it slowly up the inside of her thigh.

Love can also look like this.

He knew she was revolted by the sight of his ageing, flabby body, by the unpleasant smell of old man given off by his hair and skin. Now he set her free from the obligation to experience all this too close, and was rewarded with the gift of feeling her sex swell and grow warm and wet beneath his anxiously kneading fingers.

Who was she dreaming of, there behind her closed eyelids?

The story of a lie can also be told like this:

He told the residents of the ghetto he had not said all he had said, and everything that had happened had not actually happened. And those listening believed him, because he was the Chairman, when all was said and done, and there weren't that many others to listen to and put your faith in.

He told the demented women from Pabianice and Biała Podlaska that he had assurances 'from the very highest authority' that all was well with their husbands and that he would intervene on their behalf to ensure their children were brought back to Łódź immediately.

And he told his brother Józef, who had been agonising ever since the deportations began, that he enjoyed the full confidence of the Reich Governor, and nothing bad would ever happen to the chosen Jews in the ghetto.

And the great Chaim went about in his lie like an emperor in his palace. In every doorway there were attendants who dropped to their knees and asked if there was anything else they could do for him. What happens to a lie then, if it is a natural extension of one's whole being?

Despair and scepticism, said Rumkowski, are for the weak.

On the Sabbath, Regina lit the candles and set out the loaves, and every Friday evening when they were seated at the table he read the Sabbath prayers, since that was what was required of a good Jew in a home that would, he intended, set a good example to the whole ghetto. On Sunday they went by *dróshke* to the hospital in Wesoła Street. There he had paid 'out of his own pocket' for places and two full meals a day for Regina's two unmarried aunts and her troublemaking brother Benji. They spent the entire visiting time sitting with the two old spinsters in their room, and Regina boasted that Chaim had recently arranged for a *permanent telephone link* between him and *the powers that be in Berlin*, and her charming, mild-mannered husband said the negotiations had gone better than expected, and he was hoping for a decision before too long on his request to expand the ghetto: *Soon*, he said, *very soon you will be able to take the tram all the way from here to Paris!*

And the old ladies laughed, their hands held self-consciously in front of their mouths:

Oh Chaim, you cannot expect us to believe that –

Chaim, tylko nie wystaw mnie do wiatru.

Yet they still closed their eyes and allowed themselves to dream a little. With the great Chairman, nothing seemed impossible.

Only one thing was lacking to make the lie complete, but

230

although he hoped and prayed, Regina did not get pregnant. Biebow informed the Chairman at this time that the authorities would not be satisfied from now on with the removal from the ghetto merely of the elderly and infirm. Soon *all* who could not work – even the youngest – would be forced to leave.

Perhaps he should have heeded the warning in those words.

But the Chairman still dwelt in his Lie, and in it there was a Child, just one, that would be strong enough to survive all the misfortunes the Lord chose to visit upon them, and he would be able to confide in this, his only Child, all the things he had hitherto not dared to say to anyone.

But if his wife remained infertile, despite her youthful years, how could this child come into the world? How, and from where, could it be acquired?

He tried to save the rest of the children of the ghetto in a more tangible way.

It was quite a simple equation, after all: the more he could get into work, the more the authorities would spare.

As early as March 1942, he had begun setting up special apprentice workshops for boys and girls aged between ten and seventeen. This was where the older children from the Green House and the other orphanages in Marysin had gone.

In May of that year, after the collectives of German Jews had been moved out, he had the old elementary school building in Franciszkańska Street converted into a vocational school with twelve separate classes and fifty children to each class. There were classes in cutting out, in hand- and machine-sewing, in materials. Even simple bookkeeping was taught.

After a few weeks' training, those showing the most aptitude were given shifts in manufacturing at the Central Tailors, where they worked under the supervision of inspectors who went round and picked them up on any mistakes, or for wasting time. The children's task was to make special camouflage caps for the German army, with an outer layer of white fabric for winter field warfare, and a grey top inside for fighting in normal terrain. The Chairman went from bench to bench, saw the material run in broad lengths through the children's nimble fingers, saw the teachers bending down to help hands hold pieces of fabric straight as the sewing-machine needle tacked along them, panel after panel, and he was overcome by a feeling of pride in spite of everything: that despite the chaos and starvation all around, it was still possible to maintain such order and discipline.

From July 1942 he was able to get permanent sewing jobs for some 700 of the children in the ghetto over ten years old. If he only had time, he would without doubt be able to create jobs for – and thus save – at least as many again.

But while he was fortifying the walls of his worker city in this way, the disintegration proceeded unabated:

Back in April, news had started filtering through of the massacres in Lublin.

Then (in June): *Pabianice* and *Biała Podlaska*.

Forty railway carriages full of women and children had left *Biała Podlaska* and disappeared without trace.

Sometimes as he sat behind the closed doors of the Secretariat, he felt there was a landslide happening outside. As if something holding together the seams of reality itself had burst apart.

Dawid Gertler came to his office and told him straight out what he had lately heard of the mass deportations about to be carried out in Warsaw. There were three hundred thousand Jews being held in Warsaw. According to Gertler, the authorities there intended to spare only a tenth of them; barely thirty thousand would be kept on to work in the factories of the Warsaw ghetto.

At the same time, the English were intensifying their air

raids on strategic cities in the Reich – *Cologne, Stuttgart, Mannheim*. On 26 June, British radio broadcast news of the massacres of Poland's Jewish population for the first time. The BBC bulletins named towns such as *Slonim, Vilna, Lwów*.

But also *Chełmno* – the city of *Kulmhof* in the district of *Warthbrücken*:

> *Thousands of Jews from the industrial city of Łódź and surrounding towns and villages are believed to have met their fate in this otherwise insignificant place.*

This news from the other side of the wire reached the ghetto via the hundreds of illegal radio receivers, swiftly turning what had hitherto been a macabre suspicion into certain knowledge.

Outwardly, of course, nothing happened. The starving men and women of the ghetto continued to drag their gaunt bodies from one distribution point to the next; already bent backs became still more bent, if that was possible. But there was a certainty where there had been none before. And that certainty changed everything.

The morning after the BBC's news of the massacres in Chełmno, the Praeses carried out an inspection of the Department of Statistics in Plac Kościelny. Together with Neftalin the lawyer he went through all correspondence that had been kept and made sure to burn all documents which might make it appear to posterity that he had been too ready to comply with, or had indeed acknowledged, the true significance of, the authorities' orders. This applied, for example, to the question of dealing with the excess baggage that had been taken from the Jews as they were deported from the ghetto, for which Biebow refused to pay the additional freight costs. Rumkowski asked Neftalin to replace all record of this with a special archive entry showing not only who had been deported but also who had been granted *exceptional leave to stay*, that is, all individuals he had personally intervened to save or had otherwise vouched for.

Everyone who came into contact with the Chairman at this time could testify to a change in the smell of his body. He seemed to secrete a sharp but sweetish odour that clung about his clothes like stale tobacco smoke and followed in his wake wherever he went. But most who saw him in those days also said he carried himself with great determination and dignity. As if it were only now, with all this practical management of large groups of people, in assembly camps or columns of statistics, that he could set a course worthy of the enormous task he had imposed on himself.

*

On 24 July, the news comes through of Czerniaków's suicide in Warsaw:

> The cowardly man would thus rather die than be involved in the evacuation of the Jews of the Warsaw ghetto. And yet, as far as I understand it, thousands of Jews are still leaving Warsaw every day. So if that is the operation Czerniaków wanted to stop, his suicide has altered nothing. It is just a vain and meaningless gesture.

So reads his summary of the situation that has arisen for the other members of the Council of Elders.

Nothing like what is now happening in Warsaw will be allowed to happen here, he assures them. This is not a ghetto, after all – it is a city of workers, he says, unintentionally using the same phrase as he did the day he received Himmler outside his barrack-hut offices at Bałuty Square:

This is a city of workers, Herr Reichsführer, not a ghetto.

*

He admits to his private physician, Dr Eliasberg, that his heart has been giving him trouble again, and asks if he could possibly get him some more of the old nitroglycerine. Eliasberg not only procures more nitroglycerine, he also brings other medicine for the heart: little capsules, white and shiny like the saccharine pills that little children used to sell on street corners.

For someone who is starving, even a tiny amount of sugar like that on their tongue can mean the difference between life and death. The thought arouses him strangely. He keeps the little cyanide tablets in a metal case in his jacket, and is always putting his hand in his pocket to check they are still there.

He never thinks about what it would be like to take the tablets himself. Instead, he sees himself stirring two of them into Regina's tea. She'll pull a face at the bitter taste, but that's all she'll have time to do. Death is instantaneous. Dr Eliasberg has assured him of that.

How could he even be contemplating such a move, he who loved her so dearly? The answer was that it was precisely because he did love her so dearly. He could never endure the shame of standing before her destitute and humiliated. Like Czerniaków, chairman of the Jewish Council of Elders in Warsaw, who had not understood what obeying orders meant.

'Czerniaków was weaker then me,' said the Chairman. 'That's why he's dead now.'

That was as he lay there, letting Dr Eliasberg listen to the rhythm of his heart.

'He took his own life rather than send his brothers and sisters east.'

Dr Eliasberg said nothing.

'That will never happen here,' said the Chairman.

(*My children are making camouflage caps for winter field warfare. It can't possibly happen here.*)

Dr Eliasberg said nothing.

'But if it did happen here, I want your assurance, Dr Eliasberg . . .'

'You know I can't give any assurances, Sir.'

'But if I were to die . . . ?'

'You will never die, Praeses.'

*

On the big area of worn grass behind the Green House, the children from the Marysin orphanages gather and play games.

Their laughter echoes beneath the hard, black sky.

The children form two rows, holding hands, then raise their hands high above their shoulders and walk towards each other. The two lines join to form a circle and they start to move round, circling first one way and then the other.

He sits in his carriage, following them with his eyes. He does not want to reveal his presence immediately and spoil their game.

The younger children stumble and fall; the older ones laugh. Samstag, the German boy he noticed last time he was here, is leaning against a rusty old car chassis without wheels. He is wearing shorts that would have fitted a child ten years younger and a short, ribbed pullover that reaches to just below his navel. He smiles all the time, but without any visible sign of pleasure: as if his mouth were detachable and flopping about at the bottom of his big face. All over Marysin, the grass grows high and lush. In back yards, behind wooden sheds and latrines. The children eat the grass. That is why they are all black and sticky round the mouth.

He must remember to have a word with Miss Smoleńska about it. There could be poison in the grass.

He waits. They still have not noticed him. The clouds gather in the sky above and merge into thin veils of Scotch mist, slowly thickening. There is a distant rumble. Thunder is on its way. Soon the first raindrops will start to fall.

The children look up –

He puts his hand in his jacket pocket, prises the case of cyanide tablets open with his thumbnail and stirs them with his fingers.

The frequency of the drops is increasing now. There is dull grumbling from the wall of thunder as he asks Kuper to drive closer. The children stand with their fingers in their mouths, staring at the horse and carriage, and at the old man with his hand in his jacket pocket, like a vision from another age.

He sees that they see, and is clearly embarrassed.

Well carry on playing then, he cries, *off you go*, he says, and laughs – and when the children, at a nod from Miss Smoleńska, rather unwillingly start to move again, he pulls the tablets out of his pocket and throws them all up in the air –

Heave ho, here we go –

A child detaches itself from the throng. He is maybe ten years old; stocky, with solid thighs and broad shoulders, but quick. He whirls like a tornado across the ground and brings the palm of his hand down wherever a white tablet has landed.

There, and there, and there! chuckles the Chairman delightedly.

But as with Samstag, only the Chairman's mouth is smiling. In his eyes there is a piercing, lethal glint. Apart from the energetic boy hunting down the sugar pills, none of the children dare to come closer. They just stand timidly with their fingers in their mouths.

The boy's name is Stanisław. He arrived at the start of May with a transport from Aleksandrów. His mother and father, sisters and brothers (there were at least seven of them) are all dead. But he probably does not know this. Or does he?

Hej ty tam, podejdź tutaj.
'You there, come here!'

He says it in Polish, immediately indicating that he has identified Staszek as one of the new children.

And when the boy reluctantly approaches the barouche, he reaches down and cups the boy's chin firmly in his gloved hand.

Powiedz mi, ile żeś podniósł?
Show me, what have you found?

Staszek opens his fist and shows a handful of white pills. It is impossible to tell which of them are cyanide tablets and which are ordinary sugar pills. Completely impossible: even he could not tell the difference. And the Chairman laughs his big laugh. He wants it to be seen from far and wide how impressed he is with the boy's efforts.

At that moment, a violent clap of thunder shakes the landscape, and within a minute torrential rain is falling on them.

The operation began at five in the morning on 1 September 1942, on the anniversary of the German invasion of Poland.

Police chief Leon Rozenblat was given orders to mobilise his ghetto force just half an hour beforehand. By then, the army transport vehicles had already driven into Bałuty Square: heavy, open lorries like the ones that had carried shoes and sacks of bloody, dirty clothes to the ghetto on recent nights. And in addition, half a dozen tractors with two or three trailers attached.

In the pale dawn light, some of the wooden fences and barbed-wire barricades across the exits from the square into Zgierska and Lutomierska were taken down, new barriers erected and the standard Schupo guard supplemented by members of the security forces.

While all this was happening, the Chairman of the ghetto lay sleeping.

He slept, and dreamt he was a child.

Or to be more accurate: he dreamt he was himself and a child *simultaneously*.

The child and he were competing, aiming stones at bottle tops. The child threw his bottle top, and he himself followed suit with his stone. After a while, he noticed it was getting harder to see. The child threw the bottle top further and further in the full, blazing sunshine, and the stone he was about to throw grew as huge and heavy as a skull in his own hand, so big that in the end he could not grasp it, even if he used both hands.

A wave of anguish swept over him. The game was not a game any longer, but some grotesque test of strength between these two who were both himself.

At the very moment he tried to hurl the giant stone, someone grabbed his arm and said:

Who do you think you are? Aren't you ashamed of your arrogance?

By then the roar of the lorries' diesel engines could already be heard, along with the loud clanking of the metal chains that were pulled taut as the towing vehicles slowly moved off down the streets of the ghetto.

*

He said afterwards that what grieved him was not the purge per se; the authorities had in fact prepared him for it in advance. What grieved him was that an operation *on that scale* could begin and be in progress for hours *without anyone thinking of ringing to inform him.*

It was *his* ghetto, when all was said and done. It was their duty to keep him informed.

Miss Fuchs explained later that when the Secretariat received the order, everyone assumed that the Chairman had already *agreed to it*, and that the fact he had not come into the office was simply explained by his preferring to draw up his plans and guidelines in the security of his home.

But that was not the impression he got when he arrived at Bałuty Square and was met by a delegation of his own staff outside the row of office huts. On the contrary, their staring eyes gave him the feeling they were making a laughing stock of him, as if he had gone from being the highest authority in the ghetto to being pilloried, someone everybody could laugh at:

But Mr Chairman – DON'T YOU KNOW WHAT HAS HAPPENED?

The child throws the bottle top – but he can't throw his stone that far.

The bottle top is white and shiny, vanishing through the air like a stroke of lightning. There was no stone in the world that would have enabled him to hit it.

He ought to feel angry that the stakes in this battle are so clearly weighted against him. Everything should really speak in his favour: the heaviness of the stone, his superior body strength; the fact that he is so much older and more experienced and wiser than he was as a child. He should be able to throw that far *but it is still beyond him.*

And what is left is shame. At the fact that he, having amassed so much power, can still achieve so infinitesimally little.

*

When he finally got to the hospital in Wesoła Street it was after eight in the morning and the frantic relatives who had gathered outside the cordon threw themselves at him as if he were their only salvation.

At last, cried the crowd, or that was what it seemed to be crying:

At last he is here, the man who will free us from this scourge . . . !

At the hospital's main entrance, SS-Hauptscharführer Konrad Mühlhaus stands supervising the deportation of all the sick and confused patients Rozenblat's men are now herding them, out of the building. SS-Hauptscharführer Mühlhaus is one of those men who feels he must be permanently in motion, so other people won't notice how short he is.

He tramps round and round on the spot as he shouts orders like:

Rauf auf die Wagen! Schnell, schnell, nicht stehenbleiben!

Aware of the expectation that he will do something, he grasps his stick more firmly and strides up to the squat Mühlhaus.

Chairman: What is happening here?
Mühlhaus: I have orders to let no one pass.
Chairman: I am Rumkowski.
Mühlhaus: You could be Hermann Göring for all I care. I still can't let you through.

Then Mühlhaus is gone; he hasn't the patience to stand discussing anything with a Jew, no matter who he is or what he calls himself.

And the Chairman is left standing there alone. For a moment he looks as lost and powerless as the poor, broken men and women being carried or led from the hospital entrance to the trailers and the backs of the lorries. And yet he is not one of them. It is clearly discernible: a sort of vacuum, forming around him. Not only the German soldiers but also Rozenblat's men fall back as if he had the plague.

On the back of the lorry nearest the main building, about a hundred elderly patients are crammed in together, standing up; many of them are half-naked or wearing faded, tattered hospital clothes.

He thinks he recognises one of Regina's aunts, whom they used to visit on Sundays. He isn't sure which of the old ladies it is; but he vaguely remembers having boasted to her that they would be able to take the tram all the way to Paris together, and that she laughed delightedly behind her bony hand: Oh Chaim, you can't expect me to believe that . . . ! Now the woman is stripped naked of everything but the grey hair on her head and her terrified white eyes. Through the hubbub and crush that divides them, the woman shouts something to him and waves her matchstick arms, or perhaps her cries are directed at someone else. He is not sure, and he has no time to make sure, either. The soldier who has just shoved the last batch of patients up onto the truck hears her making a noise just beside him and takes aim at her face with his rifle butt in a wide, swinging action.

The blow lands right in the middle of the woman's jaw, and something large and messy flies out of her mouth in a spurt of blood.

He turns away, nauseated.

That is when he notices that the hospital entrance is unguarded. The guards stationed there earlier have all rushed to cut off the escape route of a patient trying to get out through a first-floor window. The escapee is wearing a blue-and-white-striped nightshirt far too big for him, which hangs like a curtain over his face and the top part of his body as he falls forward, flailing his arms frantically. (The only reason the man does not plummet straight to the ground is that someone in the room behind him has swiftly leant out and grabbed his ankles.)

He himself seizes his opportunity and slips in through the half-open main door of the hospital, and suddenly the screams and deafening shouted orders are shut off.

Broken glass crunches under the soles of his boots.

He goes slowly up the broad sweep of the spiral staircase, his steps echoing beneath the high, vaulted stonework above him; goes on down the dark corridors, taking a look here and there into the now deserted wards on either side.

When he last came visiting with Regina, there were at least two hundred patients to a ward, two per bed, head to tail like the kings and knaves on a playing card. He remembered how their toothless, two-stalked heads had all smiled, and greeted him as if with a single mouth:

GOOD MORNING, MR CHAIRMAN –

Only Benji had opted to stay silent. He had been standing over by the window, his chin resting in his hand in a studiedly thoughtful pose. Now he was trying desperately to remember the number of Benji's ward. But in all this upheaval, it is as if the hospital has been turned into an alien place. Unknown, impossible to navigate.

More or less by chance, he spots a doctor's office at the far end of one of the corridors and steps inside with a sense of relief. On a shelf just inside the door are files of purchase lists and medical notes, and on the desk a telephone, still on the hook.

As he looks at it, the telephone, absurdly, begins to ring.

For a moment he is nonplussed. Should he lift the receiver and answer? Or will the ringing just attract German officers who will throw him out of the building as soon as they see him?

He ends up backing out into the corridor again. And Benji is standing there.

He spots him out of the corner of his eye long before he realises who it is. The ward doors are all open and the light is penetrating the corridors in long, mote-filled columns or tunnels. The light that draws Benji to his attention, however, is coming not from the side, but from above – from the ceiling – which is impossible of course: there are no windows there. Benji is wearing a blue-and-white-striped nightshirt like all the other patients, and leaning forward slightly, wielding a chair, its four legs pointing down the corridor, as if to defend himself from something.

From whom? From him? The Chairman takes a few steps into the impossible light:

Benji, it's me, he says, and tries to smile.

Benji backs away. From his twisted lips comes a strange, inarticulate singing or whining sound.

Benji . . . ? is all he says. He wants his voice to sound full of anxiety and concern, but by the time it gets out of his mouth, it just sounds dishonest and false:

Be-en-j-ii, I've come to get you out of here, Be-en-jii . . .

Then Benji hurls himself forward. The four chair legs hit the Chairman full in the chest and Benji immediately drops the chair, as if it he has burnt himself on it, and runs off. But comes to a halt just as suddenly.

It is as if he had run straight into a wall.

Then the Chairman hears them, too. The sound of loud voices – *German voices!* – comes up from the stairwell below, followed by the scraping echo of energetic, booted footsteps. Now Benji does not know which way to go: forward, towards the inexorably advancing German officers, or back, towards the Praeses he fears if anything even more.

But the Chairman, too, is withdrawing, hastily taking cover behind the door of the doctor's office.

SS-Hauptscharführer Mühlhaus and two of his subordinates walk briskly along the corridor outside, and the next moment, the mechanical creaking of boot soles and rattle of weapons against leather shoulder-belts is swallowed up by the echoes from the stairwell. As soon as the sound of footsteps has died away, the Chairman goes over to the medicine cabinet in the doctor's room, takes an enamel jug from the bottom shelf and fills it with water from a tap over the sink. Then he reaches into his jacket pocket for one of the white tablets he always carries, puts it in a glass and pours in some water.

When he looks out into the corridor again, Benji is gone. He finds him again in the big ward nearest to the stairs, crouching against the whitewashed wall behind a mountain of ripped mattresses and screens that have been tossed aside. Benji is trembling from shoulder to foot, but he does not look up. The Chairman has to say his name several times with different intonation before he finally looks up through the thick fringe hiding his face.

Here Benji, drink this . . . !

Benji gives him the same drained look of terror that he had when the German officers were close by. The Chairman has to get down on his knees to put the glass to his mouth. Benji presses his lips to it and takes big, urgent gulps, like a child. The Chairman gently puts a hand to the back of his neck to support and help him.

And it is simple. He thinks of his wife. If only everything with her could have been that simple.

Benji looks up at him once, almost with gratitude. Then the poison does its work and his eyes glaze over. A long spasm runs through his body, starting at his head and ending with his heels, which jerk convulsively for a moment, then somehow stiffen in mid-movement. Without really knowing when or how it happened, he finds himself sitting with his brother-in-law's dead body in his arms.

Of the six hospitals in the ghetto, Hospital No. 1 in Łagniewnicka Street was the largest. Its ground plan was square, with two wings extending from the main building round an open courtyard. So the building could be approached from a number of different directions.

In a desperate attempt to make contact with her father, Věra went in the back way, through dense shrubbery between some huts and a shed, to the separate entrance for the maternity wing. Many of the vehicles were already in place, parked there with their trailers. SS soldiers in field-grey uniforms with leather belts and tall, shiny boots were idling away their time round the drivers' cabs or on the backs of the lorries. The soldiers' passivity was deceptive, however. She got almost as far as the loading bay at the back entrance to the hospital when a shrill whistle cut through the air. When she looked up, she saw a man in uniform appear at a wide-open window on the second floor. Then a naked baby was pushed out, and fell headlong, straight down onto the back of the waiting lorry.

One of the soldiers on the lorry – a young man with bright blond hair and a uniform that looked several sizes too big for him – stood up and waved his rifle to his colleague on the second floor. The sleeves of his jacket were so long that he had to turn them up before he could attach his bayonet. Then he stood there, legs planted wide apart, while more squealing infant bodies came raining down from the window. Whenever he skewered one of the babies on his bayonet, he lifted it high above the end of his rifle, the blood running down his rolled-up sleeves.

Somewhere in the building above, people must have noticed what was happening, for other windows opened, and from inside came the sound of screaming in Yiddish and Polish:

Murderers, murderers . . . !

Věra didn't know what to do. As if spurred on by the commotion, even more German soldiers appeared on the second floor. They were all cradling infants at their uniformed chests.

Then Věra started screaming herself.

The face of the laughing soldier on the back of the lorry changed to an 'O' of astonishment. In an instant, he had torn the bloody bundle from the tip of his bayonet and turned the sights of his rifle on her.

The sudden volley of rifle fire sent leaves and chips of wood flying from the roof of the hut, just above her head. She ducked and ran, and out of the bushes around her other running figures also appeared. Some in hospital gowns, others almost completely naked, mostly women and elderly men. Her sudden scream, and the shots that followed it, had driven them out of their temporary hiding places and now they were all running – frightened out of their senses, lifting their feet in high, stalking steps – as the salvoes of rifle fire carried on whipping up gravel and grass from the dust in front of the figures that had not yet fallen.

*

At the midday break, she stood in the queue for the soup kitchen in Jakuba Street with her tin mug, the heat of the sun burning and stinging her unprotected head as if there were a huge, open wound under the skin.

Almost everybody in the soup queue had family members in the various ghetto hospitals, and they almost all had similar stories to tell: of children thrown from maternity wards straight down into the waiting lorries; of infirm old people who had come tottering out of their wards to be run through by bayonets or shot dead. Only a few of those returning from the hospitals had managed to bring their relatives home with them.

It was rumoured that the Chairman, after protracted negotiations, had persuaded the authorities to exempt some particularly high-ranking individuals among the sick, but only on condition that others would be deported in their stead. A new Resettlement Commission had been set up to go through the patient registers to identify former in-patients who had been discharged, or people who had previously applied for places but been turned down for lack of the right contacts; anything or anyone would do: as long as they could take the places of the *few irreplaceable* individuals that those in charge said they could not do without.

It's a disgrace, an utter disgrace . . . ! Mr Moszkowski could be heard muttering as he walked in the clouds of fluff among the looms. It was as though someone kept poking him in the side with a big stick. As soon as he sat down, he was up on his feet again.

In the evening, news came through that the Chairman's father-in-law and various relatives and close friends of Jakubowicz and police commissioner Rozenblat had been 'bought out' by *substitutes* stepping into their places. The only person the Chairman had not managed to bring down from the trailers was his brother-in-law, young Benjamin Wajnberger, for the simple reason that nobody seemed to know what had become of him. There was no sign of him at the hospital; nor had he been seen in any of the temporary assembly camps. Had he tried to escape and fallen foul of some German patrol? Regina Rumkowska was broken-hearted, and said she feared the worst.

The very first evening, the Schulz family received a visit from a certain Mr Tausendgeld. He was the one charged with arranging to get them out.

Much later, when the story came out of his violent death at the hands of the German torturers, Věra tried to remember his face. But the image of Mr Tausendgeld remained as indistinct as it had been then, as he sat with them in the kitchen alcove next to Maman's little room. She remembered a face covered in lumps and bumps, and in it a mouth with small, sharp, pointed teeth that he bared every time he smiled. With his long, slim, strangely stalk-like hands, he spread what looked like long lists of names on the table and made a show of marking off names as he talked.

From inside her chamber, Maman called out to Věra and asked her in a hoarse voice to run down to Roháneks on the corner to buy some thread. She had decided to take up sewing again. She had made things for Martin and Josel when they were little. Those had been 'troubled times', too.

At the table, Mr Tausendgeld was all eyes and ears.

'She must think she's back in Prague,' he said, smiling almost approvingly through the growths on his face.

It soon became clear that he knew 'everything worth knowing' about Maman and her illness. Mrs Schulz, he said, was a person of the highest rank who must be saved at any price. And as if this were something that could only be divulged in the greatest confidence, he leant forward and whispered to Professor Schulz that the Secretariat was in the process of setting up a special enclosed camp for all those enjoying the authorities' protection. The camp would be opposite the now evacuated hospital in Łagiewnicka Street. The move there would be carried out under the protection of the ghetto's own forces, under the command of Dawid Gertler himself, whom they had to thank for the successful negotiation of this unique agreement with the German authorities.

What does it cost? was all Professor Schulz said; and Mr

Tausendgeld – without hesitation, without even looking up from his paper, where he had already noted down the sum in the margin – replied:

Thirty thousand! They are demanding even more for what might be called notables, but in your family's case I think thirty thousand marks will do.

Věra had often seen her father's face turn pale with anger, seen the knotted veins on the back of his hand bulge as if they were about to burst. But this time, Professor Schulz managed to keep his anger in check. Maybe it was because of Maman's confused voice, which persisted in calling out to Věra from the cubbyhole. Her illness hung like an incomprehensible punctuation mark in the thick, stuffy air above their heads. Or was the situation, as Věra would subsequently write in her diary, so absurd that it could be understood *only by acknowledging that the whole world had gone mad*?

In actual fact, Věra realised later, Professor Schulz had already made up his mind. They would wall up the opening to Maman's room. Martin had an idea for what he called *false wallpaper*: an ordinary roll of wallpaper, glued to a wooden board and slotted into the tongue-and-groove wall, over the opening beside the kitchen sink. The side of the false wall could be prised up with a knife and moved aside, then slotted back in place. This wouldn't put Maman's health at risk, because the air vent was still there in the ceiling, and since Papa was a doctor, he would be able to get a *Passierschein* and come and go as he wanted, no matter what happened.

'It'll be all right, Věra, you'll see,' he said.

She wondered where he got it from, this unwavering conviction of his.

But it all had to be done quickly. The new Resettlement Commission had almost finished going through its lists of those required to come forward as replacements for the people who had been 'redeemed', and the Sonder were already going round looking for them in factories and living quarters.

On the afternoon of the third day of the operation, the Chairman had a new proclamation put up outside the Department of Statisitics in Kirchplatz. From now on, it said, the recruitment section at the Central Labour Office would also accept applications from children *aged nine and up*.

That could only mean one thing: *all children under nine were also to be deported!*

The mad chasing around began all over again. Not to the hospitals and clinics this time, but to the Central Labour Office in Bałuty Square, where people queued for hours to get their children registered for work before it was too late.

Everyone was asking for the Chairman.

Where is the Praeses in this hour of need when we can least do without him? Tomorrow, they were told, tomorrow, in the fire-station yard in Lutomierska Street, he will make a speech to the residents of the ghetto that will answer all your questions.

*

In the early evening, Věra went into Maman's little room one last time. Maman was talking about the Hoffmann family, who had been their neighbours all those years in Mánesova Street. *We're in Łódź, Mama, not in Prague*, Věra said. But her mother went on insisting. Night after night she could hear their youngest girl walking up and down the hall outside the sealed apartment, crying for her deported parents.

Věra brought in the bedpan and fed Maman pieces of bread soaked in water. After a little while, Martin and Josel also squeezed in beside her. By then, even Maman realised things were not as usual. Her eyes went from one child to the next, with a glassy, unsteady look. Arnošt gave her the injection, in one arm, and her head fell into his hands like a rag. Then Martin and Josel walled her in. Arnošt had already prepared a death certificate. He said the best thing would be not to think of Maman as a living person, at least not for the next few, critical days.

But Věra could not stop hearing her heart beating behind the closed-up wall. That night, and on all those that followed, it was as if not just the wall but the whole room where they lay was bulging and pulsating with Maman's invisible heartbeats.

On the afternoon of 3 September 1942, the authorities summoned the Praeses again. He stood before them as usual, head bowed, hands at his sides.

He faced Biebow, Czarnulla, Fuchs and Ribbe.

Biebow said he had given careful consideration to the Chairman's suggestion that the old and the sick would be let go if the children were spared.

> *There is, of course, a certain logic to your proposal, Rumkowski, but the orders we have received from Berlin leave us no room for such an accommodation. All ghetto inhabitants who cannot support themselves must, of necessity, leave. That is the order, and it also applies to children.*

Then Biebow set out a number of calculations he had asked to be made, and said these showed there should be a total of at least twenty thousand non-workers, the majority of them old people and children. If they could free themselves of these *Unbrauchbare*, Berlin would no longer find reason to involve itself in 'internal' ghetto affairs.

Rumkowski replied that this was an order no human being could carry out. No human being voluntarily gives up his own children.

Then Biebow replied that Rumkowski had had his chance but he had missed it.

> *You've had weeks, months, Rumkowski, but what have you achieved? You've taken every opportunity to get round the*

rules. You've set children to work who scarcely know what
hemstitch is. You've turned the hospitals into rest homes . . . !
And all this has been going on while our administration does
everything in its power to secure the ghetto's food supply.

Then Fuchs said:

You must consider the nature of our heroic war effort, Herr
Rumkowski. Everyone is called upon to make sacrifices.

Then Ribbe said:

What could possibly make you imagine we would expend
time and energy on support for miserable Jews at a time when
Germans are being forced out of house and home by the Allies'
cowardly air raids? Are you really so naive that you thought
we would continue dispensing this sort of charity indefinitely,
Rumkowski?

Rumkowski asked them to give him time to think it over and
consult his colleagues. They said there was no time. They said
that if he had not handed over comprehensive lists of ghetto
residents over sixty-five and under ten within twelve hours,
they would initiate the operation themselves.
Czarnulla said:

The ghetto is a plague zone, a boil that must be lanced.
If you do it now, once and for all, you may hope to survive.
If you don't, there's not a chance.

The public meeting in the fire-station yard in Lutomierska Street is due to start at half past three in the afternoon, but people have been gathering in the big, open space since two. At that time of the afternoon, the sun is at its highest, and the whole expanse of stone between the buildings on either side of the yard is turned into a well of scalding hot, white light. Only later in the afternoon does a narrow shadow start to edge from the long row of sheds and outbuildings running along the exterior of the crumbling stone wall. Those just arriving all cluster in the thin strip of shade. In the end there are so many of them jostling together along the wall that the chief of the ghetto fire brigade, Mr Kaufmann, feels impelled to emerge from his cool office and push or pleadingly pull on reluctant arms to make the crowd space itself out a little.

But nobody willingly stands in the broiling hot sun.

When the Chairman finally arrives, it is half past four and the area of shade has spread halfway across the inner courtyard. But it is by now such a huge gathering that only a fraction can stand in that shade. The rest have either moved to the gable end, deeper into the courtyard, or climbed onto the roofs of the sheds and outhouses. The people up on the roofs are the first to catch sight of the Chairman and his bodyguards.

At the sight of the old man, a ripple runs through the crowd. He does not walk with head and stick held defiantly high as usual, but with hunched shoulders and eyes on the ground. In an instant, the yard falls completely silent. It is so quiet that you can even hear the birds chirruping in the trees on the other side of the wall.

The podium this time consists of a rickety table. On top of that, somebody has placed a chair, so the speaker can at least be a head taller than the crowd. Dawid Warszawski is the first to climb up onto the improvised platform. The microphones have been mounted a little too far forward, so he has to stretch to reach them, which makes him look as if he is permanently about to lose his balance and fall off. Even so, somehow he gets too close to the microphone, and every word he speaks sends an echo billowing back and forth between the loudspeakers, as if it were constantly trying to interrupt him.

Warszawski says how ironic it is that the Chairman, of all people, has been forced to take this difficult decision. After all the years the Eldest of the ghetto has devoted to bringing up the Jewish children. (*CHILDREN!* The echo reverberates back off the walls.) In conclusion, he tries to appeal for the understanding of all those gathered to listen.

There is a war on. Every day, the air-raid sirens whine above our heads. Everyone has to run for cover. At times like these, the young and the old just get in the way. That it is why it would be better if they were removed.

After these words, which merely generate restlessness and anxiety in the crowd, the Chairman climbs onto the table and leans forward to the microphone. By his voice, too, people can tell that he has changed. Gone is the shrill, slightly hysterical tone of command. The sentences follow each other slowly, with a dull and sustained metallic tone; as if it were a torture to produce each word:

The ghetto has been dealt a terrible blow. They demand that we give them the very things most valuable to us – our children and our old people. I have never had the good fortune to father children of my own, but I have spent the best years of my life among children. So I would never have imagined that it would be I who was obliged to take the sacrificial lambs to the altar. But in the autumn of my years, I must now reach out my hands and ask:

Brothers and sisters, give them to me. Give me your children . . . !

[. . .]

I had a premonition of this. I was expecting 'something', and was constantly on my guard to try to prevent it. But I was unable to intervene, because I did not know the nature of the threat we were about to face.

When they seized the patients from the hospitals, it took me completely by surprise. Believe me. I had friends and relations of my own in those hospitals and I could not help them. I believed what happened there meant it was all over, and now we would have the calm I had worked so hard to achieve. But fate proved to have something else in store. That is the lot of the Jews: when we suffer, we are forced to suffer still more – especially in times of crisis like these.

Yesterday I was ordered to deport more than twenty thousand people from the ghetto; otherwise, they said, they would do it themselves. The question was whether we should take on this odious task ourselves or leave it to others. But since our guiding principle is not 'How many will disappear?' but 'How many can we save?', we decided – we: that is to say, my closest colleagues and I – that however hard it might be, we had to implement the ruling ourselves. I had to carry out the cruel and bloody operation myself. I had to amputate the arms to save the body. I had to let the children go. If I did not do it, then maybe yet more would have to go –

I have no words of consolation to offer you today. Nor have I come to try to calm your fears. I have come like a thief, to take from you what you hold dearest. I did everything in my power to make the authorities retract this order. When that did not work, I tried to make them reduce their demand. I tried to save at least one more age group – children between nine and ten. But they refused to yield. There was only one thing I managed to do. Children above ten are saved. Let that at least be some consolation in your great pain.

We have many tuberculosis patients in the ghetto; their days, or at best weeks, are numbered. I do not know – perhaps this is just a wicked and malicious thought, perhaps not – but I still cannot help putting it before you. Give me these patients, and I will be able to save healthy people in their place. I know how much it means to you to nurse your sick relatives at home. But when faced with a decree that makes us choose who can be saved and who cannot, common sense dictates that the saved must be those who can be saved and those who have a chance of being rescued, not those who cannot be saved in any case . . .

We live in a ghetto. We live in such destitution that we haven't enough to provide for the well, let alone the sick. We all care for our sick at the cost of our own health. You give them what little bread and sugar you can spare, but in doing that, you make yourselves ill. If I had been forced to choose between sacrificing the sick, those who can never recover from their illnesses, and saving the well, I would choose without hesitation to save the well. That is why I have ordered my doctors to surrender the incurably ill, with the aim of saving in their place healthy people who are still capable of living . . .

I understand you, mothers. I see your tears. And I hear your hearts pounding, you fathers, who will have to go to your work the morning after I have taken your children from you, those children you were playing with just the other day. I understand and feel all this. Since 4 p.m. yesterday, when this ruling was announced, I have been a broken and tormented man. I share your powerlessness and feel your pain; I do not know how I can go on living after all this. I must tell you a secret. Initially they demanded I sacrifice twenty-four thousand, three thousand people a day for eight days, but I managed to negotiate the number down to twenty thousand or less, on condition this would include children up to the age of ten. Children who have turned ten are out of danger. Since the number of children and old people combined amounts to thirteen thousand, the rest of the quota must be filled with the sick.

I find it hard to speak. My strength fails me. But I must ask you one last thing. Help me to carry out this operation. The prospect of them – God forbid! – taking the matter into their own hands makes me quake with terror . . .

It is a broken man you see before you. Do not envy me. This is the most difficult decision I have ever had to make. I raise my trembling hands and implore you: give me these sacrificial victims in order that I may save others from being sacrificed, in order that I may save a hundred thousand Jews.

That was what they promised me, you see: if you hand over these people yourselves, you will be left in peace –

(Shouts from down in the crowd:

'We can all go'; and:

'Mr Chairman, don't take all the children; take one child from families with several!')

But my dear people – these are all just hollow phrases. I cannot discuss it with you. When the authorities come, none of you will say so much as a word.

I know what it means to tear limbs from your body. I begged them on my knees, but it was pointless. From towns that formerly had seven or eight thousand Jews, barely a thousand reached our ghetto alive. So what is best? What do you want? For us to let eight or nine thousand people live, or look on mutely as all perish . . . Decide for yourselves. It is my duty to try to help as many survive as possible. I am not appealing to the hotheads among you. I am appealing to people who can still listen to reason. I have done, and will continue to do, everything in my power to keep weapons off our streets and avoid bloodshed . . . The ruling could not be overturned, only tempered.

It takes the heart of a thief to demand what I demand of you now. But put yourselves in my shoes. Think logically, and draw your own conclusions. I cannot act in any way other than I do, since the number of people I can save this way far exceeds the number I have to let go . . .

Bekanntmachung Nr 391.

Betr.:

Allgemeine Gehsperre im Getto.

Ab Sonnabend,
den **5.** September 1942 **um 17 Uhr,**
ist im Getto bis auf Widerruf eine

ALLGEMEINE GEHSPERRE.

Ausgenommen hiervon sind:

Feuerwehrleute, die Transportabteilung, Fäkalien- und Müllarbeiter, Warenannahme am Baluter Ring und Radegast, Aerzte und Apothekerpersonal.

Die Passierscheine müssen beim Ordnungsdienstvorstand – Hamburgerstrasse 1 – beantragt werden.

Alle Hauswächter

sind verpflichtet darauf zu achten, dass keine fremden Personen in die für sie zuständigen Häuser gelangen, sondern sich nur die Einwohner des Hauses dortselbst aufhalten.

Diejenigen, die ohne Passierscheine auf der Strasse angetroffen werden, werden evakuiert.

Die Hausverwalter

müssen in ihrem Häuserblock mit den Hausbüchern zur Verfügung stehen.

Jeder Hauseinwohner hat seine Arbeitskarte bei sich zu halten.

CH. RUMKOWSKI
Der Aelteste der Juden in Litzmannstadt.

Litzmannstadt-Getto, 5. September 1942

Between the block of flats at 22 Gnieźnieńska Street and number 24, there is a gap or opening a few metres wide. It is as though both buildings, which have been standing on this spot for years, have leaned closer and closer to each other but never quite got all the way. In the middle of this shrinking space between the two blocks stands a partially collapsed brick wall, and on it sits Adam Rzepin, keeping guard.

It is the Sabbath. It is the day of rest. The factory gates are closed.

The wooden bridges linking the various sections of the ghetto, which are usually black with the crush of people crossing over them, are as empty as scaffolds. No traffic anywhere. All Adam can hear is the metallic drone of the flies taking off from the rubbish dump behind him. The sound of the swarms of flies rising into the air, which then dies away; beyond that, nothing but his own pounding heartbeat.

From the top of the wall, he has an uninterrupted view of the entire south-western section of the ghetto. He can see over to Lutomierska Street and to the plank and barbed-wire wall at Wrześnieńska Street where the old people's home is, and Judge Jakobson's *gericht*.

Posted at strategically important points all over the ghetto are other lookouts like him, and they send runners between them to report on what they have seen.

It is from them Adam learns that the operation has begun.

*

Although they must have known from the outset that they

would never be able to do it, the Jewish police had initially tried to carry out the whole operation themselves.

Just after dawn, as the sun still hung low and swollen over the worn cobblestone streets of the ghetto, men from Gertler's Sonderabteilung sealed off parts of Rybna Street. Then the concierge in each block was ordered to go ahead with the master keys and unlock not only the doors to attics and storerooms but also any doors the residents had not opened voluntarily.

Most people seemed to have tried to barricade themselves into their rooms.

Jewish *politsayen* carried out screaming women and children, who struggled wildly to fend them off, while the old people clutched the doorposts of their homes with a convulsive, unspeaking determination, as if they were trying to take root in the very walls. Old men could be seen pulling in their skinny, spidery legs as they attempted to hide under bedsteads, or sitting with covers or prayer shawls over their heads, rocking back and forth.

Ten or so women, their children balanced precariously in their arms or on their hips, tried to escape through the windows of Rybna Street flats facing into the courtyard. Crazed and screaming hysterically, they threatened to let themselves and their children drop if the policemen in the flats took so much as a step towards them. Two men – one in a flat up on the third floor, the other on the latrine roof, down in the yard, had tied together some sheets and blankets to make a long rope, and shouted encouragement to the escaping women to climb down the rope. The women lowered their children down first. A number of them had time for an ungainly scramble to safety, over the far side of the latrine roof. But only a few minutes later, Gertler's men came charging out into the yard and hauled down the children who were still on the roof, before the very eyes of their desperate parents, leaning helplessly out of the windows above.

Not only had the police been ordered out that morning, but also Kaufmann's firemen and the men who carried the sacks of flour from the depots to the ghetto bakeries: the so-called White Guard.

According to one of the rumours that had reached Adam as he stood at his post on the wall, all the firemen, transport workers and unloaders who had agreed to back up the police in carrying out the authorities' bloody handiwork had been given guarantees that their own children would be safe. Sometimes the victims and the perpetrators even knew each other:

What have you done with your own son, Schlomo? a man was heard to ask as his child was dragged down from the latrine roof by men never seen there in uniform before. *How much blood money did you get, you traitor . . . ?* Such exchanges were generally followed by a scuffle. A few blocks further down Rybna Street, a group of men started improvising barricades. As soon as the Jewish police and firemen showed themselves, they were pelted with stones –

Gayt avek ayere nakhesn, mir veln undzere kinder nisht opgebn . . .*

This was the point at which the German authorities decided to take matters into their own hands.

The security forces again deployed the commando units they had used for emptying the ghetto hospitals. The soldiers came running down the street in tight formation, as if to generate terror by their very appearance; lorries and tractors came after them with grating gearboxes and loudly revving engines. Soon the improvised barricades were tossed aside, vehicle entrance gates broken in or blasted open, and soldiers came pouring in through archways, rifles at the ready.

Behind the gates, the terrified concierge would at best have

* Hand over your own children, we are not going to give up ours . . .

persuaded the families living in the building to venture out of their flats and down into the yard.

While the officers went round shouting orders, men and women attempted to gather up their children and other relatives and hand over health certificates and workbooks to the SS commanders inspecting them. In some cases, Jewish police officers accompanied them, as a silent escort. There were rumours that Dawid Gertler himself had been seen on his way in and out of addresses where various prominent people lived.

By no means did all the SS commanders who had been called out bother to check the workbooks or consult the lists of names handed over to them. They went by how young or old, well or poorly nourished the lined-up Jews looked. Children and feeble, emaciated old people were shoved ruthlessly to one side, ready for loading onto the waiting vehicles. While this was going on, Gertler's *politsayen* had extreme difficulty in stopping desperate mothers and fathers from hurling themselves onto the long trailers and trying to rescue the children who had been wrested from them. There were at least two SS soldiers posted by every vehicle, and they showed no mercy, opening fire on anybody who got too close.

*

By about five in the afternoon, the German commando units and their lorries and trailers reach Gnieźnieńska Street. Just as Adam anticipated, they pull up first outside the old people's home. From his vantage point, Adam sees men from the White Guard helping old men and women up onto the trailers and backs of the lorries. The majority of them can scarcely walk unaided, and reach out imploringly to their executioners, who carry them across their shoulders or sling them from one to another like sacks of flour.

But by then, he has already decided to hide Lida. In the yard, there are two coal cellars. One has a wide metal hatch at ground

266

level through which the coal is tipped in. Adam assumes that if the Germans look for runaways anywhere, it will be here. The other cellar served as a tool store in the past. Coal shovels were kept there, along with brooms and snow shovels and the old wheelbarrow in which Adam often used to wheel Lida round.

At the very back of the now empty tool shed he has dug a hole in the ground, deep enough for the person standing in it not to be visible in the strip of light from the open door.

Into that hole he puts Lida.

She resists at first. She doesn't understand why she has to stand still in an ice-cold mass of earth, shared with spiders and old coal dust. But he stands in the hole with her for a while. He sings to her, and that makes it better.

They are there much sooner than Adam had expected.

He can hear the concierge, Mrs Herszkowicz, warbling her agitated summons across the yard:

The Germans are coming, the Germans are coming . . .
Assemble in the yard everybody, all down to the yard . . .

Today is Mrs Herszkowicz's big day. She is wearing a dark brown velvet dress with a creamy lace trim around her generous decolletage; and with it a cartwheel-sized hat with a complicated feather arrangement tucked into a ribbon round the crown. As she runs to and fro across the yard, clucking, she reminds Adam of a garishly painted pheasant.

He holds Lida's face between his two hands. He wants to force the song within her to fall silent. After a while, they shift a little so they are standing together in the hole the way they always stand: he with his arm around her body, she resting her head on his shoulder. Brother and sister. Since she is taller than him, she has to bend her knees to be at his level; and the moment she does that, and stretches her neck to nuzzle her head against his

267

collarbone, he knows that he loves and always will love her, with a love that is beyond what anyone will understand.

The Germans are under the command of the same undersized Mühlhaus who led the purge of the hospital in Wesoła Street. Because of the heat, he has removed his peaked cap and gloves and is holding them in one hand as he moves briskly along the row of tenants Mrs Herszkowicz has lined up.

Adam's father, Szaja Rzepin, is among the last to join their ranks.

Standing next to him are Moshe and Rosa Pinczewski and their daughter Maria.

Maria Pinczewska looks petrified. On paper, she has nothing to fear. For the past three months, she has been employed at a tailor's workshop that makes decals and uniform insignia for the Wehrmacht. If she had possessed merely a fraction of the ingratiating approach displayed by Mrs Herszkowicz as she shows the German soldiers round the building, she might have asserted her own usefulness and got away with it. What is more, Miss Pinczewska is still young and beautiful; blonde and blue-eyed, almost like a real Aryan.

Samuel Wajsberg and Mr and Mrs Frydman from the flats across the yard are far less favourably placed. Mrs Frydman has put a headscarf on her daughter, which makes her look significantly older than she is. Beside her stand Mr and Mrs Mendel and their daughter. Not even the normally punctilious Mühlhaus bothers to look at Mr Mendel's workbook, merely gestures impatiently to a space to the right of the stump which is all that remains of Fabian Zajtman's great chestnut tree. That is where those selected for deportation have to stand. The Frydmans' children are also escorted there. As they go, Mrs Frydman sinks into her husband's arms.

Samuel Wajsberg calls out to his wife Hala, who has not yet appeared.

It sounds more like a cry for help.

Hala! he screams.

The echo reverberates in waves up the tall, crumbling facades.

Adam comes to his father's side.

Szaja Rzepin just stares straight in front of him, head down.

Where's Lida? he asks finally, without raising his eyes from the ground.

Adam does not reply. Szaja does not repeat the question.

HA-A-A-LAA! cries Samuel again.

No answer; just the echo rolling back down.

Mrs Herszkowicz smiles a smile far too wide, and plucks nervously at the frills and flounces on her bosom.

Now, finally, Hala Wajsberg comes out into the courtyard. She is shepherding her younger son Chaim. One step behind them comes Jakub. She has dressed both her sons in freshly ironed white shirts, dark trousers with turn-ups, and carefully polished black shoes. Hala, too, is soberly attired in a straight, long-sleeved dress. She has her hair scraped back into a bun. The high bun makes her normally powerful neck look strangely vulnerable. Her cheekbones are high and shiny, almost as though she had polished her face with a glossy cream.

No more than a few minutes have elapsed since Adam came to his father's side. Mrs Herszkowicz is already back. Task completed, she can proudly inform the handsome SS officer with the tall black boots and glinting collar insignia.

Mühlhaus is now standing in front of Samuel Wajsberg, who at his full height is almost a head taller than the German officer. Mühlhaus does not even attempt to meet his eye, just holds out his hand and waits for Samuel to give him the family's workbooks.

But the fact that the officer is taking no notice of her despite all the trouble she has gone to on his behalf is suddenly too much for Mrs Herszkowicz. Unlike most of the others in these blocks of flats, she comes from a good family and has had a good Polish education, despite coming from Jewish stock. She has, moreover, carried out the task assigned to her with aplomb. She has got all the tenants to evacuate their flats in time. Here they all are, lined up with their workbooks in their hands. Yet the German officer has not so much as glanced at her.

There's one family member missing over here, she therefore announces loudly and clearly in German, pointing over to Szaja and Adam Rzepin.

SS-Hauptscharführer Mühlhaus looks up from the documents in his hand. Only now does he seem fully to appreciate what this dolled-up woman is trying to say to him, which makes Mrs Herszkowicz nervous: *Fräulein Rzepin hat sich vielleicht versteckt*, she clarifies, with something that could have passed for a full curtsey if her frilly dress had not got in the way.

Mühlhaus nods. With a distracted wave, he sends the two Jewish *politsayen* he has brought with him to hunt for the missing person; then returns to checking Samuel Wajsberg's documents. Within a couple of minutes, Lida is brought out. She is twice as tall as the two policemen carrying her; her legs are dangling floppily from her body and her face is all black with soot and soil.

Guten Tag, meine Herren, she says casually, swinging her arms to and fro.

Mühlhaus stares at her.

Wo hattest du dich versteckt . . . ? he roars, suddenly inflated by his own rage.

Lida carries on swinging her arms. It is as if she is getting ready to take off and fly away.

Mülhaus moves closer. In one rapid movement he grabs her by the hair, pulls her head down to his own and yells straight into her dissolving face:

WO HATTEST DU DICH VERSTECKT?

But Lida just carries on smiling and swinging her arms.

Mühlhaus fumbles for his service pistol; then with an expression of unbounded disgust on his face, fires two shots straight through the girl's head.

Takes a swift step back.

And Lida falls. It is her final crash.

Blood and brains spurt from the back of her head.

After the shots, utter panic breaks out. The women scream out loud, the men scream even louder. The two carefully separated groups – those waiting on one side to be taken away on the trailers, and the rest – converge again, so the two Jewish policemen step in on their own initiative and start clumsily hitting and shoving people to make sure they remain apart.

As if suddenly losing patience with the whole thing, Mühlhaus takes a couple of steps back; then with his blood-stained hand he points out a further handful of people who are to be pushed to one side. His hand falls on old Mrs Krumholz, and, as he gives a quick little smile, the blonde, blue-eyed Maria Pinczewska.

After her, Chaim Wajsberg.

It is all completely random. He has not even bothered to look at the lists Mrs Herszkowicz has given him.

Gertler's two *politsayen* take hold of Chaim Wajsberg and propel him towards the rest of the group for deportation. Hała is already on her way after her son. But Samuel intervenes. With a cry that no one would have thought his ruined lungs capable of, he throws himself at his wife and knocks her to the ground.

Jakub Wajsberg is left standing there alone. He watches in bewilderment as his father crawls up over his mother's body, as if trying to cover every inch of it with his own. A few metres from them, Adam Rzepin sits cradling his sister Lida's bloody head in his lap.

The last morning in the Green House, Rosa Smoleńska got up at four as usual, to fetch in the water that Chaja Meyer then poured into the big washtubs in the kitchen; and Józef Feldman came on his bicycle as usual, to fill the coal boxes and light the stoves. As usual; for the sake of the children, they did all they could to make even this last day begin the same way as all the others. The sun had not yet risen above the horizon, but the sky was already bright and transparently blue, and a few stray swallows were flitting about in the air, as if to announce that this September day, too, would be hot and sunny.

The evening before, Superintendent Rubin and Dr Zysman the paediatrician gathered everyone together in the *świetlica* of the children's home. Superintendent Rubin told them the authorities had decided that their stay in the ghetto was now over and that some children would be going home, while others would be looked after in 'ordinary' children's homes outside the ghetto. He said those who were moving out should not be sad about it. There was a world beyond the walls, too, he said, and it was bigger, much, much bigger than any ghetto.

He laughed again. There can surely never have been so much laughter heard in the Green House as there was that evening. But the children were grave and quiet behind their smiles. Then Nataniel asked who was to take them out of the ghetto, and how they would be travelling, by train, or perhaps by tram (all the children had seen the tram that had been taking the deportees to Radogoscz since the start of the year), and Superintendent Rubin's smile grew even wider, and he replied that they would find out tomorrow; now it was time to go and pack their things, and they should only take what they needed for the journey, and be sure to put on their very best clothes and not forget to bow or curtsey to the German soldiers who came to show them the way.

A woman from the administrative office in Dworska Street, a Mrs Goldberg, had been entrusted with taking the children to the designated assembly point. Mrs Goldberg had vivid red lipstick and was dressed in a very close-fitting, tailored suit that meant she could only take short steps when she walked. She kept her eyes fixed straight ahead, as if afraid her gaze might get snagged on something, and when she spoke it was always nervously, out of the corner of her mouth.

While Mrs Goldberg and the two guards who were to escort them waited outside, Rosa Smoleńska went round the corridors of the Green House and clapped her hands, and the children lined up in exactly the same order as they had been taught to do whenever the Chairman came to visit: the youngest at the front, the older ones rising in steps behind. On the stroke of seven, as instructed, all the children and their nurses set off to march to the assembly point on the big Ghetto Field; Rosa walked at the front with the youngest children Liba, Sofie, Dawid, and the twins Abram and Leon holding her hands; while Chaja Meyer and Malwina Kempel brought up the rear with the older ones.

Children from the other Marysin orphanages are already standing in scattered groups around the sloping, muddy field; and more are on their way. Deep tyre tracks in the loose clay show which way the lorries came in. They have backed in to form a star pattern, radiating out from the centre where the children and their supervisors are to congregate. Two cars driven by orderlies have pulled up about ten metres away, one of them with the inscription GETTOVERWALTUNG on one side. Rosa sees Hans Biebow himself walking over from that direction. He is dressed as if he were on a hunting trip, in big, baggy *Stiefelhosen*, with a rifle slung on a strap over his shoulder.

He seems agitated about something. He keeps turning round, shouting and gesticulating. Too many children are arriving at the same time. It's all going too fast.

Some of the Jewish policemen, who have been standing about in bewilderment in their peaked caps and tall, shiny boots, suddenly leap into action and start to shove the growing numbers of bodies backwards and pack them closer together.

The children are to be counted.

Then they all have to form up again. Each children's home separately. Six groups.

But by now, the alarm has begun to transmit itself to the children. They squeeze anxiously between each other's legs; some try to slink away, but they are caught by Jewish policemen, who even allow themselves to break into a run to retrieve them. A girl in a worn-out grey cardigan suddenly bursts into tears. Rosa casts an anxious glance at her own group. Staszek looks terrified. And Biebow is approaching with two SS men in long, black officer's coats.

One of them, a man with round, steel-rimmed glasses like Himmler's, has a sheaf of papers in his hand. From over by the rows of children come angry German orders for the count to be done again.

The sun is high in the sky now; she feels it burning the back of her neck, making it sweat.

Mrs Goldberg from the Wołkówna Secretariat, in her tight skirt with the slit at the back, is standing just in front of her, trying to sort out someone further back. Biebow and his men are getting closer.

All at once, a little boy in shorts and a beret sets off at a run across the stubbly grass. From where Rosa is standing, it is obvious where he is heading. In the heat haze on the far side of the Ghetto Field, there are tantalising glimpses of the shiny, corrugated tin roofs of the potting sheds along Bracka Street. If only he can make it that far.

A soldier next to her lets out a loud yell. She hears the rattle of his shoulder strap as he unhooks and raises his submachine gun. She sees the rucksack bouncing about on the boy's back, his legs beating like drumsticks beneath it. A second later, a dull shot rings out. But it is not the soldier with the submachine gun who has fired. Looking past the soldier's suddenly wavering rifle sight, she sees that Biebow has his rifle raised, too; he fires again – and far ahead of them, the boy falls from sight behind the grass bank.

Suddenly she is engulfed in a sea of running legs and struggling bodies. She keeps a tight hold on Staszek with one hand, and on the screaming Sofia with the other. Afraid of being trampled, she dare not turn round, but just carries on moving forward, her neck and shoulders held stiffly erect, like all the others now being herded along in the great crush. Of the children whose hands she is not holding, she can only catch sight of Liba and Nataniel. The twins are nowhere to be seen. Then she spots them: a couple of policemen with Jewish armbands lift first Adam, then Leon, onto the back of an already crowded truck. The children's faces have dissolved into tears. She frees one arm to signal her presence, if nothing else. At the same moment, she feels a hard blow to her back. One of the German soldiers is brutally shoving her forward with the butt of his rifle, and yelling to her from under his shiny helmet – *Vorwärts, vorwärts, nicht stehenbleiben* – and without knowing how, she too finds herself gripped round the waist and hoisted onto the lorry. As the vehicle moves off, she is thrown headlong into a jumble of children and sharp-cornered rucksacks.

Nothing in her thirty years as a nursery nurse ever prepared her for a situation like this. For what is happening now, there are no words, no instructions. Lorry engines throb and rumble all around the shuddering truck in which she sits. They pass streets which she remembers filled with people, which are now so empty that they seem unreal. Every so often, the convoy passes a German guard post; the guards stand motionless in their sentry boxes, or clustered for a smoke by the barriers at the crossing points.

Then there is a jolt and the lorry comes to a stop again. Hands release the catches at the back of the lorry, lower the tailgate, and soldiers' faces come into view at floor level, shouting at them all to get down. On the far side of the gravel forecourt where the lorries have pulled up she can see the stone steps leading up to the main entrance of the Drewnowska Street hospital.

The hospital is right on the ghetto boundary – but where once a barbed-wire fence ran, only a watchtower now remains. All forms of barrier seem to have been cleared away, and the German army vehicles have free access across the formerly impassable border. And the hospital is not a hospital any longer, either. It is more like a warehouse or transit camp. The soldiers herd them into a narrow, empty hallway, its floor covered in broken glass. The stairs to the upper floor are littered with soiled clothes and torn sheeting. The corridors run off the hall like dark, gaping tunnels. There is no electricity. They blunder around in the dark for a while and are then pushed into a large room that must formerly have been a ward. But there are no beds in it now, just a dirty floor and a window through which what remains of the sun is seeping in, thick and sludgy.

She does what she can to muster the children entrusted to her.

Staszek is still with her, as are Liba and the twins. She goes out into the corridor and calls out to Sofie and Nataniel, who have ended up in another ward.

Soon the sunlight has vanished from the window and the

pitch black of the corridors is slowly invading the echoing wards, too. The temperature drops. The youngest children are stiff and cold, their lips white with thirst. But nobody brings them bread or water. She has half a dry loaf in her bag, which she tears up so they can all have a little piece. Then they sit in silence in the gathering gloom. From outside they can hear the noise of the overloaded military trucks arriving again. It swells into a roaring wall of sound, then slowly recedes. German officers' voices can be heard shouting their horrible commands along the empty corridors, which close around the sound, as if around something obscene. She hears dragging steps encased in their own echo; the sound of shrieking, crying children somewhere close yet out of sight.

But it is not only children who are here; there are adults as well. From the sleeping space she has claimed under the window, she thinks she can make out Rumkowski's confidant Rabbi Fajner, with his big white beard. Beside him, another rabbi stands praying, the bones of his white, beardless face carved out like a bird's behind the hanging fringes of his prayer shawl. And all around them she can hear other adults dragging their heavier bodies into the room, then falling silent (or exhorting the children to do the same), almost as if they were entering a holy place.

And all at once, the last of the light is gone. And cold: from the bare stone floor, the chill is drawn like a tautened string right through their bodies.

All through the night and long into the early hours, they hear the roar of trucks pulling up and driving off again without ever switching off their engines, and soon the room is so crowded that Rosa has to sit squashed in under the window with her knees drawn up. With Sofie on her lap and Liba's head cradled in her arms, she still somehow manages to steal some rest.

*

In the crush and chaos on the lorries the previous day, Mrs Goldberg seemed to have vanished into thin air. But this morning, she is back again. Still wearing her tight suit and bright red lipstick, she stands in the faint, grey light of dawn in the hospital ward and motions to Rosa to get up and bring the children with her.

Rosa has Staszek and Liba holding one of her hands, Sofie and Nataniel the other. They walk through corridors that are now filled with a silent, naked, somehow trembling light. Through doorways she sees children sitting waiting, cross-legged, or with their knees tucked up to their chests and chins. Some are clutching their soup mugs or knapsacks. Others are slowly rocking back and forth, their heads clamped between their drawn-up knees.

In the thin, quicksilver light down in the yard, the lorries are already waiting. There are more vehicles today; there must be ten, maybe fifteen, of them. Leading down from the wide stone steps at the hospital entrance, the soldiers form a long wall of rifles.

As she makes her way with the children past the wall of soldiers, she sees Rumkowski. His carriage is parked right at the foot of the steps, so all the children have to pass him before they are lifted onto one of the lorries. And the closer she gets to him, the more she is aware of the minutely appraising look he is giving each and every one of them. The Chairman's eyes pass swiftly over the skinny, the lame and the deformed. He is looking for that single, *perfect* child, the one who can act as redress for the thousands he has been forced to sacrifice. And then she sees his face suddenly break into that smile she has so often observed before but never been able to make out.

He is smiling, but it isn't a smile –

From behind her, someone wrenches Staszek's hand out of hers, and she is left not knowing which way to turn. To go after Staszek, whose cries of protest electrify her, or after the other children, who have been swept on ahead and are calling out to her. Some of them have already been put on the lorry; and it is too late for her to get back to Rumkowski.

She sees the old man bend down and tell his driver to help Staszek up into the coach. *It's me*, she hears him say to the child, like a parody of the voice she has listened to all these years, *pan Śmierć*. The driver has already turned the horse and the carriage is gliding away, in a different direction from the loaded German lorries driving out past the barriers of barbed wire that have been pushed aside: back to safety in the ghetto.

II

The Child
(September 1942–January 1944)

May it be Your will, You who hear the beseechings of Your petitioners, to hearken unto the heartfelt sighs and pleadings that emanate from our hearts each and every day, evening, morning and afternoon. Our endurance is under strain; we have neither a leader, nor source of support, nor anyone to turn to and rely on, save for You, our Father in Heaven. Our Father, merciful Father, you have visited upon us a daily torrent of retribution, famine, sword, fear and panic. In the morning we say, 'If only it were evening,' and in the evening we say, 'If only it were morning.' No one knows who among Your people Israel, Your flock, will survive and who will fall victim to plunder and abuse. We beg of You, our Father in Heaven, restore Israel to their precincts, sons to their mothers' embrace, and fathers to sons. Bring peace to the world and remove the evil wind that has come to rest upon Your creatures. Unlock our shackles and remove our tattered, befouled clothing. Return to our homes those who have been abducted, deported and captured. Have mercy upon them and protect them, wherever they may be, from all evil afflictions, disasters, disease, and all manner of retribution, and extricate us from woe to relief, from darkness to great light, so we may serve You with our hearts and souls and keep Your holy Sabbath and festivals joyously and happily. Illuminate us in the light of Your countenance and make your signs evident, so that we may witness plainly as the Lord returns the captivity of his people. Then Jacob will rejoice, and Israel will take delight, and may all who seek refuge with You experience neither shame nor disgrace. May God redeem the righteous summarily, promptly and speedily, and let us say: Amen.

From a prayer written on one of the walls in the prayer room in Podrzeczna Street (at the approach of Rosh Hashanah and the Day of Atonement, 1941)

Today at 10 a.m. in the former preventorium at 55 Łagiewnicka Street, the Chairman celebrated bar mitzvah for his adopted son Stanisław Stein. Some thirty guests, people close to the Chairman, were in attendance. When the boy read from the Prophets, he used the Sephardic pronunciation. In the year that has passed since the adoption, the Chairman has made sure the boy has received a thorough Jewish education.

At the modest reception that followed, Moshe Karo made a speech to the assembled guests.

Among the ladies present were as always Mrs Regina Rumkowska, Mrs Helena Rumkowska, Mrs [Aron] Jakubowicz and Miss [Dora] Fuchs. Despite the modest refreshment, the Chairman was able to create a warm and intimate atmosphere among his guests.

This is the picture –

In the middle of the photograph stands a twelve- or thirteen-year-old boy with a yarmulke on his head and a candle in one hand. He is wearing a suit, clearly new and tailor-made, which looks several sizes too big for him, baggy across the shoulders, its sleeves drooping over his wrists. To his right stands an elderly man with thick, white hair, combed back, a lined face and spectacles with round, 'American' frames. The spectacles must have taken a knock, or perhaps they merely slid down his nose in the course of that awkward gesture of attempted blessing, raising his hand above his son's head. On the boy's left is a youngish woman, quite small but holding herself erect, shoulders pulled back as if she might be able to grow a centimetre or two in the picture. Despite the smile with which she is trying to dazzle the photographer, her face is gaunt and tired, and between the bridge of her nose and her cheekbone there is some kind of deposit or swelling on her skin, unless it is just a shadow cast by the bright light suffusing the whole scene at the instant the picture was taken.

Only the boy seems unruffled. Heedless of his father's clumsy movements or his mother's rigid posture, of all that has happened or is going to happen to him, he just stares inquisitively straight into the camera. As if the only thing of interest to him at that moment is *how it actually works* – how events and things that would otherwise scarcely exist suddenly become real and are arrested for all time.

There is another picture, too. It is a copy of the X-ray the Chairman had done to satisfy himself that the child he had decided to adopt was 'entirely healthy'.

This is the only real picture of yourself you will ever see, Professor Weisskopf told the boy as the overhead light was turned off.

The examination room was plunged into complete darkness, and as if it had been waiting for just such an opportunity, the peculiar, box-like thing they had fastened to his chest slowly began to move up towards his chin and head, then back down again. It made a faint rustling noise.

Then everything went quiet, and a few minutes later, Professor Weissman came out from behind the curtain. He was holding the plate, eager to display it.

The picture was like nothing the boy had ever seen before. Against a dark, shiny background, pale half-arcs rose in a regular pattern. They looked like a temple with tall pillars, floating on bright, airy clouds high up under a dark sky. Did everyone have a temple of light like that inside them? Or was it only inside him it looked that way, since he (as the Chairman often told him) was different.

It was a question that preoccupied him a great deal at that time.

What distinguishes one human being from another? How do you become *a chosen one*?

This was what he and all other schoolchildren were taught in those days:

When Wilhelm Röntgen conducted his first experiments with what were then called cathode rays in the autumn of 1895, he covered the tube and the device that generated the rays in black cardboard; then he blocked all the openings. Despite the total seal on the tube, an intense, flickering light immediately appeared on a bench he had positioned a few metres away.

Though he moved the bench further back, the light did not diminish. Nor did it gradually start to fade, as light from other sources did.

From this experiment he concluded that the new light he had discovered could also penetrate solid objects. The lower the density of the object, the easier it was for the rays to get through. They could, for example, easily penetrate a book of a thousand pages, a pack of cards, wood or hard rubber; but they could not pass through harder substances like lead or bone.

It is not possible to see the soul itself, wrote Röntgen, *but if one holds up a hand in front of the screen, the shadow picture clearly shows every bone in a finger joint, with the tissue visible as a faint outline around it*. As proof, he prepared a number of photographic plates. One of them showed the bones of his wife's left hand, complete with ring.

In June 1945, six months after the Red Army liberated

Litzmannstadt, chest X-ray pictures were found in the basement of the former preventorium at 55 Łagiewnicka Street* of thousands of the children who were taken away in the *szpera* operation of September 1942 and murdered by the Nazis.

The X-ray negatives were found in bundles up to about twenty centimetres thick, tied up with string. Some of the chest X-rays clearly showed dark areas of fluid, which in a young person causes a hunched, jerky gait with a noticeably protruding or raised shoulder. In others, darker shading within the shimmering white covering of bone is a clear indication of advanced stages of tuberculosis. But all the pictures are anonymous. If there was ever a name, a date and place of birth, or a registration number that could have identified the individual negatives, it has long since been lost.

The only feature by which the pictures can now be identified – retrospectively given a body, a name, a face – are the abnormalities themselves.

---

* Full name *Preventorium No. 2 for the Control of Pulmonary Tuberculosis.*

The other person entrusted with young Mr Rumkowski's education, apart from Moshe Karo, was Fide Szajn. The Chairman was said to have a soft spot for the ghetto's Hasidic Jews, and Fide Szajn was one to whom learning came easily. At any event, it was not anticipated that he could do any harm.

It was Fide Sjazn who carried the front end of the stretcher when Reb Gutesfeld took Mara the paralysed woman round the ghetto. Staszek, who had still not seen very much of the ghetto, was told by Szajn in interminable detail about the way the three of them had moved from place to place. In all winds and weathers and at any time of day or night they were forced to move on. At night they sought refuge in the old Bajka cinema, now used as a prayer house, or in the synagogue in Jakuba Street where the Talmud Torah School had been, and where the few Torah scrolls and prayer books saved from the Nazis' acts of arson were kept in utmost secrecy. They had also found sanctuary in the basement storeroom of the shoe factory on the corner of Towianskiego and Brzezińska Streets, because the *kierownik* who ran the place was a deeply pious Jew. They had spent a few days in the ruins of a dilapidated tenement house in Smugowa Street. The authorities had decreed that the streets in that block were to be incorporated into the Aryan part of Litzmannstadt; the residents had already been forced to move out and the demolition team had begun its work. But the house was still standing, though only the girders and parts of the frontage remained, and it rained on them incessantly as they sat huddled under a bed headboard and a few old armchairs that the wood plunderers still had not found, while the woman lay under a dirty blanket on the floor in front of them, mumbling incomprehensible strings of Hebrew prayers.

Back then there had still, believe it or not, been places in the ghetto where you could stay unnoticed. Then came the dreadful September operation, and the Jewish police forcibly ejected Reb Gutesfeld from the simple, rented room where he lived with his wife. Fide Szajn, too, was obliged to go into hiding. He could have been deported if Moshe Karo had not arranged just in time for a *tzetl* to be written out in his name, and he was transferred to a place called *optgesamt*, home to a thousand Jews that the authorities had seen fit to spare. But once he got there, and even with the passage of time, hardly a day went by without his thoughts turning to the woman they had had to leave behind them. Her name and the memory of her remained his great torment. Perhaps, he speculated to young Mr Rumkowski, she had flown over the wire again, back the way she first came, and perhaps she would return one day when the Jews once more blew the *shoifer*. Then, if not before, it would be seen that the Lord, despite all the signs to the contrary, had still not abandoned the people of Israel.

Fide Szajn was an obstinate soul. Admittedly he had had his hair cut off because the Kripo had issued orders for the arrest of anyone daring to show themselves in religious apparel. But he stubbornly persisted in wearing his long coat and big black hat. The hat looked comical perched on top of his long, emaciated, shaven head. His body looked comical, too, as if it was several sizes too large for the clothes he wore. His trousers ended at his calves and the sleeves of his over-tight jacket left his thin wrists exposed.

His face was bony and white, and his gaze darted this way and that, as if it could never decide in time where it wanted to go. Unlike everyone else's gaze, it seemed not to want to rest for a minute more than necessary on young Mr Rumkowski. Fide Szajn's own copy of the Torah had Polish text on one side and

Hebrew on the facing page. He made Staszek cover the left side with his hand, and then read and interpret what was written on the other. If Staszek got even the tiniest Hebrew word wrong, or could not remember the words he had just read, Fide Szajn rapped him over the back of the neck with his open hand.

He did not care that it was Rumkowski's very own son he had as a *talmid*. It was the words that mattered, and always would.

Fide Szajn came every day except the Sabbath, and he always began his lessons by eating. If there was one thing Fide Szajn revered more than the books he would insist on lugging with him, it was the food the Chairman's housekeeper put in front of him, and he always ate in absolute silence, as if every crumb demanded his total concentration.

After the meal, the teaching began.

Fide Szajn went in detail through the order of service, how the reading of the Torah was done, and the best ways of learning the selected sections of the text so the Holy Scripture could simply flow out of you by its own divine force. Fide Szajn invested particular care in teaching Staszek Hebrew. He dealt thoroughly with every letter of the alphabet, explaining why they looked as they did, and the divine origin of every word. A single word could serve for a whole afternoon's lecture. *Help me explain*, Fide Szajn might say (he often put it that way, as if he were the one who needed help in solving a problem and not Staszek): *help me explain why the words for fear and faith have the same root*. When Staszek could not answer, Fide Szajn would counter with a story. When Jacob, waking from his long sleep, finds the ladder leading up to Heaven in Beer Sheva, reaching out over the place where the temple lies, he is seized by fear that the place where he lay down has suddenly become another.

'The Lord is surely in this place –
how dreadful is this place . . .'
And he called the name of that place Bêt El, the house of God.

So says Rabbi Ezrael in Rabbi Ben Zimra's name:

To learn to feel fear is to learn to know the true essence of God.
God has struck fear into us that we may seek him, his name
made manifest, his origins.

This was one of Fide Szajn's favourite subjects. There were false prophets who drew a distinction between *faith* and *fear*, and called themselves the emissaries of God because they considered that they were the only ones who could put the words back together. They were thus guilty of blasphemy, for only God can heal the rift that runs between words and people.

Then Fide Szajn told the story of Sabbatai Tzvi from seventeenth-century Smyrna, who had himself proclaimed Messiah. Having been thrown out of Smyrna, Salonica and Jerusalem, he went to Constantinople to depose the Sultan. The Sultan gave him two alternatives: either to convert to Islam or to be put to death. Sabbatai Tzvi chose the former, and by this apostasy proved himself a false *shoyfet*. The word was still cleft in his sermons, so when he spoke of faith he was really only speaking of his own fear. Men like that are all too eager to run the Sultan's errands.

Fide Szajn did not need to say it out loud; it was still apparent that he viewed Chaim Rumkowski as a self-appointed redeemer of the same kind.

A man who had learnt to put his fear above his faith.

After *di groise shpere*, as the September action was now known, the Chairman was obliged to move out of the hospital. He moved into private accommodation in an ordinary block of flats. The new flat at 61 Łagiewnicka Street comprised two small, adjoining rooms, with a narrower room rather like a corridor between the other two rooms and the kitchen. This room had a tall window running the length of one side, looking out over an enclosed inner courtyard where all manner of old junk had accumulated, and where what seemed like every pigeon in the ghetto came to breed.

Though you didn't call the Chairman's rooms mere *rooms*: you said *city apartment*.

The city apartment also had a little box room at the far end of the landing, to which the Chairman held a separate key. He called it his office but seldom spent time there. He spent most of his hours and days exactly as before, in his Secretariat down at Bałuty Square, or in his residence out at Marysin.

Two rooms. The Chairman slept in one of them, and his wife Regina was supposed to do the same. But Mrs Rumkowska seldom slept there. Since the disappearance of her beloved brother, she either stayed in 'her' flat in Zgierska Street, to which no one else had access, or sat pale and listless at the desk in the other room, which everyone referred to as Mrs Rumkowska's room, even though she refused to move any of her possessions into it or even to lie on the bed the Chairman finally and reluctantly installed there. She generally locked herself in. When Mrs Rumkowska did occasionally emerge, it was as if she were stepping onto a stage. She smiled broadly and touched things distractedly. If anyone addressed her – usually the housekeeper, Mrs Koszmar – she assumed as painless an expression as she could muster, or gave a forced laugh.

But then there was that *third* room, somewhere between the Chairman's and Regina's. Though Stanisław never really knew whether it was an actual room, or one that only *came into existence* when the Praeses wished it to.

Every so often, the Chairman took him in there. And then Stanisław would realise that what looked like a narrow corridor from the outside was in fact quite a large space.

Big and cramped at the same time: cluttered with bits of old, wooden furniture that were never used. And then that window, admitting something that might have been light if the panes had not been so plastered with dirt and mud. And there was no proper air in there, either. Staszek tried to breathe, but every breath felt like having a thick, foul-smelling sock forced down his throat. He closed his eyes, and all that was left apart from the smell was the cooing and the delicate rustle of the pigeons' wings as they rose and fell in the glazed-in courtyard; and then that hateful, wheedling, paternal voice bending down to speak to him, with the same evil breath as the furniture had: a strange blend of pigeon droppings, rotting wood, stale, ingrained cigarette smoke and the particular kind of wax polish with which Mrs Koszmar regularly polished all the cupboard doors and chair arms:

This is a place just for you and me, Staszek, a holy place:
so we need to be able to make ourselves comfortable!

Everyone said he was a Rumkowski now. Princess Helena said it, and Mr Tausendgeld; and Miss Fuchs; and the key man and Fide Szajn who turned up punctually each day, eyes glazed with hunger. As well as the man they all called his benefactor, Moshe Karo.

But nothing could make him think of himself as a Rumkowski. To himself, he had always had only the one name – Stanisław Stein – even though he no longer remembered very well what his real mother had looked like. Just that she used to wear her hair in two long plaits, and that those plaits were done so tightly that looking down from above, you could see the white skin of her scalp. That was what he did when she made him stand straight and still by her while she sewed the Star of David onto the front of his jacket. Then he had to turn round and stand with his back to her while she sewed another star firmly into place. He remembered the smell of her hair. Fresh and soft, with a warm, spicy scent that was all hers. No one else had her smell.

At the Green House they had constantly asked him what he remembered of the time before he came to the ghetto, but he could not answer. It was as if the very effort of remembering blotted out whatever was somehow still there to be remembered.

The Germans. He remembered *them*. And the shame; running like an eager dog by the first jeeps in the column; laughing at the lovely sheen of the vehicles' matt steel and the soldiers' helmets; and being grabbed by the scruff of his neck by Krzysztof Kohlman, the cantor of the synagogue, and sent home with a slap on his backside.

Later, the German soldiers had hoisted the cantor up into the big chestnut outside the Catholic church, a tree so old that its bark had been worn and rubbed away so the bare white wood shone through; and at first he had thought it was a punishment because Mr Kohlman had been so nasty to him. But when Mrs Kohlman came out and pleaded and begged for them to let her husband down from the tree, they went to his shop and came back with hammer and nails. They propped a ladder against the tree; one of the soldiers climbed up, tied both Mr Kohlman's arms to the trunk, and forced his fingers back to hammer nails right through his hands. Then they left him hanging there.

And all the time he could hear his mother saying, sometimes calling out, sometimes in a hoarse whisper:

My children are Christian, my children are Christian, my children are Christian –

Why did she say that? All the Jews in the village had been rounded up on the big grassy area in front of the church, but the church door was shut, as was the door in the churchyard wall; and outside, the fine, cold rain turned everything that had been firm ground into thick, viscous mud. There were soldiers everywhere. They had big black military coats, and you could see shiny droplets of rain dotting the fabric and their helmets, and the rifles they carried on straps slung over their shoulders. Every so often one would take a quick step forward, drag a man or two out of the crowd and set about them with rifle butts, batons or their bare hands.

They went on beating even when the men were on the ground.

And when the men could no longer move, they were dragged off to the far end of the churchyard wall, from where shots continued to ring out, hour after hour.

It was after midnight when the group of women was ordered to move.

Shiny steel helmets and leather coats shouting *schnell* and *raus*, and the wailing chorus of women began to howl louder, and he stumbled between bodies now so saturated that all he could see were big, heavy, stockinged feet, squelching through the mud and missing their footing at every step; and the women talking in loud indignant voices over each other about the children they were being parted from. And about food. And what they could survive on if they had nothing to eat. He had been awfully afraid, and because the fear was everywhere, whatever he saw or touched had also turned to fear. The buses waiting for them turned into nervous, malevolent beasts, juddering with the rage pent up beneath the clattering metal covers of their engine compartments. He tried to keep his eyes straight ahead so as not to feel sick, as his mother had told him to do, but inside him and ahead of him everything was black. He had wet himself. They went on one bus, then another or it might have been the same one again, and the bus bumped around so violently amid the soft and oily warmth of its engine sounds that he felt as if invisible hands were kneading him. And he hadn't been able to hold on any longer. And his pee-soaked garments had frozen onto the lower part of his body. His teeth chattered, despite his mother holding him clasped tightly to her. And he remembers his mother saying *I wish I had a blanket to keep him warm . . .*

But somewhere between the intense desire for a blanket and the blanket's appearance, as sudden as it was unexpected (quick, nervous hands winding it round him in lots of thick layers), his mother had simply disappeared.

He never saw her again.

*

Those tucking a blanket round his cold body that morning

when the buses arrived included Malwina Kempel and nursery nurse Rosa Smoleńska from the Green House. Not that he knew it at the time. In fact, it was several months before he realised he was no longer in Aleksandrów but in *Litzmannstadt Ghetto*. (He wrote in the gently rounded hand that Miss Smoleńska taught all the children:

Litz-mann-stadt Ghet-to –)

The deported women had initially been taken to a building called Kino Marysin, which was not a cinema at all, but some kind of warehouse with draughty wooden walls and a smell of old potatoes and earth. There he sat with the label that identified his transport number hanging round his neck and the blanket they had wrapped around him, with nothing to eat but a few slices of dry bread and the soup that was brought in clanking vats every day and tasted bitter and nasty, like water you had scrubbed the floor with. After a week had passed, his *benefactor* Moshe Karo came in with a woman in the blue uniform of a nursery nurse, freshly ironed, and read out a whole list of names, and the children whose names were read out had to get up and go with her.

So he had already been in the ghetto when Rosa came to fetch him?

Ghet-to Litz-mann-stadt.

Miss Smoleńska nodded.

So what *was* it then, this ghetto?

Miss Smoleńska had no answer to that. The ghetto was what was *out there*. But he was *in here* now. Saved, as Miss Smoleńska put it.

Were there steel helmets in the ghetto, too?

He had told her before about all the Jews having to go to the square in front of the church, about the rain that meant nobody could see how many of them there were; and about the steel helmets, going around beating everyone they had herded together, only to separate them again. He was scared of those steel helmets, he said; and when he said that, Miss Smoleńska looked as she always did when the children's questions were too close for comfort or she didn't know what to answer. Her face lost all expression, and her hands found themselves suddenly very busy.

The Germans are here, but they generally stay outside. As long as we don't do anything bad, they won't come in.

They won't *ever* come in again?

When the war's over, they'll never come again.

When will the war be over, then?

But that was a question not even Rosa Smoleńska could answer.

But there was an out there, and it looked the way the Praeses had decided it should look. The General stood up in his carriage and pointed, and whatever he pointed at *came to be*. The things that sprang up like that before the two of them as they went on their *royal inauguration visit* through the ghetto were: a hospital that had been converted into a tailor's to make uniforms; a children's hospital that had become an exhibition space; a bolted and barred (and closely guarded) charcoal store; a vegetable market; and *resorty*, of course, *lots and lots of resorty. Here!* said the General, and pointed, and a wide square spread before them with barriers and gates and sentry boxes and policemen in tall, shiny boots and caps and yellow-and-white-striped armbands with Stars of David. *Here*, said the Chairman, *there are thirteen thousand men and women working every day just to look after my affairs and the ghetto's business!*

Stanisław would have liked the Praeses to ask him about his brothers, his mother, even Rosa Smoleńska and Superintendent Rubin at the Green House; he would have liked to talk about anyone and anything other than what the Chairman was pointing at and ordering into being.

'And what happens to all the people in the ghetto who are going to die?' he asked in the end, mainly to have something to say. But the Chairman did not reply. He raised his stick and commanded forth another shower of factories from the long row of tumbledown buildings and said *all this will be yours one day*.

Staszek finally plucked up his courage.

'Is it you who decides who's going to die? – Miss Smoleńska says it's the authorities who decide who's got to die!'

But the Chairman still obstinately made no reply. He was slumped so deep in his carriage seat that his kneecaps were touching his chin. Along the street through which they were driving, knots of people had gathered, a mix of policemen and ordinary workers. Some smiled and waved; some tried to climb into the carriage; and others ran alongside, attempting to keep pace for no particular reason. The Chairman did not appear put out by these tributes from the masses; on the contrary, they seemed to put him in high spirits. He leant forward to the coachman and shouted: *Faster, faster*; and then he shouted to Staszek, too:

Do you want to hold the reins?

But the reins the Chairman was offering him were not real ones, just an excuse to lift him into his lap; and there he sat now on a stiff, uncomfortable Chairmanly knee and tugged and flicked and said *whoa* and *gee up* and anything else he could think of to distract the attention of the regal General until the Praeses pressed his vast body against his own and panted like a steam engine right down the back of his neck:

*Ty jesteś moim synem, moim drogim synem –**

*

It always ended with them going to the room with the dirty light and the pigeons, where the air was so thick it felt like a woollen sock in your throat; but that was only after everyone else in the flat had gone to bed.

The Chairman would have asked Mrs Koszmar to get everything ready. There would be platters of sliced cheese and fat-edged ham, rolled so they could be filled with radish halves and bunches of parsley and dill. Flanked by two gleaming

* You are my son, my beloved son . . .

slices of lemon were wafer-thin cuts of smoked, marinated meat which the Chairman speared on the point of a knife and proffered to his Son, to watch him snap them up in his mouth like a fish. The Chairman liked to watch while Stanisław was eating, and when Stanisław was eating, it was as if the Chairman could not control himself, but plunged his fingers into a jar of sweet, black plum jam and told him to lick and suck the jam from his fingers like a goat (*tsig*, said the Chairman, making goat-like slurping noises of his own, with his tongue in the back of his throat, *tsig, tsig, tsigerli* . . . !); and the cloying taste of ripe plums was so overwhelming that it almost suffocated him, with the alien Praeses fingers finding their way in, and even deeper in, so deep that he almost choked and had to grab the Praeses by the arm and squeeze tight to make him stop. Something that did not seem to trouble the Praeses in the slightest. He merely smiled, a smile filled with satisfaction and distaste like a surgeon just embarking on a demanding operation.

But there were also times when the Chairman came back in after the two of them had just been in the Room, and then he was like another person. He swept all the platters and plates off the table and roared that Staszek was *A DISGRACE TO THE WHOLE HOUSEHOLD* and would have to learn to keep the place clean and stop leaving it like a pigsty, and he would often finish by calling Regina or Mrs Koszmar in to tidy up so it looked *RESPECTABLE* again.

The worst of it was that you could never know who the Praeses would be from one moment to the next. Or to be precise: in which guise he would reveal himself.

What baffled Staszek was not how the different parts of the Chairmanly body could be combined in one figure, but what happened to the other parts in the meantime. Where, for example, did the *happy and high-spirited Praeses* go, the one who slapped his knee and broke into loud, shrill laughter, like a mechanical toy? And what happened in the interim to the *troubled Praeses*, who talked to Staszek as if to a little adult about war and *ghetto business*? Or the *cunning Praeses*, with the cold, calculating, shifty eyes of a predator? And where did his *hands* go? Those hands that were the most active part of the Praeses's body, moving of their own volition, though Staszek made his back stiff and straight and pulled his head into his shoulders to escape. The hands still always found their way in somehow. The Chairman smiled with black teeth, his eyes were glazed and Staszek dared not do anything for fear that the *wrathful Praeses* would grab him up from the sofa and start to cuff him about the head and shoulders until his head was swimming, and Staszek threw up and was left sitting like an animal in his own vomit, which was as grey and colourless as the pigeon droppings piling up against the outside of window to the courtyard.

You disgusting little pig, said the Chairman, smiling his warmest smile.

Staszek eventually came up with a different strategy. He made sure to catch the hand *before* it started hitting; caught it and held it as you would hold a jumping frog on your lap. Then he brought it lovingly to his face and stroked the rough knuckles against his neck and cheek and chin. At first, the Chairman seemed entirely nonplussed by this sudden display of dog-like devotion, and if there had been a blow lying ready in the Chairman's hand, it was put entirely off its stroke.

As indeed was the Chairman: who sat there with his son's tearful head between his hands, as if it were an object he had no idea what to do with.

That was another way of doing it.

The doors to my rooms are always open, the Chairman would say.

I live a community life. At heart I am just a simple, ordinary Jew.

I have nothing to hide.

In the Chairman's room, plates piled high with food were set out in rows and on tiered stands: beautifully cut triangular sandwiches with smoked meat and creamed horseradish, eye-wateringly large portions; and cakes, *real* cakes and buns made from *real* flour, sugar and eggs. At the far end of the table, the wine bottles with their pouring spouts stood as if to attention, elegant white cloths tied round their necks.

It was always the same people picking their way round the table. *Resort* heads and administration chiefs, the managers of the Chairman's many offices and secretariats; Miss Fuchs, Mr Cygielman and Miss Rebeka Wołk. There were also uniform caps with various 'stripes'. In the crowd he could see Rozenblat's and other police officers' caps with red bands, while Commander Kaufmann from the fire brigade had a blue band and the head of the postal service had green. And Princess Helena's merry laugh hung like a glittering garland over the uniformly grey carpet of male noise. There was much huffing and puffing over the glasses and plates set out on the table. For Staszek, who was expected to keep to the back of the room with the Gertler and Jakubowicz children, it was like watching a play. The General in the middle, loud and purple with alcohol and exertion; and around him this court of invited dignitaries who not so much spoke as delivered lines. Grandiloquent cascades of words, or small, thin, pointed words that tumbled out of them like coins, and hung in the air or were beaten or trampled to pieces by sudden steps, unwarranted backslapping and exaggeratedly loud laughter.

Since the doors were always open, Staszek seized his chance – grabbed a fistful of squishy sandwiches, and took a stroll through the high-ceilinged reception room and on down the stairs to where the key man was keeping guard. Staszek normally only saw him from behind as he sat in his cubicle, his uniformed back and then his neck with its three rolls of hippo flab, topped by a *proper* police cap with a red band. So the key man wasn't just a key man – he was a policeman, too! Around the sleeve of his jacket he had a white armband with a blue, six-pointed star in the middle, and within the star a white circle enclosed in a V-sign.

The only way in which he could get past this colossus was to slip behind the cubicle down a narrow set of stairs to the cellar. Staszek had already made sure there was a way out from there, along a narrow basement corridor into what must once have been a laundry. There were tubs for washing and rinsing propped along the wall, some with big patches of rust where water must once have gushed into them from taps long since removed. By climbing up onto the edge of one of the empty tubs, he could reach a high window which had been left slightly open. With one hand he undid the hasp that was stopping the window opening fully, got a grip on the outside of the window frame and then forced his head and shoulders as far through as he could. And miraculously enough: before the washtub toppled over, there was someone *out there* to take him under the arms and pull and tug until his whole body was through.

Outside stood the strangest apparition he had ever seen.

A boy of about his own age, face bent forward with a grimace of seemingly constant pain. On his back he carried a cross, made of two beams, one fixed across the other. From the lengths of wood hung bottles, jars and tubes that knocked and chinked together as he tried in alarm to straighten up again But the gaze from beneath the wooden cross was no longer resting on Staszek; it had alighted on the sandwiches he had dropped as he squeezed through the window, which now lay scattered in the dirt. The boy fell on them and stuffed them into his mouth one after another, dirt and bread together, while the bottles, jars and glassware jangled and chimed over him like a tower of ringing bells.

Once he had wolfed them all, he rested back beneath his two beams of wood, patted his stomach and announced in a pompous voice:

I am the Chairman's son!

Staszek stared at him. Two ulcerated legs, blue with cold, stuck into a pair of muddy *trepki* – how could *this* be the Chairman's son? But it seemed the bottle boy did not mean it quite as literally as he had made it sound:

In the ghetto, we're all the Chairman's children.
That's what Bronek says.
So I must be the Chairman's son as well.

Then he began to howl in a loud and harrying hawker's voice:

EL-I-KSIIIR, EL-I-KSIIIR
Buy yourself a lovely new life

It belatedly dawned on Staszek that the bottle boy was a mobile chemist's shop. From his wooden cross hung not only bottles and jars but also twists of fabric, shards of mirror, scissor blades and little bits of soap, tied on with rope and string. Above this contraption, the boy's small, pale face had the look of one scared to death by everything dangling all around him.

'There's no chemist's here any more,' the Chairman's *real* son said firmly, in a voice that he tried to make like the Chairman's, authoritative and dismissive.

But the bottle boy refused to let himself be deflated.

'It makes no difference,' he replied. 'Better to stand where people *think* they're going to find a chemist's than anywhere else. That's what Bronek says, anyway!'

Staszek began to suspect there was something not quite right about the boy. There was something about his eyes; they didn't seem able to focus on what they were looking at. 'Do you want something else to eat?' asked Staszek, fishing a chunk of bread out of his pocket. (He had learnt always to have some food with him – so he had something to pop in his mouth even on days when the Chairman was not entertaining guests.) The bottle collector grabbed the bread and took a big bite. It was only when he had wolfed the whole thing that it struck him as strange for a child he didn't know to turn up in his territory, and what was more, with his pockets full of food.

But by then, Staszek had made off –

Wait for me . . . ! cried the bottle boy, and dashed after his benefactor; but with the weight of the wooden crossbar on his back it was not easy to run, and the next time Staszek turned round, the whole, huge bottle rack was out of sight, with only the gentle tinkle of glass audible somewhere behind him.

Staszek went on at a more leisurely pace down a potholed, hilly road with low houses and dilapidated wooden sheds on either side. There were people standing selling things all along the street. A windowsill or a doorstep served as a shop counter, with a few scraps of material or metal objects laid out for sale. The house window apertures had no frames in them; some were boarded up with chipboard or had a loose bit of material hanging over them. In a front doorway sat an old man with the stumps of his amputated legs wrapped in coarse sacking.

Between his wooden crutches he had spread out a realm of ironmongery, pots and pans with or without their lids. As protection from the raw autumn air he had a curly sheepskin like a waistcoat round his body, and a cap with earflaps, tied under his chin. His eyes were hidden behind a big pair of dark glasses, from behind which he was helplessly scanning the scene.

Staszek stood in front of the blind man and dropped another bit of bread into the lap between the two crutches, and the blind man must have seen the bread fall as clearly as if it were manna from Heaven, for his hands were there at once, feeling around among saucepan lids and handles, and a low *ohhh-hhh* of surprise ran through the crowd that had by then gathered around them. The boy was not only well dressed and apparently clean and healthy; he was also giving alms to the poorest of the poor.

The child himself had forgotten his earlier caution.

'I wanted to ask the way to the children's home in Okopowa Street,' he said in the politest Polish he could muster.

'*Op-kwa*?'

The man pointed in all sorts of directions, until Staszek realised that this extravagant gesturing was just to hide the fact that behind his dark glasses he was still trying to find out who was asking. Meanwhile, other curious bystanders had come closer, and were no longer in distant, isolated pockets but formed an angry group of people, all with questions to ask:

Who are you? – What are you doing here? – Where have you come from?

Staszek ducked between the shafts of a handcart full of old scrap metal and set off down the road, keeping moving until he thought he was safe.

When he turned round, the crowd was still standing around the blind man, but the man with the cart had been joined by two policemen, and Staszek saw the man raise one arm and point and then all of them, the two policemen included, looked his way.

But no one made any attempt to follow him.

Slowly, all the colour leached from the sky. The buildings became more widely scattered; trees and stone walls took a step back from the edge of the road. There was no electric light to be seen. As darkness started to fall, the temperature dropped. What Staszek at first took to be his own frosted breath turned out to be increasingly thick mist in the air. All sense of feeling began to ebb from his feet and fingertips.

He thought of the Chairman, presumably already out looking for him. He would go with his bodyguards from house to house, asking if anybody had seen *the chosen one*, and before long he would get to the man with the handcart and people would be scared and maybe admit that they had *seen him*. Maybe they would hope to earn some kind of reward that way, or they might say they didn't know anything, in order to keep out of trouble. Miss Smoleńska always used to say the less you knew, the better. Where the authorities were concerned, at any rate.

Now and then he caught sight of other people in the darkness. Some of them had armbands and uniform caps. What would happen if he stopped them and told them he was the person they were looking for? But they might not believe him, since there were others going around saying they were children of the Praeses. Maybe it would be better to tell it the way it was. That he didn't know what or who or where he was. The last thing he had done was to sit on a bus with his mother and there were other people there, too, and somebody had come and put a blanket over him because he was wet and cold. But they were strangers, everybody he met in the ghetto was a *stranger*. He had experienced many things with them, but now they had to help him get back home, or at the very least to the Green House where Miss Smoleńska would be sure to tell them who he was, and he needed somewhere to sleep, after all.

But he carried on being nobody; and the darkness that had been out there, outside him, was now inside. Once it had risen up to his eyes, it would be like water. Dark water, deep enough to drown in. He was afraid of the darkness inside himself. It was like when he tried to get to sleep in the evenings. He dared not move because he didn't know if it was him moving in the darkness, or the darkness moving in him.

When he turned round, he saw a face looming out of the mist behind him. No body, just a pale oval with no recognisable features, hanging in mid-air like a balloon, or the reflection of a candle in a window. The face also had a voice, a very calm, clear, firm voice that asked what someone like him was doing out after curfew. He repeated what he had said about looking for the children's home in *Oko-powa* Street.

It's here, just around the corner, answered the face.

They had stopped outside a gate. Behind the gate, a house stood wreathed in mist. But was it really the Green House?

He didn't recognise it. He tried to remember. That time all the children had had to line up on the stairs while Super-intendent Rubin and Miss Smoleńska counted them all, ten, twelve, fourteen (he was number fourteen?) and then get them to march off to the Big Field where the German soldiers were standing guard around their mud-spattered lorries, their submachine guns raised. It had all been just like that time they had to stand by the churchyard wall and the Nazis had come and taken away all his brothers. He couldn't remember. It was as if what was happening now had already happened more than once already.

Who are you looking for? asks the voice.

Staszek shakes his head, and starts to make his own way over to the gate. But the face stops him. The voice is gentler still as it asks again:

Do you want me to ask for anyone in particular?

Staszek is momentarily at a loss. He hasn't thought that far.

Miss Rosa, he says eventually. *Miss Rosa Smoleńska.*

Rosa, says the face, and dissolves into the mist. After a while there is the sound of fists knocking hard on a door: I was to ask for a certain Miss *R-r-r-osa*, he hears the voice say in an exaggeratedly eager voice, and from inside the house comes an equally loud, shrill voice, not answering the face's question but exhorting someone else:

Miss Roo-osa? Mis Roo-osa? Is there any Miss Roo-osa here?

From inside the house he hears a burst of loud, high-spirited laughter. Male laughter.

When the laughter dies away, all is silence. Some time passes. It is as though everything around him – the white face, the voice and the house – has dissolved into the mist and simply disappeared. From within this void, he hears the slow sound of clopping hooves. For a long time, the white horse is all he can see. The carriage and its occupants are taking their time. They are very close before Mr Kuper's crooked back and the Chairman, sitting hunched under the closed hood, come into view.

Kuper has already folded down the step, and with an indescribable feeling of relief, Staszek allows himself to be helped up into the carriage. Once again a blanket is wrapped around him. Throughout all this, the Chairman has not turned round or touched him or said so much as a word. With a gentle creak, the carriage moves off again.

After Staszek's 'little outing', as it came to be called, the Chairman's behaviour towards him changed. It was as if he stopped addressing him directly, and began to talk instead to someone standing beside him, another Staszek who looked the same and did the same things but was separate from him.

And the Chairman seemed to be a little afraid of that *other* Staszek.

Sometimes that fear became so intense that the Chairman's eyes took on a dark, feverish look. As if the other Staszek were constantly hounding and harrying him, but he could not explain how or say anything about it at all.

He and the Chairman still went together to that other room, where there was nothing to breathe but old dust and pigeon excrement.

When they had been in the room before, the Chairman had insisted they make themselves 'comfortable'. He had dragged armchairs out from the wall, brought an ashtray and lit cigarettes. Sometimes he had even started telling him things. He sometimes got so carried away by these stories that he even forgot his hands, lying there on his lap, ready for use. But nowadays he mostly just sat there, regarding Staszek with a mute and watery look in his eyes, and inwardly smiling.

The first time I saw you, you were so big and strong and clever, said the Chairman, and Staszek sat beside him, waiting.

It was as if they had the bars of a cage between them. The Chairman was on one side of them, Staszek on the other. At that moment, neither of them knew *who was master and who was slave*, as the Chairman himself would have put it.

But to be more precise: Staszek knew.

The Chairman was the one *behind* the bars.

Not that it afforded the boy any kind of relief. It was the times when the Chairman was in his cage that Staszek feared most. Then all this was no longer about the Chairman and Staszek, but just about the Chairman and the cage. The Chairman paced and paced. All night long he paced, measuring the distance from one side of the cage to the other. Or he stood alone in the cage, praying. Rumkowski prayed every morning and evening; either in the old preventorium two blocks down the street where they lived, or in the old Talmud Torah School in Jakuba Street that was used as a synagogue. When Rumkowski prayed, it was in a loud, piercing, insistent voice, as if making demands even of the Almighty. And he spoke to him the same way:

Why, Stasiulek? I received you so that you could be among the pure. That was why I let you come to me instead of all these other ganovim who just set themselves against me and jeer and humiliate me. Why do you persist in hurting me?

But there were other times when the Chairman wound his fingers around the bars of the cage one by one and pleaded: *Staszek!* He cried; *Stasiu, Stasiulek, Stasinek . . .* And stretched his arms through the bars and took his Son's head and pressed it to him.

Then he kissed him.

Then he crowned him.

And the Son was dressed for the coronation in big, red clothes the Chairman had had made, and for his feet he had tall, shiny shoes of real leather, a protective covering into which every toe had to be curled with the care and precision of which only the finest nobleman was capable. (The Chairman

313

demonstrated: *Not too fast, not too slowly; keep it all supple and smooth.*) And once the coronation was complete the King, the high General, stood alone in his cage and bore witness to the creation on the other side, and the tears ran down his cheeks. (Why are you crying, Father?) Perhaps he was crying because however much he dressed and ornamented his son, he still could not touch his Innermost Being, whatever it was that made his toes move as light as feathers within the points of the fine leather shoes, made his shoulders tremble beneath the weight of his gleaming red mantle, and his heart pound and beat inside his broad breastplate.

And the Chairman beheld his beloved and perfect Son and said:

Staszek, Stasiu, Stasiulek – my precious little one: what has become of you, and what has become of all the other precious children?

But Staszek carried on meeting the other boy, the one with the portable cross and the chemist's glassware. These days they met in safer places, out of range of the key man. One of them was a little way down the yard at the back, where there was a tannery that cleaned and prepared the leathers needed by the ghetto's shoemakers. Each time they met, Staszek fed the boy with bits of bread that he first moistened in his own mouth and then rolled into little balls, and the boy opened his mouth wide and swallowed just like a tortoise, and told him stories of what had happened in other parts of the ghetto.

One was about the Chairman, who had paid a visit to the simple room with the iron stove that the bottle boy and his uncle Bronisław shared with the boy's older cousin, Oskar, who was blind and so could not take care of himself or contribute anything to the family's livelihood.

This had been in the hard winter of 1941.

Bronek, who in order to pay the rent had taken on extra work as the caretaker and odd-job-man in their building, had decided that rather than sitting in front of the stove warming himself, the boy should go out and hack at the ice outside the front entrance. Bronek came up with ideas like that sometimes. Not because anything necessarily needed doing, but just so his nephew was *earning his keep*. So the boy had been standing there outside the entrance with pick and shovel, when suddenly an army of carriages pulled by snorting horses came along the street; the whole lot of them drew up in front of Bronek's nephew, and the Chairman stepped out of the one at the front, and *just look* – he stepped out and shook the insignificant boy's hand, and said that if *he* had had such a hard-working, conscientious son, he would have been proud to call himself his father, and then he gave the boy a fistful of food coupons and sweets.

From that moment on, Bronek ralised that his nephew was a real *glik*, one of those people from whom 'money ran like shit', as he put it to blind Oskar.

So Bronek put two lengths of wood on his nephew's shoulders and sent him off with as many of Mr Winawer's black-market drugs as he could hang on him; and since that day the boy had been walking the ghetto as an itinerant pharmacist, hung with Vigantol, Azetynil and Betabion; and ordinary sugar pills (who noticed the difference if they put their faith in their own hopes?); and tablets you might take for the foul-smelling, acid reflux the factory soup gave you; and an extract of bark with added *Kaffeemischung* that was said not only to contain 'extra nutrition' but also to improve potency, known by the people of the ghetto as 'Biebow's blend', since Biebow was rumoured to have been a coffee merchant in a past life.

(Uncle Bronek based this on a theory he had, namely that in these hard times, there is only one thing ordinary folk want to do, and that is to get out of the ghetto – and if they can't do it 'naturally', then they try pharmaceuticals!)

Look at this . . . ! yelled the bottle boy, and thrust a bottle into his mouth pulling the stopper out with his teeth; and before Staszek could blink, flames were licking gloriously from his mouth, making all the other bottles and jars glint like a starry sky. The bottle boy smothered the flames by covering his mouth with both hands, and when Staszek looked up again, his gaping little tortoise mouth looked like a big, black crater, above which two white eyes were gazing out in alarm.

This is how it was –

Once when Rosa Smoleńska was teaching history and

arithmetic to the children in the Green House, she went into a little room beside Superintendent Rubin's office and came back with a pencil box with a sliding lid and flower garlands along the sides, which she gave to Staszek. Draw me a map of Palestine, she said, and then put in all the cities, rivers and lakes in Judaea and Samaria you can remember, with their names. Staszek started on Palestine, because he knew what that country looked like, of course – *Eretz Israel* – but within its borders he did not draw lakes and cities but jackals and scorpions and desert rats, and other animals with horns and tails and sharp teeth.

Then he drew Germans – *lots* of Germans, because there were so many.

Their external attributes were easy: the police guards with their field-grey military overcoats and steel helmets that came right down the backs of their necks; and then the *other* soldiers, the ones who came in the shiny, black cars and stood laughing when they nailed Cantor Kohlman up in the tree – the ones with death's heads on the front of their caps and pips instead of stripes on their collars.

From Zagajnikowa Street, the wide and dusty exit route below the Green House, they had been able to see the Germans patrolling and keeping guard at Radogoszcz Gate every day. He drew barbed wire, a tall watchtower and the two or more Germans who checked papers and raised and lowered the barrier every time goods had to come through. He tried to recall what it had been like, that time the rain had hung in the few street lights that still worked, and all the Jews in the village had been fetched out of their houses and herded down to the square in front of the church. But all he could really remember was the man the soldiers accused of trying to escape, and dragged into the middle of the church square, and he remembered the face of the soldier who beat and kicked him, and carried on beating and kicking though the man lay there unmoving. And the face of the soldier who was beating and kicking looked just the same as the face of the man lying on the ground being beaten and kicked. They were both wet and shiny in the rain, and somehow twisted and hooded in shadow. That was why the only things that really showed up clearly in the picture he drew were the naked white soles of two feet sticking up out the bundle of clothes which was all that was left of the man: naked white soles and a body kicked to a pulp, and a furious, dissolving soldier face, looking as if somebody had kicked it, too.

After meeting the bottle boy and hearing all the fantastical stories he had to tell, Staszek started drawing other things besides Germans. He drew a host of angels, flying over a city of barbed-wire fences and tall walls. The angels were invisible to the German soldiers in their watchtowers, though the sky above them was filled with the flames of vengeance. Some of the angels in the heavens were even holding *shoifer* horns, which they blew, bringing both fences and walls tumbling down, but still the soldiers noticed nothing.

Sometimes when Staszek was sitting drawing, Miss Smoleńska would come by and stroke her hand across the back of his neck. Mrs Rumkowska never did that, though she followed what he was drawing just as closely as Miss Smoleńska had done, and she, too, had a big, swollen smile that she smiled all the time. But she never touched Staszek or said anything to him beyond what was strictly necessary and what duty demanded – such as what he had learnt at school, or whether he had behaved himself so his father or Moshe Karo, or for that matter, Mrs Koszmar the housekeeper (*Madame Cauchemar*, as Mrs Rumkowska called her) had no need to be ashamed of him. Everything Mrs Rumkowska said had to do with shame.

In the middle of the room where the Chairman held his receptions, there now stood a large tailor's dummy with no head, and the dummy had a private tailor named Master Hinzel to go with it, a dry little man with wax in his ears and a mouthful of pins, who had come to make Staszek a suit for his bar mitzvah. Master Hinzel pinned different materials onto the dummy, and Mrs Rumkowska and Princess Helena walked round it, considering them. Sometimes Staszek had to model them himself, and they pinned and pinioned him as if *he* were made of fabric.

Mrs Rumkowska and Princess Helena could not stand each other. Regina called Helena a *crazy hysteric*; Helena called Regina a *fanatical parvenue who had turned the head of an old man*. When other people were there, they exchanged fixed smiles with scornfully staring eyes. When they were alone, they argued incessantly. *You have the taste of a common barmaid*, Princess Helena might say of some opinion Mrs Rumkowska had expressed, and then the smile on Regina's face was snuffed out and she dropped whatever she was doing and withdrew to her room with the blackout curtains. Princess Helena, never wanting to be outdone, collapsed on the sofa just as Mr Tausendgeld came in with a cup of tea. *Mein Gott, ich halte es mit dieser einfältigen Person nicht mehr aus*, said Princess Helena in a German that was intended for polite company but sounded coarse and awkward in a room where there was no one to listen but Mr Tausendgeld, who of course only spoke Yiddish.

The last time he met the bottle boy, he was wearing Master Hinzel's suit for the first time, and he had put the leftover bread in jacket pockets that felt far too deep and big for the scant pickings Mrs Koszmar claimed she could spare.

It was the day the fire in the timber-processing factory in Wolborska Street broke out, and almost sent the whole ghetto up in flames; and Staszek had told Master Hinzel to make the pockets extra roomy because all his Hanukkah money would have to fit in there.

(He said things like that because he knew it amused people.)

He and the bottle boy had arranged to meet as usual in the yard by the tannery. There was a little hole in the brick wall, where Staszek left the food if the boy did not turn up for any reason. When he got there that day, the bottle boy was not there, but someone had taken out the brick he always slotted into the hole and left it on the ground. Had the bottle boy been there, seen that the hiding place was empty and gone away again? Or was it a *signal*?

Although he now knew danger to be lurking, Staszek could not resist going up to the wall. Just as he bent down for the brick, an arm was flung round his throat and a fist forced him to his knees. The panting behind him proved to be coming from a man with rotten black teeth and his cap pulled right down over his forehead, almost concealing his eyes. Other men appeared, ripping and wrenching at his clothes, emptying the pockets of anything edible. He held up his open hands to protect his face, but between his fingers, all he could see was the bottle boy, standing terrified beneath a sky that had meanwhile grown huge and unnaturally red.

Thus treachery, too, assumed a tangible form.

But the worst part had been going back with his new suit in tatters and all its generous pockets torn out: a crowned king, cast into the gutter.

Mrs Rumkowska assembled all the proof. The drawings and pictures he had been so careful to hide were now laid out for the Praeses to see. Regina also gave the Chairman back the pencils and sketchpad, and said anybody who sat drawing Germans in his spare time undoubtedly had nothing against taking orders from *them*. Not only from Gertler, who in her view had shown an *unhealthy* interest in the boy, but also from all those in Gertler's pay: Miller and Kligier and Reingold. They had seen that the boy was the Praeses' *weak spot*, and by corrupting the boy they had tried to get at *him*.

This all tumbled out of her so fast that she hardly paused for breath, and the Chairman leafed quickly through the sketchpad, stopping at one picture which he showed to Staszek:

What's this? he demanded.

It was a picture of a boy bearing a square, wooden cross on his shoulders It looked like the control bar for working a puppet, though this one was resting on his shoulders and the strings were dangling down, and hung with lots of little bottles and jars. It was the bottle boy. But he could not tell the Chairman that, of course. Nor could he say that the bottle boy had claimed he, too, was the Chairman's son. For a moment he toyed with the idea of saying it was the *other* Staszek, but in the end he just said he had been trying to draw his tailor's dummy. The Chairman saw through this lie at once:

You impudent wretch, was all he said, and then he bundled him into the other room, not even bothering to close the door behind him before removing the belt from his trousers, and started to beat Staszek before he had even bent over the back of the armchair.

And the Chairman's beating went on and on, as it usually did; and Staszek cried out and tried to twist aside. After a while he grabbed the punishing hand of the Praeses and stroked it across his tearful face, as he knew the Chairman wanted him to. With no belt to hold them in place, the Chairman's trousers had slipped down, and Staszek could see his male organ swelling and stiffening in his underpants, and when the Chairman put the boy's hand to it, he raised the engorged, red head of the penis to his face instead, and started rubbing his hand up and down it as the Chairman had taught him.

Turning round, he saw Regina standing by the half-open door, looking at them. In the cloudy, brown light from the little enclosed courtyard, her face was pale and puffy, and it was impossible to make out her features. She said nothing, just stood there brushing the side of her face with one hand, as if there was something sticky or itchy on it that she could not wipe away. The next instant, she was gone.

He was kept in for a whole week, tied up in the room, which was like a gigantic asphyxiation.

At night, birds fell from the yard and dragged their dry, outstretched wings across his face. In the mornings, Mrs Rumkowska came in to check that his arms and legs were still firmly lashed. He cried out, shouting that his mouth was full of blood and feathers, but she did not hear, just bent towards him slightly and said it was all for his own good. Then she left him, locking the door behind her, and all that was left were the dreadful birds, whose shadows crawled like insects across the lead-grey walls.

It was not until near evening that the light in the enclosed yard had dimmed enough for the reflections of the fire at the timber processing factory to bring the room out of its suffocating shadow again. At that point, Mrs Koszmar came in with a tray with some food on it, lamented extravagantly at seeing *the young master in such a state*, and loosened his wrist bonds a little, so he was at least able to eat.

It had been a 'deceptive' fire, they said later.

The two policemen who had been on fire-watching duty that night did not notice anything, although they passed the former hospital building several times when it was already in flames. Its grounds were covered in a thin layer of snow with a frozen crust; the piles of timber outside the entrance also had snow on them. The policemen had seen the film of snow on top of the platform of timber slowly receding, and heard melt-water dripping and running as if 'spring had come in the depths of winter'. Only then had they looked up and seen the smoke, which was escaping 'in great volume' from cracks in the hospital's now bricked-up windows. One of the policemen got hold of an axe, and they smashed the lock and the two iron bars across the front entrance, and as if of their own volition, the double doors burst open and the liberated sea of fire swept over them.

The fire in the factory raged for twenty-four hours. During that time, there was a constant stream of people in and out of the Chairman's flat, bringing reports and receiving new instructions.

Staszek lay there with his ear to the wall, listening to Commander Kaufman issuing orders to his firemen. Kaufman also spoke on the telephone to his 'Polish' colleagues in Litzmannstadt. He reported to them that adjoining houses and outbuildings had also caught fire, among them a timber store, and that it would be impossible for them to put out the fire if they were not given access to a hydrant twenty-five metres beyond the ghetto boundary, on *Aryan territory*. Could such a request possibly be granted and an order issued?

Half an hour later, the answer came. Kaufman's request had been granted.

And once another half-hour had passed, the wooden barriers and barbed-wire fences along Wolborska Street were pulled down, and very soon afterwards a massive gasp ran through the hundred or so *dygnitarzy* who had gathered in the Chairman's flat:

The Germans are helping put out the fire . . . !

Staszek could see in his mind's eye the German firemen setting about burning doors with crowbars and fire axes, and leading whole armies of other firemen in under beams that were collapsing in on them in showers of sparks. For the first time in nearly four years, the ghetto borders were open and German, Polish and Jewish firemen were fighting side by side.

The cause of the fire was eventually established:

When the hospital was converted after the September operation into a timber-processing plant and furniture factory, it did not occur to anybody that the patients' lift could not be used for goods and materials without installing a heavier duty electrical system. The overloading damaged a cable, generating the spark that ignited the whole factory.

From there, the fire spread to a warehouse where 3,500 brand new children's cots were awaiting transport to the Reich. The fire chief of Litzmannstadt later acknowledged that without the Jewish firemen's resourceful intervention, not only the tumbledown wooden settlements of the ghetto but also vital civil and military installations in his city centre, worth millions of marks, would have gone up in flames. At a ceremony at the House of Culture two months later, those firemen who survived were awarded a specially embossed outstanding service medal showing the Chairman's profile superimposed on a stylised image of the tallest wooden bridge, and in the speech that followed, the Chairman made sure to highlight each individual fireman's contribution in saving the ghetto and ensuring its future:

The Lord God of Israel constantly visits new trials upon His People. There are some who survive the trials they face, and there are those who perish . . . Thus shall all Jews in the ghetto be tested; and those who are found worthy shall be there on the day the temple of Jerusalem rises once more from the ruins . . . !

Staszek liked being with the men who gathered at the Chairman's home for the Jewish festivals. Men like Jakubowicz, Reingold, Kligier and Miller. He liked their decisiveness and gravity, their muted hums and haws and reserved tone behind other people's backs. Above all he liked Moshe Karo, the man who was said to have rescued him that time the transports of children and 'mad' mothers had arrived from Brzeziny and Pabianice, and the Germans had threatened to take them all away and shoot them.

One day, just a couple of months before his bar mitzvah, Moshe Karo took him along to the old Talmud school in Jakuba Street where the holy books were kept. Mr Karo was handed a bunch of keys by Rozenblat's men, who guarded the place round the clock, and then he led Staszek up a narrow side corridor to a gallery on the second floor, with wood-panelled walls. A black velvet curtain concealed a tall door with an iron grille. Karo drew back the curtain and tried several keys in the door until he finally got it open. In the glare of a naked light bulb, shelves running along the walls of the room could be seen to contain long rows of Torah arks and prayer books. Some of the Torah scrolls were so badly burnt that they were impossible to open. Two of them, Karo told him, had come from the Altshtot synagogue in Wolborska Street; others from the so-called Vilker shul in Zachodnia, one of the oldest synagogues in Łódź, and a seat of learning to which students of the Talmud had come from all over Poland. The day before the hired arsonists came, the Germans had almost everything of value in that synagogue taken down and carried away – from menorahs and candelabras to reading desks. They also emptied the Torah arks. But the cantor of the synagogue realised what was going on, and was able to hide some of the most precious items under a stone shelf on the facade of the building. Then the books were transferred to the ghetto in strictest secrecy.

Moshe Karo was a calm, quiet man, who moved slowly and with great dignity. His face, too, had a fixed and unchangingly benevolent expression, with which he looked on all those to whom he spoke, and which Staszek imagined not to alter even when he was asleep. But from time to time, some inner agitation seemed to take possession of Karo. His eyes would glaze over and look inwards, and his voice, normally so gentle and conciliatory, would suddenly sound hard, anxious and admonitory:

In my misery and distress, I often think of our time here in the ghetto –

I think of all the holy places they have destroyed, the way they have made us eat treyf *and we have no longer been allowed to keep the Sabbath commandments. But there is one thing they cannot take from us – the teachings of the Talmud and the holy wisdom of the prophets.*

'If you do not stand fast in your faith, you will be found wanting . . .'

So says the Lord, and time and again he has shown the same severity towards his people, punishing them for not following his decrees; he has annihilated their cities and driven his people out into the wilderness.

But however great the tribulations he has made us endure, some remnant has still been left, to build the walls of Jerusalem anew, and faith has been that remnant. The prophet Isaiah knew this. That was why he baptised his son Shear-Jashub, the one who will return. Our dearly beloved Praeses knows this, too. He, the humblest of all, knows what it is to be called upon as a tool.

That is why he has decided all that remains of power shall be transferred to you, and you shall be that remnant.

So your name shall be Shub, he who returns, whom nothing and nobody can destroy, he who will survive us all –

Staszek pondered what Moshe Karo had said. He pondered most of all of what Moshe Karo had said about the Chairman being merely a tool, and though he had no paper or pencil to hand, he drew himself sitting on a tall throne with his father crawling helplessly at his feet. And the sight of his powerful father in this submissive state gave him a feeling of such deep satisfaction that he was oblivious to everything else until Moshe Karo – once more an ordinary, modest man, shutting and locking the door with the iron grille and pulling the curtain back over the holy books he had been instructed to show – said in his normal voice that he had to hand the keys back to the police guards.

*

Then it happened, of course, the thing everyone knew would happen and absolutely anybody could have predicted. The Chairman, too, was taken away to Litzmannstadt by the authorities.

When Regina heard the news, she stood stock still, as if everything around her, including the air she breathed, had suddenly turned to glass.

The Chairman asked me to tell you particularly that there is no need to worry about him, said Miller, who had been driven all the way from the Secretariat to their new home in Łagiewnicka Street to deliver the message. *It's not like what happened to Gertler. The authorities only want to interview him about the distribution of food.*

But Staszek could clearly see how Regina started at the words: *It's not like what happened to Gertler.*

*

Most of the Chairman's various heads were to do with the exercising of his authority. These heads had staring eyes and the skin under his cheeks and sagging chin was as rigid and unmoving as if it were made of plaster. But there were also heads that were as round as moons, with slanting little slits for eyes and a mouth that was open, smiling craftily as if there were someone sitting inside it ready to jump out and strike the speaker, the minute that person said anything the Chairman did not want to hear.

The Chairman's smiles were like his hands: the smiles were tools with which he told people what to do.

Unless, that is, he was smiling just to make a show of being pleased. Then he would slap his knees emphatically and twist the upper part of his body into sudden contortions. At such moments, that *look* of his was always there – the complicit look, from the kindly and ingratiating head Staszek had learnt to fear more than anything else.

Only twice had Staszek seen the Chairman entirely headless.

The first time was when the Chairman was in his cage, looking at Staszek as if he wanted him to come and unlock the door. The second time was when the Germans came to take Gertler away. That day, by mistake, Staszek went over to the other side of the landing, to the room the Chairman used as his home office. There he saw the Chairman lying on his back on the sofa with his mouth open and his knees drawn up to his chest like a child. His face had been so rigid and immobile in sleep that Staszek had been sure the body and face could no longer be those of a living person. Not that he thought the Chairman was really dead, but this is what he would look like when he was.

That was why Staszek was now moving among the serious men who had gathered in his flat as soon as the Chairman was arrested, crying:

My father Praeses, is he dead now?
My father Praeses, is he dead now?

In all the Chairman's rooms, small groups of people stood repeating in low, whispering voices the soothing message Doctor Miller had brought. That the authorities only wanted to know how the food distribution was going; that there would definitely be no question of further deportations. So it took quite some time for the assembled dignitaries to become aware of the child wandering among the adults, screaming improprieties.

Mrs Rumkowska swiftly grabbed him by the arm and hauled him into the Room –

Staszek resisted with all his strength.

I want my father Praeses back, he screamed.

He was no longer 'himself'. All there was left of him was this one, utterly unbridled wish:

I want my father Praeses back, he screamed, over and over again.

Meanwhile, negotiations were in progress in the bright, open room. They were already discussing who could possibly be appointed the old man's Successor.

With the help of Mrs Koszmar, Regina tore off a piece of sheeting, which she twisted into a firm, hard rope, and together they forced it into his mouth to make him stop screaming. It was the second time Staszek had been restrained. But this time he could not move any part of his body. Not even his mouth. His tongue was like a suffocating ball in his gullet, which he had to struggle not to swallow and continually gagged on.

But the scream was there inside him, even so.

And the source of the scream was this terrible state of being someone yet no longer existing.

He saw himself lying in the bottom of a wardrobe alongside a head that was not his yet still somehow belonged to him.

And somewhere nearby, the Chairman was gathering up his scattered body parts and advancing towards him through the darkness, and the leather apron he had round his waist was bloodied by all the body parts he had been forced to cut off to get all the way there: to his only, most beloved Son.

The Chairman was gone all that day and half the next. It was half past ten the next morning before Miss Estera Daum telephoned from down at the Secretariat to say that he, the Most High, had been seen returning unharmed. He had come from the city on the 'Aryan' tram that passed through Bałuty every day, still in the suit and overcoat he had been wearing when the Gestapo came for him. His first action on resuming his duties was to lock himself in his office, Miss Daum reported, and he was still sitting in there now, having called in his closest associates one by one.

In his darkness, Staszek imagined himself lying with his back to a wall.

The wall reminded him of the brick wall outside the tannery in the yard, but without any loose bricks you could pull out. He was lying with his back pressed against the cold, hard surface of the wall, and standing there in front of him in the gloom was the boy with the cross of wood, with all the bottles and jars of medicines and tinctures dangling from it on lengths of rope and string.

As when a marionette's strings become entangled, they began mournfully knocking and rattling and chinking against each other. It was like the sound of water, if there could have been water running there; or like the sound of hooves and carriage wheels way off along a cobbled street. The women the bottle boy was telling him about were lying along the side of the road, or in the inner courtyards: some still hugging their children protectively; others with their legs parted wide, like animal carcasses, and nobody took any notice of the way they were lying or what they looked like, just took the dead bodies and swung them up onto the back of the lorries like sacks of flour.

There is such sorrow in the bottle boy's thin voice as he says all this that Staszek starts crying, too. He is not crying for the bottle boy or for his dead mother or for all the other dead people; he is crying for himself. He is crying because he is lying with his face to a wall. And because that wall is dividing him from what he once was, and because the wall is so high that nothing can be seen, nothing can be heard from the other side of it; nothing but the empty bottles clattering and jingling every time the insignificant body given the task of carrying them gets up and falls again, gets up and falls; and Moshe Karo's voice intones the Lord's promise to the Diaspora as it was spoken of by the prophet Ezekiel, the text he himself will read at his bar mitzvah:

Neither shall they defile themselves any more with their idols, nor with their detestable things, nor with any of their transgressions; but I will save them out of all their dwelling places, wherein they have sinned, and will cleanse them, so shall they be my people, and I will be their God.

He must have fallen asleep, because the next moment the clatter of the bottles has evaporated and the smell of tobacco smoke hangs heavy in the air. A faint streak of light has found its way into the room. Without turning round, he knows the Chairman is in the room and has presumably been there for some time. Like so many times before, he is wearing his crafty, observing head, and Staszek sees this and starts to cry again. Crafty as he is, the Chairman chooses to misunderstand. The bed springs give a little as the Chairman sits down and cups Staszek's chin in his hand so carefully that you might have thought he was handling the most precious jewel.

Don't be sad, boy. I've brought some food for you.

Look at this lovely food.

Paper rustles as the parcel is unwrapped. Soon the Chairman's teat-like fingers will be pushing their way into his mouth with the first bits of bread. He swallows quickly to quell the spasm of nausea washing over him.

I've been talking to Moshe Karo.

He says you are making real progress.

I'm proud of you.

The Chairman smears big dabs of slightly rancid butter over Staszek's lips and follows them with bread, candied peaches, jam. The boy is crying tears of loathing and disgust, but he sucks and licks and swallows obediently. Thickly whipped cream, too. The Chairman has a whole handful of it, and presses it to his mouth for him to lick off.

On the first Sabbath after Hanukkah, we shall celebrate your bar mitzvah.

The Chairman is now lying down on the bed, with his sticky hands round Staszek's chest and waist. They feel their way down his backbone, applying and rubbing the viscous butter in long strokes between his thighs, to the constant accompaniment of thick, panting breaths, like a piece of heavy machinery working away behind him; and then he has two buttery fingers stuck up his anus, and two even more slippery fingers stroking and massaging between his testicles and the base of his penis, and despite the pain and the shame he cannot help going hard, and the sudden pain makes his whole body twist aside, but –

Don't be afraid, says the flat, damp voice against the back of his neck, Staszek suddenly enveloped in an rich haze of alcohol and old tobacco smoke –

I shall never let them take you from me.

You are everything to me.

Then there is an inarticulate grunting sound: as if the Chairman is crying to himself or even laughing. Or perhaps it is just the sound of air being expelled from his body. Or perhaps it is their two bodies, the friction between them; and with a kind of snorting exultation, the Chairman heaves his weight on top of him and clings there, and lets his big, heavy, grateful head glide down over Staszek's neck, the bones there, his shoulder blades, and with his swollen lips and great, wet tongue begins to suck and lick all the greasy, oily residue of what he had previously rubbed onto the skin. And bit by bit, thrust by thrust, Staszek's body is pressed harder against the wall. He is plastered there, like an insect somebody has killed: exactly like the mute impression left by his dead body. And now there is no wall any longer – no tears, no pain. Just a body with no head. And who can be afraid of a body with no head?

And the Chairman leans forward and slaps his knees, and begins his story:

There was a boy named Kindl who had the keys to all the houses in the whole city. Magic keys. There was no front door lock that Kindl's keys couldn't pick. His keys fitted the mayor's house up by the castle just as they fitted the rabbi's simple abode behind the synagogue. And he had access to the miller's store of sacks of flour, and all the rich merchants' dwellings down in the city, too. He could go in and take whatever he wanted, but he was not the sort of boy to take from other people.

He could enter human hearts, as well. He was often frightened by what he saw when he opened the door to a person's heart. There was so much evil, deceit and envy. (But when he turned the key in the lock of his mother's heart, all he saw was that she loved him . . . !)

Kindl went about the city as he usually did, opening doors with his keys. People were used to him coming, and would often leave food out for him. Many people in the city took it as a good omen if Kindl visited their homes. Doors are not for keeping shut and bolted. They are there for people to come and go through. Why else would there be doors?

Many people in the city were very fond of Kindl.

Then one day, he came to a house he had not seen before. A great mansion, many storeys high, with towers and pinnacles. The front door must have been at least three metres tall, and small and insignificant as he was, Kindl found it hard to reach up to the keyhole with his key.

But the key did fit, and with some effort he got the door open.

Behind the door, however, there was nothing but a great, desolate darkness and a mighty voice saying: Do not be afraid, Kindl, come in!

But Kindl was afraid. The darkness behind the great door was like no darkness he had ever seen before. It was like a night sky without stars. It was vast and cold. There was not even any wind blowing through all that darkness; everything that fell into it was swallowed up as if it had never existed.

For the first time in his life, Kindl dared not enter. He closed the door he had just opened and went home and lay on his bed, and lay there sick for many days and nights, while his mother sat at his side and prayed to the Lord to spare his young life.

When Kindl had recovered, many weeks later, he noticed something strange. None of his keys fitted any of the houses any more. Not the mayor's residence, not the rabbi's room; not the miller's house or the merchant's: nowhere were his keys able to pick the locks. He realised there was only one thing to do. To go back to the great mansion and not be scared, but accept the voice's invitation to enter.

Once again, Kindl faced the grand door, and found that his key still fitted. It was as if no time had passed.

Again he faced the great darkness, and from the darkness came the same mighty voice as before, saying: Do not be afraid, Kindl, come in!

And Kindl plucked up his courage and stepped into the vast, black darkness.

And he was not blinded, as he had feared he would be. Nor was he swallowed up by the vastness and blackness and darkness, as he had thought he would be. He did not even fall, but floated there in the dark as if supported by a great, safe hand. And he understood that the mighty voice that had spoken to him from the darkness was the voice of the Lord God, and that God had only wanted to test him. From that day on, Kindl was at home wherever he went in the world. And he did not need to be afraid of anything, for he knew that whichever way he moved in the darkness, God would be there to lead him on the right path.

Five days after the eighth and final day of Hanukkah, the Chairman of the ghetto held bar mitzvah for his adopted son, Stanisław Rumkowski. The ceremony took place in the former preventorium at 55 Łagiewnicka Street, where Moshe Karo used to hold his *minyens*, and where rumour had it that the Chairman had met the Hasidic Jews. Moshe Karo walked at the head of a little procession, carrying the Sefer Torah scroll from the locked gallery at the Talmud Torah School in Jakuba Street right through the ghetto; and he carried the Torah scroll openly, fearing neither informers nor unbribable Kripo men.

It was a cold and frosty winter's day. The smoke rose as straight as an arrow from chimney stacks to a sky that neither received nor turned away anything.

In addition to close members of the family, thirty of the ghetto's *honoratiores* were invited; apart from people close to the Chairman such as Miss Dora Fuchs, who ran the General Secretariat, and her brother Bernhard, the guests included Mr Aron Jakubowicz, head of the Central Labour Office, Judge Stanisław-Szaja Jakobson, Mr Izrael Tabaksblat and, of course, Moshe Karo, whose resourceful action had once saved the young boy's life, and who was perhaps more of a father to him than the Chairman had ever been – though naturally such a thing could not be said on a day like this. As a sign of the special affinity between them, however, it was Moshe Karo who had given the boy the gift of the prayer shawl he was now wearing for the first time as he sat waiting on the podium.

Then the Torah scroll was brought in, and since there was no rabbi to officiate at the ceremony, it also fell to Moshe Karo to go round with it to the whole assembly, so each and every one of them could kiss the tassels of their prayer shawl and touch the scroll. A warm and intimate atmosphere spread among those assembled in the chill hall, an atmosphere further emphasised by Mr Tobaksblat reading the day's text from the Torah. According to the calendar, the reading from the Prophets for that day was taken from Ezekiel, and young Rumkowski read in a clear, distinct voice the text he had been taught to read.

For thus saieth the Lord:

Behold, I will take the children of Israel from among the heathen, whither they be gone, and will gather them on every side, and bring them into their own land.

And I will make them one nation in the land upon the mountains of Israel; and one king shall be king to them all; and they shall be no more two nations, neither shall they be divided into two kingdoms any more at all.

Neither shall they defile themselves any more with their idols, nor with their detestable things, nor with any of their transgressions; but I will save them out of all their dwelling places, wherein they have sinned, and will cleanse them, so shall they be my people, and I will be their God.

Staszek faltered only once. That was when the ceremony called on him to turn to his parents and thank them for making it possible for him to receive the knowledge with which he could now be taken into the congregation. The Chairman was sitting with his wife, brother and sister-in-law right at the front by the improvised reading desk, with his head bent forward and his legs crossed, as if the impatience he felt had merely made him sink more deeply into himself.

Staszek looked at him and the words stuck in his throat. Then Moshe Karo stepped forward and said them for him to repeat. The prompt came in a swift, fervent whisper, and nobody seemed to notice anything. Regina just sat there with the big smile she now wore day and night, and beside her sat Princess Helena, who had now arisen from her 'bed of pain' to – as the *Chronicle* reported at about that time – resume charge of all the soup kitchens in the ghetto. Her replacement, a woman who remained unnamed, had had to step down for what were termed 'political reasons'.

Up at the desk, the holy words died away and the congregation started to leave, stepping from the holy space to find themselves beneath the vaulted white sky which resembled a vast hole into which all the light was gushing. It was just a few hundred metres from the preventorium to the Chairman's new apartment, where a 'spartan' reception was held, with bread and wine and a vast array of presents.

*

The photograph was taken by Mendel Grossman. Mendel was one of a group of five or six photographers employed by the ghetto's Office of Archival and Population Statistics. He was the one, for example, who took the photographs for the workbooks that from the summer of 1943 onwards the ghetto residents were obliged to carry with them wherever they went. This picture is no different from those in the way it is posed, lit or taken, with a sort of delayed exposure that makes the people in the picture appear to be stepping out of their own movements, as others might step out of their clothes.

Regina Rumkowska, all dressed up inside her wide but anxious smile, as if she is standing behind a cracked or broken pane of glass, trying desperately to convey her goodwill to someone on the other side;

Chaim Rumkowski, on his way forward or into the centre of the picture, one hand clumsily outstretched in something that might be a blessing or a gesture of reconciliation;

And *Stanisław Rumkowski*, the son: wearing a yarmulke and the prayer shawl that was a present from Moshe Karo, and holding a candle in one hand.

The only thing is, it isn't a candle (as we can see now) but a bird, struggling free of his fingers and taking to the wing, vanishing up out of the picture so swiftly that the camera cannot keep up. And behind the three of them, in what in a photographer's studio would have been a painted backdrop or possibly a piece of artistically draped fabric, we can make out something like a ribcage or the colonnade of a collapsing palace, row after row – the bars of the cage that is holding them all captive.

III

The Last City
(September 1942–August 1944)

There was a stage. On the stage, a ghetto. There was even barbed wire round the stage, to show where the ghetto started and where it finished. An actor picked his way around the pieces of scenery, lifting up the wire to demonstrate, pointing. '*Here's the wire. Don't try to get past it or you'll be in trouble. Don't try to take it with you, either, or you'll be in even worse trouble . . . !* And the audience in the House of Culture hooted with laughter. Regina Rumkowska had never seen an audience laugh so much as when it was shown its own little world by a collection of third-rate revue artistes. Then figures were lowered from wires up at ceiling level; simple figures of card, with backs of thicker cardboard. She recognised every one of them, though their faces were so crudely drawn that you could scarcely tell one from another. Here came the Chairman in his carriage; here was Rozenblat, Chief of Police, on patrol and wielding his baton; and here came Wiktor Miller, *der gerekhter*, with his white doctor's coat flapping around his wooden leg, and here was Judge Jakobson, a nodding puppet, sitting in his courtroom swinging his club up and down as ranks of thieves and criminals paraded past the bar.

But above them all hung a single Face. The face was smooth shaven; it had sleek, dark, pomaded hair and a smile as frank and open as a child's. And on the stage below, a choir assembled, and one actor after another ran on stage; they linked arms and began to sing:

Gertler der nayer keyser
Er iz a yid a heyser

Er zugt indz tsi tsi geybn
Men zol es nor derleybn
Poylen bay dem yeke
*Men zol efenen di geto**

Gertler . . . ?! Of course the song was not about Gertler! Regina could scarcely imagine what had made her entertain such an irreverent thought. It was her husband who was the Praeses of the ghetto, and of course it was to him the actors on the stage were paying their satirical tribute. And yet Regina knew she was far from alone in the audience when she mentally exchanged the mask of the old man's sagging face for the younger police chief's considerably more handsome portrait, visible on a cardboard placard in the background.

Chaim Rumkowski was a steward, who made people feel secure despite their hunger and degradation. But there was something else about Dawid Gertler. It was something almost magical. He moved so easily, was so relaxed when he talked to people. And then of course there were his outstandingly good relations with the German authorities. He was said to have Biebow literally eating out of his hand! That alone was enough to make people believe Gertler was part of another world entirely.

At the party after the performance, she saw him standing in the middle of the group of admiring men he always had around him, explaining that the Germans were human beings, too: *Yes, the day the Jews learn to treat the Germans like human beings, we will have come a long way,* he said, prompting gales of laughter. Men bent double; they slapped their thighs; they laughed so much they nearly choked.

She remembers thinking:

* Gertler is our new emperor | He is a Jew and a hot one | He says we should give way | We must just live through it | If Poland endures the Germans | The ghetto will be opened.

Only a man who feels no fear can talk like that.

But these were days when fear was everything. Fear numbed your limbs and made the breath halt in your throat. Fear made people don their expressions carefully every morning and anxiously follow everything that was going on behind their backs. Fear made those men and women sitting in the audience laugh so wildly at the caricatures the revue artistes portrayed that their laughter bordered on hysteria. Finally they had a chance to move out of their wretched bodies and faces. And afterwards they all talked so loudly and affectedly to each other that only the voices could be heard, not a single word of what anyone said, assuming anything was said at all.

Everybody was talking. Except for Gertler.

He stood quietly outside the circle of light and was the only one who knew where the secret exits from the ghetto were, and her longing to go through them with him was so great that it felt as though her heart would burst with pain.

*

There was not much to say about Chaim's relationship with Dawid Gertler:

At first, he mistrusted him. Then he came to rely on him. Ultimately, he learnt to fear and hate him.

Before the mistrust turned to hatred, however, Gertler had been a frequent guest in their home. He would present himself at any conceivable time of day or night for long, confidential talks with his Chairman. He had also been known to turn up just to speak to her. *I've heard you have not been in the best of health recently, Mrs Rumkowska*, he might say, sitting with her hand in his and staring deeply and earnestly into her eyes.

Naturally she knew he was just putting on an act:

If Gertler came to visit when the Chairman was not at home, it was because he needed to find out something that the

347

Chairman would not or could not tell him.

Regina could not stop herself confiding in him, even so. Once she even let slip *the worst thing of all*. She intimated to him in various ways that Chaim was unhappy with her for not getting pregnant. Then Gertler had looked at her with his big eyes, and asked what made her so sure a child would be the right and only solution for her. 'In times like these, children can actually be a burden,' he said, and then, apparently casually, started talking about some of his confidants in the German ghetto administration.

He often spoke of German figures of authority in that way, preferably with some kind of concrete qualifier to highlight the nature of his relationship with them, like *old* Josef Hämmerle or *my good friend* SS-Hauptscharführer Fuchs, and he asked what made her think these high-ranking individuals treated all Jews the same. They had eyes to see with as well, didn't they? Only last week he had been sought out by Biebow's right-hand man, that stripling Schwind, who wanted to hear about the two engineers Dawidowicz and Wertheim who had so successfully repaired the X-ray equipment in the ghetto. 'In Hamburg they are crying out for competent X-ray technicians at this very moment,' Schwind had informed him, 'and it might be possible to get a ticket for them'. 'To Hamburg?' Regina asked. And Gertler: 'Not even the *master race* can master *everything*; and to acquire the knowledge they need, I know there are one or two Nazis willing to bend the odd rule.' There's a *list*, he confided to her on a later occasion; an *unofficial* list circulating among the authorities in Litzmannstadt, with the names of the *very few* Jews the German administrative staff considered *absolutely indispensable*. But for your name to be added to that list, you first had to make it plain to the authorities that you were *available*; that you would be willing to place yourself *at their disposal* at any time. And: 'Is Chaim on that list?' she couldn't help asking, only to see him shake his head with a regretful smile: 'No, unfortunately not, Chaim isn't on the list; to be honest with you, they view him as a touch *simple*, and he's far too closely linked to the ghetto.' But on the other hand, there were people, people like her for example, who could very well end up there, with the right preconditions; he could see very clearly that Mrs Rumkowska, unlike certain other people, was a woman of a certain rank and stature.

It only dawned on her much later that this was how the Devil had chosen to speak to her. In a place like the ghetto, where everything else stank of excrement and refuse, the Devil was well dressed and sweet-smelling. She confided in him that for her, the ghetto was not the walls that surrounded her, the ghetto was not the wires, the ghetto was not the curfew, the hunger or the sickness, but something in her, like a bone caught in her throat: a slow suffocation; and that she had got to get away from what was starving her of air, or she would not be able to live much longer. And the Devil leant towards her and took her hand in his and said:

'Be calm and patient, Regina.

If there's no other way, I shall buy your freedom.'

In September 1942, the authorities announced their curfew, *di geshpere*, or just *di shpere* as it came to be known. The curfew lasted for seven days, and while it was in force, the upper echelons of the ghetto's ruling elite were ordered to remain in their summer residences and on no account to come into the centre of the ghetto.

From the kitchen window under the lilacs – their flowers now over – in Miarki Street, Regina could see long columns of open army vehicles moving in. They carried German soldiers in heavy gear, sitting with the barrels of their rifles between their knees, their faces under their helmets bored or childishly grinning.

The Schupo had set up a roadblock at the entrance to Miarki Street. She was not quite sure if it was to stop those confined up here from getting out, or those down there from getting in. There were occasional concerted bursts of gunfire from down on the big, open field on the other side of Próżna Street.

More convoys of SS troop vehicles were coming along the road all the time. But there was no sign of the children everyone had been talking about.

The days that followed were chaotic.

Everyone wanted to see the Chairman, but the Chairman claimed he was indisposed, locked himself in the bedroom upstairs and refused to see anyone.

They banged on the door. They called through the keyhole. Miss Dora Fuchs even went down on her knees in front of it and loudly listed all the people who wanted to see him. It's a matter of life and death, the ghetto's very survival, you simply can't abandon us now! Regina was urged forward to the door. She was his wife, after all. For Benji's sake, she said. But where her brother's name would previously have unleashed a hail of oaths, this time there was no sound from inside the room. *Is our Praeses actually in there at all?* Helena Rumkowska asked disingenuously. Józef Rumkowski suggested they should just break the door down. But everyone else was against that. Mr Abramowicz said they must exercise restraint. The Praeses had simply retired to gather his thoughts at this crucial juncture. He would be out soon enough.

Eventually, even Gertler came, neatly dressed as always in a suit and tie, but he had some kind of smear (was it blood or dirt?) on his face and the back of his hand, and a putrid, slightly sickly smell, like chemicals or burnt oil, hung about his clothes.

He arrived in the company of Shlomo Frysk, head of the voluntary fire service in Marysin, and Isaiah Dawidowicz, police commander for District No. IV. They had two police officers with them, carrying a huge platter covered with a white linen cloth, and the five of them staggered up the stairs with the platter between them to the Chairman's room, where Mr Gertler knocked and then announced solemnly to the closed door:

You've no idea what luck you are in, Chaim; my wife has just taken some baked apples out of the oven for you – with sugar and cinnamon!

Then they went down to the kitchen and started tucking in themselves. Gertler's men were in a strange mood altogether. They were boisterous, and laughed all the time, as if to avoid looking at or speaking to each other. But the minute Gertler made the slightest movement, they all fell silent, as if waiting for precise orders.

Gertler seemed to be taking it all very calmly. He repeated the authorities' assurance that the exclusive aim of the operation was to clear the ghetto of elements unfit for work. No one whose papers are in order will have anything to fear.

But my brother . . . ! objected Regina.

Others, too, wanted to know what had happened to the relatives they had been forced to leave behind inside the ghetto. Gertler raised a hand to ask for silence round the table. The authorities, he said, are naturally the first to regret that there has been violence. They naturally attribute the blame entirely to our own police forces, which were not able to carry out the task they had been given in time.

'What we would have needed at a time like this is someone to take a firm and resolute *grip* on the situation; a person with some sort of *Praeses temperament*', he added, with the most fleeting of smiles. As the Chairman chose not to be on the spot and shoulder his responsibility, he had himself in the meantime, along with Mr Jakubowicz and Mr Warszawski, set up a makeshift 'emergency committee' to raise funds to buy the freedom of *the hard core of intellectuals* considered indispensable to the continued existence of the ghetto, not all of whom had the liquid capital required. The committee had also, with the tacit support of Biebow and Fuchs, been able to set up a protected area which they were calling 'the enclosure', where the men and women to whom the amnesty applied could be brought to safety. 'And their elderly relations and children, too, of course,' he added.

'Where is this enclosure?' somebody asked.

'Opposite the hospital in Łagiewnicka Street.'

'Is it true what they say, that the patients have been taken from all the hospitals?'

But Gertler did not answer. He rested his bloodstained hands on the table and got slowly to his feet. *I insist on seeing my father; and my brother Benjamin*, said Regina. *I know they're still down there.*

'I'll give you a lift,' was all Gertler said.

He had, as it turned out, already arranged a means of conveyance. A delivery truck of some kind from Litzmannstadt, with big white mudguards, was parked outside with one of its front wheels in the ditch. The driver had a cap with a shiny leather peak, like a common delivery man, and his eyes took on a shifty look when he saw the yellow Stars of David on their chests. *They asked me at the guard post if I was a Volksdeutscher, I said yes, but really I'm a Pole*, he said, looking furtively at Gertler, who told him to stop talking crap.

Regina had never heard a Jew speak to a Pole or Aryan like that; but presumably the driver was just another of those people Gertler had 'bought'.

She sat beside the reluctant driver with Gertler on her right. Two men from the Sonder helped Dr Eliasberg up into the back. Eliasberg was coming with them because Gertler said there was an acute need for doctors in the zone. Then the driver engaged an angrily grinding gear, and reversed the truck fiercely up onto the rutted road.

She had not been in the centre of the ghetto since the curfew came into force. Then there had been a desperate crush in every street as people tried to get hold of enough food for more than a couple of days. Now it looked like a war zone. Front doors and courtyard gates stood open wide, and the worn and shiny cobblestones were littered with books and prayer shawls, and bed bases and bloody mattresses with protruding springs. She saw no German guards on duty; just remnants of barriers that had obviously been cleared aside in haste.

They got all the way to Łagiewnicka Street before they were stopped by a Schupo officer, who as the van approached had one of his guards step out into the street and hold up his hand. After a quick glance at Gertler, whose Star of David he could not fail to notice, he turned to the driver and asked to see their documents. The driver, his function only now apparent, handed paper after paper through the wound-down window. The guard stepped away to check the documents, then came back again and addressed a question to Gertler, who rattled off an answer in surprisingly authoritative German:

Der Passierschein ist vom Herrn Amtsleiter persönlich unterschrieben.

'With the Lord's help, you'll see that we have managed to save most of them,' he said to Regina in Yiddish, as the documents were returned to the driver by the guard, who for some unfathomable reason saluted as he let them through.

They drove slowly to the area Gertler had referred to as *optgesamt*, the enclosure. It consisted of a fenced-off forecourt surrounded by tenement blocks, some in such a poor state of repair that parts of their walls had collapsed; where no sheets or blankets had been hung over the holes to keep out the heat and the flies, you could see straight into the overcrowded flats, as if into a beehive. Flocking on the other side of the fence that ran along the street side were the former *Funktionsträger* of the ghetto: administrative staff from the social department and the ghetto *Arbeitsamt*; *kierownicy*; police and fire-service officials with their wives and children; surprisingly quiet and subdued, they were all clustering round the gates, looking at the devastation beyond them.

Opposite them was the hospital – or what had once *been* the hospital – which was being stripped of its contents before the eyes of the trapped Jewish functionaries.

Drip stands, examination couches, benches, medicine cabinets – anything that could be carried – were being taken out through the front entrance by soldiers whose evidently inebriated commanding officers went round pointing and issuing orders. Some of the big carts used by the White Guard for carrying flour and potatoes stood ready outside, and with

354

the help of what remained of the hospital staff, a company of Jewish labourers recruited for the purpose heaved the equipment into them. *Vorsicht bitte, Vorsicht . . . !* shouted one of the officers attempting to supervise the proceedings, though he was far from careful himself as he staggered around on the broken glass.

That pungent, nauseatingly oily smell Regina had been aware of on Gertler's clothes earlier was tangible in the air here; a burnt smell, like something chemical that has evaporated on heating. Maybe the stench was coming from the looted hospital opposite, or it could be some substance in the fire someone had lit in a pit over by one of the sets of cellar steps inside the enclosure. Around the smoke, billowing darkly into a sky so mercilessly blue it seemed almost colourless, bored and hungry children were milling, boys in jackets and knee-breeches, and girls in what were undoubtedly once-immaculate white dresses, with sashes at the waist, and big, stiff bows in their hair. In every available space there were towering piles and stacks of suitcases and travelling bags, and groups of adults were sitting or lying in the shade of these luggage mountains. Her father was sitting, or rather slumping, in an old deckchair, his face turned to the surging black smoke. Someone had taken pity on him and tied a handkerchief over his head to protect his bald pate from the sun. But his face was already sunburnt, and one hand – lying palm upwards on the armrest of his chair, had swollen to double its usual size.

He must have got his arm caught somewhere, her father told her, or perhaps somebody trod on it when they were loaded onto the lorries and trailers that awful morning, he couldn't remember. He could only recall that half a dozen shouting German soldiers had suddenly rushed into the ward. They came at dawn, long before the nurses started coming round to empty the bedpans. Some of the patients had tried to escape – those who could walk unaided – but they had been intercepted straight away by soldiers, or maybe Jewish *politsayen*, who were posted in every corridor. Then all the patients still in the wards, whether they could walk or stand or not, were bundled out of the front entrance and up onto the trailers.

That was all he could remember. Except that Chaim had come in the end. It had been such a relief when Aron Wajnberger finally caught sight of his son-in-law. *Chaim, Chaim . . . !* he had called out from the high trailer behind the tractor.

But Chaim Rumkowski had neither seen nor heard. Having negotiated briefly with one of the SS commanders present, he merely turned and vanished into the hospital building.

And Benji? Regina grabbed her father by the shoulders, almost shaking him.

But beneath his white kerchief, Aron Wajnberger still had eyes for no one but his son-in-law. *It was as if Chaim had become a stranger to us. It was as if he wasn't seeing us any longer. Can you explain it, Regina? How is it possible for him to stop seeing us . . . ?*

Gertler, meanwhile, had remained at the barrier across the entrance to the enclosure, exchanging jokes with the Jewish guards on duty there, but when two non-uniformed members of the German ghetto administration approached him, he was again obliged to 'step aside' for discussions. While Gertler was talking to the Germans, Regina grasped her father under the arms and tried to lift him. She asked the driver to help, since her father could not walk on his own, but the driver drew back nervously. He dared not do anything as long as the Germans were there.

Then Gertler came back. Once they were sitting in the car again, she asked if they could drive on to the hospital in Wesoła Street. Gertler shook his head; that would be impossible. The whole area was shut off.

But Benji, she implored.

He said he would make enquiries. There was bound to be

someone who knew where he had been taken. He would do his very best.

When they drove back to Miarki Street, she saw that the ladder Mr Tausendgeld had propped against the wall so he could peer into Chaim's window had been taken down; Mr Tausendgeld himself had returned to Józef and Helena's *działka* and was standing in the aviary with hundreds of winged creatures circling his outstretched right arm. And suddenly she saw how small and meaningless the world they inhabited out here in Marysin was: a doll's house world perched on the edge of an abyss. Chaim had descended from his self-imposed isolation and was sitting at the kitchen table, propped on his elbows. Opposite him sat a *ganef* about eleven years old, with cheeky little slits for eyes. The eyes fastened on her the minute she stepped over the threshold, and at the same instant the boy opened his mouth for the Chairman to shovel in another bit of the cinnamon-sprinkled, icing-sugar-dusted apple dish that Mrs Gertler had baked, which Chaim, to be on the safe side, had first also dipped into a bowl of fresh, whipped cream.

Regina hated that child from the very first moment, with a silent, dark, irrational hatred she would never acknowledge, still less understand or try to explain.

It was not for anything the child said or did. It was enough for it merely to exist. Something that *ought* to have been inside her was now outside, but it was no fruit she had borne, and from the first moment the child's gaze latched onto her face, it did not waver from her for a second. She could not bear to have anyone look at her that way. Suddenly, the smiling screen she always held up to others to avoid their intrusions was no help or protection at all.

But *who* was it he saw?

What was it he saw?

*

Once the state of emergency had been lifted, the authorities let them move from the former office space in the Central Hospital to some pretty basic rooms a few blocks further up Łagiewnicka Street. Opposite their new flat they had one of the few chemist's shops still operating in the ghetto, and the Chairman used it as a *dietka* for obtaining items like milk and eggs that were normally only available on prescription. The chemist also supplied the nitroglycerine tablets he said he took 'for my heart'.

For the first few months after the child came, he complained constantly of pains in his chest, and claimed the only thing that brought him any relief was being with the child, and then she would find herself lying awake for hours, listening to their

358

semi-stifled, whispering voices and Chaim's fake, high-spirited laughter.

People came and went in the new town apartment, as they had done in the old one in the now derelict hospital building. Dawid Gertler, too, continued to visit with his children and his wife. Even so, it was apparent that relations between the Chairman and his former protégé were not what they had once been. Gertler took every opportunity to point out it was entirely thanks to him they had been able to set up *optgesamt*; that in the regrettable absence of the Chairman, he had not only had to take charge of the tricky negotiations with the Gestapo, but had also had to pay *out of his own pocket* the sum required to buy the freedom of those whose names had not already been taken off the list:

There wasn't a single złoty of public money available.

Chaim had initially tried to defend himself by adopting a jocular tone: *Watch out for this man!* he would say, putting a paternally protective arm round Gertler's shoulders.

Gertler seemed on the surface to put up with these reprimands, but everyone knew that even if the Chairman had not chosen to be invisible during the days when *the ghetto was going through its worst ever crisis*, he would still never have been able to negotiate with the authorities. Only Gertler had that power. That was the way it had always been. What riposte did the Praeses of the ghetto ever have other than his never-ending, self-glorifying speeches?

But when the audience was over, Regina noted that the young chief of police had left two men from his own personal security force outside the front entrance of their new apartment. Two extra bodyguards in addition to the six the Praeses already had. From that point on, she knew that everything she or Chaim did would be reported straight to Gertler's central command, which in turn reported to the Gestapo in Limanowskiego Street. Though she did not like to admit it, this was of course also the reason for Gertler calling on her so often. The Chairman now had a guardian. That was the sole outcome of all his efforts to 'save the children' at any cost.

*

Only madmen believe in the possibility of dialogue with the authorities! Benji used to say when he was standing in the market place to address the crowd.

Death is no less of a death because it happens to be wearing uniform!

What wouldn't she have given to have her Benji back, even for a few hours.

In the afternoons, Gertler sometimes excused himself from his many urgent duties and came to take tea with her in what she and Chaim had agreed should be *her* room in the new apartment. And Mrs Koszmar served it in the real tea service, just as she had done in the good old days when they had 'real' parties.

And in fact, everything could have been real. If only it hadn't been for the child.

All the time she was chatting to Gertler, it would be prowling round the walls of the room.

She told Mrs Koszmar to give the child something to keep it occupied, but the boy was back after only a few minutes. She could hear his panting breath behind the back of her armchair, and saw him sitting there, squeezed into the cramped space between the seat and the floor. There, right under the seat of her armchair, he had tied both their shoes – hers and Gertler's – to the chair legs with a couple of short, hard lengths of rope.

The Queen can't walk!
The Queen can't walk!

he crowed, in a voice she took to be an imitation of Benji's. That was the way Benji had screeched at her when they were little: in a voice so shrill that it almost turned falsetto.

For a moment, her eyes saw black.

She could not remember if she had called Mrs Koszmar, or if Mrs Koszmar had come rushing into the room of her own accord. At any rate, a few moments later the child had been whisked away and Gertler was standing awkwardly in the hall, drumming his fingertips uneasily on the brim of his hat:

And as far as your brother is concerned, Mrs Rumkowska, rest assured I shall do my utmost to persuade the authorities to inform me where he could have been taken!

*

It was obvious to her, of course, that Chaim loved this child with a love that was not the sort a father usually feels for his child.

So what kind of love was it?

He would sometimes spend hours in the room he reserved for the two of them, and would sit or lie there stroking and feeding the child. But on other occasions the child constantly displeased him, and he would do nothing but scold and beat it. The strange thing was, the child seemed to adapt even to the Chairman's beatings. The child absorbed the Chairman's stern moods and constant suspicion of his character.

The child became the image of his father in every respect. When the Chairman was not there to pamper and spoil it, the mollycoddled child lay haughtily in its bed with the pictures it had drawn of its beloved father draped over its chest and stomach, whimpering *where's my Praeses, where's my Praeses?* until she was at her wits' end and wished she could go in and finish him off, once and for all.

But in the end the front door opened and the Chairman was back, and the two of them could lie there again, enveloped in their perverse love.

The two of them.

And she – rejected, excluded – longed only for someone who could take her away from it all.

*

But the child did have a life of its own.

However disgusting it might seem, there was an inner will there.

The drawings were proof of that.

When he was not lying there with them spread around his bed, he kept them in a little casket Chaim had given him, and was very secretive about them.

One day while he was having his lesson with Moshe Karo, she took the casket out of its hiding place under his bed and forced the lock with a screwdriver.

She thought it her right.

Inside she found not only paper, pencils and crayons but also a collection of little chemist's bottles with indeterminate contents, and several parcels wrapped in cloth or paper and tied up with coarse string. She opened the parcels. They contained a number of the crumbly little honey cakes Mrs Koszmar had served at their last party.

She ignored the glass bottles for a moment and stared at the drawings. One of them showed Chaim with three hairy growths sticking out of his body in place of arms and legs. He had a face like a swollen red pumpkin, and was lent a distinctly feminine air by the long hair that reached right down to his waist. Beside this Chairman figure was a picture of her, with her queen's crown on her head, but surrounded by a sea of licking red flames.

At that instant it dawned on her that the glass bottles must contain poison, and the little honey cakes must be poisoned ones that the child intended to put back on the table when no one was looking. The drawing of her head wreathed in flames must be a picture of her burning in Gehenna.

That was it, of course. That was the secret.

The child planned to kill them all.

But where had he got the poison?

She showed Chaim her evidence. But Chaim looked from the chemist's bottles to the pictures and could see no connection.

What have I always said? A gifted child.
Maybe our son has a real artist inside him?

It was the Sabbath. She had lit the candles and read the blessings over the two loaves, and the child sat at their table with his gaze fixed on hers as usual.

Chaim read the prayer of thanks and the song of praise to the woman and then, with particular feeling, *Ye'simcha Elokim ke-Ephraim ve'chi-Menash*, adding in the pompous, didactic tone he always adopted when addressing the Child: . . . *as Jacob when he lay dying once told his sons Ephraim and Manasseh that they were to set an example for all Jews, so you too will grow and make sure you become an example to all Jews here in the ghetto . . .*

It struck her that Chaim had never spoken to her in anything other than this lofty, high-flown, apocalyptic tone. Even the Sabbath – the only real, only *living* moment they had together – had been turned into a stage for artificiality and death.

Here they sat behind their Faces, and Chaim was the Chairman and told the Wife he had heard rumours *that the Germans had been forced into a major retreat on the Eastern Front, and that if the Highest Lord willed it, there could be Peace by springtime*; and the Child was Evil itself, tossing Scheming Looks from the Wife to the Father; and the Father smiled and said he could remember lying there in his bedroom in Karola

363

Miarki Street, agonising over all the children he had been forced to send away from the ghetto, but at that very moment, an Angel sent by the Highest Lord Himself had come to his chamber and told him – *yes, the Angel of the Lord had told him, Mordechai Chaim Rumkowski, IN PERSON that this was where the house was to be built, and even if only one of them were to survive, they should still continue building that House*; and when he, comforted by these words, had stepped forth from his Temple of Suffering, he had been telephoned, yes he, Rumkowski, had actually been telephoned by Gauleiter Greiser *IN PERSON* to be told that *just as, say, the free city of Danzig once lived under the protection of the surrounding powers, so this Jewish state, too, might very well have a future existence within the current borders of the Third Reich*; and Gauleiter Greiser had used Herzl's own phrase, *your Jewish state*, he had said, and why go to the trouble of building that state in the land of Israel when all the *human material* was already in place here in the ghetto, all the machinery and all the equipment? When it came down to it, everything still hung on the work you were prepared to put in. Yes, that was what Gauleiter Greiser had told Rumkowski (Chaim said), and then he winked at the child (and the child winked back); and then Chaim got up from the table and said he intended to go and lie down and enjoy his Sabbath rest for a while, and would the child like to come with him; so then both were on their feet and going into their Room. And just as if this were some gangster film at the Bajka cinema, the slim outline of Gertler's body leaned out of the wings, and Gertler said in a sarcastic voice *why are you planning to leave the ghetto, you must know you'll never have it so good as you do now . . . ?* She sees him urbanely blowing smoke out through both nostrils, and then he bends forward and stubs out his cigarette in the ashtray she has put ready, and adds in a sober, businesslike tone, reminiscent of Benji's (and their feet are still tied to the chair legs):

He won't spare a single one of you, Mrs Rumkowska, not a single one; he's going to kill you all . . .

And it is the Child he's referring to now. There can be no mistake about that. It is the Child.

Three months after the *szpera* operation, as a first indication that a glorious new age would soon be dawning, the authorities staged a big Industrial Exhibition in which the ghetto's various *resorty*, by then 112 in number, could put their formidable productivity on show.

The now 'sanitised' children's hospital at 37 Łagiewnicka Street had been converted into exhibition galleries. In the wards and consultation rooms on the ground floor there were glass display cases and stands with examples of a range of ghetto products, and someone had put a long banner up on the wall with the Chairman's famous motto **UNSER EINZIGER WEG IST ARBEIT!** stencilled in big black letters in German and Yiddish.

And all round it, a montage of photographs from various factories:

Young women at a long bench, all at work with flat irons and lengths of cloth. Superimposed on the pictures of the women was a bar graph showing the continuously rising rate of production in the tailoring workshops of the ghetto. The higher the bars on the graph went, the more of the picture of the women was revealed, bench after bench of women, heads bowed over their irons or their Singer machines from an angle that made them stretch into eternity:

Trikotagenabteilung: – Militärsektor: 42 880 Stück.
                                          – Zivilsektor: 71 028 Stück.
Korsett- und Büstenhalterfabrik: 34 057 Stück.

Three years of slavery, three years of submission to a tyrannical power with no aim but the total obliteration of the ghetto: of course that was something to celebrate.

According to the *Ghetto Chronicle*, which sent a number of its correspondents to report on the proceedings, the exhibition opening was divided into two parts. The official, first part consisted of 'speeches by a series of departmental heads', followed by a tour of the galleries. After the tour, the whole event moved to the House of Culture, where the programme comprised: 1) a musical impromptu; 2) a speech by the Praeses, with presentation of medals; 3) a banquet with a ceremonial menu specially devised for the occasion by *Frau Helena Rumkowska*. The banquet and the performance at the House of Culture were the unofficial part of the programme. Preparations had been in progress for weeks. Since the banquet was intended as a *mixed* event – in other words, eminent members of the German ghetto administration or security forces might well drop in – nothing could be left to chance.

Like the Chairman's *Kinderhospital* and indeed all the other hospitals in the ghetto, the House of Culture had recently had a thorough refit. The scenery from Mr Puławer's Ghetto Revue had been taken down and removed from the building, and massed standards had been put up instead, one for every *resort*. On the wall behind the standards there now hung a large portrait of the Chairman. It was the classic image that showed a smiling Rumkowski standing with his arms full of flowers, meeting all the happy, well-fed children of the ghetto. Next, the foyer was adorned with garlands and flower arrangements made of rags and scrap paper from the ghetto's *Altmaterialressort*, and the finishing touch to the whole effect was added by the unfurling of yet another long banner:

UNSER EINZIGER WEG . . . !

אונזער איינציגער וועג איז–ארבייט

The opening of the exhibition was set for a day in early December, a Wednesday.

It was a very cold day with a strong, blustery wind. The sky as grey as cement, with snow being driven in fierce flurries over the ridges of the roofs. Beneath the criss-crossing tram-wires across Łagiewnicka Street goes a long line of *dróshkes*, their hoods opening and shutting like mouths in the squally gusts of wind.

The bosses of the various *resort* departments are arriving.

Divisional chiefs, heads of operation, administration, supply services. And after them it is the turn of those representing that vague class of people which in the Ghetto Encyclopedia goes by the title of *ghetto engineers*: factory bosses, master mechanics, supervisors. With one hand clutching the brims of their hats, the other the tails of their coats to stop them blowing up, they are heading in a steady stream into the converted House of Culture, now stripped of all the varnish of culture, and are received in the foyer beneath the streamers and garlands by those elevated by the circumstances to the rank of important dignitaries, men like Aron Jakubowicz and Dawid Warszawski, who have learnt that the best way to deal with the demands of the new age is not to join the power struggle in the ghetto (a battle they had no prospect of winning, after all) but to behave as if it were the same as any other industrial centre, open for trade, and where any means of satisfying your employer are permitted. Also to be found among these, the true architects of the Ghetto Exhibition, is Dawid Gertler, chief of police, not in uniform but sporting a big **W** (for **Wirtschaftspolizei**) on his armband, to show his affiliation in a manner appropriate for the day.

The blare of a trumpet fanfare is heard from the brass players at the entrance; the gentlemen of the reception committee click their heels and straighten their backs:

The Chairman, comes a whisper from the front edge of the crowd, has arrived; and what's more, he's brought his whole family.

So here we have him. Rumkowski. Silent, dogged, he walks slowly forward, his eyes on the floor as if his primary task were to keep his legs under control. His wife, Mrs Regina Rumkowska, is walking with her permanent, desperate smile and her arm in his. His Son has come, too! And all at once there is enough collective elbow-room along the route of the procession for everyone to see The Adopted Child, pale and surly, standing there among all the besuited gentlemen wearing a monstrous child's suit with broad lapels of quilted silk and some kind of brocade shirt with a big, eighteenth-century-style ruffle at the neck. Of all those in the company, he is the only one who looks relatively relaxed. He stares indifferently at the garlands on the ceiling while stuffing himself with sweets from a twist of paper that the Chairman or some obsequious official has pressed into his hand.

Most of those present have by this time realised something is amiss: the Praeses is far from steady on his feet, his hand groping for a wall that is not there. Someone even says it out loud:

Isn't that man a bit the worse for drink?

But by then it is too late. The trumpeters have finished their fanfare and Rumkowski is on the podium starting the award ceremony, even though there are no medals to hand out, still less medallists to receive them. But now a pair of strong, young female arms is apparently holding out the tray of medals, after all. The medals lie like fish, with all their ribbons pointing in the same direction. And Miss Dora Fuchs, clearly concerned about her Chairman's wayward behaviour, has pressed a sheet of paper into his hand and is pointing first at the text and then over to the ranks of men in suits or uniforms – all with **W**-armbands on the sleeves of their jackets – lined up with expectant smiles on the steps down from the foyer. They are the medallists.

The Chairman nods, as if he were seeing them for the first time.

Gentlemen, he says indistinctly.
(Miss Fuchs makes a hushing gesture to the audience.)
Gentlemen and ladies – brothers and sisters!
You are all familiar with the GOOD news.
Of 87,615 Jews remaining with us today, no fewer than 75,650 are employed in full-time production. THIS IS AN IM-PRRESS-I-I-VE ACHIEVEMENT.
There are not so many of us in the ghetto as before.
BUT WE HAVE CARRIED OUT OUR TASK.
Those who come after us – our children and children's children (those who have survived!) – will rightly feel proud of these men and women who by their hard, self-sacrificing labour have given them – given us all – the right to a continuing existence.
I would go so far as to say that it is these men they have to thank for their lives.

Gentlemen, he says again, still turned to the expectant men on the steps. But his face bears an expression of one who to his consternation has just forgotten what he was about to say. The girl with the medals misinterprets his confusion as a signal to step forward with the tray again. An impatient murmur rises from the audience, only to be interrupted by one of the trumpeters, who can no longer contain himself but plays a long, slowly falling note, straight out over the sea of people. As if the silvery blast has struck up in him, too, the Chairman suddenly starts to recite:

LABOUR, LABOUR, LABOUR!
Time and again I have told you

Labour is the ROCK OF ZION!
Labour the FOUNDATION OF MY STATE.
HARD, PUNISHING LABOUR –

And from down in the hall they watch everything go flying into the air: sheets of paper, tray and medals – fanning out from the Chairman's rhetorically extended right hand. The sheets of paper come sailing down, preceded by the tray, which describes a gallant arc in the air before hitting the floor with a dull crash, and followed by the medals and their ribbons, which come pattering down all around like little rockets decked with pennants.

In the midst of this rain of medals, the Chairman has gone down on all fours and is crawling around looking for the pieces of paper he has dropped. Someone towards the back of the hall starts to laugh. At first discreetly, with their hands over their mouth. Then (as a few more people join in) more openly.

Two police officers have made their way up to the podium to try to help, but are stopped by Gertler, who abruptly gets to his feet in the first row and says:

There, you see;
This man has completely lost it!

At that moment, the doors to the foyer are slammed open and Amtsleiter Biebow comes striding down the aisle, bodyguards in his wake. The sharply issued commands and stamping, rapping boot heels send all the functionaries in the first row swiftly back to their seats, and they huddle there as Biebow – having appraised the situation for a few moments, hands on hips – resolutely climbs onto the stage, grabs hold of the Chairman who is still crawling around, pulls him up into a standing position and then slaps him sharply with his gloved hand, twice, across the face.

Rumkowski, who still does not seem to have realised who it is, just stares straight ahead, saliva running from the corners of his mouth.

Biebow picks up the items scattered across the stage floor and presses them into the Chairman's arms; then he puts his own arms around him to keep everything in place (the diplomas, the medals and the Chairman himself): *You are an old man now, Rumkowski,* he is heard to say, and those in the front row with their ears anxiously pricked up think they hear him murmur almost lovingly:

You are an old man from an obsolete age, Rumkowski.

You thought you could buy yourself power and influence, that you could go on extending your perverse and filthy nest within the walls of a Greater Power and then carry on embezzling and misappropriating just as people like you have done so many times before throughout history, as it is in your nature to do.

But let me tell you something, Rumkowski: that age is now past. That age is auf ewig vorbei. *What counts now is* Entschlossenheit, Mut und Kompetenz.

This last bit he says not to Rumkowski, but turned to the audience. And he smiles as he says it: a smile that is trying to be complicit and indulgent at the same time.

And apparently it succeeds, for suddenly everybody (except Miss Fuchs, who looks shaken, and Mrs Regina Rumkowska, who sits fiddling with her handbag as if looking to hide inside it) starts to laugh. Everyone in the hall, from the ranks of dignitaries at the front, all the way to the foremen and master machinists at the back. Some even put their hands in the air and start to clap and cheer as if they were at some crude variety performance, and once the tension in their arms and legs has relaxed, others join in too, and whether from relief or recklessness, begin to stamp their feet and boo and heckle.

But this is no variety performance. Perhaps it takes a little while for people fully to register that it is in fact *Herr Amtsleiter* standing there with the Eldest of the Jews like a child in his arms, reaping the applause. One member of the brass ensemble at least had the presence of mind to realise there was a way to defuse this potentially lethal situation, and on his own initiative played the opening notes of the *Badenweilermarsch* –

Vaterland hör deiner Söhne Schwur:
Nimmer zurück! Vorwärts den Blick!

What happened after that remains unclear. Led by the men of the new age, and in particular by Gertler and Jakubowicz, who had both tired of the protracted ceremony on stage, the dignitaries made their way out to the foyer, where the Sumptuous Buffet was laid out.

The Sumptuous Buffet was famous even before it saw the light of day. The question is, whether the Sumptuous Buffet was not more widely discussed, more minutely evoked, already in one sense sampled and tasted, than the Exhibition itself had been.

The reason for the authorities' allowing Princess Helena to lay on a Buffet was so that the food products of the ghetto could also to be put on show. So there were sausages and salted meats from the ghetto's own butcheries, sadly not kosher, but they had long since been forced to give up that sort of dream; there was bread from its bakeries; there were even items of confectionery and sweet cakes with jam made in Shlomo Hercberg's former fruit-canning plant in Marysin. Red wine was also served, in tapering glasses. The wine came from Litzmannstadt and was a *Geschenk* from Biebow, but the glasses were real crystal and arranged so artistically on mirrored trays that the business leaders reaching greedily for the platters of food could not help thinking back to the golden days when *di sheyne yidn* could sit in a café in Piotrkowska Street eating *szarlotka*, drinking tea or sipping a good Rhine wine from tall glasses, like anybody else.

As for the Chairman, he seemed to have rallied after all the inspiring speeches and was now walking among the buffet guests, leaning on what little he had left of his dignity.

Most of those in the circles gathered round Jakubowicz and Gertler discreetly turned their backs at his approach. Others were not so choosy. Soon the Chairman, too, had a little group clustered around him, insignificant officials and recording clerks, waiting for some favourable word to fall from his lips that could later be cashed in, in the form of a better position; and perhaps it was the competition – men like Jakubowicz, Warszawski, Gertler or Reingold were attracting crowds double the size of his – that made the Chairman unusually liberal with his promises and undertakings that evening:

Ah, Mr Schulz, it's you! he exclaimed as he spied Dr Arnošt Schulz and his daughter at the far end of the Sumptous Buffet:

This, gentlemen . . . he explained to the Retinue following restless and anxious on his heels. (After the incident at the medal ceremony, no one dared let him out of sight for a second.)

This is Professor Schulz – aus Prag, nicht wahr?! – the only one of my doctors who has dared to tell me from the heart what he thinks.

You are a man of enlightenment, are you not, Herr Professor Schulz?

Věra Schulz could later clearly recall the first and only time she stood face to face with the tributary king of the ghetto, the self-proclaimed steward of the fates of a hundred thousand long-settled and newly arrived Jews. *An automaton* – she wrote in her diary afterwards – *a man lacking all outward life, whose energetic walk, loud speech and apparently entirely gratuitous hand movements seem to be triggered by a mechanism hidden somewhere inside his body. His face dead, pale, puffy; his voice as shrill as a factory whistle.*

For several long minutes, the Chairman stands with Věra Schulz's hand in his, as if he has come into possession of a precious object and does not know what to do with it. Věra notes the beads of sweat along his hairline, beneath his swept-back mane of white hair.

But how . . . he starts, then breaks off and tries again (with apparently genuine surprise):

How can you work with a hand like this?

Perhaps that was the very moment at which the Stomach Upset, of which so much would later be written, began to make itself felt.

Opinion was divided on the causes of 'the incident'.

Either the ghetto butchers had had to draw too deeply on their basically limited supplies of raw meat, and in order to produce the required number of sausages been obliged to turn to the inferior meat that was usually buried as soon as it arrived at Radogoszcz. Or the special delivery of *gut gehacktes Fleisch* that the ghetto administration had promised proved to consist of the same putrid horse flesh the Germans always sent, which stank for miles around from the moment it was delivered: pale green and so foul and decomposed that it virtually ran out of the wagons into the tubs when it was unloaded. But this time the meat distribution department had not dared to report the sub-standard raw materials for fear of (as they put it afterwards) 'spoiling the whole occasion'. So the sausages were delivered to the Buffet, fatty, unwholesome, the slimy intestines used for their skins distended by the soda and fermenting substances within . . . !

Another possible explanation was that – as most people thought – the sudden, unexpected abundance of lard at the party was more than even normally well-exercised directorial digestions could withstand; particularly as all the invitees to this lavish Buffet knew that an event of this distinction would in all probability only happen once in the history of the ghetto, and the important thing was to eat now, while they had the chance and the sausages were lying there, all red and tasty and contented in their sheen of glossy fat . . . !

By midnight, the first festively dressed dignitaries had started tottering out to the inner courtyard, where they braced themselves on the sooty brick walls and threw up behind hunched shoulders. In the foyer, people milled about in confusion. Some sought cover behind the great buffet table or the chairs and small tables that were still dotted about, while the kitchen and adjacent service corridor were occupied by Gertler's bodyguards, vomiting without any inhibition into the first crate or pail that came to hand, and even the saucepans and serving dishes containing the sausages that had not yet been brought out.

Having watched glassy-eyed as his whole Retinue went down, the Chairman picked his way with proud, heron-like gait out to the courtyard, where he, too, fell to the ground. Miss Dora Fuchs, who had spent the whole evening going round moistening lips with a handkerchief, now waved it vainly in the air as she shouted for a doctor – so Dr Schulz had to spend even this jubilee the way he had spent every day since arriving at the ghetto. He grabbed the doctor's bag he always had with him, asked Věra to fold a chair cover under the back of the Chairman's neck, and went down on his knees to check the ageing man's pulse:

Chairman (faintly, with his eyes on the distant ghetto sky): Who are you?

Schulz: Schulz.

Chairman: Schulz?

Schulz: We have met.

Chairman (to Věra): And this exquisite beauty at your side?

Schulz: This is my daughter Věra. You were talking to her just a few minutes ago.

Chairman: But what have you done to your lovely young hands, young Miss Věra?

Schulz: You said yourself that they were no good for work any more, Mr Chairman.

Chairman: Whoever heard of such a thing! Everyone who still has hands will naturally be given a job, and I see you have nice, clean hands, Miss Schulz.

Schulz: Clean or not, those hands are nothing to do with you . . . !

Just then, Herr Amtsleiter ordered his escort to clear the premises. Those who could still stand were forced to their feet by baton blows and rifle butts, and herded out into the back yard. There they lay, officials, policemen and ordinary ghetto dwellers, all jumbled together until they recovered sufficiently to make their own way out. On the way back to the Red House afterwards, a German officer was heard to mutter something about filthy Jewish pigs who hadn't the sense to hang on to even what little food they were given.

But of course there was nothing to eat. They could pretend or delude themselves that there was enough food or that they had enough money or valuables to buy or barter for something, and that it was just a matter of scrimping and saving and making things go further.

But the fact remained: there was no food.

The black-market price of a loaf of bread was three hundred marks, but since not even the vendors would venture out into the terrible cold of that winter, there was no bread to buy. On the bottom shelf of the larder were a few frost-damaged potatoes with scabbed skins. That was all they had. Every morning, Věra dissolved some potato flour in lukewarm water and sprinkled in some flakes of rye. That was the 'soup' they had fed Maman every morning. If her father had not been able to get Maman a bed in the clinic in Mickiewicza Street, none of them would have survived. Since she had been in the clinic, Maman had at least been getting free soup and bread, and if there was any left over, Věra sometimes got a bowlful. In thanks for this food, she had to sit with her Olympia typewriter on her lap all day, helping her father by typing out case notes and filling in registration cards. On Rumkowski's express orders, Dr Schulz had not only assumed responsibility for what was once the tuberculosis clinic but also for the former out-patient clinics in Dworska Street, and hundreds of patients were now crammed into a space that previously accommodated ten beds at most. Even the cellar and the damp laundries below the clinic building now had patients lying in them, and the corridors were full of what were called day patients (though they lay there round

378

the clock), people who were not considered ill enough to need a bed: men with blood poisoning or chronic diarrhoea; with legs swollen with hunger or acutely paralysed; or simply with frostbite. Věra registered a hundred such cases a week, most of which went for amputation, whether it was necessary or not, since Dr Schulz considered sepsis *a far worse evil*, and one for which he had no resources in current circumstances.

In the bed next to Maman's in Dr Schulz's department lay an elderly man, as bald as an egg but with bushy eyebrows, still black, which knitted in the middle like an animal's whenever he was watching someone.

The nurses called him Rabbi Einhorn or just *Mr Rabbi Sir*, and moved around his bed with the greatest reverence. Several times a day, Rabbi Einhorn took out his prayer shawl and *tefillin*, which he kept with his books in a dented little suitcase. Since he was so weak that he could hardly sit upright, Věra had to help him wind the leather straps round his arm and fasten the little leather box round his forehead, but he always wanted to find his books himself, and afterwards he did not want them touched by her or anyone else, but lay in bed with them pressed to his thin chest.

She often saw him lying there watching her as she wound paper into her typewriter or pulled it out, or tapped out an entry in some notes, or an address.

He wanted to know where she had acquired this commendable skill.

She replied that at the school of commerce in Prague there had also been courses in shorthand and typing. He wanted to know which languages she spoke, and she replied that she could express herself tolerably well in English and French but unfortunately not in Yiddish or Hebrew; then he offered to help her, took out his book and read her some prayers, first in Hebrew and then in Polish, explaining in German as he went along what he was reading. Over the following days, they read

379

several prayers together. He read first, and then she had to read the same thing. When they got to the end, he would complain long and loud about her ignorance. *It seems to me that you young people go into a room and bemoan the fact that it's so dark everywhere that you can't see anything, even though the light is shining into every nook and cranny.*

But by then he had already taught her several words in the new language. He had taught her how the syllables looked and were pronounced, and how they were put together and taken apart again to form new meanings. Three simple-sounding syllables were enough to create a whole world of words. One of the many Hebrew words he taught her was *panim*. The original word for *face*, which depending how you took it apart and put it back together could mean anything from to *be confronted with*, to *lay oneself open to*, or to be *shone through* by the Almighty.

So perhaps you understand, Fräulein Schulz, that the act of praying consists not of gabbling words from a book but of turning one's face to the Lord so that he can illuminate each and every one of his holy words from within . . .

Once when they had been reading together, he grasped her hand and asked if she could help him when the time came. In her naivety, she thought he wanted her to help him die. But when she intimated as much, he shook his bald head emphatically. What he wanted was something much more concrete than that. He said a letter would arrive, addressed to her. And when the letter came, could Fräulein Schulz do him the favour of at least giving the offer contained in it her careful consideration?

*

In May 1940, when the ghetto was set up, the Jewish ghetto administration had a hundred employees at most. Three years later, in June 1943, more than 13,000 ghetto residents made a living from one of the many offices and departments, divisions, labour offices, control bodies and inspection units presided over by Rumkowski.

Since Rumkowski's administrative machine had become so confusingly large in the course of those three years, people just said *the offices*.

Or *the Chairman's offices*.

Or *the Palace*.

It was of course a palace with no visible towers or parapets, but with many subterranean passages where employees sat keeping account without knowing what they were keeping account of, or merely dozing behind nightly inspection hatches. The Palace was an edifice built on very vague foundations, and its extent was always in doubt. Departments and offices would suddenly sprout in ordinary blocks of flats, only to vanish again as if they had never existed. But this palace did have a clear entrance. The entrance was the Chairman's secretariat on Bałuty Square. It was there everyone had to go if they wanted to get into or progress up, or further through, the hierarchies of the ghetto.

Those seeking sanctuary under the Chairman's patronage were known as *petitioners*, and the Chairman had taken in thousands of these petitioners since the ghetto was formed.

Back then, the petitioners outside the Bałuty office were given special dispensation to be in the zone cordoned off by the Germans for short periods. After the *szpera* operation, however, Biebow decided to put an end to *all this running back and forth*, and therefore barred anyone not employed by the administration from Aryan territory. Which in no way prevented the Chairman from receiving petitioners. A watchman's hut in Łagiewnicka Street was pressed into service instead. They managed to squeeze in a desk, behind which the Chairman would sit with all the personal files in front of him, and Miss Fuchs devised a primitive appointment system, handing out numbered slips to the applicants, who had to queue up outside and be called in one by one.

People petitioned for all manner of things.

Many, like Věra, asked for a hospital bed for their relatives. Others appealed for milk rations for their children. Or allotments to cultivate, now the growing season was approaching.

Many applied for permission to marry. Getting married was one of the few legal means nowadays of getting extra food rations. It was the Chairman who made these food rations available, out of his own extra quota. It was the Chairman, too, who conducted the marriage services themselves, as all religious ceremonies in the ghetto were banned, and almost all the rabbis had been deported. Some people were heard to say that the old man was absolutely *shameless* in taking such liberties, playing at being a holy man and a man of law, when he was suspected of having blood on his hands! Others said they could to some extent understand the old man adopting this role. How else could he demonstrate his power, now that Amtsleiter Biebow had not only publicly mocked and ridiculed him, but also put an end to any say he had in production and food distribution in the ghetto, not to mention 'police matters'?

According to the *Ghetto Chronicle*, in one of the wedding ceremonies regularly held at the old preventorium in Łagiewnicka Street the Chairman married no fewer than thirteen couples simultaneously; and there was a tray to hand with thirteen individual wine glasses, which were filled from a bottle fitted with a special 'sanitary' spout. It was Dr Miller who insisted on this practice, to minimise the risk of transmitting epidemic diseases. Dr Miller himself stood hidden behind the bridal canopy and used his stick to satisfy himself that everyone drank from *their own* glass and every glass was then wiped and put back on the tray without being smashed.

Much was said later of the profane version of the Jewish marriage service taking place in the Palace, of how the bridal canopy was nothing but an ordinary curtain rod draped with tulle, which on Dr Miller's orders was afterwards taken from the ceremony to the sanitary station at Bałuty Square for immediate disinfection. One could almost hear Benji's voice again, going round the streets swearing and cursing:

A jester king is what he's let himself be reduced to, that Mr Rumkowski; with that gaggle of clowns at his heels and all his ludicrous ceremonies!

But the food coupons that Miss Ejbuszyc of the approvisation department wrote out for the thirteen bridal couples were genuine, at any rate, and could be exchanged for real bread and enough extra starch in the soup to last, and keep them full, for at least a couple of days.

*

It should have been a 'happy' day, the day Josel pulled away the wallpapered panel and finally freed Maman from her incarceration. Věra would never forget the sight of the stranger that awaited them on the other side: her body as thin as one of the pins she had directed Věra to run 'round the corner' and buy, but smiling and straight-backed, holding out her *Ausweis* as if she had been sitting there for weeks anticipating this very opportunity. But Věra saw at once that there was something sticky round Maman's lips, and the walls around her bed were black with blood and dried excrement.

Arnošt, who had taken a look behind the false wall several times in past days, said that Maman's state of health was no worse than was to be expected, for all that. He took the cannula out of the back of her hand, and for a few days she even sat with them at the table when they were eating. Věra soaked cubes of bread in the soup and put them in her mouth, and her mother sucked in her thin cheeks and turned her gaze inwards to investigate this strange find that had landed under her tongue. But she swallowed it all down, and for a while even seemed satisfied with what she was being fed, and the noise and bustle around her.

But appearances were deceptive. Perhaps they were all misled by the fact that she had survived 'behind the wallpaper' at all. It soon became evident that Maman's kidneys could not cope with the food they were giving her. The primitive dialysis Arnošt had set up was not working, the wound in her abdomen where the dialysis liquid went in grew swollen and her peritoneum became inflamed; Maman grew feverish.

Věra sat up all night, waiting for the 'crisis', after which her temperature would with any luck come down. But no 'crisis' ever came. Maman's fever did recede a little, but she never woke up. Her pulse was weak, her breathing jerky and her heartbeat irregular.

They were all at her side when she died. Věra spoke to her mother of the last time they had walked in Rieger Park together, of the birds taking off from the treetops at dusk and forming a second sky above all the forest of tall roofs and copper steeples; and Maman almost seemed to smile weakly for a moment, and the fingers Věra was squeezing seemed to squeeze back. Then her breathing slowed to a stop. Maman cast off her body as you might cast off a grubby old outer garment you didn't really want to touch again, and when that act of undressing was complete, her face lay there completely calm and still, as if no one had ever touched it.

They buried Maman eighteen days into the new calendar year of 1943, one clear and frosty morning with the burnished sun suspended low and smoky above the tops of the walls in Marysin. The main gate to the big cemetery had formerly been on Bracka Street, at the north-east end of the ghetto, but as that was now on Aryan territory, the undertakers' association had opened up a smaller entrance in the brick wall on the western side, at Zagajnikowa Street, and it was through this that they entered with the cart Professor Schulz had hired.

Within the enclosing walls, the city of the dead spread before them. To the left of the path that led from the little mortuary building, banks of earth, now glittering frostily in the swollen, bluish-white sunlight, stretched out in long rows.

Each bank of earth concealed rows of graves, some of them filled in, others still awaiting their dead. To keep up, they had had to start digging back in November, Józef Feldman told them as they lifted the washed and shrouded body from the cart onto one of the low barrows on which the dead were transported in this place. Everybody remembered what it had been like the year before, in January and February when the deportations had just started and people were crammed into unheated warehouses and froze to death waiting for transport that never came. That time, the frost in the ground went to such a depth that even a crowbar made no impact, and they had no choice but to pile up the corpses and wait for the thaw to set in.

Józef Feldman told them this in the unconcerned yet still tender tone peculiar to those who have daily dealings with the dead, but Věra was scarcely listening to what the old man said. Walking behind the rhythmically creaking barrow with its metal-rimmed wheel, behind the rabbi who had conducted the ceremony and her father and two brothers, she saw in the far distance a handful of other gravediggers with a wheelbarrow, pickaxe and spade. The outlines of the figures had almost dissolved in the cold, frost-white haze, so they seemed to be hovering a few metres above the ground, and suddenly everything blurred together: the rhythmic squeak of the barrow wheel, the endless rows of unmarked graves, and the icy wind that bit her cheeks and drove painful tears from her eyes.

Perhaps it was because she was unused to all this open space. She had been in the ghetto long enough now for everything in it to seem equally dark and cramped; wherever you went, you had to crouch down or make way for others. By contrast, the distances here in the burial ground seemed to her almost unimaginable; and it was certainly unimaginable that the dead already amounted to so many.

*

The typewriter was still there on the little side table when she got back after the mourning period, but in the bed that had been Rabbi Einhorn's there was now another man, who lay looking at her with blank, expressionless eyes. Beside her typewriter stood the little metal suitcase containing the rabbi's prayer shawl and books. She would subsequently often wonder what would have happened if she had not opened the case that day. There were so many people dying and leaving useless objects behind them. In the end the whole concept lost its meaning: how could you talk of personal effects when not even death was personal any more?

But she opened the case – perhaps out of respect for the old man. Inside was a little note, written in German in the same type as that on her machine:

Meet me at the foot of the wooden bridge, corner of Kirchplatz/ Hohensteinerstrasse, Friday 9 a.m. Please bring the typewriter!
A.Gl.

With this letter, written by a stranger on her own typewriter, began what in her diary she later came to refer to as her *Unterirdisches Leben*, her underground life.

So it was that on a damp, grey-misted morning in early February 1943 she first stepped over the threshold of the Palace. Where the ghetto ended and the barbed wire began, the big black wooden bridge should have risen powerfully five metres above the street, but all that could be seen of it in the mist was the people gathering at the foot of the steps and disappearing up into it as if climbing straight up to Heaven. From above came the interminable tramp of shoes on wet wood, the loud breathing of thousands of human beings hurrying unseen – unseeing – to their anonymous jobs.

Fräulein Schulz? – The man behind her must have known who she was at once, in spite of the feeble light; or perhaps he had been guided by the Olympia typewriter that seemed to be in such demand, which she was carrying in its case under her arm.

Sind Sie dann für den heutigen Arbeitsinsatz bereit, Fräulein Schulz?

She turned round, as if an actual German were addressing her.

But he did not look as if he meant her harm. His face was smiling. Under the damp brim of his hat were big eyes that grew bigger still, the longer he stared at her. Still without the slightest idea what work he was talking about, she went with him through the mist, first into a poky inner courtyard, then down a set of cellar steps as narrow as a well-shaft. At the bottom of the steps, a solid red door with a big padlock was waiting. The man undid the padlock and pushed the wooden door, which creaked open.

If there had not been shelves or at least props enough to hold them in place, all the books would have poured down over her there and then –

There were books shelved or lying everywhere: on long, sagging bookcases propped against the walls, or on planks of wood or pieces of cardboard that had been laid on the bare stone floor, stacked beside and on top of each other in tall piles, with thicker volumes stuck in below the thinner ones like uneven blocks of stone in a wall.

All this is Rabbi Einhorn's work, he explained. The rabbi's own books are only a fraction of what's here. The rest come from Jewish homes here in the ghetto. We've been collecting them since the day the deportations started. The very thought of them ending up in the wrong hands prompted Mr Neftalin the lawyer to secure an acquisition order from the housing department. It requires every concierge or block caretaker to go through all flats, basements and attics vacated by Jewish deportees and see to it that all books and other documents found are brought here, to the archives; and when we say all, we mean literally *everything*, he said, and smiled. We don't just have books here, but all sorts of other manuscripts and publications. But no one has been able to count them yet, or catalogue them, or find out the names of the people they once belonged to. All that's still to be done.

Somehow they had managed to wedge in a desk for her among the teetering piles of books. Mr Gliksman brought a couple of warm blankets. Then a light bulb, which he produced from his mouth like a circus clown and screwed into a light fitting high on one of the cellar walls. He clearly took delight in performing such tricks. When she asked for a pencil, he plucked one from behind his ear, and then drew two pieces of carbon paper from the sleeve of his shirt for her to put between the sheets of paper she wound into the typewriter. Every title was to be entered in

388

at least two places: first on standard catalogue cards, then on long lists which would also include the former owners' names.

In a slanting column of light, full of dry shadows and particles of dust from the stone, she made a first attempt at putting the stacks of books into some sort of order. On some of the shelves, the books were already sorted – either by subject or in piles and bundles by the premises they had come from: tatty, well-thumbed copies of the Tanak; old prayer books, some so tiny that they could easily be sewn under the facing of a shirt or into the folds of a kaftan; photograph albums with pictures of men and women in their best clothes at long tables set for meals, or of schoolchildren on outings, in short trousers and knee-socks; schoolbooks with sums; grammar books in Polish and Hebrew; almanacs going back several decades; railway timetables; translations of novels by Lion Feuchtwanger, Theodor Fontane and P. G. Wodehouse.

She scrupulously entered all the names and titles on the index cards she had been given.

The problem was that not all the items could be classified as books. What was she to do, for example, with private account books – there were hundreds of them – ordinary notebooks with oilcloth covers, in which housewives had entered and totted up the cost of everything they bought?

Aleksander Gliksman came and went, but so quietly that she scarcely noticed him. She would look up from what she was doing and find the cellar empty; but the next time she looked up, he would be standing beside her again, looking at her with those big eyes that seemed to grow bigger the longer he looked. Sometimes he brought food, perhaps in addition to the daily midday soup a slice of bread with a scraping of margarine, or some wafer-thin radish slices. Sometimes they ate together, and once she asked him why it was so important for her to use the back entrance, and to come and go without being seen.

She had expected an evasive answer, but he was surprisingly

candid. 'The archive is the heart of the ghetto,' he said. Only people who enjoy the highest level of patronage are given positions here. Věra was not one of those, and if it ever got out that she had not got her position by 'the usual route', there was a risk that someone else would lay claim to her job (even though the head of the archives, Mr Neftalin, entirely approved of her appointment there). And in her case there were also special circumstances, he said, making a clumsy little move, as if to lift her arthritis-crippled hands into his lap. But there was no need for him to spell it out. Everyone knew the dangers of harbouring or employing a person classed as unfit for work.

Even so, Mr Gliksman did occasionally take her up 'into the open air'. After long days in the dark confines of the cellar, the great archive room on the first floor was a miracle of light and space. In the middle of its wide floor stood a big wood-burning stove, its flue running across the ceiling and out through one of the wide windows. The stove clearly threw out a lot of heat, as the archivists all worked in their shirtsleeves or blouses. There were five rotating card indexes. They stood in a row, like big, tombola drums, with doors in the sides that opened outward, like cupboards. Inside were the index cards for all the residents of the ghetto, sorted both alphabetically by name, and by residential address. The archive drums were locked and sealed every night, and it was said that the only person with a key to the safety lock apart from the Chairman himself was Mr Neftalin, lawyer and head of the archive department. It was Mr Neftalin who solemnly unlocked the drums again each morning. The rest of the archive staff sat at long workbenches round the constantly clattering and rotating drums, sorting copies of letters and minutes into envelopes and brown folders.

The four windows of the archive room looked out over the Church of the Most Blessed Virgin Mary and the bridge across Hohensteinerstrasse. With every passing day, the light from the sun as it rose behind the bridge and the church's double spires extended further across the floor of the archive room, and the blinds were gradually lowered until the whole room was sunk in a curious, dark-grey, almost unreal half-light. But every morning and evening the blinds were wound up again, and once more there was no boundary between the great room with its archive drums and the square with its huge wooden bridge. The people making their way up or down the bridge steps sometimes passed so close that they looked as if they were on their way straight through the room.

*

No. 1 Worker FRIEDLANDER, DAWID (sixteen) is sentenced to four months in the HOUSE OF CORRECTION for potato theft. Proof in this case provided by three potatoes intended for Kitchen no. 9 (Marysińska), found to be unlawfully in the trouser pocket of the accused.

No. 2: Tailor's apprentice KAHN, LUBA (nineteen) is sentenced to three months in the HOUSE OF CORRECTION for theft of reels of thread and darning wool to a total value of 45 ghetto marks. Wool and thread were recovered during a body search, unlawfully concealed in the shoes of the accused.

It's built to last for an eternity, the Chairman's Palace, says Aleks, showing her the copy of the report of court proceedings he is about to insert into one of the brown archive files.

One week's verdicts are summarised on two carbon-copy pages; a total of nineteen sentences passed, in cases varying from theft and burglary to attempted embezzlement. But Aleks is so indignant that his hands are shaking.

What's the point of handing down a sentence of four months or more if you don't believe the ghetto will last that long? Aren't we, with our imbecilic judicial system, just reinforcing the will of the authorities: that we stay here behind their barbed wire until the world goes under and we Jews are wiped out to the last man?

– No, go on you poor fellow, steal your potatoes! By quelling your hunger, at least you've proved you are a free man!

Aleksander Gliksman has a very strange way of talking. Whenever he is agitated or even just eager, he thrusts his head forward like a tortoise from its shell, and stares at her with an obstinate, persistent glare, as if challenging her to contradict him.

Really it's a wonder he hasn't been deported yet, Věra often thinks. Unless the secret lies in his hands. As soon as Alex has his fingerstall on, the archive documents whirl through his hands. There was something boyish, formal, almost ceremonious in the way he counts and weighs up facts. When they are alone down in the cellar, he shows her in confidence the world map he has been piecing together over a number of years on sheets of waste paper. In the archives, as everywhere else in the ghetto, paper is strictly rationed, and the various sections cannot be allocated fresh supplies until Mr Neftalin makes a formal application to the materials office. But somewhere in the vaults, Gliksman has come across discarded registration lists from the time when this part of Poland was under the administration of the Russian Empire and the Tsars: documents tied up with coarse string which have lain so long in draughty, damp conditions that the sheets have stuck together, creating bales as thick as bricks.

Now, on documents covered in old Cyrillic script, he sketches out for her with broad pencil strokes what has happened to the Russian front line since Stalingrad.

– Six top generals taken prisoner and the Wehrmacht in retreat on all fronts, he says, and shows her on his map sections how the battle for Kharkov unfolded; then indicates with thick pencil lines how General Zhukov went on to send his troops in a wide pincer movement down into the Caucasus.

Because the map is made up of loose sheets of paper, identifiable only by a number code at the top of each, it can be taken apart after every revision and hidden away. Gliksman uses a special code. He calls the German army *Paulus*, or just *Pl*, after General Friedrich Paulus who was forced into such ignominious capitulation at Stalingrad. (Aleks has come up with the idea that they ought to institute a new public holiday, a *Pauli Day*, to commemorate this battle.) *Azbuk*, or *Az*, stands for the Russian army, after the old Slavic name for the Cyrillic text flowing in dense, even greyness down the sheets of waste paper reused for the map. Larger towns or fortifications are labelled *VG* – an abbreviation of *Velikiy Gorod*: 'big city' – followed by the three letters *pad*, for *padat'*, to 'fall'. It was always the Germans who fell. If the Germans did *not* fall, or if the Wehrmacht mounted a counter-offensive and regained lost ground, Alex simply crossed out the three letters *pad*. For Gliksman's map was a *biased map*: Russian losses were only marked in the form of missed or postponed victories.

Where did you get all this from? But Aleks has no answer to questions like that. He stretches his hand wide in a gesture of helplessness and looks like a schoolboy caught scrumping apples. On another occasion, he thumps his temple with his hand and says:

You keep it all in your head as a rule . . . !

And then does his usual trick of playing with the words:

You have to keep a cool head . . . !

He has drawn the whole North African coast on four or five sheets, the background Cyrillic text a brownish smudge running through the deserts of Libya:

(Since Kasserine, Rommel's been reinforcing his armoured divisions in North Africa. The battle for Tunis is going to be decisive . . .)

But of course his maps were based on others. She realised later that this was a sort of test, a loyalty test. After that, newspapers and other documents start turning up in the room in the cellar, along with all the books. Every morning when he unlocks the door for her, she finds more bits of newspaper tucked under or between the piles of books or the boxes of index cards. *Litzmannstädter Zeitung* mainly: copies abandoned by, or stolen from, German police officers or administrative inspectors who have had reason to visit the ghetto. In them, the Wehrmacht's retreat is described as just a tactical ploy to 'straighten out' certain sections of the front. But not even propaganda minister Goebbels's proclamation of 'total war', filling two whole pages on 19 February 1943, can conceal the Germans' desperate situation.

There was other material to study. Documents, official communications, proclamations: pages torn out of illegal newspapers, sometimes so soggy and decaying that they could scarcely be read at all. (Presumably they had been in the bottom of a vegetable box or a crate of potatoes for so long that they had taken on the same colour and texture as the rotting greens.)

A few documents, however, were intact, such as a copy of the Polish resistance movement newspaper *Biuletyn Informacyjny*, in which he showed her an appeal, designed to look handwritten, with capital letters and big spaces:

JEWISH YOUTH, DO NOT BELIEVE
THE LIES THEY ARE TELLING YOU . . .
They took our parents before our very eyes,
They took our brothers and sisters.
Where are the thousands of men recruited as labourers?
Where are the Jews deported at Yom Kippur?
Of those taken out through the gates of the ghetto
NOT A SINGLE ONE has returned.
ALL THE GESTAPO'S ROADS LEAD TO PONARY,
AND PONARY MEANS DEATH . . . !

This is from Vilna, he observed, with a dry matter-of-factness in his voice that was even more chilling than the contents of the document. – It's near the border, some of the Jews there have already fled; but they've no weapons to defend themselves with, not like the ones in Warsaw.

Where's Ponary? is all she says.

He does not reply. He talks about Warsaw as if he's lived there for years:

In Warsaw, of course, they have *kanalizacja* in the whole area covered by the ghetto. That means you can get weapons in through the sewer tunnels. The smugglers on the other side take fifty złoty for a German army pistol. The hard part is the ammunition. My informant in the ŻOB complains because the Polish home army won't give them any. It's just like here: the Poles in Warsaw refuse to put weapons into Jewish hands. They sometimes seem to be more scared of the Jews than they are of the Germans.

It suddenly felt as though the books all around them in the cold, cramped cellar room were borne up by nothing but a thin column of air and would come crashing down on them at any moment. Her first reaction was to put up her defences. How dare he tip all this knowledge into her lap, without first making sure she was ready, or even *wanted* to know? The suspicions that the deportations had in some places led to mass executions of undesirable Jewish elements: she has already heard those. Every employee in every *resort* did nothing but speculate on what the Germans' real intentions were. But the fact that somewhere, in Warsaw or Lublin or Białystok, there was organised *resistance* to the German occupying forces going on – she had had no idea of that. And if that really were the case, she said, how could he stand there with that popeyed look of his and just *talk about it*? How could he, or how could they, not *do something*?

All that he did once she had blurted that out was to carry

on staring at her, calm and assured. For the first time, she saw that there was something fanatical in his look, too: though well masked by hunger, there was a long-nurtured fury there:

Who wouldn't *want* to? He said. But where would we get our weapons; *and however would we go about getting the Chairman's permission to use them?*

He laughed at his own joke. The laugh was perhaps what surprised her most. It was coarse and rasping, as if it was being drawn out of him on long chains. Then he sat there dumbly, staring down at himself with the same pale consternation in his eyes, as if startled from sleep, that he used to have when he looked at her.

She dealt with the forbidden documents he brought her in the way she had realised he wanted her to, and perhaps had intended her to from the start. Two pages of *Trybuna* were fixed inside a book about fire engines; she stuck articles from *Biuletyn Informacyjny*, *Dziennik Żołnierza* and *Głos Warszawy* between the pages of annual reports from the Mosaic congregation of Łódź. A monograph on that eminent son of the city, cloth manufacturer Israel Poznański, was thick enough to accommodate several pages of front-line reports snipped from the *Völkischer Beobachter* and *Litzmannstädter Zeitung*. As a way of marking which book and which shelf housed the forbidden texts, she thought out a simple code system with a combination of letters and numbers, which she wrote in pencil in the top right-hand corner of every typed index card.

After a couple of months' work, the inner walls of the Palace were papered over with signs and messages of this kind. They ran invisibly but alive, back and forth across all the piles of books, in and out between spines and folders. But rather than propping up the sagging library as she had hoped, this simply made the remarkable book edifice seem even more fragile and unsafe. When that sensation was at its strongest, she had the strange feeling of being sucked down through the bottom of the cellar: like the powerful little eddy in a washbasin when the water runs down the plughole. And the sense of being sucked down was sometimes so intense that she had to hang on to the edge of her desk with both hands to stop herself being washed away.

It was the usual giddiness of hunger –

She recognised the faintness, the feeling of everything solid around her dissolving. Like the beer and soda labels did when she put the bottles to soak in the big washtub Maman reluctantly let her use.

(She could feel Maman's fair hair tickling the back of her neck, the warm maternal body bending forward and enclosing her as she helped with careful fingers to tease the wet labels from the slippery bellies of the bottles.)

Everything around her was damp and porous. The light from the bulb Aleks had screwed into the fitting up by the ceiling shone with a bloated glare. She heard Aleks coming down with some food, heard the tinny clatter of the old milk can he brought the soup in. (Or was it a bit of dry bread rattling around in a shiny tea caddy?) One day he brought a glass jar of pickled gherkins. *My father's a klayngertner*, he explained, in that slightly injured tone all the native Jews of Łódź seemed to adopt when speaking Yiddish.

But however much she ate, it didn't help with the hollow suck of hunger, the sudden swirls of light-headedness and weakness. Or was it the claustrophobia of the place itself that was making her ill? The raw damp trickling out of the walls and rising in her painful neck and shoulder joints? The fact that she never got out into any proper light; or any proper darkness either: everything reduced to the same watery, dirty grey substance, a mixture of sludge, stinking coal smoke and dust.

She asked Aleks several times if she could come up and sit in the archive room a bit more often. He occasionally let her, though with reluctance, as if against his better judgement. But one morning he forbade it entirely.

The Chairman's here, was all he said, extending his head so far forward that he looked more like an angry watchdog than a harmless tortoise.

That day, Aleks hung about down in the cellar for an unusually long time. As if to reassure himself that the barked military orders and angry stamp of jackboots in the stairwell above would not be coming all the way down to them, to this 'archive within the archive' as he called it, which the two of them had built up together.

But even Aleks's visits down to her were blurring round the edges. The next time he came, she did not for the life of her know whether he had just left or been gone for several days, only that she had noticed nothing. It was as if some imperceptible yet gigantic subsidence had happened inside her. Great swathes of time had vanished unnoticed.

She saw clearly now that she would not be capable of carrying out the task Rabbi Einhorn had asked her to perform. There were simply not enough books to describe all the catastrophes occurring daily on the other side of her over-cluttered cellar walls. When she explained this to Aleks, she tried to joke about it. She said it was 'funny' to think that she had got through almost everything in the ghetto – she had survived the crush and the hunger and the filthy conditions in the collective, Maman's long illness, and their attempts to hide her from the Nazis' purges! – and then she found herself in a warm, cosy basement room, doing a job that by ghetto standards must be considered light work, and what was more, with 'lots of food' – and suddenly it was all slipping from her grasp. It was in actual fact a single piece of news that had tipped the balance, a single page of newsprint that Aleks had put on her desk one morning. The tone of the article was defiant, mutinous; but that only made the true situation that much harder to conceal. She understood at once that the uprising in Warsaw that Aleks had told her about was now over and everyone who lived in the ghetto was dead; assuming, that is, there was a ghetto left at all:

Year after year, the Germans have portrayed themselves as representatives of a proud and invincible master race, and then a single night showed them to be nothing but a collection of mortal men who fall when a lethal bullet is directed at them.

They are not invincible! Nor will they win!

Now that the fortunes of war have turned in the East, resistance to Frank and his occupying forces will also grow here in Warsaw, and across Poland. Thanks to the resistance on the streets of Warsaw, not a single one of the murderers dared to return to the cellars and tunnels of the ghetto where their chosen victims were hiding. The supermen did not dare. *The supermen were scared.*

(J. Nowak)

That was the last newspaper article she archived – dated 19 May 1943.

And from that moment on, she remembers nothing more.

In her dream, she is standing with Aleks on the porch steps of the front entrance of the archive. Hundreds of other people are also crowded onto the steps, as if they, too, are waiting for the rain to stop. Věra has never seen such rain in all her life. It pours onto the shiny cobblestones and sluices down the roofs and fronts of the buildings. Every so often, the thunder sends dull tremors through the ground, shaking the whole foundation of the ghetto.

She and Aleks are standing side by side, as if the rain has wrapped them both together in a single warm coat. After a while she actually stops being aware that they are standing there at all. She is so warm with him.

Then it brightens up. A channel of clear blue sky opens up above them.

But only above the ghetto. On the other side of the barriers and barbed wire, the thunder goes on and the sky is thick and smooth and black with rain.

Through the pale, watery light, peacocks come strutting. At the foot of the wooden bridge, a tree has taken root: a giant ash, its roots bursting out of the hard paving-stones and its branches winding far above the parapet of the bridge. On the facades all around, which still bear the marks of the rain, greenery blossoms like shimmering butterfly wings. Striped blinds are wound up, window panes nudged open into the fresh air. In shady archways and in the courtyards, activities take place that could only happen in secret before. Horses are hitched, gleaming lengths of cloth are carefully rolled out or laid on wide tabletops; plates and glasses are set out. In Wiewiórka's barber's shop, the customers sit still unshaven, their faces all turned the same way, as if all listening to the same voice. But the only thing that can be heard from the loudspeakers mounted everywhere in the ghetto is the amplified sound of rain: a hurricane of rain, gushing and running in gutters and pipes.

She walks across the wet paving stones, but can feel that she no longer has a body. Or has the whole ghetto suddenly parted company with all that weighs it down on the ground? Doorways and house fronts go flicking past as if they were pages in a book, and – as if she too were entering the pages of a book – she slips past, through the archway and into the wide inner courtyards where the children are standing. It strikes her that she has never seen the ghetto courtyards like this before. They used always to look much more like deep shafts or fillers between the buildings, meaningless cavities full of clay, broken tiles and dumped rubbish. Now the well and the outhouses and the rows of privies are all clear and distinct; the pump and its handle are painted, the outhouses have trellises covering their walls and the tar-paper roofs of the privies have acquired low containing walls made of wood, and been filled with soil and turned into patches of garden, with cucumbers and tomatoes in long, industrious rows.

And then there are all the children . . .

They are standing in loose groups, as if they have come wading through tall grass and have suddenly stopped, the whites of their eyes empty and their faces as pale as leafless flower shoots.

There weren't usually any children in the ghetto. There weren't usually elderly men sitting beneath their prayer shawls, with the leather straps of their *tefillin* round their arms and their prayer books held open against their faces.

And there wasn't usually rain, either; nor such a deep silence within that rain.

Behind all she is seeing now, behind the children and rain

and silence, there is a sort of gorge of light: an internal channel without end. And she realises with utter clarity, and without a hint of fear, that this is what dying is like. All she has to do is let her paper-light body rise straight into the inexplicably clearing sky. And she thinks she must at all costs fight against this temptation; hang on in that disgusting, dark and evil dimension which is earth and body and weight and ghetto.

But things have already gone too far.

She finds no footing within herself any more. Even the light finds no footing.

Aleks scraped thin air from an old tin can, and since the spoon seemed to be coming all the way to her mouth, she decided to bite it. The spoon tasted of metal and air. Aleks moistened a crust of bread in the soup and dabbed her sore lips gently with the bread, as you might with a cloth or a sponge. At first she did not know what he was doing there. But obviously, she must be alive. She was lying in the little 'wallpaper room' in Brzezińska Street, on the dirty mattress where her mother had also lain, and above and around were the walls her mother had smeared with faeces, and way above was the little vent with the grille that could be pushed open or pulled shut with the rod from below. Aleks was adjusting that rod now, so the light would not shine too brightly in her eyes, but even though the light stung them, and she was so weak she could hardly move her arms, she wanted the light to stay, and she sat there in the light as if down in a bottomless well, while he went on scraping out the tempting tin can with the spoon:

'Well at least you're eating,' he said, sounding pleased.

The remarkable thing was not that she had survived, but that she seemed to have been able to make other people believe she could carry on indefinitely. When her father managed to get a bed for Maman at Mickeiwicz Street, Věra carried her on her back all the way downstairs from the flat. That meant nobody saw how thin and worn out Věra's own body had become, and at the hospital she had been perpetually running around changing soiled sheets and emptying bedpans. As if trying to outrun her own exhaustion.

Josel said she must have caught the infectious disease at the hospital. But this was categorically denied by Arnošt, who said they had not had a single case of typhus fever since they moved to Mickeiwicz Street – *the typhus vanished along with the lice*, he said – and placed the blame instead on her work with the books down in the dirty cellar archive.

She was still so weak she could neither stand up nor raise and swivel her arm without her whole body starting to shake, but Aleks arranged to borrow a wooden cart, like the one Kajsar Franz, the rag-and-bone man from Franciszkańska Street, used for transporting his goods, and in this Josel and Martin towed her out to Marysin.

Aleks Gliksman's father was not just a *klayngertner*, as his son had modestly said, but the top lawyer in the ghetto's *Landvirtshaftopteil*, the department of the Palace responsible for allocating all the land in the ghetto that was not built on or in use by a *resort* or a materials depot. In the early spring of 1943, the Chairman had decided to divide the land in the ghetto once cultivated by the former collectives into allotments to be allocated for private use. The idea was that this would boost the 'domestic' production of fruit and vegetables; but although Ehud Gliksman worked in the department, and although this was the first time for several years that new plots had become available, it was far from self-evident that he would have anything to do with the actual distribution of the land. In the complicated system of dependence and debts of gratitude, called in or as yet unexploited, that prevailed in the Palace, there was always someone else who took priority. But presumably Aleks had been very persistent. Věra could imagine the tenacity and insistence in his voice as he spoke in support of the Schulz family from Prague, and their father was a doctor, as well; so one day, as Věra was lying there in the wallpaper room at the height of her illness – and even the ever-optimistic Arnošt seemed to have given up hope – a small, grey form had arrived from the Department of Agriculture, notifying the Schulz family that they had been selected to 'responsibly tend and take charge of' a vegetable plot. The formal address of the plot was 11:4 Marysińska Street (plot no. 14), and it comprised fifteen square metres of stony soil right on the corner, where Marysińska Street met Przelotna Street. The lease was for a year, with a notice period of a month.

Aleks had experience of his own in agricultural work. In the first years of the ghetto, he had been a member of the Hashomer Hatsair collective, which ran a large-scale pioneer operation out in Marysin. The *shomrim* of the ghetto had grown potatoes, beets, white cabbage, carrots and sugar peas. And not just for *hazana* – the collective distribution of food – but for the *future*, to *prepare themselves*, because in those days, Aleks pointed out, everyone believed the war wasn't going to last long and we'd soon get to Palestine, the lot of us.

That was our place, he said, nodding towards a stone building further down Próżna Street, its roof now caved in; we used to lie there at nights and listen to the bats; there were loads of bats up under the rafters. In those days, the Praeses often used to come and visit. We set long tables and he would be the guest of honour. He was a different person back then, you might almost say keen to please us; he would have dinner with us and then we'd sit there and sing songs all evening, even love songs, said Aleks, and then he sang (in a somewhat rasping voice, not particularly attractive, but penetrating):

In the land of Israel we must suffer.
I love and I suffer,
But you have no feelings
I will pick flowers for myself
*For flowers can heal my painful heart.**

* *B'erets jisrael muchrabim lisbol / Ani ohevet vesovelet / Ve'tach eincha margish / Prachim li liktof etse / Ki baprachim et libi arape.*

405

Later, the Praeses came back to us, but he had completely changed:

It was at the time of the strikes at the carpentry workshops in Drukarska and Urzędnicza that triggered off disturbances and hunger riots, and he had to call in the Germans to crush the demonstrations. And the Praeses was convinced it was in socialist circles, among us, the *shomrim* and in the other collectives, that the agitation against him had started. So he decided all the collective farms in Marysin would be shut down, and anyone who didn't report for other work would have their workbook withdrawn.

That was in March 1941. We had two choices. We could either join one of Praszkier's digging teams and start burying the dead out at Bracka Street; or we could help with the bricklaying work for the extension of the Central Jail. Shlomo Hercberg was in charge of the prison then, and he was as vile to the workers as he was to the prisoners. So neither option was particularly tempting.

What happened next? asked Věra.

I should have resisted, of course. Like some of the others wanted to. Maybe we'd have got rid of him then. But nobody did anything. And he did at least have the sense, the Praeses, to listen to my father's protestations of my innocence and let me start at the archive. I'd always taken the minutes for Hashomer, and when it came down to it, there weren't that many people in the ghetto who really knew how to write.

*

Allotment number fourteen turned out to be a little way off the road behind a grey stone wall. Under the wall there was a dilapidated wooden shed, its walls displaying more holes and cracks than solid wood. The whole of Marysińska Street was lined with these ramshackle huts, a few of them with a couple of windows to each wall and a brick chimney stack or a very basic stove flue sticking out of the window. Some of the plots that went with the sheds were small, some only an arm's length wide; others were the size of fields, and marked off by tall fences and gates.

All that spring, the Schulz children went out there whenever they got a chance: on Sundays, but also after work if they had the energy, and enough food at home to eat. Even Aleks turned up occasionally. He said he couldn't afford to lose her, and it must have been the work on the books he was referring to, because he wasn't much help with hoeing and digging and weeding, despite all the experience he claimed to have. Josel and Martin had made their own tools. Martin had bent a bit of old sheet metal from a roof ridge to make a simple spade. A wooden pole with some nails stuck through it became their rake. They sowed spinach and radishes, potatoes of course; but also white and red cabbage, and beetroot, which also had edible tops. They were known as *botwinki* in the ghetto. For watering they had a sprinkler system consisting of a few lengths of iron piping running from a metal tub Martin had managed to buy from the foreman of one of the ghetto's *Altmaterialressort*. He got it for a reasonable price, presumably because it had a gaping hole in the bottom. They heaved it up onto a tall wooden trestle they had found in the shed, and Martin plugged the hole in the bottom with a spare saucepan lid. Then they bored a small hole in the underside of the trestle, and inserted the metal piping. Then all they had to do was fill the tub with water they got from troughs and butts outside the other *działky*. When it was time to put the sprinkler on, Martin clambered onto the wall with a long metal rod with a hook on the end and nudged the saucepan lid a centimetre or two, sending water gushing down the pipe from the tub, leaking from every little hole and non-watertight join as it went.

As time went by, children took to coming to watch them at work. Youngish children, aged from about five to no more than ten; some of them were astonishingly clean and well dressed. There was one particular boy of eight or so, who was dressed in a rib-knit woollen sweater that scarcely reached his waist, knee-length shorts and worn-down *trepki* of the kind all the ghetto children wore in all seasons and weathers. He had half a dozen companions of varying ages, who clustered around him as though he were their natural leader. 'They're "rich people's children",' said Aleks when he came out to visit one Sunday, 'children of the *kierownicy*. Their parents have already saved their lives once. Now they daren't keep them in the centre of the ghetto any longer.'

One day, when the children were as usual standing in a circle round the garden wall, two men from the Sonder appeared and asked to look at their workbooks, lease and licence. Martin handed over the letter from the Department of Agriculture, and the two policemen bent over it, hummed and hawed and swung on their heels. 'That seems to be in order,' said the elder of the two, folding and handing back the sheet of paper. 'But your seedlings won't be left in peace for much longer.' This last comment with a nod back towards the wall, where the boy in the ribbed sweater was popping his head up to try to see what the secret bit of paper was the policemen were passing between them.

'The Fifth Police District is a big one, it's hard to keep it all under surveillance,' said the other policeman. 'Especially the little *działky* like this, they have problems unless they get extra protection.'

'How much?' asked Martin, who had realised straight away the direction the conversation was taking.

The elder policeman cast an appraising eye over the wall and frowned deeply as he did the calculations.

'For a plot that size, generally around fifty marks.'

'A season?' Martin asked.

'A week,' said the policeman. 'We don't commit ourselves to

anything longer-term than that. After all, neither you nor I can say for sure what will happen in the ghetto next week, can we?'

But in the end they agreed to a slightly lower price, and although they grumbled quite a bit about it being too low, the policemen duly put in an appearance all through the autumn, and even helped to weed the plot and turn the soil, and then to dig up the first of the potatoes. One of them called himself Górski, and told them the wages were the main reason he had joined Gertler's Sonder – they got eight hundred marks a month and two lots of soup a day – and those wages had enabled him to escape *di shpere* and hang on to all his children. He had three, he told them proudly, all girls.

All through that long, mild autumn, caravans of hungry city dwellers made their way out to Marysin each work-free Sunday. Most were ordinary employees of the ghetto offices and departments, who like the Schulz family had been favoured by the powers that be and become responsible 'landowners'. Many of them pushed wheelbarrows; others pulled little wagons or handcarts containing their spades, buckets, forks and rakes, clearly home-made just like Josel's and Martin's. It was a race against time. Winter, *der libe vinter* as the song called it, would soon be here, and anything growing that had not been taken out of the ground by then, when the frost came, would have to stay there until long into the following year. Always assuming a new spring came at all.

The Gliksman family had a plot of their own, not far from the Schulzes'. From there, Aleks brought them pumpkin seeds, which they sowed by the wall once they had harvested the potatoes.

When they were working together at the archive, Věra had never particularly noticed what Aleks looked like. He had always had that way of creeping up on her, sideways and on the fringes; you hardly ever saw him come or go. Now she could see how skinny he was. He had a long scarf wound round his neck, and his ears protruded above it like a pair of red pot handles. Only the eyes looking at her were still the same. Calm, unwavering and curious.

They walked up Marysińska Street in the dusky October light, and just as if it were an ordinary day in the archive, he told her all the rumours he had snapped up. The Allies had taken Naples and got a firm foothold on the Italian mainland. The Russian forces were nearing Kiev and might soon retake the Ukrainian capital. And if Kiev fell, if the Ukraine fell, then as everybody knew, it could only be a matter of time until the Red Army reached the banks of the Weichsel.

We could have the liberators here before Hanukkah!

He smiled, but somehow the smile didn't make it all the way up to his eyes. There was something stern and vigilant in that way he had of watching her, as if trying to read the effect his words were having on her.

Her father had repeatedly warned her not to confide in anyone in the ghetto. Don't even trust those you know. *Hunger makes informers of us all!*

But at that moment, as they made their way through the avenue of fruit trees behind Praszkier's workshop in the strangely smoke-hued October twilight, Věra found herself telling Aleks the dream she had had when she was ill: how in the depths of the dream, she thought she had seen once more the block of flats in Brzezińska Street where the young engineer Schmied had lived. There had been an old barrow there, its wheel taken off but its handles propped against the wall of the building; and just as there used to be all over the ghetto that once was, the whole area was swarming with children. They were either standing in the courtyard with their elbows raised above their shoulders, as if they were on their way through tall grass, or sitting in the dark entranceways where steps led up into the two stairwells: hundreds of children squeezed between the walls and handrails, wearing trousers with braces and torn blouses, with shaven heads and their thin, scabbed knees drawn up to their chins.

Then she knew this was *the place*.

She knew it with an absolute, unerring certainty, just as she knew into exactly which book she had glued the sheets of newspaper Aleks had asked her to archive; for one vertiginous moment the whole ghetto metamorphosed into one huge archive, the vaulted interiors of the stairwells and the courtyard walls with scraps of text and secret messages stuck all over them, and at the very top of the block Schmied had lived in, the light was still on in the attic with the loose bricks behind which she had seen him conceal the radio receiver he had put together.

But the children on the steps blocked her way. It was impossible to get past them. And even if she *could* have got past, she would have lacked the strength to do so. Maybe that was what prompted her, despite her father's warnings, to tell Aleks everything. She would never be able to get all the way up there on her own.

'But you've still got the key?' he asked.

His eyes were so big they seemed to be glued onto her.

'Yes, I've got the key,' she answered, and clenched her hand, just as she had in the dream: her fingers closed tightly round what she had promised herself nobody outside would ever see.

So in the ghetto there were: *the living and the dead*.

But the thing was, the living were not necessarily among all those who tramped daily up and down the tall wooden bridges of the ghetto. Nor the dead necessarily among those who had formerly tramped the same worn steps but had now been taken out and deported, nobody knew where.

Pinkas Szwarc, or Pinkas the Forger as he was known, was employed in the Department of Statistics, where his work consisted of preparing workbooks and passes for all the Jews the Germans still kept at work. It was Pinkas the Forger, too, who back in the days when the ghetto was young was given the task of designing the worthless coins and notes that were to serve as its internal currency. As well as the ghetto's equally worthless postage stamps. On the stamps, the Chairman is smiling benevolently, in front of a stylised wooden bridge set into a giant cogwheel. The ultimate symbol of work, power and prosperity in the ghetto.

Unser einziger Weg, et cetera.

As well as producing legal tender, Pinkas the Forger also painted the scenery for Moshe Pulawer's Ghetto Revue. The designs may have looked innocent at first glance: traditional scenes of birch trees and pastures, and ghetto exteriors of alleyways with ramshackle hovels crowding in, and leaning street lamps. But closer inspection revealed curious, unsettling details. From behind a rural earth closet peered the head of a devil. A chariot of angels blowing *shoifer*-horns swept over a roofscape of chimneys, in billowing clouds of smoke. The Chairman, too, appeared here and there in various incarnations. Disguised as a rabbi, he stood outside a bathhouse stuffing protesting children into a big bathtub, or waded out into a river with a fishing net in his hand, full of people thinly disguised as fish. The Ghetto Revue was performed in a total of 111 variations between May 1940 and August 1942, and on each of those evenings the ghetto potentates sat through it listening out for indecent jokes or insulting allusions from the actors, concentrating so hard on each line that they never noticed the restrained insurrection going on in the pictures behind them.

When the call came to design the exhibits for the big Industrial Exhibition, Pinkas the Forger saw it as the chance of a lifetime.

The authorities had decided to make the old children's hospital at 37 Łagiewnicka Street available as the venue for the big Industrial Exhibition, but a lot needed to be done before the building could serve as an exhibition hall. Pinkas arranged for his two younger brothers – both carpenters – to be commissioned to do the work, and together they set about breaking up the ground floor of the hospital and shifting out all the rock and earth.

Now it might be assumed that a project like that ought to arouse suspicion; piles of sand and rubble, larger than expected and all in one place, point to there being something untoward brewing. But the German guards keeping an eye on the building site took it for granted that everything was in order. Everything happening inside the hoardings had, after all, been decided and approved at the highest level. So when the first delegation of officers from the Wehrmacht came to inspect the gleaming glass display cases full of muffs and earmuffs and snowshoes and camouflage uniforms, they did not know there were already some twenty Jews crouching in the three underground chambers Pinkas the Forger and his brothers had excavated beneath their feet.

That was the start of what in the ghetto came to be known as the bunker – a place where the ghetto's dead could dwell, and not be confused with those who were still alive. A place, too, where those who, like the piano tuner, were constantly moving between the realms of the living and the dead, could pause and rest between journeys.

The piano tuner was used to confined spaces, anyway.

In all the years that had passed since he first set foot in the ghetto, he had not grown to a size that would prevent him climbing inside a piano if the need arose. He turned up at the House of Culture one morning. Pinkas the Forger was standing on a stepladder painting scattered clouds on a backdrop of unchangingly blue ghetto sky when the piano tuner came onto the stage with his two threadbare bags of tuning instruments and his by now equally worn-out question, and Pinkas did not even bother to take the brushes out of his mouth to reply, merely pointing in the direction of the concert grand belonging to conductor Bajgelman; and like an animal that has finally found its way home, the piano tuner opened the lid of the grand piano and climbed in.

His task accomplished, he tried to make himself useful in any way he could. He carried Miss Rotsztat's instrument for her every time she had a solo evening performance, and helped the Schum twins get in and out of their stage costumes. He clipped tickets, showed the high-ranking guests to their reserved seats in the front row, emptied ashtrays, and chatted to anyone who happened to linger in the foyer.

But then came *di groise shpere*, and when musicians and actors reconvened at the start of October, only half the orchestra members were there, the children's chorus was no more, and of the stage hands only Mr Dawidowicz and his assistant, clumsy little Herzel (whom everyone used to tease) remained. The House of Culture, they were informed, would from then on be used exclusively for prize-giving ceremonies and other such serious events, not for scandalous revues. Bajgelman was preparing to disband the orchestra. And the musicians were either too tired or too debilitated by hunger and illness even to think of carrying on playing.

But the piano tuner refused to give up. If the *resort* workers could no longer come to the theatre, he said, then couldn't the theatre come to them?

*

Although there were no longer any children's homes in the ghetto, Rosa Smoleńska was still in the employ of the Health and Social Department. She sat all day in a dingy corner of Miss Wołk's secretariat in Dworska Street, recording applications for milk substitutes for pregnant women or extra allowances of rationed foods for tuberculosis patients. But from time to time she also taught languages, arithmetic and Jewish history to the children of top ghetto officials, at selected factories. She and her pupils had to make do with whatever space they could find: dusty stock rooms or some box room the director had made available; and they had to put up with constant interruptions, like the sound of the factory whistle, or the arrival of a sudden extra order that meant all available labour had to be mobilised immediately.

But there were some moments of light relief. One was when the theatre coach came trundling through the factory gates during the dinner break and parked itself, to universal cheers, right outside the watchman's hut where the factory supervisor liked to lurk with the foremen.

Obviously it was difficult when 'on tour' to perform more than a couple of the acts from the Ghetto Revue; so they padded out their *plotki* with a selection of songs.

Mrs Harel sang the song of Berele and Braindele, accompanied on the violin by Mr Gelbroth. Out in the open air, the pitch of the violin was thin and brittle, like a thumbnail running down a pane of glass. The next item sounded better, as the whole troupe broke into the patter song *Tsip tsipele*, with new words by Mr Bajgelman himself, all about the Soup Lady – *pani Wydzielaczka*. Everyone knew her! It was the fat, short-sighted woman behind the serving hatch on the first floor, who dispensed soup to them every day: just skimming the surface of the soup for people she mistrusted, but dipping her ladle in gloriously deep for those who had somehow won her respect. Greatly touched to find themselves featuring personally in the spectacle presented by the unfamiliar band of players, the whole audience joined in: two hundred women in headscarves, all together –

Pani vidzelatske: Ich mayn nisht GELEKHTER
– A bisele tifer, A bisele GEDEKHTER*

– rattling and beating their spoons in their soup mugs until director Stech put his hands over his ears and asked the caretaker to sound the factory whistle to shut them up.

Rosa Smoleńska recognised the piano tuner straight away. The last time she had seen him, he was sitting on a stepladder tampering with the bell on the kitchen wall in the Green House. Now he was perched in just the same position on the baggage rail atop Bajgelman's theatre coach, balancing there like a fly on the rim of a jam jar.

When the performance was over and Mr Gelbroth was going round with his violin case to beg for coins or crusts of bread, the piano tuner hopped down from the roof of the coach and walked briskly over to Miss Smoleńska. There were a few things he had to tell her. About the piano in the Green House. Which was still there, and in good condition, he was able to inform her. The problem was, he couldn't get to it any more, because the house had been converted into an *Erholungsheim*. Not for

---

* Soup Lady, Soup Lady, this is no JOKE, / Filling your ladle won't make me CHOKE.

the children of the Praeses this time, but for Mr Gertler's *own people*, who you could hear singing in there, bellowing at the tops of their voices, and they couldn't play, either. How could he get at the piano when the whole place was full of Sonder? Could Miss Smoleńska tell him that?

He had hardly uttered the word Sonder before a ripple of unease ran through the crowd, and the youngest female factory employees started shrieking:

Loyf, loyf! – der Zonderman kimt!!!

Inside the watchman's hut, two of the foremen became aware of the danger, and came dashing out, flapping the skirts of their aprons. *Shoo, shoo!* they cried, as if the women were a flock of hens that could thus be driven back to their work benches.

This particular unit of the ghetto Sonderabteilung was led by a tall, thin man wearing a slightly grubby-looking chalk-stripe suit, at least two sizes too big for him. The face beneath his peaked cap was smooth and pale, every bone and muscle visible, from his hairline down to his pointed chin.

Dokumente! he shouted at Gelbroth, who was clutching his violin case as if it were a life jacket or a babe in arms to be defended with his life.

Some of the assembled women were certainly surprised that this Jewish *politsajt* insisted on addressing the theatre troupe in German. But not Rosa Smoleńska. Since that early Sabbath morning when the Kohlman brothers from the Cologne collective had knocked at the door with young Mr Samstag dangling between them, she had never spoken anything but German with the Green House's eldest and, one must suppose, most difficult child. She knew that Samstag had subsequently taught himself to affect both Polish and Yiddish. But *affect* was precisely the word. It was the same with the German he was now pretending to speak to Mr Gelbroth. It sounded exactly like the bombastic German of command and authority, strewn with the odd word of Polish or Yiddish, that the *dygnitarze* of the ghetto employed when they were trying to make themselves seem important. But he couldn't fool Rosa.

– *Beruf? Oder hast du keine Arbeit?*
– *Ich bin Schauspieler.*
– *Was machst du denn hier – du shóyte – wenn du Schauspieler bist?*
– *Ich habe hier meine gute Arbeit!*
– *Hörs mal oyf zum shráien, wir sind nisht afn di stséne!*

The piano tuner was hanging wide-eyed on Miss Smoleńska's arm.

Samstag, he whispered, with something like reverence in his voice. From his newly attained height of someone in command, Samstag looked down at the piano tuner with a smile which resembled a sack full of shiny teeth.

Samstag ist leider im Getto kein Ruhetag, was all he said before handing the documents back to Mr Gelbroth and leaving the factory yard, his men following in his wake.

They had made a decision after all, then, the Sonder: *not* to disperse the crowd, despite the fact that they very well could have done, and that the regulations required it. Nor had they taken the fleeing theatrical troupe into custody; they had let Bajgelman's coach move on, as it would for the months and years that followed. More than one *resort* would be cheered up by these *badchonim* who came and drove away the constant pangs of hunger with a few dissonant chords on the violin and songs you recognised and could join in with.

But the piano tuner suddenly looked very small, huddled there on top of the theatre coach's mound of props:

Just imagine Samstag – der shóyte! –

But then, as he formed his lips to find the tune for a song about how a lonely orphanage boy came to be a *politsajt* in the army of Gertler himself, his body and face began to tremble, and not a note emerged. The piano tuner was to make many attempts at that song, in different keys and registers; but even the ghetto's own cement-grey key – hollowed out and emptied of all resonance – did not seem able to generate the right tune.

Rosa Smoleńska had done everything she possibly could to find out what had happened to the Green House children. In the Secretariat in Dworska Street there were several grey files to which technically only Miss Wołk had access, but Rosa had crept in now and again to take a look inside them. Once she had been caught at it by Miss Wołk herself. *If I see you nosing into the Adoption Committee minutes again, I shall personally see to it that you are deported*, Miss Wołk had said, as Rosa gathered her skirts around her legs and stood bolt upright, arms at her sides with her eyes on the ground, as she had learnt to do whenever anyone in authority accused her of anything. *No, Mr Rumkowski, I wasn't standing there listening*, she said, that time the Chairman locked himself into the office with the 'naughty' girls in Helenówek; she said the same thing now:

> *No, Miss Wołk, there must be some misunderstanding. Miss Wołk, I've never seen any files like that.*

Only to return to Miss Wołk's office day after day and painstakingly, file by file, memorise all the names.

First and foremost, the Praeses children. This was the name given to those for whom the Chairman had found apprenticeship places as part of his great campaign to 'save the children of the ghetto': either in the newly established apprentices' school in Franciszkańska Street, or straight in at the Central Tailoring Workshop. The youngsters had become model workers, and the Praeses children were therefore in great demand among those who wrote to the Secretariat after *di shpere* and applied to adopt.

It was also apparent that the people applying had often lost children of their own in the events of September.

Kazimir's new parents, former tram driver Jurczak Topoliński and his wife, had lost both their boys, one aged six, the other four. Nataniel's foster parents had lost a daughter, born the very day the Germans entered Poland, 1 September 1939. I always thought, her mother said, that the fact she shared her birthday with the war would protect her, but the Germans came on the very first day of the curfew and took her away from me. Can you explain that to me, Miss Smoleńska? How can anyone expect a little girl of three to cope all by herself without her mummy?

There were tales of survival, too. There was much talk in the ghetto of the *well children*. There were several versions of the story. One was about a girl of two who was put in a sling made of sheets and lowered into a well on the chain usually used for sending down the buckets. When the Germans came, the girl's parents said she had died of typhus and they had had to burn all her clothes and bury them in the yard, because of the risk of infection. The girl was kept down in the cold well in her sling of sheets for seven days. Every day they lowered food and water for her, until the curfew was lifted and they could haul her up again. She was cold and exhausted, but alive.

And she was still alive. Because the remarkable thing about these well children was that once the *szpera* operation had raged its last, nobody cared about the fact that they had been on the deportation lists. The bureaucratic apparatus of the ghetto enfolded them anew, and the girl in the well got a new set of bread coupons and ration cards.

Debora Żurawska, the child who was perhaps closest of all to Rosa, would also have got an apprenticeship place in

Franciszkańska Street, except that after the Chairman's visit to the Green House and what happened to Mirjam, she refused to have anything more to do with the Praeses of the ghetto. Rosa knew no more of her present life than what was in the files in Miss Wołk's office.

Herrn PLOT, Maciej, FRANZSTR. 133

In Beantwortung Ihres Gesuches vom 24.9.1942 wird Ihnen hiermit das Kind ŻURAWSKA, Debora im Alter von 15 Jahren zur Aufnahme in Ihre Familie zugeteilt.

Litzmannstadt Getto, den 25.9.42 –

No. 133 Franzstrasse/Franciszkańska turned out to be a row of wooden shanties by a shallow ditch with sewage and rubbish floating in it. There was no door on the street side, and the only window in the row had long since been boarded up and sealed with mortar. When Rosa attempted to make her way across the stinking ditch and round the back of the building, she was confronted by a bunch of men who audibly and with much wild gesturing assured her that no Debora Żurawska lived there, nor any Maciej Plot for that matter, whatever the documents claimed.

When Rosa Smoleńska went to the Department of Statistics, she was informed by a weary clerk that there certainly had been a person named Maciej Plot in the ghetto, but that his name had been deleted from the register. Maciej Plot had been employed at the sawmill in Drukarska Street. In January 1942 he had been put on the Resettlement Committee's list of 'undesirable elements' in the ghetto, and in February he had been deported. Someone had accused him of stealing offcuts from the sawmill's plank store. The accusation could have been genuine, or it could have been trumped up to save someone else's skin. That was the winter, after all, said the clerk, when it was so cold in the ghetto that everybody stole; and those who for whatever reason had no chance to steal just froze to death before they even got as far as the waiting trains in Marysin.

But if Maciej Plot had been deported or was dead, who had filled in the adoption papers in his name? And in that case where, and with *whom*, was young Miss Żurawska now?

What Rosa still did not know was that there were two ways for a Jew to leave the ghetto. You took either the 'interior' or the 'exterior' route. In both cases, the relatives you left behind had to hand in your workbook and ration cards, which were then cancelled by the authorities in question, who stamped them with the word **TOT** or **AUSGESIEDELT** – depending which route had been chosen.

But the fact that a workbook had been stamped was not the same as its former owner being entirely out of circulation. There were artful men who bought up ration cards that had been left behind, or bribed employees of the Central Labour Office not to put their stamp on the identity papers of the deportees. As soon as the availability of a new consignment of rations was announced, they went round with the dead people's cards and used up the vouchers left in them. Bread, rye flakes, sugar. Since there were so many moving out, tens of thousands of men and women in the course of just a few months, this meant a considerable amount of food ended up on the black market, where it could be bought by those who had *gelt genug* – that is to say, who had already done well out of other sorts of business.

One of the individuals raising the dead like this was a known ghetto thief and swindler named *Mogn* – The Belly. The Belly was even craftier than the rest. He took the workbooks and ration cards of the dead to the *resort* bosses in the ghetto and persuaded them to take on their previous employees again. This admittedly meant they would be obliged to pay out wages to people who had been deported, but The Belly swiftly offered to bear that expense himself. The point was that the dead could then carry on drawing their benefits and getting their ration cards renewed, basically for ever.

An empire built on nothing, a shadow empire; but The Belly was a rich man:

When he received guests, he sat in an armchair two metres tall, his rump and back supported on soft, silken cushions and his enormous paunch, slack but majestic, hanging down between his two flabby forearms. A good and dutiful Jew who kept the Sabbath holy, followed all the prescribed rituals and even thought he could afford to keep kosher. What was more, he did charitable works. To show his piety and his charitable zeal, he decided to apply for the guardianship of some of the poor orphaned children forced out of their *ochronki* after the *szpera* operation, who were now being auctioned off by the Wołkówna Secretariat. A flock of his most deserving dead people – among them former sawmill worker Maciej Plot – filled in the adoption forms, and they were all completed so correctly that not even Miss Wołk and her colleagues in the Adoption Committee could find any fault.

So it was that Debora Żurawska, too, found herself in the kingdom of the dead, although she was still among the living.

She naturally had to surrender her workbook and ration cards as soon as she set foot in The Belly's home. In exchange for a very modest share of her own rations, she scrubbed the floors in the row of shanties in Franciszkańska Street, or ran around after one of the many 'wives' The Belly had acquired over the years. Still being pretty, she had to put in some hours in one of the 'rest homes' which Gertler had taken over from the Chairman, and which The Belly had now populated with the dead so he had something to offer the jaded policemen who came in for a rest. In one of these homes there was a piano, and since Debora Żurawska was rumoured once to have played the piano, she also had to provide musical entertainment for The Belly's guests.

Rosa Smoleńska had been back to the Population Registry to make further enquiries, and been told that The Belly had arranged a temporary job for Debora at the hat and cap factory in Brzezińska Street. It was the one that made the earmuffs for the German army. Day after day, Rosa waited outside the gates in the hope of catching a glimpse of her former protégée. In the end, one of the other workers took pity on the patiently waiting figure and told her that if it was Debora she wanted, there was another way out, which the girl always used. So Rosa switched her attention to the back of the factory, where there was a small loading bay, and at the end of the shift the next evening she saw Debora coming out that way with a handful of other young girls. Waiting at the base of the loading platform like some sort of escort were two men she recognised from their encounter outside the shanty row in Franciszkańska Street.

Debora is another person, yet still the same.

Thinner, but with her stomach as distended as so many of the other hungry children, and a face as lean as an animal's. And she walks with a strange, crab-like gait, one shoulder hunched up towards the back of her neck. Rosa recalls she used to walk like that when they were carrying the water up from the well together, but that was because her body was counterbalancing the weight of the full bucket they carried between them; icy cold autumn or winter mornings with the dark earth like a bowl formed of two cupped hands with the lightening sky between them. Debora had told her about all the things she would do when the war was over: apply to the Warsaw conservatoire, maybe go to London or Paris; and after each confidence, she would change hands on the bucket handle. Debora is walking the same way now – but there is no bucket. On her feet she has a pair of *trepki*, their soles so worn that she has to lift one leg as she turns, or is she in fact *limping*?

Rosa sees it now. They must have beaten her up.

She runs after her:

I've found you a job, she says, or rather shouts, since Debora
Żurawska is doing her utmost to drag her awkward, twisted
body after the other factory girls, who have hurried on ahead.

In the packing shed at Tusk's china factory.
You'll be packing fuses. There are plenty of jobs in the packing
hall there!
Any number of them!

But Debora does not turn round.

Instead, Rosa finds one of The Belly's guards on either side
of her. They have the peaks of their caps pulled well down and
are smiling through immobile faces. They smile even as they
grab Rosa round the waist and fling her to the ground.

The girls have got as far as Franciszkańska Street now, and
The Belly is standing outside waiting for them. He is even
bigger than in real life than the rumours suggest. So fat in the
stomach that he can scarcely walk without others to support
him. Two youngish women and a man who looks like a younger
version of himself – his son (if that is what he is) even has the
same kind of Phrygian cap on his head as his father. The bunch
advances as one across the dried mud. The paunch that has
given The Belly his nickname hangs between his thighs like a
loose, shapeless sack. One might have expected The Belly to
be parading all the full bellies he has enjoyed, but The Belly's
stomach hangs empty, and maybe that explains his fury. He
starts to speak even before they reach her. He knows who she
is, he says. She works at the Wołkówna Secretariat doesn't she?
Parasites, he says. That's what you are, drawing your wages
for interfering with the rights of upstanding citizens, because
your precious Praeses only has eyes for the children, of course,
for the *little ones*, he gives them oranges and *chocolates*, but
we adults, *capable* men who do their jobs and support their
families, what do we get, oh yes, he thanks us by sending

people like Miss Wołk, not to mention you – *Smoleńska* – that's not even a proper Jewish name!

And all the time The Belly is spitting forth his contempt, Rosa Smoleńska can hear an insistent ringing in her head, just as she did that time the Chairman locked himself in with Mirjam and the piano tuner climbed the stepladder and put his tuning fork to the bell in the hall. And just as it did then, the noise seems to drive away all the light and space around them. Everything is swallowed up or dissolved in that appalling noise, which stops them thinking or breathing, or doing or saying anything at all.

And Rosa sees that Debora's once slim piano fingers are ruined, inflamed and red and sore, as if they have been dipped in lye; and stuffed into, or rather wrapped in, a pair of gloves that look more like a bundle of rags. She automatically takes the girl's hand, and Deborah cries out in pain and tries to pull away, and someone (is it The Belly again?) starts up again:

'Who actually are you, Miss Smoleńska?' And Rosa replies: 'I am the girl's mother.' Debora immediately says: 'I have no mother, I never have had a mother.' And The Belly: 'Get this woman out of here right now, you lot.'

*

The ghetto's Sonderabteilung had its headquarters on the other side of Bałuty Square, looking out on the back yard of the building at the corner of Limanowskiego and Zgierska Streets that housed the Gestapo offices and the First District of the police. All visitors to the Sonder had first to present themselves to the German guard manning the barrier, and if he found their papers in order, they then walked round the barrier and in through a little gate to the left of the actual Gestapo building.

There were no lights on behind the barred windows, but a cluster of men were standing outside, warming themselves round an improvised brazier in the yard: a big, wide-bellied metal drum, long since blackened, from which sulphurous black smoke billowed and fumed. All the air in the yard was permeated with a faint smoke haze that made bodies and faces pale and indistinct.

Samstag did not say anything as she approached, but turned away with a slight smile – as if she had caught him doing something shameful. On his arm he wore the Sonderabteilung's armband with the Star of David. The peaked cap that went with it had been laid aside with the others on the window sill, but she could see that the sweatband inside had left a clear mark on his forehead, a narrow stripe, shining like an inflamed wound in the reflected gleam of the fire. The only thing that was still the same was that row of sharp, even teeth, shiny and wet with saliva when they were bared by his smile.

Are you his bit of skirt now? was all he said, and then in Polish, so the others would hear as well: *Czy jesteś jego kochanką?*

At the expression *bit of skirt*, the other men drew closer to the brazier and eyed Rosa impudently, with big smiles on their faces. The smoke from the burning drum forced tears from her eyes, and suddenly her whole body was shaking helplessly.

Samstag stepped forward and held her.

There there, he said. *Don't cry.*

The hands that held her were firm and calloused. She could smell the sweat and the ingrained, stale smoke in his clothes, and something else besides, sweet and cloying, and suddenly it was all too much, and she felt something give way. Like the feeble, rambling old woman she has been reduced to, she tells him about her visit to Franciszkańska Street; about Debora who only came out to turn her away; and about her hands: 'she'll never be able to apply to the Conservatoire with those' (these were her exact words); and about the repulsive Belly, who couldn't walk unaided and whose once bulging stomach now hung like a limp bag of flesh between his legs. She does not know if Samstag is listening or not. Maybe he is. At the mention of The Belly's name, however, the smiles of the other policemen fade. The Belly is a powerful man from whom many of the Sonder have taken bribes. She sees them turning their backs, suddenly indifferent.

But Samstag carries on comforting her – ever more mechanically and persistently:

Nie płacz, kochana, nie płacz . . .

The roles are reversed. Inconceivable that this is the body she once lifted out of Chaja Meyer's bathtub in the kitchen of the Green House: the rangy teenager who had tried to cover himself when the coarse, frayed towel got down to his private parts. She thinks about the children in the well. How long can they stay down there in the cold, dead water without something changing irrevocably inside them, so they come back up as another person?

Two days after her visit, a unit of Gertler's Sonderabteilung went to The Belly's overpopulated residence in Franciszkańska Street. Reports disagreed on what actually happened next. Some said Samstag had led the operation in person. Others were sure he had held back, to let his men deal with the matter on their own.

The witnesses were all, however, in perfect agreement that the police had entered the house without warning. They had swung their batons to drive out all the women and children, and set about body-searching all the men they had seized. A large number of knives were confiscated, along with fat wads of Reichsmarks and American dollars. In cases like this, the unwritten rule was that the police officers on duty pocketed the bundles of notes they confiscated. Seeing them do this, The Belly was shocked out of the temporary paralysis induced by the unexpected raid, and with his head drawn into his shoulders, he charged the police.

Certain people said that the Belly's vast paunch was just a common oedema. That The Belly was as starving as everyone else. But be that as it may, he was still possessed of a brute strength never before seen in the ghetto. It took several men to wrestle the immense body to the floor, and The Belly almost broke free several times. According to some sources, while all this was going on, Samstag pushed his way through the knot of battling policemen, bent back The Belly's mighty bovine neck and beat him with his baton until the blood spurted from his smashed nose and the resisting body finally slumped back.

It was said that The Belly then tried to run away.

But he didn't get far with his eyes full of blood and a body he could not hold upright on his own.

Outside the house, he was brought down in yet another tussle.

In the middle of the yard, just as in all the other yards in the ghetto, there was a pump. On the pump was a curved iron hook, for hanging a bucket on while you pumped up the water. The Belly was lying on his back on the ground by the pump, his face a furious mask of blood and mud. There were six men sitting on his arms and legs to stop him getting up again. Some witnesses said Samstag then stepped forward to the felled figure. From the depths of his smile, shiny with saliva, he asked The Belly if he knew what the punishment was for men who assaulted the children entrusted to their care.

It is doubtful whether The Belly understood what Samstag was talking about. His jawbone had probably been smashed by the baton blows Samstag had already dealt him, for his mouth was hanging slackly and a growing froth of saliva and blood was forming over his cracked lower lip.

Two of Samstag's men forced The Belly's arms behind his back to make him get up. The Belly presumably thought they were trying to arrest him, so he made his body as heavy as he could. Samstag took advantage of this, and with the men still holding on to The Belly, he took a firm grasp on his head and brought it down on the pump so that the protruding iron hook plunged straight into The Belly's left eye.

The Belly let out an almost animal bellow.

Samstag's men kept their grip on both his arms. As the blood flowed, the gouged-out eye dangled on its string like an egg, coated in an oily, brownish membrane. Samstag siezed hold of The Belly's head again, countered the heaving and thrusting of his body with calm, careful, almost affectionate manoeuvres – and forced the head down onto the pump handle again. It was done more slowly this time. The Belly struggled against it with everything he had: arms, legs, shoulders, back. But Samstag was patient. Unimaginably slowly, punctuated by short, intense jolts as The Belly seemed on the verge of tearing himself free, the bloodied pump hook eased into his right eye, too.

And there he lay, the once almighty, like a bull in a slaughterhouse with blood coursing from his blinded face.

While all this was in progress, a curious crowd had gathered. First those who lived under The Belly's own roof, about a score of them, women and children; then passers-by, who had heard the commotion from the street and dashed in to investigate. Debora realised that if she wanted to escape, she would have to do it now, before the police withdrew and The Belly began to wreak his terrible vengeance. She went back into the house, packed what few possessions she had in her old rucksack and then waded through the wide, sludge-bottomed ditch out into the street. Then she wandered for hours in the streets around Bałuty Square, asking everyone she met if they could possibly tell her where Rosa Smoleńska lived.

The ghetto clock at the corner of Zawiszy Czarnego and Łagiewnicka Streets showed almost five. In the encroaching winter darkness, the slushy pavements were crowded with people leaving factories and workshops. One of the passers-by thought he knew of an old schoolmistress by the name of Smoleńska who lived in the same block of flats as his sister in Brzezińska Street. She would have no trouble finding the place.

It had a bay window at the front.

It was on the front steps of the building with the peeling bay window that Rosa Smoleńska found Debora Żurawska many hours later, when she got home. The girl was sitting huddled at the top of the steps, right outside the front door, shivering with terror and cold. Rosa put her to sleep in her bed, while she slept rolled up in some thick blankets on the dirty floor in front of the stove. In the grey dawn light, Debora got up, packed her rucksack and disappeared off to work without a word. But she was back in Rosa's flat that evening, bringing with her all her ration cards, and as a signal of her intention to stay, she let Rosa lock them in the kitchen drawer where she kept her own card and coupons.

This is a city of workers, Herr Reichsführer, not a ghetto.

In 1943 and the early part of 1944, Hans Biebow could look out over an empire that was the closest a ghetto could get to a fully functioning city of workers. Ninety per cent of the population worked in the factories and workshops Rumkowski had established on Biebow's orders. Production was efficient, proceeds were high. The previous year (1942), the Gettoverwaltung as a whole had made a net profit of almost ten million Reichsmarks, a prodigious sum.

But if you ran a *Musterlager*, it made others envious. So far, the ghetto had been under civilian administration, but the SS, which under Himmler was looking more and more like a state within the state, was making ever more audacious moves to get its hands on the lucrative ghetto. If the Litzmannstadt ghetto became a labour camp, it could be run much more efficiently under a military regime, the SS argued. A concrete proposal had already been submitted by the organisation's so-called Wirtschaftsverwaltungshauptamt to move the whole ghetto, heavy machinery and all, to Lublin, where the ghetto (in terms of numbers of Jews) was almost as large but only a tenth as productive. If the ghetto industries of Lublin and Litzmannstadt were merged, the profit generated by the rationalisation would run into millions. The SS had worked it all out.

Biebow did what he could to keep the SS and Reichsführer Himmler at bay. He went to Posen to make sure he had the continuing support of the civilian administration there. He went to Berlin and met Speer and representatives of the army's Rüstungskommando, which despite the massive retreats in the

East continued to fill the order books of the ghetto with orders for uniforms and war equipment. As long as the war effort continued at the current highly intensive level, the Wehrmacht would never accept any moves or changes that might threaten a stoppage or interruption in the supply chain. But Biebow knew everything was hanging by the slenderest of threads; if there were any more setbacks on the Eastern front, the Führer might suddenly start listening to Himmler again and order relocation or restructuring of the ghetto.

The war, which had made Biebow's fortune in so many ways, was ultimately a double-edged sword. At times, a dreadful suspicion came over Biebow that the ghetto he otherwise considered so stable and secure had no solid foundation at all, that everything he had built up was mere show, and a single word – a single stroke of the pen on a despatch from Berlin – would be enough to bring it all crashing down . . . Like when the new mayor of Litzmannstadt, Otto Bradfisch, claimed at their recent meeting that the ghetto was not a *Musterlager* at all, but on the contrary, *a disgrace, Herr Biebow, a disgrace . . . !* The normally self-controlled and chilly Bradfisch thumped his fist on the police reports that had piled up on his desk. Biebow knew very well what these contained; they were reports of Kripo employees bribed to turn a blind eye to 'losses' from the factories, and of officials in his own administration who had, in exchange for a generous private commission, agreed to set the workers to producing women's underwear for Neckermann's in Berlin instead of fulfilling existing orders for the army on time; and *how can it be possible that to this very day, officials in your own administration are letting themselves be bribed by Jews, how can it be possible, Herr Biebow?*

And what help then are Biebow's attempts to explain that corruption is in the Jewish *nature*, which he repeats over and over again (he blames the Jews even though it was his own administrative staff who did the stealing). *Then see to it that this nature is suppressed once and for all!* Bradfisch retorts. Biebow is trapped in a vice. No matter what he does or does not do, he is simply giving the SS more arguments for taking charge of the ghetto.

*

Here's Biebow again. It is high summer. In the grass, the crickets send arcs of scraping sound up to the high sky of hunger. Below it, thousands of parched, crook-backed men and women are in constant motion. With carts and barrows, they are making their way out of the stinking back alleys of the ghetto or bent over picks and shovels in the mud and grit by the side of the road.

But Biebow does not see them. His vehicle has stopped by the dilapidated wooden hovel known in the ghetto as Praszkier's workshop. His driver has parked the vehicle a little further on and opened both doors; the bodyguards have sought the shade of the tree. As for him, he is sauntering around with his hands behind his back, watching the dust he has kicked up slowly settle on the toes of his shoes.

On the other side of the road, by the corner of Próżna Street and Okopowa Street, two elderly men are mowing a field. Despite the baking July heat, they are wearing thick jackets, the linings fully visible in the seams on the back and chest where the star-shaped yellow patches have been sewn on. Their scythes glint in the sunlight. They have a can of water, which they keep passing back and forth between them. Then one of them shouts something to Biebow.

What's going on? Something is proffered. Biebow reluctantly makes his way towards them.

One of them has a toothless smile between sunken cheeks. Raises the can. Offers Biebow some water. I thought you might be thirsty in this heat, Sir.

This is naturally something quite unheard of in the ghetto.

A Jew offering a drink to an Aryan, and the first in command at that; not to mention something as insanitary as a communal can of water. Biebow looks from one to the other – they are standing beneath the blades of their scythes; there is a sort of expectant look to their smiles – so he has no choice but at least to uncork the container and wipe his mouth with a grimace (though God knows he's thirsty).

And then it comes, of course. One Jew, feigning tact and discretion, asks if the high-up gentleman can spare a little bread.

What's that? – Bread? –Bread is a rationed commodity. – Any decent man will have been issued with coupons so he can get bread from his local shop.

I've a bookful of coupons, the man persists, but what good are they, if I drag myself round to the distribution point and they say there's no bread to be had – *Es ist kein Brot da*. He makes his voice honeyed and fawning, the way he thinks Germans in authority expect Jews to speak, and says:

I haven't eaten a meal for three whole days.

But Biebow concedes nothing: *Here in the ghetto, there is bread for all who are willing to work.*

At this, the hay-maker plucks up his courage and points out that he jolly well does work, the high-up gentlemen can see that with his own eyes, he and his friend Icek have mowed a whole meadow to provide feed and seed corn for dairyman Mr Michał Gertler and his cows. But there are some people who've never done an honest day's work in their lives. They come and go, those *shiskes*! – Oh yes. – He knows all right. – Some of them even travel in *limouzz-iines*.

He says the word as if it is a warm egg he is holding in his mouth.

All of a sudden, Biebow is listening. *Who*, he says.

The man gives a vague wave of his hand.

Biebow: *And where to?*

The hay-maker: *Where to?*

Biebow: *Where do they go, these people in limousines?*

The hay-maker: *To that place over there.*

Biebow: *What sort of place is it?*

The hay-maker: *They used to call it the Green House. Now I don't know what--*

Biebow: *What? Speak up, man!*

The hay-maker: *A pensie.*

Biebow: *A what?*

The hay-maker: *A boarding house.*

Biebow: *Well, well, a boarding house, is it? For whom, if I might ask?*

And the hay-maker, with a shrug – as if to say: *What do I know? For the people in power? For people with broad shoulders? For people who think they deserve a rest between breaths?* But he says none of this. Nor does he need to. For Herr Biebow is already off, striding up towards the Green House. And the two scythes follow. This could get interesting.

A year after its evacuation in the *szpera* operation, not much is left of the old children's home. The last vestiges of the colour that once gave the orphanage its name flaked off long ago; some kind of rot has started spreading upwards from the heavy stone base of the building, turning the wood into a foul, spongy mass of timber. The roof has caved in, and several of the window frames have been taken out, leaving gaping black holes in the walls. Yet curtains have been put up at some of these holes, and from behind the curtains, a collection of frightened or angry faces is peering.

Biebow bangs on the door lintel with the side of his hand, and, as if the house were a living being, a loud wail suddenly issues from its depths.

Crazy, mutters the old hay-maker, standing close by, *completely crazy*, and what happens next is crazier still. For

437

hardly has Biebow withdrawn his hand than the door is wrenched open and ten or so chickens flap wildly up in front of him. *Yes, real chickens – real, live chickens,* the hay-maker later declares, of the sort not seen in the ghetto since before the Germans came. Biebow must have been equally startled himself. He puts his hands up to his face to protect himself from this fluttering onslaught, and it takes him a while to notice the enormous man sitting in a trolley on the far side of the flapping wings, his mouth open in a scream as crazed and deformed as himself. Yes, some people would certainly have found it hard to recognise The Belly. Not least because of this scream, which he now directs at anything and anyone coming near him in his sightless degradation. How was he to know it was the Amtsleiter himself standing there on the other side of the frenzied chickens? For he could not see a thing. And what Biebow saw was a grotesque, misshapen monster, thrust into a rickety wooden contraption, his body overflowing from its sides, with a belly in the middle, a smooth, blue-veined belly scantily covered by cloth rags, and above it a disfigured face with bloody, crusted scabs where the eyes should have been, and a mouth – gaping, wobbling flesh – screaming at him like a madman.

Mechanically he took two steps back, fumbling for the gun in the holster inside his jacket as if desperate for something to hang on to; and when he finally drew it, he instantly emptied the whole magazine into the repulsive Creature, which was hurled backwards by the force of the bullets and hit the wall with a sort of squelch; and as if they, too, had been hit by a ricochet, the chickens scattered in all directions: the air is filled for a moment with a cloud of blood and fluttering feathers.

Then something very strange happened. A silence fell that unified them all. Biebow was right at the front, with his emptied magazine, his head and shoulders covered in chicken feathers; and beside him, also in chicken suits, stood

The Belly's two guards, who had pushed The Belly's trolley to the door when the knock came because he, despite the risks involved, always wanted to open the door himself; and after the guards came two of the young prostitutes The Belly had insisted on bringing with him to the Green House, who were now displaying themselves at the door, and then, outside said door, the two hay-makers who had joined the walk up from Prazkier's workshop.

At that moment, they were many – and Biebow was alone. One of The Belly's sidekicks could have gone for one of Chaja Meyer's big cook's knives that were still in the top kitchen drawer. And the hay-makers still had their scythes, as well.

Right there and then, somebody could easily have got rid of the highest representative of the tyrannical power that made their lives a daily hell.

But this apparently did not occur to any of them at that precise moment. The Belly's bearers and attendants seemed virtually paralysed by the sight of their master dead; while the hay-maker whose name was Icek had only one idea in his head. The white vestment of feathers had scarcely settled on Herr Amtsleiter's shoulders before Icek took one of the cackling chickens under his arm and dashed off with it down the hill. It meant food for himself and his family for at least a month. Halfway down Zagajnikowa Street he met Biebow's chauffeur and bodyguards, who had heard the shot and come rushing to see what the matter was.

*

Nobody in the ghetto could seriously claim that everything which subsequently happened – the fall of the Palace, Gertler's arrest and the attempt on the Chairman's life – was the result of a common pimp and petty thief called The Belly having his eyes poked out and then being shot by a German. But in Wiewiórka's barber's shop, where these events were the subject of lively discussion, the general conclusion was that in the ghetto, pride went before a fall. That applied as much to petty thieves as it did to *shiskes*. And once a stone had been set rolling . . . !

Mr Tausendgeld, who was the one who had rented out the Green House as a safe haven for the fleeing Belly, was feeding the birds in Princess Helena's aviaries when the first shot rang out from down in Zagajnikowa Street. He was so startled that he almost fell off the ladder; then he ran into the house with his long right arm flailing in front of him:

The English are coming, the English are coming . . .

But it was only the Kripo who came. There must have been about ten of them, and halfway up the stairs to the first floor, where Princess Helena lay on her sickbed, they caught up with him and dragged him back out to the courtyard, where one of their cars was waiting. Half an hour later he was hanging with his arms tied behind his back from the infamous meat hook in the basement of the Red House, while half a dozen men from the prison section admired the comical oddities of nature that had created Mr Tausendgeld's elongated right arm. His body hung very obviously askew, so much askew that his lumpy face pointed *down* to the floor, whereas the prisoners usually had their heads *up*. Custody officer Müller therefore had to swing his rubber-sheathed wooden club up from underneath to land a blow to the head, almost as if perfecting his golf swing. But the blow hit home nonetheless; and Tausendgeld screamed – and his body cowered as it hung there, even though there was nothing to cower behind. But the only name the Kripo interrogator got out of him was Gertler's, which was not the name they wanted to hear at that time.

Meanwhile, Biebow had got back to his office in Bałuty Square. He still had chicken feathers on his lapels when Rumkowski was brought in. Rumkowski stood as he always did, head sunk on chest, arms at his sides. It was almost as if you could hear the whole mighty palace come thundering about his ears.

Biebow: I thought we had an agreement.

Chairman: We did, and we still do, Herr Amtsleiter.

Biebow: And yet provisions for a sum equivalent to 126,263 Jews have been brought into the ghetto and entered into your books, despite the fact that by your own calculations, there are currently only 86,985 Jews. How do you explain that?

Chairman: There must be some mistake.

Biebow: Mistake? We make no mistakes here. 38,278 Jews must therefore have found the situation in the ghetto so over-whelmingly attractive that they have made their own way here to help themselves from our loaded tables. Can you tell me where these Jews are now, Mr Rumkowski?

Chairman: If incorrect information has been filed or supplied, I shall immediately –

Biebow: And how did they get in? Perhaps they made sure to sneak in when I was asleep or at some other time when my back was turned?

Chairman: I shall go and get to the bottom of this unfortunate situation at once.

Biebow: You will have to do more than that, Rumkowski! I order you here and now to carry out a new census. *Every head must be counted!* And for every Jew, address and *Ressort* must be clearly stated. From now on, no address is valid unless it is also a residential address and the one at which the Jew in question is registered. Do you understand? And that includes your own stupid head, Rumkowski! To achieve this, new workbooks must also be issued. Each book will, in addition to the holder's name, date of birth, residential address and *Ressort*, also have a photograph, certified as authentic by Jakubowitsch at the Central Labour Office. This identity document will be shown every time provisions that require coupons are handed over, and every time premises are searched. – *Ist das verstanden worden*?

The first raid began immediately. Through the half-open bedroom window, Princess Helena saw the policemen who had so recently dragged off poor Tausendgeld standing down in the garden by her bird cages. She could just about put up with them taking away Mr Tausendgeld, but what possible justification could they have for touching her birds? She threw the window open wide, leant out into the lethal white light and shouted:

Don't touch my linnets!
Take whatever you want, just don't touch my linnets!

Every year it was the same story where Princess Helena's liver was concerned:

Summer came, bringing with it fatigue and malaise, and a headache that made it almost impossible for her to open her eyes in the mornings. On palpating her abdominal organs, Dr Garfinkel discerned, just as he had the year before, a certain swelling of the liver, and he therefore prescribed a strict diet consisting of white meat in a delicate broth, and above all rest in complete darkness, since jaundice patients risked serious eye damage if exposed to direct sunlight.

That was why Princess Helena was standing in the middle of the room with her hand over her eyes when the Kripo came in, overturning everything in their path. Wicker cages of frightened, fluttering birds. Boxes and trunks of shoes and clothes; her writing desk with all the letters and invitations and thank-you cards. Even the abundantly plumed hat she had worn to the Sumptuous Buffet, where men such as Biebow and Fuchs had been among the guests, was pulled off the hat shelf in the wardrobe to be trampled and soiled beneath the heels of boots. Princess Helena screamed and tried to hide behind the curtains. When that did not work, she sought cover back in bed, just as Detective Superintendent Schnellmann passed her a telephone receiver and demanded that Mrs Helena Rumkowska ring her brother-in-law. When she refused, and carried on screaming and thrashing her arms about, Superintendent Schnellmann made the call himself, and took the opportunity of reporting to his superior at the same time:

Wir haben noch ein paar Hühner gefunden – while irritably batting away a pair of disorientated starlings who, freed from their cages, were flapping about between the bed and the fluttering curtains.

In normal circumstances, it would now have been high time for Mr Tausendgeld to come in and start to parley. He might have popped some small gift into the assiduous detective inspector's hand. He might have said they could help each other sort out this little difficulty to the satisfaction of both parties. But now Tausendgeld was hanging from the hook in the basement of the Red House and being forced to answer questions about his 'clandestine' links with the Sonderabteilung of the ghetto, and there was unfortunately very little room for compromise. When the Chairman finally realised that this time there was no way out, he ordered a carriage to be sent to Karola Miarki Street to rescue her from the siege.

Now it just so happened that a large number of carriages had been ordered in Marysin that day; a lot of people suddenly wanted to move from 'the country' to 'the town'. The Chairman had only his own barouche at his disposal, but after arguing the toss for quite some time he was finally able to supplement it with a very ordinary, basic rack wagon, the sort the two men mowing the field used for their grass.

When the whole equipage arrived, however, Princess Helena was less interested in being evacuated herself than in finding safe refuge for her birds. She stood at the bedroom window directing Kuper and the other coachmen until they had filled the whole carriage from the driver's seat to the hood with cages of starlings and finches. Then she returned to her bed and refused to budge, despite all threats. In the end, the coachmen had to carry the bed with Helena in it down the narrow, creaking staircase and lift it into the wagon, where they tied the whole lot down securely so the vast lady would not tip out. Then trunks, boxes and bags were also put aboard, and the procession moved off.

It was on the afternoon of Saturday 10 July 1943: a close and clammy day with the sky hanging as taut and blue-glistening as a cow's udder over the dustbowl streets of the ghetto. All the way in from Marysin to Bałuty Square, The Belly's prostitutes could be seen walking, their arms as thin as sticks and their stomachs distended by hunger. They called out to the deposed princess lying in her bed on top of the swaying, lumbering wagon. But behind the length of material someone had compassionately tied round Princess Helena's sensitive eyes, she was almost as blind as The Belly had once been. She could hear nothing, either. The racket the caged birds were making drowned out everything else.

Once at Dworska Street, the procession turned and proceeded without pause towards the Chairman's town residence. If they had made an unexpected stop there, they would have seen Mr Tausengeld's broken body floating in the pool of raw sewage on the corner. He was lying face down, the longer of his two arms stretched sideways at a crooked angle, as if trying to reach even in death for something he would never quite be able to grasp.

*

For her part, Regina Rumkowska would always remember the last time she saw the Gertler family, dressed as if straight out of some popular weekly magazine: his wife in a light cotton dress and coat, and a hat with a veil; the boys in shorts with knee socks and short tweed sports jackets; the little girl in proper shoes with laces, like her mother's, and a hat that was also identical to her mother's except for the two pretty red ribbons dangling from its brim, parallel with the long plait hanging down her back.

The Praeses is not at home, was all Regina could say to this miraculous family that had suddenly appeared on her doorstep. But Gertler merely lifted his hat urbanely and said the family had just popped round to ask if young *Mr Stanisław* or the *Son of the House* might perhaps like to accompany his wife and children on a little carriage ride. He himself, he said, would be glad to stay a little longer. He had a matter of some urgency to talk to her about.

There had been people coming and going all day, an endless stream of people discussing the evacuation of the summer residences in Marysin, and who had been taken by the Kripo and who had as yet been 'spared'. They had been able to erect screens around Princess Helena's bed, so she would not have to hear the worst of it; but as soon as she recognised her husband's voice above those of the other men, she started crying out and shouting orders again.

> *Józef, can you bring me my tea that Dr Garfinkel prescribed?*
> *Did you remember to bring the morello cherries from Miarki Street;*
> *and the bowl of cream Michał's wife brought?*

(Nor did the screens around Helena's bed do anything to lessen the cacophony of starlings, goldfinches and other birds singing and calling and twittering in their cages: a whole zoo that suddenly seemed to have been substituted for the living, human guests.)

> *We're going to Sosnowiec, not Hamburg after all. But maybe it will be just as easy to find out what has become of your*

brother from there, Mrs Rumkowska, I think I may have picked up the trail.

Dawid Gertler leant forward and offered her a cigarette from a slim silver case, which he opened with his little fingernail. She stared at him. It had suddenly hit her why Gertler and his wife and children were dressed up. They were about to leave the ghetto, all of them.

You must be patient and wait, Mrs Rumkowska.

That was the last time she saw him. It was 13 July 1943.

Soon after they had left, she packed her suitcase with the few possessions she still had, including her passport and examination certificates, and prepared to wait.

The next afternoon, 14 July, two cars with Poznań number plates drove up to the security hut outside Gestapo headquarters in Limanowskiego Street, where the Sonderabteilung also had its base. Once past the barrier, the cars stopped but kept their engines running. Gertler was brought out immediately, between two plainclothes policemen. Several officials from the security service followed with armloads of cardboard boxes, files, drawers and other clearly confiscated material. Some of the staff of the Praeses's Secretariat, who witnessed the event, heard Gertler, just as he was climbing into the car, ask one of the non-uniformed policemen if they had enough material or would like to search his home as well, and heard the German police commander say loud and clear that he and his men had all they needed for the time being. Minutes later, the two cars swept out past the Bałuty gates, past the obligatory salute of the duty guards; then on down Limanowskiego Street and out of the ghetto.

In the days that followed, people converged on Bałuty Square in the evenings, because every day rumours circulated that Gertler was about to return. Every evening for two weeks, people flocked there to receive him. And the numbers continued to swell; there were days when up to five hundred hopeful faces stood waiting under the ghetto clock at the corner of Zawiszy Czarnego and Łagiewnicka Streets. Rumour had it that Gertler would be coming back in the same Poznań-registered car that had taken him away, and that the moment he 'entered the gates of the ghetto' he would give a special 'sign' through the back window of the car.

The rumours of Gertler's return seemed at times to have more staying power and detail to them than anything being said about why he had been forced to go.

Regina Rumkowska, too, dreamt several times of Dawid Gertler's return. In most of these dreams, Gertler was already dead. She could not explain how she had established he was dead, but she knew straight away it was a dead man sitting behind the gleaming window of the SS limousine that came purring under the wooden bridges one night with its headlights switched off; a dead man who then climbed out and saluted the guard of honour from his own Sonder commando that had come to welcome him back. The men in the guard of honour were dead, too. In actual fact, everybody in the ghetto was dead. The bodies of the fourteen thieves and troublemakers the Germans had put to death were still hanging in Bazarowa Street (each with a placard round its neck saying *I am a Jew and a traitor to my own people*), and the dead Gertler pushed the corpses aside as you might sheets on a washing line, and went in to sit down and confer with his closest advisers in the offices in the Limanowskiego Street building: the lights from the office windows on the first floor facing the courtyard in the Gestapo complex were the only lights on in the ghetto, and they shone all night. (And even as she was still dreaming this dream of herself and a quarter of a million other dead people, she would think that this perhaps explained why Gertler could move with such ease across the ghetto border, day or night. Why his family had always seemed so well dressed and sophisticated. Perhaps this was also the reason for his finally claiming to be on the trail of her vanished brother.

Gertler was dead. Perhaps he had been dead from the very start.)

But Regina Rumkowska was still there, left behind to wait.

She sat in the hall of the flat at 61 Łagiewnicka Street, her case packed with only the bare essentials, just as Gertler had instructed, waiting for a car or a carriage or whatever was coming to fetch her. All around her, the Palace was collapsing. The inspection of all the office staff ordered by Biebow was already under way, and people from many different departments were coming and going, all seeking audiences with the Chairman to appeal to him to 'spare' some son or cousin or father-in-law or niece. Among the many supplicants was the head of finance at the ghetto's *landvirtshaftopteil*, Dr Ehud Gliksman, who had come about his son. In the ghetto archive and registry, healthy young archivists were now being rounded up into labour brigades which, on Biebow's orders, would be put to 'useful' work in Radogoszcz or wherever useful work was called for. Pinkas Szwarc, the forger, was enlisted to rush out the new workbooks with photographs that Biebow demanded each of these new workers should have, and as soon as they had been issued with their new identification papers, they were marched off to Marysin in long columns under the command of Jewish *politsayen*, who taunted them, shouting with great relish:

Ir parazitn, vos hobn gelebt fun undz ale teg,

Itst iz tsayt tsu groben in dem shays!
Rirt zilh af di polkes, ir khazeyrim!*

(*Mr Gliksman*: But my son is an intellectual, he is not made for hard, physical labour. *Chairman*: Believe me, Mr Gliksman, not even I can do anything in the face of the authorities' decision, *not even I*, Mr Gliksman!)

*

After just a few hours, the child was back from the diversion of the carriage ride with Mrs Gertler, but no one had had time to take any notice of him. Miss Dora Fuchs had somehow managed to organise two independent queues for the petitioners who had troubled to come all the way from the Secretariat to the Chairman's 'private' office. In the sitting room, Princess Helena lay behind the screens that had been put up around her bed. Dr Garfinkel had administered a dose of morphine, but it did not seem to be helping her much. She lay on her back flailing her arms, trying to fight off real or imaginary birds, while Mrs Koszmar stood on a stool with a dustpan, attempting to dislodge the specimens that were roosting in the curtains.

Princess Helena finally fell asleep. Staszek peeped between the hangings and saw her head lying there by itself on the pillow, the long, pointed nose sticking up between the two puffy cheeks as if from two balloon sails. He would have liked to pop those cheeks, but didn't dare. He wandered off round the room instead. The birds had gone strangely quiet – as if they had only just realised someone had moved them.

In one corner of the room stood the tailor's dummy, with an almost finished suit hanging from its headless shoulders; Staszek pulled out one of the long pins that were fastening

---

* You parasites, living on us all this time, / Now it's your turn to dig in the dirt! / Stir your stumps, you layabouts!

some of the pieces of fabric together. He squatted by one of the cages. In the cage sat a white parrot, a cockatoo, its crest erect. He tried saying something to it. But the bird just stared at him from under its white fringe, and then turned its back with a disdainful waddle. Staszek stuck the long pin through the bars and to his surprise saw its point glide in just below its head. The bird gave a start and tried to flutter away. When Staszek pulled the pin out again, a thin trickle of blood drew a pretty brushstroke across the ruffled, white feathers. The bird itself seemed to be staggering; then it tried to raise its wings as if to fly, but could not lift the right one properly. Its eyes stared at him in alarm but without reproach, and its beak gaped wide, as if it had suddenly decided to start talking.

Staszek cast an anxious look back towards the screens, but behind them, all was quiet. Princess Helena was still asleep. He opened the cage door, suddenly unsure what to do with the bird, which was now just lying there pointlessly on the floor of the cage with its beak open and its wings pulled up under it. After a bit, he reached in and lifted it out. For some reason, he found the feel of the spool-shaped body, still warm, intensely unpleasant. He dropped it at once, and then tried to deal with the sticky mess of blood in his palm, which also had feathers and some yellow stuff stuck in it. He would have to go out to the kitchen and rinse his hand in the bucket, but he did not dare; Mrs Koszmar was still in the hall, trying with Miss Fuchs's assistance to show the petitioners to the Chairman's office; and what would Princess Helena say when she woke up? And how would he explain the dead bird?

In the meantime, he prowled from cage to cage – to see if there was anywhere he could deposit the dead cockatoo. But there wasn't. The other birds had woken up now, in fact, and were circling their cages frenetically, as if they could scent the smell of death he carried with him.

Every so often, he made a lunge at some particularly noisy

cage, straddling it and sticking the pin in from above, just for the satisfaction of seeing what squirted from the bird inside as it clung frantically to the bars of its cage, unsure where the pinpoint was coming from.

From behind the bed drapery, a voice suddenly rang out:

Stasiu, Stasiulek . . . ? it said, in a surprisingly soft and silky tone.

Princess Helena was awake. She still knew nothing about Mr Tausendgeld, but she was starting to feel restless and impatient, and wanted to talk to her wonderful, beloved nephew – *Staaa-siooo?*

He sat astride another cage. Inside it was a thrush with a lovely yellow beak. He clenched his thighs so tightly that he felt a pleasant little tickle in his groin, and then plunged the long pin between his legs with a deep, digging action. He looked down and saw the thrush dragging a damaged wing. Round and round it dragged the wing, as if standing in for the second hand on a clock. The shrill outcry from the other cages was terrible now: a wall of sound in his ears.

Princess Helena realised something was up. She called through the din of the birds.

Stasiu? Come here please! What are you doing? Come here, pleee-ase . . . !

He moved quickly from cage to cage, knocking as many to the ground as he could, and stabbing at the birds inside, which were trying to hang in mid-air with helplessly fluttering wings. The pin slipped in his sticky palm. He had to keep changing his grip. In the end he abandoned the pin entirely, pulled open a cage door and put in his whole hand.

Two wood pigeons flew from his touch; he felt the rustling wing quills of one of them brush the outside of his wrist; the other pecked between his knuckles.

He pulled back his hand and looked up to see Regina Rumkowska standing in the doorway. She was fully dressed and had a suitcase in her hand, but an expression on her face as if she had been standing there for a long time, waiting for him to look in her direction.

You are evil, evil, evil, was all she said, and smiled, as if she had just been given confirmation of something she had known for a long time.

Dead birds lay everywhere. Where the rugs were ruckled under the chairs and table in the sitting room, along the skirting boards in the corridor, in the kitchen doorway. Just inside that doorway stood the child, looking at its foster mother. The hands holding the dead parrot were smeared with blood. The boy also had blood on his neck and cheeks and round his mouth, and this mask of blood distorted his facial features, lending him an air of slight dismay that could almost be taken for innocence.

But there was no innocence in his gaze. The child was observing her with the same expression of defiant, almost impassioned hatred as it had before. Regina grabbed the boy's hand before he could put it to his mouth again – looked for a few moments at the bloody form of the bird, its pathetic little legs pressed into the downy feathers of its abdomen, then threw it to Mrs Koszmar who was on her way from the room where Princess Helena lay. She was still brandishing the dustpan:

There are more petitioners arriving, Mrs Rumkowska! What shall I do?

Regina did not answer. She took the boy by the arm and shoved him into the room where the Chairman usually took him, where he kept his little casket with the loathsome pictures. She locked the door carefully and slipped the key into the pocket of her dress. When she came back to the hall, Chaim was standing on the landing, his face as white as a sheet; behind him stood Abramowicz and the rest of the staff. It fell to Abramowicz to express what Chaim, his jaw gaping, was clearly trying but not being able to say:

They've taken Gertler; may the God of Israel have mercy on us –
They've taken Gertler!

They had also brought with them the body of Mr Tausendgeld; and Dr Garfinkel immediately pulled back the screens to give the howling Princess Helena another shot of morphine. But Regina could think only of Gertler. She sat in the hall with her suitcase, waiting for the man who would never return, yet who was the only one that could have reunited her with her dead brother.

In his office, the Chairman sat crying:

He was like a son to me, the closest thing to a proper son I've ever had . . .

And in its room, the child sat laughing among all the pictures it had drawn of dead and mutilated birds.

Speech by Hans Biebow to factory directors and commissioners of the ghetto, held at the House of Culture, 7 December 1943 (reconstruction)*

Functionaries, Ressort-Leiter, *workers of the ghetto –*
   (*Mr Auerbach! Do please be seated.*)
   It has long been my intention to address you, but various difficulties have arisen to prevent me doing so before now. I shall speak slowly and clearly so that those who do not speak German can nonetheless understand, or be helped by others to understand, what I say.
   It has come to my notice that there has been unrest in the ghetto. This unrest is primarily the result, as I understand it, of certain irregularities regarding food distribution. It is self-evident that where food supplies are concerned, the German people must be provided for first, then the rest of Europe, and the Jews last of all.
   Since I took charge of the ghetto and its administration three-and-a-half years ago, one of my main tasks has been to make provision for food supplies. You have no idea what a strain it has been for me to find sufficient labour for the ghetto every day. Only labour can ensure the continuing transport of food to the ghetto.
   I readily admit that some of the methods of distribution introduced by my Jewish representatives have unwittingly benefited those who already have food at the expense of others who do not. There have been some appalling cases of improper practice in which individuals have greedily helped themselves or even, in the worst cases, sold on what limited provisions there were. To clamp down

---

* 'Amtsleiter Biebow was led on stage in the House of Culture from the wings by Commander Leon Rozenblat, and as soon as he was on the stage, he called on all the representatives of the ghetto police in attendance to take their places behind him. So these officers sat behind him on stage and then kept a watchful eye on the gathering throughout the speech. In other words, there was no way round Biebow's express order prohibiting any kind of shorthand note-taking; so the text that follows [below] is a reconstruction based on written accounts made from memory by some of those present at the event.'

on this criminal trade once and for all, I have declared the current coupon system null and void, and brought in a single system for the allocation of extra rations. From now on, those who work at least 55 hours a week will have their workbooks stamped with the letter **L** *(for* **Langarbeiter***), and I am announcing here and now that it is the duty of every* Ressort-Leiter *to enforce the new regulations, and I assure them that any attempt to abuse this certification system, or to produce certification in the names of people who are no longer resident in the ghetto, will have repercussions they could not have dreamt of – they will in fact be forced to step down from the stage of Life.**

This applies to Ressort-Leiter *but it also applies to every level of decision-maker involved in the testing process [die Prüfungen] or assessment of continued validity for all work permits.*

Workers, representatives of departments and secretariats –

For almost four years now, you have lived incarcerated behind barbed wire. In the course of those years, some of you have speculated as to whether this situation will change. I can assure you that this will not happen. The leadership [die Führung] in Berlin is firm and resolute, and we will win this war which the enemies of the German people have forced us to wage.

In this regard I must underline very clearly that the supervision of the ghetto is a police matter, the primary responsibility being that of the Kripo and Herr Auerbach, and whatever authority he and the SD choose for delegation to the ghetto's own forces of law and order. We used to cooperate very well with Dawid Gertler. Unfortunately Dawid Gertler has been forced to leave the ghetto. His successor will be Marek Kligier. Kligier is in continual contact with us and with the security services. Let me remind you that when the Special Section [Sonderabteilung] searches a property – which will happen increasingly often in future – this search has

---

* His actual words were: *Ein solcher Leiter würde etwas erleben, woran er nicht im Traume denkt: er würde nämlich von der Bühne des Lebens abtreten müssen* . . .

been ordered, or at the very least approved – by us, and it is the Sonder's unconditional duty to confiscate or take charge of both objects and individuals found to be outside the rules applying to all production in the ghetto from this moment forward.

In the matter of production, let me mention the additional demands and measures that have been imposed on us. The so-called testing process [die Prüfungen] – that is, the recruitment and registration of former clerical and departmental employees for the labour commandos inside and outside the ghetto – which has already begun will proceed at the required pace. In the immediate future we will need five thousand workers for a project assigned to us by the department of Speer's Ministry [the Ministry of Armaments and War Production] responsible for emergency housing in war-damaged areas of the Reich, and our factories will be producing moulded Heraklite boarding for all this prefabricated housing.

For any of you who might happen to have objections to these measures – or see this labour effort as temporary or of short duration – I emphasise that recruitment will continue.

We will continue to need workers.

We will need workers ad infinitum, for as long as the war effort lasts.

The Chairman's fall from power after the *szpera* operation seemed to go on almost indefinitely. Like a madman being stripped of garment after garment, he had one absolute power after another taken from him. He no longer had any influence over production or the conditions of production in the ghetto. He no longer had any say in food distribution – except the tiny two per cent that was his to allocate 'personally', which he persisted in using for ex gratia gestures, like giving all the workers in the ghetto coupons equivalent to a plate of *tsholent* at Yom Kippur. After the purges of the summer of 1943, he was not even in charge of his own appointments. The names of all those he wished to see promoted, or for that matter, dismissed, had to be approved by the German ghetto administration. Ultimately, it was Biebow who pulled all the strings. The Praeses of the ghetto was a lord of misrule, a ragged spindle-shanks whose power amounted to nothing more than a style he had adopted, and whose world could be reduced to a few ceremonies, marrying and divorcing people, and going on pointless 'inspections' of factories or soup kitchens. Not even the bodyguards who had always been at his side seemed to form up in such numbers any more.

But at the very moment the fall seemed almost complete, the humiliation total, something happened to give the Chairman, at a stroke, if not his power and authority back, then at least some kind of rehabilitation.

They said he was a traitor to the ghetto. But perhaps treachery, like heroism, is something that requires a long period of preparation before it can be crowned with success.

In that case, the treachery was already there on the first day of the *szpera* operation, when Rumkowski acted his part most heroically and refused to carry out the actions the authorities had ordered him to carry out. But hero or traitor? Saviour or executioner? Perhaps it made no difference in the long run. Rumkowski *was* the ghetto. Whatever actions he took, whichever or however many Jews he saved or did not save, the only stage prepared for him was that of the traitor. His only task was to step up onto that stage when the time was ripe and the powers that be commanded it.

<u>From the</u> Ghetto Chronicle
<u>Litzmannstadt Ghetto, Tuesday 14 December 1943:</u>

At 11.30 this morning, a rumour ran like wildfire round the ghetto: *The Chairman has been taken away by the Gestapo.* The course of events is said to have been as follows. At 9.30, a vehicle from the Geheimen Staatspolizei in Posen arrived at Baluter Ring. Two men, one in uniform and one in plain clothes, announced themselves in the Secretariat outside the Chairman's office.

'Are you the Eldest of the Jews . . . ? What is your name?' The Chairman gave his name, and then the two policemen said: 'Let us have this conversation in private,' and went into his office. The two men the Chairman happened to have with him, Moshe Karo and Eliasz Tabaksblat, immediately left the room.

The Chairman's meeting with the two officers lasted for about two hours. Then, at about 11.30, the Chairman went off towards the city centre in the company of the two men from the security services.

At first, no one in the ghetto was really aware this had occurred. It was only at about seven in the evening, when the Chairman had still not returned, that the ghetto's heart began to pound. Everywhere, people congregated in groups to talk about what had happened.

The Chairman's horse and carriage stood outside his office as usual, and they were still there late that evening, no reports having been received. Many were convinced the Chairman had been taken to Posen.

As he left Baluter Ring, the Chairman just had time to say to Dr [Wiktor] Miller, who happened to be there: 'If anything should happen, remember the food distribution is the only thing that matters. Nothing else.' The Chairman appeared very composed.

In these difficult hours, many recalled the Gertler affair. But there is a great difference between the two. Gertler was a popular personality in the ghetto, but this incident – everybody agreed – involved the father of the ghetto himself. The horror of it ran in the bloodstream of every single one of them. Never had people been so acutely aware of the inescapable fact that *Rumkowski is the ghetto!* – hardly anyone could sleep that night. And there was further cause for alarm: Amtsleiter Biebow had been called to the city and nothing had been heard from him, either. In a situation like this, what was there to do but wait and see?

The Chairman only ever told a select circle of people close to him what happened in the course of the twenty-four hours he was away from the ghetto. He initially thought the two security men were taking him to the offices of the German administration in Moltkestrasse, but when he recounted what had happened afterwards, he was not so sure. The only thing he could remember clearly was that the doors through which he was led were so tall that he could not see how close they came to the ceiling, and that the stucco ornaments at the top were gilded. He was taken into a large room, where five 'top men' were seated at a long table, with green lampshades above it, hanging so low that the smoke suspended in the lamplight obscured the faces behind it. He was not able to make out a single one of them, despite the fact that they all (he said) had their eyes fixed on him at that moment.

An adjutant clicked his heels and barked his *Heil Hitler!* For his part, he stood as always with his hands at his sides and his head bowed:

Rumkowski!
Ich melde mich gehorsamt!

Out of the corner of his eye, he nonetheless saw one of the security officers bring in the account books he had been ordered to bring with him, and the books passing between the Germans sitting at the table. There was a sound like one of them clearing his throat, or perhaps giving a low laugh:

We know who you are.
You are the Elder of the Jews, the richest Jew in Łódź.
The whole Reich is talking about you.

The account books had finally reached the man seated on the far left. He leafed through a few pages distractedly, and then went back to observing him through his thick glasses, while continuously moistening his lower lip with the tip of his tongue. I found out later, said Rumkowski, that it was SS-Obersturmbannführer Adolf Eichmann; and the man to his right, with the horn-rimmed glasses, was SS-Hauptsturmführer Dr Max Horn of the SS's Wirtschafts- und Verwaltungsamt, whose initiative this whole committee was; and next to him was SS-Oberführer Dr Herbert Mehlhorn, with responsibility for the Jews at the Reichsstatthalterei in Posen. But none of these top men introduced themselves, naturally; none of them did or said anything at all except create a tinkle of glasses and carafes, or clear their throats or smack their tongues. (It was as if, Rumkowski said later, they were all perfectly happy just to have cast an eye over me.) A few moments later, the tall doors were opened again, an orderly came in, gave the Hitler salute and announced Amtsleiter Biebow. But by then, Rumkowski had already been asked to leave the room, and all he was able to catch before the door was closed behind him were a few quick questions from the far side of the table, to which he heard Biebow reply that the production of the Heraklite boards was in full swing. *Genau, Herr Hauptsturmführer*, and the 'ghetto laboratories' had even developed a special mixture of cement and wood chips that was displaying quite *unique* qualities in all the durability tests. Nowhere else in the Generalgouvernement or the Warthegau had they succeeded in manufacturing such an *exemplary product*.

Und so weiter. Filtering out through the crack between the door and its frame – or perhaps somewhere higher up: through the gap just below the soaring entablature – came the sound of Biebow's ingratiating voice as he continued to boast of the ghetto's working capacity and outstanding productivity.

Rumkowski was shown out to an anteroom. Along the wall, under a portrait-sized picture of the Führer, ran a row of wooden benches. Rumkowski perched on the edge of one of them. His audience had been so brief that he was convinced for some time he had only been brought out temporarily and would shortly be called back into the room. But time passed, and nothing happened except that the voices on the other side of the door grew more strident. Then he also heard a chink of glass and the sound, light but firm, of boots crossing the creaking wooden floor. The eyes of the SS guard, too, kept swivelling from him to the door, as if he did not know what to do with this Jew his superiors had dumped on him. And he had no cigarettes on him, Rumkowski said later; all he had were a couple of dry biscuits he had managed to grab from the tin Miss Dora Fuchs kept on her desk, but he dared not get them out for fear of giving an unfavourable impression: 'a poor Jew, eating.'

Then a sudden burst of laughter came from within, the door opened, and Biebow's face looked out – first uncomprehending, then horrified:

Are you still here, Rumkowski?

Biebow closed the door behind him with both hands and put a shushing forefinger to his lips. Then he led Rumkowski across a landing and down a long, dark corridor to a small room where the light was on, and shot Rumkowski a conspiratorial look as he closed the door behind him.

What happened next was hard for Rumkowski to explain even to his closest associates. Perhaps he lacked the words to describe the sudden sense of intimacy that seemed to have arisen between him and Biebow. It was almost like the old days, before there was any 'production process', before there were any *resorty* to speak of, when they would sit in Rumkowski's office together while Biebow went through long lists of tenders without finding the product he needed anywhere, and Rumkowski would suddenly come up with the name of a person or a company and Biebow would exclaim:

Why, that's brilliant, Rumkowski!

Except the news they were discussing this time was not so cheering, said Rumkowski, and he tried to repeat Biebow's confidences as best he could. Namely that a decision had been taken in Berlin to the effect that the demands of the continuing war effort made it no longer feasible to retain a ghetto administration of the present size, that the administration would be reorganised and even previously 'irreplaceable' people like Ribbe and Czarnulla would be obliged to leave Litzmannstadt to serve in the army.

But that's not the worst thing, Rumkowski; the worst thing is that the whole ghetto, the entire section of ghetto production working for the armament industry, is going to transfer from

462

civilian administration to the SS's Ostindustrie-Gesellschaft –
in short, the ghetto's going from the Gau to the SS!

The room they were now in was what Rumkowski called Biebow's 'city office'. It was dominated by a big, wide desk, with a blotter and inkstand of imitation marble. Along the edge of the table stood telephones, arranged in order of size. Biebow took a glass from a wall cupboard and poured himself a drink, and then took a cigarette from a case on the desk; he did not offer one to Rumkowski:

> *They're taking a break now, but this much is clear: if Dr Horn gets his way in the negotiations, I shall have to leave my post in the administration as well, and I'm sure you can imagine very vividly what that will mean for the autonomy I have given you Jews all these years, Rumkowski.*

That was the moment at which a stage that had lain shrouded in darkness until then suddenly revealed itself to him, Rumkowski said. By reaching down his hand and smiling accommodatingly, Biebow was now bringing Rumkowski up onto that stage in a considerate, almost comradely fashion:

> *But I won't leave the administration, of course, without paying tribute to the excellent spirit of cooperation in which we have always worked, you and I, Rumkowski.*
>
> *And I may have the option of taking some of your most capable workers with me. But then they must be really capable workers, the sort I know only you can generate.*
>
> *I have great plans, Rumkowski. They're trying to tempt me with the offer of taking over a big textile exporting company with depots and warehouses in Hamburg and Kiel, and of course I've still got all my contacts in the coffee and tea business.*

And as for you and your family, Rumkowski, I shall at any event make sure you are offered a secure and dignified exit from here.

Gute Geschäftsbeziehungen vergisst man doch nicht so schnell.

But now you must go, Rumkowski; Dr Horn is punctuality itself, he holds people to account if they are so much as a minute late.

This last was said as he took hold of Rumkowski's arm: Rumkowski, who was expecting some kind of embrace to follow – a drunken test of loyalty like those he had had to endure in the old days – adjusted his stance accordingly. But Biebow was only trying to get to the coins in his jacket pocket. He pressed a few pfennigs into Rumkowski's hand and slapped him chummily on the back:

This should be enough for your tram fare, Rumkowski!

And remarkably enough, that was how Rumkowski the 'rich' Jew, who except for that time he went in the Gestapo's lorry convoy to Warsaw had never once stepped outside his allotted *Gebiet*, found himself standing entirely alone and unguarded in the Aryan part of Litzmannstadt, waiting for a tram to come and take him back to the ghetto.

Grey dawn. At the tram stop in Podolska Street, a group of ordinary Poles and Volksdeutsche had formed. They all stared at the yellow star he wore on the breast and shoulder of his jacket. Was a Jew coming on the tram with *them*? And what was a Jew doing outside the walls and fences of the ghetto, anyway? But Herr Amtsleiter had not only told him to take the tram but also given him money for his ticket, so when the tram came, Rumkowski did that most forbidden of things. He – *a common Jew!* – got into one of the Polish carriages and nobody stopped him. He sat right at the back, staring at the doors as they opened and closed with an almost miraculous smoothness to let other Poles on or off. The car was soon completely full. But at the back, where he was, it was empty. He was hungry. He still had in his pocket the two biscuits he had taken from Dora Fuchs's old tea caddy. But he didn't dare touch them. He didn't dare move a muscle.

Then the barriers of wood and barbed wire gradually began to close in on them, and the tram started to climb up the 'dead' Aryan corridor that ran along Zgierska Street. One of the passengers must have spoken to the driver by then, because against all the rules, the tram stopped at Bałuty Square, and the Chairman got off. And the tram gave a ding of its bell and set off again with terror-struck faces staring out of its illuminated windows, and the Chairman walked towards his ghetto, thinking of Biebow and the promise the man had given him:

Aber guter Arbeiter – Musterarbeiter müssen es sein.

Opinion would subsequently differ as to when the last wave of deportations from the ghetto actually began. Whether it was in June 1944, when Mayor Otto Bradfisch gave orders for the final evacuation of the ghetto, or at the start of February, as soon as the authorities suddenly demanded that 1,500 strong, fit men register for 'work outside the ghetto'. (An order which, when not immediately followed, was raised to 1,600 men and then to 1,700.) Or did the deportations in actual fact start as early as that chill grey, misty December morning in 1943, when the Praeses presented himself to the German guards at Bałuty Square after having vanished from the ghetto without trace for a whole day and night?

He came empty-handed, but he still had something with him that he had not had when he left.

That was what some people thought, anyway.

Now Rumkowski was not known for slacking when there were things that needed to be done. Scarcely two hours after the tram deposited him at Bałuty Square, he paid a visit to *Betrieb Sonnabend* at 12 Jakuba Street. The cobblers there had just downed tools to protest against their dreadful working conditions, and refused to eat their soup despite Director Sonnabend's entreaties. Rumkowski was scarcely through the factory gates before he went up to one of the strikers and knocked him to the ground. He punished the other cobblers by extending their working day by two hours every evening, and he took the ringleader to the Central Jail where he had him flogged in front of all the other prisoners.

It was a pattern that would be repeated all through that

spring. If you stole the tiniest stump of hemp rope, or even just a couple of nuts or screws, you were mercilessly hauled off to the Central Jail. In previous years it would have been a disaster to have so many able-bodied people in the ghetto behind bars. But not any more. On an inspection of the jail just a few weeks into the new calendar year, the Chairman referred to 'his' prisoners as a *store of usable human material* that could serve as a *reserve* in bad times. There was much deliberation in the ghetto over what the Chairman could possibly mean by this, and in particular, which bad times he had in mind. It was not long before the announcement was made that everyone had somehow known to be coming:

<u>**Proclamation No. 408:**</u>
1,500 men for work outside the ghetto

On the instructions of Amtsleiter Biebow, 1,500 men are to be sent away for manual labour outside the ghetto. The workers in question shall have physical and mental capacities that will expedite their training for various purposes. No large items of luggage are permitted. The workers in question are, however, to bring shoes and winter clothing.

Exemption from this summons is granted to workers at those factories and workshops deemed by the Trades Commission to be indispensable for the production of goods in the ghetto, and to the following sectors:

1./ Dry-cleaning and cleansing
2./ Gas department
3./ Empty bottle depot

Workers in all other sections are to report from tomorrow at 8 a.m. to the former out-patient's clinic at 40 Hamburgerstrasse for examination and inspection by a medical commission appointed for the purpose.

Litzmannstadt-Ghetto, Tuesday 8 February 1944
M Ch. Rumkowski. Eldest of the Jews

No one reading this proclamation could avoid thinking back to the *szpera* operation, eighteen months previously. Admittedly the Chairman came round and assured them it was all different this time, and *only* to do with work (what had it been before, then?), that all those who went would be *out of danger*. But if he had not told the truth last time around, why should anyone believe him now? What was more, persistent rumours insisted that the ghetto would no longer be under civilian rule, and that all the industries in the ghetto were going to be bought up by a newly established, SS-run company called Ostindustrie-Gesellschaft, which intended to send away all the Jews unfit for work, regardless of age, meaning in practice they would turn the ghetto into a concentration camp. The Praeses of the ghetto had, moreover, apparently agreed to this plan, in fact he was even said to support it, since it gave him the chance to get rid of his enemies once and for all and to take charge of the ghetto again.

That was why nobody responded to the summons when it actually came.

Two days later, the morning of 10 February 1944, only thirteen of the required 1,500 workers had come forward for medical examinations at Hamburgerstrasse.

Two days later, the number had risen to fifty-one.

The rest failed to appear.

The workers involved did not arrive at their places of work either, not even turning up to fetch their daily soup ration. The Chairman threatened to withdraw their workbooks and block their ration cards. But even that did not help.

On the morning of 18 February 1944 it was reported that a total of 653 men were now interned in the Central Jail. Even if one included all those who were already incarcerated there for other reasons, it was still not enough to fill the first transport of 750 men that the authorities were demanding.

The same day, the Chairman declared a ghetto-wide curfew. Overnight, all the factories were sealed, all the distribution points were closed, and the men of the Sonder went from house to house. Apartments, cellars and attic storerooms were broken into and searched, and those who were not on any of the exemption lists, or who could not produce any valid work permits, were summarily taken away to the Central Jail. People said it was just like it had been during *di groise shpere*. Only this time, the Jews themselves had done all the dirty work. There was not a single German soldier, not a single German weapon to be seen anywhere.

*

There had been a time when Jakub Wajsberg had had no other way of earning his keep than to dig for coal on the site of the old brickworks on the corner of Łagiewnicka and Dworska Streets, where he had to compete not only with hundreds of other children but also with starving adults who prowled the site, hoping to steal the coal sacks from the doggedly labouring children. (Sometimes Adam Rzepin helped by keeping watch for him from the roof of the works, sometimes not.)

But all that had changed now.

Because for the past couple of months, Jakub had been the fortunate owner of a small barrow: a simple cart with two stiff wheels that could only be moved by means of a shaft or a trace. In the barrow he kept the tools his uncle Fabian Zajtman used before the war in his puppet-making workshop on Gnieźnieńska Street. Awls, hammers and chisels; everything you could possibly need to sharpen a knife or bend a piece of metal into a crowbar.

Jakub Wajsberg went from yard to yard offering such services for sale. He also carried with him the glove puppets and marionettes his uncle had made. His original intention had been to sell the puppets, or at least the material they were made of – the fabric, the wood, the wood shavings and the metal wire would certainly have their uses. But then he did not need to, because with the help of the barrow, his father had managed to get his *Ressort-Leiter* to agree to let Jakub help transport things for the carpentry workshop.

It was all thanks to the barrow.

This was the time, the late winter and early spring of 1944, when the ghetto began production of the *Behelfshäuser* ordered by the armaments ministry in Berlin. These were to be houses for German families whose homes had been reduced to ashes and rubble during the Allied bombing raids. All the parts for the emergency housing were to be prefabricated in the ghetto. Not only the famous Heraklite panels (whose miraculous mixture of cement and wood pulp had been eulogised by Biebow) but also the doors, gables and roof trusses of the houses. Never before in the four-year history of the ghetto had the pace of work been so intensive or the production rate so high. The factories involved introduced a three-shift system; saw-blades and planing machines were not still for a single hour of the day; and once the stamp of the Central Labour Office had landed in your work log, nobody asked who you were or where you came from; you were thrown straight into the job. Since Jakub had a barrow, he was put to work at the timber yard at Bazarowa Street, from where, every day, hundreds of cubic metres of timber had to be taken first to the sawmill at Drukarska, then to the various cabinet-makers in Pucka and Urzędnicza Streets.

These were the strangest of days in the ghetto.

The ghetto Jakub had grown up in was a crowded, noisy place. Now it was as if sheets of ominous silence were spreading across whole areas. Jakub might stop with his barrow in the middle of a normally overpopulated street, and all he could hear was the hollow sound of raindrops pattering against a tarpaulin awning, and then the rain itself, rising like a whisper from the wet ground beneath. When had it ever been so silent around him that he had been able to make out the almost inaudible murmur of falling rain?

The only people outside on days like these would be the men of the Sonder. They were posted on every street corner, standing guard with their hands behind their backs and their tall boots planted far apart. Sometimes singly, sometimes in groups of four or six – as if they were preparing to storm a whole neighbourhood. Quite often they would be dragging someone, a man, or something that had once been a man but that now looked more like one of Zajtman's puppets, with legs dangling limply from its body: yet another of the many thousand who preferred to stay hidden in woodsheds and coal cellars rather than report for labour duties as ordered by the Chairman.

And if Jakub happened to stop with his barrow in a place where a police raid had just taken place, the Sonder would overpower him, too. Their faces were wrecked by the violence to which they daily subjected others, filled with dictatorial scorn and an obscure brand of shame:

Rozejść się, rozejść się –
Get yourself off home! Go home!

To him as an eleven-year-old, this was incomprehensible. How could it be that spots of such unreal silence could exist in the very places where the shrill scraping and cutting of saw-blades and planes continued without a break, hour after hour, and people ran themselves breathless getting from one work station to the next? How could two workers bend down in unison to lift the two ends of a wide pack of boards, just as a third man was carried out between them, a battered, bloody head between two strong, uniformed arms? And nobody saw, nobody took any notice at all.

From out of this unfathomable landscape of noise and silence, Bajgelman's carriage came grinding into view on its reluctant wheel axles.

The piano tuner, who had as usual been perched precariously on top of the mountain of props at the back, jumped down into the sawmill yard and whisked the tarpaulin aside with the same exaggerated flourish he might have used to open a stage curtain. Under a red cloth cover stood a piano, and piled on top of it and lying all round it were tubas and trombones, their mouthpieces stifled by mattresses and old sofa stuffing, and their shiny valves and keys tucked up in dirty rags like children with colds. A double bass in an oilcloth shroud. Violins in their cases, stacked one on top of the other like coffins.

There was something predatory about the piano tuner's face as he told them about the German youth orchestra, its members drawn exclusively from the Hitler-Jugend, which had been set up a few weeks back in Litzmannstadt, and that its leaders had demanded that their instruments come from the city's rich *Judengebiet*. As soon as he received this 'offer', Biebow had ordered the Chairman to issue a decree that all musical instruments were to be handed in immediately to the compulsory purchase centre at Bleicherweg. An official German valuer had then been sent in from Litzmannstadt. He had divided the instruments into three categories – worthless, unusable and acceptable – and only agreed to pay a few symbolic marks for the third group; and never before had conductor Bajgelman cried as much as he did when a violin made by an apprentice of the eighteenth-century master Guarneri, worth at least several thousand marks, was taken out of his hands for about twenty worthless rumkies.

The fact that people are starving and dying or being rounded up and deported you can endure. But what do you do with the silence, what do you do with all this dreadful silence?

*

The ninth of March is Purim. It is also Chaim Rumkowski's birthday. But the Praeses of the ghetto stays in bed that day and lets it be known he will not be receiving visitors, though he will accept birthday greetings by post. These should bear the

472

special stamps that Pinkas the Forger has produced to mark the double celebration.

It seems the Chairman is reverting to some of his earlier airs and graces.

Bajgelman's theatre troupe will have to refrain from instrumental birthday tributes this year, as there are no longer any instruments in the ghetto. Mrs Grosz will have to perform her song of congratulation to the accompaniment of whatever is to hand: wooden mallets, vibrating saw blades, *menażki* and clattering broom handles. Afterwards, Jakub Wajsberg stages an improvised Purim play with some of Fabian Zajtman's puppets. He uses the edge of the cart as a stage and the vivid red camouflage cover from Bajgelman's piano as a curtain that can be raised and lowered.

The Hungry Rabbi of Włodawa is given the role of *loyfer*, the one who introduces the whole show. The Hungry Rabbi of Włodawa was one of Fabian Zajtman's favourite puppets. Wherever he went with his puppet theatre, he would always take the Hungry Rabbi with him; sometimes the Hungry Rabbi would introduce the whole performance, while at other times he just took one of the roles in the play.

The Hungry Rabbi of Włodawa lives at the very top of the town's synagogue, in an attic room with a sloping roof, a bed, a small table and a wood-burning stove. From this elevated position (on stage he is now seen climbing in through the attic window) he explains he served as rabbi in Włodawa for twenty years and has not been given a crust of bread to eat since. When he asks the Eldest of the Parish why he has never received any bread, the Eldest replies that it is because the rulers of the *kehillah* do not like what he preaches. But the Hungry Rabbi of Włodawa is carrying a sack. It is the same sack that Jakub always carries, the one in which he keeps all Fabian Zajtman's puppets. And now the Hungry Rabbi asks the audience if they would like him to open the sack to see what's inside. And the audience laughs and shouts and calls out *yes, yes . . . !* (they know Jakub and his sack); and from the sack the Hungry Rabbi of Włodawa produces a rare oriental plant which, when burnt, gives off a special kind of smoke that works as a *vundermitl* (meanwhile Jakub has started a fire to illustrate this, and smoke is billowing up from under the cart). When people stick their heads into the smoke it is as if their minds are being distorted, Jakub explains, making them believe that everything they are told is true, that the Persian king Ahasveros wishes the people of Israel well, and that they have nothing to fear from the evil Haman.

And the people in the audience who recognise the classic Purim story are now shouting indignantly: *What sort of rabbi is that?*

Out with the false rabbi!

And so the rabbi is thrown out, the poisonous smoke clears, the scene changes and the real Purim play can begin:

Esther has married the Persian king Ahasveros and the king's servant Haman is skulking in the wings, concocting evil plots against the Jewish people. For the king's servant Haman, Jakub uses one of Zajtman's old glove puppets, which he has dressed as a *politsay* with a cap and tall boots, and a Sonder armband. A deep shiver runs through the audience as they catch sight of Haman dressed in a police uniform, and here and there, people begin to shout agitatedly and clatter their tin soup mugs.

But now Mordechai comes on stage to save the day, and of course, it is the Hungry Rabbi of Włodawa again, only in a different guise. And once more the Rabbi has his sack with him. And again, the sack is full of *vundermitl. Come, come . . . !* says Mordechai. *If you stick your heads in the sack, you will get bread galore. And I shall take you to the land of Israel . . . !* And, as if to show them who he really is behind all his disguises, Mordechai has one hand raised in the gesture of blessing that

474

the Chairman uses when he marries the bridal couples of the ghetto.

And: *Chaim, Chaim!* cry the onlookers, who recognised their Chairman from the very start. And the air is filled with billowing *vundermitl*.

And the great Haman falls on his back, choked by all the dreadful smoke.

And the scales fall from the Persian king Ahasveros's eyes. He recognises Haman for the instrument of the Devil that he is, praises Mordechai for his cunning and swears eternal loyalty to the Jewish people ever after. But the audience still only has eyes for the disguised Chairman with his sack and his *vundermitl*. They stamp their feet, clatter their soup mugs and shout by turns:

> *Chaim, Chaim!*
> *Give us bread!*
> *Chaim, Chaim!*
> *Give us bread!*

*

The following day: a Friday.

It would soon have been the Sabbath, if the authorities had not banned all keeping of the Sabbath in the ghetto.

Instead, a mist has swept in over the ghetto, and all that can be seen of the buildings are their footings, rotting in the mud. Samuel Wajsberg has got right to the entrance of the carpentry works before he sees the policemen forming a human chain in front of the factory gates. An officer stands in front of the row, flicking through the identity documents of the workers as they arrive.

Once their documents have been checked, the workers are told to line up in the yard, and then a kind of inventory begins.

Sonder men walk to and fro among the planing machinery

and crosscut timber saws, counting loads of timber and noting them down. Samuel stands next to Jakub. Jakub shifts a little uneasily, but shows no other sign of anything being wrong.

The mist lifts a little. A pale, watery light finds its way through the clouds, lending the factory roof a dull, rigid gleam, like quicksilver. It is so quiet that you can hear the sound of melting snow dripping and running from the underside of the roof, down into the muddy yard.

All of a sudden, a quick exchange of words rattles from inside the office and a Mr Kutner is escorted out by stiff police guards. Samuel Wajsberg said afterwards that he knew hardly anything about this Kutner – other than that he was employed in the section of Serwański's carpentry workshop that made door lintels and window frames. The chain of policemen has taken a few steps forward as if to quash any attempt by the other workers to protest against the arrest. But no one protests, and after a while the employees are urged to get back to their work.

A short distance from the workbench where Samuel is feeding wood into the big planing machine, a small cluster of workers has formed. They are talking among themselves and pointing in his direction. To judge by the snippets he can hear, they are talking not about him but about Jakub and the theatre troupe's performance the day before.

He hears them wondering where Jakub could have got hold of all the cloth and material for his puppets when wood and fabric remnants are so scarce in the ghetto.

Samuel then asks the police guard for permission to leave the plane for a moment, and goes out into the yard to look for Jakub. The mist has burnt away now. The sun glares down on all the timber lying sawn and naked, resin oozing from the cut surfaces.

But no Jakub.

Samuel concludes he must be out with his barrow again, and his heart contracts inside his chest. He waits for five minutes, but to no avail, so then he goes back to his place at the planing machine.

They walk home together, father and son.

Samuel asks Jakub whether, after the performance, he was ordered to answer questions about wood going missing. Jakub shakes his head. But he walks on in silence, his head bowed. And he is not carrying the sack of puppets thrown casually over one shoulder as usual, but has it tucked between his legs, almost as if he were ashamed of it.

The next morning, Samuel is called in to see the factory manager.

The last time Samuel dared to cross the threshold of Serwański's office was when he pleaded for a job for Jakub. On that occasion, he had said he was proud of Jakub, of his skills with hammer and chisel. He had undoubtedly inherited it from his uncle, the well-known puppet-maker Fabian Zajtman.

Neither of them recalls that conversation now.

Serwański clears his throat and proceeds to tell Samuel that he is going to set the exact situation before him. Mr Kutner, whom the Sonder has just taken into custody, is one of his best workers, a very capable engineer, whom he *cannot contemplate losing under any circumstances.*

That leaves the problem of young Mr Jakub and the 'embarrassment' his Purim play has caused the other carpentry workers, and if Mr Wajsberg could consider an exchange; if his son Jakub could take Engineer Kutner's place?

You must try to understand, Mr Wajsberg, he says, and looks at Samuel as if he really does expect him to understand, *that the authorities are demanding that I make forty strong and healthy workers available for the Labour Reserve in the Central*

Jail. How can I do without forty men with the hectic production schedule we have now? I don't know what else I can do.

There is an ache in Samuel Wajsberg's lung, round the imprint of the boot that once kicked him. He does not know what to say.

But I have already lost one child, Mr Serwański.

(You simply cannot say such things.)

But Serwański has an answer even for what is unspoken:

If you don't send your son, you will have to take Kutner's place yourself, Mr Wajsberg. And besides, you also have that problem with your lung.

Mr Serwański is smiling now; the difficult part is over. He explains that papers will be arriving. There will be no need for any 'bothersome dismissal' of Mr Wajsberg. What is more, working conditions in Częstochowa, where the authorities say the workers are to be sent, are supposed to be quite tolerable. And the war will soon be over, at any rate. And then they will all be reunited again, the whole family. Mr Wajsberg can also console himself with the fact that he is not alone. Worker exchanges like these happen all the time.

*

When Chaim was taken from them on one of those hateful *szpera* days, something changed for ever inside Hala.

Jakub's brother Chaim had been more loved and cherished than most other children, and Hala had always known she had a special bond with him. She alone had been able to get through to that intractable, quiet strength of will which she knew to be hiding behind his seemingly dull and lifeless eyes; and that connection between mother and son was not broken when Chaim was taken from them. On the contrary, it grew even stronger. Every day, Hala believed she knew exactly where her youngest son was, what he was doing and what he was thinking. She could shape her body and soul around his

478

as effortlessly as some people put on a pair of socks or a glove.

But Hala was also a woman of a practical disposition.

The remaining child must be fed, even if there was scarcely any food to be had.

She went to work at the Central Laundry every day, ate her daily *resortka* together with the other women. When new consignments of rations were announced, she would jostle in queues for hours to get what little extra was on offer, a bag of beets perhaps, or half a kilo of *botwinki* they could use for making soup.

But all that time there was also this other world, where she lived with Chaim:

She would sometimes cry when she was thinking about him, and when the crying was at its most intense, it turned into a consuming pain in her breast. Then he would appear to her again. First his eyes, the unwavering grey gaze. From that gaze, his whole, miraculous body would then materialise. The broad, taut neck; the shoulders, already as square as a man's on a boy of only six; the shoulder blades as straight and sharp as knife blades. Hala touched the boy's strong, slender body and the moist, soft folds in the armpits, crotch and backs of the knees that were like a part of her own body.

His body, she soon realised, had never really left hers.

Between the outer and the inner world, between life in the ghetto and her dreams of Chaim, a chasm opened up inside Hala. On the other side of that chasm were Samuel and Jakub. From the side where she and Chaim were, Hala called to Jakub and forbade him from going out with his barrow, even though the barrow was all Jakub had; and that expression on Hala's face that made her look as if she was calling from the far side of a chasm never changed. Every evening, she held Jakub in a vice-like grip while she scrubbed his urchin's ragged fingernails to get rid of all the dirt.

Having endured four long years of hunger and misery in the

ghetto, Hala Wajsberg knew one thing for certain:

never stand out from the crowd

– If Samuel had not attracted the attention of the German guard at the crossing on Zgierska Street that time, he would never have been kicked in the lung and been crippled for life.

– If Adam Rzepin had not been so stubborn and hidden his sick sister during the curfew, the German officer would not have been driven into such a rage and her beloved Chaim would still have been among them.

– And as for this puppet business, she had always maintained, even in Fabian Zajtman's lifetime, that a Jew should consider graven images beneath his dignity. A good Jew keeps the Sabbath holy, keeps kosher (if he can) and above all, does not play the clown. Nothing but evil can ever come of blasphemy and idolatry.

She sat ladling the thin beetroot soup out of the pot, and all she could see was the thing that deviated from the norm. On the cloth, either side of his soup plate, lay her son's hands, rubbed raw and dirty after a whole day in the ghetto; and beside her husband's hands lay the letter from the Resettlement Commission addressed to *Hr Samuel Wajsberg, Gnesenerstrasse 28, Litzmannstadt Getto*. She could see the address clearly written at the head of the letter. How was it possible for such a loathsome document to have wormed its way into their home?

You're not reporting to any resettlement commission, was all she said.

Without a single gesture, but with a kind of ringing fury to every syllable, as if the words she was now pronouncing were the first she had uttered for decades:

You're not going there, whatever you do you're not going there . . . we'll have to hide you!

480

Samuel had not even considered hiding, even though hundreds of men in the same situation as him were already lying low. The Chairman was threatening reprisals. Women who protected their men had their work permits withdrawn. And everyone in the ghetto knew what that meant. No work equals no food.

Even so, Hala did not hesitate for a second. They had taken her most beloved child from her. She was not going to let them have anyone else. She would rather they took her.

Neither of them was eating now. Neither of them dared to meet Hala's eyes, either. (If they had, they would have noticed a pale line running below her high cheekbones towards the corners of her mouth, a mask cut as tightly as any worn by Fabian Zajtman's old puppets.)

There was an old storeroom, previously used for coal, attached to the washhouse in Łagiewnicka Street. Nowadays the coal deliveries came, if they came at all, so sporadically that there was never any need for storage. But Hala still had the key. She took it out of her apron pocket, put it down on the table and stood up.

It would be Jakub's task to take his father there. As for her, she would go and pack his things. She would also pack enough food to see him through. She said nothing about what food, or where it would come from; but neither of them dared to ask.

One of Fabian Zajtman's favourite stories was the one about a bear tamer, who went from market place to market place with his dancing bear. The bear tamer had no name, but the bear was called Mikrut. And what was special about this bear, the way Fabian Zajtman told it, was that even when they were walking from town to town, Mikrut did not take his paws from his tamer's shoulders.

They went journeying from place to place, as inseparable as a tandem.

Jakub felt like that tandem, walking through the ghetto with his father. Up and down they went, up and down familiar streets that the curfew had made utterly alien. Not so long ago, thousands of people had been jostling between the sheds and stalls. Now there was nobody here to jostle at all. Nor any light leaking through the cracks between the blackout curtains. From eight o'clock in the evening, there was a complete blackout in the ghetto.

To stop workers from hiding at their places of work, the Chairman had ordered all the factories to shut and lock their doors at the end of the last shift. The coal store of the Łagiewnicka Street laundry, however, was not in the same building as the laundry, but in the cellar of the building opposite. Jakub unlocked the door with the key Hala had given him. The door was rusty and squeaked alarmingly.

Is there anything you need?
No. Nothing.
I'll come back tomorrow.
Come when you can. I'll be fine.

Jakub stands with the door in one hand, the key in the other. His father's face in half-light, body bent, eyes fixed to the ground. Jakub knows he must shut and lock the door right away, or it will become unbearable. But it feels all wrong to shut the door. A son doesn't shut the door on his father. And besides, how will his father find his way around in this disgusting hole? Will there even be enough air? Where will he sleep?

Samuel does not move, and neither does his son. They stand there, each in his own indecision, until something clatters in the street outside, something metal caught by a passing boot. Then a sharp voice calling out in Yiddish. The Sonder.

Shut it now, says his father.

And Jakub shuts the door. It is so difficult to turn the key in the lock that he has to brace his whole body against the door.

But still he locks his father up, waits until he thinks the Sonder patrol has passed and then creeps back out into the street.

*

Jakub is walking with his bear through the forest. The forest is full of dense thickets. The bear tamer can hardly see the path in front of him. But at least he has his bear's paws safely on his shoulders.

Then something happens. The bear tamer turns round, but even though he can still feel the bear's paws on his back, the bear has gone.

He knows he must walk on regardless.

He walks on and on, and as he walks, he can feel himself turning into a bear. But if he is a bear – then who is his tamer?

Jakub stands there with his innocent bear paws in the air, and has no answer.

Where's your tamer? They ask him again and again.

There are four of them, Sonder men, and they have spaced themselves out, as if about to launch themselves at him from four directions at once. And of course it is not the bear tamer they are asking about.

Where's your father? they ask him.

There is one policeman in particular. He is blond and blue-eyed, with an oblong face and a mouth composed entirely of teeth. Time and again, the smiling policeman steps in, as if to take cover behind his back; and each time he does so, one of the others steps forward and hits Jakub hard in the face with a baton or an open hand.

Where've you hidden your father? asks the blond man with the shiny teeth, now standing so close behind Jakub that he can feel the man's hot breath on his neck. There's something odd about the Polish word order, but Jakub has no time to work it out before the man lets go of his back again and the three others step forward to strike.

483

After four hours, they let him go.

Somehow he makes it home to Gneźnieńska Street.

His body is whole, at any rate. Nothing is broken. But it is as if his body has lost all its strength. He manages to get as far as the front entrance, but making it upstairs is beyond him. Hala finds him at the foot of the stairs when she comes home from the laundry at about seven that evening. She hoists him onto her back and carries him all the way up the stairs, as if he were a common sack of potatoes.

In the flat, she lights the stove, heats a pan of water and washes his face with a rag. Then she sprinkles something that looks like salt into the water and washes his face again. It also stings like salt, and Jakub cries out and tries to turn his face away. But Hala wedges his head between her legs and carries on rubbing and scrubbing his face. When she finally lets him go, his face is burning as if something has corroded away all the skin. He struggles free, and remembers nothing more. He must have fallen asleep.

That same night, the same four men come and drag them out of their beds.

Was he even sleeping in a bed?

He can't remember. Only that strange men are pinning him against the wall. They have their batons with them again, and the blows land in his side, the curving part between his chest and his hipbone where it hurts the most. The pain is so acute that it leaves no room for a scream in his windpipe. Instead he throws up: a pale, watery mess. But they do not care. They push his face down into the vomit and press what might be knees or elbows down onto his neck and shoulder blades until he can no longer breathe.

Don't kill him!

The scream comes from Hala.

Despite the pain, he manages to turn to one side. And he

484

sees his mother reeling back with blood gushing from her nose. One of the men is forcing her body against the wall.

They stand there for a long time, seeming not to move, the policeman's body pressed against his mother's, almost as if in gentle embrace. Slowly, the man starts to move the lower part of his body in short, stabbing thrusts. Only then does he see Hala's face. All that can be seen are two helplessly staring eyes above the hand pressed hard over her mouth and nose.

Jakub makes an attempt to free himself from the paralysis of pain enveloping him, to reach his mother who is lying curled up against the wall.

But no matter how hard he tries, he cannot get out of himself. Then the pain evolves into a dreadful, nauseating numbness – and he throws up again.

*

Jakub unlocks the door to his father's hiding place.

The darkness of the coal cellar has been absorbed into his father's face. Around and between them is the acrid smell of freshly produced liquid excrement, so strong that it overpowers even the pungent odour of damp and mould.

It is the smell of total degradation.

For the first time in his life, Jakub Wajsberg is afraid of his father. He is afraid of what the darkness and isolation may do to him. May already have done.

So he takes his time before he unpacks what he has brought. A small candle, which he puts on the floor between them.

When his father asks what the candle cost, he replies that it was only a few pfennigs. In actual fact it cost one and a half marks at the market on Pieprzowa Street. The compulsory blackout has turned the wax candles sold by the children into a desirable commodity. – Then the bowl of soup, on which Hala has put a lid, to keep it warm. – And the bread.

His father drinks the soup greedily and stuffs the bread into his mouth with trembling hands, even though he knows he shouldn't. The food is useless if it runs through your body too fast. But in his degradation, Samuel cannot see his own black face; he can no longer see what his own hands and lips are doing.

Finally, they can start to talk.

'They've raised the quota to sixteen hundred men now,' says Jakub.

Samuel says nothing. Jakub has to fill in for him.

And how many have reported?

'They haven't managed to fill the quota,' he says in answer to his own question.

A couple of nights later, Jakub says:

'They've raised it to seventeen hundred men.'

And what total is the Labour Reserve up to now?

Jakub presses his fingers against the cold stone floor.

And how many have volunteered? his father fails to say, but Jakub says:

'Women can come forward for the Labour Reserve now, too.'

Samuel Wajsberg's face is impassive as he hears Jakub say this. Then it is as if the face with its darkness unfolds and pulls itself together.

And Jakub can't contain himself:

Please, Dad, don't let them take Mum.

'Go now,' says Samuel, turning his face from the light.

The next day, his father is already standing ready behind the door when Jakub turns the key. He has already packed his few belongings, and he does not let his son across the threshold; he just barges out clumsily, making Jakub stumble backwards.

Where are you going?
That's enough.
But Mum's sent some food for you.
I don't need any more food.

But his father is not nearly as furious and strong as he seemed the minute before. They walk a few hundred metres, then his father staggers and has to support himself against the wall of a building. After another couple of hundred metres, he collapses completely. Jakub grabs him by the coat sleeve and tries to drag him back onto his feet. But it's no good. He has to get down on all fours and put his arms around his father's body before Samuel allows himself to be shifted out of his terrible, petrified state.

Slowly, the tandem sets off again.

It is scarcely eight hundred metres from the laundry in Łagewniecka Street to the main entrance of the Central Jail. It takes them a good hour to get there. And as Jakub supports his father, he can't help but wonder at how it is possible to become so weak. He has brought food every day, hasn't he; his mother has even been more generous with his father's portions than she used to be when Chaim was still alive. The slices of the carefully saved loaf have been cut thicker every day.

Hunger weakens. But the darkness is worse. Once it gets hold of a person, it slowly hollows out the strongest of bodies. Jakub thinks that it may not even be his father walking beside him any longer, just some sort of terrible, blind effigy.

At the entrance to the Central Jail stand two German policemen, and alongside them two Jewish police guards posted at the prison gates. One of the guards approaches them with suspicion as Jakub walks up with his father. Jakub tries to think of some suitable words to say, but his father is quicker:

My name is Samuel Wajsberg.
I have come to report for the Labour Reserve.

The face of the distrustful prison guard lights up. He raises one hand and signals to his colleague who is approaching from the other side. *So we've decided it's time to report now . . . !* says

487

the colleague, clearly addressing the German police officers, and as if to show those in power how powerful he is himself, he swings his baton and brings it down heavily across Jakub's father's neck. His father flops down like a marionette as its strings are cut. The German police do not bat an eyelid. The suspicious guard prods the body with the toe of his boot. It is as though he dare not quite trust what his colleague has done. Then he takes a short step back.

You've done your job, he says to Jakub. Go home now.

Adam Rzepin had moved in with Józef Feldman at the old nursery business in Marysin the year before, in March or April. Neither of them could have said subsequently exactly when or even why it happened that way. They simply agreed it would be more practical for them both like that. Józef cleared a space for him to sleep between the buckets and troughs in the far corner of one wall of the greenhouse. This was where customers in times past would have wandered round choosing from the selection of apple and pear saplings, their root balls wrapped in sacking. He put an old mattress down on the stone floor, and added some jute sacks and a horse blanket, and here Adam Rzepin lay, watching day break over the low garden wall and send shards of light cascading from the broken glass vessels on the shelves above him. The light was returning.

On paper, Adam Rzepin was still officially living with his father in the ghetto, but Szaja now only had the kitchen, another family having laid claim to the living room. Adam would go and visit his father in Gnieźnieńska Street every few days. Adam normally only carried his workbook around with him. He left his bread coupons in the bureau drawer in Szaja's kitchen. And it was Szaja who saw to exchanging them for the small ration that was available. His father insisted on weighing everything on the scales each time Adam came, and made sure each loaf was divided exactly in half, even though Adam often brought his own food: potatoes skimmed from the carts, turnips, cabbage and beets that had been dug up during the winter months. The new lodgers eyed them enviously from the living room. Rzepin's son must have links at the very top, with

489

di oberstn; how else could he breeze in with all these precious things?

Adam had learnt to be cautious. The place was crawling with Sonder, all the way out to Marysin. To be on the safe side, even when he was walking the short stretch from Feldman's to the Radogoszcz Gate, he always tried to stick with some of the others in his work brigade, generally Jankiel Moskowicz and Marek Szajnwald, and the latter's two younger brothers, who also did loading and unloading work in the railway goods yard.

Jankiel was fourteen, fifteen at most; with hair like a scrubbing brush and a wide band of pale freckles across the bridge of his nose that made him look even younger. Jankiel still had not learnt how to stay unobtrusive, and also save energy, by keeping quiet as he worked. He had theories about everything, and missed no opportunity to give them an airing. 'This lot's all come from the Eastern front,' he declared, for example, when a convoy of military material came jolting up Jagiellońska Street; even some whole tanks with mud in their caterpillar treads, and whirring gun turrets. 'They're lucky they managed to get their artillery out, but if they think they're going to be able to set up a new front here, they think wrong. Stalin'll just drive straight over them with his armoured division.'

But it wasn't just retreating German artillery that was being taken out via Radogoszcz, it was also most of the material produced in such breathtaking quantities by the ghetto industries all that winter and spring. Door pieces, window panels, gables, sometimes whole roof trusses were lashed to the backs of the lorries that made their way to the goods yard in a steady stream. A whole city in motion.

And there was the constant demand for more labour.

A few privileged workers came on the tram, and its two coupled carriages could be seen gliding in over the wide, muddy flatlands every morning. But most of the new recruits came on foot, some of them still in their shirts and sleeve protectors, as if expected back at their office and counting-house desks later in the day.

(Some of those recruited by force had wild stories to tell of Biebow turning up in person to make sure all the office employees left their places of work. He went to the coupon department. And to the Chamber of Trades and Inspection he had set up himself, where he announced to a shocked assembly of accountants that either their boss Józef Rumkowski must put thirty-five fit and healthy workers at his disposal immediately, or Herr Rumkowski would have to come out to Marysin himself and break bricks.)

'They're making cement board,' announced Jankiel proudly one day, '*Hera-klite!*'

Jankiel had tried to talk to some of the Palace employees – *the lawyers* as he called them – in the hope of getting messages via them to Communist comrades who still worked in the ghetto. But it was a strained, tired and sickly bunch that was sent to Radogoszcz that winter; few of them would be any good as couriers. Mr Olszer had hardly had time to put them on his books before they collapsed with hunger and exhaustion, and had to be cared for in the makeshift cottage hospital the Chairman had been given permission to set up on the site.

Not even Harry Olszer had his own office. He didn't even have a desk until Oberwachtmeister Sonnenfarb, on the orders of the stationmaster himself, lent him the little 'radio table' he had in the security hut out by the loading platform. Mr Olszer now sat at this table registering new arrivals, with one arm shielding his eyes from the rain or whirling snow.

Eventually some experienced construction workers from Drewnowska put up a hangar-like wooden structure a little bit further down the goods yard. The hangar was ninety metres long and three metres tall, with overhanging eaves five metres wide or more. Some of the Palace workers were ordered to the warehouse, where they had to take sand and carry crushed bricks to the pit where the cement mixers stood. The cement mixers were under the supervision of Polish workers who were brought in by train every morning. Adam recognised some of them from when they worked in the loading bay; some had even been in the habit of smuggling cigarettes and medicines into the ghetto. But none of the Poles gave any sign of recognising him now. They just went on feeding and tipping the cement mixers, and did not raise their eyes even when it was time for the compound to be poured into the prepared frames.

Moulding Heraklite boards was what the hangar had been built for. A mixture of cement, crushed brick and wood chips was poured into wooden moulds. Then men came forward with long rakes and smoothed off the top. After a couple of hours, the foreman and engineers came along to test the compound with wooden sticks to see if it had set.

It was important to the Germans, this! In the first two weeks of March alone, while the hangar was being built, no fewer than four delegations came out from Litzmannstadt. Biebow and his men came to inspect progress. Then the special commission of *Fachleute* that Biebow had set up, led by Aron Jakubowicz. Even the Jewish engineers were brought by car, remarkably enough. Adam could see their terrified faces through the back and side windows as the motorcade drove by. As if they were being somehow taken hostage by the Germans.

And in March, it was the Chairman's turn.

Adam had every reason to remember that day, not only for the consequences it had for him personally; but also because that was the day it really dawned on him that the war was nearing its end. Nothing but what happened to the Chairman could convince him of that. Not the panicky building of *Behelfshäuser*; not the whine of the air-raid sirens echoing across the empty sky every night; not the trenches being dug behind the walls of Bracka Street; not even the now almost daily rumours, spread by Jankiel and his comrades, that Russian liaison officers were secretly gaining entry to the ghetto at night for meetings with the Communist resistance. But when they turned round and went for the *highest of the high*, the Chairman himself; when things had *gone that far*, then he knew . . .

By that stage, the Poles and the German engineers had a prototype house ready. As the finished houses would, the prototype measured three metres by five metres and was built of Heraklite panels, painted blue, the windows inserted as if someone had simply walked past and stamped them in place on the walls. Sonnenfarb fell in love with it from the first moment. He at once shifted all his old kit there from the security hut on the goods yard platform, had Olszer's 'radio table' brought back, and fixed the old yard bell to the outer wall. He called it his 'show house', perhaps in part because of its dazzling blue colour.

The German security team at Radogoszcz had never changed over the years – at least not since Adam started. Two Schupo guards, Schalz and Henze; three if you counted Dietrich Sonnenfarb, who however made a point of showing himself among the rabble as little as possible. But when the soup cart arrived – or when it was time for a change of shift – Sonnenfarb condescended to stick a hand out of the window to ring the bell. Apart from that, he only emerged to go to the privy, which he did as a matter of course after eating the lunch he brought with him. Adam and the other workers would stand there fantasising about what delicacies he might have in his clattering tins and containers every morning, and they always paused in their work to watch Sonnenfarb, after his meal, roll his vast bodily bulk in the direction of the goods yard's 'Aryan' latrine, marvelling that a person could take in so much food at one sitting that he was obliged to 'empty himself' to make room for more.

On the way back, Sonnenfarb would always kick some

worker who happened to be standing in his way, or stick his freshly wiped backside in the air and pretend to fart out his contempt.

Adam had long since learnt to put up with this routine dishing out of physical and verbal abuse. He hardly noticed it. Nor did he hear the shouted German commands any longer, the hysterical Germanic *issuing of orders* which went on constantly over their heads; over the screeching of wagons switching into the siding; the clang of hatches being opened; metal against metal. The only thing worth keeping your ears pricked up for was the announcement of the midday soup. When Sonnenfarb stuck his big, podgy hand out of the window of his blue show house and started tugging at the clapper of the bell (which had been screwed to the wall in exactly the same position as it had been on the former guard hut), Adam, too, paid attention.

One of Jankiel's theories was that the food transports they had to unload were only for the powerful, well-placed residents of the ghetto; that even the soup they were fed each day was thinned down so the concentrated version could go to *them*. *Let's see if the soup's taken a detour past the cabbage today*, he would say, as Sonnenfarb yanked on the clapper.

Then Schalz walked by and smacked him on the head, so he spilt his soup in front of hundreds of shocked workers. But Jankiel was never one to show his fear. He just gave a slight bow. As if the German guards had, by knocking the soup out of his hands, given him the opportunity for yet another circus trick to display the consummate contempt *he* felt for *them*.

It had been decided that the Chairman would conduct his muster that day: *eine Musterung des nach Radegast zugeteilten Menschenmaterials*, as the *Chronicle* puts it.

The workers of the so-called Labour Reserve were standing in Kino Marysin, huddling up as the snow and rain drove through the gaps in the ill-fitting boards that constituted its walls.

494

There was disquiet among the group. A representative of the office workers Biebow had ordered out demanded that all the women workers be allowed to return to their 'normal jobs'; or at least work indoors or with some protection from the wind. One of the male workers complained that their hands and fingers were being cut to shreds by the chips of brick; that the soup they were served was so thin you could see a coin in the bottom of your tin (if you'd had a coin to chuck in).

Dear Jews, dear fellow-sufferers, brothers and sisters began the Chairman, but even by then, some of the workers had had enough and started to elbow their way out of the crowded barn. Though Sonder men ordered out to police the event made a half-hearted attempt to block the way, the first workers were soon followed by more. People went back to their workplaces, and the officials from the Central Labour Office who were supposed to be keeping a written record of the muster stood there helplessly with their long lists of names.

Strike, muttered someone; *this amounts to a withdrawal of labour . . . !*

But what help was that?

The weather had been extremely changeable for some days. One instant the sun would be shining from a sky clearing so rapidly from grey to brilliant blue that it almost hurt your eyes. The next second, banks of driving rain or snow swept in from the wide plain all around. Within a minute, the fields on the other side of the barbed-wire compound and watchtowers were brushed as white as zinc, and suddenly there was nothing to see but the snow, which at that moment – as the workers bent once more over their hods and wheelbarrows – seemed to be swirling up from inside the ground itself.

In view of the weather, the Chairman had been expected to return to the electrically heated security of the office in Bałuty Square after the abortive muster. Instead, he made Kuper turn the carriage and head to Radogoszcz in a cloud of driving snow.

495

Insisted on inspecting the cement factory, too, as Jankiel put it later. *Though none of it was anything to do with him. It was Biebow's and Olszer's project!*

The snow that had fallen in such volume a short time before had turned to thick, heavy slush, being made slushier still by all the barrow wheels, boots and clogs constantly moving around the building site. Two men carrying hods of sand slipped, one of them pulling the other down as he fell. At the same moment, one wheel of the Chairman's carriage stuck fast in the mud, and Kuper got down.

That was when Adam saw that something was not as it should be.

The bodyguards who always surrounded the Chairman were nowhere to be seen. The Chairman had risen to his feet in the carriage, but sat down again when he saw how alone he was.

From up on the wooden scaffolding that supported the hanger roof, someone suddenly shouted:

Chaim, Chaim!
Give us bread, Chaim!

It was not an aggressive shout; on the contrary, it sounded almost friendly. Adam saw the Chairman glance up with a look that momentarily appeared full of expectation.

Then the first stone fell.

Inconceivably enough. And all the workers in the vicinity tensed.

Though it must have been one of their own number who threw the stone, nobody seemed to be expecting it. It was as much of a shock to them as to the Chairman, who now did what he had been planning to do before: stood up to dismount from the carriage.

Then the second stone came flying.

Adam saw it describe a distinct arc through what was left

496

of the sky, before landing somewhere behind the carriage; and suddenly the air in front of him was filled with stones, and not just stones but also chunks of brick; old metal rods; bits of wood wrenched off the moulds, still spattered with cement. The snow was coming at them horizontally now, and suddenly there were shouts and yells everywhere, but most of all it was the Chairman crying out, in a hard, shrill, almost piping voice, like a little animal being unintentionally squeezed to death.

That was when it happened. A powerful blow knocked him to the ground.

He never saw where the blow came from or who delivered it, just curled up round the intense pain and shuffled his arm helplessly through the slush and mud. He felt something wet running out of his trouser leg and had time to think *as long as I don't bleed to death*, when a kick came out of thin air, thudding into his side. Two strong hands took him under the arms, and for a moment it was impossible to distinguish the mud running through the snow from the eyes staring straight into his; and under them a row of white teeth glistening with spittle in a mouth wide open round a voice that kept on shouting:

Du SHÓYTE – how long did you think you could escape me?

According to various people of high station who witnessed the event, the 'bad weather' made the Chairman slip and hit his head on a cement trough, and he had therefore been obliged to seek temporary medical care. Others said Biebow had taken pity on the poorly Eldest of the Jews and had him taken to an 'Aryan hospital' in Litzmannstadt to receive attention.

Neither of these statements is true.

It is not true that the Chairman slipped over, nor that he sought or received care outside the ghetto. He lay in the bedroom of the summer residence he shared with his brother in Karola Miarki Street in Marysin with a bloodstained bandage round his head, dreaming that it was spring and the water was rushing and rising as it always did in Russia at this time of year, and all around him in the water stood his children, watching him drown. Then his young rescuer came wading towards him, lifted him into his arms and carried him resolutely to the shore.

Chairman: Who are you?

Samstag: *Ich bin Werner Samstag. Leiter von der Sonderabteilung, VI:e Revier.* I have come to tell you that liberation is near. I have also come to tell you that I have just saved your life.

Chairman: Naturally, I am eternally grateful to you for this trial of strength!

Samstag: *Ssschooo, mein Herr,* do you know it's true what they say about the Russians? I saw one yesterday. He was standing in the queue at the distribution point and he turned round and said to me – *Ne bojsja, osvobozjdenieje blizko* . . . Don't be afraid, liberation is near! (That's what he said. Those were his very words.)

Chairman: If I were to take any notice of these constant rumours I'd never get anything done. What self-indulgence!

Samstag: No, *to dobreze* – now you're starting to sound like yourself again at last – *Baléydik nisht dem eybershtn er vet dir schlogn tsu der erd!*

Chairman: Who are you?

Samstag: Who am I? – I'm not you!

And yet: the person in the ghetto most like you!

Chairman: It sounds like a riddle! Did I invent it . . . ?

Samstag: At any event, they can't stand your likeness any more. *Oyf mit den altn*, they say. You drive past in your swanky carriage and *your own people* turn their backs and pretend to be doing something else, just so they don't have to see you. In actual fact, the whole ghetto is one big conspiracy against you. You're the only one who can't see it.

Chairman: What else are the people saying about me?

Samstag: The people are saying that you are their only shield against the darkness –

Jest szczęściem w nieszczęściu.

Chairman: That's true. I am.

Samstag: They say you handed over the children, the sick and the old –

They say of the defenceless, you sacrificed them first –
They say of those who thirsted most, you let them die of thirst!

Chairman: Are you one of them by any chance? *Bist du ein Praeseskind . . . ?*

Samstag: Legitimate or illegitimate? *Freund oder Feind?*

Samstag oder Sonntag?

Ich bin der Sonstwastag – ein sonniges – ein glückliches Kind!
Ober hot nisht keyn moyre. S'z gut!

I wasn't on the list. That's all.

Chairman: What list?

Samstag: The list of all the children – your legitimate children!

Ich bin ein eheliches Kind, ein echtes Ghettokind!

(You can see that, can't you: I've no skin left, I've no nose or cheeks – I'm like you! Nobody who saw me would be able to tell for sure –

If I am a friend or a foe.

Gut oder Böse?

Ob man von einer guten Familie stammt oder nicht.

Ob man ein Jude ist – o d e r   n i c h t!)

You too, Mr Praeses, must learn to tell Friend from Foe –

You can't appeal to everyone and anyone at the same time.

That's why there has to be a LIST. Who will have the privilege of coming with you, and who will be left behind?

Chairman: And if I die? If somebody murders me on the way?

Samstag: You can't die – you're my father! (I have also personally taken measures to ensure that those behind this obnoxious plot against you are arrested and imprisoned.)

And anyway, dead or not – what difference does it make?

Those who wish you their worst say you were dead from the very first moment you stepped into this ghetto –

Pan Śmierć? Is that you?

In that case, we're all Death's children here in the ghetto.

We're standing here waiting for you to lead us out.

We cry: *Father! Give us proof of your immortality!*

Save our children – and you will also save yourself!

Adam Rzepin thought they would accuse him of attempted murder, or at least of inciting agitation, and if they did not kill him straight away they would take him to the 'cinema' of the Central Jail and then extract the truth from him bit by bit, the way Shlomo Hercberg used to. But Shlomo Hercberg's methods were not in favour with the new prison chief. Werner Samstag was known to go into the Pit himself, and even to fraternise familiarly with his prisoners. But on these visits, he always had a swarm of *politsayen* with him, all so keen to make a good impression on their superior that this time they did not even wait for their commander's order before pressing the Praeses's would-be murderer up against the wall, kicking and kneeing him in the stomach and genitals until he was lying on the floor, fighting for breath.

It was these *assistants*, as Samstag called them, who informed Adam that Polish and Jewish doctors were fighting to save the Chairman's life. That Biebow had even conferred with Bradfisch about sending in the special units of the SS, as they had in August 1940, to nip the rebellion in the bud, and that if they did, young Rzepin would not only have the Chairman's life on his conscience but also bear ultimate responsibility for whether the remaining eighty thousand Jews in the ghetto would be deported or not.

All this was pure fabrication, but Adam Rzepin naturally did not know that.

Only after the assistants had made these accusations did Werner Samstag enter the cell. All Adam could subsequently remember of the interrogation was the shiny smile the new prison chief directed at him. Just teeth, no mouth. It was like being questioned by Death himself:

Samstag: Are you big or little, Rzepin?

Adam: Pardon?

Samstag: Are you a big or a little Rzepin?

Assistants: Is your name Adam or Lajb?

Adam: My name's Adam . . .

Assistants: We know what your name is. Are you big or little?

Adam: . . . Rzepin.

Assistants: You've already told us.

What's your uncle called?

Adam: Lajb. My uncle's called Lajb . . .

Samstag: When did you last see him?

We want to know where he is, who he's got on his list.

Assistants: Give us the names of those Bolsheviks – those murdering German lackeys – give us those and we'll let you out of here!

Samstag: We already know all about you –

The price you were prepared to pay last time you came out.

Do you remember that, Adam Rzepin?

Your uncle Lajb came and bought you out that time.

And the price was your own sister.

Assistants: When did you last see your uncle Lajb?

Samstag: You're in this up to your neck, Adam.

We've got it all on paper: the letter from the Resettlement Commission;

Shlomo Hercberg's exemption warrant – made out in your name;

the document your uncle signed when he came to fetch you –

Assistants: We know the price you were willing to pay to get out last time. Your own sister.

Samstag: Tell us where he is, your uncle Lajb. Give us the names of the insurgents and subversives on your uncle Lajb's list, and I'll give you back your freedom.

*

He lay with his head on the ground, just by the bars where the long row of cells began, and all around were the sounds of steps and boot heels crunching and scraping on gritty stone. Even at night, Samstag's men were bringing in new volunteers for the Chairman's Labour Reserve in the Central Jail.

They were never referred to as anything but *volunteers* – regardless of how long it took them to respond to the summons, or whether the Sonder had had to go and fetch them.

The man on the barrack-bed beside him said there were three thousand in the Reserve now: all of them men fit for work. He said this with obvious satisfaction, even pride; and added that he was looking forward to getting to the munitions factory in Częstochowa, where rumour had it only the *best* workers were sent. Then he leant forward and, as if confiding in Adam, said that admittedly Hitler's days were numbered, but the Germans would never let the Litzmannstadt ghetto be liberated. The Jews would have to leave the ghetto first. Only then would the Russians or British come and relieve them.

There seemed to be a good deal of optimism among the 'volunteers' generally. Adam soon realised this was very largely Samstag's work. Since Samstag had taken over, all the cell doors of the Central Jail stood open, and prisoners in the so-called 'outer' Reserve could come and go as they pleased (some of them only had makeshift beds or barrack-beds along the corridor of the cell block, as if they were on their way somewhere else and had just made camp there temporarily); and early in the mornings when the soup cart came out with its cheerfully clanking vats and billy cans, who was the first to reach it but Samstag himself, like a proper soup lady, shouting in his peculiar, foreign-sounding idiom:

There's food here for anyone who wants to work!
FOOD FOR ALL! FOOD FOR ALL!

Adam found himself being moved deeper and deeper into the passages as 'volunteers' continued to arrive and the cell block got more and more crowded. Down in the passages was where they put people rejected by the Reserve, those who had some deformity or injury they did not like others to see.

On his last stay in the Pit, it had been warmer down here. There had also been that high, whining note he had been instinctively drawn to, though he could never explain why. As if there was a hole or opening somewhere lower down, letting in air through some vent or hatch. Though that was completely impossible, of course. That would have meant the solid rock on which the ghetto was built was hollowed out at the base.

The strange note was still there, but it was broader and more diffuse now: not as keen and piercing. And just as before, there seemed to be some sort of acoustic low pressure that gave you a sucking, dragging feeling in your head, like a whirlpool.

Deeper down in the Pit, Adam saw, too, that the passages did not lead out of the cell block, as he had previously assumed, but carried on down through the ground in a rough spiral: so at a level perhaps five or ten metres below the one he had been in before, he could hear the same sounds above him that he had heard minutes or days before – but more faintly: the rattle of keys being turned in pointless locks; doors being opened or unlatched; the slightly manic laughter of the men in the Reserve who were so relieved at finally having something to eat when nobody else in the ghetto was getting anything that they forgot they were about to be deported.

– Rock upon rock, in distinctly defined layers.

(and between and below all those layers of rock:

these passages winding and going on winding, down and down) –

When did he realise that he had crossed a threshold and was no longer in the realm of the living? Perhaps it was the way the rejects sat. Huddled and turned away, as if they no longer even had faces to show.

But the song remained the same. A long-drawn-out note, which at this depth in the earth sounded more like a rumble that vibrated not only in your forehead and temples but also in your whole jaw cavity and at the base of your skull. And there were still the running, gushing sounds from the latrine trench along the side of the rock passage, with the additional inflow of the water that seeped from the cave roofs and walls and even seemed to rise from the uneven stone surface under him. In some stretches of the tunnel, he had to wade through deep pools of cloudy, stinking waste water.

But he could stand up straight now as he walked, and when he raised his eyes it was as if the darkness in the cave shaft was more porous, or at least easier for the eye to penetrate. A dark landscape spread before him. The roof of the cave passage became a rock sky, and in front of him the latrine trench ran out into an underground sea that the wet conditions had created and widened, with waves moving against the distorted rock walls in a long, oily swell.

The dead surrounded him now on all sides –

Some of them had their travel bags and mattress bundles with them, as if they could not be parted from their possessions even here. But most simply sat alone or in pairs, their arms stretched out from their bodies as if even their own limbs had suddenly become alien objects.

And of course, Lida was among them. She was sitting on a rocky projection, dressed in the pale cotton shift she used to pull on over her head each morning, with her angel's wings on her back, the ones she had always dreamt of wearing. And beside her sat Werner Samstag, with one foot in the latrine trench and dark glasses covering his eyes, as if to protect himself from the overpowering, now ever-present, light.

Samstag didn't need to say anything. Perhaps he had

never been as easy to understand as he was now. *A father*, he declaimed, putting his arm theatrically round Lida's thin shoulders, *never abandons his own children.*

But not even Werner Samstag could stop Adam touching Lida one last time. He took her hands, near the tips of her fingers, and waded out with them into the brown mess of sewage under the dead white light. Her body floated up behind her as if it suddenly weighed nothing, and her sleeveless dress filled out like a balloon or a shining white sail; just for a little while, before the black sewage water was absorbed into the fabric and her body was weighed down by the strange, underwater currents. But for an almost imperceptible moment, she lay floating there – and the most fleeting of smiles passed across her face. Almost like those times he had pushed her round in the wheelbarrow: a smile born of the bliss of moving freely without constantly falling.

And so he finally lets go – and allows her to glide out into that open sea that is nothing.

Treachery is something you carry with you constantly, like a knife held close against your heart.

When Adam Rzepin returned from the Reserve after three weeks, Olszer initially refused to put him back on the books. *We've no use for defective workers; I don't know why they persist in sending us these defective workers!*

Administrative superintendent Olszer had once been Elder of the Jews in Wieluń; that had taught him (he said) how to handle people. The head of the German Schupo unit that supervised Radogoszcz, Abteilungsführer Dietrich Sonnenfarb, also thought he knew how to handle people. He must have stood at the window of his blue show house for a long time watching what Olszer and Rzepin were doing, because as soon as Adam set off to limp back to his work in the sandpit in the hangar, he came out and attached himself right behind him. And they walked a farcical tandem walk, with him dragging his leg behind him just as Adam did – a stiff, rolling movement of the hip, impossible to distinguish from the hunger gait so prevalent in the ghetto.

The German guards laughed – as they were expected to.

Everyone else averted their eyes.

Adam had suddenly become one of those people nobody talks to. It was the fact that he had come back from the Reserve. If you were in the Reserve, you were in a sense already *outside* the ghetto, even if the transport had not yet taken you away. Anybody who came back from the Reserve must have been rejected on some grounds. Or could he have been recruited as an informer?

Since military loads kept arriving for transfer from road to rail, Adam was sent back to the loading bay at regular intervals. And all of a sudden, enormous quantities of cabbage arrived for the ghetto. Ordinary white cabbages, their outer leaves so pale and immature that the heads looked as if they had been wrapped in bandages. Since large areas of the former vegetable depot were under water, Adam and his work gang had to sign out tools – iron bars and hammers and clumsy little wooden mallets, which they used under the supervision of Schalz and the other guards to erect small wooden crates on poles, in which the cabbages could be stacked while awaiting the final stage of their journey into the ghetto. It was a measure of the authorities' confusion, or at any rate, of the general disarray that was creeping in, that they let their Jewish workers sign out these potentially lethal tools. They would never have done that before.

But then, the ghetto was experiencing a very unusual wintertime thaw. They had to wade through foul, smelly waste water even to get to the hangar; and every day when their shift was over, Olszer ordered them to stack the Heraklite boards up on blocks, so they would not be damaged if the water rose any further during the night. Adam certainly seemed to be the only one in the gang who wasn't worried about the water. He knew where it had come from, after all. He knew where the tools had come from, too. As soon as he felt the weight of a knife and chisel in his hand, he understood that a higher power had put the tools into his hands.

He spotted Jankiel, Gabriel, the Szajnwald brothers and the others first when the soup cart was brought in. They all avoided his eyes, except Jankiel, who never gave way to anyone. As soon as Jankiel sat down beside him, Adam knew he would have to ask him about Uncle Lajb. But he didn't say his name, just described how he looked: the high-browed, thin face, the shape of a cycle saddle, with little slits for eyes; and went on to describe the look from those eye nicks, which stared straight

508

at you but still didn't really seem to be seeing what they were seeing.

Jankiel knew at once who he meant. In return, he could have asked what Samstag and his men had done to Adam in jail, asked why they suddenly let Adam go, asked why he hadn't been taken into the Reserve like everybody else the Sonder 'took a fancy' to. But Jankiel didn't. Instead he said:

Is it true what they say, that Lajb's your uncle and it's thanks to him you got the job here?

And when Adam looked away –

And is it thanks to him that you got the job back again, as well?

*

Many of those at Radogoszcz remembered what it was like the last time there was a soup strike in the ghetto. That was in June 1943, and also in Marysin: in the cobbler's workshop known as *Betrieb Izbicki*, where they made clogs and basic wooden sandals that were really no more than a wooden sole and an insert with a strap across, which could be produced by the hundred thousand at a negligible cost.

The man in charge, Berek Izbicki, was known in the ghetto as a real tower of strength. When the authorities were looking, he did all he could to appear a model of efficiency, but as soon as the Central Labour Office inspectors' backs were turned, he cut corners all over the place and what was more, treated his workers worse than animals. Izbicki's *resortka* were put through the strainer daily. While foremen and managers, including Izbicki himself, always got a rich, nourishing stew with vegetables and chunks of cabbage that could be fished out with the ladle, the ordinary workers had to make do with a boiled-to-extinction, watered-down affair that tasted worse than latrine water.

This went on for months, and eventually one of the workers had had enough, threw his soup dish aside and cried:

This is bloody undrinkable, I'm not drinking it.

His outburst was unplanned. Even so, the worker's comment was passed from mouth to mouth like a secret message, and in the end it reached Izbicki, who was sitting eating his dinner of soup enriched with pickled beetroot and potato. Incandescent with rage, he strode along the line of workers queuing at the soup counter and said:

Who's been complaining about my soup?

When the cobbler who had thrown down his soup somewhat awkwardly raised his hand, Izbicki grabbed him by the shoulders and slapped him across the face with the back of his hand.

But then the unthinkable happened:

Instead of submitting to his punishment, the recalcitrant cobbler raised his hand and hit Izbicki so hard that the man fell flat on the floor.

In the general amazement that ensued, a handful of local police came charging in, batons raised; but instead of dispersing as usual, the workers just stood there, as if glued to the ground, and when Izbicki struggled back to his feet and tried to push and shove his workers towards the counter where the soup ladies were waiting, first one, then another responded by simply slipping out of the queue and returning empty-handed to their work place.

The first soup strike was a reality.

This was considered such a grave crisis that the Chairman was summoned, and he took several on-the-spot disciplinary measures that were supposedly 'fair' because they included all parties. First, Izbicki was reprimanded for using physical violence on one of his employees. Then the recalcitrant cobbler was threatened with the withdrawal of his workbook and ration card if he continued his attempts to incite rebellion. Nor were there any further obstructions. The cobbler obediently swallowed down his soup, hung on to his workbook, and so he and his family were able to keep body and soul together for a little while longer.

But in the ghetto, the little words 'soup strike' had taken hold. And the workers had something to remember.

For even if it is the case that a worker has nothing he can stake, not even his own life, and nothing to bargain with since his employer has nothing to give anyway, there is nonetheless power to be won from that simple little act of *sitting down and refusing your soup* . . . A last little window of possibility suddenly opening, even after his final bit of strength has been exhausted. Even young Jankiel was heard to say day after day:

Think, if we could just sit down and say no . . . !

The soup strike at Izbicki's in the summer of 1943 followed a long, hard winter, and in Marysin and at Radogoszcz nobody cared about the workers' conditions: everyone was busy toiling and carrying and heeding the supervisor's orders. But then spring came again, another wartime spring. And as if there was some form of diabolical intelligence squatting on the far side of the barbed wire that had devised it all expressly to torment the residents of the ghetto, food suddenly began arriving in the railway goods yard.

For four whole years, the ghetto had been crying out for potatoes; not the rotten, frozen, slimy, stinking tubers that used to turn up every so often, but proper potatoes. A few patches of rot didn't matter, as long as they were firm and hard, by all means with traces of *real* soil on their skins, so you at least had some conception of the rich, firm, loose yet slightly moist topsoil from which they had been dug.

No one had seen such a potato for four years. But now here they were. First it was all the cabbage, at least a tonne of it; every wagon full to the brim of plump, palest green globes, looking like 'children's heads you felt like scrubbing behind the ears'. And then the potatoes, real potatoes; enough wagonloads of them to fill up the old storage bins in Jagiellońska again. And lots of other greens and vegetables: spinach, French beans, turnips.

Shouts from down at the loading bay: *The Germans have reinvented the onion at last!*

And pickled beetroot. Inconceivable amounts of pickled beetroot.

By then, altercations had already broken out among the unloaders as to who should take the first batch to the depots. Unloading inside the depot, out of sight of the supervising steel helmets, was the first point at which skimming could start.

As they queued for their soup, too, the mood was one of cautious but well-founded optimism, and the tired old jokes were delivered in an unusually lively tone:

be interesting to see if the soup's taken a detour past the cabbage today
or if the cabbage happened to end up in the soup on its way out of here by mistake,
if so, it's Praeses cabbage, you know the flavour:
tastes as if it's gone off, but you fart gold, genuine article –

But there was no cabbage in the soup. No sign of any potato either. Just the usual tepid, starchy slops, as foul as ever. Jankiel was standing behind Adam, and behind him came the rest of the soup-cart queue, stretching interminably. Here and there an optimistic head craned, trying to assess from the reaction of the people at the front what the soup tasted like today. Then Jankiel turned to face them, raised his billy can over his head and dashed it to the ground with full force.

I'm not eating this shit . . .

Strike: everyone stared as if bewitched at the young man with the freckles and the scrubbing-brush hair. His eyes were wild but there was a hint of something else deep inside. What? – Defiance? Hope? – Sonnenfarb had immediately crawled out of his showy blue coop. He was followed in the usual sequence by Schalz and Henze.

Someone here refusing his soup . . . ?

Sonnenfarb did not need to wait for the answer to know who the culprit was. Jankiel's billy can was still lying where he had hurled it – just in front of him.

Like a hammer thrower, Sonnenfarb cast the weight of his enormous bodily bulk backwards; then his hand came round and Jankiel fell as if he had been clubbed. Schalz followed this up with a rifle barrel to the fallen boy's head: *Sieh zu, dass Du deinen Arsch hochkriegst und deine Suppe verputzt sonst mache ich dir Beine . . . !*

If Adam at that moment could have got his own skinny body between the rifle barrel and Jankiel's naked head, the skin quivering like the surface tension on a bowl of water, he would have done it. Schalz slowly put a bullet into the bore of his rifle. Jankiel grimaced, baring the teeth in his bottom jaw. But no shot was fired. Suddenly everyone in the queue, both ahead of the boy and behind him, dropped their soup cans on the ground. The clatter of hundreds of billies hitting the ground at the same time was so deafening that even Schulz lost his head and turned round, his rifle barrel raised.

There was panic in his eyes.

Keine Mittagspause mehr, keine Mittagspause, he bellowed, waving his rifle in the air. *Los zur Arbeit . . .*

The crowds went back to work. But everything was sluggish now. More trains were arriving in the siding, but despite the angry shouts of the German guards, the unloaders moved extremely slowly towards their work stations, and after a couple of hours, Sonnenfarb rang the bell to mark the end of the shift.

By then, rumours had already spread to the centre of the ghetto that soup strikes had broken out. They had stopped work in Metallager I and II in Łagiewnicka Street, and at the saddlery at Jakuba.

And the water in the ghetto rose, and went on rising.

Night after night, the meltwater rose from the dead earth.

Adam took care of the tools that chance had put in his hand. Now he had a knife, a chisel, a mallet and a hammer, and carried them with him, hidden in the waistband of his trousers the way he had once taken medicaments and messages to Feldman. Nobody suspected anything, because of that rolling hip movement he has been putting on since his stay in the Pit. One of those useless individuals, unserviceable for future labour, who for some unexplained reason have found favour with the authorities and been allowed to stay. One of the survivors, or perhaps just one more of the living dead? One day, he decided he had had enough of all the limping, and broke out of the marching column when it was on its way back into the ghetto.

Where're you off to? Jankiel called after him.

(He kept his eyes peeled, that Jankiel.)

They'll shoot you if you go that way!

But he went anyway.

At Radogosccz Gate, the melted snow came halfway up the watchtower and the soldier at the top looked out over his own mirror image onto a roving, disintegrating expanse of water. The boundary fence that divided ghetto from city was a fence no more, just a piece of wire stretched across nothingness.

At nights, the searchlights were sometimes switched on: a scoop of bright light rose from the ground to the drenched sky, as the solitary guard up there in the tower raked his machine gun over anything that moved out there:

tra-atta-tata-tatta-ta-ttaaa . . .

It was said that under cover of night, Jews tried to swim across those sections of the wire that were now under water. In actual fact, the duty guard was shooting rats. The guards with a sense of humour said things had got so bad now that even the rats in Litzmannstadt were trying to escape the 'Bolshevik invasion'.

In the light from the two mirrors, water and sky, Marysin looked rather like an ancient face, its features alternately protruding and being smoothed flat again. The telegraph poles along Jagiellońska and Zagajnikowa ran across the watery mirror like long wheel spokes. Spread among the spokes, the tin roofs of houses and workshops drifted between wind-ruffled floes of water.

What was left of the Green House was keeping itself passably well wedged up on its slope, and the cemetery was still behind its walls, and Józef Feldman's nursery with its toolshed and glasshouse gables lay a little further along.

But the old willow outside Praszkier's workshop, at the crossroads where Okopowa met Marysińska, was nodding there like a Medusa head with its long, delicate green branches floating on the surface of the glassy water. If you could have seen the whole ghetto from above, you could have drawn a line from the cartilaginous willow all the way over to the cesspits where the latrine carriers unloaded and emptied out their barrels.

Everything in between had been dissolved by water.

Adam thought at first that the stench was coming from the cesspits, but this smell was unlike the harsh, austere, saltpetre smell from the faecal beds: it was thicker, with the addition of something musty, something nauseously sickly.

The forecourt led him up onto more solid ground. This was

where what had once been the 'workshop' stood. A long row of wooden buildings with stables and outbuildings ended in a larger, free-standing building that was originally a coach shed. The big vehicle access door of one of these weather-bleached wooden buildings had come unlatched and was banging in the wind.

Adam thought as he approached it that someone should have oiled the hinges.

Then he realised the hinges were not the source of that loud and piercing sound. The source of the stench also became clear. It was rats.

Lajb had aged in the few years that had passed. From a distance, you could have taken him for one of those Polish farmers who spent all day out in the fields, until their skin was burnt black by the sun. But this was not sunburn. At close quarters, the skin looked swollen, as if there was some discharge beneath it, and that discharge was on its way up. The eyes that used to be naked and pale grey were now embedded in puffy, bulging skin, and his bald pate was a shiny red, and wet, almost like a grindstone.

Lajb sat at a long table he had dragged into the middle of the coach shed, and in cages all around, rats ran up over and under and along the walls, or clung to the bars with claws and sharp teeth, hissing.

Treyf . . . ! was all Lajb said, and it was unclear if he meant the rats or Adam, who had stopped in the doorway, overcome by the formidable stench.

In the sludgy, dirty-grey half-light, he saw Lajb get up from the table and stuffed his hand into a big, black glove. In his other hand, he picked up a wooden pole with a claw-like fluke at the end, and used it to unlatch the door of one of the cages. The rat inside clung instinctively to the underside of the pole. Then Lajb made a lightning grab for the creature with his other

– gloved – hand; he turned the rat's body over and slit open its belly with a single violent thrust of the blade.

He opened the belly wide over a slop pail he had slid into position with his foot. The other rats were like creatures possessed as soon as they scented the blood and guts; and for a moment it was impossible to see, still less hear, for all the rattling and screaming whipped up by the caged animals. With a long, precise manoeuvre involving both hands, Lajb then chucked out the contents of the slop pail, letting blood and intestines splash the bars of the cages; next he put his blade into the still quivering body of the rat and skinned it with a single, practised stroke.

Then he turned his burnt and naked face towards Adam:

I know you've come for the list of the people who tried to kill the Chairman –
Take it now, there won't be much time later . . . !

Adam had already seen the money Lajb had laid out on the table in neat bundles and piles: coins in one pile, notes in another; like in a bank or a counting house. Proper currencies, too: złoty and Reichsmarks and green American dollar bills. Some of the notes were so creased that they looked as if they had been crumpled up in pockets or coat linings for decades before being retrieved and smoothed flat by careful fingers.

Lajb wiped the blood from his hands on a rag he seemed to keep under the seat of his chair for the purpose, ran his bloody hand over his mouth and took out a bundle of notebooks with oilcloth covers, which he laid out and then straightened up on the table, just as he must have done with the money. Or the parts of his bicycle when he used to take it to bits, laying everything out separately, down to the last little nickel-plated screw or frame component: scrupulously, with the same restrained, precisely judged movements as a rabbi setting the Seder table or a kosher butcher jointing and cutting up his meat.

(And when the authorities issued the order for all the bicycles in the ghetto to be handed in, Lajb had been first in the queue at the collection point in Lutomierska Street to hand his in. That was the month of the first soup strike, and Lajb had naturally also been there at Izbicki's just before, noting down the names of all the troublemakers in his black books. Adam could remember the look on Lajb's face, the day he had to surrender his bicycle. Vaguely apologetic, subservient; but above all, *proud*. As if it gave him satisfaction, even though this time it was a blow to him personally, to see once again the forces of law and order triumph over unbridled, unregulated disintegration.

And then there was the reward: *the money* he got in return: and it made no difference how small or insignificant the sums were, or that there was nothing to buy with them –)

But Adam was not looking at the money on the table. He was looking at the wall of cages: behind each row of bars a tangle of twisted, tormented animal bodies; and for a minute he wondered what would happen if he were able to unlatch all the cages simultaneously. What would happen if – maybe only for a moment – all this arduously contained chaos were set free?

But the restless creatures are moving so rapidlyly that it is impossible to hold on to the slightest thought; and the smell is so disgusting that he can't even imagine about anything beyond it – however fleeting and transient it may be.

Adam no longer sees the cages and bars. All he is aware of is a wave of trembling animal bodies moving from one end of the room to the other.

And even Lajb's face, as it bends over the wads of notes on the table, is like an extension of this choking wave motion. Lajb head on rat body. Over and over again, the head loses its shape, widens into an ingratiating smile at one moment, only to be encveloped in an expression of blood-suffused, violent hatred the next. Lajb himself – or what is left of his voice above the screech of the animals – is speaking in a calm, almost paternally intoning tone. As if it all came down to a bit of practical management. And *tired* – yes, even the constantly alert supervisor Lajb is tired when it comes to handing over the results of his work so someone can carry it on after him:

Adam, listen carefully now –

When your name comes up on the list of those to be deported, don't obey, but take this money and try to find a safe place to hide.

Ask Feldman – he'll help you.

They'll say all the ghetto residents have got to move to another, safer place. They'll say the ghetto's too close to the front. That it's not safe here. But there's no safer place than here. There never has been.

There is nowhere else at all but here.

Adam tries to put down the bundles of notes and the handwritten notebooks Lajb has given him. But there are no unoccupied surfaces here to put anything on. And by the time he realises this, he has hesitated too long.

When Adam gets out after him, his uncle Lajb is already halfway down to Zagajnikowa Street. Only now does Adam see what he has been seeing all this time but not had time to register. Lajb is walking barefoot through the water. He has no longer even got the shoes that he was once so proud of.

Later that same evening, once Józef Feldman has rolled himself up in his sleeping furs out in the office, Adam gets a lamp and reads the names on Lajb's list.

There are twelve notebooks, covering a dozen factories and workshops in the ghetto, referred to by street name and number. The Central Tailors in Łagiewnicka Street is *The Central*. The tailoring workshops in Jakuba are *18 Jakuba* and *15 Jakuba*, and the hosiery factory in Drewnowska is *75 Drewnowska*. Lajb has entered the information in blunt pencil on the coarse, ruled pages. In the margin he has sometimes noted the contacts who supplied the information. His letters are small and concisely formed: as if he was aiming for maximum clarity in minimum space.

Each resort name is followed by a long list of workers' names in alphabetical order. In some cases the workers' home addresses are also given, along with notes on family circum-stances and political and religious affiliation. *Bolshevism* is the most frequently used designation; the abbreviation *PZ* stands for *Poale Zion*, *O* means Orthodox (*Ag I = Agudat Israel*), while the Bundists are marked simply with a *B*, with a bold central stroke.

Adam leafs through the full pages of the notebook; past the saddlery where Lajb must have worked after he finished at the cabinet-makers in Drewnowska; past the nail and tack factory and Izbicki's shoe factory in Marysin, until he finally reaches the loading and unloading section in Radogoszcz. But what name was Lajb employed under there? And how had he been able to work there for month after month, maybe year after year, without Adam or anybody else recognising him?

On the Radogoszcz pages of the notebook there are a good fifty names, and Adam knows most of them well:

> _Marek Szajnwald_ – aged 21–25 Marysińska; called 'M with the club foot'; also called 'The Tartar' (Adam had never heard him called anything but Marek or Marku)
>
> _Gabriel Gelibter_ – aged 34 – called 'The Doctor' (because he once helped bandage up a man who caught his hand in a screw clamp), former member of PZ
>
> _Pinkas Kleiman_ – aged 27 – known Bolshevist; previously at the Clearing Committee; got to know Sefardek there

And then Jankiel, of course:

> _Jankiel Moskowicz_ – aged 17 – former Gordonia activist, now Communist, 19 Marysińska. Lives with father and mother. Known stooge of _Niutek R._ No brothers or sisters. (Father: Adam M, foreman at 56 Brzezińska – low-voltage factory)

Adam stood up on the loading platform watching as the vehicles and guards of the Gettoverwaltung processed past the goods sheds and came to a halt in front of the part of the railway-yard building where the stationmaster and the supervisors had their offices. It was the second day of the strike, and Adam's first thought was we've had it now, they're coming to deport us. But unlike on previous occasions, when Biebow had 'shown round' SS personnel and delegations of visiting businessmen, this time there was only one staff car in the procession; the rest were police outriders on motorbikes, or members of Biebow's personal protection squad. What was more, it was obvious this visit had not been announced in advance. It took half an hour from the arrival of the motorcade for Dietrich Sonnenfarb to come rushing out to them, frantically gesturing and shouting to everyone to assemble in the railway yard, where Biebow was going to give a speech to the ghetto workers.

But Herr Amtsleiter did not have the patience to wait for the stationmaster to find him to a suitable place. Outside Sonnen-farb's show house there was a trailer on wheels. It was parked rather on a tilt, but Biebow managed to climb up onto it, and stand upright with a helping hand from two of his bodyguards.

Workers of the ghetto!

I have come out here to speak to you directly, to make sure you fully understand the gravity of the present situation.

Many of you are seeing me for the first time – so I ask you to take an extra good look at me, because I shall not say again what I am going to say now.

The situation in Litzmannstadt has changed. The enemies of the Reich are already dropping bombs on the outskirts of the city. If any of these bombs had fallen on the ghetto, none of us would have been standing here today. I can assure you that we will do our utmost to guarantee your safety, and will continue to secure your source of livelihood.

This also applies to you railway-yard workers.

But you must take responsibility for your own safety as well.

I have today ordered two extra brigades of workers to dig trenches. A line will be drawn as rapidly as possible from Ewaldstrasse to Bernhardstrasse; another will be dug at Bertholdstrasse, from Kino Marysin outwards.

You will receive immediate instructions on where the digging battalions are to assemble. For those who may perhaps be considering not presenting themselves, I would like to remind you that the Häftlingskommando already instituted in the Central Jail is still accepting workers. I have been informed only today that labour is needed at the Siemens works, at AG Union and the Schuckert works, wherever ammunition is being made, workers are required, as well as in Tschenstochau, where I understand a good many of your number have already been taken.

It has also been brought to my notice that many of you have complained about the food, and even refused to eat it because you have decided all of a sudden that the soup you are served is of inferior quality. I understand that you want to eat and live, and that you will do. But it is crucially important that foodstuffs be provided primarily to those who need them. What makes you think people are any better off elsewhere? Every day, German cities are being bombed. Even in the centre of Litzmannstadt, people are starving. Even native Germans are starving. It is our duty and obligation to provide for people of our own stock first and foremost.

But we will naturally take care of our Jews, too. In all my

years as Amtsleiter, not a day has passed without my doing everything in my power to ensure stable conditions for my Jewish workers. Although it has periodically been politically disadvantageous I have, by winning large and important orders for the ghetto, secured employment for Jews I would otherwise have been obliged to deport. Not one hair on your heads has been harmed. You yourselves can testify to that.

Let me therefore remind you that it is vital that every order be met to the letter, exactly as directed, and that all transports of materials leaving Radegast be despatched promptly and swiftly; and that every order issued by the officers in command be obeyed instantly. Those who do as they are told will be treated with the greatest goodwill.

I AM NOT STANDING HERE TO DELIVER A MESSAGE THAT WILL FALL ON DEAF EARS!

If you persist in your intractable behaviour, which is detrimental to all, if you carry on dragging your feet and refusing to carry out the tasks set you, I can no longer guarantee anyone's safety. So do your duty – pack your things and present yourselves at the stipulated place.

Without waiting for any reaction – as if the aim of the precipitate visit had simply been to utter these words, and nothing more – Biebow was quickly helped down from the trailer and accompanied back to the car by his attendants. On the loading platform and round the hangar, the workers who had been rounded up to listen stood waiting for something *else* to happen – for them to be assigned to the requisite digging gangs; for the door to the materials store to be unlocked, so picks and spades could be passed out.

But nothing of that kind happened.

Sonnenfarb stood there at a loss for a while in the middle of the crowd. Was that an order Biebow had just given him, or not? Then returned, apparently impotent, to his show house. From its wide-open window, the radio blared. At first it sounded something like marching music.

Those working in the vicinity of the goods yard had heard Sonnenfarb listening to the radio before, but then the sound had filtered out through closed windows and the volume had always been conspiratorially turned down as soon as the door was opened. But now the volume was being turned up and up. An excited male voice hurled its metallic-sounding exhortations straight out into the dead light:

A war of such vast historic importance as that into which we now find ourselves drawn naturally brings with it unprecedented sacrifices and burdens. There are some who are not able to see these sacrifices in their wider historical context. The more people who fail to do so, the likelier it is that future fighting generations will misunderstand the sacrifices we were forced to make, or even begin to view them as negligible.

But viewed from the perspective of time and eternity, our conception and evaluation of particular historic events changes.

History provides us with numerous examples.

It is unintelligible to us today, for example, why the contemporaries of Alexander the Great or Julius Caesar did not appreciate the true significance of these men. For us, however, none of their greatness is hidden.

I know people who listen, Adam heard Marek Szajnwald muttering, *but hardly to that loudmouth . . . !*

Adam turned round. Henze and Schalz had both made their way over to Sonnenfarb's house; but as the door was closed and their superior did not deign to show himself, they had no idea what to do. It was an indisputable breach of regulations for the radio to be on at all. The stationmaster had also decreed that those Jews involved in the unloading work were not in any circumstances to be anywhere near radio receivers or other communication equipment. But could you penalise your own commanding officer? And then it wasn't just anybody speaking, it was Goebbels, and on Hitler's birthday as well! Attempting to get the set switched off would be tantamount to trying to silence the Führer himself.

At that moment, the door of the house was flung open. Sonnenfarb appeared in the doorway, and announced that Herr Biebow had telephoned from the Sixth Police District to inform him that all workers were to be given an extra helping of soup *in honour of the great day*.

The soup cart seemed to come trundling up out of thin air. All at once, there were things to do. Schalz and Henze dashed off to try to get the workers into an orderly line. But the soup queue was a straggling affair, stretching many listless metres. People seemed reluctant to come up at all.

Sonnenfarb had retired inside again, and from the open window came more of Goebbels's bombastic diatribe, followed by thunderous applause. No one in command at the station seemed to feel the need to put a stop to this highly irregular broadcasting.

HEIL HITLER! rang out triumphally from inside the house, clearly in response to the corresponding salute from the radio. Then once again, a soup can was thrown to the ground – a gaggle dispersed – workers strode deliberately away from the soup cart, which was left standing on its own in the middle of the loading bay, shiny and almost unreal.

Sonnenfarb appeared at the door once more.

Provocation? Again?

– and suddenly there were armed German guards all round them. Where had they come from? The deceptive lethargy that had descended on the goods yard transformed totally and was all running boots, jangling shoulder straps, hoarse German voices shouting *Halt!*

Someone from the knot of workers turned and shouted:

It was HIM, it was HIM . . . !

Adam saw Jankiel turn towards Schalz, who had already raised his rifle. Jankiel held up his soup can in one hand, as if to show that it was brimming with Hitler's delicious birthday soup. Or was it just another scornful gesture?

Adam turned round, and at the same instant, Schalz pulled the trigger and fired. The echo of the shot rang out in a silence that was one great cavity.

They all stood round the cavity, stunned. Jankiel lay sprawled on the ground in front of them. The blood was pumping from a wound in his neck and spreading in a big pool around him, as his eyes stared blankly and uncomprehendingly over to the place where his soup can was lying – impossible to tell if he had thrown the can as far from him as he could or if now, even in death, he was doing all he could to reach out for it.

But the soup can was empty. Not a drop of soup had landed in it.

*

Adam walked home along empty roads. The sun was burning out of nothing. In the splinters of light and shade from the greenhouse, he saw the same cars that had brought Biebow to Radogoszcz standing waiting outside the nursery, but none of them contained Biebow. The only person who had stepped out of the motorcade was Werner Samstag. It was the first time Adam had seen him wearing the new uniform that the Sonder had commissioned: grey-green jacket with the red-and-white insignia of the local police on the lapels and shoulder straps, a cap of the same colours, and tall, black boots.

Samstag was smiling as usual, but when Adam got up to him only a grimace remained: a greyish-white row of teeth stuck in a face that looked as if it was coming unhinged.

Where's the list? was all Samstag said.

Adam couldn't keep his body still. The constant, nagging hunger, the exhaustion and the terror sent cramps running in long spasms from his legs right up to his chest and shoulders. He attempted to shake his head, but only set his teeth chattering, which enraged 'the new' Samstag.

Adam found himself pressed hard against the wall:

Where? shouted Samstag, the spittle spraying from his lips.

We know you went to see Lajb, where's the list . . . ?

And before he could even reply:

You're lying! Why are you lying?

Adam's first impulse was just to give way at the knees. Jankiel was dead anyway. What did it matter if his, or for that matter any other workers', names were on somebody's list? Why not just give Samstag the list he wanted?

But Samstag's rage didn't seem to be in proportion to what he was asking for. And moreover – wasn't it strange that the authorities were escorting their Jewish police superintendent? If the authorities didn't trust their cowed subjects, who *could* they trust? And who should Adam trust, in his turn?

In the office of the nursery, Feldman had lit the stove. Through the cracks in the rusty metal, the licking flames looked pale and lifeless, set against the dull sunshine.

Samstag was bent forward, raking around with the poker among the glowing logs. Adam stood with his back to the wall, watching the young policeman's leaning, still boyishly slim body. He simultaneously saw himself, standing alongside and waiting for the punishment that would now be meted out. And the greenhouse wall behind him was a solid wall, and the solid wall (he thought) will continue to exist, and it will be the same wall everywhere, and no matter what happens, those in authority will always have some threat to use. Deportation, assault, red-hot iron in your face.

But there was another thought in him at the same time, awoken the moment he saw the line of cars parked outside the nursery, and Werner Samstag beside the front car, all dressed up like a chauffeur in old-fashioned livery.

What *resort-laiter* (he thought) would agree to make uniforms for a Jewish special unit that might no longer even exist by the time they were finished? And why would the authorities care about uniforms if there wasn't going to be anybody left to police?

They're scared.

(That was what he thought. Just the one simple thing:)

Something's happening, but they don't know what – just that all the power they once had is slowly slipping out of their hands. And as he stood there with the certainty of their fear at his back, Adam told himself he was not going to give them anything more. Let them beat me to a pulp, but from now on I'm not giving them anything more.

Samstag stood before him with the hot poker raised.

Then Józef Feldman stepped out of the soil-reeking pitch darkness and put a hand on Samstag's shoulder:

Don't bother, Werner; he hasn't got anything . . .

Samstag's and Feldman's eyes met fleetingly, but still long enough for the glow of the poker Samstag held in his hand to fade. Then the grimacing leer on Samstag's face turned to an expression of unspeakable distaste and ennui, and with a practised jerk of his head, he ordered his men to let go of Adam.

What followed was an orgy of random destruction.

First Samstag's men pulled all the aquariums down off their shelves; then they set about the sides of the greenhouse, swinging their batons high above their heads and shoulders and smashing the panes one by one. Then they went into Feldman's 'office', wrenched down cupboards and mantelpieces, and smashed plates and dishes. Even the solitary hotplate Feldman had installed, though there was scarcely anything to cook on it, was pulled loose from the wall and thrown to the ground.

Samstag stepped forward from all the unspeakable devastation as if through a sky-blue haze of broken glass. He was holding some of the wads of notes Lajb had given Adam.

Are these your squealer's wages? he said – it wasn't clear if he meant him or Feldman – but he didn't wait for an answer before sitting down on the edge of Adam's mattress and counting up the cash he had found. When he was satisfied with the total, he stuffed the bundles of notes in the pockets of his new uniform and strode out with his men after him.

A minute or two passed; then there was the sound of car engines starting outside, one after another; then they were gone again, the line of vehicles in close formation, down towards Zagajnikowa Street.

Adam stood amid the destruction. Glass cases that had each at one time held a world of their own lay in fragments all around them.

'I'm sorry,' said Adam.

'It's not your fault,' said Feldman.

The fire was still burning in the stove with the same, faint flames. Adam took Lajb's notebooks out from the interior of the mattress where he had hidden them, took up the poker Samstag had threatened him with, tore out page after page and pushed them in through the stove door with its pointed end.

And so they all burnt up: Marek with the club foot, Mr Gelibter, Pinkas Kleiman; and Jankiel, of course. Then Adam shut the stove door, unsure if he had now saved them or merely condemned them to an even worse fate.

She saw him growing out of the quivering streak between the flooded earth and the blindingly bright sky – a lump of clay swelling and stretching until it became a person of flesh and blood, slowly moving towards her.

Věra had not seen Aleks for almost ten months, not since the day Biebow gave the order for the Palace to be destroyed. But Aleks hadn't changed much. He had always been thin, and now he was even thinner, his face indented around his brow and cheek bones. But his eyes were the same. They stared at her in growing wonder, as if he were the one most surprised that they had met each other again.

For ten months she had been more or less locked in the cellar beneath the archive, puzzling together all the pieces of news that she or the others in the group had managed to get from the radio. Even when she found out nothing, she forced herself to note something in her diary. She noted rain or snowfall and the colour of the sky. She noted the number of air-raid warnings they had been woken by that night. The sirens wailing through the ghetto and the illumination of the German anti-aircraft defence's huge, swinging searchlights, falling from the sky and suddenly bringing a roof, a gable wall, a deserted street out of the ghetto darkness that always enveloped them.

But above all she noted what the newsreaders said. The voices coming out of the radio were as thin and pointed as needles, and constantly awash in a roar of static: high, whining, oddly undulating ebbs and flows of sound that made her think of big, vibrating hoops swirling towards her through the air.

But still in the end she was able to make out at least something in the vast flood of information flowing by, and to get the words down on paper. She used the quotation code she and Aleks had agreed in advance. The day the Allied troops landed on the Apennine peninsula for the first time – September 1943 – she got out an old Baedeker atlas, and was then able to mark the places where the battles took place, including those at Monte Casino. In a volume of well-known quotations from Latin poets, she wrote lines by Ovid, Seneca and Petronius that would make it possible to chart the progress of the campaign from a distance:

Omnia iam fient quae posse negabam.

'Everything I used to say could never happen is happening now.'

Anyone wanting to find out what she knew would have had to take every book off every shelf and extract sheets from every file and folder in the entire basement library. And that would still not have been enough, because all the words and sentences were coded, and the maps Aleks had drawn were divided up into so many little fragments and pasted into so many different volumes that it would have been impossible to piece them all back together again even if you had known what the whole thing looked like. It was a painstaking construction process. By building it up in the strictest possible way, she hoped to make it look so much like reality that the boundaries between the world outside and the ghetto she lived in would, if not disappear, at least be less visible than before.

An impossible project, of course.

But the walls were getting thinner and thinner.

One morning she heard Maman playing the piano again. She was playing the old Pleyel piano. That was the piano they had had in the apartment by Rieger Park in Prague, before they got the grand piano. Věra recognised the dry tone with the same instant clarity as she did the faint rustle of her mother's dress as she bent over the keyboard and the inner side of the arm of her dress brushed against the bodice. They were simple practice pieces: *Papillons* and *Kinderszenen*.

*

There were four listeners in the group Věra was part of. She knew the others' names but little more. She usually did not know when they would be listening until she was called. The listeners had few set rules, but they did insist on one thing: if you were listening in a group, you only gathered when the group leader called you.

There were also people who listened alone – so-called *solitaires*.

Solitaires were people who had had a radio in their basement even before the war, or had been able to bring a small set with them when they were deported here, and had then not handed it in when ordered to do so, even though this could mean paying with their lives. Věra was sure there were several such solitaires at the archive where she worked. She thought she could see the same flash of joy in their faces that she felt every time the Allies advanced or took some stronghold of strategic importance. Many of the solitaires kept what they heard to themselves. But some were persistently indiscreet. That was how news of the war leaked out into the ghetto. If there was one thing Chaim Widawski and the other 'real' listeners feared, it was not the Sonder's informers – who were now lurking at every corner – but that all the careless talk about the war, about the Russians and where they were and what they were doing, would sooner or later lead the Kripo to those who knew *more* but said nothing.

Chaim Widawski and Aron Altszuler were in a group with Izak Lubliński and the three Weksler brothers. Out in Marysin, Aleks Gliksman was part of another group; and round the set in Brzezińska Street were the third group: Věra and two Polish

534

Jews named Krzepicki and Bronowicz, and a 'German' called Hahn.

And then there was the lad, Shem, who was their *goniec* and took messages if anyone was sick or couldn't come, or if they had to change the time or maybe even the place, if the 'station' where they listened was under surveillance.

All the groups had messenger boys, who were not necessarily in the know about what the listeners were up to. The less they knew, the better.

Věra never found out how much Shem did or didn't know. The lad had a stiff leg, or perhaps he was handicapped in some way. When he walked, he pushed his healthy hip forward and dragged the bad leg after him, which gave him a generally hunched-up look, his head tucked down into his shoulder, giving him an air of perpetual subservience. But he smiled all the time, his eyes screwed up as if in a state of crafty or knowing expectation. (Věra knew scarcely any more about Krzepicki and Bronowicz – did not understand very much of what they said, since they only spoke Yiddish or Polish. She didn't know anything more definite about Hahn, either, though he had been in one of the transports from Berlin, so he ought to be 'the same type of person' as her.)

It was mainly the Polish-language broadcasts from London they were able to pick up, and sometimes the ones from Moscow. On those occasions it would be Krzepicki wearing the headphones. But locating the right frequency was far from easy. The German transmitters in Posen or Litzmannstadt broke in with a 'symphony concert', or the German newsreader with his voice high in his throat reported new successes on the Russian front, where the proud German army had engaged in fierce fighting – it was always 'fierce fighting' – and succeeded in repulsing the Bolshevik attack.

Věra tried to keep note of all the places mentioned, so she could add them to Aleks's loose-leaf map, but she normally only got a few of them before the newsreader went over to something called *Aussenpolitische Berichte*, which was always about diplomats and ministers meeting in Berlin, and always led up to some extended, indignant haranguing of *der Totengräber des britischen Imperiums* or *der gemeine englische Gauner*, as Winston Churchill was known, and Věra listened, hoping to get at least some hint of what Churchill's *Lügen und Betrügereien* amounted to in concrete terms. But she never did. The newsreader would start talking about fleet manoeuvres in the Baltic, or the programme moved on to an item with an experienced nurse giving advice on the hygienic cleaning and dressing of wounds.

Afterwards, they would discuss what they had heard. Whoever had been wearing the headphones in that session would translate for the rest of them. None of the other listeners wrote anything down. It was an unspoken rule that there was to be no written evidence of their activity – all news was to be passed from mouth to mouth. But when Krzepicki did manage to pick up the BBC, and Věra had the headphones, they could all see Werner Hahn nodding and biting his lips as if mentally trying to note every word that had been said.

Perhaps Hahn was building up his own internal archive of what was happening on the main sections of the front.

Just as she was. Or the legendary Chaim Widawski.

Widawski. At the start of 1944, he had just turned forty, bachelor; lived with his parents in a cramped flat in Pozdrzeczna Street, along with two of his cousins.

Widawski was given employment as an inspector in the ghetto's card and coupon department (*Wydział Kartkowy*). He found himself quietly stepping into one of the most important posts in the whole ghetto. Bread, milk, meat and vegetable coupons to a value of thousands of marks passed through his hands every day, but strangely enough it never seemed to occur to him to exploit his position to gain influence and power.

But he did keep records. In spring 1943, in the margin of the big office ledger where he had to enter the authentication numbers of the coupons as he checked them, he started to write number and letter codes describing the front-line positions of the German and Russian forces; how far particular armies or corps were from certain strategic points; and notes of the armies' relative strengths – for example, how well armed the German tanks and artillery were when they were sent out after the defeat at Stalingrad to meet General Zjukov's counter-offensive.

This exposed a remarkable paradox. Though Widawski's coded war diary was kept entirely secretly, everybody in the ghetto knew that Widawski was the one to ask if you wanted details of what was happening on the various sections of the front. If anyone had *war news*, it was Widawski. Yet still no one seemed to realise he was among the listeners. Everyone was *taken totally unawares* when this fact was revealed.

It was as if there were two different sorts of knowledge in the ghetto; two worlds existing side by side without ever coming into contact with each other.

But the walls between those worlds, too, were now starting to get thin.

*

Es geht alles vorüber
Es geht alles vorbei
Nach jedem Dezember
Kommt wieder der Mai

That was what he had written, the letters squashed up together so he could fit them onto the greasy brown wrapping paper that was presumably all he had to hand; his characteristic handwriting, sloping forward slightly, seemed as yet unimpaired. The scrap of paper had been on her desk one morning at the end of the month, and was just one of the countless ways in which Aleks proved that he shared that escape artist's ability to get through any number of chained and bolted doors to deliver his message. She knew that, because Mr Szobek, an Orthodox Jew who had been the archive caretaker for many years, and who apart from Věra was the only one with keys to the cellar, had finally succumbed to tuberculosis and been admitted to the Dworska Street clinic.

But there was something special about this particular popular song that she, and doubtless Aleks too, had heard several times on the German radio stations:

Even long after the Germans arrived (Aleks once told her), the *shomrim* of the ghetto used to sing German songs in the collective in the evenings; and further, they sung in *German*, as if to send the message that the longed-for liberation applied to people of all nationalities. If Aleks had wanted to appeal to her to come and visit him in his far-flung banishment, he could not have put it in any better or clearer way.

Marysin in May. The contrast between the noise and frantic activity in the centre of the ghetto, where every *resort* was now involved in the production of Speer's emergency housing, and the old garden suburb, which after the night-time rain had awoken to new life beneath the blossoming cherry and apple trees, could not have been starker. Only a few hundred metres from the puddles of Dworska Street, where the 'city' formally ended, stretched one perfectly straight row of carefully measured and parcelled-out allotments after another. The whole route, from Marysińska Street out along Bracka Street and Jagiellońska, was like one big garden with green sprouting all around, each allotment with neat rows of canes supporting the delicate plant stems. Some of the plots were so small that they were entirely taken up by little cold frames, stacked on top or alongside each other in some ingenious system that would ensure maximum sunlight for each frame.

She would later look back on that day, as one of the last she and Aleks spent in the ghetto together.

Aleks had inspected her parcel, as he jokingly called their plot, hers and her brothers', and the watering system that Martin and Josel had built, which now watered not only their plot but also a number of neighbouring allotments. Then they took a walk, just the two of them, up along the narrow streets of Marysin.

The sky was a sail of dazzling blue. Larks beat the air, as if they hung quivering on invisible threads.

The grass was warm.

(When she came to write about her 'day out' in her diary, she would think that she had never before – not even in Prague, when she and her brothers went walking in the hills outside Zbraslav – thought of the natural world as having human qualities. Like hair or skin or discarded clothes. But that was what the grass was like that day, what was left of the grass in the ghetto. It was *warm*; body temperature, almost lukewarm.)

Aleks told her how work at the cement and woodchip factory out at Radogoszcz was going; how he and the rest of the labour brigade were fetched by the local police every morning and marched back every evening. By some coincidence that might well have been pure chance, the team of workers was billeted in the very Próżna Street building that the *shomrim* had used. That was where Aleks was taking her now. It was Sunday, the only non-working day of the week. Among the workers they passed, Věra recognised several former archive employees, and post office staff whom she sometimes used to run into on the steps or in the queues at the distribution points round Baluter Ring; they were thinner than ever, if that was possible, their clothes were torn and more or less ruined, and their shoes were basically just wrappings of dirty rags. By no means all of them in Próżna Street were committed Zionists, Aleks studiously informed her even before they got there. As if that mattered! Here they were, anyway, workers from *all* over the ghetto, jammed in under a single leaky roof. Věra took out some of the produce she and her brothers had been able to grow on their plot: some hard potato tubers, gherkins, radishes; and some vegetables she and Martin had bottled and put aside for what they called winter use – beetroot and white cabbage. Other brigade members brought out what they had. There was bread; and something they called *babka* or *lofix*, which was ordinary instant coffee, mixed with some kind of thickening agent, left to set and then cut up like a cake.

In the glow of the kiln in the middle of the huge room, they sat talking afterwards about the campaign the communist goods-yard workers had started. It had a code name, passed from mouth to mouth whenever more loaded wagons arrived:

Pracuj powoli . . . ! 'Work slowly.' The aim was to plod through every extended or delayed shift.

The order had also gone out for them to refuse to queue for their dinnertime soup.

There was complete bewilderment among the German goods-yard command. The stationmaster had gone to Biebow and complained that the Jews had grown sluggish and valuable cargoes had just been left. They had even discussed the possibility of increasing the nutritional content of the soup – no longer *straining* it, in other words. Biebow had even gone out there himself one day to try to talk the workers round. The authorities had even suggested that playing march music through loudspeakers might increase the work tempo!

This made them all laugh, until Aleks piped up and said he had decided to join the Communists, anyway; Niutek Radzyner and his associates were the only ones in the ghetto successfully putting up at least a bit of resistance to the Praeses. Someone else chimed in, arguing the opposite case, and a heated discussion ensued, continuing until the darkness had emptied the insect-humming, early summer sky of all its light, and the kiln was sending sparks high, high in the draught and up into a column of smoke almost invisible in the dusk. And suddenly, quite spontaneously, someone took up a song, and someone else joined in a little hesitantly, and all at once, everybody was singing, quietly at first but then louder and louder, with more and more conviction:

> *Man darf tsi kemfn*
> *Shtark tsi kempfn*
> *Oi az der arbaiter zol nisht laidn noit!*
> *Men tur nisht shvagn*
> *Nor hakn shabn*
> *Oi vet er ersht gringer krign a shtikl broit**

That night, wrapped in Aleks's heavy grey overcoat with its acrid smell of cinders and stale sweat, pressed tightly against his body to keep warm in the cold, she whispered to him and tried to look into his eyes, those eyes that were so tired sometimes, but so alert and attentive, too.

When he saw she was looking at him, he gave a little smile and said her name, once, very quietly. Věra was all he said, as if the two syllables of her name were something that could be gently taken apart, and just as gently put back together again. Instead of answering, she leant over and cupped his face in her hands. That way, she thought, he was finally within the circle of her arms again: palpable.

And she felt intensely at that moment that it was not just all his secret words that she longed for, all the forbidden messages

---

* Now we must struggle / Hard is the struggle / O that the worker not be in need! / We must not lose heart / But toil and do our part; / O that he could only get a bit of bread.

he slipped into piles of paper and into the books he secretly brought down to her basement room. But all of him, all that he was – his pale face and implausibly narrow shoulders – she took hold of them now – and she held his back, too, and his hips and waist. She could not help it. She wanted to possess him. If the Bolsheviks ever came and liberated them, this was still the only thing she wanted. She wanted to desire him as she had desired no one else in her whole life, and as she had not thought it possible to desire anyone at all in this land of hunger and exile.

*

They called him 'the boy Shem'; he was their bodyguard and rat-catcher, and the one – Věra was subsequently quite convinced of it – who saved them all, just in time.

On the first floor of the block in Brzezińska Street, where they still kept Schmied's radio in the drying attic, lived a certain Szmul Borowicz. At one time, boasted Borowicz, he had been a senior official in the food-distribution department, had a three-room flat and been able to afford a maid. But then the Palace fell, and Borowicz had had to relinquish his 'nice' job, and like so many others in those uncertain days he had joined the Sonder, where he quickly rose through the ranks, and now insisted on being addressed as 'Captain'.

Every so often, the Kripo came round to question Borowicz. There was much slamming of doors; the Germans made Borowicz dash around with keys, opening storerooms in the basement and cupboards in the flat, to show them what he had inside. But at the end of the process, they never arrested Borowicz or even took him in for further questioning. From this, everyone in the block concluded that Borowicz was working as an informer.

That was how the boy Shem came into the picture. Shem lived with his father on the second floor of the block, in the flat above Borowicz's. Whenever the Kripo came to visit, the lad observed Borowicz's doings in a pocket mirror he had mounted outside the window, or by pretending to set his home-made rat-traps outside the concierge's flat, and listening under the door. He once saw in his mirror the plainclothes Kripo men gathering round some papers Borowicz put on the table for their perusal. He also saw one of the Kripo men hit Borowicz across the face. But then the German fished in the pocket of his coat and offered Borowicz a cigarette.

Inquisitive as he was, Shem also crept up to the drying attic with his rat-traps and watched wide-eyed as Věra and her fellow listeners crouched over Schmied's old radio receiver; and Krzepicki said: 'We either rope in the boy Shem, or we forget all this right now.' That was how the boy Shem first became their *goniec*. While they listened, he kept watch outside, or down on the stairs with his traps.

At Krzepicki's suggestion, they put Schmied's radio in an old trunk they had brought up to the attic lumber room. It was the trunk Werner Hahn had brought with him in the transport from Berlin: a travelling trunk with old-fashioned mountings, which could stand either flat on the floor or on end. Krzepicki thought it could actually be an advantage to have the Sonder living in the building where they listened, but it did mean they had to be prepared to get out quickly, and from that point of view it was better to keep the radio in a trunk than behind a hearth, where precious minutes were wasted digging it out and hiding it again.

His observation proved correct. Just a couple of weeks after they put the receiver in the trunk, the boy sounded the alert: Borowicz was on his way upstairs with two German policemen. They slammed the trunk shut, got the boy Shem to lie on top of it, and carried the whole lot down the stairs with the lad clinging on and shouting and bellowing; and Mr Borowicz turned round after them and shouted:

I knew that boy was epileptic, I knew it –

The Germans just stood poker-faced.

But which of them would have touched a Jew with rabies of their own free will?

That was how they saved themselves and the receiver. Though it was a 'close shave', as Szmul Krzepicki put it afterwards.

So they moved to a disused coal shed in the yard of a building in Marynarska Street, opposite Borowicz's block but with a wooden fence, which did little to prevent people from seeing in, but at least gave them some semblance of security.

They were sitting in there when the morning news of the landing came through. Outside, warm, heavy rain was falling, beating on the wooden roof and fence planks. Věra later often recalled that sound, and how hard it had been to make out the voices in the headphones through the continuous rattle of the rain. Through the slatted walls of the shed she caught a glimpse of the boy Shem's top half, soaked through, and thought please let him sit still for a minute so I can get this, just as the voice at the other end said *This is the BBC Home Service. Here is a special bulletin read by John Snagge*:

Early this morning the Allies began the assault on the north-western face of Hitler's European fortress ... The first official news came just after half past nine when Supreme Headquarters of the Allied Expeditionary Force, usually called 'SHAEF' from its initials, issued COMMUNIQUÉ No. 1. This said, 'Under the command of General Eisenhower Allied naval forces supported by strong air forces began landing Allied armies this morning on the northern coast of France ...'

At that moment, of course, Shem stood up.

Every detail seemed etched on her memory: them crouching round the trunk, Krzepicki and Bronowicz beside her, with that tensing of the back and shoulders you see in children who think they can make themselves invisible to adults; and Werner Hahn's eyes growing inside his skull as the significance of the words Věra was translating from English into German slowly dawned on him.

But how much did Shem understand? Věra could never work out whether that oddly staring, boyish face with the sort of perpetually seething look was expressing fear or expectation. Whether the cramp in his deformed body was stopping the immense pressure bulging and bursting in there from getting out. Or whether it was in fact fear that fettered him. At any rate, she could see him standing there, taut as a coiled steel spring on the other side of the wooden planks of the shed wall. The next moment, she could not. And the expression on Krzepicki's face was now one of real horror:

Sshhh! Mir muzn avék, di kúmt shoyn!
We have to go they'll soon be here!

But it was already too late:

The boy Shem had dragged his paralysed leg after him (they could see the marks in the yard, as it turned to mud in the rain, trailing all the way out to the street), and he was standing at the intersection of Marynarska Street and Brzezińska Street, shouting out loud. People came rushing, arms outstretched, from gateways and buildings. In a dizzying moment of clarity, Věra realised they were listeners, the whole lot of them – solitaires who had heard the same news and were rushing out to share it with each other. Somewhere at the bottom of the heap of people whooping and hugging and kissing each other was the boy Shem, squashed down into the mud by his own unwieldy weight and the laughing crowd on top.

*

But it was not the boy Shem who gave them away.

In the torture chambers of the Red House, he didn't say a word. Nor in the confrontation in which they lined up a handful of entirely innocent people in front of him and told him they would kill them all if he didn't tell them who the 'traitors' were. Not even when he was taken out into the yard with his hands tied behind his back and forced down on his knees in front of the bodies of the other listeners they had already executed.

You've got one last chance! said the Kripo inspector, cocking his pistol against the boy's temple. *Give us the names of your accomplices and we'll let you go.*

But behind his anguished, chewing face, the boy Shem stubbornly held his tongue.

The one who informed on Widawski was in fact a man called Sankiewicz. Widawski and Sankiewicz had been neighbours for some years in the house in Podrzeczna Street. They were not close friends, but had always said hello to each other and exchanged a few friendly words. Sankiewicz had been one of the many who tended to rely on Widawski to hear the latest on the 'world situation'. He had carefully observed from his window the times of day Widawski came and went, and who he came and went with. But although everyone in the block knew Sankiewicz was a Kripo *Spitzel*, nobody ever thought he would be the one to inform on Wadawski.

It was those two worlds again.

At six in the morning the day after the Allied landing in Normandy, the Kripo swooped. Moszje Altszuler was sitting eating breakfast with his sixteen-year-old son when the police came storming in, and naturally he denied any dealings with listeners. Then the Kripo took his son Aron into the next room and waited until he could stand the screams no longer and produced the parts of a Kosmos radio receiver from an old sewing-machine case. Moszje Altszuler, a trained electrician,

546

had made the headphones himself from copper wire that he would later be found to have stolen from the low-voltage works that employed him.

From Altszuler's in Wolborska Street, the police went on to Młynarska Street, where the concierge let them into the flat of one Moszje Tafel, whom they caught *in flagrante delicto*, as it were. Tafel was sitting there with his headphones on, listening intently, and glanced up only briefly as the police surrounded him.

After Moszje Tafel, they seized a man named Lubliński in Niecała Street; then three brothers named Weksler – Jakub, Szymon and Henoch – in Łagiewnicka Street. And then there was Chaim Widawski, whose name seemed to crop up in all the interrogations.

On the morning of 8 June, Detective Superintendent Gerlow and two of his assistants go to Widawski's home in Podrzeczna Street, where the young man's terrified parents tell him that it is true their son has not been home for some days, but that he is an honest, upright individual who has most definitely not had the slightest thing to do with any listeners. At the coupon department, too, Widawski's fellow workers have to admit they have not seen young Mr Coupon Inspector for a few days, but say he has probably just taken a few days off because he is ill. Then the police tell Widawski's colleagues to spread word that if the fugitive traitor does not immediately give himself up, they will arrest not only Widawski's mother and father but also the entire staff of his department, and kill them one by one until all the illegal listeners have been caught.

Then they go on to the next name on the list.

*

Věra is writing. She sits all day down among the piles of books and files and albums, writing. She writes without a break, and as fast as her aching fingers will let her; on clean sheets of paper or the backs of sheets already used; on catalogue cards, in the spaces on the title pages of books or in the margins of old notebooks. She writes down everything she has ever heard, or thought she heard, the newsreaders say.

Every time she hears the scraping sound of footsteps on the steps outside, or thinks she sees the shadow of a moving body, she huddles down as if to make herself invisible. When she hears the clatter of the soup cart, she goes up to the archive and takes her place in the queue, and stands there waiting for her ladleful, looking neither right nor left, afraid that the least glance in any direction might be enough to give her away.

She thinks about Aleks. About whether they have heard about the raids on the Altszulers and Wekslers out in Marysin, too, and been able to find somewhere safe, as Widawski has. But where would Aleks go, if so? They live in a ghetto. Where could there possibly be any safe places to hide?

When five o'clock comes and the working day is over, and the Kripo still have not turned up, she packs up her things. But instead of turning into the yard of her own block, she carries on along Brzezińska Street.

At the crossroads were she last saw Shem, as he was mobbed by joyful solitaires, a knot of people is standing, backs turned. She pauses a little way from them, to check none of the backs belong to anyone living in that building, who might recognise her and give her away. After a while she cautiously takes a man by the elbow, draws him out of the crowd and asks him what's happening. The man looks her up and down suspiciously. Then he suddenly appears to make his mind up, and in a voice outwardly quivering with indignation but inwardly bursting with pride at being able to tell her, he confides to her that one of the listeners the police are looking for – the ringleader himself! – committed suicide that morning. – Someone called Chaim Widawski, if that name means anything to her. People who lived round there had seen him standing outside his parents' flat all night, not being able to decide whether to make his presence known or not. Towards morning, somebody saw him get something out of his pocket, and thought: he'll give up now, he'll finally go into the house and up to the flat; but he only made it halfway to the front door before the poison took effect and he fell to the ground; *prussic acid*, says the man, with a knowing nod, he had the poison with him all the time. Died before his parents' very eyes, he did; they both saw him from the window.

Věra asks if there have been any arrests in the building outside which they are now standing, and the man tells her the Kripo were there and found a radio in a coal shed in the house on the other side of the road, cunningly hidden in an old trunk. They'd caught two men so far – one a slim, acrobatic type; and the other a German Jew already identified as the owner of the trunk. His name and former address in Berlin had been on the inside of the lid.

But from Aleks, not a word.

If they hadn't caught him, there was only one place he could be: the old Hashomer building in Próżna Street. Halfway out to Marysin, hunger makes her go all light-headed again. The world starts to sway in that familiar way, her knees buckle and her mouth goes all dull and dry. She sits down on a big stone at the roadside and unwraps the bit of bread she always carries in her handkerchief for times like this. But she is overcome, not only by weakness but also by the feeling of having lost all control and direction. Before, there had been an *inside* and an *outside*, and a firm, unshakeable, albeit intangible will to get the world out there to penetrate *here*, into the ghetto, and in that way (almost like turning a piece of clothing inside out) somehow get *out* herself. Now there is nothing here – no outside, no inside. All that is left is sun, behind a film of bright cloud, a pale sun, slowly melting into the whiteness, and suddenly everything dissolves around her into a hot, white, shapeless haze.

When she gets to the collective in Próżna Street, it is milky-white twilight already, and exhausted workers have curled up in their sleeping places under the roof and its holes. When she crawls at last to the spot she shared with Aleks, the mattress and blankets are cold and undisturbed. She lies awake all night, listening to the bats darting about on rapid, invisible wings in the vast darkness under the roof; but he does not come.

Litzmannstadt Ghetto, Thursday/Friday 15–16 June 1944:
<u>Commission in the ghetto</u>. The ghetto is once again in a state of great agitation. In the late morning, a commission came to the ghetto, made up of head mayor Dr Bradfisch, former mayor Wentske, regional parliamentary president Dr Albers and a senior officer (bearing the insignia of the Order of Knights), probably from the air defence forces.

The commission members made their way to the Chairman's office, where Dr Bradfisch had some minutes' conversation with the Praeses. Then Gestapo Commissars Fuchs and Stromberg came to Miss Fuchs's office. No sooner were these visits over than the ghetto was full of wild rumours. They all tended in one direction: resettlement [*Aussiedlung*]. Nobody in the ghetto yet knew what had actually been said in the Chairman's office, but it is believed that it had to do with large-scale resettlements. Earlier this morning, a figure of 500–600 men was being bandied about, but later in the day thousands of people were understood to be involved, possibly the majority of the ghetto population – in fact some even claimed to know that a total liquidation of the ghetto lies ahead.

[...] The aim is for a number of large transports of workers to leave the ghetto. It is said that an initial group of 500 will be taken to Munich for clearing-up operations after the recent bombing raids. Another group of 900 or so will leave the same week, probably as soon as Friday 23 June. Then 3,000 people a week are to leave in the following three weeks. A supervisor, two doctors, medical staff and police will be ordered to accompany these transports. The police will not be recruited from the ghetto's existing forces but from the people in the transport. [. . .] It is unclear where these major transports will be going.

*

Proclamation No. 416
<u>Re: Voluntary Labour Outside the Ghetto</u>
<u>ATTENTION!</u>

It is hereby announced that men and women (including married couples) may register for labour outside the ghetto.

Parents who have children who have reached working age may also register these children for labour outside the ghetto.

Those who register will be supplied with all necessary items: clothes, shoes, underwear and socks. Fifteen kilograms of luggage per person are permitted.

I would like to draw particular attention to the fact that that these workers have been granted permission to use the postal service, and will be able to write letters. It has also been confirmed that all those who register for labour outside the ghetto will have the opportunity to collect their rations immediately, and not need to wait their turn. Registration for the above will take place in the ghetto at the Central Labour Office, 13 Lutomierska Street, from Friday 16 July 1944, daily between 8 a.m. and 9 p.m.

Litzmannstadt Ghetto, 19 June 1944
Ch. Rumkowski, Eldest of the Jews in Litzmannstadt

*

Memorandum
<u>(written copy of order issued verbally)</u>*

Each Monday, Wednesday and Friday a transport will leave for labour outside the ghetto. Each transport will consist of 1,000 people. The first transport will leave this Wednesday, 21 June 1944

* Written down by D. Fuchs in the Chairman's diary, Sunday 18 June 1944.

(*c.* 600). The transports will be numbered with Roman numerals (Transport I, etc). Every worker who is leaving will be issued with a transport number. Each individual will wear this number on his/her person, and attach the same number to his/her baggage. Fifteen to twenty kilograms of effects per person are permitted; this should include a small pillow and a blanket. Food for three days is to be taken. A transport supervisor will be appointed for each transport, and ten assistants; a total of eleven people per transport.

The transports will leave at 7 a.m., and loading must therefore begin punctually at 6 a.m. A doctor or field surgeon and two or three nurses will accompany each group of 1,000. Relatives of medical staff may accompany them.

Effects not to be wrapped in sheets or blankets but to be packed as compactly as possible for ease of stowing on board the trains.

Regarding the eleven accompanying persons: these are all to wear the caps and armbands of the local police force.

*

Tagesbericht von Donnerstag,den 22.Juni 1944.   Tageschronik Nr.173

Das Wetter: Tagesmittel 19-3o Grad,sonnig.

Sterbefälle: 28,   Geburten : keine

Festnahmen: Verschiedenes: 1,   Diebstahl: 1

Bevölkerungsstand: 76.4o1

Selbstmordversuch: Am 21.6.1944 versuchte die Sachs Gerti geb.22.8.1905
in Brünn,durch Einnahme eines Schlafmittels Selbstmord
zu begehen.Die Genannte wurde durch die Rettungsbereit-
schaft ins Krankenhaus überführt.

Tage snachrichten

Der Präses befindet sich noch immer in Spitalspflege.
Ausreise.
Das Getto steht ganz unter dem Eindruck
des Aderlasses,der ihm jetzt bevorsteht.Man glaubt allgemein,dass es si..
jetzt um den Beginn einer allmählichen Liquidierung des Gettos handle und
man befürchtet,dass nach Absolvierung d r vorgesehenen Transporte,vielleicht
nach kurzer Unterbrechung,eine weitere Evakuierung vor sich gehen wird.
Gegen diese Annahme spricht der Umstand,dass die Gettoverwaltung nach wie
vor Aufträge für die Ressorts hereinnimmt und dass man bestrebt ist,die
wichtigen Ressorts,durch die Aussiedlung,in ihrer Produktion nicht zu störer

Abtrennung von Gettoteilen. Heute fand am Baluter-Ring eine Besprechung zwischen Vertreter der Gettoverwaltung und einigen jüdischen
Abteilungsleitern statt.Gegenstand der Besprechung war die Frage,unter wel-
chen Umständen gewisse Partien des Gettos abgetrennt und der Stadt einver-
leibt werden könnten.Es handelt sich um die Wohnblocks an der Hamburgerstrasse,am Bach,Holzstrasse,Altmarkt und Rauchgasse.Bei Kassierung dieses
Teiles des Gettos würde eine Umsiedlung von ungefähr 1o.000 Juden in andere
Teile d s Gettos erforderlich sein.Im Zusammenhang damit nahm auch der Leiter des Wohnungsamtes Wolfowicz an der Besprechung teil.Ing.Gutman soll
ein entsprechendes Gutachten über dieses Projekt ausarbeiten.

Zur Arbeit ausserhalb des Gettos.In der Nacht auf heute wurden durch weitere
Polizeistreifen Personen sichergestellt,und ins Zentralgefängnis gebracht.
Es handelt sich zunächst um die Sicherung des Kontingents für den 2.grösse-
ren Transport,der voraussichtlich Montag,d n 26.ds.Mts.abgehen soll.
Gestern wurden ca 600 Menschen für den 1.Transport bestimmt.Es heisst,dass
ca 5o Menschen hievon,separat über Baluter-Ring,zum Torfstechen abgehen sol-
len.Alle Reisefertigen erhielten heute 1 Brot,25 dkg Wurst,25 dkg Zucker
und 25 dkg Margarine.
Allmählich erfolgt die Deblockierung der Lebensmittelkarten von Personen
die die Aufforderung erhielten,von der Kommission jedoch befreit wurden.
Der Vorgang ist ziemlich kompliziert.Die Listen aus dem Zentralgefängnis
gehen zunächst an die Kartenstelle,die zufolge ihrer Mitarbeit an der Ak-
tion von der Stellung eines Kontingents befreit ist,und an die Approvisa-
tionsabteilung wo sich sämtliche Register befinden.Dort werden die Eintra-
gungen vorgenommen u.zw.unter Kontrolle der Sonderabteilung,die die Listen
ebenfalls erhält.Die im Laufe des Tages erfolgten Deblockierungen werden
dann d n Verteilungsläden bekanntgegeben,bzw.ersehen diese aus den Register

./.

From the *Ghetto Chronicle*,

Litzmanstadt Ghetto, Thursday/Friday 22–23 June 1944

This is how it was reported in the *Chronicle*:

At five in the afternoon on Friday 16 June 1944, the day head mayor Otto Bradfisch came to Rumkowski to inform him that the ghetto was now to be cleared definitively, Hans Biebow had also arrived at Bałuty Square. In a highly intoxicated state, he barged into the Chairman's office, ordered all the staff to leave the room; then hurled himself at the Chairman and set about him with his stick.

This was the second time in swift succession that the Chairman had been attacked in what was clearly an act of madness, and his body and face bore the clear marks of the blows. Where he had previously been firm and steady in his bearing, he was now bent and fumbling, and the once proud and unsullied face beneath the mane of white hair, the face that once adorned walls and desks in all the offices and secretariats of the ghetto, was now a mask of wounds and swollen bruises.

The two colleagues who had accompanied Biebow, Czarnulla and Schwind, realised that if they did not restrain Mr Biebow, something highly regrettable might happen. Even some of the Jewish employees, Mr Jakubowicz and Miss Fuchs, tried to talk to Herr Biebow and calm him down. But nothing helped.

You bloody well keep your hands off my Jews! shouted Biebow from the barrack-hut. Then the window smashed in a shower of broken glass, and Biebow's voice echoed loud and clear across the square:

The Devil take you, you pathetic coward – I can't spare a single man, but when Herr Oberbürgermeister comes and says you've got to send three thousand men out of the ghetto every week, you just say – jawohl, Herr Oberbürgermeister – of course, Herr Oberbürgermeister – because that's all you know how to do, you Jews, say your hypocritical and fawning yes and Amen to everything, while they're literally stealing the ghetto from under my nose.

You tell me: how am I supposed to send off all my deliveries if I haven't got any workers left to rely on? How shall I survive here in the ghetto if there aren't any Jews any more?

Once he had had the splinters of glass removed and the wounds to his face patched up with some stitches and dressings, the Praeses of the ghetto had, at his own request, been taken 'home' to his old bedroom on the top floor of the summer residence in Karola Miarki Street. By this juncture, everyone thought the Chairman's last hours had come. Mr Abramowicz bent down to the old man's sickbed and asked if he had a final request, and the old man said he wanted them to send for his faithful servant from the old days, former nursery nurse Rosa Smoleńska.

There was a good deal of fuss about this afterwards. Despite all the sacrifices made by the Chairman's many faithful servants and close colleagues all those years, the only person he wanted to see when he was dying was a common nursery nurse. But Mr Abramowicz duly went with Kuper in the barouche to the bay-windowed flat in Brzezińska Street where Miss Smoleńska lived with one of the Praeses children who had been adopted; and Miss Smoleńska put on her old nursery nurse's uniform again, and the two of them were taken in the carriage out to Marysin; and Mr Abramowicz let her into the sickroom where the dying Praeses lay, and discreetly shut the door; and the Praeses looked her up and down, and gave a vague wave of the hand to indicate she should sit down at his side, and then said *the main thing now is the children*; and from that moment on, everything was as it was before, and always had been.

Chairman: The main thing now is the children! You, Miss Smoleńska, are to gather them all at a special assembly point that I shall not give you details of until later. NOT ONE SINGLE CHILD MUST BE MISSED. Do you understand, Miss Smoleńska? A special transport has been arranged for the children. Two doctors will accompany it, and two nurses that I shall select myself. What do you say, Miss Smoleńska?

Would you like to go with the transport as its nursery nurse?

Rosa Smoleńska had long since lost count of all the times over the years she had been summoned to offices and bedrooms where the Chairman lay 'sick', or perhaps just 'feeling the effects'. (If it wasn't his 'heart', which was a constant preoccupation of his at that time, it would be something else.)

This time he did look genuinely ill, his face red and swollen, clotted with blood where the wounds on his temple, on both cheeks and near his eye had been stitched. But the dreadful thing was that underneath that mess, the old face was still there. And that face now smiled and winked at her, just as slyly and shamelessly colluding as it always had been; and the voice from inside the bandages was the one that had always ordered her about, or pretended to accommodate her wishes as long as she (in turn) accommodated his:

Chairman: Because you'll want to come with your children, won't you, Miss Smoleńska? In that case, I want you to make it your responsibility to bring all the children to the assembly point that will be specified.

Can you promise Rumkowski that?

He had taken her hand between his. His hands were bandaged right up over her wrists, and his fingers looked like little lumps of dough as they protruded from the bandage. – *But it was the same hand!* – And just as so many times before when he had

557

tricked her into touching him, the hand was trying to find its way in and reach places where it had no business to be.

And how was she to tell him then that all the children he insisted she gather together were gone?

That there were no children left to save!

He had helped to send them all away, hadn't he!

She couldn't do it. Behind that mess of a face, his heartless gaze was entreating her again, and she could not let him down. And she said, *Yes, Mr Chairman, I shall do what I can, Mr Chairman*. And under the freshly ironed nursery nurse's uniform, the doughy, bandage-impeded fingers groped their way over her thigh and between her legs. And what could she do? She smiled, and cried with gratitude, of course. As she had always done.

The last deportations from the ghetto were done in two stages. A first, more orderly operation lasted from 16 July until the middle of the following month. Then there was a break of two weeks, when most things seemed to go back to normal. Then the deportations resumed, and this time there was no question of transports to places outside the ghetto any more; this was a total *Verlagerung*.

The whole ghetto, people, machinery and everything, was to be moved elsewhere.

The front was very close now. The air-raid sirens regularly howled for several hours each night, and as she lay awake behind the curtain in Mrs Grabowska's flat, Rosa Smoleńska could feel the detonations of distantly falling bombs, dull tremors through the walls of the house and up through her own body.

In these last weeks, Debora Żurawska had been working at Tusk's factory on the corner of Lwowska Street and Zielna Street. The factory made porcelain casings for fuses and insulators, and was one of the few activities classed as *kriegswichtig* by Biebow and thus allowed to remain in the ghetto even after the evacuation had begun. Debora worked right at the end of the cold, crowded shed, where she and some other girls stood packing the finished fuses in little square boxes made of card. Twelve plugs to a box, and then the flaps at the top and bottom of the boxes had to be tucked into the little diagonal slots on their sides. Then the boxes were packed in bigger cardboard boxes, twenty in each.

Day after day Debora would perform these simple operations.

Then one day, she did not come home. Rosa had to admit afterwards that she could not say exactly *when* Debora had gone off: whether it was that morning on her way to Tusk's, or during the night, or even the evening before. It had happened quite often recently, Debora going off, or 'forgetting herself' as they said at the factory. She would leave the packing room at the *resort*, wander off and get lost in one of the streets behind the factory that were simultaneously familiar yet utterly strange. This could happen in the middle of the day, or in the evening after the factory whistle blew. If it was the middle of the day, she usually only got a few blocks before the Sonder stopped her and demanded to see her workbook. But if it happened at the end of the shift, she had sometimes gone quite some distance before a neighbour or acquaintance alerted Rosa to the fact that they had seen 'her girl' in the district. Once she even went over the wooden bridge at Bałuty and wandered round among the workers at the cabinet-maker's in Drukarska Street, and it was sheer luck that Rosa got to her before the Sonder did.

But there were times when Rosa was simply too tired. Ten hours a day at the uniform-making workshop, where she had a job sewing linings into gloves and winter caps; then three hours queuing every evening for some meagre allocation of rations, or carrying water up from the gas collective, or washing clothes, or scrubbing the stairs and floors. Sometimes she was so exhausted she just fell into bed. When she woke up the next morning, she sometimes found Debora sitting fully clothed on the floor outside the sleeping alcove, starring transfixed at the flies moving around on the reverse of the fabric Rosa had put over the window, where the sun was shining through it: the way the flies' shadows enlarged, the moment before they attached themselves to the fabric, then shrank as they let go again and flew off. That generally meant she had been out all night, and Rosa shuddered to think what might happen if she ventured too close to the wire in her confusion, and one of the bored German sentries suddenly took it into his head to fire.

But Debora not only 'forgot herself' in the ghetto, she also tried to disappear behind the goodwill of others, or behind her own or other people's words.

'Let me help you,' she would say with enthusiastic kindness as Mrs Grabowska came along with the coal bucket, and go down on hands and knees to light the fire in the stove. *This* Debora was as swift to aid and come to the rescue of others as the girl that Rosa had come to know in the Green House; but *this* Debora forgot the bucket of coal or pail of water the instant she had gone to get it, or merely stared at Rosa in disbelief as she tried to explain the best way home from the factory. The words fell off her as the flies and other insects fell off the back of the fabric at the window. They were only shadows, and just as irrelevant.

In fact, it was only when Mrs Grabowska came in with the coal to light the stove the second morning and stood there with the rake and shovel and suddenly remembered – *oh yes, there was someone here asking for young Miss Debora the other day* – that Rosa started to worry. She asked who it was, but Mrs Grabowska had no idea, of course. How could she know? There were so many people coming and going these days. Youngish type – Sonder or something like that – was all she could remember.

*

The story is still told in the ghetto of the mute and paralysed woman Mara who was found in Zgierska Street outside the barbed wire one day, and who was rejected by the Orthodox rabbis and was therefore taken care of by the rabbi of the ghetto's Hasidic Jews, one Reb Gutesfeld. Day after day, Reb Gutesfeld and his *helfer* were to be seen parading round with the paralysed woman on a sort of pallet, a rudimentary stretcher, and people had come to her in secret in the prayer house in Lutomierska Street or in the synagogue in the old Bajka cinema, as a rumour spread that she was the daughter of a *tsaddik* and therefore had healing powers.

But she never spoke, nor moved so much as a limb.

Then the Nazis brought in the *Gehsperre* and people sat in their homes, terrified, waiting for the Sonder and the SS men to come and take their old people and children from them. The last of the ghetto's ageing rabbis were sent away from the ghetto, and the righteous woman would have been, too, if she had not already been summarily shot.

But then a rumour went round that somebody in the ghetto had seen her. It must have been the third, or possibly the fourth, day after the curfew was imposed, and the policemen from Gertler's Sonderabteilung who reported the sighting were terror-struck. For the paralysed woman had been seen walking upright, on her own two feet, not always straight, but tottering from one house wall to the next; every so often she collapsed, but soon got up again. And once this rumour started to spread, it turned out that other people had seen the woman, from inside their flats. And this time she was even alleged to have got into houses through closed front doors, and on every floor she came to, she was said to have touched the mezuzah on the doorpost, and some people were even rumoured to have let her in, and it was said she told them that the God of Israel is with his people at the hour of departure, whether it is to Babylon or Mitsraim. And if a single one of the tribe of Israel should perish on the way, then as the prophet says, all will have perished. Yet one who perishes cannot destroy them all. For if it is so that a single stone cannot be hewn from a rock without harming the whole rock, then it is equally so that even if a stone is hewn from it, the rock will still endure. The tribe of Israel is indestructible. That was what she was reported to have said.

As departure faced them again now, there were again people finding their way from house to house by night. But they could certainly not be considered holy men, and they spoke inspiringly, not of the indestructible rock of Zion or Eretz Israel, as the woman Mara allegedly did, but of the chance for everyone to be well fed and satisfied for at least one day before the transports left. Rosa had heard them herself, standing whispering with their silky-smooth voices behind the piece of red cloth she had put across the window –

Drai . . . ! They might say.

Or:

Drai en a halb . . . !

The longer Debora was away, the more convinced Rosa was that the girl had fallen prey to one of those whispering buyers of souls.

This was how it was:

Since Biebow had insisted that as many factories as possible continue production, all *Ressort-Leiter* had the task of drawing up lists of which workers they considered indispensable and which they could do without, if strictly necessary. On the basis of these lists, a special *Inter-Ressort Komitee* then decided which workers would go in the next transport and which would carry on working. A *resort* could also 'buy' workers from the committee if there was a specific need for them, or if Biebow had decreed that production in that *resort* was of particular importance.

This meant there was a continuous trade in people.

Some factory bosses could pay as much as ten 'dispensables' in exchange for one skilled mechanic.

Thus the need for all these 'souls'. These were often very young men or women, who in return for bread or food coupons agreed to be deported in place of the person in demand, so the quota of deportees would remain filled and steady.

It was like a machine; a gigantic sorting mechanism at work:

Those who had enough money to pay for it bought themselves a bit longer in the ghetto. Those who did not have money at least still had their 'souls', and could sell those.

By early dawn, Brzezińska Street is already filled with a noise so intense it seems to form a body in its own right, a body of sound floating high above the mass of people moving sluggishly up and down the whole length of the street.

There are two streams running though the ghetto. One on its way up from Plac Kościelny. In it are the paid-for, the freed, the exceptions, those who still have jobs to go to, with rucksacks on their backs and *menażki* clattering inoffensively at their waists. Another stream is on its way down to Plac Kościelny. In it are all the others: those who have been given written notice to leave or been forced to sell themselves as souls.

By dinnertime, the crowd has assumed almost incredible proportions:

People are standing in the middle of the street with their loads of furniture and kitchen equipment; just standing: trapped in an apparently never-ending caravan of carts and barrows that have tipped over or got stuck, and people are trying to get them up and running again by pushing from behind or trying to drag them with rope harnesses and straps.

On her way down towards Bałuty Square, Rosa passes the so-called purchase point: a large enclosure that starts right down by Kron's chemist's shop at the foot of the wooden bridge and runs all the way up to Jojne Pilcer Square. Anything that could possibly be sold has been brought here: tables, dining suites, cabinets, doors; used, even damaged suitcases and bags that might still be serviceable in some way; clothes, too, above all warm coats and overcoats, and winter shoes and boots. The ghetto will buy back certain household goods; but few of those who have made their way here to dispose of their last possessions want payment for them. And certainly not in money. The ghetto rumkies are worthless now. People preparing to leave want food: bread, flour, sugar or tinned food, anything they can take with them to eat.

And disputes have broken out all over the place, because people think they have not got what they were promised, or not for the right price. The scuffles are observed by forty or so policemen, who form a loosely linked chain up from the wooden bridge. But the police do not intervene, or they just make an occasional, token intervention to break up a few of the particularly violent fights. Perhaps they have had orders to keep out of it, or perhaps they don't dare get involved. Or they could just be guarding their own property; they might have relatives of their own in nearby buildings or districts.

Every so often Rosa thinks she catches a glimpse of the Chairman's carriage amid all the chaos, the Chairman's dis- figured face beneath the brim of his hat or inside the hood of the carriage as it passes. The Praeses of the ghetto is tirelessly active in these final days. He issues proclamations. He makes speeches. He appeals to the ghetto residents who are still in hiding to give up and come out.

Yidn fun geto bazint zikh!

Sometimes he and Biebow appear together. It looks most peculiar – the aggressor and the aggressed standing side by side. To crown it all, Biebow still has the hand that hit the Chairman bandaged and in a sling, and the Chairman wears his blood-encrusted cuts and his closed and puffy eye like a mask over his real face. They even prompt each other, like the comedy duo in Moshe Pałtwer's Ghetto Revue. First the Chairman says a few introductory words. Then Biebow speaks.

My Jews, says Biebow.

He's never said that before.

One day there is a rumour that there is food available down at the old fruit and vegetable market. White cabbage. Three kilos per ration. An almost unimaginable amount for a ghetto that has been living on rotten turnips and fizzing, fermented sauerkraut for several years.

Scales and weights stand ready in the middle of the market square, and people push forward, ready to fill their empty bags. Then comes the sudden sound of revving tractor engines; then the loud clink of trailers being attached, metal on metal. A terrifying sound for those who remember the *szpera* days of eighteen months before. People instantly drop what they are doing and make a run for it, but get no further than a block or two before helmeted soldiers come charging into the square from all directions. Reinforcements in the form of truckloads of German police come in from Łagiewnicka Street; they move so fast that they almost seem to *flow* off the backs of the lorries; they seize those in flight and bundle them unceremoniously up onto the trailers.

Then suddenly the Chairman and Biebow are there again – the aggressor and the aggressed; the German and the Jew – standing on the back of one of the trucks. Biebow even raises his bandaged hand as if appealing to the crowd, while shouting: *No, no, no . . . !* And beside him stands the Praeses with his disfigured face, and he too raises an arm in the air and shouts *no, no, no,* like some sort of echo; and Biebow speaks:

My Jews, he says.

This is what we c o u l d have done.
  We could have loaded you into lorries and deported the lot of you.
  Aber so machen wir es nicht! Nein, nein, nein . . . !
  We do not want to use violence. There is no need.
  All the Jews in the ghetto are safe and secure in our hands.
  There is plenty of work in Germany, and there are still spare places on the trains.
  Go home and think it over in peace and quiet, and then bring your children and other husbands or wives and report

to Radegast Station first thing tomorrow morning.

We promise to do our best to make existence as tolerable for you as possible.

Rosa Smoleńska stands among the others who have gathered around the back of the lorry to listen to the two men. She has in her hand the list of the Praeses children she has compiled by referring to the prohibited adoption files in Miss Wołk's office. The list includes not only the names of the children themselves, but also the names of their 'new' parents, or their next of kin; and the names of the factories in which either Wołk or Rumkowski has been able to get them jobs, plus the names of the *kierownicy* who, like Mr Tusk, had been instructed to act as the children's guardians.

She goes with her list from *resort* to *resort*. But the factory managers have long since lost track of which employees they have or do not have. The workers they once had have been exchanged for others long ago; either they, too, have been sold as souls; or they have been sold but then come back under a different name, or in another guise, because someone with greater power and influence has bought their freedom; or they have simply stopped turning up. There is a transport leaving the ghetto every day now. People think that if they can just stay hidden a bit longer, liberation may come. But in these last days, even the distinction between the dead and the living is dissolving. There are people who claim to have seen *neshomes* walking about the streets of the ghetto as large as life, neighbours or work colleagues who sold themselves and were deported from the ghetto, and whom everyone thought dead and gone for good, but who have now come back to demand what is rightfully theirs.

It is the eighth of August. Rosa Smoleńska is on her way back from the glove and sock factory in Młynarska Street when shots are fired close by. It is not the first time, but it is the first time it has sounded so close.

At first it does not seem too bad. A bang here and there, not continuous firing.

Then she sees that the whole street below is full of people. They seem to be issuing from everywhere: a viscous mass of human beings. For a time, the human mass appears to be at a complete standstill in front of her. Not because people are not moving fast enough, but because everyone is trying to move at once and therefore nobody is succeeding. People are pushing, barging, trying to elbow their way through. Some have their possessions with them. A basket of clothes and shoes; an enamel bowl full of household utensils; a dangling milk can, swinging to and fro like a cowbell. In the midst of all these silent or shouting, open-mouthed or grimly dogged faces, she catches sight of Mrs Grabowska, making her way forward a few metres at a time, lugging an enormous suitcase.

It is from Mrs Grabowska that she hears that the Germans have finally moved into the ghetto.

Not from the fringes as everyone had feared and been talking about for months, but straight into the heart of the ghetto: Łagiewnicka, Zawiszy Czarnego, Brzezińska and Młynarska: all four streets in the middle of the ghetto are blocked by German military vehicles. The police have set up provisional *Schutzpunkte* and rolled out barbed wire, running east from Bałuty Square, and special SS units have already started to enter the blocks of flats in Zawiszy Czarnego and Berka Joselewicza Streets.

'We can't get back,' says Mrs Grabowska.

And who is the first man to enter the cordoned-off zone but Biebow's henchman, the Praeses? The soldiers standing guard let him pass, as a mine-clearance company would let through a seeker dog. He walks alone, without bodyguards this time, as if to underline the gravity of his purpose. Mrs Grabowska saw him herself, standing in the doorway of someone's home, pleading. As if in some farcical reversal of the story of the paralysed woman Mara – upright, perverted and proud – he tells the waiting families that this is their last chance to leave. He says he can give them his *personal* guarantee that not a hair on their heads will be harmed.

*

Rosa spends the night with someone Mrs Grabowska knows, who lives at the top of one of the old tenements in Młynarska. From the window of the flat, she sees German army vehicles arriving from Litzmannstadt to reinforce the ghetto roadblocks. File after file of heavy lorries drive in with wire mesh fencing and rolls of barbed wire on the back.

She is with some twenty people who have not yet reported for departure, sitting in a single room, all with their faces hidden behind hunched shoulders and drawn-up knees. None of them have anything to eat or drink. Many of them have not even had time to grab their cooking pots.

All Rosa has is the list of Praeses children, along with a few photographs she has saved. One of them was taken in the kitchen of the Green House. At one end of the long row of shiny saucepans and vats of soup stands Chaja Meyer in her cook's hat and white apron, and behind her sit all the children in a row, also wearing white, the youngest with bibs; all bent over their bowls of soup, as if the aim of the picture were to display their deloused heads. In another photograph, the children are lined up in front of the fence out at the Big Field. They are all seen in profile, standing with their hands on each other's shoulders like a ballet company or as if about to march off.

But they are just pictures. Shaven-headed boys; girls with plaits.

They could be any old children.

That morning, Rumkowski has had a new proclamation printed. Copies of it have been pasted up on every house wall from Młynarska Street all the way down to the sewage pools in Dworska:

Proclamation Regarding Relocation of the Ghetto

<u>All factories to remain closed:</u>
From Thursday 10 August 1944, all factories in the ghetto are to remain closed. A maximum of ten people may stay behind in each factory to pack and ship goods.

<u>Clearance of the western section of the ghetto:</u>
From Thursday 10 August 1944, the western part of the ghetto (on the far side of the bridge) is to be cleared of all residents and workers. All its residents and workers are to move to the eastern part of the ghetto.

From Thursday 10 August 1944, no provisions will be supplied to the western parts of the ghetto.

Litzmannstadt Ghetto, 9 August 1944
Mordechai Ch. Rumkowski
Eldest of the Jews

Watching from the window the following day, she sees long columns of people on their way out to Radogoszcz. They look peaceful, despite the enormous burdens they are carrying. Somewhere from under the forest of rucksacks with blankets and mattresses bound to them, and collections of pots and pans all tied together, a woman steps forward and grabs a bunch of parsley from an allotment as they go by, and passes it to another woman, a friend further back. She wonders where they have all come from, these people; whether the authorities have begun emptying whole factories. She also wonders if she dare run down and show the names and pictures of the Praeses children to the people marching by, in the hope that someone may recognise a name or a face.

But she does not dare. The marching column is accompanied on either side by local police, keeping strict watch. The police did not stop the woman picking parsley, but they would definitely react to someone who came and disturbed the pace and order of the march.

It is another whole day before she feels bold enough to venture out. This being summer, darkness falls late. And when the daylight has faded enough for the street below to be visible only as a thin ribbon through the bluish gloom, the moon rises into the sky and once again it is almost as bright as day. She tries to stay close to the walls and shadows of buildings, to keep out of the light; but down in Zgierska Street there is no more darkness left to hide in. The full moon straddles the narrow gap between the two halves of the ghetto, and beneath its huge disc, the wooden bridge is black with the jostling crowd of people crossing it. As she gets closer, she can also hear the sound: the drumming of thousands of *trepki* tramping across the bare boards of the bridge.

She knows at that moment that there is no point looking for the children any more. At the western end of the bridge at Lutomierska Street there are guards, and they grab and haul aside anybody trying to push their way over the bridge against the tide of people. And there is no point asking those who are emerging on the eastern side with their bags and packs.

She sits down on the worn stone steps of a building entrance in Zgierska Street and tries to think. What is she to do if she no longer has freedom of movement in the ghetto?

And what is she to say to the old man if she can't bring him the children?

They were there, they were all there, but they disappeared.

Or: *they were all there; but I couldn't reach them.*

She simply can't say it.

*

New day, new dawn. Once more she makes her way out to Marysin. All along Marysińska Street she passes a line of trailers, stationed at neat, twenty-metre intervals. Halfway up to the Chairman's residence, the Germans have erected a road block, where a handful of SS men stand joking with the guard. A few individuals and bunches of stragglers, mostly elderly men and women, are walking up the road with their luggage. They look so much more vulnerable to her now they are no longer part of the marching convoy, and the SS men notice it, too. One of the police officers suddenly breaks into a run (his long coat opening like an umbrella over his tall boots), shoulder belt jangling, to catch up with one of the Jews on the road. – What has he done? Has he brought too much baggage? Is he too close to the edge of the road? – Then all at once, all five policemen are bunching round the now prone Jew. Through their laughing, jeering voices come the dull thump of boot toes on a soft body and the man's desperate cries for help.

At that moment there is a strange, whistling sound, and all the air is torn from her lungs. She sees the sentry at the barrier ahead take two steps forward and hold up both hands as if to ward something off; the whistle grows to a roar, and beneath her running feet, the ground she was standing on becomes a shaking board.

She sees herself lying in the ditch on top of the battered man; sees the smoke from the explosion rising above the soft straps of his rucksack. Then someone reaches down to her from above, grasps her under the arms and pulls her out onto the road again. It is Samstag. (She would have known him even if he had emerged from her deepest dreams.) What is he doing here? That is all she has time to think.

Run, is all he says, pointing to the houses further down Marysińska Street.

Somehow she finds her feet. She still feels as though she is on the deck of a ship that is constantly tilting and pitching beneath her. The buildings on either side of the road seem to be sliding to and fro, too; one moment they are enveloped in a cloud of thick, billowing smoke, the next they are fully visible again. Once she gets in through the front entrance, she realises it is the place she stayed the night before.

Then, the stairwells and flats had been full to overflowing with people. Now there is not a soul to be seen, only some of the things they have left behind: blankets, mattresses, pots and pans. She goes upstairs to the room on the second floor. The windows of the flat are wide open. When she looks out, she sees the long row of trailers she passed earlier, and it dawns on her that the trailers are not waiting there ready for the operation, but that the operation *is already complete*. The SS commandos must have come through and cleared the whole district that night, while she was gone. That is why there are no people left.

That is why the road block is right at the top of the street.

Werner Samstag materialises again, in the doorway behind her.

With an expression of sympathy so lofty and distant that it seems more like sarcasm, he looks down at the blood all over the front of her dress.

Then he bends down to her. For a moment she is convinced he is about to kill her, but he just takes her under the arms again and slings her over his shoulder with surprising ease. Only now, hanging head-down over his shoulder, does she become aware that she is still holding the list of Praeses children in one hand. In the other, clutched equally tightly, she has the handkerchief containing the scraps of bread she was saving in case she came across any of the children again. She finds herself being carried down the cluttered stairs and out into the ghetto once more.

But it is a ghost town now.

All around, doors hang open, banging to and fro. Empty, gaping windows.

It is as if a great wind has surged through everything, but a wind of no defined dimensions or direction, a wind that simply shapes the emptiness all around without touching anything.

Although it is now lighter, the dawn sky is entirely black –

Clinging to Samstag's back, at the edge of her field of vision she glimpses houses, fences and walls, flickering past with an even rhythm. They take the back way through everything. Samstag moves with animal litheness, loping between rows of outhouses and latrines, where the horrible smell hits her, only to be wafted aside a moment later by the sickly scent of once-flowering lilacs. For a minute or two, she thinks she can see the barbed-wire-topped walls of the Central Jail, and the cell block inside them. Then all at once, she knows where she is. They are in the forecourt of what was once the children's hospital of the ghetto, and up on the crumbling wall of the building, the sign confirms it:

KINDERHOSPITAL DES ÄLTESTEN DER JUDEN

There is still evidence of the Central Labour Office's big industrial exhibition. In the entrance hall, the display cases are still standing on their plinths, and on the floor, surrounded by broken glass and bits of torn curtain fabric, drifts of posters showing statistics form piles and fans: pathetic now, with dirty footprints clearly superimposed on the beautifully ordered columns of figures.

From the back building, a basic, single-storey affair with rough planks over the windows, a set of stone steps with un-bricked walls plunges virtually straight into the base of the building; then a narrow basement passage seems to run like a tunnel under the building itself. Rosa can feel the dank draught of cold from the stone-and-earth walls and instinctively ducks her head to avoid hitting it on the ceiling. But Samstag is careful. As if she were no more than an oversized doll, he shifts her down onto one arm. In his other hand he has an arc light. He must have reached for a switch without her noticing, for suddenly the walls and ceiling and floor of the cellar passage around her are illuminated by a blindingly sharp light. Pots of paint, jars of solvent on shelves; tools laid out, sorted by shape and size. The remains of Pinkas Szwarc's big printing press stands brooding in the middle of the floor. However did they get that great thing down here? And beyond the printing press, in a shelf beneath the low roof, there are musical instruments of very imaginable kind: a tuba, a trombone and (suspended from hooks screwed into wood panels) violins hanging by their necks from loops of finest piano wire.

But by then she has caught sight of the children from the Green House.

Their faces, lined up alongside each other like beads in an abacus, look pale, dazzled by the glaring light. She sees the piano tuner's wizened face first. Behind that, like a copy of the photograph taken in the kitchen of the Green House: Nataniel; Kazimir; Estera; Adam.

All the children on the list are there. Including Debora Żurawska.

Rosa sees the girl look up quickly, and lower her eyes again in shame. And Rosa wants to say something, but the words she is groping for are now far out of reach. So she squeezes herself between low shelves, the mouthpieces of the hanging brass instruments, the sharp edge of a grinding machine. She has to do the last bit crawling, with her head drawn in, as loose sand and little stones from the roof above are trickling down the back of her neck. When she finally gets there, she opens out the handkerchief with the chunks of bread she has saved. She gives one of the crusts to Debora, who is sitting at the end; then tears up the rest of the bread with trembling hands and passes over roughly the same amount to each of the other children in the row – Nataniel, Kazimir, Estera – still incapable of uttering a single word.

Behind the children runs a low stone wall, with rocks jutting out of it that must once have been plastered over with cement. The cement must have come loose long ago. The mortar between the bricks underneath is also crumbling. The whole wall behind them will collapse before too long.

Samstag came, says Nataniel, his voice as husky and rasping as the cement.

Samstag works for the police force now, Estera fills in, a bit officiously (as always): as if the word *police* still had some value as an explanation.

But then, perhaps it does – *for them*.

She remembers a game the children used to play when they lived in the Green House: the forbidden game, Natasza used to call it. In the game, the children all pretended to be getting on with their usual activities. Natasza would be bent over her sewing basket, Debora playing the piano. One of the children was chosen to go out into the hall and shout: *Someone's coming*. Whenever Kazimir was chosen, he would come back in and yell: *Churchill's coming!* If Adam were the one chosen, he would come back in and shout *Roosevelt's coming!*

And they all had to go and hide. She remembers one occasion, before Dr Rubin put a stop to all such goings on: Kazimir had rolled himself up in the floor rug under the piano in the Pink Room, and then Werner Samstag came stumbling in with a saucepan on his head and a fish slice in his hand:

The Chairman's coming . . . !

All around him, the children were sitting as if transfixed.

So *he* had always been the one who came and saved them at the last minute. When she finished handing out the bread and looked up again, she saw the cone of light from the arc lamp still hanging above the door, but there was no longer a body behind the light. The children must have seen Samstag go, but none of them seemed to have reacted. Samstag continued to come and go as he always had.

Debora took a handkerchief from the bodice of her dress, twisted it into a thin string, dampened one side of it with spit; then roughly clamped Rosa's head between her own two, drawn-up knees, and began firmly but carefully wiping away the blood and dirt from her face. Rosa tried to wriggle free. She felt an urgent need to explain. The children did not know what the ghetto looked like outside this cramped cellar space; they did not know that all the streets round about were blocked off and that the Gestapo would soon be coming with their dogs. She tried to tell them this, but at the sight of Debora wiping her face with the expressionless look you might have while washing a cooking pot or saucepan, she gave up. Overcome with fatigue, she let her head sink impotently back into the girl's lap.

'You've got to trust me, Debora,' she said. 'Why don't you?'

But Debora did not answer. Debora will never answer.

Debora takes the coal shovel out of Mrs Grabowski's hands or reaches out for the handle of the bucket of water they are carrying back from the well outside the Green House. But she will never answer:

Let me do that, is all she says. *Seeing as I'm already up*.

Words that she lays before you just as one might produce an object, any old object behind which she can make herself invisible. Just as Debora left her rucksack with the comb and the mirror wrapped in linen cloth by the window in Brzezińska Street; or left behind the music for the musical revue at the Green House. Just as everything ever owned by anyone in the ghetto has been left behind, now and for evermore. Or just as Werner Samstag left behind – what? A big, white, blinding light still burning inside the cellar door that has been closed on them.

So in the end, only Rosa Smoleńska was left, as Debora bent over and wiped the blood and the pain from her face.

And so in the end, Rosa closed her aching eyes.

And so in the end, Rosa Smoleńska's face was left behind as well.

They had been told the authorities would send a car to take them to the station, but still no car had turned up. While everyone in Miarki Street including Miss Fuchs and her brother sat there on the furniture they had carried out, Staszek climbed up into the cherry tree, in the crown of which Mr Tausendgeld had hidden Princess Helena's money the day before the Palace fell. Now Helena Rumkowska is insisting the money be brought down again. Uncle Józef has propped a ladder against the tree trunk, but even the top rung of the ladder is not high enough for him to be able to reach into the crown itself. The only person who could reach that far into the huge tree was Mr Tausendgeld with his by then legendary right arm; and having been roundly scolded for his incompetence, Józef Rumkowski has returned to the ghetto to find a pole or a fishing net or some other long, thin object, so the money can be retrieved before they leave. But while they are waiting, who should climb up into the cherry tree if not Princess Helena's own *líbling*, her *Stasiek*, her *Stasiulek*? He climbs like a child, his grazed, red-raw knees sticking out and his thighs clamped tight around the trunk, and is soon aware of the delightful friction of his member against the rough bark.

In the very top of the crown of the cherry tree, beneath the leafy patchwork, dangle the bags of Reichsmarks hung there by Mr Tausendgeld. The bags look the same as his face once did, as if they have been sewn together both from top to bottom and from edge to edge. When Staszek squeezes one of the bags, he can feel something moving in there like a chewing jaw. Way below, under the blotches of leaf where the sweet fruit hung, everything they have brought from their homes in Miarki and Okopowa Street stands waiting for transport. Beds and dining tables, chaises longues and chests of drawers; the Chairman's 'private' escritoire, and Princess Helena's *credence* (but without its glassware and sets of china – Józef Rumkowski has had to pack those) and her birdcages, those she still has, full of chattering winged creatures shuffling around and clinging on to basketwork sides and cage roofs.

Beyond the canopy of leaves, the ghetto spreads away. Clusters of low buildings and wooden shacks, with the occasional taller building sticking up like a crooked tooth. If Staszek reaches out his hand, he can grab the whole ghetto and turn it round in a single movement. He spreads his fingers wide, and in the middle of the ghetto – in the middle of his own palm – his father stands waiting.

The father, too, is waiting for the promised transport.

It was promised for three o'clock at Bałuty Square, and it is now *past* three, and Rumkowski has long since lost patience and gone out onto the square to keep a lookout for the vehicle. As at his Miarki Street home, the furniture and filing cabinets that he has previously selected as absolutely indispensable have been brought out. This is the last transport. He is alone in the row of barrack offices. Not even the employees of the German ghetto administration are still there.

He is alone, and the sky above him is so wide and desolate that he feels he could plunge down into it, as if into a well.

Several times in recent nights, he has been dreaming of plunging into the sky like that, and every time he has then found himself lying in an open place like this. It is dark, and all around in the darkness were the remains of human bodies, chopped to pieces. Black birds come out of the darkness to settle on the corpses. Sometimes they come so close that he can hear the rustle of their soft wings against the stitches in his face, still painful. And as he lies there shackled to the ground in this holy place, they come to cut him up too, and take him to pieces. And he understands at that moment that if he has been captive, it has never been because he was shut in, mankind is by nature shut in; nor because it has been dark around him, it is always dark around us; but because in this way he has been continually separated from what was rightly his.

The insight had brought him relief, a moment of growing clarity in the darkness that was still turbulent with the wingbeats of the great birds.

Lord, of what have you pieced me together –
that I may not recognise myself even in my own image?

Just as he thinks this, the transport arrives. It is the big carriage, the hearse that was once built to deal more efficiently with transporting the dead, with no fewer than thirty-six different compartments and sections on a single chassis (most of them sliding, like desk drawers or oven shelves). It is not Meir Klamm up on the box, however, but Amtsleiter Biebow; and he sees at that instant how huge the hearse is; its roof is taller than any one of the collapsing buildings around the square.

Are you coming or not? The very last transport will be leaving shortly . . . ! calls Biebow from up on the box, and the men he has with him from the clean-up commando have already started loading chairs, desks and cabinets. While up in the tree, the great cherry tree where the gifts of money to the Eldest of the Jews hang like big, black fruits, the Child windmills its arms to signal to all those waiting below:

OUR TRANSPORT . . . !
OUR TRANSPORT'S COMING . . . !

*

Regina is aghast. *I'm not travelling in that thing,* she says, her eyes wide and her cheeks flushing with shame.

But she has to, of course. What choice do they have?

Staszek sits in the rear, leaning back against all the trunks and cases stacked behind the driver's seat and watching the ghetto disappear into the hot, dry cloud of dust stirred up by the carriage wheels. Empty buildings against a meaningless sky. Streets that are not streets any more, just cleared routes for easier access to tucked-away sheds or outhouses. A coal depot, its security fence ripped down and set on fire; rows of chicken coops with broken bars; a pump with no handle.

The banks of the sewage-oozing ditches are strewn with things people have dropped or abandoned. Everything from kitchen equipment, blankets and mattresses to suitcases that burst open as they hit the ground, disgorging their contents of threadbare clothes and worn-out shoes.

Every so often, they come across files or small knots of people. Most are on their way from the assembly point at the jail, and marching up to five abreast with a local guard about ten metres from each group. The guard yells the occasional order, but the people give no sign of having heard. Only once the big carriage has overtaken the marchers, slowly and with much creaking of its warped wheels, do they stop and stare. From his lofty vantage point, Staszek can see their gaunt faces slipping by without so much as a smile or a hand raised in greeting.

Radogoszcz is jammed with people. People are sitting or standing outside the warehouses in the goods yard with piles of luggage. Irascible German guards move constantly among the waiting crowd, swinging their rifle butts to make anyone sitting down stand up again.

An officer sees their vehicle arriving and shouts an order. The barked command also draws the attention of the station commanders and the goods-yard workers several hundred metres away with their stacks of timber and stocks of metal. A sudden whisper seems to run through the crowd, subdued at first, then rising in volume:

The Praeses is coming . . . ! Praeses . . . ! Praeses . . . !

Staszek sees the faces open wide in amazement as the hearse passes. No one expected to see the Praeses of the ghetto here, and certainly not in a conveyance like that! But he *is* here. Staszek thinks of the document his father once carefully got out to show him, telling him it had been signed by *Bradfisch personally*. He solemnly indicated all the official stamps. This document, he explained, would grant them safe conduct wherever they wished to go.

'So don't be afraid, Staszek . . . !'

But Staszek is not afraid. It is the Chairman who is afraid. From the top of his luggage mountain, Staszek can see him repeatedly patting his jacket pocket to check all the documents are still there.

The carriage has stopped at the far end of the track, where the platform would have ended if there had been a platform. In fact there is just a little shed with an overhanging roof where the freight supervisors generally gather when the big goods transports come in. The train is already in, and Dora Fuchs and her brother Bernhard are waiting by one of the open wagon doors, as if unsure about getting on board. An open lorry with a tarpaulin canopy has been driven up to the carriage, and all the party's luggage is on the ground beside it, including a few of the wooden and cane cages Princess Helena keeps her birds in.

As the Chairman arrives, Princess Helena seems to awake from some kind of trance. *They promised us a transport of our own*, she says accusingly, *and now they insist we get on one of these . . . !*

Her husband is standing beside her. He has a look of confusion on his face, as if incapable of collecting his thoughts around a single word. But there is no need for him to say anything. The soldiers on guard suddenly click their heels to a muted *Heil Hitler* as Biebow squeezes to the front of the crowd.

He has both his colleagues with him, Ribbe and Schwind; all three look guiltily amused, as if they were not in a goods yard but at some obscene fairground.

But Biebow's step and tone are determined.

Biebow: So it's time to go, then.
Chairman: But it was agreed we would have our own transport.
Biebow: This is the transport.
Chairman (digging in the inside pocket of his jacket): But it was agreed . . . ?
Biebow: I don't know what agreement you are talking about. There is a transport leaving Litzmannstadt now, and this is it.

The Chairman stands there, holding out the letter, with an air at that moment of almost schoolboyish innocence. But when Biebow continues to ignore it, the surprise in the Chairman's face slowly gives way to dismay. Something is happening in direct contravention of anything he could have conceived. In his awkward and inadequate way, he does what he can to retrieve the situation.

'If we could at least have our own carriage . . .' he says, carefully folding the document back up again; and Biebow changes tone, as if on command: *Why yes, of course!* he says, gesturing to the men with him, who in their turn gesture to the soldiers on guard to accompany them into the wagon.

Agitated voices are soon heard from inside, and out come a bunch of elderly men who have apparently been in the wagon all the time. They look at Rumkowski with reproach and then start hauling their trunks and bundles of sheets along the train, heading for wagons further down, into which deportees are swarming by the hundred.

584

Dora Fuchs vanishes into the wagon to inspect it. She emerges with a look of vague distaste, but shrugs her shoulders. A group of goods-yard workers is ordered by the German guards to load the party's luggage, and begins to do so. Some SS officers come past. They, too, have that furtive, slightly embarrassed smile on their lips, as if they were watching some kind of fairground attraction.

Staszek is one of the first to climb aboard. The wagon is a standard luggage van, divided in half by a solid partition wall. There is sawdust on the floor.

'I apologise for the perhaps slightly primitive conditions, but you will be able to change to a more comfortable carriage in due course,' says Biebow. But he does not raise his head to look them in the eye as he says it. The Chairman, too, has now realised that the promise he was given is worthless. He goes out after Biebow and makes one more attempt to show him the letter signed by Bradfisch. But Biebow will not so much as glance at the document this time, either.

Looking out of the wagon window, Staszek sees a big cluster of workers, all in ragged trousers far too big for them, approaching at a smart pace, driven on by Jewish policemen with their batons raised. At the front of the hurrying group are several of the men previously ejected from the compartment. German guards approach, and with much shouting and waving of arms, a mass of people is squashed in through the door of Rumkowski's wagon.

Inside, Rumkowski and his brother get to their feet to protest, but before they can take more than a couple of steps they are forced back by the pressure of the crowd. The last ones aboard have to hang on to the backs of those ahead of them to avoid falling back onto the ground, where the Jewish policemen are using hands, elbows and batons to keep them all squashed inside. From the wagon comes a loud clatter as the toilet bucket in the corner is knocked over and kicked aside.

Then a reedy voice shouts:

Let me out, let me out . . . !

It is the Chairman, determined to get to the door at any cost. But there are maybe a hundred starving, desperate, screaming, weeping men and women in his way; they could not have let him through, even if they wanted to.

Staszek is still by the window. Outside he can see a couple of goods-yard workers walking along the track. One of them has a shovel, and his eyes are fixed on the ground in front of his feet, as if he is looking for something he has dropped. Behind the man with the shovel, the scenery begins to slip slowly backwards, almost as if it were that – the scenery – and not the wagon starting to move. He turns away, to the darkness and crush of the wagon interior.

IV

Seeing in the Dark
(August 1944–January 1945)

All are sleeping, the dead now rise from their graves and come alive again. And I do not do even that, for I am not dead and so cannot come back to life, and even were I dead I could not come to life again: for I have never lived.

Søren Kierkegaard

A thin sliver of light: that is all he has to go by.

When the sliver of light is gone, it is night. When the sliver of light returns, it is day.

The sliver of light is a luminous top step, floating elusively above the rough angles of the worn steps leading up out of the earth cellar.

Earth cellar may be the wrong name for it. Back in the days when Feldman had his nursery business, he used it as a place for keeping bulbs and seeds and other things that need protection from light and heat. But it is so cramped down here that he feels more as if he has been pushed down a well. He can hardly get his shoulders through the opening. It is impossible to sit or lie down. He has to stand, or slump with his hip or hindquarters pressed against the earth wall. Right at the bottom – there are four steps, each about half a metre in depth – the cellar-well ends in a narrow chamber just over a metre long and about half the height. That is where he opens his bowels. It is so shallow that he has to do this lying on one side with his face towards the shaft and the lower part of his body forced as far into the hole as it will possibly go. His motions are soft and warm and run down the inside of his thigh, and he has nothing to wipe himself with but some dry grass he took down there with him.

And even though it is unbearable, he has to bear it.

From this moment on, you're dead, Feldman said before he slid across the heavy wooden cover that constitutes the roof of the earth cellar.

Feldman promised to bring him food whenever he could.

That is: whenever the clean-up unit he belonged to was sent out to Marysin. It would be easier to slip away then. He might be able to, he might not. Nobody knew. But if he could hit on some excuse for coming to the earth cellar, he would knock three times on the cover. That would be the signal telling Adam there was food waiting outside for him.

Before he left, he handed over what little he could spare:

A bit of bread, two shrivelled onions, a head of cabbage that had already started rotting from the centre.

At least Adam was not cold. A little of the lingering heat of late summer found its way down into the dark, earth shaft, and he knew that even if some length of time passed, the soil would carry on keeping him warm.

The light came, and went.

He tried to keep count of the days, but found that after a few days he no longer knew if this was his third or fifth day and night down there, or if he had been there even longer.

He stood mostly, or perched, head bowed (so as not to hit the roof) on one of the carved-out steps.

If he slept, he did it in short bursts, and deeply, as if he were unconscious. His sleeping and waking states blurred into each other, and soon it made no difference whether it was light or dark. The one constant was his hunger. The hunger hollowed him out from within, just as the light would have done. It lit up his mouth and gullet and belly. The light of his hunger was dry and white, without substance, but as sharp and blinding as a wound to the eyes.

He wondered how long it would be before Feldman came.

He counted slivers of light, so utterly exhausted now that they multiplied before his eyes. One sliver became a thousand slivers, a single day and night down here became thousands. He realised that if he stayed beneath his covering of earth a single day more, he would lose all concept of what was what. What was inside, what was outside. Space, time.

But still he stayed there.

He thought about the dogs.

Sooner or later, the Gestapo's hunt for fugitives would bring them out to Feldman's nursery. They had their lists; they knew who had responded to their resettlement orders and who had tried to hide. They would start in the middle of the ghetto and work their way out towards Marysin.

And when they got there, where would they start looking?

Feldman had been convinced they would content themselves with the house-cum-office and the cellar. That is, the proper cellar. The one under the house. If there was nobody in the house, they probably wouldn't bother much with searching the garden, and he would be all right. So Feldman thought.

Adam, too, thought the police probably would not find him. But he was less sure about the dogs. That was the thought preying on his mind, day after day –

If they had dogs with them:

Was there any way of covering over that sliver of light which was also his source of air? Would it help, anyway? And how would he cope with being in total darkness, day after day? The thought obsessed him to the point where he thought he could already hear the dogs, panting and tugging at their leashes, hear their claws scraping and scratching at the edge of the wooden cover. How long would it be before he thought he could hear Feldman's magical three knocks, as well?

He decided to keep his chink of light for now.

Feldman did not come, and he realised in the end that he would have to emerge.

He was frantic with hunger and thirst. If he stayed there a day or even an hour more, he might not even have the energy to push the cover aside, in which case he would have to stay there until he suffocated to death and slowly rotted away.

He observed the chink of light carefully. As the light gradually began to fade, he went up to the top step and heaved up the cover with the back of his neck and both hands.

Outside: mild, damp September evening.

The air: the first breaths: harsh and raw in lungs grown accustomed to dank earth and stone dust. He could hardly propel his legs forward. He was quivering like an eel all over, and when the quivering would not stop, he had to let himself go.

He let himself fall into damp, cold grass and lay there for a while, completely still, breathing and looking up at the darkening sky.

It was so damp that he could hardly see the stars, just a vaguely floating grey mist across the night sky, so indistinct that at first he was not sure if he was seeing anything at all. Perhaps he was seeing light mirages after spending so long in the dark.

After a while, he thought he could make out voices.

There was something strange about the voices, too. They came and went in waves. Sometimes they were close, sometimes they drifted further away. But though at times they seemed very close, he never managed to identify any individual one.

He could not even hear what language they were speaking.

The clean-up commando was based in the old tailoring workshop at 16 Jakuba. According to Feldman, there were a hundred men billeted there. Then there was another collective in Łagiewnicka Street, where Aron Jakubowicz was rumoured to be, under the protection of Biebow. That would mean another two to three hundred men. Apart from that, there was no one left in the ghetto. Unless there had been an order to dig trenches, it was doubtful whether anyone from the clean-up commando would have been sent all the way out to Marysin at this time of day.

So whose voices could they be?

Germans'?

Feldman had warned him there was a risk they might decide to use the old nursery as some kind of camp, though he himself did not think it all that likely. The kitchen and office were unusable, and the glasshouse was not exactly suitable accommodation for policemen. It would be safer for them to keep their forces all together in the centre of the ghetto and just come out to Marysin in daylight, to carry out specific tasks.

Or were the voices coming from Radogoszcz Station? Were they still unloading things out there? If so, then why?

Adam walked round the glasshouse a number of times without getting any clearer idea of what he was hearing. Everywhere was dark. But the voices were still talking to each other. Well, more than talking. They seemed to be in some state of agitation that was making them interrupt, or constantly try to make themselves heard above, each other. Still without a single word being distinguishable.

He opened the door of the main building. It gave as he grasped it, as if its hinges were loose or it was starting to rot away. Beneath him the brittle crunch of broken glass. The shards had been lying there since the day Samstag and his men went berserk among the objects in Feldman's private collection.

The interior was bathed in a peculiar light, softly greenish as if still being filtered through the musty layer of dust and mould that had coated the insides of the aquariums.

He took a teapot from the kitchen in Feldman's office and filled it to the brim with water from the pump over by the outhouses. He used the water he still had left after quenching his thirst to wash with. First he washed his crotch and thighs; then his torso, armpits and face.

But he did not dry himself. If they came with dogs – and surely it was only a matter of time – then any towels or rags he had dried himself with would put them onto the scent.

Naked and freezing cold, he went back to the office and looked through the ragged bits of clothing Feldman had left behind. When it started getting cold and damp in the autumn, Feldman used to don a pair of broad, baggy sheepskin trousers. They would be too short for Adam, but since they were so wide in the crotch area, he ought to be able to get them on. He found a coat, too, and a blanket that would be good to have as a head and backrest when he leant against the bare stone.

He rolled his own clothes up into a big bundle. He would have to take them back down into the cellar hole with him. Everything he used up here would have to accompany him back down. But he still could not quite bring himself to climb down into the cramped, stinking shaft again. While he was above ground, he had to find something to eat. He rolled himself in Feldman's blanket and sat there trying to visualise the formerly well-guarded orchards. Which fence led to which orchard enclosure. After all, the evacuation of the ghetto had happened so fast. There was bound to be fruit left unpicked on the trees somewhere.

He waited until it was dark. There were no voices now. The

idea came into his head that the whole damp expanse of space out there was holding its breath, ready to cast itself down onto him as soon as he stepped outside. He tried not to tread on any gravel or stones. But the swishing sound as he strode through the damp grass was as loud as a scream to his ears. A low stone wall ran down the hillock from which the earth cellar had been excavated. On the other side of the wall was an area that had been given over to growing beets. He remembered there were some apple trees in a narrow strip of stony ground running between the ploughed beet field and the road past Praszkier's workshop. He boldly climbed over the wall, and then a wrought-iron fence he did not remember being there before, but it was there now: rusting ironwork protruding like a cage from waist-length grass and thickets of wild raspberry bushes.

He was under the trees now. Their crowns vanished up into the nocturnal haze above him. He could see where the branches started, but not where they ended.

It was deathly quiet all around him. Not even a startled bird, taking off with a rattle of wings. He thought he could see the hanging apples as blobs of deeper darkness within the darkness. Or was he just imagining it, because the thought of there being fruit left on the trees was so intoxicatingly vivid that it vanquished all others?

Grasping the thick trunk with both hands, he tried to shake down the apples. The branches closest to him scarcely moved. Then he gripped the trunk between his legs, managed to get hold of a low-hanging branch, and heaved himself up. But what he had taken for fruit turned out to be nothing more than thicker leaves; the apples were further in, small and unripe. They tasted sour and musty; his palate was soon smarting and his jaws ached. But he carried on eating nonetheless, and then made a tuck at the waist of Feldman's thick, sheepskin trousers and filled it with all the fruit he could reach.

He stood there, back on the ground under the tree,

surrounded by a silence he had cracked apart. But not a sound once the last branch of the tree swung back into place after him. Not a movement beyond his own breathing and the surging of the blood behind his eyes.

Where had all the voices gone?

That night he dreamt he and Lida were trapped inside one of Feldman's many smooth glass cases. There was so little space between the glass sides that neither of them could move. When he finally succeeded in forcing his head round and his chin down, he saw that his arm and Lida's breasts and chin were also made of glass, and that their bodies below neck level had fused into a single glass form. Breast, stomach and trunk were glued tightly to each other; their translucent shoulders and heads were just separate enough for them to be able to make out each other's features.

And neither of them could move.

Mucus, or maybe just unusually thick saliva, was running from Lida's mouth, and as it ran it set, and froze into glass. He wanted to stretch forward and lick the cold mucus from her lips, but all he could do was turn his face, and then he hit his fragile head on the side of the container.

He licked the green coating on the inside of the container instead.

The coating was unexpectedly thick and rough, but even though it left a nauseating, sweetish aftertaste on his tongue, he could not stop licking the green deposits.

The hunger was aching and tautening in his abdomen now, as if his body when it grew together with Lida's had swollen into an enormous nodule of glass: a ball of hunger, bulging inside him with its sharp glistening surfaces.

He awoke in the darkness with terrible cramps in his stomach, and manoeuvred himself just in time into the ledge he used as an earth closet before the liquid motion squirted out of him.

In spasm after spasm until his head was swimming.

He wiped himself in a rudimentary fashion with the clothes he had, but knew as he did so that he could not stay down there in his cellar well, however risky it was to climb out.

From then on, he spent at least a few hours a day 'up there'.

The days were mild. The moisture that enveloped sky and landscape in a cocoon of impenetrable mist in the evenings and overnight lingered on in the daytime as a slight veiling of the sunlight. The houses and wooden shacks with their walls of unpainted timber and roughly jointed corners, the fences and stone field boundaries, the trees with their crowns of autumnal foliage, wet and heavy: everything was softening. The grass faded beneath his feet. Presumably his faintness and hunger were contributing to this sensation of everything mellowing. He felt as if he himself were being dissolved. Or rather being released: into a sort of unreal suspension.

One day he thought he heard distant gunfire. Isolated shots at first, followed by a rattle of machine-gun fire.

The firing went on for perhaps twenty minutes, with interruptions of varying lengths. He listened intently to hear whether the echo was dwindling and the firing getting closer. But that didn't happen. After a time, everything went quiet and he forgot what he had heard almost immediately.

Another day he thought he saw some figures moving, out on the open field next to the cemetery. About a dozen men: they seemed to be walking in single file. In the pale haze of the sun, the outlines of their bodies blurred together, and eventually they were completely gone.

He thought about Feldman.

Why didn't he come? Were the Germans keeping him shut up all the time, or under such strict supervision that there was no chance of slipping away? Or worse still: had they caught him trying to get out to Marysin again and shot him?

He knew he couldn't discount the possibility.

If Feldman didn't come, he would have to fend for himself.

Day by day, to the extent his strength allowed it, he widened the scope of his exploration.

The area on the far side of the earth cellar, where he had struggled in the dark to wrench down the wizened, unripe apples, was one of smallish wooden houses and shanties, gradually submitting to overgrown oblivion. Many of them were previously occupied by proper 'city dwellers', people with *plaitses*. If they did not live there themselves, they had 'rented out' their properties to people with even better contacts. A man called Tausendgeld had acted as intermediary.

The doors and windows of some of the houses were now open wide to the autumn light.

Abandoned rooms: bedrooms with overturned beds, the coils sprouting from their sprung bases; wardrobes with open doors and half the contents spilling out; trampled articles of clothing and bed linen littering the floor. In the kitchens, however, little or nothing of worth.

Of worth meant edible. In an unlocked kitchen cupboard, he found a bit of dry bread, mouldy, and so hard he could hardly get his teeth into it. He tried holding the whole thing in his mouth, but even that failed to soften it.

In another house he found a tin of beans. It took him several hours' labour with a stone and a big chisel to get it open, only to see the putrid, fermenting contents fizz up over his wrist in a poisonous foam. The smell was so nauseating that it persisted even after he had washed his hands in cold water from the well and scrubbed them with sand.

In a third house he came across some money in the bottom of some drawers. Rumkies. The three drawers of a cabinet had all been lined with oilcloth, tacked into place, and under the oilcloth layer were banknotes, hundreds of them, carefully smoothed flat so not even the tiniest bulge showed. He stood there with the worthless ghetto marks in his hand, and when he thought about somebody scrimping and saving year after year to amass all this ridiculous paper currency in the belief that they would be able to buy something with it one day, he began to chuckle. He tottered from room to room for a while with the worthless notes in his hand, hooting and cackling with laughter. Eventually he made himself calm down. If he carried on like this, wasting his energy on hysterical outbursts, he would soon have no strength left.

He had got right down to Marynarska, to the corner of Zbożowa Street. On the other side of the block was the Central Jail, where the mighty Shlomo Hercberg once reigned supreme, and where those consigned to the so called Labour Reserve were later taken. He was standing there wondering whether the jail could possibly still be in use, perhaps as a barracks, when the sky was suddenly rent by a tremendous crash.

Three planes in close formation at alarmingly low altitude.

He fell headlong to the ground and covered his head with his arms.

The next second, almost as an afterthought, the air raid sirens began to wail over Litzmannstadt. The noise went on, as piercing as saw blades. Then the sky was cut apart by another violent crash, and the three planes climbed steeply from the rooftops straight up into the sky again; this time followed by the heavy, somehow lagging rat-tat-tat of air defence batteries somewhere far away.

He lay there in the middle of the road, where the pressure wave had thrown him. He had never seen foreign fighter planes at such close range before. A kind of euphoria spread warmth from the pit of his stomach right out to the smallest finger joint. So their liberators must be very close by, perhaps only a few kilometres away.

After a while the sirens stopped, as if the sound had furled into itself, and excited voices began shouting all around him in Polish and German. He turned his head and saw two Wehrmacht soldiers come running out of a building at the corner of the road, some two hundred metres away. Seconds later, a tank emerged into the road, presumably from a hiding place in the courtyard of the Central Jail. It stopped for a time with its gun barrel pointing straight at him. Then there were soldiers' bodies moving in front of and behind the tank, and its gun swivelled to one side, slow and dignified.

He knew the German soldiers would have seen him if they had not been in such a hurry, and so frightened themselves. And if he had not been lying down. As soon as they were out of sight, he chanced it: stood up, and made for the nearest building at a crouching run.

He should have realised what risks he was taking.

The stillness of the ghetto – the deserted streets, the empty blocks of flats – it was all an illusion.

In each and every one of the apparently empty buildings he passed, there could be a German soldier lurking, tracking him with telescopic sights or the barrel of a rifle.

He must never let himself forget that.

The last time he was in the old children's home in Okopowa Street was when he helped Feldman bring in the coal for the stove in the basement. By then, the Green House had already stopped being a children's home and been transferred to the vague body that also ran the 'rest homes' for the *dygnitarzy* of the ghetto. If there was one place in the ghetto where you might find food hidden away, thought Adam, it was here.

Even so, it felt as though the Green House was surrounded by invisible walls or fences.

He walked past it several times, unable to bring himself to go in.

He was sure Lida had never been held captive there. But there was still something about the visual memory of her naked body, blue with cold, in the doorway of an unfamiliar house, which changed the image of this house, too. Or it could be the thought of all the children who had lived here. He remembered the way they used to stand motionless with their fingers gripping the wire fence round the big field at the back. Pale, shadow-like faces. And yet it was a peacable house. He recalled the shrill sound of children's voices, shouting and laughing, that used to be audible far and wide around it.

At last he plucked up his courage and went in.

The stench inside almost stupefied him.

Somewhere, he had always been expecting this. One of the buildings would have to contain dead bodies.

People who were too weak to get to the assembly points unaided. People who decided to hide at the last minute. People who, like him, had not had enough food or water with them to keep themselves alive. Unless, of course, the Germans had already searched these houses and killed whoever they found there on the spot, forgetting to take the bodies away afterwards. Because what point was there in dealing with the bodies when the last transports had already left the ghetto?

If the other houses showed clear signs of hasty departure, then the Green House looked totally vandalised. In the kitchen, all the tables had been tipped over, what kitchen equipment was left – saucepans, lids, dishes – had all been pulled out of the cupboards. In the narrow corridor between the front hall and the little room Feldman used to call the Pink Room, the floor had been taken up, leaving a gaping hole in the middle. There was no trace of the piano that used to be in there. It had presumably been confiscated when Biebow decided all the musical instruments in the ghetto were to be handed in and sold; if it had not been chopped up for firewood long before.

Even in here, there was no escaping the smell.

He tore a bit off the curtain that had been tossed onto the upended sofa on the far side of the room, and tied the fabric round his mouth and nose as a mask.

Then he went up the stairs.

He went slowly, pausing at every step to listen.

The last people staying there must have relieved themselves on the stairs, as he encountered dried deposits of human faeces. Along with tattered bits of cloth, pages torn out of exercise books; here the remains of a shoe, a male shoe, with both the heel and the upper torn off.

Upstairs, there was no doubting where the smell was coming from.

With one hand pressing the improvised mask to his face, the other held out to steady himself against the wall, he made his way along the corridor to the superintendent's room and opened the door with his elbow.

Werner Samstag was lying on his back on the little sofa beside Dr Rubin's desk. There was no doubting it was him. He was dressed in the newly made but now badly soiled police uniform he had been wearing the day he turned up at Feldman's house to try to get Lajb's list of potential assassins and resistance men out of him.

His head must have been resting on the arm of the sofa, but after the shot was fired (or perhaps as a result of the shot) it had slumped down and was now hanging halfway to the floor. It was this, the fact that the head and top half of the body were hanging down while the rest of the body was still lying on the sofa, gave the face a most peculiar look. The left side of the head, where the shot had entered, was black with clotted blood. The rest of the face was puffed up and almost blue in colour, and the tongue was protruding between the lips, so the dead head seemed to be pulling a face at him.

He took a cautious step into the room, and swarms of flies buzzed up from the swollen, stinking body. He saw insects crawling in the open, brown wound in the head, and at the neck. But what interested him most was the pistol still grasped in Samstag's right hand.

Where had he got the gun?

It was unthinkable that Samstag could have become powerful enough to be able to go around the ghetto armed, like any German.

Someone must have got him the weapon – or used it against him.

Adam was very close to the corpse now. The position of the body had made the blood from the gunshot wound to the head run down the shoulder and the underside of the arm, under the jacket sleeve, emerging from the cuff to run in rivulets down the wrist, which was resting heavily but stably on the floor. The fingers clenched round the pistol butt were also encased in thick, coagulated blood. He wrenched the piece of cloth from his face, wrapped it round his hand to make a glove and tried to prise up the corpse's fingers one by one, in the hope of removing the pistol.

A sigh ran through the body, as if it was defending itself even in death against any assault. It took some time, but he eventually managed to straighten out the fingers and release the bloodstained weapon.

He carefully wrapped the pistol in the cloth and took it down to the kitchen, where he put the chairs and tables back something like the way they used to be. At least now he had somewhere to sit.

With water from the well in the yard, and another piece of curtain fabric, he cleaned the bore and the butt. It looked like a perfectly ordinary German Luger pistol, the kind all German officers carried in their holsters. Adam Rzepin knew no more about guns than what they looked like and how the people carrying them behaved.

But there were no cartridges left in the magazine.

The bullet that killed Werner Samstag must have been the last.

As a weapon, the pistol was therefore worthless, unless he could find any other magazines hidden up in Rubin's room somewhere.

He sat there, weighing the gun in his hand, trying to imagine how much he could have got for it if he had been able to sell it on Pieprzowa Street, several thousand marks for sure, assuming anyone had dared to touch it or sell it on. If the Gestapo had got wind of there being real guns in circulation on the black market, they would undoubtedly have blown the whole ghetto sky high.

But really it was of no importance whether Samstag had been given the pistol, or had bought or stolen it. What was important was that he – Adam – now had it in his possession.

And he also had Werner Samstag in his possession.

Two things came home to Adam at the same time:

If the body could be left there, it was possible he might escape detection. The dogs – when they came – would locate the dead body straight away. The Germans with them would immediately have the body brought out and buried or burnt. With any luck, they would then take no further interest in the Green House.

Sitting in the Green House kitchen, as the light faded quickly in the windows around him, he decided to move in with Samstag, who had chosen to come back home in the end. Samstag was welcome to stay on in the Superintendent's room. As for him, he could live in the cellar.

And just a few days after he installed himself in the Green House, they came. They had dogs with them, as he had suspected they would. The only thing that took him by surprise was that they came so early, before he was awake, and he always woke up long before dawn. He could hear the squeak and scrape of jackboots on the floorboards above. Voices shouting. Loud thuds, the crash of objects being pulled out or knocked over. Someone cursing, long and hard, in German.

He implored Lida to please calm down.

He realised as soon as he set foot in the Green House again that Lida would not tolerate it. The discovery of Samstag's body had hardly improved matters.

All day she had been constantly on the move, and in the evening she had come crashing towards him again. He was kneeling in what was left of the Green House kitchen, looking through the saucepan cupboards. Dusk had set in, it was dark right up to the shiny tabletops, and all he saw was her outstretched hands, coming through the darkness with the fingers hooked like claws, as if she wanted to scratch his eyes out. Again her face was made of glass, the lips and cheeks petrified into an expression that was not an expression any longer, just an unbearable mask or grimace. He quickly crawled under a table and held up one of its shiny leaves as a shield in front of him.

He never understood where Lida's fury came from. He had never experienced that hatred while she was alive. Something must have happened to her since she crossed the boundary to the world of the dead, if it was not the mere fact that there was still a boundary between the dead and the living.

Now he is beseeching her, deliberately keeping all his movements gentle and restrained, so as not to awaken the fury in her once more.

But the Germans are right overhead.

The dogs bark and yelp, and their claws scratch at the wooden hatch to the basement.

He hears boots tramping round in circles.

Presumably they are looking for the staple so they can pull up the hatch.

Inside her face of glass, Lida is holding her breath, just like him.

The hatch opens with a creak, immediately above him. A roving beam of torchlight captures bare brick walls, and he sees their veined pattern of cracks for the first time.

Then there is a shout from behind the bright glare of the light:

Franz! Komm zu mir hoch! – and the asthmatically panting canine jaws that were just leaning over the edge are jerked back on their leads, and the hatch comes down with a loud bang and wreathes him in a cloud of sawdust and old coal dust. In the darkness, he and Lida are once again bodies without weight or dimension.

The Germans rummage about on the floor above for a while longer. He hears wood creaking and squeaking beneath the weight of slow, heavy steps. They are probably on their way down the stairs with the dead body. Then suddenly they are outside the building. There is a different ring to their voices, quickly erased by wind and distance. He thinks he can hear the faint sound of sharp shovel blades. Are they going to bury Samstag here? And what does that mean for himself? Can he stay here? Can the dead hear?

From then on, he carries the weapon with him, stuck in the waistband of Feldman's trousers. The trousers are so big that the pistol slips down between his legs whenever as he makes any sudden movement. He would never be able to run any distance with the weapon on him. But he likes having it there, and he likes taking it out from time to time, to hold it and study it more closely.

Just think. A Jew with a gun.

Every so often, he pretends to put its muzzle to the head of one of the Germans Lida had to dance for. Here, have a taste of your own medicine! he says, screwing the harmless pistol muzzle against a wall or a tree trunk or whatever happens to be to hand. But the right words will not come, and if it is a German temple to which he is pressing the pistol muzzle, it refuses to explode into gunpowder and smoke and blood once he fires the imaginary shot. There is something missing.

It has grown noticeably colder.

The damp is rising from the ground.

In the streets beyond Miarki Street, where the Chairman had his summer residence and the guards from the Sonder's protection squad once patrolled, oak and maple are ablaze. The maple burns with a brighter flame against the oak's muted rust-brown; the leaves gleaming with moisture after days of rain or fog, bordered with a touch of silver after clear, frosty nights.

Yes, the frost is coming. He knows he will have to light a fire before too long. If only he can find something to light it with.

613

For the time being, he is sleeping on some boards he has torn up from the floor of the Green House kitchen and laid out in its cellar; wrapped up in an old horse blanket he retrieved from Feldman's. But soon it will not be enough. The moisture in the walls is inching higher with every day that passes. It eats into everything it can reach: into elbow creases and groins, under your skin. In the end, it feels as though it is eating into the very marrow of his bones. He can feel it taking hold of his backbone; even clamping his skull in a vice-like grip.

His frosted breath glistens in front of him like a deadly mist.

He has no concept of the day or date. But he can tell by the way the light lies across the fields, brushing out the contours of the remaining foliage between tree trunks and stone walls, that it must be late October or early November.

The overnight frost comes more frequently now, as do the long white streaks of cold fog in the mornings, which sometimes persist until late in the day, as thick as syrup.

He looks at the sun, which is suspended over the horizon as if hanging inside an enormous sheet, swollen and tied at the top. Birds take off from behind stone walls, screeching as they circle in the air; they look like vast, eccentric cartwheels rolling through the sky.

Sitting on the edge of the well outside the Green House one day, he sees a man making his way on foot up Zagajnikowa Street.

Although the man is still so far away that he can make out no more than the outlines of the body, he knows it is Feldman. There is something about the way he bobs into every step and incorporates his whole body into a long, dogged, mechanical jog. No other human being walks that way.

He releases the safety catch of the pistol and puts his left hand under his right arm for support as he takes aim. Keeps his arm stretched out until Feldman is close enough to see what Adam has in his hand.

Feldman stops, stares straight into the muzzle of the gun. Mute, uncomprehending.

Adam does not move either.

Feldman deviates slowly sideways, out of the line of fire. Adam tracks his movements with the pistol. Feldman looks so alarmed that Adam can't help laughing. He lowers the weapon into his lap.

Where on earth did you get hold of that? says Feldman when he gets closer at last. He seems even more wizened beneath his coat and cap than usual; but he's the same Feldman.

What took you so long? says Adam.

Feldman explains that they have been kept in their quarters in Jakuba Street the whole time. Some mornings they were divided up into work brigades and marched to various places in the ghetto. Mostly it's been a matter of clearing out offices and departments. Every day they cleared vast amounts of paper out of filing cabinets and desk drawers and then burnt it all in big braziers. He'd no idea the ghetto had produced so much *paper*, he says.

Then they moved on to the workshops. They dismantled and took away the cutting and sanding machines from the furniture factories in Drukarska and Bazarowa. Some of them even had to demount the big steam-powered washtubs in the laundries, the mangles and the sheet presses. The whole lot was taken out to Radogoszcz and loaded onto trains heading west, away from the front.

So that explains the noises in the night. The convoys of marching men he saw at the limits of his visual range were on their way to the station goods yard.

'Is there anybody left out there?' he asks.

'Out where?'

'At Radogoszcz.'

Feldman shakes his head.

'There's only us, from the special unit. A hundred men at most.'

'Jankiel.'

'Don't know. Jankiel's dead. Most of them are dead.'

Adam is not convinced. He finds it hard to keep track of

616

who is dead and who is still alive. Szaja, *his father* – he has a vague image in his mind of him in the ranks of a group of men being marched out to the station from the Central Jail. And Lajb? All he can see of him now are rats behind the rusty bars of cages. Even Lida looked more alive than Lajb.

'I've brought you a bite to eat,' Feldman says.

He unwraps a bundle he has had tied inside his coat, a dirty handkerchief containing dry bread, chunks of sausage amounting to a few hundred grams, two shrivelled potatoes. Adam sees himself touching all these desirable things, not in a rush, not greedily, but like an insect exploring a piece of fruit, slowly, tentatively. It must have taken Feldman weeks to assemble such treasure, saving a little of his own meagre ration every day.

'How did you know I was here?' says Adam.

'I didn't. I was ordered to come and fetch some spades.'

Adam forgets the simplest things. This time he has forgotten to swallow. The saliva is running down the side of his chin. Feldman reaches forward and wipes it away with the back of his hand.

'There's no spade here,' says Adam. 'I've already looked.'

They sit in silence for a while.

Then Feldman asks him how things are going. Adam says he's getting by. He goes from house to house. He takes whatever he finds. There's still fruit in most of the gardens: frostbitten and maggoty apples with a sharp, musty taste. There are also beets to hack out of the ground at the old allotments. He even found a patch of fresh onions. Can you believe it, Feldman? Fresh onions. In one house he found a paraffin stove. But no paraffin. He's been wondering if he could try lighting it with oil. The can of fuel oil he skimmed from the station is still at the nursery, but he hasn't dared in case it attracts anybody's attention. Apart from the Germans, he hasn't seen a soul the whole time, he says.

All the time Adam is talking, Feldman can't take his eyes off the pistol on his lap. So Adam has to tell him about Samstag after all. He does not really want to, but he knows he has no choice.

Feldman sits there for a long time without saying a word, so long that Adam thinks he is not going to respond at all. But eventually he says they've been talking about Samstag in Jakuba. Some claim to know he went on the very last transport, the one Rumkowski and his family took. Some of his own men say that they were ordered to go and look for him. That the Germans, too, were hunting all over the ghetto for him. That they are scared of him. Biebow most of all. Biebow was even said to have offered a reward for anyone, singular or plural, who could catch him alive.

Adam holds up the pistol.

Feldman just shakes his head.

'And Biebow . . . ?'

Spends most of his time staggering round the ghetto, drunk. Indulges in his own special brand of sharpshooting. Bare-headed, with his sleeves rolled up, bottle in one hand, service pistol in the other. They have got into the way of saying: *Biebow's coming*. And taking cover as soon as he comes round the corner. The only one of the former ghetto *dygnitarzy* left is Jakubowicz. He's been given responsibility for what's left of the Central Tailoring Workshop, downgraded to *kierownik*, but at least he avoided being deported like all the other top dogs. But now even the Central has been shut down and taken apart – the machinery's going to *Königs Wusterhausen*; they spent all last week moving it – and Biebow has lost his last confidant, presumably the only Jew in the ghetto to whom he felt he could speak entirely openly.

At length, Feldman gets to his feet.

'And when are the Russians coming?' says Adam.

He asks as a child might have asked. With words in poster-print letters, and his hand held out as if he expected Feldman to drop the answer into it.

But Feldman just shrugs his shoulders inside his big overcoat. As if the question has been asked so often that it has become irrelevant. – Maybe they'll have second thoughts when they get here. Maybe they'll take the Balkans first. Bulgaria's already declared war on Germany. The Allies have taken Belgium and Holland, are marching on Paris. It's only a question of time now. But time, time: what can happen over time?

'I shall freeze to death before they get here,' says Adam.

He has no other way of expressing it.

'You won't freeze to death, Adam,' says Feldman. 'People like you don't freeze to death.'

Then he turns and heads on down to the old nursery to fetch his spades.

He lies alone on the bits of board in the cellar of the Green House.

He thinks of the time when he worked at the railway goods yard. Everything that was loaded and unloaded. First people were brought in, then they were taken out. Machinery was transported in, then transported out. He thinks about the long freight trains of machine parts that came in by night; about how they had to carry the packing cases in the frigid glare of the searchlights: carry them on their backs to the backs of the waiting lorries. For the heaviest machine parts, they had to construct cradles to be lowered into the wagons by cranes.

And now it was all being transported out of the ghetto again.

How many could there be left in the clean-up commando down in Jakuba Street? Feldman thought there were five hundred at most; women and men held separately.

Were five hundred enough to obliterate the memory of a city of several hundred thousand at its peak?

He thinks about Jankiel's head lying there in the gravel like a dirty apple, grit and cinders caught up in the spreading blood. Lida is squatting beside the prostrate body, her long, thin arms dangling lifeless between her knees.

Her eyes are fixed on her brother.

Behind her come all the others – Gelibter and Roszek and Szajnwald with the club foot – the shapes of backs and shoulders he so often saw being hoisted in under heavy wooden crates, with small, precise movements. He would have recognised those backs in his dreams if he had seen them again, one by one, bent or crooked or proud, arched, like Jankiel's backwhen he stood up, stomach out and tailbone in, as though he never tired of showing off what he had hanging there in front. And always smiling. That was why the German guards felt the need to go up and hit him, over and over again. To wipe off that cheeky, freckled smile.

Where are they being taken now? And why isn't he with them?

Lying there in the darkness of the cellar, he thinks there must be a tipping point somewhere, like when you put weights onto a pair of scales and it suddenly dips.

When the exiled and the dead outnumber the living, it is the dead who start talking instead of the living. There are simply not enough of the living left to be able to maintain a whole reality.

Now he understands. That is where the voices are coming from.

When it is dark and cold and the damp erases all the boundaries, the balance shifts and the sky above is not his sky any longer, but *their* sky. The sky *they* march under on their way from the jail in Czarnieckiego Street all the way out to Marysin, three or five abreast with the policeman a little way out on the left; and the Green House children standing watching from behind the orphanage fence, their hands hanging forgotten in the bars of their cage.

Then there had not been a sound from the marching column. Now he can suddenly hear all the men singing. All the backs are singing. A voiceless, mighty, rumbling earthsong, growing and expanding inside him. For the song is in him, too. The whole world is booming and shaking with it. He puts his arms up to his ears to shut out the song, but it is no use. When the dead sing, their song has no constraints or fetters, and there is nothing to hide or muffle it with.

When he finally wakes up, only the echo of his scream remains. But it reaches a long way, that echo: far beyond and outside himself, as if he had personally unwittingly drawn a line round all the absent and the dead within a radius of many thousands of kilometres.

So what is left of him, then, of himself? Alone and undelivered among those who are still alive.

He could not recall having ever wept in his whole life. Not even when they took Lida from him had he wept. But now he wept, mainly, perhaps, because there was no one left to weep for.

Winter is coming. It cannot be put off any longer.

The year is like the wheel of an old watermill, tipping on round with its heavy paddles. Sometimes fast, sometimes less so. But never letting itself be stopped.

One morning the long, gentle slope running down from the Green House is brushed with snow. It is the first snow of the year. The wind whisks the snow along with it in thin, white veils, or makes energetic little snow brooms of it that sweep off round the fields, white on green.

He knows he hasn't got much time if he is to find enough food and fuel to last him all winter.

Feldman has been back up a couple of times.

The lax discipline creeping into the collective in Jakuba Street seems to have got even more casual. The clean-up commando is marched out more and more sporadically. The German officers spend most of their time drinking and playing cards. Food is increasingly hard to get hold of, and it is impossible for Feldman to bring him any quantity of coal or wood without being seen.

Adam has already rummaged around in the old tool shed and found two empty wood sacks. There is not even the tiniest bit of wood left in them, but he does find a little fine, damp sawdust in the bottom. They must have held offcuts from some sawmill; maybe a gift to Feldman on some occasion. He stuffs the two empty wood sacks under his coat and goes out into the drifting snow.

Part of him must have been sure this was just a passing snow shower. The wind seemed to indicate it. Strong and gusty, biting into face and hands.

But the wind dies down and the snow does not stop falling. It comes down more and more heavily. Everything goes quiet. He walks through a pillared hall of thickly falling snow.

It strikes him that his tracks in the snow could give him away, but he is already too far down Marysińska Street for it to be worth turning back.

He must have something to show for his trip. Otherwise he will have expended all this energy for nothing.

He thinks about previous ghetto winters. As soon as the snow fell, it was dirtied and despoiled. By ashes, excrement and rubbish. And the endless paths people forged through it: like narrow black corridors through snow no plough has touched.

Within the curtains of falling snow it is now so white and quiet and still as to be almost unreal. No tracks.

He walks, but it is as if he is not walking at all. He walks as if he is being carried or lifted through the increasingly dense sheets of gently falling snow.

The central coal depot is in Spacerowa Street, just along from the corner with Łagiewnicka, a hundred metres or so from Bałuty Square.

He has not dared to come so close to the heart of the ghetto before.

The coal depot used to be one of the most strictly guarded places in the ghetto. Jewish policemen stood outside the entrance day and night. All along the fence of the compound, too; and at the back, in case anybody tried getting in from the street running parallel, on the north side of the square. The high fence is still there, but the gate is open and there are no guards to be seen.

As he crosses the street, his footsteps leave deep impressions in the snow. He wonders if he should try to smooth over his tracks as he goes, but thinks he would probably just make things worse. The snow is wet now; he can see water pooling in his footprints. It can only be a matter of time until the snow turns to rain, and then it will have been pointless anyway.

He goes further into the compound. Whenever new fuel rations were announced, thousands of people would come and queue up for their five- or ten-kilo allocations of briquettes. He remembers the long, snaking queues that started right inside the little storehouse, a barrack hut almost identical to the one the ghetto administration had at Bałuty Square, and then stretched out into Łagiewnicka Street. Queue-jumping was a popular sport: invoking some imaginary auntie who you said was keeping a place for you up by the counter. Any attempt to butt in like that caused uproar among those behind. People protested loudly and the officers on duty would race over and plunge in, dealing out baton blows to anyone who looked as if they might be hiding a queue-jumper behind their backs.

Now there is nobody here. The compound lies open and empty beneath the snow falling from the sky.

He has no real hopes of finding anything. If there was any coal left here after the last marching column left the ghetto, other hands would have laid claim to it long since.

The door of the warehouse is half open, as well, and can no longer be locked, because (he sees now) the bolt and door handle have been removed. He advances into the gloom, his tentative footsteps echoing dry and cold against the ceiling and bare walls. He can hardly make out anything in the darkness. A bench at the far end, and behind it, a door that must lead into the store itself. This, too, is unlocked, but inside the room it is darker still. He can hardly see his hand in front of his face; moves forward blindly, bumps into a wall, and then a short set of steps is descending under his feet. At the bottom there is a door, and it opens. He is in some kind of small, inner courtyard, perhaps twenty metres square, covered in a thick layer of pristine snow, and enclosed on the far side by a tall wall. This must have been where they kept the briquettes. Over by the wall, which marks the boundary between the coal depot and the blocks of flats beyond, there is a small shed, a tool shed perhaps. He goes over to it and gives the door a half-hearted tug.

There are no tools inside – if that was what he was expecting – but there are wood offcuts piled against the wall. Two decent-sized piles, each about a metre high, and better still, tied up with rope, as if they have just been stacked there to wait for someone like him to come and carry them away. Basic bits of board, different lengths, building timber presumably; most of them broken off at the end. But he is already calculating things in his mind. He should be able to get two or three bundles of wood in each sack; he can carry two or three more under his arm. If the worst comes to the worst, and it's all too heavy, he can hide a couple of bundles on the way, and come back for them later.

He does not hesitate, but opens the sacks and starts to fill them. He has just started on the second one when he hears something behind him.

It is a thin, delicate, scraping sound. He would not have noticed it, had it not been for the absolute silence in the falling snow.

Steps on a cold stone floor; exactly the same sounds that amplified around him as he went into the storehouse.

Someone is following him, probably after seeing his tracks in the snow.

He stuffs the last bundle of wood into the second sack, drags both sacks back across the snow-covered yard and presses his back to the wall on the other side.

There is a German soldier in the building. He can tell by the harsh, solidly booted, albeit slightly uncertain footsteps across the floor. The metallic jangle of a rifle being unhooked from

626

its strap and sliding slowly down over the belts and buttons of the uniform. Soon he can also hear the soldier's long, hesitant breaths. Now the soldier sees what Adam himself has long been aware of: the confusion of footprints, crossing each other out in the yard, overlaid with the drag marks left by the two sacks. The soldier takes a few steps out into the yard; it is as if he has to get closer to have any way of understanding what he sees. As he does so, Adam also takes two steps forward, and raises the pistol in both hands.

The young soldier turns round, his face blank and wide open. *A Jew with a pistol.*

This is so inconceivable that he has no conception of how to react.

Adam takes a couple more quick steps forward, forces the pistol muzzle into the man's face and indicates that he should put his rifle down.

Inconceivably enough, the man obeys.

Adam grabs the rifle strap with one hand, gets the butt into his lap and aims the long rifle barrel. Before the man realises what is happening, Adam has put a finger under the trigger and fired.

The shot must have hit the very edge of his neck, for his body is spun half a turn, blood spraying from the side of the head. The German lands on his back in the snow, arms wide as if preparing for an embrace. Adam is there again, with the rifle muzzle pressed to the man's head, but there is no need. The blood is gushing from the neck wound as if from a tap. The man is not moving, except for his mouth, which is gaping fishlike, as if seeking for words. But nothing is said, or if it is he does not hear, as the echo of the shot continues to reverberate around them, and Adam knows that in the quietness of the ghetto, the report will have been heard everywhere.

He slings the soldier's rifle over his shoulder by its strap and lugs the two sacks of wood from the inner yard, through

627

the storehouse and out into the compound. Then along Łagiewnicka Street, plodding with his sacks in the middle of the road, an open target. Anybody who sees him will be able to take aim and shoot him.

But nobody sees him – nobody shoots.

The snow has turned to rain, and a faint haze is thickening in the rain, taking on the colour of the twilight that is developing around him. The last thing he sees before turning off Łagiewnicka Street is the big ghetto clock that has always been there. *Ghetto time*: a very peculiar time, different from all the other times in the world. Now, the hands are pointing to 4.40 on the pale clock face.

Twenty to five. Snow turns to rain. A Jew has just killed a German.

A few blocks further on:

He has carried on up Młynarska Street; keeping as far to the right as he can, to the side of the street in the shelter of the trees. That is when it strikes him that the most stupid thing he could do right now is to go back to the Green House. It is obvious the Germans will look there first. And if they start questioning the clean-up commando, Feldman may very well be forced to tell them about the Green House and the nursery.

On the other side of the road: a long row of standard blocks of flats. There is nothing left of the snowfall but light rain. The tracks he has left will be obliterated within an hour at most. He goes into one of the dark stairway entrances, dragging the wood sacks after him. He goes up as far as he can. First floor, second floor.

The door of a flat: he shoves it open with his shoulder.

Two rooms, wallpaper drooping, peeling off in long lengths from the damp-stained walls; a window looking out on the street; a sooty stove.

He lies down on his back on the ice-cold bed, tries to make

himself breathe more calmly.

Right across the middle of the ceiling an intricate pattern of cracks as the plaster has come away in the damp.

So he has wood – two sackfuls. He could even have got a fire going if he had had anything to light it with, and were it not for the fact that they would instantly discover him if he did.

Just like the pistol, not to mention the rifle, the wood, too, is now completely useless.

He stays three days in the room in Młynarska Street. In that time, the rain turns back to snow several times over, and on the morning of the third day the temperature plummets. He is woken by the cold long before it is light. The cold is surrounding his body inside Feldman's sheepskin coat like a ring of repelling metal. Encased in this ring of steel, he can scarcely move. He cannot feel the skin of his face when he touches it. He has lost all sensation in his fingers and toes. He has experienced severe cold before – but never like this. Hauling himself with great effort into a slumped sitting position, he sees that the moisture has covered the inside of the window with a stiff chequering of ice. Everything is steaming frostily. Not just his mouth as he breathes, but also the ceiling, walls and floor. He reluctantly leaves the bed to find something to eat. In one of the flats, the snow has blown in through the window and built a barrage half a metre high between the bed in the corner and the grimy stove. The ill-fitting window is banging to and fro on its squeaky hinges, the air all around filled with that senseless straining, whining, squealing – sounds without any human meaning.

He knows with utter certainty that if he stays in here a minute longer he will die. He has already searched every flat in the block and found nothing to eat. He knows he needs to think rationally:

In the Green House he has hoarded away what little he has been able to spare. Leftover bits of dry bread; a few spoonfuls of cornflour and rye flour he scraped out of the bottom of some old storage jars; some frozen beets and turnips he dug up at the abandoned allotments. Apples: rotten on the side that has been lying on the ground, but quite edible otherwise.

Those provisions should last him at least a few more weeks. But if the cold continues he will have to have a fire. So does it make any difference if he lights one here, or in the wood-burning stove in the Green House? If the Germans are anywhere nearby, they will smell the wood smoke wherever he is. In that case he'd be better off going back at the Green House. Once there, he also has more chance of getting away or staying hidden if they turn up again.

And what makes him think, strictly speaking, that they are looking specifically for him? Or that they have time to look for anyone? Or reason to? They may have heard the shot but not been able to work out where it came from. Maybe the body is still there – unseen – in the foul, frozen water in the cramped inner yard of the briquette store.

Not particularly likely. But he has to admit it is entirely possible.

So as dusk sets in, he gathers up his few things, puts the German soldier's rifle across his body on its strap, takes his two sacks of wood and lugs them out with him.

The cold continues. He finds himself crunching slowly over ice. The wind slaps a burning mask of freezing cold to his cheeks and forehead.

Before long, his fingers grasping the sacks have gone entirely numb.

He is so faint with hunger that his legs will hardly carry him. The will to keep moving is still there, but that will is struggling in a vacuum.

He can't sit down, either.

He thinks of what his father used to say, about it once being so cold in the ghetto that the saliva froze in people's mouths. Would they find him here, then, the way he had found Samstag?

Where he dropped, on his way home with his pathetic sacks of wood. Stolen goods, what's more.

So he pushes on. The night sky is like a helmet, pulled low over his brow. Beneath it, his gaze opens only a narrow tunnel ahead of him. He moves through it without stopping or looking round to check there is no one else out there in the darkness, beneath the sky helmet, to see him and follow him.

He goes past Praszkier's workshop, turns into Okopowa Street and is back at the corner of Zagajnikowa. Along the roadside and behind the garden fences are mounds of snow that have thawed and frozen again. But the snow looks untouched. No remains of footprints anywhere, as far as he can see. If he is still capable of seeing anything at all. His gaze is clouded; it seems to swell up as soon as he tries to fix it on anything.

He is so weak that he has to lean on anything he can.

Garden gate, house wall; then the door into the front hall, and from the (thank God!) dark hall down into the protection of the cellar.

He has already gathered up all he needs. Some tarred roofing paper, for example, to line the bottom of the stove so the damp does not stop the wood burning. He feeds in some oak twigs, still with leaves on, and then builds a little tower of bits of wood. The fire takes almost immediately; first he lets it burn up in the cross-draught, then he carefully closes the stove door, so the warmth will spread round the room and not just evaporate.

The smoke from the fire can no doubt be seen for several kilometres.

But he doesn't care. The fire in the stove sucks and crackles away, serene and majestic; he even starts to sweat inside Feldman's big coat. Sweat pours out of him; even the stiff, frozen skin of his face is sweating. It trickles down his ears and lips and eyes.

And this pleasure he has created around himself, as unexpected as it is seductive, makes him feel almost like a devil in his earth or den. Utterly hateful in his irresponsibility.

Let them come.

But nobody comes.

Eventually, the flames behind the bars of the stove die down. The fire goes out, and with astonishing speed the cold takes possession of the room again.

Lying there semi-naked and shivering, listening for any sound, he steps forward once more to the German soldier he killed.

He has seen much of death, but this is the first time he has killed another person.

A German, moreover. Some people would no doubt say the swine deserved to die.

But for him, the action is still too huge to be grasped in word or thought.

First he thought: he killed someone. So they will come after him. They won't give up until they have exacted their revenge. They will flay him as they did that Jew Pinkas or whatever his name was, who had the goldsmith's shop in Pietrkowska Street before the ghetto was set up, and when the Germans came he tried to hide away all he owned in various places around his flat, and with friends and acquaintances. When Pinkas refused to reveal where he had hidden the gold, they beat him up, stripped him, tied a rope round under his arms, fixed the rope to a motorbike and sidecar and then dragged Pinkas's naked body up and down the length of Piotrkowska Street from the Grand Hotel to Plac Wolności until all his skin was gone, and the arms and legs sticking out of the bloody remains. In the end, only his head and trunk were left.

That was what they would do to him, too. Or so he imagined. But when they still did not come, he was less sure.

Maybe what had happened somehow hadn't happened. Maybe he had only dreamt it, the way he sometimes thought or dreamt that Lida was with him.

She was there, but she wasn't really.

And maybe the soldier he had killed wasn't really dead, either, since he was German and it was a known fact that Germans couldn't die. He saw the spray of blood that had issued from the torn carotid artery flowing back into the body again. He saw the soldier get up, regain his composure; grip his rifle again and turn to him indignantly:

Die? If anyone was going to die here, it was surely him – *the Jew.*

It had been decreed from the very beginning that it was the Jew who was going to die, and since it had been decreed, then so it had to be in the end. Who did he think he was, anyway? The master of history? Not even a German could go so mad that he believed he could rule over everything just because he was all alone in the world.

Fresh snow falls, and lies on within its darkness.

And the darkness stops and thickens around him, too.

He is in the heart of this winter, embedded in it like a stone in the stomach of some large, hibernating animal.

The cold persists; but the snow is also an insulator, remarkably enough.

It is no longer as raw and damp in the Green House.

He pulls up the hall floor and saws the floorboards up for firewood. He uses a rusty old iron grate he has found to spread the ashes from the fire more evenly and make the heat last longer.

Slowly, oh so slowly, the Green House starts to become inhabited again.

One night he thinks he can hear piano music from the Pink Room.

But the shell of the music has been peeled away. All he can hear are the dry, mechanical thuds of the wooden hammers hitting the steel wires in the vast belly of the instrument. A music from *within*. And the thuds come harder, faster. In the end, the noise is deafening: a cacophony of cold hammering that transmits itself into a shaking of his whole frame.

He realises he is sick.

The fever washes through him in waves, alternately hot and cold. There is a dangerous drowsiness in his body that he instinctively senses he must not give way to. To stop the drowsiness getting the upper hand, he starts shouting. He shouts out loud, with the full force of his lungs. He shouts Feldman's name. He shouts his father's name. He shouts Lida's name. When he can't think of any more people's names, he starts shouting the names of places he has been, of streets in the ghetto.

Do his shouts really get out to echo round the room, or do they escape him merely as faint, whispered exhalations? He dare not trust his own hearing any more. Impossible to say whether what he hears is also what is heard in the room around him.

In the end, all the voices abandon him as well, and he succumbs to his weakness.

In his fever, he is crawling around on the floor like a baby.

There are other children crawling on all fours around him.

The room is full of children. All is as it should be.

Lida is a child, too. An enormous head with a warm, wet, dribbling mouth. She is swathed, as she used to be, in a dirty sheet with small holes for her arms and legs, so she can't reach to smear herself with her own faeces.

And every day her mother took the sheet off her, washed it and dried it and put it over her head again.

But Lida is clean now. She drags her long body after her as if it were nothing but a bulky and constricting cover, the case from which the pupa is about to emerge.

And she smiles from her wet mouth. A bright, open, trusting smile.

I'm never dead, she says.

He has been hearing sporadic gunfire for several days without understanding what he hears. Not the solid carpets of noise as the Allied planes flew over, not the whine and violent detonations of falling bombs. Not the recoil of trench mortars – not even the concentrated rattle of automatic weapons.

No, *mechanical* firing is what he can hear.

A swift, sporadic grazing of what is his external sky now, the sky he wears around his head and shoulders like a helmet, every time he wakes up.

The sky above the cemetery is enamel grey above the low walls and mutilated trees. He cannot believe it is the same landscape, the same landscape returning day after day, and his first impulse is to go and lie down again: defy the hunger by at least trying to sleep. In the end, the firing becomes as ingrained a sound as the patter of rain or the sound of water dripping and running down off the roof as the night's heavy snowfall starts to melt.

Only when the shots are accompanied by voices does he really rouse himself.

The voices are sometimes close, sometimes far away, and again it is hard to tell whether they are coming from inside him or outside.

To be on the safe side, he straps the rifle over his shoulder and goes out.

After a long period of inactivity, unhampered movement is difficult. It feels as if someone has fixed heavy wooden cuffs round his arms and legs. His head is pulled, or at least tries to slump, downwards all the time. Anyone who saw him would have said he was a shadow of his former self.

And perhaps that is true. At any rate, he has survived his own self.

Against all the odds, he has survived.

A dazzlingly white winter light over fields and arable land still covered in snow.

But not entirely: bits of the dark soil beneath are slowly burning their way through. The world is white and black, with strands of snow running across the black fields like reflections of the vast whiteness of the sky.

Against the white, he sees figures moving. They are following the same route the marching columns used to take to Radogoszcz Station. But these people are moving more freely, as if refusing to be kept together by any officer's command. Every so often, one of the figures stops and shouts something or waves his arms above his head. Whenever this happens, the whole column stops, and others start shouting and waving their arms too. Impossible to hear what they are saying. Their voices merge into an acoustic wall, as sharp and repelling as the wall of light, the sky.

Are they trying to signal to him? Is he the intended recipient of all this shouting and waving? But in any case, how can they see him, since he can hardly make them out? In all likelihood, the distance is too great.

Then a few of the figures break away from the group and start running towards him.

Three people running. Józef Feldman out in front. He can plainly recognise the rapid, springy strides that always seem to be throwing his body forward. The head protruding from his coat is bright red – excited and anxious at the same time – as if he is finding it hard to assemble the various parts of himself into one coherent face.

Feldman shouts something, and individual words detach themselves from the shout.

He pieces it together as:

. . . Russians . . . are . . . here . . .

Then, as if Feldman's words were a covert stage direction, the first of the Russian armoured vehicles turns into Zagajnikowa Street. They are proper tanks: KV tanks on caterpillar tracks, mud splashed right up to their guns, the red hammer-and-sickle flag fixed at the back, above the din of their engines and the belching exhaust fumes. There are two or three men on each gun turret. Some of them are singing. At least he thinks he hears something like singing, rising and falling around him.

In the singing and the racket of the engines, Feldman tries to shout something else, but the singing overpowers him. Adam can't contain himself: he runs down towards Zagajnikowa Street, from which one convoy after another is emerging; tanks and supply vehicles with radio equipment.

Halfway to the Russian tank units, he turns and waves.

Feldman waves back. With big, emphatic swings of his arms.

Come here . . . here . . . it sounds as if he is saying.

But Adam ignores him. He has got to accept this wonderful moment of liberation with his whole body. Otherwise it will never be real.

And now he sees it, too. At the far end of Zagajnikowa Street, the barbed wire and fencing have been torn down, the sentry box where the German ghetto guard used to stand with his submachine gun on his stomach has been thrown on its side. On the other side of the boundary, the landscape is just the same as here. The same flat sunlight, the same dirty slabs of melting snow. He can't restrain himself any longer. He runs past the barbed wire that has been tossed aside, straight out into the open field, and starts dancing round – whooping with joy – with his arms stretched up towards the boundless white sky.

Then the first shot finds its target. And another, straight after it.

He can't understand why the legs beneath him suddenly refuse to obey. In a wave of panic, he realises they are shooting at *him*.

Where are the shots coming from? Who is shooting?

He turns round to wave again, to somehow make it clear that it is all a misunderstanding. They have been liberated. He was never anyone's enemy.

But then another shot echoes out over Marysin and his body is thrown face-first into the sweet, black clay.

He tries with all his strength to raise his face from the mud and turn it up to the light.

And the sky is fixed at that angle. Now it no longer exists.

Afterword

Many of the characters appearing in this book vanish out of history with the final evacuation of the ghetto in August 1944. But there are exceptions. One is Dawid Gertler, who features particularly in the third part of the novel. Though Gertler's contemporaries ascribed to him an almost mystical capacity for survival, it was generally assumed that he was murdered by the Nazis after the Gestapo took him from the ghetto in July 1943. Contrary to expectations, however, Gertler turned out to have survived both his interrogation and his subsequent detention in a concentration camp. He surfaces in Hannover in 1961 as a witness at the trial of Günther Fuchs, which was then in progress. Fuchs was chief in command of the department within the security forces that dealt with what were known as 'Jewish affairs', in the ghetto set up by the Germans in Litzmannstadt. It was therefore Fuchs who was in practice responsible for the mass murders committed from January 1942 onwards, and for the so-called *szpera* action in September of the same year, which had such catastrophic consequences for the population of the ghetto.

In his evidence against Fuchs, however, Gertler paints a somewhat different picture of the events of those dramatic days than the one that had been painted previously.

He asserts, for example, that after Rumkowski made his speech of 4 September 1942 – in which he informed the ghetto inhabitants of the Nazis' decision to deport all old people and children under ten – he was seized with indecision. According to Gertler, after making his speech, Rumkowski went in person to Fuchs to inform him he could not carry out the order and then withdrew from the public eye, basically not being seen again until seven days later, when the curfew was lifted. For the ten days and nights of the curfew, the so-called *szpera* days, it fell instead to David Gertler to mitigate the effects of the Nazis' decision and to attempt in this, the ghetto's 'most critical hour', to save as many lives as possible:

> *I approached Fuchs and Bibow* [sic!] *to try to negotiate with them about buying the children's freedom. I had already taken Bibow into my confidence, as he could otherwise have put obstructions in my way. The Gestapo, so in practice Fuchs, were responsible for the transaction itself. I was thus able, on behalf of those in the ghetto who had money, to buy back large numbers of children. Since the Gestapo, and Bibow too, were practically eating out of my hand, various people in positions of authority even agreed in the course of these transactions to release children without demanding any payment at all. This meant that the total number of people transported [from the ghetto] amounted to 12,300 or 12,700 rather than the 20,000 that was the original target . . .*

Whatever weight one may attach to this testimony – Gertler's principal concern was naturally to enhance his own reputation – it still offers a rather different image of Rumkowski as a person than that which had previously emerged (through historians such as Isaiah Trunk, for example).

Most of the testimonies of people who outlived Rumkowski, and there are in fact quite a number, portray him as an unscrupulous careerist and collaborator who would go to some lengths to implement the decisions of the Nazi powers. And yet there was clearly a point at which even Mordechai Chaim Rumkowski felt obliged to look away and say no. This novel revolves around that moment. What did it take to make even the strong man of the ghetto refuse to obey? What made him do it? And what price did he have to pay for his (as Gertler still

– paradoxically enough – calls it during his cross-examination) irresponsible submission?

In broad outline, but with some additions, the course of events in this novel follows developments in the ghetto as described in the *Ghetto Chronicle*.

The *Ghetto Chronicle* is a document of some three thousand pages which was the collective work of a handful of employees in the ghetto's archive section. The archive was a section of the *Statistische Abteilung* set up by Rumkowski in the spring of 1940, and later also oversaw the ghetto's population register (*Meldebüro* or *Meldeamt*). Over time, these sections merged and expanded, and by 1944 consisted in total of '44 employees, 1 director, 23 secretaries and office staff, 12 draughtsmen and printmakers, 4 photographers and 4 odd-jobbers [*sonstige*]', as stated in a report reproduced by the *Chronicle* at the time.

The Statistics Department had clearly defined functions from the outset. It was to produce

> *daily briefings to the state police and other relevant parties within the ghetto administration on the population's state of health (including births and deaths), along with detailed studies of a demographic nature of the condition of the employees, production in the factories, and anything else requested by the Elder of the Jews.* [It was also] . . . *to make compilations of this statistical material available to other interested groups, produce visual presentations of statistical data and photomontages for the purposes of teaching and propaganda, and also . . . produce and collect illustrative material for archiving and various practical uses.*

In addition to these specific tasks, there was also a more general role, which called on it 'on the quiet' – those are the actual words! – 'to collect material for a future presentation (= history) of the ghetto and to keep personal notes for this purpose'.

From the day the first observation is recorded in the *Chronicle* – 12 January 1941 – through to the last entry a month before the ultimate liquidation of the ghetto, the *Chronicle* is thus primarily conceived as a testimony for *future* readers.

This may not initially be apparent to today's readers. Until September 1941, the *Chronicle*, at that time written in Polish, was less a collective diary and more a kind of standard, open form on which certain, regular events were repeatedly recorded. In that respect, it is reminiscent of the *pinkas* or *Gemeindebücher* previously kept over several generations in Jewish communities in Poland, and in Eastern Europe generally. The *Chronicle* contains, for example, columns for the day's weather and for the number of births and deaths; there are extracts from police reports, details of consignments of food and fuel that have arrived or are due to do so; notes of changes to working hours and working conditions in the factories of the ghetto, and so on. The *Chronicle* also reproduces most of the official proclamations emanating from Rumkowski's headquarters or the German ghetto administration, and also (in shorthand) virtually all the Chairman's speeches.

This documentary role had an important function. By reference to the *Chronicle*, Rumkowski was able to monitor the history of his reign as it was being written.

Gradually, however, the form and content of the *Chronicle* change. This is most noticeable from the autumn of 1941 onwards, when some of the newly arrived, so-called 'western Jews' are taken on by the Archive Department of the ghetto and start writing in the *Chronicle*. At least two of them, Oskar Singer and Oskar Rosenfeld, are established authors and journalists with many years' experience of operating under various forms of bureaucratic censorship. From this point on, the *Chronicle* is less formulaic and more polyphonic; other genres are introduced, and even critical voices begin to make themselves heard (often in the form of satire). It is important to note, however, that it nonetheless continues to reflect (and subordinate itself to) a version of ghetto events sanctioned by Rumkowski.

The *Chronicle*'s character as a repository of tradition and a contemporary testimony, yet also a mouthpiece for Rumkowski, means it is concrete and exact (in its detail) and yet simultaneously unreliable on a more general level as a source of information about what was actually happening in the ghetto.

Anyone reading the *Chronicle* today must also learn to distinguish between what posterity (*now*) knows for a fact and what the chroniclers (*then*) could only suspect. Today we may not in all respects know *more* than the inmates of the ghetto did. But we know *in a different way*: with a historical transparency and clarity of detail that those incarcerated there did not possess.

As early as February or March 1942 there was unambiguous evidence available in the ghetto that most of the 'transports' that had left since the turn of the year had gone directly to death camps. Rumkowski undoubtedly knew from an early stage, if not from the very start, that the population of the ghetto was being murdered before his very eyes. But far from everybody knew, and the lack of absolute certainty created the strange grey zone, hovering between hope and despair, to which all the entries in the *Chronicle* subscribe. Despite all the evidence to the contrary, there were still those who persisted in believing there was a life beyond the ghetto, somewhere and in some form; and this refusal to abandon all hope of survival characterises the authors of the *Ghetto Chronicle* to the very last day. It also characterises to the very last the image the *Chronicle* presents of Chaim Rumkowski, the man who elevated uncertainty to the level of a state ideology, enabling him to continue unhindered his delivery of the raw material required by the Nazi extermination machine.

Beginning as late as January 1944, some of the *Chronicle* writers attempted to encapsulate life in the ghetto in a *Ghetto Encyclopedia*. The *Encyclopedia* can be seen as an appendix to the *Chronicle* or as yet another attempt to leave a visible record of *the time of the ghetto* for posterity.

The *Ghetto Encyclopedia* is a collection of little catalogue cards recording large numbers of people and phenomena from everyday life in the ghetto, its management and administration. The *Encyclopedia* provides not only definitions and derivations of various words and phrases in common use in the ghetto, neologisms and loan words (usually from Polish, or from the Austrian bureaucratic jargon brought in by the 'foreign' Jews), but also a handful of miniature biographies of leading men and women in ghetto society. The influential individuals whose cameos appear there include Aron Jakubowicz, head of the Central Labour Office, Dawid Gertler, and Gertler's successor as head of the powerful Sonderabteilung, Mordka Kligier.

But not Mordechai Chaim Rumkowski.

There could be several explanations for the absence of a card for Rumkowski. Either there never was a card for him, which seems unlikely – he was the most powerful man in the ghetto, after all. Or the card was removed at some juncture and destroyed. If that is the case, then the *Encyclopedia* bears out the indirect evidence offered by the *Chronicle* that the fiction, or perhaps rather the *editing* of the fiction, of the ghetto had begun even before the German occupation came to an end.

So although most of what happened in the ghetto is unusually well documented, there are gaps in the recording of events, places where reliable evidence is thin on the ground. This applies, for example, to the days of the *szpera*, when Chaim Rumkowski chose to 'submit' for a number of days and allow authority to pass to Dawid Gertler. It applies also to the exact circumstances surrounding Rumkowski's adoption of a child from one of the ghetto's children's homes, and his relationship with that child. The fact that Rumkowski systematically abused the orphans is exceptionally well substantiated, given the circumstances. In her book *Rumkowski and the Orphans of Łódź* (1999), Lucille Eichengreen sees these assaults, which she not only witnessed but was herself subjected to, as manifestations not so much of Rumkowski's sexual predilections as of his constant need to assert his power and authority at all levels in the ghetto. In a world where the only options were survival and subjection, the role of sexuality is hard to define but should not be underestimated. The fictional character Věra Schulz calls Rumkowski 'a monster' in her diary, but her words are actually taken from Eichengreen's book. I have made similar use of the testimonies of many other ghetto survivors. The long description of the 'western' Jews' initial encounter with the Łódź ghetto is largely based on Oskar Rosenfeld's account of the journey from Radogoszcz Station into the ghetto in *Wozu noch Welt: Aufziehungen aus dem Getto Lodz* (1994).

Unlike Rosenfeld, who retains his anonymity throughout the book, most of the officials and functionaries of any importance appear here under their own names. This is mainly because their deeds and misdeeds are so well documented, not least in the discussions of their backgrounds and actions in the *Chronicle* and the *Encyclopedia*, that inventing names for them would have seemed like providing superfluous disguise. In any case, I am of the view that the nature of the events that took place in Łódź in 1940–44 makes that sort of camouflage morally dubious.

Finally, a few words about the photograph on the cover of this book. The photograph is one of a total of four hundred taken by the chief accountant of the German ghetto administration, an Austrian named Walter Genewein. In all his photography Genewein used colour film, unusual for that time, which he ordered from the laboratories of IG Farbenindustrie in

Switzerland. No one knew of the existence of these pictures until 1988 when, soon after Genewein's death, one of his relatives offered the negatives for sale in a second-hand bookshop in Vienna. Genewein, a convinced Nazi, worked as part of the German administrative machine in the ghetto for virtually as long as it existed, and was therefore probably commissioned to take the photographs. Someone within the administration, possibly Biebow himself, gave amateur photographer Genewein the task of documenting the reality of the ghetto. What is striking about these pictures is how little of the *actual* reality of the ghetto they nonetheless show: how little of the hunger, the sickness, privation and poverty. Even death, ever present in the ghetto, is invisible in Genewein's work except perhaps as a stylisation of clouds and tram wires above crumbling houses and workshops.

What we see in Genewein's work is, rather, the history of the ghetto as he and the other Nazi officials saw it – or persuaded themselves it would look when it was eventually written. Genewein intends his images for the eyes of *future* observers, just as the writers of the *Chronicle* and *Encyclopedia* (albeit for completely opposite reasons) address their diary entries and miniature biographies to 'later' readers, who are 'unfamiliar with the reality of the ghetto'. There is nothing in Genewein's pictures, however, to indicate that he consciously arranged, or sought to create a flattering image of, the reality he was capturing. He himself probably saw the ghetto the way it appears in his pictures. It is apparent from a letter he wrote to family members back home in Austria that he saw the ghetto as a completely neutral part of the city of Łódź/ Litzmannstadt, albeit shut off and under police surveillance, where impoverished Jews lived and earned their keep more or less honestly in workplaces provided for them by the Germans in their infinite generosity.

Whether Rumkowski is to be viewed as saviour or traitor,

hero or scapegoat (a question that has preoccupied writers of the ghetto's history from the very first) is thus, at one level, wholly theoretical. It all depends on the perspective one adopts. It is entirely possible to imagine alternative courses of history in which things could have turned out differently for Rumkowski. If von Stauffenberg had succeeded in his coup against Hitler in July 1944, for example, or if Stalin had not agreed to halt the Red Army offensive at the River Wisła. Then Poland might conceivably have been freed from German occupation six months earlier, and Mordechai Chaim Rumkowski could have stepped from the ruins of the Jewish ghetto of the city of Łódź as what he perpetually strove to be, the liberator of his imprisoned people, and not, as history now generally paints him, as one of the most obedient tools of the Nazi executioners.

Main Characters

Gettoverwaltung (the German civilian ghetto administration)

Hans Biebow, Amtsleiter, head of the German civilian administration

Joseph Hämmerle, the ghetto administration's head of finance and central purchasing

Wilhelm Ribbe, responsible for the deployment of Jewish labour, exploitation of confiscated goods and factory management within the ghetto administration

Erich Czarnulla, in charge (within the ghetto administration) of all production of metal goods and of deliveries to the Wehrmacht

Heinrich Schwind, in charge of materials and stock control at Baluter Ring and Radegast, also responsible for supervising the supply of foodstuffs to the ghetto

Other German officials (including military and police administration)

SS-Oberstürmbannführer and Regierungsrat *Otto Bradfisch*, from 21 January 1942 Leiter der Stapostelle Litzmannstadt, with responsibility for the deportations from the ghetto to Chełmno beginning at that time; previously with the SS-Einsatzkommando in the Ukraine. From 2 July 1943 Oberbürgermeister of Litzmannstadt (successor to Werner Ventzki)

SS-Hauptsturmführer *Günther Fuchs*, head of Referat II B 4, later IV B 4, the Department of 'Jewish Affairs'

SS-Sturmscharführer *Albert Richter*, head of the Gestapo headquarters in the ghetto (1, Limanowskiego), and deputy head of the Department of 'Jewish Affairs'

SS-Hauptscharführer and Kriminaloberassistent *Alfred Stromberg*, working at Referat II B 4, for 'Jewish Affairs' at Gestapo-Dienststelle Getto Litzmannstadt

The Eldest of the Jews in Litzmannstadt (The Jewish ghetto administration)

Mordechai Chaim Rumkowski, Eldest of the Jews, Chairman of the ruling 'Council of Elders' (*Beirat*), taken in the last transport to Auschwitz on 28 August 1944 and murdered there, with his whole family, probably the same day

Dora Fuchs, Rumkowski's (senior) secretary and head of all the Chairman's secretariats (also responsible for contacts with the German 'authorities'). Dora Fuchs survived the war and emigrated to Israel

Mieczysław Abramowicz, secretary and personal assistant to Rumkowski

Józef Rumkowski, Rumkowski's brother, ran the ghetto's largest hospital, and was also head the Chamber of Highest Control (later renamed the FUKR – Fach und Kontrollreferat), set up to combat corruption in the ghetto. Was in the last transport out of the ghetto in August 1944 and was murdered with the rest of his family

Rebeka (Regina/Renia) *Wołk*, head of Rumkowski's 'Presidial Secretariat', later (until spring 1944) the Dworska Street Secretariat, also called Sekretariat Wołkówna

Dr *Wiktor Miller*, head of the health authorities in the ghetto (succeeded Dr Leon Szykier in the position)

Leon Rozenblat, chief of the regular police force of the ghetto (known until September 1940 as HIOD, Hilfsordningsdienst), later overshadowed by the Sonderabteilung; held the largely symbolic position of 'Deputy' Elder of the Jews over an extended period of time

Shlomo Hercberg, Chairman of *Forshtand Marysin*, classed for administrative purposes as a separate enclave within the ghetto; also commandant of the Central Jail and of District VI (the Marysin district) of the ghetto police. Deported from the ghetto and murdered with his whole family in March 1942

Aron Jakubowicz, head of the Central Labour Office (Centraler Arbeits-Resort); taken from the Litzmannstadt ghetto to one of the special labour units set up by Hans Biebow in Sachsenhausen. Jakubowicz survived the war

Stanisław (Szaja) *Jakobson*, Chairman of the Jewish Court in the ghetto; deported to, and murdered in, Auschwitz in August 1944

Dawid Warszawski, head of the Central Tailoring Workshop; murdered in Auschwitz in 1944

Henryk Neftalin, Head of the Department of Statistics and Population Registration (Meldeamt, statistische Abteilung) and the Archive; murdered in Auschwitz in 1944

Szmul Rosensztajn, manager of the only printing works in the ghetto; in that capacity also appointed head of the Chairman's 'Propaganda Department'. Szmul Rozenztajn was also editor of the 'Geto-Tsajtung' that was published for the first nine months the ghetto was in existence

Dr *Michał Eliasberg*, the Chairman's personal physician (was among the thirteen doctors recruited by Rumkowski in Warsaw, who came to Łódź in May 1941)

The Special Department

(Sonderkommando, known from September 1942 as the Sonderabteilung)

Dawid Gertler, arrested in the ghetto on 12 July 1943

Marek (Mordka) *Kligier*, appointed Gertler's successor in July 1943

Rumkowski's family (and staff)

Mordechai Chaim Rumkowski, Eldest of the Jews

Regina Rumkowska (Ruchla), Rumkowski's wife (married in December 1941)

Stanisław Rumkowski (born Stern, 1927), adopted as Rumkowski's son in September 1942

Józef Rumkowski, Rumkowski's brother

Helena Rumkowska (Princess Helena), Józef Rumkowski's wife, put in charge of soup kitchens and other communal feeding points in the ghetto after these were 'nationalised' (including those run by various parties, interest groups and voluntary aid organisations)

Jakub Tausendgeld, lawyer, and entrusted with the management of the Rumkowski family's 'assets', including Chaim Rumkowski's private resources

Icek Fajnsztajn, Princess Helena's personal secretary

Dr *Herz Garfinkel*, Princess Helena's personal physician

Lev Kuper, head groom and coachman

Dana Koszmar, housekeeper to the Rumkowski family

Estera (Etka) *Daum*, secretary and chief telephonist at Rumkowski's Secretariat at Bałuty square. She survived the ghetto and returned after the war to the city of Łódź. In 2008 her personal diaries were published in Poland

The Gnieźnieńska Street families

Ada Herszkowicz, concierge, block supervisor

Adam Rzepin, unskilled labourer

Lida Rzepin, Adam's sister

Szaja Rzepin, Adam and Lida's father

Lajb Rzepin, Szaja Rzepin's brother; employed at the time of the 1940 general strike at the cabinet-maker's in Drukarska Street – subsequently informer and spy for the Sonderabteilung and Kripo

Hala Wajsberg, niece of puppet-maker Fabian Zajtman

Samuel Wajsberg, carpenter

Jakub and *Chaim*, their children

Moshe and *Rosa Pinczewski*

Maria Pinczewska, their daughter

Jakub and *Rakel Frydman*

Feliks and *Dawid*, their children

Staff and children of the Green House (the children's home in Okopowa Street)

Dr *Józef Rubin*, superintendent

Malwina Kempel, nursery nurse; also Dr Rubin's secretary
Rosa Smoleńska, nursery nurse
Dr *Adrian Zysman*, paediatrician
Chaja Meyer, cook/housekeeper
Józef Feldman, caretaker, boiler-man
Older children:
Debora Żurawska
Kazimir Majerowicz (The Blackamoor)
Nataniel Sztuk
Mirjam Szygorska (died February 1942)
Estera Lubińska
Natasza Maliniak
Adam Gonik
Stanisław Stern (later Rumkowski)
Younger children:
twins *Abram* and *Leon Moserowicz*
Dawid, Teresa, Sofie, Natan (from Helenówek)
Liba, Chawa (and others)

The Schulz family (from the collective at 27 Franciszkańska Street)
Arnošt Schulz, doctor
Irena Schulzová (Maman), his wife
Věra Schulzová, their daughter
Martin and Josef (Josel) Schulz, their sons

The Archive (technically a subdivision of the ghetto's Department of Statistics)
Henryk Neftalin, head of department and member of the ruling Council of Elders
Dr *Oskar Singer*, Dr *Oskar Rosenfeld* and *Alicja de Buton* (invisible in the text but present throughout as writers for the *Ghetto Chronicle*)
Aleksander (Aleks) *Gliksman*, archivist

Rabbi (technically 'engineer') *Itzhak Einhorn*
Pinkas Szwarc, artist, graphic artist, set designer
Mendel Grossman, photographer

Listeners in Brzezińska Street
Werner Hahn, Schmul Krzepicki, Moszje Bronowicz, 'the boy' *Shem*

Labour brigade at Radogoszcz
Harry (Herry) *Olszer*, 'Verwaltungsleiter' (engineer), in charge of the
    construction site at Marysin

Workers
Marek Szajnwald, Jankiel Moskowicz, Gabriel Gelibter, Simon Roszek,
    Pinkas Kleiman, Herz Szyfer (and others)

The German station guard (at Radegast station)
Oberwachtmeister *Dietrich Sonnenfarb*
Lothar Schalz, Markus Henze

Acknowledgements

Thanks to Helge Axelsson Johnsons Stiftelse in Stockholm and to the Institut für die Wissenschaften vom Menschen (IWM) in Vienna for grants and opportunities for writing and research.

Particular thanks to Dr Sascha Feuchert and his colleagues of Arbeitsstelle Holocaustliteratur at the Institut für Germanistik at Justus Liebig University in Giessen, Germany, and to the late Julian Baranowski of the city archives in Łódź, for allowing me access to as yet unedited sections of the *Ghetto Chronicle* and other unpublished material including official proclamations, photographs and correspondence.

The *Ghetto Chronicle* is now available in an unabridged, five-volume German edition of over three thousand pages in length, published in November 2007: *Die Chronik des Gettos Lodz/Litzmannstadt* (Wallstein Verlag). Its principal editors are Sascha Feuchert, Erwin Leibfried and Jörg Riecke, assisted by Dr Julian Baranowski, Joanna Podolska, Krystyna Radziszewska and Jacek Walicki. Thanks to the staff of the Vienna University Library (Departments of Judaism and Contemporary History) and to the Jewish Library in Stockholm; to Zbigniew Janeczek for permission to reproduce the map on p. vi.

Many thanks also to Andrea Löw, Dirk Rupnow and Klaus Nellen (Vienna); to Jakub Ringart and Artur Zonabend (Stockholm); thanks also to Magnus Bergh, Anders Bodegård, Sarah Death, Aimée Delblanc, Stephen Farran-Lee, Carl Henrik Fredriksson, Peter Fröberg Idling, Joakim Hansson, Dagmar Hartlová, Tora Hedin, Lars Jakobson, Mariusz Kalinowski, Lennart Kerbel, Charlotte Kitzinger, Gisela Kosubek, Irena Kowadło-Przedmojska, Ola Larsmo, Paul Levine, Magnus Ljunggren, Karin Lundwall, Johanna Mo, Birgit Munkhammar, Joanna Podolska, Helena Rubinstein,

Björn Sandmark, Kaj Schueler, Caterina Pascual Söderbaum, Tomasz Zbikowski and Andrea Zederbauer for advice, recommendations, reading and help with translations, and much more.

To Katerina and Sasha.

Glossary

Some Yiddish spellings in the text reflect contemporary dialect

Aleynhilf (Yidd.)   Jewish self-help organisation

Approvisation (Austrian Ger.)   officialese; term used in the ghetto for food distribution; the head of the Approvisation Department was Maks (Awigdor Mendel) Szczęśliwy

badchen (Hebr./Yidd.; plural *badchonim*)   jester, entertainer (at weddings, etc.)

Beirat (Ger.)   another name for the 'Council of the Elders' appointed by the Germans, with Rumkowski as its chairman

bocher (Yidd.)   Talmud student

botwinki (Pol.)   beetroot tops (plural)

Bund (Yidd.)   the Jewish socialist party; full name: United Jewish Socialist Workers Party, in Poland, Lithuania and Russia (argued against both 'assimilation' and 'emigration')

dybek (Yidd.)   evil spirit

dietka (Pol.)   special ghetto shops selling such restricted items as dairy products (on prescription)

dygnitarze (Pol.; plural *dygnitarzy*)   an official, a (high-ranking, Jewish) ghetto functionary

dróshke (Yidd.)   hired carriage; Pol.: *dorożka*

działka (Pol.)   garden plot, allotment

eved hagermanim (Hebr.)   slave of the Germans

feldsher (Yidd.)   surgeon carrying out basic operations, barber-surgeon

ganef (Yidd.; plural *ganovim*)   young rascal, thief

Generalgouvernement (Ger.)   the part of Poland not directly incorporated into the German Reich

goniec (Pol.)   'prancer' (literally: horse); ghetto slang for a runner, messenger boy

Gordonia (Yidd.)   Zionist youth organisation; founded by Aharon David Gordon (1856–1922), a progressive Zionist

grober (Yidd.)   gravedigger, digger

hakhshara (Yidd; plural *haksharot*)   agricultural collective for young people on their way to Palestine

Hanukkah   Jewish midwinter festival, commemorating the rededication of the temple in Jerusalem

Hashomer Hatsair   Zionist youth organisation with Marxist tendencies

helfer (Yidd.)   teacher's assistant

Kaddish (Hebr.)   funeral prayer

kapote (Yidd.)   long coat formerly worn by male Jews of eastern Europe

kashrut (Hebr.)   (religious) rules governing the preparation and consumption of food; kosher

kehila (*kehile*, *kehal*) (Yidd.)   Jewish community council. Before the Second World War, all such community councils in Poland came under a central, ruling body, *Vaad Arba Aratzot*, which constituted a Jewish parliament equivalent to the Polish one (sejm = *sejmik*) with administrative and legislative power over all the Jewish communities on Polish territory. (The Nazis' improper, even perverted version of a 'Council of Elders' (*Ältestenrat*) or 'Jewish Council' had its roots in this division of legislative power between the Polish and Jewish nations of Poland)

khevre (*chevre*) (Yidd.)   guild; professional association; circle of friends

kidushin (Hebr.)   wedding; *mesader kidushin* – one who officiates at a wedding

kierownik (Pol.)   head of a factory or workshop

kolacja (Pol.)   evening meal; also (after 1943) the name given to the meals to which those employed in heavy labour were entitled every other week on production of coupons devised by the Chairman; known in German as *Kräftigungsmittage*

kolejka (Pol.)   queue (for example, at a food distribution point)

luftmentsh (Yidd.)   literally, person of the air, impractical person who achieves nothing in life

matse (Yidd.)   unleavened bread, eaten at Pesach (Passover) to commemorate the flight from Egypt

melamed (Yidd./Hebr.)   schoolteacher (of young children)

menaschka (Ger./Yidd.; plural *menażka*)   a mess tin or can, usually tied round the body, for holding and transporting soup. A word of Austrian origin: in the Austrian army, the word *menage* is used to mean 'food (and drink)'; hence the word *Menage-schale* (food bowl); Polish spelling: *menażka*

minyen (Yidd.; Hebr: minjan)   prayer group

Mitsraim (Yidd./Hebr.)   Egypt

mittags (Yidd.)   ghetto slang for the (midday) soup that all workers at all *resorty* paid to receive at their places of work (also known as *resortka*)

mosrim (Hebr.)   informant, informer

neshome (Yidd.)   soul

ochronki (Pol.)   orphanage (German: *Waisenheim*)

OD (Ger.)   *Ordnungsdienst*: the Jewish ghetto police (until September 1941)

opiekuni (Pol.)   supervisor at a factory, soup kitchen, etc.

pekl (Yidd.)   bundle, pack

pleytses (*plaitses*) (Yidd.)   literally 'shoulders', protection; also *protekcja* (Pol.)

ratsye (Yidd.)   ration

rebbe (Yidd.)   a rabbi in the Hasidic Jewish community

resort (Pol.)   from the German *Arbeitsressort*, term for factories and larger workshops in the ghetto

resortka (Pol.)   (midday) soup served in the factory canteens; also *mittags* (Yidd.)

sheine jidn (Yidd.)   literally: the 'beautiful' Jews, the rich and wealthy upper class, cf: *di balabatim* (the respected, the bourgeoisie), or *proste* (the ordinary people)

shiske (Yidd.)   potentate, 'big shot'

shobecht (Yidd.)   potato peel

shoyfet (Hebr, Yidd.)   a judge

shóyte (Yidd.)   idiot

shojfer (Yidd.)   horn blown during religious festivals, such as the Jewish New Year celebration, Rosh Hashanah, and when leaving the synagogue on the Day of Atonement; the expression *Ivan blust shoifer* means that someone else (originally the Russians) has taken charge of Jewish affairs

shoklen (Yidd.)   to 'shake', to rock to and fro (at prayer)

shomer (Hebr.)   guard

shomrim (Hebr.)   members of the Zionist youth collective Hashomer Hatzair (= rescuers, protectors); most of its members were Zionists overtly non-religious and Marxist in character

shpere (Yidd.; from Ger. *Gehsprerre*, Pol. *szpera*)   curfew; *di groise shpere* was the name used in the ghetto for the SS-implemented cleansing operations and mass murders of the ghetto Jews, 5–11 September 1942

shtetl (Yidd.; plural *shtetlech*)   village or small town, sometimes referred to places where Jews constituted a significant proportion of the population

shtraiml (Yidd.)   (Hasidic) fur hat

Sonderkommando (Ger.), later known as *Sonderabteilung*   special
   force within the Jewish ghetto police; helped the Gestapo seize
   items of value, and was subsequently in charge of rounding people
   up for the German authorities, ready for deportation or forced
   labour; led until July 1943 by *Dawid Gertler*; and after him by
   Marek Kligier

świetlica (Pol.)   dayroom or living room

szarlotka (Pol.)   an apple pastry

tallit (Hebr.)   prayer shawl

talmid (Hebr.)   student

Talmud Tora (Hebr.)   (public) Jewish primary school with basic
   instruction in arithmetic, spelling, Hebrew etc; the teacher at the
   Talmud Torah school, the *melamed*, usually lived with his family in
   the schoolroom

tefillin (Hebr.)   slips of parchment containing passages from the
   Torah, worn in small, cube-shaped leather boxes strapped to the
   arm and forehead during daily prayers

tnoyim (Yidd.)   marriage or betrothal contract; a term used in the
   ghetto for the deportation order served on 'undesirable' residents

treyf (Yidd.)   non-kosher food, refuse

trepki (Pol.)   wooden clogs

tsaddik (Yidd; plural *tsaddikim*)   a holy, literally 'righteous' man,
   spiritual leader of a Hasidic communion; *tzadika* (Hebr. form)
   daughter of such a holy man

tsdóke (Yidd.)   charity

tsetl (Yidd.)   list, slip of paper

tsholent (Yidd.)   Jewish dish of potatoes, beans and meat, prepared on
   low heat for the Sabbath

tsiper (Yidd.)   pickpocket, pilferer

(*pani*) *Wydzielaczka* (Pol.)   ghetto slang for the – usually young –
   women who served soup in the factory canteens and soup kitchens

yarmulke (Yidd.)   skullcap

yeke (Yidd.)   'Eastern Jewish' term for German; ghetto slang for the
   western European ('German') Jews who began arriving in the
   ghetto in September 1941

Yom Kippur (Hebr.)   Day of Atonement